WAR STORY

WAR STORY

Sara Hely

Thomas Dunne Books
St. Martin's Press ⧈ New York

THOMAS DUNNE BOOKS.
An imprint of St. Martin's Press.

www.stmartins.com

ISBN 0-312-30532-X

First published in Great Britain by HEADLINE BOOK PUBLISHING
A division of Hodder Headline

First U.S. Edition: May 2003

10 9 8 7 6 5 4 3 2 1

For Aunt Peggie and Dita,
With Love

Part One

Early Spring
to
Late Summer
1940

Chapter 1

Lady Dulcimer had grown deaf with the years. She could no longer hear the grandfather clock striking the hours on the landing outside her bedroom. She missed its companionable voice, especially during the past few days when she could not sleep for worrying about her son Dart's divorce.

It had been a distressing week. She had expected unpleasantness. Divorce was a terrible thing, and it had been hard to get Lord Dulcimer to come to terms with what he saw as Dart's disgrace. Certainly nothing in Lady Dulcimer's experience had prepared her for the dreadfulness of the past week.

A public fight between such a well-known and fashionable couple as Lord and Lady Dartmore had been a gift to the gutter press. They relished it, and accusations and counter-charges of adultery and strange bedroom antics had been blazoned across the headlines. Even *The Times* and the *Daily Telegraph* had carried daily reports. Lady Dulcimer and her butler had gone to all manner of shifts to keep the more lurid reports away from Lord Dulcimer. And it would not do for young Quentin to read all that filth about his parents, either.

Preventing this had not been easy. Dulcimer Hall, previously shunned for its manifold discomforts, had come into fashion since the start of the war. The government had advised old people to leave London, and thousands of children from the capital had been evacuated for fear of bombs. Lady Dulcimer's two married daughters promptly despatched their children and attendants to stay in Sussex, and the shabby old east wing and all the nursery rooms were now full to overflowing. During the course of the year a steady trickle of elderly relations had come to join the wartime throng. Every cottage, stable flat and farmhouse on the estate was occupied.

Lady Dulcimer rather liked being the centre of so much bustle and life. But when it came to keeping the 'Dartmore Case' headlines from her eldest grandson, it posed a problem. She could hardly ban people from taking their usual newspapers, and if Quentin went visiting, which he did when he had nothing better to do, all her careful precautions would be undone.

The only thing to do was to keep him busy. All week long she had done her best to divert him, taking him fishing, shooting rabbits in the park, borrowing a pony for him to ride. Such a good looking boy, she thought, and remarkably unspoiled, considering how Dart and Peggy competed for his favours one minute and neglected him the next. He reminded Lady Dulcimer of her second son, Johnnie, who had died before the war began, and whose widow and three children were living at Dulcimer. Dart's case was over, thank goodness, and Quentin would soon be going back to school – a week late. She had enjoyed him, but felt worn out by her exertions. Thinking of Quentin with pleasure, Lady Dulcimer drifted back to sleep.

She might miss the sound of the clock outside her room, but there was really no need for it. Lady Dulcimer's personal maid kept better time than any manmade device. At half past eight precisely, Miss Trumpet marched into the room.

'Good morning, milady.'

'Gracious, Trumpet. It can't be half past yet, surely.'

The youngest of Lady Dulcimer's dogs bounced off the sofa where he slept with two others, greeting the newcomer with ecstatic wags of his tail. The older dogs merely raised their heads and watched. They knew the morning ritual.

'Get away, you daft thing,' said Trumpet, pushing a cold nose away and stumping across the carpeted floor to draw back the heavy curtains with a rattle and screech of brass on brass. 'Blowing a gale all night and raining cats and dogs, milady,' she announced in her penetrating Scots voice. 'It's a good thing his lordship isn't playing soldiers this week. Their tents would have been fair blown away. And you should see the lawn. Such a mess. All those cabbages and onions they planted are under water. I never thought it was a good idea to plough up the lawn.'

'Digging for victory, Trumpet,' murmured Lady Dulcimer. 'We will need to grow all the food we can, this year.'

'His lordship would have been better putting fish on the lawn, the way it is this morning. It's a shame, all that lovely grass being done away with. When I think of the church garden party we held on it last summer . . .'

'None of us have time for garden parties, with a war on.'

'There are some that always find ways to do what they want,' retorted Trumpet, coming over to arrange Lady Dulcimer's pillows at her back. The senior dog growled ominously from under the eiderdown, just to let her know that he was there. 'Lord Dartmore drove in at six o'clock this morning, and now he has gone riding with Mrs John. They came pestering Mr Vestry for a cup of tea in the pantry before they went out.'

'Dart here?' Lady Dulcimer hoisted herself up a little higher, and hugged her cocoon of shawls around her. She was pleased. 'He must have been glad to get out of London.'

'Glad to get away from those wicked newsmen, more likely. According to Mr Vestry, both his young lordship and Mrs John were full of the joys of spring when they rode off.'

Lady Dulcimer did not miss the arch note in Trumpet's voice, and she knew very well that the servants were expecting her widowed daughter-in-law Antonia and her son Dart to make a match of it, once the decree nisi came through to make his divorce final. This started her worrying again. She did not think it would be a good thing. Still less was she sure that Dart would oblige his well-wishers. Dart seldom did what people expected of him – as the events of the past week had proved so painfully.

Her breakfast tray was brought, and Lady Dulcimer peered warily under the silver cover. A poached egg looked back at her. Dart ought to leave Antonia alone. His divorce would not be final for some weeks. She wished he would be more careful.

She handed the silver cover to Trumpet. 'They cannot have gone riding. There is nothing in the stables to ride, except Master Quentin's pony.'

'Eat your egg while it's hot, milady,' advised Trumpet, tucking a damask napkin over the swathing shawls. 'That is what I meant to tell you. Lord Dartmore has brought three great horses with him, driving them down from Leicestershire through the night. It seems he means to leave them here, while he goes back to France to join his regiment.'

'Eat up, Abby,' said Nanny. 'Plenty of soldiers in the trenches would be glad to have hot porridge for breakfast.'

'Not trenches, Nanny,' said Quentin using his newly developed public school manner. 'You are out of date. Trenches were in the Great War.'

'Out of date I may be,' said Nanny, spooning sieved prunes and porridge into Jamie's mouth, and scraping half a spoonful off his chubby face and posting it in after. 'Lots of people went hungry in the Great War, and very likely will in this. I'm not having food wasted in my nursery. Come along, Abby.'

'Don't you know there's a war on, Abigail Cary?' said Quentin in a silly voice.

'That's enough of your nonsense, Quentin,' said Nanny, frowning direfully at Abby when she and her cousin spluttered with laughter. 'Leave Abby alone until she has finished eating, do. As it is, she looks like being late for her lessons with Miss Brimley.'

'It's not fair,' grumbled Abby, who detested lessons at the best of times. 'Quentin is going back to Eton late, so why can't we stop lessons until he has gone?'

5

'Because Miss Brimley came back specially to start this week,' said Nanny repressively. Divorce or not, she would be glad to be rid of Quentin. Having him here made Abby harder to handle. 'If you have finished, Quentin, why don't you go and get your fishing things ready?'

Quentin tipped his chair, and said he was not going fishing until the afternoon. 'I say, Nanny, did you know that Alice and Doris are off to join the Fire Service?'

'I wish Brimstone would join the forces,' said Abby gloomily.

'Don't call Miss Brimley that.'

'My father always did,' said Quentin cheerfully. 'He and Uncle Johnnie used to pull the hairpins out of her bun and make her cry.'

'That's quite enough, Quentin. Leave Abby alone until she has finished.' And to Abby she added, 'Give over grumbling, and eat up.'

'I just can't seem to get it down, Nanny,' said Abby, looking in revulsion at the mess of congealing porridge and prunes on her plate. 'I just can't.'

'Then you will eat it at lunchtime,' said Nanny curtly. She told the nursery maid, Maggie, to put Abby's plate in the nursery cupboard. When Abby protested, she relented slightly. 'Five minutes more then, and after that into the cupboard it goes.'

Abby could see that Nanny meant it. She took one more mouthful, and retched. 'I don't feel well.'

'Show me your tongue.'

Abby stuck her tongue out as far as it would go.

'Just as I thought. Bilious. Milk of Magnesia for you tonight, young lady.'

Abby glared, and gave her tongue a defiant wiggle. Quentin and Miles laughed, and little Jamie joined in, blowing a raspberry with his prunes and porridge, so that it spattered all over Nanny's crisp white apron. All the children fell about laughing, even Aunt Jean's little boys and Aunt Cora's two mice who sat with their strict nanny and Mamzelle at another table.

'Just look what you've done, Abby,' said Nanny crossly. 'Finish your breakfast and stop playing the giddy goat. You don't have to show off just because Quentin is here. Not another word out of you until you are finished.'

She wiped Jamie's ghastly prune mask with his feeder, scooped him out of his high chair, and tucked him briskly under one arm. 'Come along, my booty boy.'

Seven-year-old Miles was told to follow her, and Nanny marched her youngest charges out of the room, saying to the nursery maid, 'You can start clearing away, Maggie. But mind you see that Abby has a clean plate before she gets down.'

'Yes, Nanny,' said Maggie. She went to hold the door open for them, placing her substantial form between Nanny and the nursery dachshund who was polishing off Abby's breakfast. Maggie was on Abby's side over some things.

Dart and Antonia Cary came back from riding on the common wet through and exhilarated by their exertions on that stormy morning. Dart stayed behind to help the ancient groom see to the horses, then came into the cavernous front hall, casting whip and sodden gloves on a central table.

Vestry, the butler, cruised to meet him, wearing a reproachful face. 'The breakfast gong has gone, my lord.'

'I need a bath, Vestry. I've been up all night.'

'The bathwater is never hot until the evening, my lord. One of his lordship's wartime economies. I have instructed one of the maids to put hot water in your room, however.'

'Better than nothing, I suppose,' said Dart, squelching towards the stairs. 'Thanks, Vestry.'

There was a rosy-faced girl in his bedroom, putting a brass can with a steaming spout on the marble-topped washstand. He smiled at her. She smiled back, her face as bright and clean as a dewy morning. 'Watch yourself with that water, my lord,' she said. 'It's nearly boiling.'

'I'll be careful,' said Dart. He looked at her. 'Have we met before?'

Her face became brighter still, lit by sudden laughter. 'Aye. We've met before.' Her laughter spilled over because he looked so puzzled. 'I'm Maggie.'

Dart's blue eyes narrowed. She was a big girl, but as wholesome as newly baked bread in her striped blue and white dress. With her soft brown hair braided round her head like that, she had a curiously old-fashioned air. Not his type, but promising all the same. The last housemaid, Betty, had been great fun, always ready with a smile and friendly banter, but she had gone to work in a factory. He said slowly, 'So you are Maggie? That doesn't tell me much. Have you been at Dulcimer long?'

'A year since January, Lord Dartmore.' She was suddenly quite serious. 'I'll tell you another thing. Abby has been wearying to see you, ever since you sent that postcard.'

'Abby?' It dawned on him, then, where he had seen this girl. 'So you are Antonia's nursery maid? You look different without your hat.' He turned to the washstand and poured a steaming libation into the wide, flowered china bowl. 'Will you do something for me, Maggie?'

She said primly, 'I'll need to hear what it is first.'

He laughed. Definitely more cautious than Betty, this one. 'Tell Abby to come and see me in the stable yard after breakfast, there's a good girl. I've got something for her.'

7

'What does my father want Abby for?' demanded Quentin jealously.

'How should I know?' replied Maggie, busy clearing plates, and wanting rid of him. Quentin was all too given to tripping her up, or pinching her bottom when she was ironing or cleaning out the grate. 'Why don't you go along and see for yourself?'

He caught up with Abby. 'I bet it's one of those girly things. A frilly dress, perhaps, or a doll that wets itself. Serve you right if it is a doll.'

'Uncle Dart wouldn't give me a doll. He knows I hate dolls.'

'It's not fair. I am the one he should be giving presents to.'

'Then why don't you tell him so?'

'I might,' said Quentin, knowing that he would not. His father was unpredictable, sometime expansively generous, at other times accusing his son of being a demanding brat.

But when Dart led them into a loosebox and showed them what he had brought for Abby, Quentin knew such a pang of resentment that he could not help exclaiming, 'A puppy! Dad! You absolutely promised I could have one. Why is Abby getting it instead?'

Dart was watching Abby's thin, freckled face, an odd smile tilting his lips. She was cradling the warm ball of fluff in her arms, speechless with delight. Dart liked giving Abby things. A plain child, she had a worshipful way of looking her thanks that was hard to resist.

'Dad! You promised me a dog.'

'You'll get one some day,' Dart told his son dismissively.

Antonia appeared in the open doorway, looking flushed and beautiful. She was out of breath, as though she had been running. She said almost shrilly, 'What is this? A puppy for Abby?'

Abby looked up at her uncle and then at her mother, her eyes glowing. 'I love him, Mummy. Oh, I just love him already.'

Antonia looked at Dart. 'You might have asked me if I wanted my daughter to have a puppy.'

'So I might,' he agreed suavely. 'But with one thing and another, it slipped my mind this morning.'

Antonia went closer and looked. Her newly dried hair foamed like spun white gold around her face, almost hiding her carnation cheeks from his malicious gaze. 'It looks a pretty good mongrel to me.'

'Don't be a snob, Antonia.'

'I wonder that you dare land it on us after foisting all your hunters on Father Dulcimer. Besides, we already have a nursery dog. If Nanny is upset, I won't allow Abby to keep it.'

'Mummy, please!'

'I'll have it,' said Quentin, too eagerly.

'Be quiet, Quentin. You know you can't take a puppy to Eton.'

'Then it must go back to where it came from,' said Antonia, ignoring Abby's anguished look. 'Quentin is quite right. It is not fair to give Abby a dog when your own son is not allowed one.'

'Life is never fair, Antonia mia. And I have no time to take it anywhere, because I must be at Biggin Hill airfield before noon. Remember? You promised to drive me there in your ambulance.'

'Gosh, Dad! Flying? Where are you flying to?'

'Back to France. A chap I know commands a squadron at Biggin Hill and is going to land me near my unit.' Dart clapped his son on the shoulder, seeing an easy way to cheer him up. 'How about coming with us to the airfield?'

'Oh, rather!'

Antonia said, 'I am not supposed to take passengers in the back of my ambulance, Dart. It's against Red Cross regulations.'

'Such a stickler for rules, little sister-in-law?' said Dart, mocking her with his eyes. 'You must have got out of bed on the wrong side. Quentin can squash in between us.' He grabbed Antonia's hand, pulling her towards the door of the loosebox. Over his shoulder, he said, 'Leave your mother to me, Abby. All you need to do is to find a name for that puppy, and to remember to feed it four times a day. It will have to sleep in here, to begin with. And when I come back, I shall expect it to be at least twice the size.'

Abby stammered her thanks, hugging her new darling so tightly that it gave a little grunt of protest. 'But what will I feed it on, Uncle Dart?'

He told her to give it milk and porridge. When she was alone in the loosebox, Abby began a silent dance of triumph.

Maggie Dunlop the nursery maid was a heavy sleeper, and the under housemaid whose duty it was to wake the most lowly servants at Dulcimer Hall sometimes had to shake her quite hard before she opened reluctant eyes upon a new day. The morning after Lord Dartmore's sudden arrival and equally hasty departure, however, the nursery maid woke early of her own accord, fully an hour before she had to start work.

There was always a sense of excitement at Dulcimer when Lord Dartmore came, both in the servants' hall and in the nursery. The children loved their Uncle Dart, particularly Abby, who had been overjoyed with his gift of the puppy.

Maggie could hear the child shifting and turning in the adjacent bed. The postcard from Dart, Maggie knew, had given rise to quite different expectations.

Abby told Maggie what she hoped for and the nursery maid shook her braided head.

'Your mother would tell you if it was that, surely?'

'Mummy doesn't often tell me things,' said Abby. 'She did ask me the other day if I would like a new daddy. She and Uncle Dart may be planning to get married.'

'Well, don't pin your hopes on it,' Maggie advised her.

Not only the Cary children adored their Uncle Dart. Most of the female staff at Dulcimer Hall were more or less in love with him – and Maggie was no exception. Lord Dartmore had been her secret hero from the day, four year ago, when she had first seen him giving the prizes at her school sports. That had been at Glen Cary, the Dulcimers' Scottish estate, where Maggie had lived all her life. Tall, sunburned and smiling, he was like a prince in a fairy tale. Even thinking about Lord Dartmore gave her the strangest feelings, somewhere between wanting to laugh and trying not to cry. And when he had smiled at her and thanked her for bringing hot water for washing, Maggie could have lain down and died for him.

'And a fat lot of good that would have done you,' the sensible Maggie told the other, foolish one. 'Die at his feet, and he would likely send for one of the garden boys to take you away in a sack.'

She had once seen him shoot his old labrador. The dog was ill and past his work, and Lord Dartmore had decided to shoot the animal himself, rather than send for the vet. 'The old boy understands about guns and hates going to the vet,' his lordship had said to Maggie's father. 'It's better this way.'

So Maggie had watched from the doorway of her father's cottage, horrified, yet unable to look away. Lord Dartmore and her father, head keeper at Glen Cary, had walked together down the path beside the burn, the old dog limping at his master's heels. She saw Lord Dartmore turn and aim the gun at the dog's head, saw the animal stagger and topple over, even as the shot sounded in her ears. Within minutes, Lord Dartmore was driving off down the rough glen road, and Maggie's father was left to bury the body.

Maggie shivered as she lay with her face half buried in her pillows. That ruthless quality about Lord Dartmore was as much part of his fascination as his golden looks and his air of owning the earth. When they needed a nursery maid at Dulcimer Hall, she had wanted to go there very badly. She thought she would see Lord Dartmore occasion-ally, when he came to visit his parents. Most of all, though, Maggie wanted to get away from her father.

She had been afraid of Ian Dunlop for as long as she could remember. Other people feared him too. Her two older brothers had borne their share of beatings, and kept a weather eye upon the gamekeeper's changeable moods. Even Gran walked carefully when his bearded face took on that dark, inward look. But it was Maggie who feared him deep down, trembling when she heard his step on the path outside the cottage, quaking at the sound of his voice. She never seemed to do anything right where her father was concerned.

Her friend Glynis told her that she was a coward. 'You should stand up to him, Maggie. Just tell him to his face that you are going to the school outing. You are twelve and about to leave school, it's time you learned to stand up for yourself.'

Maggie shuddered. 'I couldn't, Glynis. Not possibly. My dad is that strict. I've never been allowed to act in school plays, or to go to the parties or the summer picnics, or do anything except lessons. Never once.'

'Why ever not?'

Maggie did not know. She only knew that it was so, that it had always been so. She had won the top scholarship to the Secondary, but her father would not let her go, even though Gran and the local schoolmaster pleaded with him. She turned to Glynis, and said, 'It's no good. Honestly not, Glynis. So, if you're coming home with me, don't speak of it.'

'It beats me to understand what's wrong with your going on a school outing.'

'He says I would be led astray, whatever that means.'

Glynis gave vent to a hissing little shriek of laughter. 'Small hope of that on a day trip to the seaside, with the boys penned at one end of the beach and us girls at the other. Now, if your brother Tom had been coming with us, that would have been a different matter. I would have done my best to get him to lead me astray.'

Maggie giggled, aware that giggling was expected of her. It was only in the past year that Glynis and the others had admitted Maggie to their charmed circle, and she knew that she had Tom to thank for it. She was indeed thankful, for it made all the difference. It did not matter that her good-looking younger brother was her passport to these favours. She was grateful for acceptance on any terms.

Glynis said coaxingly. 'If I walk down the glen with you, do you think your gran would ask me to tea?'

'She's out today,' Maggie said briefly. 'I have to get the tea myself.'

Glynis took this for an invitation, and came along. There did not seem to be any way of stopping her.

The cottage was quiet and empty when they got there, but almost before she had put the kettle on, Maggie heard the menfolk tramping their way into the scullery. Her face wore a shut down look as she busied herself at the stove. Teatime was an ordeal when Gran was out. However hard Maggie tried to get things right, she seldom escaped without criticism. Her father came in first, drying his hands on a towel. He looked pleased to see Glynis, which was a relief.

'Well, lassie? Come to visit us, have you? I hear that the minister is to present you with the Scripture Union prize, come Sunday. Well done, indeed.'

Glynis lowered her eyes demurely, and pursed her small mouth in a smile. 'Thank you, Mr Dunlop.'

'It's a pity our Maggie has never learned to read and revere the Bible,' he said grimly. He surveyed Maggie's tense, sturdy form as she stood waiting for the kettle to boil. 'She's little better than a heathen.'

'Oh, but Maggie is so clever,' breathed Glynis, aware that the Dunlop brothers were padding in behind her on stockinged feet. Nobody wore tackety boots on Gran's well-scrubbed kitchen floor, except the head of the house. Glynis sighed wistfully, 'I would give anything to be good at my books like Maggie.'

'A knowledge of the Lord's Word will stand you in better stead than the scholarship that Maggie's been wasting her time on.'

'Hardly time wasted, Dad,' protested Tom. 'Winning the scholarship was a credit to her, even if you won't let her take it up.'

Maggie tried in vain to catch Tom's eye, dreading his championship, for all that she was grateful. But her father merely said, mildly for him, 'I want to hear no more talk about scholarships. Hurry along with the tea, Maggie. And if your friend is staying, why haven't you laid a place for her?'

'Sorry, Dad.' Maggie would never have dared to invite Glynis, or anyone else, to tea. Her father doing so was astonishing, really, but she knew better than to defend herself. She reached up to the dresser for plates and a cup and saucer. Her hands were unsteady as she dished up Gran's thick lentil soup. She wished Glynis had not stayed. She was such a chatterbox that she might say anything. Besides, she liked stirring things up. She might say something about the outing, just to see what would happen.

'Where's Gran?' Tom asked. He could see that Maggie was in a state, though he could not guess why. She stood in Gran's place at the end of the scrubbed table, pouring out the tea with a wooden expression on her round, rosy face. 'Has she gone into town?'

'Mothers' Union tea,' said his brother Alistair succinctly.

'Old wives club, eh?' Ian Dunlop slurped up some soup, eyeing Glynis, who was daintily sipping hers from the edge of a spoon. 'Now that you girls are about to leave the school, I suppose you'll be wanting to join the Mothers' Union and the Rural yourselves?'

'I'm afraid Maggie and I aren't old enough yet, Mr Dunlop. Besides,' she added, her demureness slipping, 'I've had enough of the glen, and staying in it. Enough of school, too. I'm off to stay with my auntie in Dundee. I'm going to learn shorthand and typing, and then I'll likely get a job in an office. I don't envy Maggie, staying here and working at the manse.'

True to her word, Glynis departed to Dundee, and Maggie went to the manse to work as a daily general maid. Cook was known to be something of a tartar, but compared to Ian Dunlop and Gran, she was mild enough. And it was a relief to be out of the cottage for six days

12

each week. Maggie felt herself lucky indeed. She walked two miles up the glen early each morning, in time to clean out the fires in the minister's study and the living room, laying them ready for when they were needed. She did the rough work of the house, peeling potatoes and other vegetables, scrubbing floors, or pots and pans in the dark scullery, dashing up the stairs to help the living-in maid make the beds and sweep and polish, before hurrying downstairs again to help Cook with the midday meal. Mrs Fraser has been a widow with a teenage daughter when she married her second husband. Grown up, and now married, Dawn sometimes came to the manse with her lively small boys, and taking them on the moor, or putting them to bed, was a welcome novelty on top of Maggie's other duties. It was hard work, but nobody picked on her, or seemed to think her steeped in wickedness, and when the minister heard her singing at her work, he actually said he liked to hear it.

Maggie grew to love the minister. He was tall and ungainly, absent-minded and not a particularly good preacher, more interested in his history books and learning modern languages than reading the Good Book, Maggie's father would have said. But people came to the manse from all parts of the glen, and more often than not they went away feeling better for telling him their troubles. What was so special about him, none of his visitors quite knew. Maggie thought she knew. Mr Fraser was just good; good all through.

After a time, the living-in maid left to get married, and Mrs Fraser asked Maggie to take her place. The heavy work could be done by one of the under-keeper's wives, and it meant that Maggie's wages went up to seven shillings a week. Ian Dunlop did not object. He said that Maggie could put two shillings of it into her Post Office savings, but he would not let her live in at the manse. Maggie went on walking down the glen each day and back at the end of every afternoon, content with her lot. It was an ordeal going home after her work was finished, for she never knew what sort of mood her father would be in, but mostly she managed not to think of home until the cottage roof came in sight. It seemed to her that this state of things might go on for ever.

But it was not to be. She was nearing her sixteenth birthday when it was learned that Lady Dulcimer was looking for a nursery maid for her grandchildren. Mrs Fraser said that Maggie would be just the person.

'A nursery maid?' echoed the minister, when his lady told him what she had in mind. 'That girl has too good a brain to waste herself on that sort of drudgery. She has a really good grasp of languages. Far better than mine. I only wish that I could teach her proper French pronunciation.' The minister had been doing a French course by post for years, and finding Maggie poring over one of his textbooks, had invited her to join him. 'She ought to go to university.'

'I know, dear, and I don't want to lose her. She is a thoroughly nice child, so cheerful and willing.'

'She's more than that,' said the minister stubbornly. 'She's bright. She should be at school. I promised her that we would all go to France, but if there is a war that will be scuppered.'

'You can promise what you like,' said Mrs Fraser, 'but Ian Dunlop would never let her go anywhere, war or no war. Maggie knows it. We all know it. When he comes near her, she freezes like a rabbit with a stoat. She ought to get away, and this post at Dulcimer may be her best chance. After all, Lord Dulcimer is Ian Dunlop's employer, and his house belongs to the estate. If I tell him that I have recommended his daughter, he can hardly say no.'

Maggie's father said no without the least difficulty. He would not hear of it. The old lord and his lady were all very well, he told Maggie, but the rest of the Cary family were a godless, rackety lot – not the sort of folk for Maggie to work for. She would stay at the manse, and that was that. He could keep an eye on her there. Shame on her that she should want to go!

Maggie was downcast, but not surprised. At least he had not belted her, or gone into one of his long, terrifying tirades about sin and damnation. She went to work next day and told Cook cheerfully that it was no good.

Cook was relieved to hear that Maggie was staying on. But when Mrs Fraser heard, she had different ideas. She called to take afternoon tea with Maggie's grandmother, and by the time Ian Dunlop came in from the moor, Mrs Fraser had won Gran over. Ian was a stark man and a stubborn one, but with the minister's lady and his mother set on Maggie going to Sussex, he found his arguments wearing thin.

'England is a long way off, Mistress Fraser. Maggie's nobbut fifteen.'

'She will be sixteen soon, Ian, and besides, she would not be travelling alone. I've offered to take her to London, if she goes, and Lady Dulcimer's maid will meet us and take her to Sussex.'

'That's very good of you, ma'am, I'm sure,' said Maggie's father, though he sounded as sour as late-picked rhubarb. 'Has the lassie been misbehaving that you're wanting rid of her?'

Mrs Fraser smiled at Maggie, who was standing very still, her hands clasped behind her back. 'Nothing of the sort. I shall miss her, but Lady Dulcimer's personal maid has been on the telephone three times. Miss Trumpet is known to Mrs Dunlop, I hear, so she can be sure that Maggie will be in good hands. They are badly needing a girl to train as nursery maid – one who will stay, and give those poor children some security. You know, don't you, that John Cary was run over and killed last spring? His widow and the three children are living in Sussex with the grandparents. Maggie likes children. It will be a chance for her.'

'It's not what my mother and I planned for the lassie. I doubt she'll learn flighty ways down there in England.'

'There's no need to worry about that, Ian. Your Maggie's got her head screwed on.'

'And they'll have nothing to complain of when it comes to sewing and mending,' put in Gran, suddenly showing her hand. 'I've seen to that.'

'Yes, indeed. I told Miss Trumpet that Maggie shows real skill with her needle.'

Ian Dunlop looked at his mother resentfully. It was not often that she went against him, but when she did, there was no budging her. He turned back to their visitor. 'That's as may be, Mistress Fraser, but Maggie's my only daughter. I'll fair miss her if she goes.'

'He will miss the work she does for him, the old hypocrite,' said Mrs Fraser wrathfully when she got back to the manse. 'And he will miss having someone to browbeat. If he has ever spoken a kind word to Maggie, I've yet to hear of it. Blows and abuse is all she gets from him, and Mrs Dunlop is not much better. Ian and the two boys are all she has time for. Everything must be done for the menfolk, and Maggie does most of it. No wonder Ian's wife left him if he treated her like that.'

The minister smiled at his wife's vehemence. 'It was the other way round, my dear. Your precious Maggie's mother was a lovely, town-bred creature, and Ian doted on her. She sang in the choir, so I saw her every week – and always Ian would be there waiting so that his beloved Mary did not have to walk home alone.' The minister rubbed a hand over his bald head, thinking back on that half-forgotten episode. He had never been able to fathom it.

'It all went wrong so suddenly. I baptised little Maggie on the Sunday. Ian lived in the under-keeper's house further up the glen at that time, and I drove there with a carload of people. There was quite a gathering. The next thing I heard was that Mary had gone off with a cousin of hers – a young man who was the baby's sponsor at the baptism. Ian was like a stricken beast. We feared for his mind. Even to this day, he will not have Mary's name spoken, and the children were told that she had been killed in a car accident.'

'It wouldn't hurt him to treat Maggie better. It's not her fault that her mother ran away with a cousin.'

'He blames her all the same.'

'All the more reason for her to get away. I told Ian that you were thinking of putting his name forward as an Elder. Do you think you could?'

*   *   *

15

Maggie was the latest in a long line of nursery maids at Dulcimer Hall, following on after a string of others who did not stay long enough for Abby to remember their names.

'Girls have no stamina nowadays,' said Nanny, surprised by the way they kept leaving. One after another they came and went. Nanny bullied them. She called it training. It was hard enough getting girls in London, but in the depths of Sussex, with war in the offing, it was pretty well impossible.

'I wonder what this one will be like,' said Abby when they heard about the girl from Scotland.

'No better nor no worse than the others, I dare say, for all that Miss Trumpet acts as if she has performed a miracle,' replied Nanny. 'Are you going to get out of that bath, slowcoach, or must I wait all day?'

Nanny was relieved to hear about Maggie, really. Not that she showed it when the girl arrived at Dulcimer. Nanny looked her over and sniffed. 'My! You're a big girl! None of our nursery maid's uniforms will go round you. Can you sew?'

Maggie nodded.

'Lost your tongue, have you? Well, you can start putting a gusset into a dress for yourself and letting down the hem. You ought to manage that. What do they feed you on in Scotland?' But without waiting for an answer, she added, 'It's to be hoped you aren't lazy. I've no time for lazy girls in my nursery.'

There was no time for anything, or so it seemed to Maggie in those early days at Dulcimer Hall. The house was vast to her eyes, more than three times larger than the shooting lodge at Glen Cary – and there were so many strange people in it. She washed and ironed the children's clothes, cleaned the nurseries, carried coals, laid fires, blackleaded the grates. Trying to find her way around the stone labyrinth which led to the kitchens was a dreadful worry at first. She would stagger up the back stairs with laden trays for the nursery, and Nanny would more than likely chide her for dawdling. It was one long race, from the moment when she was woken at a quarter to six until she fell into bed at nine o'clock at night.

She slept in the second night nursery with Abby, creeping out to the bathroom in the cold dawn to avoid waking the sleeping child. There was a daily routine of cleaning to be done before she took Nanny her cup of tea at seven. All day and every day, things had to be done to Nanny's pattern, strictly to time, to an accompaniment of admonition and criticism. 'Not that cloth, girl. That's for the shelves.' 'How many times must I tell you to wash the glasses first?' 'These nappies aren't properly aired. Put them back on the fireguard.' 'Hurry up with that ironing. We haven't got all day.'

So it went on. Maggie despaired of pleasing Nanny in those early months. She was tempted to give in her notice, like the others – but the dread of being sent home to her father at Glen Cary kept her going.

And it got better. Little by little, the house did not seem quite so vast, and the people grew more familiar, some of them even quite friendly. And the Cary children were a help. She loved the stout, cheerful baby Jamie, and six-year-old Miles was the most beautiful and good-natured little boy. Abby was different. She was thin, freckled, often rebellious and bad-tempered. She was eight when Maggie first met her. But it was Abby who was to make all the difference.

When Maggie came to Dulcimer to work, she thought the Cary children were spoiled rotten. They went through their days without lifting a finger, their clothes changed twice a day, new ones laid out each morning. No shivering in the cold dawn for the Cary children when Maggie first knew them. Fires were lit in their bedrooms an hour before they set foot out of bed. Meals were cooked downstairs and put down before them in their upstairs nursery. All the same, it did not take Maggie long to see that Abby got most of the scolds and very little of the spoiling that was meted out to her brothers. Before long, united by Nanny's tyranny, Maggie and Abby became friends.

'A pity Nanny is too old to be called up,' said Abby when she had been sent to bed for smacking Miles. 'Then you could look after us, and things would be better.'

'Likely you would have to learn to look after yourself,' retorted Maggie, who was brushing Abby's straight fawn hair. 'That would be a change for you, that would. As soon as I'm old enough, I'm off to train as a nurse.'

'It's not fair,' said Abby. 'War is no fun for children. Everybody is going away to join up. Soon there will be nobody left here except Granny and Grandpa and the dogs.'

Abby felt thoroughly let down by the war. She had been pleased when it broke out, scenting change, a break in the stodge of nursery routine – and about time. She enjoyed going to the church hall to get fitted out with a gas mask. They had a horrid rubbery smell, and made farting noises when you spoke or laughed inside them. Butter rationing was fun to begin with too. They had their own dishes with a week's dollop. On Sundays the children and Nanny had lunch in the dining room with the grandparents, so Maggie was sent downstairs with a flotilla of little flagged dishes.

But the newness and the excitement wore off. By the New Year of 1940 all that had happened was that her mother had got a job in the local Red Cross, and life at Dulcimer went on its humdrum, totally predictable way. Lessons in the mornings with Miss Brimley, lunch in the nursery, a rest after lunch and then the inevitable, boring walk in the afternoon.

'Such fun for you to be in the country, now that all the cousins have come to join us,' said Antonia, trying on her new Red Cross uniform, specially made for her at Huntsman's. Goodness knows how she would pay for it, but she did not worry about that for the present. Surprising how becoming navy blue could be, if you were fair. The hat was a horror, of course, but she need not wear it much. She twisted sideways to make sure about the back of the jacket. 'You'll be able to play with Joan and Betty and Aunt Jean's boys every day.'

'Nanny is on non-speaks with Mamzelle,' said Abby gloomily. She did not bother to tell Antonia that Aunt Cora's prim little girls were the last children she would want to play with, and Aunt Jean's boys were too young. 'We only see them at meals and on Sundays going to church. I wish I could go to boarding school like Quentin.'

'Quentin is a boy,' said Antonia. 'Boarding schools give girls thick legs. You're much better off doing lessons with Brimmy.'

'I hate Brimmy. And she hates me.'

'Of course she doesn't hate you,' said Antonia irritably. Why did Abby argue so much? 'Miss Brimley is devoted to all of us. She taught Uncle Dart and Daddy their lessons, long before you were born.'

'Don't I know it! She goes on and on about them. If I can't go to boarding school, I'd like to go to the village school.'

'No. Miles must be properly grounded for his prep school.'

'I don't mean Miles. I mean me.'

'Try not to be self-centred, darling. It's too drearily off-putting.' Antonia focused her mind resolutely on her uniform coat and skirt. Yes. It really was a shade long. It was no good having good legs if you did not show them off. An inch off the hem would help.

'Run and fetch Maggie, darling. She can take it up for me.'

Antonia had never really forgiven Johnnie for making her a widow. So careless and unnecessary of him to get drunk at Boodles and be knocked down by a taxi, of all things. And to do it just when war was in the air and all her friends were having such fun, joining the forces or getting jobs or throwing parties in their newly built air raid shelters. And it was worse than that. Johnnie had somehow gambled or muddled away their money, and there was practically nothing left. It had been a terrible shock, being widowed and penniless at one and the same time.

The pretty house near Peter Jones had to be sold, and for months and months Antonia had been stuck down in Sussex with the children and her in-laws – buried alive, just as surely as Johnnie was buried and dead.

Shattered by the loss of their younger son, and embarrassed by his improvidence, Lord and Lady Dulcimer could not do enough for his widow and three children. Poor little Antonia. They told her that she was not to bother her head about anything. Their kindness was stifling. There was no escape – not when the alternative was to be bogged down in Ireland with her own impoverished and far from doting parents. However, she persuaded the Dulcimers that she ought to do her bit for the war, and driving an ambulance for the East Grinstead Red Cross did give her a measure of escape. But sometimes she came close to screaming with boredom.

Two things kept her going. These were her occasional trips to London, where she had her hair cut, or lunched with friends or with cousin David Vorst. David adored her, and his boyish adulation was a refreshment to her spirits.

And sometimes, all too rarely, Dart came to Dulcimer Hall on leave. He had been so good to her after Johnnie died that they had grown very close in the past year. Once or twice they even managed to get away together for sweet stolen hours. Antonia had lived for these hours; but lately, with his divorce so nearly finalised, Dart had been elusive. He said they must be careful – a remark at which anyone but Antonia would have laughed. Antonia did not laugh. She missed Dart too much. Besides, she meant to marry him when he was free and felt a need to keep in touch.

The children saw little of Antonia now, what with her war work and her little trips to London. She slept late at weekends, and somehow they stopped going down to the drawing room to be read to. Maggie read to Abby, sometimes, though on many evenings she was too busy doing things for Nanny.

When Abby complained she was bored, Maggie advised her to stop moaning. There was no time for Maggie to be bored. None at all. She grew busier and busier, because so many of the servants had gone to join up, or to work in munitions factories. Before long it really did look as if there would be nobody young left to do the heavy work.

'You'd better watch out, Maggie,' said a blithely departing parlour maid. 'Cook and Mr Vestry and Mrs Hawkins will have you doing all their dirty work, not to mention Miss Trumpet, who thinks she owns you. You will have to learn to say no.'

'No need for me to say it,' retorted Maggie cheerfully. 'Nanny doesn't like me doing things for Downstairs. And if I do a job for Miss Trumpet, I don't mention it.'

This was true. Nanny declared that she was not going to have Maggie put upon. If she needed more work to do, Nanny would find it for her. All the same, it was rather harder to stand firm when Lord or Lady Dulcimer wanted to borrow her.

'Nice gal, that nursery maid of Antonia's,' said Lord Dulcimer, surprised that anything connected with his beautiful but idle daughter-in-law should be so obliging. 'Met her in the garden, and she said she would give a hand with the weeding. She says she would enjoy it.'

'Maggie is good with the Boys,' said Lady Dulcimer, whose life and thoughts were centred on her motley pack of male dogs. Their leader and her favourite was a Dalmatian called Walls. The second footman had recently joined the army, and nobody else wanted to take Walls for walks. The three other dogs were manageable, but Walls was nervous and aggressive. Sudden noises like bicycle bells or car horns sent him rushing into the attack.

'Maggie could take him on a lead when the children go walking.'

'It wouldn't be fair to ask her, Effie. Ten to one Walls would bite someone, or get into a fight.'

'Walls never bites people unless he feels threatened,' said the countess, getting to her feet. She was deaf enough never to hear things that did not suit her. 'Come along, my darlings. Let's go and see if Cook has got some bones for you.' She called the Boys out of their respective armchairs and sofas, and made her way out of the library on a wave of warm doggy smells.

'If only something would happen,' groaned Abby. 'I wouldn't mind what it was. Just something to change things.'

Maggie was unsympathetic. She was feeling low. Her brother Tom had just left.

Tom had enlisted in the Royal Navy, and when Lord Dulcimer heard that he planned to visit Maggie, he invited the young man to stay at the Hall. 'I'll lend him a rod, and he can go fishing. There's plenty of room in the attics nowadays.'

So Tom came, and even Nanny seemed to approve of Maggie's favourite brother. He ate his meals in the nursery, and treated Nanny with cheerful respect. But Tom's leave was over too quickly, and Maggie was in no mood to listen to Abby's latest grumbles.

'Changes are not always what you expect,' she said bluntly. 'Be thankful that you aren't a Norwegian child, with the Germans marching down the street and taking over everything.'

'I bet Norwegian children don't have to go for walks. They couldn't, could they, with all those fjords?'

Chapter 2

The sirens were wailing as David Vorst stepped off the darkened train into the cavernous gloom of King's Cross Station. One of the women behind him said something about 'moaning minnie', and the crowd of weary travellers shuffled towards the ticket barrier. Tin-hatted men with faintly glowing torches emerged out of the smoke-filled gloom and advised them to go down to the nearby shelter until the All Clear

The warden nearest to David was like a stage colonel with a loud hectoring voice. He was reminded of his Uncle Bernard Dulcimer in Sussex, who had been enjoying himself hugely during the past months, assembling and organising a private army of Defence Volunteers. Most of the weary band of travellers turned meekly towards the nearest shelters, responding to the voice of authority.

David withdrew behind a loaded trolley of crates and waited for them to go away. After stifling in the train for nearly twelve hours, he had no inclination to follow. It was more than likely that the raid was just another scare, caused by a single German reconnaissance plane, or someone in command of air raid precautions having a try-out. Since Dunkirk there had been quite a few of what David's Air Force friends called 'flaps' – air raid warnings without anything coming of them. Londoners were growing impatient with these false alarms, and some said they wished the Germans would stop messing about. This waiting was trying to the nerves.

David shouldered his leather grip and made his way out of the station. Outside in the deserted street the summer night was cool. Blacked-out houses loomed darkly on either side, and above the buildings searchlights from the parks probed the night sky. A barrage balloon flowered into view, trapped between two swords of light.

David drew several deep relieved breaths, savouring the freshness of the night air. He set off to walk home to the London Vorst Hotel, swinging along with the ease of one who could find his way blindfold if need be. There were few people about at this late hour. A policeman recognised him as he crossed Hyde Park Corner, and a lady on very high heels undulated hopefully out of a doorway in Piccadilly, but he merely nodded to each of them and walked on. He had pushed his way past the sandbags flanking the night door of the hotel when it was opened to him from the inside.

'Mr David! We was getting worried, Mrs Cornberg and me.'

'I told you not to stay up, Stebbings. My train was five hours late. Full of troops and people standing in the corridors, and nothing much to eat.' David had shared his picnic with a young mother with two tired children and some Tommies returning to their units after post-Dunkirk leave. 'Will there be anything in the icebox upstairs? I'm starving.'

'There's a chicken salad and a thermos of coffee in the drawing room, sir. Mrs Cornberg wanted to wait up and make you coffee, but I told her you'd like it left, knowing as how you don't like to be fussed.'

'Smart man,' said David. Mrs Cornberg was the elderly housekeeper at the London Vorst Hotel and, like the hall porter, one of David's oldest friends and allies. Weary as he was, he could still feel amused by the night porter's smug air of triumph. These two retainers had fought over him, scolded and cosseted him for as long as he could remember.

He waited while the old man locked up and made sure that the blackout screens were in place, and then strode towards the lift with his bag before Stebbings could wrest it from him. 'Thank you, but I'll manage. And I guess I can remember how to work the elevator. Go to bed, for Pete's sake.'

But there was no stopping the old man riding up in the lift, giving him a blow by blow recital of how worried he and Mrs Cornberg had been at his delayed return. There was no way of stopping him from coming into the spacious rooftop flat, fussing with the tray of food, switching on the electric fire. David had been managing director in charge of Vorst Hotels UK for the past year, was twenty-three years old and about, he hoped, to become a fighter pilot in the Royal Air Force – if only the red tape merchants would get a move on. But in the eyes of Stebbings and the older members of staff in the London Vorst Hotel he was still the boy who had been left in their charge while his parents were busy with other things. They thought of him as someone to be guarded, guided and looked after, and reminded to take his pocket handkerchief with him.

There was a small pile of mail, but nothing from the Air Ministry. Nor was there any letter from Antonia. 'No other messages for me?'

'Just two Western Union cables from the chairman, sir. And Mrs Kennedy's secretary phoned from the embassy. It seems the ambassador's lady would like you to ring when you get back.'

David grunted. Both his parents had been pulling out all the stops, raising hell, trying to get him to go back to the United States. His mother had always known Mrs Kennedy – 'that dearest Rose' as she called her – and was in constant communication with her. At a luncheon party at the embassy, a week or so back, both his host and hostess had taken him aside separately and told him how worried his parents were about his lingering in England when all the world knew that a German invasion was imminent. He owed it to them and to his country to return home. No need to get mixed up in the British war, they said, particularly when it was going so badly.

Still, David was not thinking of his parents. His thoughts were all for Antonia, and whether or not she would decide to marry Dart. His unease about this had been like an ache in his belly all day – ever since he had seen the newspaper report about Dart's decree nisi coming through. With an edge to his voice he said, 'Now, Stebbings, stop finding things to do, and go to bed. You've remembered to put a hot bottle in my bed, I hope?'

The old man's bald head jerked up, and he gave David a startled, rheumy look. Then he broke into a wheezing chuckle. 'Nearly got me that time, Mr David! All right, I'm just going.' With his hand on the knob, he added, 'There was a packet come this morning by special delivery. Mrs John Cary rang up from Sussex. She said we wasn't to leave it with your other letters, sir, so Mrs Cornberg put it on your dressing table next door. Mrs Cary said she wanted it to be a surprise.'

'Is that so?' David's thin, dark face showed no sign of his inner feelings. 'Well, see you in the morning, Stebbings. And thanks.'

A buff-coloured envelope lay on the polished mahogany. It was smaller than David's hand. It felt feather-light when he picked it up. He opened the envelope and slid the tissue-wrapped packet out. He held it in his hand for quite some seconds, knowing what it must contain, and dreading to find out beyond doubt.

He felt very little, just an odd sort of blankness, when Antonia's 'surprise' slid from the paper onto the dressing-table top. He stood looking down. It was a red satin rosette, the kind that they awarded to children in gymkhanas. In the middle he saw the words '2nd Prize' embossed in gold letters. Antonia had promised to tell him if ever she made up her mind to marry his cousin, Lord Dartmore. Evidently she had decided to do so.

David had warned Antonia that he was a bad loser. 'I'm a transatlantic savage, remember. In our schools nobody teaches us to lose gracefully, like you British in your sleepy games of cricket. We scream and yell at the umpire, and hate to be beaten.'

Still, when Antonia saw him waiting for her in Victoria Station the following morning, she thought he looked as usual – dark, thin as a wire and very pleased to see her. She knew a qualm of unease. Had he got her coded message? Perhaps he had not understood it.

He picked up her large cream hide suitcase and the smaller, matching dressing case. 'Travelling light, as usual?' he said. He always teased her about the amount of luggage she needed to take wherever she went. 'Are you sure it's enough for one night?'

23

He handed her into the front of his open car, before putting her cases in the dicky-seat. His car was a low-slung sports model with huge headlights and an engine that purred like a leashed tiger. It had been a twenty-first birthday present from his mother. Lately, due to petrol rationing, it had been penned up in the garage below the hotel. It had a most unpatriotic thirst.

'What's this, David? Have you become king of the black market all of a sudden?'

He glanced sideways at her, his eyes glowed, and his lean dark cheeks creased as he smiled. 'I decided to blow my last three months' coupons. I'm going to take you out to lunch. Is there anywhere special you want to go?'

Antonia looked at him uneasily. He really was looking extraordinarily cheerful. She said quickly, 'I don't mind where we go. You choose.'

'Fine,' he said, letting in the clutch. 'We'll go to Maidenhead and feed the swans. I booked a table at that hotel you like overlooking the river.' He glanced at her again. She was sitting tensely, a tendril of hair flying like gold silk against the brim of her close-fitting, exceedingly modish hat. He laid a brown hand on her tightly folded gloved ones and said gently, 'Take that pretty thing off your head and relax, honey. I got your message, and there's no need to say anything. Come and spend today with me, and I'll have you back in London well before Dart arrives.'

They ate expensively and well at the famous riverside hotel, which by a miracle had fresh Dover sole and strawberries to offer. They talked of all manner of things, of a play Antonia had been to, of her work in the East Grinstead Red Cross, of the discomforts of living at Dulcimer Hall with her in-laws. He asked about her children, which led her to tell him about the latest bad behaviour of Lady Dulcimer's dogs. They talked, indeed, of anything but what was uppermost in their minds.

Time passed. A group of red-tabbed army officers got up noisily and went out into the garden. More guests arrived, to be told that half the things on the menu were off. Green lawns sloped away gently to the paler green willows that fringed the sliding waters of the Thames. The sun shone golden. A muted clock-clocking of croquet balls came to them through the open French windows.

At length, a little tipsy with champagne and lack of sleep, David rose and held out his hand to her. 'What next? Shall we take a rowboat down the river, or drive on somewhere else? Or do you want to play croquet with those colonels? They looked as if they wanted to have you join them.'

She laughed up at him, her laughter like a chime of silver bells. Heads turned at nearby tables, and people smiled at the sound. Her enormous blue eyes were fringed with dark lashes. She was so lovely.

His bones seemed to melt in his body. He felt an anguished sense of loss, for he knew that for him this was the end of an idyll.

Antonia was feeling happy and full of goodwill towards the whole world. David was such a dear. Far too young to be taken seriously, of course, but there were times when she could almost believe herself in love with him. If it had not been for Dart . . . She smiled up at him. 'Anything but croquet, darling. We have croquet morning, noon and night at Dulcimer.'

'How come?' He pulled her to her feet and led her through the open windows onto a terrace. 'You told me that Uncle Bernard had ploughed up the lawns to plant vegetables – "digging for victory".'

'They play croquet on the tennis court nowadays. Dart brings his army friends when he gets leave, so that makes croquet part of the war effort. Comforts and recreation for the troops, you know.'

'Sure.' David's tone was dry. 'I only hope you're not marrying Dart just to help the war effort.'

'Oh, no.' Antonia, at her ease, was eager to talk about herself and Dart. She had spoken to David of her hopes before, for she was like a child in many ways, with a child's need to confide her hopes and fears. David was a good listener.

He handed her into a cushion-lined rowing boat, which the hotel kept ready for clients, and as he settled himself opposite and picked up the oars, she said seriously, 'All the people at Dulcimer have been expecting us to marry – the in-laws, the servants, all of them. As for my children, they absolutely adore their Uncle Dart. Now that he is free of Peggy, there really isn't any need to wait. It will make everybody happy.'

David looked at her. 'And are you so sure that Dart will make you happy, Antonia?'

'Of course.'

'He never had much success with Peggy.'

'Peggy didn't understand him.'

'Oh, Antonia . . .'

'No. Listen! Peggy tried to make Dart into something he could never be. She wanted to stop him gambling, from riding races, from having fun with his friends. American women take life so seriously.' She looked up guiltily, to find that David was laughing at her. He just could not help himself. He loved her more than ever when she was seriously silly. She said in a nettled tone, 'It's nothing to laugh at. I know you try to defend Peggy because you are both Americans, but you must admit she was a disaster.'

'She was spoiled and set on having her own way. But then, so is Dart.'

She smiled and blew him a mocking kiss with one slender hand. It was not often that she could goad David into criticising his rival, and she felt pleased. It showed that he was properly jealous, for all that he hid it so well. 'Dart needs me,' she said seriously. 'He's changed a lot since the war, you know. He looks gorgeous in his uniform, too! Oh, and did I tell you? He's been awarded the DSO.'

'Is that so?' In fact, David knew this already. His uncle, Lord Dulcimer, had rung him up to boast about his son and heir's latest achievement, brimming over with pride and the need to tell everyone. David had responded suitably. He was fond of his uncle, so he kept his thoughts to himself. Trust Dart to win a gong for dashing and foolhardy behaviour! There was an Errol Flynn quality about him. How many luckless people, David wondered cynically, had been killed taking the enemy-held farmhouse which had earned Dart his decoration for gallantry?

He pulled on an oar and the boat moved out into the faster water. 'So when is the wedding?'

'Soon, I hope.'

Antonia's thoughts slid away into a happy reverie. She considered what she might wear when she married Dart. Being a widow, and it being wartime, made the whole thing a bit of a puzzle. One thing was certain. She was not going to rig herself out in her Red Cross uniform, as one of her colleagues had done last month.

She was rather quiet on the way back to London. David made no attempt to distract her. Last night's train journey was beginning to catch up with him, and he needed all his willpower and concentration to keep awake.

Antonia's thoughts came to her in flashes, like lights going on and off in her mind. No need for white satin and a veil. Those old wedding photographs showed her as looking a positive dowdy on the day she married Johnnie Cary. Goodness. That was nearly twelve years ago. How long ago it seemed – another world. Dart had been best man at that wedding, and now he was to be her bridegroom.

It might be fun to be married in London and throw a party that evening. But would people come to a party, now that the blackout was making it so difficult to move about at night?

A country wedding? They could have a dance at Dulcimer. She loved dancing, and so did Dart. Their steps went so well together. And her little boys could be pages, and Abby a bridesmaid. A pity Abby was so skinny and freckled. She wondered if there would be time to have a wedding dress made. Material was hard to get, but she was sure that Stiebel would do something for her when he knew she was getting married again. It would be fun to come out of purdah, to start going to parties as Dart's wife!

She wondered where they would live. Until this moment she had not given it a thought. During the past months, Dart had stayed at his club when he was not with his regiment, so they would have to start afresh. She was glad. They might rent one of those flats in Marsham

26

Court. They were service flats, so there would be no need for any tedious housework or cooking.

In no time at all, it seemed, they were passing through Hyde Park – a strangely altered wartime park with no bright flower beds or nannies and nursery maids pushing prams. Instead, there were trenches and shelters, and anti-aircraft guns and trucks tucked in behind barbed wire. Two fat barrage balloons nodded high above the trees, and a group of tin-hatted men in khaki were getting ready to launch another, busying themselves round it as it lay wallowing, half deflated, like some stranded monster beside its anchoring truck.

'Such a shame, spoiling the park,' said Antonia. 'Nanny would have a fit, seeing her favourite haunts full of soldiers and bomb shelters.'

'It will be good to hear the guns when the bombs start to fall.'

Antonia shivered. 'You think there will be bombs?'

'Sure to be. It's just a matter of time.'

Suddenly the idea of a flat in Marsham Court lost a little of its allure.

They were drawing up in front of Lord Dulcimer's London house in Chesterfield Gardens. She turned to David to thank him for her lovely day. 'Such heaven, darling. I just can't thank you enough.'

'My pleasure, Antonia.' He was at his most formal, his face closed and unreadable. He went round to her side of the car and stood holding the door for her to get out. The fanlighted door of her father-in-law's mansion awaited her only yards away.

She felt a reluctance to go in. It had been a good day. In the past few hours, David had given her all the things she most liked and yearned for: exquisite food, champagne, admiration and a feeling of being cherished. She did not want it to end. 'Come in with me,' she said coaxingly. 'I'll give you a cup of tea.'

'I never drink tea, Antonia.'

'A Scotch and soda, then?'

'Not even that.' He waited for her to get out of his car, took the latch key from her gloved hand and went up the steps to open the door for her.

She said wistfully, 'Won't I see you again soon? Today has been so special, and I have so much enjoyed all those other times when you took me to eat at the Vorst. It's like a miracle to me, after Dulcimer, being warm and comfortable, and being treated like royalty in your lovely family hotel.'

He said gently, 'You could have it all the time if you married me, Antonia. You know that is what I want.'

'Darling David. If it wasn't for Dart, I would marry you tomorrow.'

He left her and drove back to the hotel. Her words burned in his mind, sharp as acid. If it wasn't for Dart. Damn Dart! At this moment he almost wished that his cousin *had* died on the Dunkirk beaches.

He left his car in the garage below the hotel, and went through the lobby without looking left or right.

The girl at the telephone switchboard looked after him as he strode long-legged and purposefully towards the lift. She knew that Mr David had been out in his car with Mrs Cary – just as every one of the hotel staff knew why he had been lingering in London all these months. Could it be that the widow had turned him down? Mr David had not looked at anyone else for months, even though Mrs Cary was well over thirty and far too old for him. Some people did not know when they were lucky.

David let himself into the penthouse flat and turned on the shower. People in wartime England were making a virtue of the fuel economy regulations, and he knew that he was fortunate to come home to the Vorst where the water was still kept hot. He loosened his tie, and sat down on the bed, weary and utterly dispirited. Antonia was going to marry Dart. They would go to Dulcimer at the weekend to celebrate Dart's DSO, and would declare their happiness to the world. Unbearable! Yet he knew that, for his uncle and aunt's sake, he would have to bear it. But after that he would get out.

He had been trying for months to get into the Royal Air Force. Perhaps being London-born had something to do with his strong feeling that this was his war, too. Now, for the first time, as he sat there trying to summon the energy to get under the shower, he found himself glad of the red tape that had delayed his acceptance as a fighter pilot. He would call that stuffed shirt at the Air Ministry in the morning, and tell him to forget it. Then he would cable his father in New York to say that he was coming home. The old man would be pleased, whoever else was not.

Antonia stood in the dark upper landing of the Chesterfield Gardens house, waiting for the sound of the caretaker's shuffling feet to fade away into the basement regions. The Dulcimer town house was a dismal place. She and John Cary had been married from it twelve years before. Even in those bright pre-war days, the flowers and the glittering chandeliers had done little to alleviate the prevailing brownness.

Antonia peered down the stairway – now covered with a fawn drugget – and recalled how she and Johnnie had stood there in their wedding finery, shaking hands with hundreds of smiling people they hardly knew, while Dart stood behind them making outrageous remarks.

The thought of Johnnie gave her an odd feeling. It was not guilt, exactly, but a spooky notion that he was looking over her shoulder. Johnnie had always been jealous of his elder brother, hating the way she and Dart had such fun together. She peered up the stairs where the grumbling caretaker had recently taken her suitcases, and gave herself a little shake. Johnnie was dead, buried in the family vault below Dulcimer church. This was her life now, and she was going to start living it to the full.

She ran lightly up the stairs, went into the sparsely lit bedroom, and began to pull dresses and underwear out of her largest case.

It had been beautifully easy to get away from Dulcimer. The London house was being loaned to a government department, and the insurers wanted an inventory of anything valuable that would be left. The matter was urgent, but Lord Dulcimer was too busy training the remaining estate workers to repel a German invasion, and Lady Dulcimer refused to leave her dogs. So when Antonia offered to attend to this chore, they were amazed and grateful.

'My dear! Are you sure?'

'But what about your ambulance, Antonia?'

It was hard not to laugh, particularly when Lady Dulcimer got in a fuss about her sleeping alone in the London house, and offered to send her personal maid. 'Such a dark, dreary place for you to be alone in, dear child. Trumpet could unpack for you and make sure your bed is aired.'

Antonia said seriously, 'Mother D, you're an angel. But what on earth would the Boys do without Trumpet?'

Lady Dulcimer had temporarily forgotten the all-important dogs, so the danger was averted; but the thought of a threesome made up of Dart, herself and the grim Miss Trumpet had been convulsing Antonia for days. She just could not wait to share the joke with him.

She washed quickly in lukewarm water, and was still wandering about in her new silk and lace camiknickers when she heard Dart calling her.

She hung over the banister rail, her hair fluffed up like a pale halo. Dart was standing on the drawing-room landing, his own fair head lighting up the dark stairwell, his tanned face upraised. He had a cocktail shaker in his hand and was smiling.

'Come down, Tonia The martinis are ready and I've brought a picnic from Fortnum's.'

'I won't be long. I'm just getting dressed.'

'You'll do as you are. Come down, or I'm coming to get you, and you'll miss your dinner.'

'Give me five minutes, angel.'

'Not a moment more. I've only got until midnight. After that I'll have to go. I need to be in Yorkshire for breakfast.'

She gave a squeak of dismay and rushed into the bedroom. She put on the dress with the easiest fastenings, snagged her best silk stockings which had been a present from David, and brushed her hair in feverish

29

haste. She was still dabbing on some of her precious pre-war scent when she went into the drawing room.

Dart was frowning and impatient by then. It took two martinis and her story about Trumpet to woo him back into good humour. And after that, she might just as well not have bothered to put her pretty dress on.

'Not here, Dart,' she protested, thinking of the caretaker. 'Upstairs.'

But upstairs would not do for him. Too cold, he said, tossing brocaded cushions off all the chairs and sofas and piling them in a great nest in front of the fire.

'Come and undress me, little sister-in-law.'

She obeyed him, trembling and already hot with desire, giggling at his way of addressing her. 'Johnnie would be furious if he could see us.'

'Revolving in the family vault, the bum,' said Dart, reaching behind her for the cocktail shaker. 'Now, shut up about Johnnie. You're here to think of me, and nobody else.' He topped up his glass, and then dribbled ice-cold martini onto her nakedness, bending down, teasing, probing and feathering sensitive places with his tongue. 'Mustn't waste good gin in wartime, must we?'

It was a tumultuous coming together for both of them, Antonia thought; better by far than the furtive, stolen times of the past months. They ate smoked salmon sandwiches and drank champagne and made love until the room grew shadowy with the ending of the summer day. Dart dozed, while Antonia lay beside him on the nest of cushions; wakeful, full of wonder and joyous content. She had known, of course, that Dart could be a ruthless and demanding lover. But this time, more than ever, he had shocked her, treated her like a whore, which she found immeasurably exciting. Never with Johnnie had her body been consumed by this flame of throbbing and abject desire.

'With my body I thee worship.' The words of the marriage service popped unbidden into her dreaming mind, and she spoke them aloud, pressing herself closer to him and caressing his nakedness. 'And this time, angel, it will be true. I never knew what worship was, until now.'

He opened eyes as blue as her own. 'Talkative woman, aren't you? What are you on about?'

'Just telling you that you are marvellous.'

'You're not that bad yourself,' he said, rolling over and pinning her down. His hands on her slender shoulders, he raised himself and grinned. 'You've come on a lot since the last time, Tonia. Who has been giving you lessons in that ambulance you drive so dutifully? Did he grumble about the discomfort as much as I did?'

'Don't, Dart. As if I would! You know very well that nobody matters to me but you. I adore you, and I don't care who knows it.'

Dart smiled. He believed her, smugly aware that he had a unique way with her. His narrowed eyes surveyed her flushing, imploring face. 'Little wanton, aren't you?'

'Yes,' she agreed eagerly. 'It's true. It's like a miracle. If only it could stay like this always.'

'Nothing is for always. It's different every time – or it should be. That was what went wrong with Peggy, all too soon. The first of a hundred things,' he added bitterly. 'God! How that woman hates me. Did you hear? She's taken Quentin away from Eton.'

'She can't have!'

'She can. She has. That crooked lawyer of hers has tied the thing up so tight that I haven't any say in what happens to my son. While I was choking my lungs out in the reek of Dunkirk, Peggy went down to the school and took him away on the next ship. Cabled me from Washington to tell me that she's sending him to Groton in September. The bitch!'

'Is that the American school that David went to?'

'If you choose to call it a school,' he retorted with easy Etonian arrogance. 'Apparently there's not a thing I can do about it. It may be years before I see Quentin again.'

'At least he'll be safe in America.'

'Safe!' he echoed explosively. 'That was what Peggy claimed when she took him away. In the boy's best interests, she called it. Safe from the terrors of war! Pampered and ruined by Peggy and her impossible parents, more like. He'll be taught to look on me as a villain.'

'Surely your lawyers would let you bring him back to England, once we're married and have a settled home.'

No sooner were the words out of her mouth than she felt the stillness in him. She caught her breath. He pulled away, but only to reach for a cigarette and light it. He said, without looking at her, 'I need another drink. We've finished the champagne but there's whisky over there on the table. Get some, there's a good girl.'

It pleased Dart to order her about. Half an hour earlier, even minutes before, she would have obeyed him happily, titillated by this lordly treatment. But the magic had gone, and in its place a cold trickle of doubt was seeping. She got up obediently, to gain time, reached for Dart's army jacket and put it round her shoulders. But she was shivering when she brought his whisky, and when she had handed it to him, she took a gulp from her own newly filled glass.

He patted the cushions, beckoning her to join him, but she shook her head. She stood a little way off, between him and the glowing fire, drowned by the khaki jacket, with only her slender ankles and bare feet to be seen below it.

They eyed each other. Antonia felt frozen, lost for words. She had been so sure of him, certain that he needed her as much as she wanted and needed him.

31

'Damn it, woman! What's this talk of marriage? I've only just got rid of one wife. I'm a free man. That's what we've been celebrating for the past two hours, surely?'

Her lips felt stiff. She said in a small voice, 'David said you were self-centred. I suppose he was right.'

He said impatiently, 'What has David got to do with it? Come here, and stop talking nonsense.'

'I . . . I thought you wanted me.'

'And who says I don't?' He reached over and pulled her down on her knees at his side. 'Darling Tonia. Don't spoil it. Let's enjoy each other while we have the time.'

She started to cry, silently, the tears brimming out of her huge blue eyes and running down her cheeks. She said, 'Everyone expects us to get married. You know they do.'

'I make a point of never doing what's expected of me,' he said curtly. 'Anybody who knows me at all, knows that.'

'But you said you loved me!'

'Oh, God!' he said rather helplessly. 'Don't you see? I've only just this minute escaped from Peggy. What is more, I've all but beggared myself doing it. Apart from anything else, I simply cannot afford to get married again.'

She stared at him. It had never occurred to her that Dart could ever be short of money. Johnnie had always felt bitter that the elder Cary son had everything, would inherit everything, while he was obliged to support a wife and three children on a meagre allowance. Dart, with his string of racehorses, his hunters, his habitual gambling for high stakes, had easily captured Antonia's admiration and envy; and his claim that he was actually short of money was little short of shocking. Surely he could not mean it?

He saw her amazement and pressed home his advantage. 'If you are looking for a well-heeled husband, dearie, you might do worse than one of the Vorst cousins. You could take the children to America, too. Aunt Chrissie has been writing to Mother for months, trying to get all the grandchildren across the Atlantic. Cousin Conway is a shade stodgy, but he's nearer your age than the boy David. Both of them are gold-plated, however.'

'Don't be vulgar,' she said pettishly. 'Anyway, I don't want to go to America.' She pulled one of the larger sofa cushions away from beside him, and put it back where it belonged, then picked up the empty glasses and carried them over to a tray at the side of the room.

'Oh, come on, Tonia. Stop flouncing about and sulking. We've less than an hour left. If you insist on making a scene, I'll take myself off to Yorkshire now.'

She said in a muffled tone, 'Perhaps that would be best.'

They dressed silently, like two strangers, at opposite sides of the room. Facing the fireplace, Dart knotted his khaki tie, his eyes following her reflection in the mottled glass above it. He had often teased her about being a quick-change artiste, and already she was fully dressed, putting the room to rights, plumping fat cushions back where they belonged on the long sofas.

He crossed the room and twirled her round to face him. 'Tonia, my love. Are you too busy playing the housewife to kiss me goodbye?' She eyed him coldly, refusing this mild blandishment, and he said, 'I very much hope that you'll have come out of your sulks before the celebration weekend. It won't do for you to spoil Pa's festivities with that sour face.'

She tossed her head. 'I may not be there. There are other people in my life besides you, Dart.'

'Oh?' It dawned on him why she was so put out. She had counted on appearing at his celebration as his bride-to-be. He decided to punish her for her effrontery. 'So where will you go? You can hardly shack up at the Vorst, because David will be at Dulcimer. Really, if you are so keen to get married again, you could do worse than grab David while he is so near and so devoted.'

'David is just a boy.'

'He's rich, though.'

Antonia said coldly, 'You make me sound like a gold digger.'

'There are worse things to dig for than gold, Antonia mia. You should think about it.'

Dart's words had been spoken in a spirit of affectionate mockery. He would have been surprised to know how soon Antonia began to consider his advice. That night in her chilly upstairs room, she began to wonder what it would be like to be married to David Vorst.

He was young, certainly, but on the credit side he was wealthy, nice looking in a thin, dark way, had lovely manners and an amusing turn of phrase. Most important of all, he adored her and wanted nothing more than to please and cherish her. What matter if he was a little younger than herself? Young people were more malleable than those who had grown set in their ways.

She had been so sure of Dart, sure that he would marry her the very minute he was free. He had lured her into believing that he was serious, had taken his pleasure and then dumped her, leaving her jilted like some village maiden. He doubtless assumed that she would go meekly back to prison life at Dulcimer. She fumed. Dart needed to be taught a lesson.

David. He was a dear boy. And he had asked her several times to marry him – only until now she had never taken him seriously.

She would ring him in the morning, and ask his help with Father Dulcimer's inventory. David might very well make a charming husband. And if they did get married, she was willing to bet that Dart would not like it one little bit!

Early next morning David went to his office. There were things to do before he went home to America. He would have to appoint someone to take his place, and the sooner the better.

He was sitting at his desk, feeling rather empty, when the door opened. Odette Steiner came in with coffee and the day's letters on a tray.

He smiled at her, but at the sight of her white, drawn face, got up and went over. 'What has happened? Have you had news?' He took the tray from her, and said curtly in French, 'Sit down and tell me.'

She obeyed him, seeming to crumple into a low chair. She was a small woman, usually quick and elegant in her movements. Today she looked like an old woman. Her lips parted. No words came. David had managed to get Odette and her children out of France in May, only days before the Germans came. It had been a nightmare journey, and he had more than once marvelled at her courage and the way she had adjusted since then to life in England, despite her constant gnawing anxiety for her husband, Michel. This morning she was plainly in shock.

He turned away from her and poured coffee for both of them. 'Drink this. Take your time. You look as if you need it, and I certainly do.' He perched on the edge of his desk and sipped some of the fragrant brew, while she struggled to regain her composure.

She was dimly grateful for his matter-of-fact manner and drank the coffee. In a little while she told him what she had learned.

'I went down to the transit camp.' She saw his dark brows draw together, and added quickly, 'I know you told me not to go, and you were right. It was a dreadful place. But, David, I had to. There was a man there who told me about Michel . . .' Her voice shook, but she went on, 'He met up with another Jewish family while they were waiting for a boat to take them across the Channel. They were in the hotel business too, and they had heard. They said that some men picked Michel up on the steps of the Paris Vorst, and that he was driven away in a car. Just one day before the Germans came.' For a moment, Odette bowed her smooth dark head, and put her hands over her face. Her voice was muffled. 'He left it too late . . .'

David was appalled. Michel Steiner had run the prestigious Hotel Vorst in Paris with skill and flair for over ten years. David had been sent to France to be trained by him, and had become greatly attached to the Steiners. They had taught him so much, had taken him into their family, shared their many interests with him, as though he was their own son. In some ways, Michel Steiner had behaved more like a father to him than Cornelius Vorst had ever found time to do.

34

When Cornelius had arranged for David to take over the management of the British hotels – his first important job within the business – David had implored Michel Steiner to leave France as well. But he had refused. He was a Jew, he said, but he was also a Frenchman. His place was in Paris, at the Vorst, which he had built up and nurtured over the years, until many discerning people preferred it to the Crillon or the Ritz. Michel had been adamant that he would not leave and had changed the subject.

'You will do well in London, David. Clients will like having a member of the Vorst family to welcome them. Clients are the same the world over.'

'I hope to do all right. But, Michel, you would do even better. If there is a war, you would be safer with the Channel between you and those Nazis.'

'Safety is not everything.'

The Steiners had a holiday house in Normandy, to which Odette took the children in summer when Paris grew too hot. Getting Michel to the Mas was a rare achievement, and Odette told David that he ought to feel honoured. For no one else had Michel ever agreed to leave his precious Paris Vorst for five whole days. This was to be David's last day in France. The next day he would take his car over on the ferry to Dover, and the Steiner family planned to see him off before driving back to Paris.

Only when they were on the quayside did Michel talk again about leaving France. Odette and the children had gone to watch a yacht weigh anchor, and Michel said suddenly, 'If the Germans invade France, I shall want to get Odette and the children away. You will do that for us, David, if I cannot?'

David promised. They even arranged a code word to be sent by the British Embassy, laughing at themselves for being melodramatic. The code had worked when it was needed, and David had kept his promise. But as Odette turned her ravaged face to look at him, he wondered fleetingly whether he had done her a service by bringing her away. Michel had been right. Safety was not everything.

Common sense reasserted itself. Odette needed bolstering, not maudlin sympathy. He said, with a firmness he did not feel, 'Odette, just think. What you learned today was rumour, not proof. Michel may have been picked up by friends. Anyway,' he added when she seemed about to argue, 'you must try not to lose hope. You have to think of Josef and Marie. Wherever Michel is, that is what he would expect of you.'

She said bitterly, 'Easy for you to say that. I should never have left him. You thought yourself a hero, didn't you, coming to rescue me? Two great stupid men, planning so cleverly to take me and the children out of France and ruining my life! If I had been there, I would not have let Michel stay so long.'

He did not deny it. He merely said, 'Where are Josef and Marie this morning?'

She said dully, 'With my friend in Chelsea. I left them with her yesterday, before I took the train to Sussex. She offered to keep them today, and I let her. I . . . I am a coward. I must think what to say to them, but I am too frightened to think. How do you tell two little children that their father has been taken away by the Gestapo – perhaps at this very moment is being tortured or killed by them?'

'You don't know that, Odette. When you see Marie and Josef you must try to go on as you have been doing since you left Paris. Just be your cheerful self, and tell the kids that Michel will join you soon.'

She said despairingly, 'Cheerful? It has never been anything but pretending.'

'Do you think I don't know it?' He grasped her cold hands in his own long-fingered warm ones, and gave them a little shake. 'Just go on pretending.'

'David,' said Odette wearily, 'I have no strength to pretend any more.'

'Not today, maybe. But it will come back, when you see the children again. Leave them with your friend today and try to get some sleep.'

He began flipping unseeingly through his letters, finding it hard to bear the anguished accusation in her eyes. He added gruffly, 'And as for calling yourself a coward, Odette, you have to be the bravest woman I know.'

He went out presently, hailed a passing taxi, and paid a visit to the offices of the Cunard Line. Having made up his mind to go back to America, he wanted to book his passage. But the place was crowded to the doors with people clamouring for tickets to the United States or Canada. He did not stay. He would cable his father. Cornelius Vorst would doubtless have strings to pull. For once he would ask his father to pull them.

He could not get the Steiners out of his mind. His unhappiness at losing Antonia seemed suddenly rather puny compared to what might be happening to Michel Steiner.

When he returned to his office, the telephone was shrilling. He heard his name, spoken in a thread of a whisper.

He said in sudden sharp anxiety, 'Antonia? Is that you?'

'David.' Her voice was stronger, but muffled as though she had caught a cold in the night. 'It's Father Dulcimer's wretched lists. I can't find half the things. Would you have time to help me?'

David's heart began to pound. 'Sure I'll help. But you sound terrible, Antonia. Do you need a doctor?'

'It's you I need, darling. Please come.'

'I'll be right over.'

36

Chapter 3

Lord Dulcimer's party to celebrate Dart's medal was to take place on the last weekend in June, the same weekend that a service of thanksgiving for the miraculous escape of the British troops from Dunkirk was planned. This seemed appropriate to Lord Dulcimer, since Dart had been one of those evacuated from Dunkirk.

People were urged to help with the church flowers, the ladies of the church sewing circle made coloured bunting out of scraps of material which would be hung across the village street for a whole week. There was to be a church parade, a school pageant with the Scouts and Guides and all the schoolchildren taking part. Inevitably Lord Dulcimer's Defence Volunteers would be marching with the rest. He drilled them mercilessly, and insisted that there should be a dress rehearsal before the event.

'It won't do to get the timing wrong. If we are having a parade, we must do it properly.'

'Nonsense, Bernard,' said Mrs Harriby, the most vocal of the organisers. 'It's just a simple affair. What do we need a rehearsal for?'

But there were others who thought it might be a good idea, and it was arranged, despite Mrs Harriby's complaints that it would make extra work. But what nobody had foreseen was the unheralded arrival of a score of children from the East End of London on the eve of the rehearsal.

Their arrival was far from welcome. Miss Climpson, the village dressmaker, who was delivering a dress for Lady Dulcimer, said that everyone was at sixes and sevens. 'Just fancy, Nanny,' the little dressmaker said as she sipped a restorative cup of tea in the nursery, 'more than twenty of them, and some of them with nothing but their gas masks and the clothes they were sent in. The WVS woman who brought them had ten other children to take on to Haywards Heath. She just dumped ours on the vicar and ran.'

Abby said hopefully, 'Do you think any of the new children will be sent to live here?'

'Not if I have anything to say in the matter,' said Nanny. 'Slum children, I don't doubt. They would never fit in.'

'But where will they go?' Abby longed for other children to play with, and if they were actually in the house, even Nanny could not stop her from seeing them. Not all of the time.

'I have no idea. It's none of our business.'

'Why are so many coming, all of a sudden?'

'Because there may be bombs, and Mr Churchill has told them they should.' Nanny was full of Mr Churchill these days, with hardly a word to say about Mr Chamberlain, who had been a great favourite of hers last summer. Very unfaithful of her, Abby thought.

'How I wish some of them would be sent here,' she said

'Wish as hard as you like,' said Nanny. 'If wishes were horses, beggars would ride.'

The Higgins children were the dirtiest and most tiresome of a far from appetising bunch of evacuees from the East End of London. There were four of them, and Bert, the eldest, was the most dreadful boy. His language brought some of the hurriedly formed reception committee close to swooning. Bert said that he and his brother and two sisters must stay together, and nobody wanted to have them. Not all four.

'Now, dear,' said the vicar's wife, 'be reasonable.' Her own house was full, what with a married daughter and three children, and two evacuees of pre-Dunkirk issue. 'Why not let Ivy and little Joe go with Mr and Mrs Gantry? It's only for tonight, you know. Tomorrow we will try to find you somewhere where you can be together.'

'No,' said Bert.

'Just who are you to keep saying no to everyone?' demanded Mrs Harriby. She was chairman of the reception committee and had spent the past three hours bullying people into accepting children they had never meant to have. But she had met her match in Bert. Her right hand was bandaged. He had bitten her when she had tried to manhandle him out of the way, and the wretched Gantrys were already sidling towards the church hall door in some relief. 'If you don't behave yourself I shall send for the police, and you will find yourselves locked up for the night.'

Ivy burst into shrill wails at this, and the vicar's wife said wearily, 'That's not very helpful, Constance.' She turned back to Bert and the others, and said through a descant of Ivy's cries, 'Nobody is going to lock any of you up. But you should try to think what is best for the little ones, Bert. They must be very tired after their early start and having to wait around here all morning.'

Bert said nothing. He would have died rather than admit it, but he was bone weary himself – worn out and fed up with battling against all these women who were bent on taking the girls and little Joe away. Well, he had learned his lesson the first time they had been evacuated, almost eight months before. They had gone with their school that time, and being in different classes the four of them had been split up

38

and had not set eyes on each other again until Mum suddenly turned up and brought them all back to Stepney. 'Never again,' she had said when she saw the state little Joe was in.

After Dunkirk, though, people started sending their kids off again, and she had changed her mind. But this time Bert had promised to look after the girls and Joe, and no busybodying bitches were going to stop him.

Still, Bert felt caught, besieged, and was wondering what on earth to do. He was a stubborn boy, but he was also a realist, and talk of the police had shaken him. There was not much that an eleven-year-old boy could do if the police started coming into it. He didn't have a leg to stand on really, and he felt helpless.

Mrs Harriby was feeling much the same. She had drawn a group of the ladies together, and said fiercely, 'That settles it. I shall have to ring the Hall.'

'You had better ask for Lord D, then,' said one of the women. 'Lady D won't come to the telephone. She always gets Miss Trumpet to answer it. Being deaf, you know.' It was tacitly acknowledged that Trumpet would be a harder nut to crack than either of her employers.

But Mrs Harriby knew that the earl was practising for the parade and would not be at home. 'I shall demand to speak to Effie Dulcimer. It's about time they did their bit, and so I shall tell her.'

'They took in several children last autumn, Constance.'

'No they didn't. All their evacuees were billeted with the estate workers. They never had any in the house.'

'They have all the grandchildren and their nannies staying, and several relatives from London. Quite a houseful.'

'That is perfectly true,' said Miss Climpson, the little dressmaker. 'And they are very short-staffed. Nanny told me that the housekeeper cannot get a laundry maid for love nor money.'

'Dear me,' said Mrs Harriby acidly, 'now we really know there's a war on.' This raised a titter. 'May I use the vicarage telephone?'

The vicar's wife nodded, but after Mrs Harriby had hurried away, she looked rather doubtfully at the four Higgins children. Ivy was still snivelling and running at the nose. Rita had started crying drearily in her turn, and little Joe had wet his trousers. She could not think that this family would fit in at Dulcimer Hall.

Bert slapped Rita and told her to shut her bleeding row, and bent down to mop at Joe's legs with their one towel, keeping a wary eye on the bitches all the while. They had moved a little away, and were standing in a bunch, yapping among themselves in their funny plummy voices. The head bitch had gone to use the phone.

Bert slid his eyes around cautiously, without turning his head. There was a door near them. It was open, and through it he could see trees and green grass; greener even than Green Park which he had been to once, when Mum took him and Rita up west to see the coronation parade. He decided not to stay for the police to find them. No sense in that. He grabbed little Joe and Ivy by their sticky hands, and jerked his head at Rita to follow. All four sidled towards the open door.

Mrs Harriby came back and reported disgustedly that there was no answer from the Hall. It was only then that someone noticed that the Higgins children had vanished.

Next to mealtimes, walks were the bane of Abby's life.

Every single afternoon, rain or shine, they walked down the beech avenue to the great iron gates, turned right down the main road leading to the village. They went through the village, in through the farm gates, past the farm buildings and up the long, steep west drive. Sometimes they stopped in the village shop, where Nanny chatted with the postmistress, or bought stamps. Occasionally there was a newborn calf to see at the farm. But essentially it was always the same old round.

This Friday they met Constable Starkey on his bicycle, looking for some lost evacuees. Had they seen them? He was the first of several people to ask this question. Some boy scouts went by at a jog trot, on their way to search the common.

At the far end of the village street, they met Mrs Harriby who was standing by her gate, looming over her ancient gardener and instructing him about clipping a hedge. She had seized the shears out of his hand, to show him how to do it. She looked hot and cross, and one of her hands was bandaged. She, too, told Nanny about the Higgins children, brandishing the shears, gnashing them together as though she wanted to chop the lost children into pieces. The vicar's wife came along in her wheezing car. She jerked to a stop beside the prams. She had been halfway to East Grinstead, and still no sign. It was a great worry.

Nanny promised to keep an eye out, and the nursery party pressed on. Nanny said that it was to be hoped that they would not meet the Higgins children. 'Running away before they've barely come, and acting so wild!' she said to Maggie, sniffing her disapproval. 'Slum children. Nits in their hair and rickets, I shouldn't wonder. That sort never settle. With luck they'll find their way back to London before anyone stops them.'

Abby trudged along, hot, uncomfortable and disgruntled in her tidy summer coat. Blue linen, it was, with stitched cream cuffs and collar. Nanny always made them dress up on fine afternoons. Country clothes were for mornings only. Nanny herself went hatted and gloved as though for Hyde Park, pushing Jamie in the high black and cream pram. Maggie sweated along in a dark blue gaberdine mackintosh, with a deep felt pot of a hat pulled over her eyes. It was her arduous

40

duty to propel the mailcart – a sit-up-and-beg affair with caned sides which had been at Dulcimer since the beginning of time. Miles and the fat dachshund rode in it when their legs got tired. Abby's legs got tired too, but nobody bothered about them.

'Come along, Abby! Don't dawdle,' said Nanny sharply, looking back over her shoulder, eyes beady under the brim of her dark felt hat with its summer trimming of navy and white grosgrain ribbon. 'Why are you walking in that silly way?'

'I need to go, Nanny.'

'Nonsense. Of course you don't.'

'I do!' Abby clutched herself, miming desperation. She added, without much hope, 'Why don't I run back across the paddock?'

'Nonsense,' said Nanny again. 'You will do no such thing.' She turned an accusing eye upon Maggie. 'You should have made sure she went to the lav before we started.'

'I told her to, Nanny,' said Maggie.

'Well, then. She will just have to wait until we get back to the house.' Nanny started pushing the pram again. Maggie hurried to catch up. With Miles and Benjie tucked together in the mailcart, it was hard enough keeping up with Nanny on the last steep stretch, without giving her a head start.

Abby trailed along, scuffing her polished lace-up shoes and kicking crossly at pebbles as she walked. Before long, she was well behind the prams, and what had started as a pretence had become a real need. She truly was desperate to go. The others were twenty yards ahead, their backs turned. Abby picked her way over the cattle grid, and without daring to look at Nanny at all, pushed her way through some dense rhododendron bushes until she reached the pine wood.

She hoisted up her linen coat, groped with hasty hands under her cotton dress to unbutton her knickers from her liberty bodice. She pulled her knickers down and squatted over a springy bed of last year's pine needles. The fawn ground darkened between her knees. Blessed, blessed relief!

A snigger. More sniggers, coming from the branches above Abby's head. She jerked upright, clutching her underpinnings and glaring upwards, face hot and eyes startled.

The Higgins family looked down at Abby, all four of them laughing fit to bust.

'Well,' said Maggie later, 'you wished for more children, and more children is what you got.'

'Nobody could wish for that awful Bert!' fumed Abby.

'Och, away! He's not so bad.'

'You just don't know!' said Abby, her face hot as she remembered. 'He's as bad as he can be. Anyway, look at the trouble he's caused.'

'He wasn't to know, was he?'

'You're as bad as Grandpa.'

Maggie gave up trying to argue with Abby. She seemed really upset. But, one way and another, it had been an upsetting afternoon. One minute Maggie had been panting and pushing along, with Nanny still a few paces ahead. Miles lolled back comfortably in the mailcart, playing with Benjie's ears. It might have been just another ordinary afternoon. The next minute, a car appeared out of nowhere. Out of this car came Mrs John, almost tumbling out of it in her eagerness.

'Darlings!' she cried, in her breathless, silvery voice. Maggie thought that she looked even lovelier than ever. She was all smiles, and wearing a pretty new hat and coat. Miles was half out of the mailcart before she reached him. A dark young man followed more slowly, unfolding his thin length out of the low-slung car. He seemed content to stand there, leaning against the bonnet, while Antonia and Miles clasped each other joyously – the fair-headed little boy and his even more silvery-haired mother. It was a pretty sight and, like the dark man, Maggie found herself smiling.

Nanny lifted Jamie out of his pram and brought him over to be kissed and hugged in his turn. 'Say hello to Mummy, there's a good boy.' Benjie was barking his head off. Then, on top of all this, Lord Dulcimer came out of the wicket gate beside the drive, looking hot and spherical in khaki battle dress and a forage cap. There was a whistle hanging from a chain round his neck.

'So, there you are! David, you young rascal! Just like a true Vorst, stealing a march on us all, eh?' He shook hands with the dark young man, looking past him at the long, dusty green car in mock disgust. 'Good God! I was sure that the war would put paid to that hideosity. It must drink petrol.'

'It certainly does,' said the man called David. He had a deep, rather slow voice – quite different to what Maggie had expected. She thought it made him sound older than he looked. 'But we thought we should travel in style, just this once, it being a special occasion.'

'You're right about that! Your Aunt Effie nearly fell off her chair when I told her your news.' The earl came forward and gave his daughter-in-law a smacking kiss and a hug. 'Have you told the kids yet, Antonia?'

But Antonia, frowning a little, was looking about her. 'Where is Abby, Nanny? She doesn't know yet, does she? I wanted to tell her myself.'

'You told me not to tell her, madam, so I didn't. Now, where can she have got to? She was here only a minute ago,' Nanny added, with a little cluck of annoyance. She looked back down the drive, past the long dark green car. 'Maggie. Run back and call her, do! She can't be far.'

But there was no need for Maggie to call. Abby was already stalking out of the bushes, pink-faced and hitching at the clothes around her middle. Following at her heels were the four Higgins children, giggling at some joke. All four carried gas masks in cardboard cases and wore identification labels pinned to their jerseys. Little Joe had discarded his wet trousers, and his legs twinkled along under his flapping shirt tails like grubby sticks of celery with boots on.

'Go away!' hissed Abby.

'Not bleeding likely,' said Bert, keeping in step at her shoulder. 'Cor! Look at that racing car!'

'Just leave me alone!' Abby walked faster. Suddenly she saw who it was, and started running. 'Mummy! You've come! Nanny says you have got something to tell us.'

'Darling Abby!' Abby was folded into Antonia's scented embrace. 'You remember Cousin David, don't you?'

Abby looked blankly at her mother, and said uncertainly, 'Cousin who?'

'No, of course she doesn't remember me,' said David. 'We only met for a moment, last winter.' He looked down at Antonia and her small daughter, and held out his hand. 'Hi there, Abby.'

Abby gave a quick startled glance from David to her mother, and shook the outstretched hand like an obedient child at a dancing class.

Antonia smiled brightly. Maggie had a feeling that Mrs John was nervous of Abby for some reason. 'I was telling David that you hated walking. How would you like a ride in his lovely car?'

'No room in the car with all your bags and packages, Antonia. Abby and Miles will have to stand on the running board.'

Abby looked from the car to David, and back. Maggie could see that she was puzzled, even a trifle wary.

'Abby!' Antonia's voice was sharp. 'Where are your manners?'

All the others were by this time looking at the four Higgins children. Lord Dulcimer was eyeing them with open curiosity, and the children looked back at him, their eyes like saucers in their grubby faces. But it was David who spoke to them first.

'What about you others? Want to come with us?'

Bert said cautiously, 'Come where?'

'Mercy me!' exclaimed Nanny, marching round the bonnet of David's car to take a good look at them. 'It's the missing evacuees. The whole village has been out looking for them. I promised to watch out for them.'

'It looks as if you've found them then, Nanny,' said David with a smile.

'Such trouble as you've caused!' Nanny went on in a scolding tone. 'Even the vicar was out looking for you. And the police, you silly children.'

43

'What for? We ain't done nothing,' said Bert, taking a step backwards.

'You call it nothing, biting poor Mrs Harriby? You ought to be ashamed of yourself.'

Lord Dulcimer gave a crack of laughter. 'Bit her, did you? Brave chap, taking on that old warhorse.'

Nanny darted the earl a look which would have quelled most people. 'Mrs Harriby was trying to find billets for them. It's no easy matter, milord, with a whole new lot arriving. And these ones . . .' She caught sight, suddenly, of little Joe's bare limbs, and said sharply, 'What's happened to that poor mite's trousers?'

'He took 'em off,' said Bert with a shrug. 'They was wet, see.'

Nanny turned away to tell Maggie to fetch a blanket out of the mailcart, and in a moment had Joe wrapped like a papoose from the armpits down. She remarked crossly, 'This child needs a bath. If they hadn't wasted all afternoon running away, he would be in bed and asleep by now.'

'What did you run away for?' demanded Lord Dulcimer.

Bert swallowed. He had caught sight of the whistle round the earl's neck. 'You a p'liceman, then?'

'Of course he isn't,' said Abby scornfully. 'You don't know much if you don't know what a policeman looks like.'

'Be quiet, Abby. Now, boy?'

Bert took a step closer, sensing an ally in the stout man in the khaki clothes. 'I promised Mum I wouldn't go nowhere without Ivy and Rita and Joe. But see, guv'nor, none of them women has room for all of us.'

Lord Dulcimer met Bert's brown eyes. He shrugged and said simply, 'You'd better hop onto David's running board, then. We'll find room for you all at Dulcimer.'

Nanny's face was a study. Maggie had to clench her teeth together hard to stop herself laughing out loud. But with the clamour and excitement of Antonia and David driving off with the older children clinging on both sides, nobody would have noticed what she did. Nor did Nanny say anything about the London children when they started on their way up the last bit of the drive. Lord Dulcimer walked beside her, and possibly Nanny did not feel up to voicing her disapproval directly to his lordship. Maggie, pushing Joe Higgins and Benjie knew that she would have plenty to say later.

When they reached the front door, the children were grouped around David, begging for another ride.

'Just one more!' Abby's face was flushed with excitement and pleasure.

'One more turn! One more!' cried the others.

But David had already switched off the engine and was handing

Antonia out of the passenger seat. He looked down at her. 'Shall I tell them, honey? Or will you?'

'Yes, Mummy,' put in Abby, coming back to things that really mattered. 'Nanny has been hinting all day. Do say what it is.'

Miles was clinging to his mother's hand, looking up at her adoringly. She ruffled his tow-coloured hair, but she looked at Abby.

'Haven't you guessed yet, darling? David is my surprise. We were married yesterday morning. I've brought you a new daddy.'

Maggie never forgot the picture they all made. She and Nanny had just heaved the heavy mailcart with the swaddled Joe in it up the steps, and they stood there together, Nanny holding Jamie in her arms. Lord Dulcimer had a finger on the front door bell, saying that they needed Vestry. Mrs John in her pert little veiled hat stood below with her hand on her new husband's arm, and beyond them Bert was fingering the bulb of the car horn. His sisters and Miles stood round him. Abby was a little apart from the rest. Her face was drained of colour, the freckles standing out clearly, her eyes dark with shock.

Nanny moved suddenly, handed Jamie over to Maggie, and started down the steps.

Antonia said in an imploring tone, 'Abby . . .'

Abby spoke slowly, as though something was sticking in her throat. 'Mummy. You couldn't. I thought . . .'

'Darling . . .'

'I just don't believe it . . .'

But that was as far as it got. Bert gave in to irresistible temptation and gave three vigorous squeezes on the bulb of the car hooter just as Vestry opened the front door. A furious horde of barking dogs plunged past the butler, led by the spotted Walls in full cry. Nanny was swept off her feet, and went down under the rampaging pack. There were shouts, screams from the children and Antonia. Maggie just managed to snatch Jamie and Joe Higgins out of the way, and heard Lord Dulcimer roaring at the dogs to behave.

'Stupid boy!' yelled Abby furiously at Bert.

It was all over in an instant, really. The dogs, bewildered by the noise, dashed off down the drive in search of prey. David went down on one knee beside Nanny. 'Are you all right? Just stay still for a moment and catch your breath.'

'Those dreadful Boys, Nanny!' cried Antonia, also leaning over her. 'They ought to be shut up.'

Nanny's face was the colour of a dirty dishcloth. She managed to say in a labouring tone, 'You ought to have let me tell Abby, Mrs John. She wasn't ready . . . she thought . . . she hoped . . .'

That was all Nanny managed to say before she fainted dead away.

Chapter 4

'Caught you with your trousis down, Westy,' said Bert, later. 'Girls are always in trouble when they need to pee.'

'Better than some people, who can't tell the difference between a cow and a bull,' retorted Abby coldly. 'Lucky for you that I was around to rescue you that time you decided to go milking.'

Bert grinned at her. 'Where I come from, milk comes decent in bottles or tins, not warm and foaming in cans, like here.'

'Ugh!' They both laughed. They hated the milk at Dulcimer, which came to the table still warm from the cow. Bert got away with drinking it in tea, but Nanny made her children drink it plain.

Bert was lucky that Abby had been there when he was chased by the bull, and he knew it. She had waved her arms and shouted to distract the animal's attention while he legged it to the fence. The fright he got with the bull made them quits. For a girl she was not half bad, he told her, for all that she needed keeping in her place at times.

There were moments when Bert caught himself looking at Abby, wondering just how differently things would have turned out if he had not followed her out of the bushes that day. If Abby had not been taken short under the pine trees, Bert felt sure that they would never have got to stay at Dulcimer Hall.

Bert was not the only one to think how strangely things had turned out. Maggie was astounded by it, whenever she had time to think. There was very little thinking time, what with coping with four extra children as well as the three Carys.

Such changes! Within the space of a day, the whole shape of their lives was turned upside down, and for Maggie more than anyone.

Lord Dulcimer had decided that the four children from Stepney should stay at Dulcimer. He also declared, with a decisiveness that he usually kept for Home Guard affairs, that it was ridiculous for the grandchildren to be catered for in the faraway nursery wing. From now on, the children and their assorted keepers were to have their main meals in the dining room, and tea in what used to be the still room, beside the pantry.

'Feed the herd together. Saves money. Saves food, too. Good farming practice, Vestry.'

'Is that so, my lord?' said the elderly butler blankly. 'In that case I shall endeavour to ascertain if there are enough extra leaves for the dining-room table.'

'Good God, Vestry! I'm not having a lot of chattering children round me while I eat. Bring the ping-pong table in and put it in the bay window at the north end. They can eat there.'

'The two sofas for her ladyship's dogs are situated in that part of the room,' Vestry reminded him.

'Then they will have to be moved somewhere else. I'll tell her ladyship that the Boys must make adjustments, like the rest of us.'

Vestry almost smiled. 'And the four new evacuees, my lord? Are they to be fed with the ... the herd?'

'Of course. What d'you think all these new arrangements are in aid of, man?'

Vestry closed his eyes momentarily. 'Just as you wish, my lord.'

Maggie very much doubted if even Lord Dulcimer would have got away with this if Nanny had been there to do battle with him. But Nanny was in hospital for three whole days.

Nanny's leg was not broken, which was at first suspected. It was badly bruised, however, and she had torn muscles and was in a great deal of pain, so she was kept in hospital until they judged she was no longer suffering from shock.

'Nothing to the shock I suffered when I got back,' Nanny told the local doctor tartly. 'I told them it was only a sprain. But those young hospital doctors think they know it all.'

'You will still have to take it easy, Miss Jones,' said the doctor firmly. 'You should try to keep that leg up as much as you can. No more walks for a month or so.'

'What heaven!' said Abby gleefully. 'Now we shall have time to do things.'

'That's not a nice way to talk,' said Maggie reprovingly. 'Nanny's leg is still hurting her badly. You should be sorry, not glad about it.'

'Well, I am sorry for Nanny, but I can't help being pleased for myself,' said Abby unrepentantly. 'Admit it, Maggie. It's much more fun eating with everybody downstairs and being free in the afternoons.'

'Speak for yourself. Nanny wants me to push her out to the summerhouse.'

'That won't take you long.'

'I can't leave her there all by herself. Someone has to keep an eye on the little ones at the sandpit, at least until Miss Brimley has had her lunch and a nap at her sister's house, and is free to sit with Nanny. After that, Cook wants me to pick strawberries.'

'Bert and I might help, if you like.'

'You ate twice as many as you picked, last time. Cook needs the strawberries for jam.'

'There's strawberry fool for lunch tomorrow,' said Abby dreamily. 'And cakes for tea. They've been saving cream and eggs and sugar for weeks because of Uncle Dart's weekend. Cook and Trumpet are sorry for him because Mummy went off and got married to that David man.'

'Stand still,' said Maggie, who had herself been feeling rather sorry for Abby. 'How can I tie your hair ribbon if you shoogle around like that? Nanny will have something to say if she sees you looking untidy.'

'Not if I don't go near the summerhouse, she won't. Bert is waiting for me.'

It had not taken Abby long to change her mind about Bert. He was more fun than Quentin; more fun than anyone Abby had ever played with. Bert and his sisters attended the village school, but on his return he usually came to look for Abby. 'You ready yet, West?'

'Why does he call you West?' Miles wanted to know.

Abby shrugged. Bert had declared that Abby was not a name at all. The only Abbey he knew was the one the King and Queen had been crowned in. So he started calling her Westminster, as a tease. Soon this became Westy, or West, which Bert thought suited her better – 'up west' being Higgins-talk for anything posh.

At first Nanny would try to keep Abby away from Bert, telling him that she had homework to do, or must clean her teeth, or was expected in the drawing room in her tidy clothes. But Bert never seemed to be put off. He would wait quite good-naturedly until Abby was free, wandering around in the nursery wing, poking his nose into cup-boards, fingering the bedlinen and the washstands, and endlessly going back to have another go at flushing the lavatory. That lavatory – and indeed many of the ones at Dulcimer Hall – were a source of wonderment and recurring delight to Bert. Mahogany thrones, they were, with a sort of upside down stirrup which you lifted up, causing a little round trap door to open and water to start circling about in the pan, slowly at first, then gushing and gurgling like the stream at the end of the shrubbery.

'The toilets here are the best.'

'Mummy doesn't let me call it a toilet,' said Abby.

'Why not?'

'Goodness knows.' There were all sorts of words that Antonia would not allow, something that Abby had long ago accepted but had never thought to question.

Not so, Bert. He questioned everything. He did not ask questions of grown-ups but tried to puzzle out for himself how things worked, why cows ate grass while humans could not, how engines worked, why people did and said the things they did. He was endlessly curious, tireless in his pursuit of information, and almost from the first he had appointed Abby as his partner in this search.

'Where does this river go to, West? Could we sail right down to the sea from here?'

Abby wondered why she liked Bert so much. She had hated him to begin with, but her determination to ignore him hardly lasted more than a day. For one thing, his delight in the puppy made her think that he was not so bad. But after that, she was simply unable to resist the flattery of his wanting her company. Boys, in Abby's experience, only played with you if there was absolutely nobody else available. As soon as another boy came in sight, they dropped you like a hot stone. With Bert, it was Abby he wanted, and he did not care who knew it.

Amazingly, even Nanny came to like Bert, once he was cleaned up and dressed in Quentin's outgrown flannel shorts and aertex shirts. He was not at all good-looking, really. He was skinny, with spiky hair and one of those bony faces that seemed to crease right up when he smiled, sending his eyes right back into his head.

'Funny looking boy, that Bert Higgins,' said Nanny. 'But he's turning out better than I expected.'

The servants' hall at Dulcimer was a hive of gossip. First thing in the morning, mid-morning, afternoon and evening, they came from all ends of the house to share in a ritual of tea and scandal. Sitting at her humble end of the table, between Lady Cora's schoolroom maid and a new girl who worked in the garden, Maggie felt her eyes growing out on stalks at some of the things she heard. There was a constant buzz of speculation about Mrs John and her new American husband. Sides were taken. Cook thought the bridegroom was too young.

'Baby-snatching, I call it,' she said.

Miss Trumpet was indignant on Dart's behalf. 'Really, I could hardly bring myself to be civil to Mr David when Mrs John brought him to see me. A nice way he has behaved! Worming his way in here because his mother and Lady Dulcimer are sisters. Him and his flashy car and his dollars. Honeymooning in London, they are, this minute. And for some considerable time, from all accounts. The Red Cross ambulance is to be sent back to the depot tomorrow.'

'Life's easy for some,' said the housekeeper with a sniff. 'It would be nice to be a voluntary worker like madam, able to drop everything and walk away. I suppose our Mrs John will be too busy for war work now.'

'Too busy spending her American husband's money,' retorted Miss Trumpet sourly. He said he was going to take her shopping in Bond Street. Being a foreigner, I suppose he has nothing better to do. When I think of poor Lord Dartmore, defending our country from the

49

Nazis, it makes me furious. Stands to reason he has no time to take anyone shopping.'

'Nor would he want to,' remarked the housekeeper. 'Lord Dartmore is not the sort to kick his heels while a lady tries on hats and dresses.'

'Better at undressing them, eh?' put in the first footman – nowadays the only one. He winked knowingly, and there was a titter from the lower end of the table.

'That will do,' said the housekeeper grandly. 'Some more tea, Mr Vestry?'

'No, thank you, Mrs Hawkins. I have had a sufficiency.'

Pouring herself and Miss Trumpet another cup, Mrs Hawkins said thoughtfully, 'Mind you, Lord Dartmore's divorce must have cost him a pretty penny, if what the papers say is true.'

'You don't want to believe all you read in the papers.' Miss Trumpet helped herself to another biscuit. 'And it was worth any amount of money to rid himself of that woman. She never appreciated him. If only Mrs John had waited. It was a real shock to my lady. You would think, with Mr David Vorst her nephew, and his own parents away in America, she would have been consulted. But no, not one word did they tell her until after the wedding! And I'll tell you another thing. My lady thinks there will be a rare fuss when the Vorst parents learn about the marriage. It's no wonder they went off and got married on the sly.'

'Someone ought to have stopped it,' said Cook, rising to her feet, which was her way of signalling the end of morning tea. 'That young man doesn't look old enough to marry anyone. You can tell that he's fair gone on Mrs John, though. Never took his eyes off her all the time they were in my kitchen.'

Trumpet frowned at Cook over her rimless spectacles. 'They should have kept out of the way until after Lord Dartmore's weekend. But what do they do? Mrs John rings up, as bold as brass, and says she wants to be met at the station. If you ask me, she means to flaunt her new clothes.'

David stood by the open window of his dressing room at Dulcimer, knotting his tie. A great wave of happiness seemed to well up inside him – happiness and sheer amazement that he and Antonia were married. He was so happy that it almost frightened him. All during the past week, he and Antonia had revelled in being together, making love, laughing at the most idiotic things. Nothing ruffled their mood of euphoria. Even the cable from David's possessive, rather managing parents contained nothing but a loving welcome to Antonia and congratulations to them both. A miracle, that, all of a piece with the other unbelievable things that had come about.

Antonia had been like a starry-eyed little girl with a new doll's house, delighting in the novelty of living in the rooftop flat of a luxury hotel. She had taken over the large main bedroom which was usually kept for the chairman and his wife. She never seemed to tire of ringing down for meals when they were hungry, of taking little jaunts to the shops, of charming the hotel staff with her smiles and her pretty gratitude. In the train, she had sat silent, gazing out of the window, upright and tense like a child on a trip to the seaside. He had just sat watching her, feeling that nothing that had happened in the past week was altogether real.

He leaned out of the dressing-room window. Dulcimer in summer. It was raining. That was real enough. The rain fell chill against his newly shaven skin, and a gust of wind shook the wet ivy and soaked his hair.

He liked it. Somehow the smell of rain and wet leaves and grass merely added to the intoxication of his mood. How wonderful to be a married man, and to be looking out upon an English garden in the rain.

He leaned even further out, so that he could just see a corner of Antonia's window next door. She had banished him to the dressing room, saying that she wanted to surprise him with her new dress.

'Hey there, Mrs Vorst!' he called out. 'You've been too long making yourself beautiful. I'm starved of your company.'

Her face appeared at the window, flowerlike, framed by shining, wet ivy. 'Was your bathwater hot, darling?'

'Mm. Sort of warm.'

'Mine was freezing.' She smiled at him. 'And while I remember, angel, don't take coffee after dinner. They make it once a year here, and it tastes of boiled mud.'

'I wouldn't want to miss it,' he assured her, laughing. But he was serious. He intended to savour everything to the full this weekend. His present incredible happiness was somehow made more believable by minor discomforts like bad coffee and doubtful plumbing.

He wondered if Dart had arrived yet. He felt a qualm of unease when he thought of his cousin, and he knew very well that Antonia was both dreading and looking forward to seeing Dart again.

A deafening clamour met David and Antonia when they made their rather belated entrance into the drawing room. All the family were assembled, happily occupied with shouting at the tops of their voices and sucking down Lord Dulcimer's vintage champagne like cattle after a prolonged drought.

Dart's two married sisters were there in full cry. Large Lady Cora Munnings and even larger Lady Jean Smith-Davies with her stout husband, were roaring with laughter at one end of the room. Dart was bellowing at Lady Dulcimer, who had her hand cupped to her ear

51

in an effort to hear him better, and Admiral Munnings, Cora's husband, was keeping his end up with his quarterdeck voice. All the dogs rushed towards the latecomers, barking, and as Lord Dulcimer pushed his way through the throng, he added to the decibels by roaring at the dogs to keep quiet. He wrapped Antonia in a welcoming hug.

'Come along, you lovebirds.' He turned to shake David vigorously by the hand. 'Welcome, my boy. Dart has arrived, and we're all drinking champagne. I told Vestry to keep it hidden until we had something important to celebrate, and this seems the right moment. A wedding and Dart's medal. That calls for something a bit special, don't you think?'

The newly wedded pair were swooped on and surrounded. Emerging from Lady Jean's capacious embrace, Antonia found herself face to face with Dart.

He put a hand under her chin and bent to kiss her lingeringly on the lips. 'I have always thought you a quick worker, Tonia mia, but never more so than now. No wonder you look like a cat who has swallowed a canary. The poor bird never stood a chance.'

'Dart . . .'

'What shall I give you as a wedding present? A packet of bird seed? A pretty gilt cage to keep him in?'

She pulled away from him, and found David at her side.

'Come along, honey,' he said, taking her hand. 'Uncle Bernard says he's starving. Bring your glass with you, and we can tell Dart our news later.'

David found himself seated next to Lady Cora at dinner. 'You've certainly given us all a fine surprise, David. George and I will be sorry to lose you but your mother will be overjoyed to have you safely back in America. Aunt Chrissie has been writing to Mother by every post, fuming and fussing at your staying in London.'

'Yeah. Don't I know it.' David's tone was distinctly unenthusiastic. 'But we're not going.'

'Good gracious! Why ever not? Isn't that why Antonia married you?'

'You'd better ask her, Cora,' murmured David politely.

Antonia, overhearing, gave a little gurgle of laughter and blew a kiss at her new husband across the table. 'No need to be rude, Cora. I married David because I love him.'

'I'm sure you did,' said Lady Cora, her face flushing to a deeper shade of plum. 'But after all, it's only sensible for you to go to America, now that there's almost bound to be an invasion. This is not your war, David.'

'Have you been talking to my father, Cora?' David asked her in a dry voice.

'Whatever can you mean?' asked Lady Cora, astonished. 'Isn't Uncle Cornelius over in America?'

'I believe so. But you sounded so like him just now that I wondered if he had been working on you.'

She digested this, and then asked curiously, 'Was he very cross about your marriage?'

'Not at all,' said Antonia quickly and firmly. 'David's parents sent us the most lovely cable, inviting us all to Maple Valley, and even offering us a house on the estate. So they can't have been cross, can they?'

'I want to see the puppy,' Dart told Abby next day.

'Oh, good. Can you come now?'

'When I've finished my breakfast. What have you called him?'

'Wat.'

'What *name* have you given him?'

Abby looked at Bert, and they both laughed. 'I've just told you, Uncle Dart. Wat is his name. You know, like Wat Tyler.'

'He's a rebel, is he? Has he grown?'

'He's so fat after his meals that I sometimes think he'll burst. And so sweet, you have no idea! Wait until you see him.'

'Don't pester Uncle Dart,' said Antonia from where she was sipping tea at the far end of the table. 'He probably has better things to do this morning than drool over that mongrel.'

'But Mummy, Bert and I are just off to give Wat his breakfast, and I thought—'

'You are not going anywhere until you've been upstairs, miss,' put in Nanny sharply.

'Oh, Nanny . . .'

'You will go upstairs and go to the lav and clean your teeth, and no nonsense. Go with Miles and Abby, Maggie. I wouldn't put it past her to dodge off, now that I cannot climb the stairs. It won't kill your little dog to wait another ten minutes.'

Bert and Abby exchanged resigned glances and went out together, having first gone round the tables to scrape out any half-eaten porridge bowls, and adding the remains of porridge from the sideboard dish. They were constantly on the scrounge for things for the puppy to eat, vying with the new landgirl, who wanted scraps for the hens. While Abby was upstairs, Bert paid a visit to the kitchen and got some milk from Cook, and some crusts of bread and potato peelings which he later bartered for an egg with the landgirl.

On Sunday morning, the parade oompahed merrily down the village street, and Dulcimer church was packed to the doors. The weather stayed fair, and there were as many people outside as there were in the

53

church. Hymns of thanksgiving were sung with fervour, and there were lumps in throats and misty eyes when the vicar prayed for those who had lost their lives at Dunkirk. They thanked God for the armada of ships of all shapes and sizes that had rescued so many men of the Expeditionary Force. It had been a miracle. God was on their side.

Coming out of church in an exalted mood, Mrs Harriby came alongside the admiral, who had donned his uniform in honour of the occasion. 'Well, George? Wasn't that inspiring? I hope you mean to tell Mr Churchill about it. I am told that you are one of his right-hand men these days.'

'Hardly that,' said George Munnings with a look of amusement. He was trying vainly to recall who in the world this woman was. However, his ignorance was not exposed, because Mrs Harriby spotted David and Antonia and surged over to offer her felicitations.

The family escaped at last, walking up the lime avenue, chivvied by Lord Dulcimer who had been pleased by the performance of his Volunteers in the parade but was now badly needing his lunch.

David and the admiral found themselves walking together. 'Cora tells me that you're staying in England. What do you plan to do?'

David hesitated. He barely knew George Munnings; he had met him once or twice at family gatherings, and that was all. Still, if he really worked in the Prime Minister's office, it might be worth asking his advice.

The admiral repeated his question.

David took the plunge. 'I want to join the RAF. If there's an invasion, sir, they'll need people to fly fighter planes, and that's what I'm trained to do. I figured that I could be useful, and I want to help. But it seems they don't want me. Not those goops at the Air Ministry, anyhow.'

'Have you applied?' And when David said he had, he asked, 'How long ago was that?'

'Months. I passed all their tests, and went for interviews. They said that I should hear quite soon, as they were short of trained pilots. I got my first pilot's licence when I was at Harvard, and unofficially, I've been flying in Scotland most weekends.'

They walked on in silence for a little way, then Admiral Munnings said thoughtfully, 'You're right about one thing. We do need pilots, and need them urgently.'

David almost groaned. He said bitterly, 'You know something? I get the feeling that I'm trying to join a club, and that someone is throwing in blackballs as fast as they can. A couple of months ago I asked my father to pull strings with Ambassador Kennedy. They were classmates, and are still friends. But that did no good at all.'

'Mr Kennedy? What did he say about it?'

David shrugged. 'Mr Kennedy doesn't want Americans to get mixed up in your Limey war, sir. He reckons you're going to lose it, and has even got my pa believing the same thing, damn it.'

'And what do *you* think of our chances?'

The young man looked down at the older one. The admiral was a small man. David said hesitantly, 'You really want to know, sir?'

'I wouldn't ask you if I didn't. And don't call me sir. It makes me feel older than God.'

David grinned. 'Here goes, then. I think we stand a good chance of beating off an invasion if we keep control in the air. From what I hear, we were sunk in France because nobody understood just how important that was, and the German pilots were more experienced than we were.'

'You're right, of course.' The admiral stroked his chin. 'I wonder if I could help. I don't promise anything, but come and see me in London next week if you don't hear from the Air Ministry by then.'

David's face lit with hope. 'I would surely like that,' he began fervently, but broke off when he saw Antonia waiting for them at the garden gate. He reached for his bride's slender hand, and squeezed it. 'Hi, darling. I've been boring the admiral about my ambitions.'

'Don't encourage him, George,' said Antonia. 'He doesn't think I mean it when I tell him that I could never marry anyone in the Air Force. But I do.'

'You're ten days too late, honey,' said David. 'At least you are, if the Air Force decide to take me on.'

Dart had been dreading the weekend, and in the event he found it even worse than he'd feared. The parade and the church service had been trying enough, with neighbours gushing all over him and asking about Dunkirk. The noisy family dinner went on far too long. When, on the following afternoon, Antonia reproached him yet again for giving Abby the puppy, it felt like the last straw.

'Dart, darling, I do so wish you hadn't. We may be sending the children to America, and I am dreading the fuss Abby will make when I tell her she must leave that mongrel behind.'

Dart looked at her with open resentment. She was flushed and looking deliciously pretty, holding onto David's arm as though in need of its support.

'So Cora was right,' he said unpleasantly. 'You did marry him to get yourself to America. When do you sail?'

'Dart, don't—'

David stilled her protest by squeezing her arm. 'Don't mind him, honey. He's jealous, and I can't say that I blame him.'

'Generous of you,' said Dart with quiet savagery. 'But then you can afford to be generous, can't you? Keep splashing out with the mighty dollar, Vorst, and you'll keep her happy and biddable – until she finds something better. It's a pity, though, that you've failed to buy your way into the Royal Air Force. Don't they want you? Or is that talk of wanting to fly fighter planes just so much hot air?'

'Please, Dart ...' Antonia came towards him, her hands outstretched in appeal, which only added fuel to his anger.

'You'll have no trouble buying your way onto a ship. Bad luck on the others who want to get out before the bombs start falling. Cabins are sure to be found for Mr and Mrs Vorst and their three pretty children.'

David said steadily, 'I would like to get the kids away, certainly. Antonia, too, if she would agree to go.'

'David, no!' Antonia's voice was low. 'You know I don't want to ...'

Dart's bright blue gaze went from one to the other. 'What's this, Tonia? Refusing to go with him before you've been married ten days? You'll be in the record books.' And before either of them could say anything, he stalked off.

When they came down to dinner, they learned that Dart had gone back to London.

Antonia was back in the social swim and enjoying herself hugely. She rang up her London friends, telling them that she was married and that she and David were keeping open house in the penthouse flat. The friends flocked along willingly. Gin and whisky were scarce in the shops, but seemed to flow freely at the Vorst Hotel.

David was never there until evening, for during the days he haunted the Air Ministry, waiting for news, demanding to see people who always seemed to be in conference, or otherwise unavailable. He met up with Air Force friends, and sought advice about how best to break this deadlock, but nobody seemed able to help.

One day he did manage to corner one of these elusive people. 'Oh, it's you again, Vorst,' said the elderly Group Captain. 'I didn't expect to see you again. We heard that you were married and returning to America.'

'Who told you that, sir?'

The officer became evasive. He shook his grey head, murmuring, 'I can't remember who told me. One hears these things. I have a good many American contacts, you know ...' He refused to say more and David felt like strangling him. At the end of this third abortive day, he rang the admiral's flat, and learned from Cora that George was still at his office, and unlikely to be home until after nine in the evening.

Sighing, he rang off, and walked back to the Vorst in a despondent mood, wishing that Antonia had not chosen to throw a cocktail party that evening. He never knew whom he might find at these gatherings, but when he saw the long black car with the diplomatic number plates, he did not need Stebbings' excited mutter to tell him who was upstairs.

In the flat he was met by the sound of voices, laughter and the clink of glasses. Hank Fuller came out of the drawing room. He was one of the military staff at the United States Embassy, and he hailed David with pleasure. 'Here comes the bridegroom. My boss will be delighted.'

David, anything but delighted, said, 'What is Mr Kennedy doing here?'

'Come to congratulate you on your marriage, of course.'

'Antonia should have warned me.'

'She didn't know. We were driving back from Whitehall, and he suddenly decided to call in.'

'Don't tell him I'm here. I need to clean up.'

'Don't worry, Dave. Antonia is keeping him perfectly happy.'

In his dressing room he found Odette drawing the blackout curtains.

'You shouldn't be doing that, Odette,' he said from the doorway. 'That's housemaid's work. You should be joining the party in there.'

She turned to smile at him. 'Mrs Cornberg is short of housemaids. You know I like to be busy, and to sit around talking and drinking, that I do not like. My English is not so good, you know.'

'It's as good as you want it to be,' he told her, smiling and recalling the occasions when Odette had been Michel's hostess in the Paris Vorst. 'If you don't want to join those chatterers next door, I quite understand. I could do without them myself.'

The Frenchwoman gave him a straight look. 'David, is it truly necessary for you to be out so much? You have been married only a short time, and Antonia must be needing you. Those people in there are not . . . not a good mixing.'

'That's nothing new. Antonia mixes all sorts together, and usually they seem to love it.'

If Antonia felt daunted by the odd composition of her impromptu party, she did not show it. She was sitting on a sofa at the roof garden end of the drawing room, thanking the ambassador for smoothing the path of her marriage.

'I think you must have put in a good word for us with his parents,' she said. 'They sent us such a lovely cable. Until it came, I was quite in a jitter.'

The ambassador patted her hand. 'No need for you to worry, my dear. I have known Cornelius and Chrissie Vorst all my life, and they'll just love you. They'll love you all the more for taking David home. Just you get him on board a ship to America. Do it soon. He'll go, if you tell him it's what you want.'

'Mr Ambassador, he still hopes to join the RAF. He won't leave

England while there's any chance of being accepted.'

'Tell him he hasn't a hope. I assure you that there is no likelihood of his being taken on.'

She turned to look at him. 'How can you know that, Mr Ambassador?'

'Let's say I very much doubt it.'

'He wants it so badly. He goes to the Air Ministry every day, and before we were married he used to disappear to some airfield in Scotland where they let him fly fighter planes ...' She broke off, looking guilty. 'Oh! I'm not supposed to tell people about that.'

'I won't give him away.'

'You see,' said Antonia seriously, 'David is convinced that they need pilots, and it's driving him crazy. He even thinks that some high-up person may be telling them not to take him.'

'Is that what he thinks?'

A note of amusement in Mr Kennedy's voice made Antonia look at him in sudden suspicion, her blue eyes wide and almost accusing. 'Mr Ambassador! Was it you?'

He smiled at her. 'Now how in the world could I tell the British Air Ministry what to do?' he asked in a reasonable tone. 'I can give you some good advice, though. Get David away. If you leave it too long, it may be too late.'

Only then did they both become aware of David standing over them. Hank Fuller was at his side, looking wooden.

After a momentary silence, Mr Kennedy said easily, 'So there you are, David. I hope you will forgive me for calling in without warning.'

'Of course, sir. Antonia and I are happy to welcome you at any time.'

'You've gotten yourself a beautiful wife. She and I have been having a delightful talk.'

'So I have just overheard, sir,' said David, unsmiling. 'It is good of you to interest yourself in my affairs.'

'Darling, you weren't very polite,' said Antonia when their guests had left. But she kissed him, to sweeten the words. 'After all, the ambassador has been very kind to us.'

'Kind?' David looked at her darkly. 'Joe Kennedy is a snake in the grass, and you know it. Darn it, I should have known. He and my father have always been as thick as thieves.'

'You cannot blame your parents for being worried about you.'

'I don't blame them, but they are not going to run my life. No one does that except me.'

'David!' She had to run to catch up with him at the door of the flat. 'Where are you going?'

'Out.'

'But it's past ten o'clock! We haven't dined yet.'

'I'm not hungry. Order what you like, Antonia.'

He did not stay to listen to her protests and went down the stairs three at a time.

Admiral Munnings waited until David's first torrent of speech had come to an end. Then he said that he would do his best, but could not promise anything.

'You see the Prime Minister most days, don't you? Just ask him to see me, that's all!'

'Not a chance. Winston cannot see everybody who has a grievance.'

'He wants more pilots. You said so last week.'

The admiral rather wished that he had never said anything of the kind. He had never seen David in this mood – taut, determined and refusing to take no for an answer. 'All right. Put your request on paper, and I will see what I can do.'

The dark eyes glowed. 'Great, George! You will give it to him? Tomorrow?'

'I'll give it to him as soon as I can,' said the admiral wearily. His long day's work was not yet over. 'Now go away, and bring your letter over in the morning.'

But his uninvited guest had already pulled a sheet of writing paper from a bureau desk, and was uncapping his fountain pen. The admiral went to stand at his shoulder. 'Make it short, or he won't read it.'

The letter was brief, clear and to the point. George put the envelope in his pocket and pushed David out of the door, cutting short his thanks. 'Go back to that pretty wife of yours, you hothead. And don't set your hopes too high.'

'I won't,' David called back, though the confident tilt of his head suggested the opposite.

The summons came at seven thirty next morning.

George's voice said, 'He'll see you. How soon can you get to Admiralty House?'

'Give me fifteen minutes.'

Antonia was asleep and did not stir when he left. Two hours later he was back, and he went straight to her bedroom. She was chattering on the telephone.

She blew him a kiss. With her hand over the mouthpiece, she said, 'It's Dart, darling. Be with you in a minute . . .' She pulled at the soft lace bedcover with one hand, and went on talking to Dart for fully five minutes before ringing off.

'Guess what, angel? Dart may get sent to Washington. Something diplomatic and secret. In one way he wants to stay with his regiment, but he thinks it would be a chance to see Quentin. Wouldn't it be fun if he visited us in Maple Valley after we get there?'

David said nothing. She reached up a hand and pulled him down, holding up her face for his kiss. 'Don't be sulky, angel. How many times must I tell you that there is no need for you to be jealous of Dart.'

'I know it,' he said gravely, sitting beside her on the bed. He was holding a folded sheet of paper in his hand. 'I'm just wondering how to tell you my news. Guess who I've been seeing this morning?'

'Gracious! How should I know? It's far too early for seeing anyone, I should think.' She smiled at Odette Steiner, who had come in with a tray of letters and newspapers. 'Isn't that so, madame? Nobody civilised talks business before ten o'clock.'

'Don't tell Odette that. Michel was always up at six in Paris. What you mean is, English women can't get going in the mornings. Now, Antonia. Try to guess who I have been with.'

'One of your friends from the embassy?' she said, humouring him. She saw his lips twitch in a half-smile. 'Did you say sorry to Mr Kennedy for turning him out last night?'

'Not on your life! Guess again.'

'I give up, darling.'

'OK.' He unfolded the sheet of paper and laid it on the tray before her. She looked at it blankly. 'That's George and Cora's writing paper ... and your writing.' She looked up at him. 'I don't see ...'

'It's not *all* my writing.' He jabbed a finger at the paper. 'Look at the darker ink at the bottom.'

She read the relevant words slowly, aloud. 'It says, "Why has Mr David Vorst been refused entry to the Royal Air Force as a pilot? His qualifications speak for themselves, and we need him. Please eliminate red tape, and admit him *immediately*. Keep me informed. W.S.C." '

'W.S.C.?' Antonia gave a small gasp, and looked at David. 'Not ... not Winston Churchill?'

He nodded.

She gave a little squeak of excitement. The prime minister! How impressed her friends would be! 'You actually saw him? What did he look like?'

'Pretty much like a gnome in pyjamas. He'd been working half the night.'

'Oh, David. Did you have breakfast with him at ten Downing Street?'

He said he had not. The Prime Minister was still living at Admiralty House, where he had lodged when he had been First Sea Lord. He had breakfasted with George at his club.

Antonia looked at her new diamond wristwatch and said, 'Gracious! I promised to meet Marjorie in Harrods. I must get dressed and fly!'

60

David caught at her hand. 'Let Marjorie wait. I want to tell you about it.'

But she would not stay. She dashed about pulling clothes off hangers, refusing to listen. 'Tell me tonight, angel. We have the Wilsons and a couple of their friends coming in for drinks, but after that nobody. Goodness! Where have I put my gloves! I shall be horribly late . . .'

'Antonia!'

The door slammed behind a small departing whirlwind. Odette's bony face was expressionless.

David picked up the letter which had worked such miracles at the Air Ministry. He said rather forlornly, 'I don't think Antonia understood.'

She looked at him, her dark eyes under their pencilled brows bright with intelligence. 'I, also, do not entirely understand, David. Is it that the Air Force has decided to take you?'

'That's it!' His thin face lit with the brilliance of his excitement. 'I start on Monday. I'm off to get measured for my uniform this morning. I've had my miracle, Odette, and just when I thought it would never happen.'

'Angel, you can't be serious about this Air Force business?' said Antonia when David came back from speeding their guests on their way. He had been in jubilant form that evening, and Antonia had exclaimed and kissed him with all the rest – all the chatterers deeply impressed that the Prime Minister had taken up his cause. This was their first chance to talk alone. She repeated, 'You're not serious, I should hope.'

'Serious? I should say not,' said David, swooping on her and kissing her rapturously. 'I am just so happy, it hurts. I start basic training in the Midlands on Monday, but they say that with my experience I should be operational within two to three weeks.'

Antonia pulled herself out of his embrace so that she could look up at his face. David had a way of saying outrageous things, deadpan, his dark eyes solemn. But this time he was far from solemn. He was behaving as though someone had given him a huge present. Surely he was teasing.

'Don't talk like that. You frighten me. You know perfectly well that we are taking the children to America.'

'Not now that they have accepted me as a pilot, honey.'

'You must write to them then and tell them that you have just got married,' said Antonia, gently smoothing a lock of dark hair off his forehead. 'Tell them that your new wife has been widowed once and doesn't want to risk it a second time.'

He looked at her blankly.

61

'They will understand,' she assured him, turning to take a cigarette out of a silver box and fitting it into her new holder. 'Flying fighter planes is bound to be dangerous.'

He swallowed. Patiently, he said, 'Antonia, you know I've been waiting and hoping for this. It's something I must do. Try to understand.'

Antonia waited for him to light her cigarette, her eyes veiled by her long dark lashes. Once it was lit, she inhaled deeply and looked up. 'And what about me and the children? Two days ago you were planning to take us all to Maple Valley.'

He said gently, 'I remember.' Odd, he thought, how long ago that seemed. 'You could still take the children. Or you could send them over with Nanny.'

'Not without you.' She turned away from him, hurt and indignant that he was prepared to let her go so easily. He had actually taken it for granted that she would share his pleasure in this preposterous idea of going into the Air Force. How selfish and insensitive men were!

'Aunt Chrissie is counting on your going home,' she told him.

'I know she is. All the same, Mother will accept my decision. She has known for months what I want to do.'

Antonia sighed, and said crossly, 'Nobody goes into the RAF. Not a single person I know. I just couldn't bear to see you in that commonplace uniform.'

He laughed and made a grab at her. 'OK. I promise to wear nothing but my birthday suit when I'm with you. It may cramp our style socially, but that won't bother me. Maybe Marjorie will stay away.'

She slapped his hands away, saying pettishly, 'Don't try to be funny, David. Your place is in America. This is a British war. Nothing to do with you.'

'I was born in London, Antonia. Right here in this hotel, and London is my home.'

'But New York will feel like home too, when you've been there a day or so. Look, angel, your parents want you back home. I want to meet them. Won't you give up this idea for my sake? To please me?'

'I would do most things to please you, Antonia, but don't ask me to give this up. I just can't do it.'

She looked at him, for the first time feeling not only angry but bewildered. She drew a breath. She was not a perceptive woman, but she could see that he was still in a state of high excitement, a mood in which opposition might make him even more determined to have his way. She had little doubt of being able to bring him round but decided that it would be wiser to go slowly. Perhaps he would be more amenable this weekend when they were at Dulcimer. Anyway, she was feeling hungry.

'Let's talk about this another time, darling. Do you think we could have dinner soon?'

The large boxes containing David's new Air Force uniform and other kit were brought upstairs to the flat on Friday morning. Antonia was out when they came, so the first she saw of them was at Dulcimer on Friday night.

'Shall I try the uniform on?'

'Not on my account,' said Antonia coldly, looking at the blue tunic with disfavour. 'It's just as I expected. Too, too middle-class. Nobody I know wears it.'

He laughed at her. 'Snob!'

'Well, it's true.'

'So what? It will suit me fine. There's nothing aristocratic about the Vorsts, you know. Solid Dutch burghers, we were, when we landed in New Amsterdam – traders and innkeepers. That's what we still are.'

'Why have you brought it here?'

'I told you, honey. I am due to start training on Monday morning. I shall need to leave after lunch on Sunday.'

Antonia, who had been holding herself in, waiting her moment to relaunch her attack, looked at him in dismay and indignation. 'You can't be serious. We're dining with Hank and Chesney on Monday.'

'I rang and put them off. I thought you'd probably want to stay on at Dulcimer, until we can be together.' He smiled suddenly. 'I told Hank that he and his boss ought to be the first to know my news.'

She opened her mouth to protest, but the brazen sound of the dinner gong came to their ears. She gave a little flounce of disgust and moved to the bedroom door. It would never do to be late for dinner. Nothing made Lord Dulcimer crosser than having to wait for his food.

Dart arrived at Dulcimer on Saturday. He went through the French windows to the terrace and heard Antonia say, 'You are utterly selfish. I wish I'd never agreed to marry you.'

'So the honeymoon's over, is it? All good things come to an end, I suppose. Or wasn't it so good, Antonia mia?'

'Mind your own business,' she snapped. She was in rather less than radiant looks after pleading and arguing and raging at David for half the night. 'I'm just miserable that we aren't going to America. I was so looking forward to it . . .'

There was a sob in her voice. Dart looked at her curiously. 'Not going? Why not?'

'Because David has this tiresome and dangerous plan to go into the Air Force. He doesn't care that I want to be in America, with no blackout and no horrible economies. David says that I should go with the children but I won't be shoved off like that.'

Dart's brows lifted. 'Do the children know you mean to send them?'

'Not yet. We thought we should speak to Nanny first.'

'Better tell them soon. It will give them time to get used to the idea,' advised Dart.

It had not escaped his notice that David had so far said nothing at all. He looked at his cousin curiously. He looked much as usual, disappointingly so – dark and thoughtful and giving nothing away. He showed none of the signs of a man who had been given a hard time by his wife.

Antonia had also been watching and wondering. She had tried everything to turn him from his purpose, and he had not budged an inch. Not one. She had chosen to marry him. So what manner of husband had she got herself? Something unexpected – and infinitely more interesting. This was no adoring boy but a man who would make up his mind and not be turned from it. A lightning bolt of purely sexual excitement coursed through her veins and brought the colour flooding into her face.

She found herself wishing that she had not wasted so much time in argument. After tomorrow, she might not see David again for weeks.

Dart, too familiar with that look for his comfort, was assailed by very different feelings. He turned on his heel and left them without a word.

Chapter 5

Nanny said that wild horses would not drag her to America.

'No need for horses, Nanny. We thought you would prefer to go by boat,' said David gravely.

'You thought that, did you, sir?' Nanny did not give Antonia's new husband so much as a glance. She was vengefully slicing bread for tea, holding the white loaf sideways against her aproned front in a manner peculiar to herself.

'Nanny, please!' Antonia was at her cajoling best. 'How could I think of sending my angels with anyone else but you?'

'You could take them yourself, madam.'

'I was going to, until Mr Vorst decided to join the Royal Air Force. As it is, I am positively relying on you, Nanny.'

This time, Nanny afforded David a look of grudging approval. 'Staying to fight the Nazis, are you, sir? I'm glad to hear it.' She turned to Antonia and said, 'The children and I will be quite all right here in the country. We've got our gas masks, haven't we? And with his lordship's volunteers, or Home Guard as we're supposed to call them, we'll be as right as rain.'

'There may be an invasion, Nanny. You would be much safer in America.'

'Mr Churchill isn't talking of going to America, is he? Well, neither am I. Running away, I call it. I stayed in England all through the last war, madam, and I'm staying this time.'

Antonia looked at David helplessly, but he only smiled at her. Maggie came in with the two Higgins girls and little Joe, and Mamzelle followed with Lady Cora's Joan and Betty, and Nanny Smith-Davies and her boys. Realising that they could hardly continue the discussion in front of all these people, Antonia and David went to have tea in the drawing room.

Abby, who had come in to hear the last part of the discussion, gave an inward sigh of relief, for once thanking goodness for Nanny. Nobody said anything more about going to America for nearly three weeks, for Antonia went to London to see David off and stayed at the Vorst until he had finished his preliminary training. Then, just when Abby was starting to feel safe, Antonia returned and told Nanny that

Miss Brimley had agreed to accompany the children to America. Abby was appalled. Miss Brimley in the mornings was hard enough to bear. If the governess went with them to America, there would be no getting away from her.

'That settles it. I'm staying here with Nanny.'

'Don't be boring, Abby,' said Antonia, yawning. It was a Saturday morning. Maggie had just carried Antonia's breakfast tray up from the dining room. The elder Cary children and the puppy had followed, and Abby scooped the little dog in her arms before they went in, in case he made a puddle. She was taken aback to find David there, opening letters near the window. She was still not used to having him around, and wished he would stay away.

Miles rushed up to Antonia's bed to kiss her.

'You will love it at Maple Valley, darlings,' Antonia said brightly.

'How do you know? You've never been there.' Abby glared at David; she was holding Wat so tightly that he began to struggle. She stroked the puppy, and when he was still, added, 'Just because *he* says so. If America is so wonderful, Mum, why don't you come with us?'

'Try to understand, Abby. David and I haven't been married very long, and I don't want to leave him.'

'And I don't want to leave Wat.'

'Of course you don't, Abby,' said David, who had kept out of the discussion so far. 'It's tough, but we all have to do difficult things in wartime. Your mother and I could look after Wat when you go to America. He'd be company for her when I am busy working for the Air Force.'

Abby shook her head, hating this American usurper for his air of reasonableness, blaming him for stealing Antonia from under Dart's nose. David was the last person she would give him to. 'Certainly not. He's mine. Uncle Dart gave him to me, and I promised to look after him.'

'Oh, Abby,' said Antonia wearily, leaning forward to let Maggie lay a cobweb-fine bedjacket round her slender shoulders. 'David is only trying to help. If you cannot be more civil, you'd better go away.'

'Don't worry, I'm going. I know you don't want me, now you've got him. But I warn you. Don't try to send me to America with Brimstone.' She felt her voice go all wobbly, and went quickly to the door. 'I'll jump off the ship if you do.'

Maggie followed Abby out of Antonia's bedroom. David put down his letters and followed. He came upon them at the bottom of the back stairs, where a door led into the garden. The puppy had gone outside, and Abby was sobbing, clasped in the plump nursery maid's arms. Maggie looked at David and shook her braided head.

He went away.

*   *   *

After dinner that evening, David went in search of the nursery maid. He found her in the kitchen garden, hoeing between rows of young carrots. She must have sensed his eye upon her, for she looked up, ceased the rhythmic swaying of her work, and waited to hear what he had to say.

He plunged in abruptly. 'What are we going to do about Abby? Does she really hate Miss Brimley that much?'

Maggie blew a stray tendril of hair out of her eyes and leaned on her hoe. After a pause, she said, 'They don't get on, the pair of them.'

'Why not?'

'Abby says that Miss Brimley doesn't like girls.'

'And what do you say, Maggie?'

Maggie took so long to answer that David was beginning to wonder if she had heard his question. Finally she spoke. 'Miss Brimley never had to do with girls before. It has always been little boys she taught. She likes everything to be just so, really, and not knowing any girls, she may be feared of them.'

'What if you were to tell Abby that? Would she understand?'

'I doubt it. Abby is too feared of what is going to happen to herself – of changes, and of losing that puppy that Lord Dartmore gave her. And she doesn't want to lose Bert Higgins either, not when she's just found him as a friend. She was lonely for a friend before he came.'

'I see.' David thought that Abby had already found a valuable ally in Maggie. He wondered if the child knew it. It was nearly dark in the kitchen garden, and the colour had drained away from the plants and the rows of raspberry canes. Maggie's rosy, daytime face was just a pale blur in the milky gloaming light, and her voice was as soft as the evening air.

'Children are a bit like plants. They need to put down roots. Abby and her brothers have had a good many changes, sir, what with Mr Johnnie dying, and the war and all. Abby hates new things, for all that she used to grumble about being bored.'

David said regretfully, 'She resents me, doesn't she?'

'Give her time, sir. She will come around.'

David felt oddly comforted by the nursery maid's words. Hardly more than a child herself, she had a soothing way with her. He was aware that Maggie worked hard, very likely harder than anyone else at Dulcimer. On his three brief visits since his marriage, he had come upon her doing all sorts of things: walking Lady Dulcimer's dogs before breakfast, helping in the pantry, in the guest bedrooms, serving at table. And here she was working in the garden. There seemed no end to the things she was expected to do, yet he had never seen her looking resentful or out of humour.

He liked the way the girl spoke, too, the clarity of her diction and the slight rolling of her 'r's when she spoke of Bert or Dart. He reached over and took the hoe from her hand. 'You have done enough for one day.' And as she stepped over a low box hedge onto the gravel path beside him, he asked curiously, 'What part of Scotland do you come from, Maggie?'

He was surprised to hear that she came from Glen Cary. Before the war David had stayed there on several occasions, always in summer, and usually for the grouse shooting. Somehow he could not imagine what it must be like to live in that wild glen all the year round. He told her that he was now done with his basic training and would be leaving for Scotland after the weekend. He hoped to escape to Glen Cary whenever his flying duties allowed.

'Perhaps I could visit your family, Maggie? I'll take a letter to your mother, if you like.'

'My mother is dead, sir. But . . . but I'd be glad if you would take a letter to my gran.'

'No problem. Can you explain to me how I shall find her?'

'Anyone will tell you, Mr David. Ask for Ian Dunlop's house. My dad is head keeper at Glen Cary.'

'Holy smoke!' David peered down at Maggie in astonishment. He added apologetically, 'Sorry, Maggie. I don't mean to be rude, but to tell the truth, your father has always scared me half to death.'

'That makes two of us, Mr David,' said Maggie on a tremor of laughter. 'But my dad would think twice before he raised a hand to you.'

He was shocked. 'You mean he hits you, Maggie?'

'Only sometimes. I keep out of his way, mostly.'

He followed her down the narrow garden path until they reached the wrought-iron gate leading into the main flower garden. People were so full of surprises. Who would have thought that the grim, bearded head keeper at Glen Cary could have fathered plump, merry, loving Maggie? Amazing. He latched the gate, and caught up with her, putting a detaining hand on her arm.

'Look, Maggie,' he said in his slow, deep voice, 'it's not fixed that the children are going away. But if we decide to send them, will you go too? It would make all the difference to Abby if she had you there.'

With his hand on her arm, he felt her shock as if it had been his own. She said in a wondering voice, 'America? Me go to America? I never thought of it.'

'Well, think about it now,' he urged, grasping her arm tighter. 'If you get there before the end of August, my family may still be on Cape Cod. There will be swimming and sailing, and picnics on the beach, and clambakes . . .'

'Clambakes!' said Nanny with a sniff. 'And what's a clambake when it's at home, I'd like to know?' And when Maggie could not tell her, she added tartly, 'All very well for madam's new husband to talk of swimming and sailing and riding bicycles, my girl. If you go to America, you'll still be one of the servants, just as you are now – and Miss Brimley will have you up and down waiting on her, worse than any child. She's handless, that woman. That's education for you.'

'Likely we won't be going to America after all,' said Maggie peaceably. Then, curiously, she added, 'I wonder what the Americans will think of us all if we go.'

'I doubt if they'll even notice you,' snapped Nanny, who was not at all pleased to learn that Maggie had been invited to go with the children. 'There will still be clothes to wash and iron, and rooms to clean. Why you should want to go gallivanting off to live among foreigners, I'm sure I don't know.'

'If we do go to America, it will be us who will be the foreigners, Nanny. Me and Miss Brimley and the children.'

'Foreigners? My children?' said Nanny, scandalised. 'Don't talk soft, my girl. The Cary children are British. Came over with the Conqueror, the Carys did. Foreigners, indeed! The very idea!'

Maggie's sailor brother came to Dulcimer Hall on leave. As she knew he would, Tom saw exactly what Maggie meant about foreigners.

'Foreigners?' he repeated thoughtfully. 'Aye, that's how they will think of you over there. And all the more reason to go, if you can. I never knew, until I joined the Navy, just how huge the world was and what a lot there is to learn. Just you go to America, Maggie. I wish someone would offer me a chance like that.'

Maggie said sadly, 'Dad will never agree to it.'

'Surely he will, if his lordship were to write and ask him?'

'You know Dad. He thinks America is a sink of iniquity.'

Tom was silent, his eyes on the brown, dimpled water. 'Then go without telling him. He'll not be able to come after you in wartime.'

'But they'll be bound to write and ask his permission.'

'I suppose so.'

Neither of them spoke. Lord Dulcimer had once again lent Tom a fishing rod, and to Maggie's delight, she had been given the afternoon off. It was a grey, breezy afternoon, perfect for fishing. Within an hour, there were three silver trout lying on the grass, and even the fanatical Tom laid down his rod and sat munching jam sandwiches and drinking inky tea from the nursery thermos flask. He said very little about the Navy. He told her that he was not meant to talk for security reasons, but Maggie thought he just wanted to put the war out of his mind for the afternoon. They talked, instead, of home things, and of the astonishing news that their brother Alistair and Glynis were married.

Gran had written to tell Maggie about it, and of how the pair of them had taken over an attic room in the family cottage. It seemed that Gran still ruled the roost, though, cooking and cleaning for them as she had always done. Glynis had a job as secretary and bookkeeper in the Glen Cary estate office. Considering how Glynis had sworn never to moulder in the glen, Maggie thought this was quite a comedown.

'All on top of one another in that cramped wee house, they must be,' she said with a shudder. 'And Glynis used to have such big ideas.'

Tom laughed at her, and told her that she should try sleeping in a hammock and living out of one canvas bag. He pointed to where the roofs of Dulcimer were just visible between the trees. 'You're the one with the big ideas after living in that barn. You never used to think home was so wee, as I recall. You'll be looking down on us all, I suppose.'

Maggie laughed, and denied looking down on anyone.

Again they sat silent. Maggie was so happy to be with him, and found herself wishing the peaceful moment could go on and on. It did not, of course, for a fish jumped under the willows at the far side of the pool, and Tom reached for his rod and got up all in a hurry. Maggie stayed where she was, watching him cast his line with infinite delicacy, his face intent, his eyes narrowed against the subdued glare of the water. Tom had always been her favourite person and, seeing him so lean and fit in his bell-bottomed trousers and heavy dark blue sweater, she felt a strong sense of pride in him.

Later, she walked with him to the village bus stop, but it was only when the bus came in sight and wheezed to a stop that Tom turned to her and said with sudden urgency, 'Maggie! Whatever you do, don't let Dad stop you from going to America.'

He gave her a hug, picked up his bag and jumped onto the already moving bus. Leaning out perilously, he shouted back at her.

'Promise you'll go if you can, Maggie! I'll be right ashamed of you if you don't stand up to Dad for once.' He took off his white sailor's hat and waved it at her.

Maggie watched, smiling and half blinded by sudden tears until the bus disappeared round a bend in the road.

They saw no more of Antonia and David after that weekend, for David handed the reins of the Vorst Hotel to Odette, and was now a pilot officer in the Royal Air Force. Antonia had gone to Scotland to be with him.

She rang up once, but the line was so bad that Nanny gave the telephone back to Lord Dulcimer with a helpless shake of her head. The only thing that Antonia did manage to convey was that all the would-be American travellers, Lady Cora's nursery party as well as her own, must go to London to collect their passports. An arrangement had been made to put all the children and their attendants on one visa which would be stamped on their passports at the American Consulate. Cornelius Vorst had secured this special concession for them.

'Trust that old robber baron,' Abby heard Dart say to his mother. 'He's a law unto himself.'

'It's very good of Cornelius,' said Lady Dulcimer, who was feeding cake to the Boys. Walls was sitting beside her with two horrible strings of dribble dangling from the sides of his mouth. Abby watched, fascinated, to see if these would land in her grandmother's lap or be sucked in with the cake. 'He has guaranteed to support them all until the end of the war, if need be. It may be a long time before the seas are safe enough to get them back.'

'Oh, God!' said Dart irritably. 'Don't I know it. Quentin may be away for years. When the War Office talked of sending me to Washington, I very much hoped to see him. But it all fell through. How will you and Father like having a gum-chewing American with a crew cut taking over this place when we are dead?'

Lady Dulcimer gave a last morsel to Walls and said calmly, 'I don't suppose that we shall take a great deal of notice of haircuts after we are dead. If we go to heaven, hopefully the Boys will be there. And if it's the other place, we shall be busy trying to keep in with the Devil.'

Dart said sourly, 'I've wished Peggy in hell so many times that she'll surely be there. What a merry party it will be!' He met Abby's serious gaze and said lightly, 'Well, Abigail. If old Cornelius Vorst manages to bribe some shipping company to take you across before the end of August, you'll probably meet up with Quentin. Peggy's mother lives just down the road from Maple Valley.'

Abby went out to join Bert and the others picking raspberries. All the children were being paid to pick fruit, as there was a bumper crop that summer and all hands were needed to harvest it.

As they worked, she and Bert talked about the American business. Apart from the unresolved problem of who would care for Wat, there were other worries. Once they had collected their passports in London, they were returning to Dulcimer to pack their cases and wait to be summoned to a ship. It might be ages, or they might be sent for soon. Either way, they would be given very little notice, for fear that the Germans might get wind of a convoy setting sail and send U-boats to intercept them. This thought made Abby shiver. Bert told her not to complain. She was bleeding lucky to be going.

'I wouldn't mind so much if you were coming. If you did, it might even be fun.'

'Wouldn't it just,' said Bert wistfully. 'But they would never take Joe and the girls, and I promised my mum.'

71

Abby sighed, and consoled herself by eating a raspberry. One thing that went some way towards reconciling her to her fate was the thought that Maggie might be coming with them: but even that was not yet certain.

Lord Dulcimer had written to Maggie's father, asking his consent for Maggie to go to America. The days passed, and still no word came. Lord Dulcimer told Maggie cheerfully that it did not matter in the least. 'Cheer up. I shall sign for you in *loco parentis*. That'll do the trick.'

Maggie was not wholly reassured, but told Abby that she wished her own father was even half as kindly and understanding as his lordship.

At her side in the raspberry nets, Bert gave a shout. 'I saw you eat one, Ivy. That'll be a penny in the box.'

'Abby has eaten lots and lots,' complained Ivy. 'It's not fair...'

'Do you want to go home to Mum, or don't you? At this rate, I'll leave you behind when the rest of us go.'

'You can't. You told Mum you'd keep us together.'

Bert had made up his mind that if Abby was sent to America, he was not staying on at Dulcimer. Not longer than he could help, anyway. All the Higginses were saving up, but even with Abby's fruit-picking money swelling the fund, she privately thought that the war might be over before they got away. Then she remembered her birthday. 'I'll ask everyone to give me money this year, if you like. That ought to help.'

'No thanks,' said Bert distantly. 'We'll manage on our own or we won't be going. I don't want your charity, ta very much.'

'It's not charity,' said Abby crossly. 'No different to your taking my fruit money.'

'That's just pennies. Your birthday money's different. Lord Dartmore will stump up, and your grandpa and your aunts. And your new American stepfather ought to be worth at least ten bob if you write and ask him.'

'I don't want his charity, any more than you want mine.'

'Huh! You're sleeping for free in his swanky hotel for two nights when you go to get your passports. If that's not taking charity, I don't know what is.'

'You're jealous. That's your trouble,' she retorted, marching off before Bert could find any more annoying things to say.

Chapter 6

Going to London was a great adventure. In the excitement Abby forgot that she was miserable and did not want to be sent away to America.

The taxi took them past their old house in Chesham Street, which she had not seen since her father had been run over and killed. She remembered that long ago, unhappy time. The house had been full of whispers, with people going into rooms and shutting her out, and when they left the house for the last time, the current nursery maid had sobbed into her handkerchief. Abby had not cried. There was just that horrid unsafe feeling in her tummy that would not go away. She remembered thinking that the nursery maid had no right to cry when she had only been with them for a short time. She knew, though, that it was the end of everything. Daddy was dead, and none of them would ever be happy again.

But this July day none of those things seemed to matter. She listened idly to Nanny telling Maggie that the nurseries had been six floors up, and how they had walked in Cadogan Gardens every morning, and in Hyde Park in the afternoons. Abby smiled to herself, surprised to find that the unhappy past had been dug up and thrown away.

A lot of serious digging had been going on in London, it seemed. They passed gardens which had been turned over to allotments, and others dotted with hump-backed air raid shelters. Nanny never stopped pointing and exclaiming, expressing disgust at seeing everything looking so shabby, with sandbags in front of many doorways, and brown strips of paper criss-crossed over window panes. And then the taxi drew up at the Vorst Hotel. They had hardly climbed out of the taxi before a small posse of hotel staff came out from behind a wall of sandbags and took them in charge.

'Just as if we were royalty,' said Nanny, much gratified.

She and Maggie were having a last cup of tea in their sumptuous sitting room before going to bed. It had, indeed, been a momentous and exhausting day. So many new faces, and everyone in the hotel so concerned that everything should be just right for Nanny. The housekeeper, the hall porter and a Frenchwoman called Madame

Odette had all been at pains to ensure this.

They had been taken up to their rooms. The children were thrilled by the huge bathrooms with their gleaming brass taps and tiled walls. They rushed in and out, turning on the showers and exclaiming until Nanny told them to give over.

At teatime they went along the corridor to find the Munnings party which consisted of, not only Joan and Betty and their French Mamzelle, but the four children of the Admiral's brother who were also going to America. Their brisk little nanny looked like a rosy-faced cottage loaf. They knew that Lady Cora was there, because they heard her voice bugling down the hall. Mr Smith-Davies and Lady Jean had decided against sending their boys and Lady Jean had taken them to Wales for the duration.

They found everybody sitting at a well stocked tea table. Two French children turned to stare at Abby and her brothers. Their mother, Madame Steiner, had been one of the first to welcome them that afternoon. There were some others whom they had not previously met: three small boys with a haughty-looking governess called Miss Fortescue, who looked down her large nose at the rest of the company. Nanny told Abby later that all these crushed little boys were lords, because their father was a duke. They sat in meek silence while their governess did all the talking. Abby felt sorry for them and from then on spoke of them as the lordlings.

Collecting passports next morning did not take long, and since they were not due at the United States Consulate to have them endorsed with visas until the following day, they could spend the afternoon as they chose.

In the event it was Nanny's choice. She swept them off to Sloane Street where they visited Hayfords and Peter Yapp, a high treat for Nanny, who had been yearning to visit both these shrines since leaving London. She set about buying clothes for the children to take to America. Dozens of cotton socks at Hayfords, silk socks for best, knickers by the dozen, gaiters for winter, new coats, and liberty bodices for Abby in two sizes. 'You'll grow into the other ones by next year, I dare say.'

'Nanny, I'm too old for liberty bodices,' said Abby in what was more of a grumble than a protest. She had lost this battle too many times. 'Why can't I have skirts with waistbands?'

'You'll get skirts with waistbands, miss, when you've got a waist to put them round.' Abby was as skinny as a pin – straight up and down. 'Until then, you will have to put up with buttons.' Nanny consulted her list and said, 'Now, what else have we forgotten?'

Peter Yapp, the shoe shop, was only a few doors down. Brown lace-up shoes were bought for all three children, house shoes with buttons for Abby, buckled ones for the boys. It went on and on.

A shocking waste of London time, Abby thought; and before Nanny's shopping lusts were satisfied, the shops were shutting, and they were too late to get into Woollands to buy the cotton material she wanted. Maggie was to make summer dresses for Abby.

'Never mind,' said Nanny when they were all sitting around a laden tea table, back at the hotel. Despite a limp and a stick to support her, Nanny seemed to have found a day on the hard London pavements marvellously invigorating. She said, 'If the children haven't to be at the Consulate until two o'clock tomorrow, there will be plenty of time to buy what we need in Woollands. We will go there first thing.'

Abby and Maggie exchanged glum looks, and went on eating their tea. It did not look as if they would ever get to the zoo.

In her dream, Odette Steiner walked through the woods, hand in hand with Michel. His fingers were warm, and although she did not look at him, she knew that he was smiling. Sunlight filtered through the leaves and somewhere birds were singing.

Then a bell rang – raucous, insistent. It went on and on.

Reluctantly, she struggled back to consciousness, sat up without opening her eyes, and reached out to turn off her alarm clock. She found that she was shaken and sweating, bitterly resentful of those recurring, sweet dreams that made sleep something to be dreaded these days. She had been a long time getting to sleep last night, tossing and turning, worrying about what was best to do.

What would Michel want her to do? Something in her shied away from the answer to this, but she forced it back on track, and admitted to herself that Michel would tell her to take Marie and Josef to America. Take the chance to get far away. If the Germans invaded, the horror would begin all over again. It made sense to go, with the Vorsts offering to care for them, and the American Embassy providing a blanket visa for any children and attendant adults who were on the Vorst family list.

But when David tried to persuade her, she told him that she could not. While there was even the faintest possibility that Michel might arrive in London, she could not leave. Would not.

'Then send the children on ahead,' he advised her, speaking on the telephone from an RAF base in Scotland. She exclaimed distressfully at the notion of parting from them, but he said, 'They'll be fine, Odette, until you and Michel can join them. They can stay at Maple Valley with Antonia's kids. They'll be well taken care of, I promise you.'

'We ought to keep together, David. The children will feel betrayed if I send them off without me.'

'Have you asked them?'

'David! Of course not. They are only ten and eight years old.'

'Go on. Ask them. They'll have each other, for one thing. I always thought they were a couple of remarkably independent kids.'

David had met the Steiner children when he was working as a trainee at the Paris Vorst. It was true that they had been full of fun and mischief in those days, but Odette knew that the events of the past months had marked them. There was a watchfulness about Josef, and Marie had woken up screaming on more than one occasion. And they had stopped asking when Papa was coming. How could she send them off to America without her?

'Tell them the truth, Odette. Say that you promised Michel to wait for him, and that you will come to them as soon as he arrives.'

He was right, she supposed, but the thought of telling her children made her quail. Words spoken can never be recalled. What would they think? How would they react? What invisible wounds would she inflict upon them?

Her decision had to be made today. The others were going to the Consulate in the afternoon, and that visit was a deadline.

Odette got up and made herself coffee in the little kitchen at the end of the hall, and carried it to the bedroom where the children slept. They were awake. She could hear them chattering through the closed door, and a gurgle of laughter from Marie. She drew a shaky breath, and went in.

'So you see, we must decide what to do,' Odette concluded, surprised to find that her voice was almost steady. Marie and Josef regarded her out of large, dark eyes – so uncannily like Michel's eyes. 'Should I send you to America? It is not what I wish, of course, but Papa must not come to London and find that I am gone. What do you think?'

She had feared this so much – had conjectured and guessed at their reactions so many times. Would Josef go white and silent? Would Marie cry and cling to her?

In the event they did neither. They rather liked having all those strange English children staying at the hotel – they had eaten with them at lunch and tea yesterday. Those children were going to America to stay with Monsieur David's family, and they envied them. But Maman was worried about Papa, and they had not told her what they wanted. So when she said that she might send them to this place called Maple Valley, they could hardly believe it.

They looked at each other. Odette held her breath, in an inward agony of apprehension, outwardly calm. 'We would like to go, Maman,' said Josef. 'You and Papa will come and find us there?'

'Naturally. Just as soon as Papa comes.'

They looked relieved, and before long their pent-up questions started tumbling out. 'Will we travel on a great ship, like the ones we saw in Cherbourg?'

'Will we go with those other children?'

'Do they have schools in America?'

'They won't send Josef away to sleep in a school, like they do in England, will they?' Marie asked anxiously.

Odette assured them that they would go to a day school, and were in no danger of being separated.

'None of those children speak French,' Marie said with a frown, 'and we can't understand their English when they speak quickly like they do.'

'Then you'll have to work hard, to improve your English.'

'We'll teach them to speak French,' said Josef sturdily.

David called up later that morning, and it sounded at first as though Odette was in tears.

But she was laughing too. She said, 'Oh David! They said they wished to go. But suddenly Josef looked tragic, and said that after all he would not go. I asked him why. I was in such suspense . . .'

'Well, don't keep *me* in suspense as well!'

'I had promised to take them to Madame Tussaud's when the summer was over. If they went to America so soon, he would never see the Chamber of Horrors.'

'I suppose,' said Nanny grudgingly to Maggie, 'that you had better go with Miles and Abby and Miss Brimley to see the waxworks. You might as well get to know those French children, because Madame Odette is still waiting for news of her husband, poor soul, and can't go with them to America.'

Maggie beamed, and said she would love to go with them.

'Well, don't go putting yourself forward. Miss Brimley is in charge of Miles and Abby, and I don't want to hear her complaining of you.'

'No, Nanny.'

'And another thing. Try to see that Abby behaves herself. Miss Brimley has only to open her mouth for Abby to contradict her.'

'I'll try.'

Abby enjoyed leading Josef and Marie and Miles round Madame Tussaud's, and pointing things out. The French children started jabbering excitedly at the exhibit 'La Belle et La Bête' and knew about Monsieur and Madame Curie in the inventors' hall. There were some more recent waxworks. There was Winston Churchill, of course, and Mr Chamberlain (pushed into the background these days) and Hitler and a group of German politicians, looking suitably evil. Miss Brimley and Odette followed the children, making rather laboured conversation.

Maggie kept at the back of the little party, 'not putting herself forward' and saying nothing, according to Nanny's instructions. This suited her well, for she could listen to what the French children were saying.

What luck to be going to America in charge of Marie and Josef! Maggie had never been much into praying, but she was praying like mad these days, imploring God to put in a word with her father about America.

Josef was getting fidgety. The Chamber of Horrors was what he wanted, but none of the younger children were allowed to visit it. Miss Brimley offered to go to the tearoom and wait for Madame Odette and Josef to come back. She beckoned to Abby.

Josef looked at Abby, scorn in his prune-dark eyes.

Abby dreaded the Chamber of Horrors but knew that she had to face it. Josef was almost exactly her age, and besides, Bert would despise her if he found out that she had been to Tussaud's and had not taken this chance.

She spoke before she lost her nerve. 'I'd like to go, please.'

Maggie gave Abby a nudge. 'You don't have to. I'm not sure that I fancy it myself.'

'Go and have tea with Brimmy and Miles, then. I don't need you to hold my hand.'

It was plain to Maggie that Abby was prepared to die rather than dodge the ordeal, so she said amiably, 'Please yourself. But don't expect me to be sorry for you if you don't enjoy it.' Then, becoming aware of Madame Odette's eyes upon her, she blushed, and looked at the floor.

Odette was amused. David had mentioned the nursery maid. He had told her that the girl could be counted on to be kind to Marie and Josef. So Odette had watched her cutting up Miles's sausages at breakfast, and fetching and carrying for Nanny and Miss Brimley. A clear-eyed girl, with lovely skin, and a cheerful way with her. Overweight, of course, but when she slimmed down, she might even be pretty. But this afternoon she had barely opened her mouth and was all but extinguished by a drab mackintosh and a truly dreadful hat. No wonder she lacked assurance if they dressed her so appallingly.

'Abby will come to no harm, I think,' said Odette, as the two children hurried down the darkened stairway leading to the Chamber of Horrors. She smiled. 'They must not admit to knowing fear, these children. Shall we go with them, do you think, even though they will not want us?'

Maggie smiled at her gratefully and nodded.

In the days when Maggie had been general maid at the manse, she and Mr Fraser used to have long, enjoyable discussions about all things French. The minister's wife had come back one day from a jumble sale, bringing with her a holdall full of old French magazines and newspapers – *Vogue* and *Paris Match* and a heap of old daily papers. She gave these treasures to the minister for his birthday, and together the two French aficionados had read and digested them until the papers were in tatters and the magazines fell to bits. When he had leisure to do so, the minister would seek out Maggie, and while she got on with whatever task was on hand, they would talk together in their laboured French – airing outdated views about French life and politics, and that mysterious thing the magazines called 'chic'. Maggie sometimes wrote to Mr Fraser in French.

To Maggie's eyes, Madame Odette was the embodiment of chic. She was fine-boned and exceedingly thin, simply clad in a black and white print crêpe-de-Chine dress, her shining dark hair swept up under a small black straw hat, pearl earrings in her ears. With her long thin face and rather prominent nose, she was not at all pretty. Abby, whose taste ran to fair-haired beauties like her own mother, said that Madame Odette looked just like one of Tom's black fishing flies. But to the nursery maid's eyes, the French lady wore her clothes with style and grace. Maggie thought she would never tire of hearing her speak and watching the eloquent movements of her hands as she explained the waxworks to her children.

As Maggie followed her around, she began to plan in her mind how she would describe Madame Odette to Mr Fraser when she next wrote. She was in the habit of planning these letters in all sorts of odd moments, while pushing the mailcart, walking Lady Dulcimer's Boys, even cleaning baths. Seeking for the right words helped to sweeten tiresome or tiring tasks, and saved time. When she got a moment to write, she would know which words to look up in her French dictionary. Besides, even thinking about Mr Fraser made her feel good. Next to Tom, she loved him best.

There were some loathsome things in the Chamber of Horrors. An elderly, uniformed attendant sat on a stool in one corner, looking sour – and no wonder. Maggie could not think how anyone could bear to work in such a place.

Abby and Josef were scampering ahead, shrieking and exclaiming like two little savages. Maggie averted her eyes from a man hanging with a hook through his ribs, only to be confronted with a tableau of two brawny villains stretching an emaciated victim on a rack, overseen by a black-clad interrogator who was smiling grimly and taking notes. All manner of instruments of torture were on display in this section.

And then, ahead of her, she heard a soft moan and a mutter of speech. Madame Odette swayed and seemed to crumple. The attendant and Maggie reached and caught her, just before she fell.

Odette came to her senses reluctantly. She did not open her eyes for some minutes, but lay listening apathetically to the voices. Someone was patting her hands, speaking to her in execrable but fluent French, telling her that everything was all right. She was not to worry. She would be better in a minute or two.

A man's voice said, in English, 'I'll need to get back. It's as much as my job's worth to leave my post.'

'Yes, of course.' The quiet voice had changed to English. 'The lady will be all right if she lies quiet for a while in your office. And would you please tell those children to go down to the tea room? We will come as soon as we can.'

Footsteps, and the sound of a door closing.

Odette opened her eyes to find that the nursery maid was kneeling beside her. Maggie was holding her hand and looking intently into her face. When she saw Odette's eyes open, she smiled in obvious relief.

'You came over faint, madame. It was the heat in that horrible place, I think. I was glad for an excuse to get out of it myself.'

Memory rushed back. Odette remembered the tortured man's face, the grim enjoyment of his interrogator, and of how her submerged fears for Michel had surged up, overwhelming, unbearable. She saw, not a waxwork figure, but Michel himself in the hands of torturers, sharing in that moment his fear and his pain. Oh, God! What unspeakable torments was he suffering at this moment, and she powerless in this foreign land?

She must have spoken aloud, for the girl gave her hand a little shake, and said rapidly, 'No, madame. It all happened long ago. Things like that don't happen nowadays.'

'You don't know. None of you English know, or want to know.' And when Maggie, at a loss for words, looked merely bewildered, she added bitterly, 'How should you? This war is still a game to you. You have lost very little, you British people – some guns, some tanks, but you know nothing of fear, or hunger, or loved ones being taken from you, perhaps dying in pain . . .'

'You may be right.' Maggie said, low-voiced. 'It is only just beginning for us.'

Odette stared up at the nursery maid remorsefully. 'I should not speak so to you, my child. You have been kind, and somehow you have learned to speak my language. But no matter. We must find the children. Where is your coat?'

Maggie smiled. 'Under your head, madame. The floor is not very clean.' Then she raised Odette's head, and held a glass of water to her lips. 'Please drink a little. It will make you feel better.'

The lukewarm water tasted horrible but it helped her to regain her self-control, and by the time a worried looking Josef put his head round the door, closely followed by a fluttering Miss Brimley and Abby, she hoped she looked much as usual.

'Madame Odette! That man said you were taken ill!' exclaimed

Miss Brimley. She always talked in exclamations, particularly when she was correcting Abby's sums. 'My goodness! Your dress is all over dust! Did you fall down?'

'Something like that,' said Odette, putting an arm round Josef. Maggie still thought she looked ghastly. Spots of rouge stood out starkly on her thin cheeks. 'But I am better. Maggie has looked after me well. And now, we should go back to the hotel.'

'But Maggie wants to see the zoo,' protested Abby, who wanted to go there herself. 'And Josef would like to come.'

Maggie shook her head. 'Not now.'

'Perhaps later,' murmured Odette, breathing deeply as though starved of air.

'Certainly not, Abby!' said Miss Brimley. 'We shall be late for lunch if we go anywhere else.' She turned to Maggie, who was looking untidy, with her mackintosh undone and covered with dust, and her hat all crooked. 'Whatever made you put that idea into Abby's head, Maggie?'

'She didn't put it in my head, I put it in hers,' Abby contradicted. 'And there's loads of time before lunch—' She broke off as Maggie trod on her foot.

After it was decided to send the Cary children to Long Island, cables had come and gone between Maple Valley and Dulcimer, and in the end several more families had been invited to join this exodus. David's brother Conway had invited the lordlings, and some acquaintances of Lord Dulcimer were sending their grandchildren, who came for lunch at the hotel. After their meal they were herded into the lobby, the children staying close to their respective grown-ups.

But when the bus came and they went out to board it, they were swept aside by a tidal wave of other people who, bursting out of several cars, came running across the street. Marshalled by a tall, bony-faced lady in a flowered cotton dress and a hat like a teapot, a crowd of young people with attendant nurses and governesses swarmed noisily across the road, laughing and calling to each other, and ignoring everyone else. The hotel party watched in astonishment as the newcomers charged up the steps of the bus, behaving as though they owned it.

Abby found out later that these Devenishes were made up of three large and separate families, all related in some way to each other. That day, however, she was just awed by their numbers, their haughty looks, and their utter disregard of everybody else. She could have done without them. There seemed to be some public schoolboys, and two girls who looked almost grown-up, as well as a crowd of smaller children, none of whom took any notice of Abby's shy smiles of greeting.

Abby had heard about the Devenishes, of course, because Nanny knew all about them and you could tell she approved. For Abby's part, it took less than a minute to decide that they were best avoided, so she turned quickly towards the back of the bus.

The French children were there, and they grinned at Abby. She smiled back, liking them. They spoke English in a funny way, but after their morning at Madame Tussaud's, Abby felt at ease with them. One thing had surprised her very much. Maggie could understand and speak French.

It did not take long at the Consulate. There was a stir after the formalities were over. Ambassador Kennedy came in with the consul and an aide, and stood talking to the Devenish head lady with the teapot hat. He seemed to know her well.

Finally they were all lined up for a photograph, with Mr Kennedy and the American consul seated in the middle, the taller children standing at the back, and the smallest ones sitting cross-legged on the floor. They were told to smile. The camera lights flashed, and afterwards the ambassador wished them luck, and went away through some tall doors.

It was while they were finishing tea that one of the hotel staff came in and whispered something to Nanny. She pushed back her chair, told Maggie to take Jamie along to the bedroom and put him on his potty, and vanished through the door. Maggie had only just finished taking the little boy's bib off and had lifted him out of his high chair when Nanny came back.

She looked at Maggie rather grimly.

'I'm just going, Nanny,' said Maggie hastily. 'His feeder strings were all knotted up . . .'

'Never mind that. I want you.' Nanny looked towards the governess. 'Give Jamie to Miss Brimley.'

Jamie was passed over to the governess, who stood holding him, looking nervously at the sticky child, as though he was a time bomb about to explode. Nanny propelled Maggie from the room.

Lord Dulcimer, wearing a city suit and a black tie, was standing by the window at the end of the passage. He also looked grimly at Maggie. Her stomach gave a lurch of alarm. What had she done wrong? Or had her father written to say that she was not to go to America?

Her father had sent a telegram, but it had nothing to do with America. Baldly, because he knew no bearable way of breaking the news, Lord Dulcimer told Maggie that her brother Tom had been killed in action off the coast of Norfolk.

Chapter 7

They brought Tom's body home to Glen Cary, and he was buried in the graveyard overlooking the loch where he had so loved to go fishing. Mr Fraser in his brief oration at the graveside said that it was a fine and fitting place for Tom to be laid to rest. Maggie would have agreed. But Maggie was not there. In the glen, women did not go to funeral services or burials.

After a brief service in the kirk, the strongest men loaded the flag-draped coffin on a horsedrawn cart from the farm, and with the minister striding ahead like a tall, ungainly bird, a sombre procession followed Tom's body up the hill to the lochside cemetery. Ian Dunlop and Alistair walked directly behind the coffin, followed by a lieutenant from Tom's minesweeper, the local schoolmaster, two elderly shepherds, and a gnarled keeper from a neighbouring estate. A handful of Tom's younger friends had also contrived to get there, having somehow circumvented the claims of duty and the difficulties of wartime travel. Estate workers were there too, men who had come out of retirement to replace the ones who had gone to war. Most of them had known Tom since he was knee-high.

The head of the cortège was nearing the graveyard when a keen-eyed mourner pointed to a moving cloud of dust on the glen road. They waited, and presently a tall figure got out of a taxi and started up the path towards them. It was Dart, in uniform, come to represent the family.

Tom's commanding officer had written to Ian Dunlop, conveying his sympathy, and giving a brief description of how Tom had died. He had been killed instantly when enemy gunfire had strafed the minesweeper's deck. He added that the boy would be greatly missed.

There was no way of knowing whether this letter, or the presence of an officer from the minesweeper, brought the head keeper any comfort. His demeanour did not change, either, when Dart made his belated appearance. Ian's face and expression were as grey as the stone walls surrounding the graveyard. But he waited for the young laird to come up and shake his hand, and there was a pause while they talked together in the gateway to the cemetery.

Maggie had been sent home by night train, straight from London, still in her gaberdine mackintosh and hat, with the striped blue and white nursery maid's uniform under it. She remembered very little about the day or the night after she was told of Tom's death. After the initial moments of shock and pain, when her whole being utterly rejected what they were trying to tell her, there followed a period when she felt most strange. Nothing seemed quite real. People were kind. They gave her cups of tea, and Nanny helped her to pack her few belongings. She remembered Abby coming and hugging her really hard, refusing to let her go until Maggie had promised to come back soon. Later she found herself in King's Cross Station without knowing how she had got there, and Lord Dulcimer and Madame Odette found her a seat on an overcrowded train. The Frenchwoman handed her a parcel containing a rug, a thermos and some sandwiches for the journey, and his lordship had patted her shoulder in parting, and told her she was a brave girl.

Maggie was not at all brave. Not after the anaesthetic effect of shock had worn off next morning and she found herself waiting outside the bleak little Highland station for a bus that would drop her at the end of the glen road. Then it was that she first realised the extent of her loss – that Tom would not be at home when she got there. That he would never be at home again, to tease and torment her, to laugh at the silly things she said or did. Tom who had been her friend always, and occasionally dared to be her champion. Tom who had been killed when his minesweeper was dive-bombed by German planes. Shivering in the morning rain, blinded by sudden tears and feeling utterly desolate, Maggie did not hear a car draw up beside her.

Her case was taken from her, and a hand touched her shoulder. It was Mr Fraser. He did not speak. He just took her in his arms and held her, and she broke down completely and sobbed her heart out on the front of his hairy tweed jacket.

The minister was wonderfully matter-of-fact. He waited for the first storm of her grief to blow itself out. Then he bundled her into his shabby car, and climbed in beside her. After that he rooted in a pocket and brought out a large tartan handkerchief.

'Here, lass,' he said, unfolding it for her. 'You've ironed enough of these in your time, so you'll know what to do with it. Have a good cry before you start mopping up. It'll do you good.'

This made Maggie laugh in the midst of her gulping sobs. Mr Fraser had always kept a drawer full of colourful handkerchiefs in his study, and generations of glen people had wept or wiped their noses on them over the years. And somehow these tartan squares always found their way back to the manse, which Mrs Fraser declared would not have happened if they had been white and respectable.

She must have fallen asleep out of sheer exhaustion, for the next thing she knew they were halfway down the glen, with the sun shining, the heather in full bloom, purple and fragrant, and the moors stretching away to the sky on all sides. The clouds had rolled away. Overhead it was blue, and the morning sun had transformed the wet spiders' webs and seeding grasses to a sea of shining beads. Presently the grey slate roof of the manse came into view, with the stark shape of the kirk beyond it.

'You'll take breakfast with us at the manse, Maggie,' said the minister, taking her acquiescence for granted. 'And then I'll run you home. You'll not have eaten much since yesterday?'

She said no, she had not. She thought guiltily of Madame Odette's sandwiches which she had given away some time during the night. She still did not think she could swallow anything, but when presently she had been embraced by Mrs Fraser and surprisingly even by Cook, she managed to eat two slices of Cook's homemade bread and drank a cup of strong tea at the manse kitchen table. Her welcome here was like being enfolded in warm velvet. Everything was so familiar and so safe. She would have liked to stay for ever.

But soon an all too familiar anxiety was knotting her innards. She refused a third slice of bread and a second cup of tea. The minister came in and told her it was time to be off up the glen. She got up, thanked Mrs Fraser and Cook, and followed him out to his car, feeling like a condemned criminal on the way to the gallows. It was well over a year since she had seen her father, but she had not grown out of dreading him.

At first it was not so bad. There did not seem to be anybody around when Mr Fraser ushered her into the bread-scented kitchen. They paused in the doorway, and in a moment Gran came out of the scullery, drying her hands on a rough towel. She looked smaller, a little more bent, and Maggie felt a rush of compassion for the old lady. Tom had been her favourite, not a doubt of it, but here she was looking essentially just as usual. Maggie forgot about everything but giving some comfort to Gran. She dropped her little suitcase, which she had not allowed the minister to carry for her, and went across the room in a rush.

For a moment they clung. Then they both seemed to remember that Gran had never been one for kissing or hugging, and drew apart.

'So you've come, Maggie?' said the old lady briskly. 'Mind you thank the minister kindly for going to meet you in his motor. It was very good of you, Mr Fraser, with petrol so short, and so busy as you are with the funeral tomorrow.'

'I'm never too busy to see my friend Maggie,' said the minister cheerfully. 'Oh, and I'm to tell you that we are sending down a cooked chicken this afternoon. Cook thought you could use it, with all the folk coming in after the funeral.' He paused, looking at Maggie's tired face. 'I'll leave you now, Mistress Dunlop. But my wife and I hope you will spare Maggie to us one evening before she goes south again. She will be weary after sitting up all night, and should lie down on her bed for a while.'

His words were kindly meant, but Maggie did not want to lie down, and said so quickly before her grandmother's dawning frown found an outlet in speech. Her limbs felt leaden with weariness, but lying down would mean thinking. Work was better, and plainly work was expected of her.

'What do you want me to do, Gran?'

'Well, you can start by hanging your coat in the passage.'

It was as if she had never been away.

It had not occurred to Maggie, until then, that her part of the funeral rites for Tom would be to clean the cottage from top to bottom. She should have known, of course, for it had always been so whenever visitors were expected. It did not matter that the incomers would never go a step beyond the front room and the hall leading to it. Gran invariably carried on as though the whole place was about to be inspected from attic to cellar.

So into the scullery Maggie went and scrubbed and scoured, and later up to the attics, armed with bucket and scrubbing brushes, polish and dusters. The three small rooms up there were where she and her brothers had slept ever since Ian Dunlop had become head keeper at Glen Cary. It was a shock to find that her own little room had vanished. A wall had been taken down between her room and Alistair's to make a larger space for him and his bride, Glynis. She was wondering if she liked the new wallpaper or not when Glynis came in.

Glynis had got out of cleaning duties that morning because the estate factor had called to say he wanted some letters typed. Gran had been scandalised. The factor ought to have known better than to ask such a thing, she said, with the family in mourning. But Glynis had felt obliged to help him, and off she had gone. Maggie, knowing Glynis's ways, rather suspected that her new sister-in-law had planned the whole thing as a way of escape from chores.

She came clattering in on high heels, wearing a neat black skirt and a white blouse. She kicked off her shoes, and flung herself full length on the high double bed.

'Oh, Maggie,' she said, in her breathy, little girl's voice, 'it's so good to see you.' She giggled. 'You never expected to find me here, married to your big brother, did you?' And when Maggie did not immediately say anything, she looked up quickly. 'What's the matter? Have you taken the huff that we didn't ask you to the wedding?'

'Not me,' Maggie assured her bluntly. 'I couldn't have got away. Nor could I have afforded the fare. But Glynis, I thought you couldn't wait to escape from the glen. What on earth got into you? And Tom was the one you liked, not Alistair.'

'Well, so I did. But Alistair fancied me, and with Tom away we began going about together. It's such a relief to see you, you've no idea! I never thought you would come home once you had managed to get away.'

'His lordship came up to London and put me on a train.'

'Well, thank goodness for that,' said Glynis with feeling. 'You see, Alistair and I have applied for jobs with the Ministry of Food in Glasgow, and now that you're home, there'll be nothing to keep us.'

Maggie gaped at her. She stammered, 'But . . . but Glynis, I'm only here for the funeral. Mr Vorst and Mrs John have asked me to go to America with the children, and I said I would.'

'Not a hope. You should've heard your dad on the subject of America. He was ranting on day after day about it. But then the telegram came about Tom, and that took his mind off it. I wouldn't mention America at all if I were you.'

Maggie sat down suddenly on the bed. Her legs seem to have gone on holiday. 'I said I'd go. I promised Abby.'

Glynis had gone over to a dressing table and was sitting with her back to Maggie, surveying her face in the mirror. 'Then you shouldn't have come home. If you'd gone off without telling him, he couldn't have done anything about it.'

'How could I? I had to come home for . . . for Tom. And . . . for Gran, too, for that matter.'

Glynis turned back to Maggie, hearing her friend's voice wobble dangerously. She said in an embarrassed way, 'It's awful, isn't it? Have you gone in to see him yet?'

Maggie gaped at Glynis for the second time in minutes. 'See him? You mean Tom is here, here in the house?'

'In the front room,' said Glynis succintly. She went on in her pretty, refined voice, 'It's such a wicked waste. I always said he was the best looking brother.' Then she added, as Maggie looked blankly at her, 'If you want to see him, you'd better go down now. They're coming at two o'clock to close the coffin and take it to the kirk for the night.'

Maggie was not sure that she wanted to see Tom's body. But it seemed to her a terrible thing that Tom had been lying there in the front room, and Gran had never told her. It was as though he was already on the way to being forgotten. Gran had only been concerned with baking scones and making pancakes on the griddle, and setting her to clean the house.

Maggie crept with thudding heart into the front room, with its drawn blinds and stuffy lavender and polish smell, and peered fearfully over the rim of the open coffin. Then she knew. Tom was not here. Not the real Tom.

87

She had been so afraid that his wounds would show, or that his face would wear a look of fear. It was almost an anti-climax to see the waxen stranger who lay there, dressed in Tom's best uniform, with a serene expression and hands crossed on his chest. Tom had never been serene. He had been ruddy-faced and vital, full of fun and laughter, always wanting to be out in the open air. Like Maggie, he had hated the front room. She turned and went quickly out, climbing the steep, lino-covered stair to the attic. She got on with her cleaning.

It was only when she went up to Tom's room that night, longing to lie down at the end of that long, long day, that she felt that he might not, after all, be so very far away. The little attic room seemed full of him. She buried her face in the lumpy pillow, and as her pent-up tears fell hotly on the flannelette cover, it occurred to her how much Tom would have laughed at all these preparations for his funeral. 'Such a fuss about nothing,' he used to say when Gran went into one of her fevers of 'redding up' for visitors. And more likely than not he would be off to fetch his rod and tackle from the shed, and go in search of a fish.

Maggie heard the men tramping past the front of the cottage after the funeral, and shivered inwardly at the sound of her father's voice in the lobby. Gran and Glynis were awaiting the mourners in the front room, Gran presiding over the teapot, and Glynis standing at her side, ready to hand round sandwiches and scones and pancakes. Ian and Alistair Dunlop would dispense the whisky, of course, for drams were on a par with funerals – a male preserve.

Maggie was in the kitchen, sweating with nerves and heat in her borrowed funereal black. Gran had insisted on blacks, and since Maggie did not possess any, and none of Gran's or Glynis's clothes would go round her, she had been loaned a coat and skirt by Cook at the manse. It was thick and heavy and prickled her skin, and by the time she had made the tea, taken the scones from the oven and handed the tray over to Glynis, she was scarlet in the face and felt she might burst into flames any minute.

She went through the scullery and opened the back door. The cool, summer breeze was like balm to her perspiring face and hands, and she would have given anything for a paddle in the burn or, better still, a bathe in the loch. But she could not leave the cottage. Part of 'showing a proper respect for the dead' meant that Maggie not only had to be swathed in black wool that smelled of mothballs, but on no account must she show herself outside the house, for fear of what people would say. Glynis had been as rebellious as Maggie at this edict, and more outspoken – but only when the two of them were safely on their own, feeding the hens that morning. But even Glynis had conformed.

'Alistair says it's important to keep in with Gran. She doesn't know about our Glasgow jobs yet, and nor does your dad. Alistair says it's best to wait until we've had a letter of confirmation from the ministry.'

'Glynis. I can't stay here. I truly want to go to America and I promised I would. We must talk about it.'

'What's the use of talking? Your dad would kill you rather than let you go. I saw him looking at you last evening at teatime.'

Maggie's first meeting with her father, dreaded for so long, had been not so bad, after all. She had trembled with apprehension when he came in to his tea, but he'd merely looked at her grimly and said, 'So it's you again.' Then he'd turned away and had not looked at her again during the meal. But Maggie had been only too aware of his brooding inimical regard since then. When she saw him, she quaked inwardly, bracing herself for the inevitable storm. But he had not so far said anything. The respite was welcome, but she knew that he was only biding his time.

She heard Glynis calling her. She went quickly back inside.

Glynis was smiling. For a bare second, Maggie wondered what was up. And then she saw Dart in the kitchen doorway. He looked tall and distinguished, and as Maggie's eyes widened at the sight of him, he smiled.

'So this is where you've been hiding.' He reached out a hand and clasped Maggie's nerveless one. 'My poor girl. I'm so sorry about Tom. We shall all miss him, but you more than anyone, I think.'

Maggie had never heard Dart speak in that warm, gentle tone, and it came close to destroying her precarious composure. She ducked her head and managed to mutter some sort of thanks, withdrawing her hot hand before it began to tremble.

Glynis said in her refined, front-room voice, 'It was right good of your lordship to come for the funeral. We have to thank you very much for your kindness.'

Ignoring Glynis, Dart asked Maggie, 'When are you coming back to Dulcimer? I told Abby that I would find out.'

'Oh?' Maggie was so touched that for a moment she forgot her doubts and fears. 'How was Abby, my lord? Was she all right? I fair miss her.'

'Abby is missing you too. Shall I take you south with me tomorrow? I won't be leaving until the evening. Will that give you time enough?'

This time, Maggie did not care who saw that she was trembling. Her grey eyes were suddenly shining with gratitude for this unexpected way of escape. Surely even her father could not gainsay Lord Dartmore. Not when he was there in person. 'I'll be ready whenever you say, my lord. And thank you.'

* * *

Dart left with the minister before the other mourners got down to serious whisky drinking. Maggie caught a glimpse of her father escorting them to the minister's car. Suddenly, Glynis was back in the kitchen. She stood there with her hands on her hips.

'You're a sly one, Maggie. I never thought you had it in you. Such big, worshipping eyes. Yes, milord! Thank you, milord! I'll be ready whenever you say. You've learned a thing or two down there in England, it seems.'

Maggie made a hasty imploring movement with her hands.

Glynis laughed, her eyes relentless. Maggie knew that look of old, and her heart sank. She said desperately, 'Don't tell my dad, Glynis. Please. It's my only chance.'

Glynis stopped laughing. Her button mouth thinned and her voice was cold. 'You've already had your chance. You've been away for long enough. Now it's my turn to start living – and Alistair's,' she added, almost as an afterthought. 'If you don't want me to tell your dad, you must swear that you won't leave. Otherwise I'll tell.'

There was a tense silence. Both girls held their breath as they heard Ian Dunlop go past the window again. They heard him speaking in the hall, and old Mrs Dunlop's voice murmuring an answer.

Gran came in. She looked exhausted, and collapsed rather than sat on one of the wooden kitchen chairs. She looked at them rather as if she hardly knew what they were doing there. Then, with an effort, she said, 'You girls had best clear the tea things out of the front room before the menfolk settle down to their dramming. There's just five of them left now, and they'll not want to be disturbed again tonight.'

Glynis and Maggie washed and dried and put away, neither of them looking at the other, or saying a word, conscious of Gran still sitting at the kitchen table. Only when Maggie had persuaded Gran to go to bed with a flannel-wrapped stone hot bottle at her feet did Maggie come back to face Glynis.

She was feeling pretty desperate by this time. 'Come outside. We can't talk here.'

'I meant what I said,' said Glynis stonily. 'Give up this idea of America or I go to your dad.'

'Don't talk so loud.'

Glynis tittered. 'What's the harm? Unlike you, I have nothing to hide.'

Maggie had not spent her last school years as Glynis's follower without getting to know her ways. Whatever she might promise, Glynis would very likely let drop about Lord Dartmore's offer to take her south, if only for the excitement of stirring up trouble.

Maggie said slowly, without hope, 'What about that job in Glasgow? You and Alistair have hidden that carefully enough.'

Glynis looked over her shoulder before coming over to grasp Maggie's arm in a painful, pinching grip. 'If you spoil that for us, Maggie, it won't be just your dad who will half kill you. Don't you dare!'

Maggie pulled away from her, rubbing her arm and trying to think what best to do. Fratching with Glynis would solve nothing. She suddenly wished that Mr Fraser was here to advise her. 'Glynis, there must be someone else who would keep house here.'

'Your gran would never let a stranger in.'

'She just might if it was the right person.' Maggie rubbed a work-roughened hand over her eyes and said, 'Give me until tomorrow. Please, Glynis.'

'How do I know you won't run away in the night?'

Maggie looked at her. Her eyes were steady and a shade scornful, but all she said was, 'You know me well enough to know that I wouldn't do that.'

Glynis looked almost abashed. She tossed her permed head and said, 'Oh, very well. Until tomorrow then.'

Dart dined with the Frasers on the evening of Tom Dunlop's funeral. But they did not press him to stay the night. When Dart came to the glen, he always slept at the Lodge. He refused the minister's offer of a lift home in the manse car. It was a fine night. As always in that Highland region in summer, it never got wholly dark. He preferred to walk.

The shortest route to the Lodge ran past Ian Dunlop's cottage, which lay in the midst of outbuildings, a capacious game larder and dog kennels. The dogs would surely start barking if he went by, and having shaken off the depression of the funeral, the last thing Dart wanted was for Dunlop to come out and offer him a further dram. He turned down the track to the lochside, and once on the flat pebbled strand that edged the water, he could see the Lodge, with its turreted roofs and sprawling bulk.

Dart loved Glen Cary Lodge. He had a way of turning up there at all seasons and times, and never seemed to notice its manifold inconveniences or its ugliness.

Fifteen years before, he had taken Peggy to Glen Cary on the second stage of their honeymoon, telling her that it was his favourite place on earth. He had been at first incredulous and then outraged to find that she compared his private heaven unfavourably with the Hotel Westminster at Le Touquet, from where they had just come. A Victorian dump, she called it, and went on to say something even ruder about the plumbing. He retorted with a jibe about Americans having no soul above the lavatory, and there followed the first of many rows. Newly wed, they had made even more furious love, and laughed it off. But only for a time. Peggy's dislike of the Lodge had always rankled.

As he passed along the lochside under the stars, he had the familiar sense of coming home. The pensioner caretaker had gone to bed, but there was a turf fire glowing on the living-room hearth, and he poked it into life before pouring himself a malt whisky. He stretched out his long legs, and sat contentedly watching the flames, enjoying the silence and solitude.

He felt that he had earned this respite. After all, he had barely known the Dunlop boy, and avoided funerals whenever possible. But Lord Dulcimer had asked him to go, and Abby had implored him with tears in her eyes. The child was convinced that she would be frog-marched onto a ship before the nursery maid could get away to join them. For some reason, the big Dunlop girl was important to Abby. 'I spoke to Mummy in St Andrews on the telephone,' Abby told him earnestly, 'and I asked her to go to the funeral. But she said she had too much to do looking after that wretched David man . . .'

Dart got to his feet, and drained his glass. He knew very well why he had come north. It was not to please his father or Abby, but because he wanted to see Antonia. He was still furious with her, outraged at her marrying the Vorst puppy to spite him. After that disastrous weekend at Dulcimer, he had seen her once queening it at the Vorst, and after that had resolved to leave her alone. He wished her joy of her worshipping boy husband.

Since she had gone north he had received a scribbled postcard from her complaining of a grim boarding house and a diet of herrings and baked beans. She would tire of that soon enough.

Now that he was in Scotland he decided to ring her in St Andrews. She would welcome a change from baked beans. He would take her out to lunch. He remembered that he had offered to take the Dunlop girl back to Dulcimer. Well, he could put her on a southbound train, before heading for St Andrews and Antonia.

Chapter 8

Old Mrs Dunlop lay with her eyes half closed, drowsily watching while Maggie moved around her bedroom. The old lady felt warmer now, and the strength was seeping back like a slow, incoming tide. Soon she would be back to normal, her old energetic self – but not yet. Not quite yet. Better to lie still and let Maggie think she was dozing.

Maggie was tidying up, hanging clothes in the dark mahogany wardrobe, straightening things, putting shoes into gingham shoe bags. The girl's movements were quiet and neat, so that other house sounds were clearly audible in the background. The rumble of men's voices from the front room, footsteps when one of them went out into the lobby, the flush of the toilet, the clatter of Glynis's shoes on the linoleum-covered stairway. Strange, thought Mrs Dunlop, that tiny, birdlike Glynis made such a noise, while big Maggie moved about with hardly any sound at all.

The old lady's mind wandered back in time. Mary used to move in just that quiet way. But Mary had been slight like Glynis, small-waisted and curved in all the right places – a real little beauty. Maggie had her mother's colouring, but there the likeness ended, for she was in every sense a big strong girl. Just as well she did not resemble her mother, with Ian being so bitterly resentful, even after seventeen years. His once possessive devotion for Mary had changed overnight to an enduring hatred.

What had made Mary leave so suddenly? Even after all these years, Mrs Dunlop had never puzzled it out. There had been nothing remarkable about the young ex-soldier called Jack; a distant kinsman who had been brought up by Mary's mother when his own mother had died, and his sister moved away. Jack had been a sponsor at the baptism. He had been younger than Mary by some years, and not much to look at.

Whatever the reason, Ian Dunlop had taken against the young man at sight. But then, Ian could never bear to see his pretty wife smiling at anyone. He sat silent at the christening tea party, watching the cousin, and glowering.

Mary took no notice of Ian's sulks – or so it seemed. When the

93

visitors had gone she just smiled at Ian serenely, picked baby Maggie out of her crib, and carried her away to be fed.

It was unbelievable, really, that Mary could have gone off like that. Mrs Dunlop could have sworn that she adored that baby. But leave she did – and without a word, except one brief scribbled note to Ian. She must have packed her bag and gone during the night, and neither she nor Jack were ever seen or heard of again.

The first thing Mrs Dunlop knew about it was next morning when she heard the baby crying. She had taken no notice, expecting Mary to pick her up. But the crying went on and on, until Mrs Dunlop could bear it no longer. After that it was all a muddle in her mind, the dishevelled bedroom, empty drawers pulled out and cupboard doors open, and neither Ian nor Mary anywhere to be found. She remembered struggling to deal with the screaming baby, who had always been breastfed and furiously rejected milk from a bottle.

There were other memories. Ian coming in from the moor, holding Mary's note in his hand. He tossed the single, sheet of pale blue paper into the fire – they cooked on an open range in those days – and looked at his mother with terrible eyes.

'Well, Mother. Mary has gone off with that kinsman of hers, God's curse upon him. They mean to sail for America next week.'

She remembered saying that he should go after Mary and bring her back, but he cut her short. 'I'd not have her back if she crawled here on her knees. A whore like that? Do you think I would let her near my sons, corrupting them, teaching them Godless, town ways? They are better off without her. I'll be away to the market tonight, and I'll thank you, Mother, to tell the boys that their mother is dead. Make up whatever tale you please, and when I come back none of you will mention my wife's name.' He stalked to the door, but not before the baby began to wail again. 'And keep that damned brat quiet. If it wasn't for her, this would never have happened.'

Mrs Dunlop heard Maggie go softly from the room and close the door. Maggie's quiet ways might well have something to do with the fact that keeping her quiet as a baby had been an utter necessity in those early years. Ian could never bear sight nor sound of his daughter. She had only to let out a whimper for his face to darken. None of them spoke of it, but the boys were aware of the need to keep Maggie out of Ian's way. Even Alistair, never perceptive, knew it. Tom had known fine, and would lead the toddling child out of the cottage, playing with her by the hour beside the burn when the weather was fine, and when she was older taking her fishing or looking at birds.

Tom. The lad had been named Thomas for her own father, and had grown up in his image. Mrs Dunlop stirred, as this renewed, inescapable pain came back to torment her. Why should Tom have to be killed? Such a waste of a fine, kind young man, to be cut off before he had half begun to live. This dreadful war! And from what you could tell in the papers, it was only just beginning.

Maggie was a good child, for all that she was clumsy and stupid compared to her brothers. People seemed to like her. Mrs Dunlop sighed, for it came to her that Maggie was neither clumsy nor stupid except when her father was there. If only they got on better, she would dearly love to keep Maggie at home. She was feeling her age these days, more than she cared to admit.

But it would not do. She would ask Mrs Fraser to take Maggie back into service. Once the Cary children had gone, Maggie would be out of a job. There was no way that Ian would let her go to America. It was hard luck, but Maggie would have to accept it.

Mrs Dunlop closed her eyes. She would tell Maggie about Mary running off. She was a kind child, and it might help her to understand why her father felt so bitter – particularly about America.

But when Maggie came in later, the old lady was deeply asleep.

It was past midnight when the last of the mourners crunched rather unsteadily away under Maggie's attic window. Alistair came past her door on his way to bed, stumbling up the stairs, fumbling noisily with the door handle of his and Glynis's room. The attic walls were thin, and there was a prolonged session of thumps, bedsprings creaking, muted speech and occasional giggles from Glynis before things grew quiet.

Maggie lay rigid on Tom's hard mattress, aware by some sense born of fear that her father had not gone to his room. As a rule, Ian Dunlop was an abstemious man. She always feared him, but when he had drink taken, he was like a devil. Twice in the past, after a dramming session, he had come upstairs and ranted at her as she lay quivering in bed, before pulling her out and taking his belt to her.

Soon she could bear the suspense no longer, so she crept out of bed and peered fearfully through a slit in the window curtains. And there he was, standing by the burn. The moonlight was full on his face as he stared back towards the house. Maggie froze. He seemed to be looking at her, and she felt his hatred. She no longer asked herself why her father hated her. She just knew that he did. Very carefully, she let the curtain slide back into place, and tiptoed shivering back to bed. It seemed an age before she heard him come in again, and even longer before he finally went into his own room and shut the door.

Ian had seen the twitching curtain. He smiled grimly to himself, aware that Maggie was in a state of terrified suspense. He had been glad to let her sweat. He owed her something for going to Dulcimer against his wishes. But at the sight of that curtain, he was tempted to go up to her and teach her a lesson for spying on him. He had told his mother that he would not mention America until after the funeral day. It was over. It was past two in the morning.

He made his way purposefully back to the house, and he heard his mother calling from her room. He opened her door and saw her sitting upright in bed, her white hair severely braided, her spectacles on her nose. She had been reading her Bible.

'I thought I heard you, son. You'll be away to your bed, then?'

'Just going, Mother. That was a fine spread you gave us. And the minister gave Tom a grand send-off.'

She nodded again. 'Then sleep well, son.'

'Good night, Mother.'

He went away. He was not deceived. She had been waiting up, to make sure he did not go near Maggie. Well, tomorrow it would be different. Tomorrow, after walking the moor with Lord Dartmore, he would have it out with Maggie, and nobody was going to stop him.

Before seven in the morning, Maggie was at the back door of the manse. Cook was up, as Maggie knew she would be, and had just re-lit the stove.

'So what brings you here so bright and early, Maggie?'

'I've brought your black costume back, Cook, and thank you kindly for letting me wear it.' She saw Cook looking disparagingly at the brown paper parcel, and said, 'I'll hang it up in your bedroom, shall I?'

'No need for that,' said Cook. 'I'm in no hurry for it this hot weather. You must have been half stewed. Now, out with it, Maggie. What else have you come for?'

Maggie blushed. 'I came to see if I could have a wee word with the minister, Cook. But of course I'll wait until after he has had his breakfast.'

'Then you'll be waiting a long time,' said Cook bluntly. 'The minister and Mistress Fraser have been up and away this hour or more. They're away to Inverness. They had word that Dawn's baby had come. It's Mrs Fraser's first granddaughter. They decided to catch the night train at Glen Cary Halt, and won't be back till tomorrow night.'

Maggie's look of stunned disappointment prompted the older woman to say, 'Is there anything I can do to help, lassie?'

Maggie looked at Cook. She did not think that there was much anyone could do to help. But she needed to tell somebody. In halting accents she explained her predicament, and when she came away half an hour later, she was in better heart.

Against all Maggie's expectations, Cook had come up with a possible solution.

She called in at the estate office. She had to talk to Glynis. But Glynis, like the minister, was not there. The factor told Maggie that he was expecting her any minute. Would Maggie care to wait in the outer office?

She waited as long as she dared, but there was still the midday dinner to get. After a full hour, and no sign of Glynis, she hurried away.

It was only when she came to the kitchen door of her father's house and heard them talking about her that she knew the worst. She stood just outside the door, trying to steady her breathing. What had Tom said about going to America? 'Don't let anyone stop you, Maggie. I'll be right ashamed of you if you don't stand up to him for once.'

She would try to stand up for herself. For Tom, she would try not to be a coward.

She heard Glynis saying, 'I knew fine that Maggie was planning to go with Lord Dartmore. But she didn't want me to tell you.'

Ian Dunlop's voice was deadly quiet. 'I'll be bound she didn't. But I'd have had it out of her even if his lordship hadn't told me.'

'Maggie is late. She said she would be back to get the dinner,' said Gran querulously, to an accompaniment of clashing saucepans – a sure sign of displeasure. 'She went down the glen early to see the minister but promised to be back in good time.'

'Maybe she's run off to the Lodge, to hide there until his lordship takes her away,' suggested Glynis.

Maggie spoke from the doorway. 'I told you I wouldn't do that. And I do at least try to keep my promises.'

All three turned to look at her – Gran by the stove, Glynis and Ian seated at the kitchen table.

To her grandmother, Maggie said simply, 'Sorry, Gran. I wanted to talk to Glynis, and waited too long at the estate office.' She crossed the kitchen and sat down at the table, opposite her father, folding her hands in her lap. She said a trifle breathlessly, 'So, Dad? Has his lordship told you that he offered to take me back to Dulcimer?'

'Aye. He did so. And I told him that you had changed your mind about going.'

Glynis was disappointed. Glancing from one to another of these two, you might think they were discussing the weather. What a comedown! She had hoped for fireworks. Gran, by the stove, knew better, and wished she had warned Maggie last night. If only she had not fallen asleep

'I'll need to go back, Dad,' Maggie said. It was hard to keep a matter-of-fact tone, but she knew it was her best hope. 'I'll need to work out my notice.'

'Aye. And slip off to America when my back is turned. That den of iniquity.'

'That's not what I've heard. And Dad, Tom said that I ought to take a chance to go there.'

'We will leave your brother's name out of this, Maggie,' said the head keeper, his voice rising.

Maggie's heart sank. If only he would listen to her. An inner voice reminded her that her father had never listened. Not once, in all her life. She said, 'I promised. Abby is relying on me, Dad.'

'Is that so, Maggie?' Slowly, Ian Dunlop came to his feet. They all saw that he was holding his bone-handled shepherd's crook. He looked at Maggie and banged it suddenly on the table top. All three women jumped. Glasses and cutlery rattled on the chequered cloth. Glynis gave vent to a small breathless shriek, half frightened, half pleasurable.

'That is one promise that you will not be keeping.'

'I must keep it, Dad.'

He paid no attention to her but cleared some glasses and plates to one side, and spread out a typed sheet of paper.

'I've a letter of resignation ready for you to sign, and you will sign it now. It's time you came home and did your duty by your own family.'

Maggie had also come to her feet. 'I'm not signing any paper. I've given my promise, and I cannot go back on it.'

'You'll put your name to that letter one way or another,' he said, in that same conversational tone. 'Will you do it now, or must I beat the daylights out of you first?'

Maggie's eyes were on her father's left hand which was fumbling at the buckle of his thick, brass-studded belt. She said, 'You'll do that anyway, I'm thinking – but I'll sign no letter.'

'Maggie!' Mrs Dunlop's voice was imploring. 'I wanted to explain to you last night. Do as your father tells you. Believe me, he has a reason for not wanting you to go to America—'

'Hold your tongue, Mother. The lass will do as she is told or take the consequences.' He raised his stick again, thwacking it sideways across the table and sending plates and glasses crashing onto the floor.

Mrs Dunlop made a sound like a whimper. 'Ian, don't . . .'

Ian ignored his mother. He merely said, 'So, Maggie? Will you take what's coming to you here and risk my breaking more of your grandmother's china, or will you take yourself to the kennel and wait for me? Just the place for a bitch, to my way of thinking.'

Maggie looked into her grandmother's pleading eyes, and to a broken cup at her feet. She said bleakly, 'I'll go. But don't bother to bring that letter with you, for I'll not put my name to it.'

She walked out quickly, her braided head held high.

* * *

David was undergoing intensive retraining at a Fife air base, learning to fly the newest Spitfires. This involved night flying as well as sorties by day. He was concerned that there was little time to spend with Antonia, but he need not have worried. She was pretty and amusing and soon became a popular member of their small, largely male community – and when he came in, often too tired to talk, he could only be relieved to find a note saying that she was dining out, or had gone off to play golf. He marvelled at the way Antonia had adapted to being an RAF wife. He found himself admiring and loving her more than ever.

At first they had taken lodgings near the air base – the home of the grumbling landlady and the diet of baked beans – but later moved to a flat in nearby St Andrews. This suited them better. The RAF had requisitioned one of the university buildings, and several of David's fellow pilot officers were billeted there. The Vorsts took over the top floor, and were content with their rooftop abode.

David warned Antonia that she was not to fall in love with any of the dashing young men who lived downstairs. But in truth he was consoled by the thought that one or other of his friends and colleagues would be on hand to keep an eye on her. Antonia swung a pretty golf club, and was much in demand as a partner in mixed foursomes.

He came home from the base one afternoon to find the flat deserted. A note on the hall table informed him that Antonia had gone out to lunch with some girlfriends. It was past six o'clock. Strange. She was not much addicted to female company. What was keeping her?

He turned into the bedroom which overlooked the street, stripping off his Air Force tie and gazing idly out of the window. Then he saw them – Dart and Antonia strolling down the street, talking and laughing.

His whole being seemed to jolt with the shock of seeing them together. It was like being slammed back against a wall, and a firestorm of jealousy raged through him. Dart! What the hell was Dart doing here, when he ought to be in England, well out of their way?

He watched them come along the street and pause opposite a parked black car. He had left it there minutes earlier. He had regretfully pensioned off the thirsty monster, and had bought a second-hand Austin, which he and Antonia shared. David drew back out of sight, in case she should look up and catch him spying on her.

He had himself in hand by the time she came in, flushed and breathless from her climb up four flights of stairs. 'Darling!' she cried. 'Just look who I found in Rusacks at lunchtime. I made him join in our girls' lunch party.'

'She made me pay for it, too,' said Dart, as the two men shook hands. 'And very expensive it was. You always were an expensive little vehicle to run, Tonia.'

Antonia smiled at Dart, choosing to take this as a compliment. 'Better than to be thought cheap, surely?'

'No doubt, but I have never before found you carousing with four other women. Quite a new departure. And none of them even half pretty.'

'If I had known you were coming, Dart darling, I would have looked out my prettiest friends to amuse you.'

'Would you, Tonia mia? How very obliging of you.'

David was not enjoying this banter. They seemed to be talking on two levels, one of them in code. He felt excluded. He choked back his resentment and asked Dart what had brought him to Scotland.

'The Dunlop boy's funeral, of course. Father twisted my arm, and so did Abby, the little wretch. I half expected to find you there, Tonia.'

Antonia said, rather sharply, 'You know perfectly well that women don't go to funerals in Scotland.'

'Well, David might have gone.'

'David hasn't got time for that sort of thing. He's been flying night and day, without a single break. I hardly ever get time to talk to him.'

David looked at Antonia, who was flushed and looked guilty. Then he turned his eyes back to Dart. 'Should I know what you are talking about?'

'Not if Antonia hasn't told you,' said Dart, frowning at her. 'Why ever didn't you?'

'There wasn't time. We've hardly had a minute together this week.' She turned to look at David, her blue eyes enormous and her mouth trembling. 'Darling heart, I meant to tell you, honestly. Maggie's brother was killed. You know, the one who was in the Navy.'

'And he was buried at Glen Cary yesterday,' said Dart, seeing David's tanned face grow still and taut.

'Tom? Not Maggie's Tom?'

Dart nodded.

'That poor kid.' David rounded on Antonia. 'You ought to have told me, honey. I'd have gone to the funeral, if only for Maggie.'

'You're as bad as Abby,' said Antonia crossly. 'Such a fuss to make about a nursery maid. It's very sad about her brother, but after all, there is a war on. And anyway, going to America will take Maggie's mind off her sorrows.'

Dart shook his head. 'The girl has changed her mind. She's decided not to go.'

'Well, she might have had the decency to let us know,' said Antonia even more crossly.

David found it difficult to believe in Maggie's defection. He said slowly, 'Are you sure about this?'

Dart shrugged. 'Her father told me. Like Antonia, I was rather annoyed. I saw her after the funeral bun fight and offered to bring her away with me.'

'I suppose you turned on the charm,' said Antonia. 'She would not have known how to say no.'

'All she had to do was to say that she wanted to stay at home.'

Antonia sighed. 'What a bore. Abby is bound to make a grand fuss.'

David looked at his wife for a long moment. Then he said quietly, 'You know something? I think it's time we all had a drink. What can I fix for you, Antonia?'

'I'll say this for you, young David,' said Dart presently, 'you make a mighty wicked martini. As good as I do myself, and I can't put it higher than that.'

'Thanks,' said David. 'But then you were taught how to mix them by my father, weren't you?'

They dined at Dart's hotel overlooking the Old Course, and contrary to David's expectations, it was a pleasant evening. Dart was at his most amiable, for once resisting the urge to flirt with Antonia. David came away thinking that his cousin could be really quite likeable when he tried. He talked about Glen Cary with knowledge and enthusiasm. David had not realised how much Dart was involved with the place. 'You ought to go there,' he told them both. 'You love it as much as I do, don't you, Tonia?'

She twinkled at him. 'Anyone who wants to keep in with you *has* to say they love it.'

'Of course.'

The Vorsts walked home through a rainstorm, and came up into their bare top-floor flat breathless, soaked to the skin and laughing. David made love to Antonia savagely that night, with no tender consideration for her wishes. It was as though he was trying to subdue and possess her utterly. She responded with fire and fervour, and some surprise.

When they lay quiet and spent, David said ruefully, 'When I saw you down there with Dart today, I felt so burned up and jealous, I could have killed you both. I am sorry, honey.'

She laid a polished fingertip over his lips. 'Hush. Don't say sorry. You were wonderful tonight. If seeing Dart has this effect on you, I must try to lure him here more often.'

'Don't you dare! You are mine. My wife. What say we go visiting at Glen Cary this weekend, honey? I'm due at least a twenty-four, and I've never been there with you. We could talk to Maggie. I just don't get it. She was so excited about going to Maple Valley with the kids.'

'I'm not sure I want to send the children with someone who changes her mind so easily.'

101

'There must be a reason. Shock? Grief? She just loved that brother of hers. She must be devastated.'

Antonia said in a bored voice, 'Do we *have* to talk about that wretched girl all night? You can talk to her when you take me to Glen Cary on Saturday. It will be nice to get away.'

Antonia got away the very next day – but to Dulcimer not Glen Cary. News came that the children might sail any day. Nobody knew the precise day or port of embarkation, because convoy movements were shrouded in secrecy, but they were already packed, and must be ready to go at an hour's notice. David saw his wife and Dart on to a train at Cupar, before heading back to the air base. His leave would have to wait.

On Friday afternoon, Glynis felt a strong reluctance to leave her work. It had been a relief to get away from the head keeper's house. She dreaded going back, even though she had worried all day about what was happening. Alistair was away at the sheep sales, and the factor and every able-bodied man on the estate had gone off to the high woods to fight a forest fire that had got out of control. There was no one she could talk to.

She had never before witnessed her friend Maggie in trouble with her father, and had wondered what it would be like. She had even expected to find it exciting.

The reality had appalled her. For what seemed like an unbearable length of time, she and Gran had sat together in the kitchen, waiting for Ian to come back. At length, unable to bear the suspense, Glynis had gone out into the yard to listen. She tiptoed nearer to the dog kennel doors, and heard the deep rumble of the head keeper's voice, and Maggie's unintelligible replies, and then sounds as of someone beating a carpet. A scream from Maggie, sharp, agonised – and then silence. Glynis scuttled back into the kitchen, getting there just in time.

Ian Dunlop stood at the kitchen door, looking in on them. He breathed as though he had been running.

'I'm off to look to the sheep, and after that to help with the fire. Don't go near Maggie, either of you. I haven't finished with her. I'll go to her this evening, and if necessary she'll stay there until tomorrow morning.'

'Ian,' said Mrs Dunlop, imploringly, 'send her up to her room if you've a mind to it, but don't leave her out there in the kennel.'

'She'll stay there until she's given in. I'll brook no defiance from my daughter. She'll sign that letter, and that's all there is about it.'

'Let me talk to her, son.'

'I've told you to leave her alone, Mother. And don't bother to look at her when I'm up the hill.'

He shut the door on his mother's protests, and a minute later they saw him stride past the window with two collies at his heels. Ian's dogs adored him.

Maggie thought she must have lost consciousness, because it was dark and cold when she woke. Through the thin wooden partition of the back kennel she heard her father's shooting dogs stirring and scratching; the sound of one of them lapping water made her aware of a terrible thirst. Ian had shouted at her that he would smash her face and break every bone in her body unless she obeyed him. She thought that he had already gone some way to doing it. But she had not given in. She hurt all over, and there was a crust of dried blood at the corner of her swollen mouth and over one eye; but she had still managed to refuse when he once more ordered her to sign the letter to the David Vorsts. But even for Abby, even for Tom, she did not think she could hold out when her dad came back in the morning.

But by some unexplained miracle, her father did not come near her. The dogs set up a frantic barking before dawn, a heavy vehicle came noisily into the yard, and there was a volley of thudding knocks at the house door. She heard men's voices upraised and talk of another fire. Her father's deep tones answered, and just when Maggie was trying to edge herself against the wall into a sitting position to face him, she heard the lorry rev up and roar away into the distance. Silence. Could it be that her father had gone with them? Or was he just keeping her in suspense?

A little later, she heard footsteps. Not her father's. She knew his tread too well. Glynis's face, looking frightened, peered at her over the half door. She stared at Maggie in horror. 'My God, Maggie! Oh, *my God*!'

Maggie tried to smile at her, but it hurt her mouth too much.

'Oh, Maggie, if I'd known, I'd never . . .' Glynis sounded close to tears. She came closer, recoiled, but said resolutely, 'Look, Maggie. I daren't untie you because your dad will be back. I don't know when. There's a second bad fire in the wood above the village, and all the men have gone to put it out, but for how long I don't know. Can I get you anything?'

Speech was difficult, but she somehow got her sister-in-law to understand about her raging thirst. In a little while Glynis was back with water and a plate of bread and butter. Maggie managed to gulp some of the water, even though a lot of it dribbled from her wounded mouth and ran down her bloodied chin, making pale splashes on the filthy, stained front of her nursery maid dress. The bread she could not to cope with, so Glynis went away again, determined to bring her something soft and manageable. Something like scrambled eggs perhaps?

Mrs Dunlop was drinking a cup of tea in the kitchen. She turned, and seeing the plate in Glynis's hand, and the look on her face, said anxiously, 'Is the lassie all right?'

Glynis stared at the older woman, hating her. She said with bitter irony, 'All right? You can ask if Maggie is all *right*? She's tied by the wrists to a ring on the wall, all over blood and dirt, can't speak or see out of one eye, has wet herself. Does that count for "all right" in this family? I never knew until now what it has been like for Maggie all this time.'

Gran stared at Glynis, and her teacup rattled on its saucer as she laid it down. 'I'll go to her,' she said.

It took Gran and Glynis some time to get Maggie back into the house. They got her to her feet, with difficulty, after they had cut through the ropes on her wrists. Maggie was taller than both women and no lightweight, and her knees kept buckling under her as all three made their staggering way across the yard and into the kitchen. They did not attempt to get her upstairs to her room, but decided to lay her down on Gran's bed. But despite their efforts to steady her, Maggie toppled and fell to the ground beside the high bedstead, and lay there, barely conscious after the effort and pain of being moved by her two far from expert rescuers.

Mrs Dunlop and Glynis stood looking down at Maggie helplessly.

'We ought to send for the doctor,' said Glynis.

'We will not. The lassie will come to herself in a little while, and then we'll clean her up and get her into bed.'

'But won't he beat her again? He said he would.'

Mrs Dunlop was silent for so long that Glynis wondered if she had heard the question. In a little while the older woman said, 'There must be no more beating. I'll speak to him. Ian usually minds me.'

Glynis doubted if the head keeper was going to listen to anyone in his present violent, frustrated, near-crazed mood. If only there was some way of getting Maggie away while he was out with the firefighters. She looked helplessly at Maggie's recumbent form. She was lying on her side, her hair loose and matted, her bloodied and swollen face mercifully turned away. Glynis had once seen a picture of a stranded whale in the newspaper. Maggie looked no less helpless and immovable.

'Don't just stand there, Glynis,' said Gran sharply. 'Fetch me a pillow to put under her head, and the quilt from off my bed. And then you had best be off to work. I'll see to her.'

When Glynis had changed her clothes and was at the door, Gran called her back. 'Now then,' the old lady said. 'Don't you go talking of this to anyone. This is a family matter, and must go no further. Just keep it to yourself. You'll promise?'

Glynis promised to keep her mouth shut, and made her escape.

She made a poor pretence of working in the office. The factor was evidently still helping with the fire. By mid-afternoon Glynis decided to close the office and go home. She was just putting a cover on her typewriter, when the telephone rang.

The glen road was rutted and uneven, but David did not slacken his speed as the Austin rattled and bounced down it. After speaking to that girl in the Glen Cary estate office – she said she was Maggie's sister-in-law – he had been consumed with anxiety. The girl had not told him very much, only that he should come, and come quickly.

'What's the problem?' he had asked her again. 'Please tell me, Mrs Dunlop.'

'Mr Vorst, I can't tell you, but please come . . .'

The manse came in sight, and he saw the minister's car turning in at the gate. He slowed down, waved. Mr and Mrs Fraser turned startled faces, and waved back.

As David wound his car window down, the minister came alongside and peered in at him. 'This is a pleasant surprise. What brings you?'

David got out to shake hands. 'It may seem odd, but I've come to see Maggie Dunlop.'

'But didn't Maggie go south after the funeral? I only came home from Inverness last night, but I think I would have heard if she was here.'

'I spoke to some girl in the estate office, Glynis or something, and she told me Maggie was at home. She sounded odd, scared, and ended up by scaring me. She said I ought to come.'

The minister studied David's face. 'You think there's something wrong? Don't try to explain. You can tell me as we go along. I'm coming with you.'

On the way, David told the minister what he knew. It sounded a threadbare story. 'Of course, people do change their minds,' he said, 'but it doesn't feel right. And that girl in the office sounded so odd. I may look all kinds of fool, Mr Fraser, but I want to see Maggie for myself. And I keep remembering,' he said, exposing his fear, which sounded sillier than ever when put into words, 'that Maggie is terrified of her father.'

'And with good reason,' said the minister soberly. 'You were right to come. And if we look fools together, why should we worry?'

The forest fire had been brought under control, and with a skeleton force left up the hill to keep an eye on it, the rest of the firefighters were free to go home. Ian Dunlop was dropped off beside his house. He was dirty, weary, his hair and beard singed in places, but like all the others he was satisfied with the day's work.

All the same, when a car turned into his road end after him, he was not best pleased. A salesman, was it? Or some man from one of the new, interfering ministries? What a time to come calling! He waited as the car drew to a halt at the entrance to his yard. He would soon send this person about his business.

It was a shock to see a tall man in Air Force uniform, and even more of a shock to recognise who it was. As the minister climbed out of the other door, Ian Dunlop's sense of dismay was almost over-powering.

'Good evening, Mr Dunlop,' said David pleasantly. 'I'm sorry to disturb you when you're just back and weary. I won't keep you long. I just wanted a quick word with Maggie if she's about.'

'Good evening, sir. Good evening, minister.' The head keeper licked his lips, tasting soot. Carefully avoiding looking behind him at the kennels, where the dogs were setting up a furious barking, he said civilly, 'Will you come away in? I'll call my mother. You'll take a cup of tea?'

'No need to stand on ceremony,' said the minister as their host made an attempt to steer them round the house to the front door. He went past him to the kitchen door and opened it. 'Mrs Dunlop won't mind if we go in this way. Oh, good evening, Mrs Dunlop,' he added cheerfully as Gran came rapidly out of her bedroom, closing the door behind her. 'Forgive us giving you no warning, but Mr Vorst has come all the way from Fife to see Maggie. Is she somewhere about?'

Mrs Dunlop looked past the visitors at her son, Ian. He narrowed his eyes at her, warning her, but with his back to the open door, all she saw was his dark outline against a red evening sky. She said helplessly, 'I'm sorry, minister. Maggie is not very well just now. Could you maybe come back tomorrow?'

'Mrs Dunlop,' said David, taking her rough, lined hand in his and holding it. 'What is the matter with Maggie? I do most urgently need to see her. We all like her so much, especially my stepdaughter, Abby. And Abby will be terribly disappointed to hear that Maggie no longer means to go to America. Why did she change her mind?'

'What's it to do with you?' demanded the head keeper, brushing his mother aside and coming round to confront his visitor. 'She changed her mind, and that's an end to it. What right have you to come into my house, trying to bully my daughter into going to America? She's not going, and that's that.'

'Oh?' said David, sounding interested. 'And was this Maggie's decision, or yours?'

'That's none of your business.'

'Oh, come,' said the minister mildly, seating himself at the kitchen table and laying his tweed hat upon it. 'Mr Vorst has been Maggie's employer ever since his marriage to Mrs John Cary. I should say that it is very much his business.' He looked up into the head keeper's soot-smeared, glowering face. He said gently, 'And as for bullying, there's no question of that. He just wants a quiet chat with her, to find out what she really wants.'

'It's Maggie's duty to stay at home and keep house for me and my mother. That is what my daughter wants, minister.'

'You surprise me, Ian. I used to get the impression that Maggie was not always happy at home. And now that Tom is dead, I expected her to have all the more reason for getting away.'

'Are you telling me,' said Ian in a stifled voice, 'that Maggie complained of her treatment here?'

'Certainly not. Maggie would never do so. Would she have any reason for complaint?'

'None at all.' Uneasily, Ian turned to David, who had followed the minister's lead and taken a seat at the kitchen table. 'You'd best take yourself off, Mr Vorst. You'll not be seeing Maggie tonight, and I'll not have her going to America. A den of iniquity, that's what it is!'

'Iniquity? Have you ever been there, Ian?' inquired the minister. He rose to his feet as he spoke and stood in front of Ian Dunlop, eye to eye. He said sternly, 'Ian. What have you done? Where *is* Maggie?'

The keeper turned away from the minister's probing gaze, and said feebly, 'Mr Fraser, I've nobbut this minute come home. My mother will know where she is.' He glared at the old lady, his red-rimmed eyes warning her.

Mrs Dunlop hesitated, torn between loyalties, and feeling far from well.

None of them heard the bedroom door open. Glynis said clearly in her high, little girl's voice, 'Maggie is in here, minister. I think you should come and take a look at her.'

Part Two

August 1940

to

June 1941

Chapter 9

Mrs Cornelius Vorst – Aunt Chrissie to all the children from Britain – was a soft-spoken woman with a happy disposition and a strong sense of family. She wanted people around her to be cheerful and contented, and it pleased her very much to fill the attics of Maple Valley House with all those little refugees from the European war. When it turned out that nearly fifty people were being sent over, not just the Cary children and their immediate cousins, it was clear that even the spacious attics of Maple Valley House could not contain them all. So Aunt Chrissie decided to delay the sale of Bellefield, her late aunt's house outside Syosset, so that all the extra newcomers could be sent there.

Mrs Sandridge, her secretary, saw to the arrangements for the second house as efficiently as she dealt with Aunt Chrissie's other affairs. It was also Mrs Sandridge who arranged for an army of workmen and decorators to abandon their tasks at the New York Vorst and to transform the top storey of Maple Valley House into accommodation for twelve British children and their assorted keepers. There was plenty of room up there.

After his marriage, Cornelius Vorst had built Maple Valley House for his bride, Christina. For Chrissie, he meant to have the very best, and after visiting England and France on an extended honeymoon, he decided on the French style for his new Long Island mansion. Chrissie would have preferred something more English. Chrissie and Lady Dulcimer were twin sisters, and though fond of Effie Dulcimer, Cornelius regarded Dulcimer Hall as the most uncomfortable house in the world, and felt no desire to duplicate it. So they compromised. Chrissie was to have her English flower garden, and a park laid out after the manner of Capability Brown, and Cornelius went ahead with building a much turreted French chateau.

It took three years to build the house to his satisfaction, and even longer to landscape the gardens and plant the thousands of trees and shrubs which were to be Maple Valley's glory. Even after forty years, Cornelius still felt a surge of pleasure as his automobile swept through the wrought-iron gates and he caught sight of the imposing façade of their family home. For a family home Maple Valley House truly was.

Chrissie saw to that. Cornelius used to say proudly that his wife could make a happy home in a covered wagon. As it was, with a Vorst hotel in most major American cities ready to accommodate her, she had never been obliged to fulfil his boast. But with her children and her dogs and her delightfully informal brand of hospitality, Chrissie turned her husband's new and exceedingly grand chateau into a place of ease and warmth and charm.

However, it was not until the summer of 1940 that the large attics claimed her attention. The architect had meant the servants to live up there, but Cornelius Vorst would have none of it. He had a fixed dislike of being what he termed 'crowded out and stared at by a lot of women', and before he moved his wife and family into their new residence, he built a large servants' annexe behind the kitchen entrance, and planted it round with concealing, evergreen shrubs. With a few privileged exceptions, the Maple Valley staff lodged down there, and for years the attics remained sparsely furnished and occupied only very occasionally by visiting lady's maids or valets. But when she knew that the English children were coming, Chrissie changed all that. It was she who chose the charming painted furniture, the wallpapers and the drapes, and nearly gave the architect a coronary when she decreed that there were to be three more bathrooms.

'Three, ma'am?' he echoed, looking as though he had swallowed a frog. 'There are two large bathrooms up there already.'

'They *are* much too large, aren't they?' agreed Chrissie, looking at him as though he had said something clever. 'The one beside the east turret could certainly be turned into two. I feel sure that you will find a way of fitting in the others.'

'But do they really need five bathrooms up there, Mrs Vorst? This is July, you know, and a lot of workmen will be on vacation just now.'

'Mr Hunter,' inquired Chrissie gently, 'would you enjoy sharing a bathroom with six or seven other people?'

'Well, no, ma'am. But these Europeans don't expect the same standards . . .'

'Some may not, Mr Hunter. But these are my family and my guests, and I want the best for them. If you really don't think you can help me, then please say so.'

'I'll do anything for you, ma'am. You know that.' She did not speak. He said carefully, 'Just when are you expecting them?'

'I have really no idea, Mr Hunter,' she said, rising. 'Not later than the end of August, I hope. The children will have to start school after Labor Day, and they will need a week or so to settle in.'

Chrissie got her bathrooms, and everything else she asked for. The keynote was to be simplicity, she said, but when the British newcomers saw their attic quarters they would think them positively sumptuous.

In the meantime, the British travellers had to spend three tedious days and nights in a Liverpool hotel. It was an exasperating time, both for the would-be travellers and those seeing them off. Nobody knew when the convoy was due to sail, and the docks were out of bounds to civilians. Abby was in a state of angry despair. Not only had Josef and Marie not come at the last minute, but neither had Maggie – although Antonia assured her that the nursery maid would come straight to the boat. Disliking Miss Brimley, and missing even Nanny's astringent company, Abby longed for the courage to refuse to embark on the *Duchess of Montrose* when they were finally driven to the docks.

But Maggie arrived just in time. Abby never forgot how she looked that day, with her battered, misshapen face and empurpled, closed up eyes.

It had been a close shave. Antonia and all the stay-at-homes had gone ashore, and the children and their various keepers were being shown their sleeping quarters. When Abby caught sight of Maggie's familiar, gaberdine-clad form, she ran past Mrs Fraser who had brought her, and could only hug and lean against her, trying not to let her see how shocked she was by her terrible face. She had been warned that Maggie had been in an accident, but it was worse than she expected.

'You've come! Oh, Maggie! You have really come!' she kept on repeating foolishly. Then she paused, aware of movement around her. Mamzelle was clucking and hurrying her children away. Others were following them up a steep companionway, and Miss Brimley came over and touched Abby's arm.

'Come along now, dear,' she muttered. Her mouth looked pinched, and her pink-lidded, fair-lashed eyes darted to Maggie's dreadful face, and away. Just as though she was looking at a dog mess, thought Abby resentfully. 'They've arranged to give us high tea upstairs before we sail.'

'Maggie must come too.'

'No, dear. The stewardess is going to take Maggie to the sick bay.'

'Then I'll go with her. I want to see where she's sleeping.'

'Children won't be allowed in the sick bay.'

'How do you know? Maggie will be lonely all by herself.'

Mrs Fraser broke in on this argument, for she was feeling bone weary, and a ship's officer was waiting to take her ashore. She had almost given up hope of getting Maggie to the ship on time. 'Go with the others, Abby. Maggie isn't feeling well, and needs to be alone this evening. But I will ask someone to come and tell you where to find her when she's better.'

No one ever knew what Mrs Fraser said to the nurse in the sick bay, or to the young officer who escorted her to the gangway, but the staff in the sick bay cosseted and looked after Maggie with more tenderness and sympathy than she had known in all her seventeen years. For a couple of days she was too wretched and ashamed of her battered face and multiple bruises to do more than accept their ministrations gratefully, crying weakly sometimes when she was alone. She slept a lot, woke and slept again, and slowly began to feel better. The ship's doctor came, looked at her cuts and bruises, and said that none of the scars would be permanent – but recommended a haircut.

The Glen Cary doctor had shorn her hair in order to tend her bleeding scalp, but once cut properly and washed, it curved like soft brown feathers around her head. Her head felt lighter without the heavy braids she had worn lifelong.

'Lucky you, to have hair that bends. And your face is better,' Abby added, though a shade doubtfully. 'Maggie. What happened? Brimmy won't tell me. She just whispers about you to Mamzelle, and drops hints.'

'I got in an argument,' said Maggie, looking down at her swathed and poulticed hands. 'And got the worst of it.'

And that was all she would say, then or later, and Abby soon learned not to keep asking. And anyway, the next day, everything changed. The storm came.

It had been brewing all evening, and after dinner the ship rolled so suddenly and heavily that several passengers were hurled down the stairs near the main saloon, and some bones were broken. By next morning Miss Brimley and Mamzelle and more than half the children on their corridor had been miserably sick for hours. The sick bay filled up with the seriously ill as well as those with broken bones, and Maggie decided to get up to see how the children were faring.

She found Miss Brimley moaning and puking in a lower bunk, and Miles lying in a pool of his own sick on an upper one. Jamie was roaring his head off, fighting off Abby's efforts to get him dressed. A weary looking stewardess came in with an armful of sheets, and at the sight of Maggie she handed over her burden with a groan of relief.

'So you're better? Thank the Lord for that! Can you manage while I see what Number Four wants?'

'I'll manage fine.'

'Good.' She looked at Jamie who had stopped bawling and was holding onto Maggie and sucking his thumb. 'I should take those kids on deck, if I were you. Wrap them up warm, and take them to C Deck. They'll be better in the fresh air.' She glanced down at Miss Brimley, who had fallen back exhausted, her eyes closed and sunken. 'I'll keep an eye on that poor woman. She's been took real bad.'

Miss Brimley was so ill that she was moved to the sick bay that afternoon, and it was Maggie who slept with Abby and her brothers in the airless, sour-smelling cabin.

All day they stayed on the upper decks. Abby was soon grumbling that Maggie was unbearably bossy, making them get dressed and go on deck when they felt so seasick. Maggie pushed Jamie along the heaving deck until he fell asleep in his borrowed pram, and then coaxed the older children to play party games on a sheltered bit of deck. She gave them glucose drinks to sip and dry biscuits to nibble. The storm clamoured on, but even Miles lost his pea-green complexion after the first day.

The Devenish clan had berths in another part of the ship, and many of them were prostrated by seasickness. The fierce Miss Fortescue and all three lordlings were laid low by the rough weather, despite being accommodated in first-class cabins on the upper deck. When Maggie shepherded her pallid brood of children into the dining room next morning, Lady Adele beckoned them over, and they joined the few surviving Devenishes. The teapot hat had been discarded, and without it Lady Adele's masterful nose seemed all the more pronounced in her sallow face with her hair pulled back in a loose bun at the nape of her long neck. Unperturbed by the storm, Lady Adele took cheerful charge and Maggie found herself appointed as second-in-command.

It was an energetic few days, and out of it grew a sense of companionship with the once haughty Devenishes. Maggie had no time to feel sorry for herself or embarrassed about her bruised face. Nobody seemed to notice her looks, and they all felt rather pleased with themselves as survivors of the storm.

But it was frightening, too, and immensely noisy, with the booming of the water, the huge height of the waves, the momentary check and shudder as the vessel poised on the summit of each mountainous crest, before crashing and rolling into the next creaming trough. Sometimes they feared that the great liner would break in half. Lifeboat drill assumed a new and terrible reality. Abby prayed fervently that they would never have to use the lifeboats, for surely they would be broken to matchsticks in that smashing, crashing sea?

But the ship ploughed on. At times the racing storm clouds cleared, and they caught glimpses of the rest of the convoy – ships of all sizes and shapes, herded by sleek, grey destroyers and corvettes, all struggling through the heavy seas at the pace of the slowest freighter.

In the cabin, they learned to wedge themselves against the wooden sides of the bunk, and by the second day Abby mostly forgot to feel queasy. There was no time for it. It took all her energies and attention just hanging on. Maggie took Jamie in beside her, lying him down between herself and the wall, so that he could not fall out.

At last the storm abated, and the dining room and the saloons filled up with querulous convalescents from the underworld. Then there was time to worry about icebergs coming too close, or a U-boat getting in among the convoy. Few of them spoke of these fears –

certainly not in Lady Adele's hearing – but they all felt relieved when, one morning, they found the banks of the St Lawrence River sliding past the portholes.

Two days later they arrived at Long Island, weary and bewildered by so many changes of scene. Abby was scared. It was like standing on a precipice and knowing you had to jump off. What would it be like? She found herself wishing that the Devenishes and Lady Adele were still with them. Adele, on hobnobbing terms with ambassadors and ships' captains, would not have been daunted by new places or unpredictable events. But the Devenishes had been swooped on in Grand Central Station and swept off to somewhere called Bellefield.

The group of British refugees stood uncertainly below the shallow stone steps which led to the imposing door of Maple Valley House. They were an oddly assorted band. The Vorsts' granddaughter Kim, peering at them from a curtained window to one side of the front hall, decided that they looked pretty drear. No fun at all. All those prim children in neat summer coats and white socks and buttoned shoes. And the odd-looking old women who were fussing round them, dressed in dowdy dark blue coats and skirts, with pot hats and even *gloves*, for heaven's sakes!

She was watching them from a side window because she had not made up her mind whether or not to join the newcomers. The only other young British person she knew was Quentin Cary, who sometimes stayed down the road with his grandmother. She liked Quentin, but he had warned her that she would very likely find her new cousins boring. They certainly looked a lot of weirdos, from where she was standing. There was a big frumpy girl who was helping with the bags. Kim wondered what was wrong with her face.

She made up her mind to duck out of meeting them, and went home across the gardens, so did not witness her grandmother's arrival at the top of the broad stone steps. Chrissie Vorst was surrounded by six barking, wagging, long-haired dachshunds. The dogs poured down the steps, swarming round the children, fawning and sniffing. For Abby, everything was suddenly much better. She was enfolded in her great-aunt's lavender-scented embrace, and Chrissie's pretty voice bade her welcome to Maple Valley.

It was a happy house. They all felt it. The dogs were not what Abby had been used to. They were yappy and given to piddling, but not wild like Granny's Boys. Aunt Chrissie was more approachable and not as tweedy as Granny Dulcimer. But Abby was time and again reminded that these two silver-haired ladies were sisters – twins who had been born in America. They dressed differently, and their houses were absolutely dissimilar both outside and in, but Abby felt comfortable at Maple Valley from the first, and loved Aunt Chrissie on sight.

The only thing that spoiled things for her was Kim. Kimberley Christina Faber was Aunt Chrissie's granddaughter – the only one. Almost the first thing Aunt Chrissie said was that she did so hope that Abby and Kim would be friends – and Kim would barely speak to her.

Kim was nine years old, almost a year younger than Abby. People talked of her as a little darling, a precocious brat, a knowing one, a little monster – depending on how she chose to treat them. She was in a disagreeable mood these days, for she was an avid eavesdropper and knew that her Uncle David was daily risking his life fighting the Germans. She loved him, and missed him, and the thought of him still in England made her miserable and angry and sometimes sick with dread. Her mother told her not to worry, and tried to keep reports of the war out of her sensitive little daughter's way.

The sensitive little daughter was a resourceful child. She sneaked into her grandfather's study when nobody was looking, and after reading lurid accounts of the air battle over England, of dogfights far up in the sky, of dive bombers strafing airfields, began to wish she had left the newspapers alone. In her frightened mind she saw David being shot down in flames, or plunging to the earth when his parachute did not open. She loved him. Why did he have to go away to fight for the horrible British?

She was comforted to discover that her grandfather hated the British too. 'It makes me so mad, Chrissie,' she heard him say, some days before the children came. 'David must be out of his mind. He marries an Englishwoman ten years older than himself, saddles you with a pack of her Limey brats, and risks his life fighting in their damned stupid war! If he comes safely out of this folly, Chrissie, I've a good mind to disinherit him for causing you so much worry.'

Kim decided to have little to do with the Limey brats after that first sighting. She resented their invasion of her grandparents' house and disliked the sound of their prissy voices. Kim lived with her parents and two small brothers in a charming white painted villa at the far end of the Maple Valley gardens. Her mother Tina had recently bought a picture gallery in Manhattan and had installed an artist friend as manager and much as she adored her good-looking husband and her children, the gallery was where her main interest lay. When they were launching the work of an exciting new artist, she sometimes stayed in New York for days. Bill Faber, Kim's father, was a golf fanatic and seldom home from his club before dark. Kim was never neglected, however, for she pretty well lived at the big house where her grandparents always made her feel special and there was plenty going on. But suddenly it looked as if having the English children there was going to spoil her fun.

She succeeded in avoiding them for nearly two weeks by going to

117

visit Quentin Cary and his mother in Cape Cod. Returning home reluctantly, she made up her mind to give the big house a wide berth. But her mother and father were away, and two days with just her little brothers and their nurse were uneventful enough to make her wonder how they were getting on over there. She went to find out.

They were getting on too well. Sure that her grandfather would be hating them as much as she did, she paid him a visit. She expected Cornelius to be holed up in his special lair where only she and Grandma Chrissie went uninvited. But when she peered round the door of his book-lined study, he was not there.

She heard his voice coming from the red drawing room next door. She crept towards the half-open double doors, and saw him. He was sitting on a gilded, high-backed chair, surrounded by all the British children. Some sat cross-legged on the floor, others on chairs, and one of the littler girls was actually lolling back on her grandfather's knee. He was reading poetry aloud and they were all listening as though spellbound. None of them noticed her glowering in the doorway.

She turned quickly, and fled.

When Kim was little she used to have tantrums. She would lie face down on the floor in those days, and scream and drum her feet and hands on the floor until they were bruised and sore. It was a good way of getting what she wanted, but she was older now. There were other ways of letting people know when you were upset.

Kim was more than upset. For the first time in her life she was consumed by an agony of jealousy. The sight of those interlopers grouped about her grandfather, littering the lovely red drawing room with its silk-covered walls and glittering chandeliers with rocking horses, drawing boards, toys, and books – made her want to kill them all. That evening she lay in her little four-poster bed – a recent present from Grandma Chrissie – with her face turned sideways on the pillow. She did not speak, or move, however much they asked her to tell them what was the matter. Tears slid slowly from under her lashes. Poor little girl, they thought. She was a picture of desolation. It was such a good performance that Kim ended up half frightening even herself.

She certainly frightened the nurse and the cook, and when her mother came home from New York, she was no more successful than the others in her efforts to find out what was wrong. Eventually the doctor was sent for. He was an old friend of the family, and knew the right questions to ask.

'So you went to the big house, Kim? Did something happen there to upset you?

Tina Faber went across to the big house to see her mother. Presently she went away, and Mrs Vorst called up her secretary, Mrs Sandridge,

118

on the house telephone. As previously arranged, the two ladies went out into the garden to pick flowers. Their progress was a familiar sight to Maple Valley people. Mrs Vorst rode in her three-wheeled electric chariot, the three oldest dachshunds tucked in around her feet, while the younger dogs scampered on ahead. The secretary followed, a flat basket containing a pair of secateurs and two pairs of chamois leather gloves on her arm. Mrs Vorst was to all appearances her usual placid self, a plump, pretty lady with exquisite ankles and tiny feet. She wore one of her pleated gowns of pastel coloured crêpe-de-Chine, with a straw hat to shield her from the sun.

She was just a little concerned about Kim, she confided presently, snipping a perfect rose and handing it to Mrs Sandridge. She explained that the child was feeling pushed out, supplanted by the visiting children. 'Such a pity,' said Aunt Chrissie thoughtfully. 'We shall have to think of some way to reassure her, won't we?'

Part of Mrs Vorst's lovability lay in the fact that she seldom gave orders. There was really no need. Her wishes were faithfully carried out by her secretary, or by her chauffeur, Mr James. On this occasion, it was Mrs Sandridge's unenviable role to act as a sort of filter for Mrs Vorst's worries.

'Don't do it, May,' advised James, the chauffeur. 'It sounds like Kim up to her tricks.'

'But who will tell them if I don't?'

'Don't look at me,' said James. 'Ten to one it will cause trouble. Leave those children to sort themselves out in their own way.'

The secretary sighed. She had promised to speak to the visitors and it was too late to draw back. She knew it was not going to be easy. But someone had to try. 'I promised Mrs Vorst. There's no help for it.'

He smiled. 'Your trouble is that you've never learned to say no.'

She raised her head and said rather acidly, 'You're a great one to say that. When have you ever refused to give Mrs Vorst anything she wanted?'

He smiled at Mrs Sandridge. 'Not often, I admit.'

'Never,' she retorted. 'Not once, in all the years I've known you.'

He grunted. 'All the same, I think it's a mistake to meddle with those kids.'

'I said I would talk to the British women.'

Mrs Sandridge did her best. She had a quiet word with Miss Brimley and the others. They listened to her politely, hiding their dismay, and agreed to have a word with their children about Kim.

Chapter 10

Miss Brimley carried her scuffed red leather writing case about with her everywhere, and whenever she had a spare moment she wrote letters to friends in England. She haunted Mrs Sandridge's office, hoping for answers. She called it 'keeping in touch', but was often disappointed, and even when a letter came it could be a mixed blessing. Letters assuaged her longing for news but they also kept her homesickness alive. There was both pleasure and pain in keeping in touch.

To Abby, Miss Brimley's letters were a source of irritation. The governess would read scraps aloud to her crony Miss Fortescue, and as this usually happened at breakfast, there was no escape.

'Who could want to know what her blessed sister did at the Dulcimer village whist drive three weeks ago,' Abby grumbled. 'And I don't want to hear what Trumpet has to say about Vestry's corns, either. Revolting! It quite put me off my breakfast.'

'Since when have you been so keen on breakfast?' asked Maggie.

Abby was brushing her hair before getting into bed. She tossed it out of her eyes, and looked at Maggie. 'It's only the toast I don't like. Brimstone makes me eat two slices.'

'So you said yesterday, and the day before,' said Maggie. 'You should try not to repeat yourself.'

'Beast,' said Abby equably, putting the hairbrush down. She climbed into bed. Joan and Betty, Aunt Cora's little girls, were already tucked up, though not yet asleep.

Later, lying in the darkened bedroom, Abby thought about Kim, and how she was still refusing to be friends. It was, she felt, a great pity that Josef and Marie Steiner had not come to Maple Valley. They would have been such a help. Josef was so sure of himself. He would not have minded if Kim despised him and ignored him by turns.

She missed Bert, too, and was cross with him for not writing. He had promised to write, and so far she had heard nothing. She wanted so badly to know how he was, and whether he still planned to take his family back to London. She could not imagine how he would earn enough, but you never knew with Bert. If only he would write!

* * *

120

Bert had not managed to write because all through the month of August he had been working in the harvest, tying up the sheaves of oats and barley, stooking them until each field was dotted with untidy golden wigwams. He helped to load the farm carts, worked with the horses, and occasionally got a shot at driving the farm tractor. He went fruit picking in the garden and the apple orchards. There was so much to do, and money to be earned. He worked from first light until dark, falling into bed at the end of each day, sunburned, scratched and too weary to think.

By the end of August, he had saved enough to get his family to London by bus. Dulcimer felt empty now that Abby had gone. He told himself that he would write to her when he was safely home in Stepney.

Then one day he found a way of reaching London for free. A lorry was coming to cart the apple harvest all the way to Covent Garden. Bert decided that they could stow away behind the piled-up crates. It was a chance in a million, and he took it. One morning the Higgins family were gone. Abby's mongrel Wat was also missing.

Cook was not sorry to lose Wat, for the dog was large and hungry and a dedicated thief. 'What a mercy! Lately I haven't dared to turn my back for fear a loaf or the week's butter ration goes missing.'

'Pity,' said Lord Dulcimer, who liked and respected Bert. 'I wish I had known he was feeling homesick. What on earth will Nanny do, Effie, with no children to run after?'

'Perhaps she would like to look after the Boys?' suggested Lady Dulcimer, though not very hopefully.

'No, thank you, milady,' said Nanny with disheartening promptitude. 'There's enough mending here to keep me busy for a twelvemonth. The linen room is a disgrace, and some of his lordship's clothes are little better than rags. Dear knows what the last sewing woman did with her time before she went off to work in that factory.'

All the same, Nanny was black affronted. Bert had been sly. 'It stands to reason he must have been planning this for weeks! Ever since Abby went off, I shouldn't wonder. But not a word did he utter, working in the harvest and the apple orchard till all hours as though butter wouldn't melt in his mouth.'

'He was a good worker,' said Lord Dulcimer regretfully. 'Worth two of those landgirls, and good with machinery and the horses.' Lord Dulcimer felt that he should have known. Bert had asked for his harvesting wages a day early, saying that he needed it for his mother in Stepney. With hindsight, Lord Dulcimer realised that this had been the exact truth. 'I shall be sorry to lose that boy.'

'It's a pity,' said Nanny. 'I was just getting Joe dry at night, and Ivy didn't whine so much. Downright unkind, I call it, dragging them off without a word.'

'Nobody saw them at the railway station, or at the bus stops. I just hope they got there safely.'

They were soon relieved of this worry. A postcard came for Nanny.

'Gone home to Mum,' Bert wrote. 'Thanks for having us and thanks to the Lord and Lady. I have taken Wat with me like Abby asked – Bert Higgins.'

Bert felt a little ashamed that he had just walked out, but the chance of stowing away behind all those apple crates would never have come again. Getting to London for free meant that he was richer than he had been in his whole life.

It was a long, hot walk from Covent Garden to Stepney, and Bert carried Joe for the last mile or so. With Wat on a lead, this was a problem. Used to roaming free in the country, Wat kept tugging away, or tangling round Bert's legs. In the end, he just had to let the dog off, and from then on Wat never left his heels.

They reached their home street at last, weary but excited. The door of Mum's house was never locked and stood open to the street in warm weather. What a wonderful surprise they were going to give her! All four children crept up to the door, Ivy trying to stifle her giggles, and one by one they slipped carefully through the open door which always creaked if you pushed it.

For a moment they stood listening in the little hall. It smelled familiar, a mixture of soup and polish, chips and cigarette smoke – but it was smaller than Bert remembered. Then he heard his mum humming a tune just the other side of the kitchen door. He held Joe's sticky paw and pushed the door open.

'Anyone at home, then?'

Mum was standing at the cooker, stirring something. She gasped, dropped the spoon and they all rushed together with shrieks and cries of excitement and happiness. Everyone talked at once, asking questions which nobody answered, jabbering, laughing and nobody even trying to make head or tail of the others. Ignored in the general pandemonium, Wat made the pleasing discovery that he was just the right height for the kitchen table, and raised a questing muzzle. Luckily, Bert saw and swatted him, saving a plateful of bread and marge from going down the hatch.

Shouting to be heard, laughing and half crying, none of them caught the sound of steps upon the stairs. Bert saw his mother glance up, and looked quickly in the same direction.

A large man stood in the doorway, his sandy hair almost touching the lintel. He wore trousers and just a vest over his hairy chest, and his feet were large and bare. He stared at them all, rubbing his eyes and frowning. Wat growled. He was wary of strange men.

Mum said rather quickly, 'Oh, dear. Did we wake you? I forgot you were trying to sleep.' Then she turned to the children. 'This is your Uncle Terry. He's the new lodger.'

It was a shock to find that Mum had taken up with a man. In the three years since his dad had died, Bert had come to consider himself the man of the house in Cotton Street, and he felt supplanted.

He tried to hide his chagrin for his mum's sake, slept without complaint on a heap of coats on the floor of the seldom used front room, and when Terry was working day shifts he tried to ignore the sounds of his mother and her lodger heaving about on the creaking bed upstairs. The girls and Joe had a slip of a bedroom above the kitchen. It felt rather crowded after Dulcimer, and Terry complained if the children made a noise when he was trying to sleep in the daytime. He was working at the docks, and was constantly switching between night and day shifts.

What his mother saw in Terry, Bert had no idea. But she was always singing his praises, perhaps hoping that by this recital of her lover's virtues, Bert would come to admire him too. No chance of that. Before a week had gone by, Bert felt a despairing hatred for the interloper. He wished very much that he had never decided to come home.

Terry did not like dogs, and sensing this, Wat growled at him whenever he came home. Then Terry said that Wat must be chained up in the shed at night. He did not hold with dogs indoors. Mum had looked so imploring that Bert had gone along with it – at least on the nights when Terry was not working. Other nights he sneaked the dog into the front room and was comforted by his warm woolly body.

But it was Wat's stealing habits that put the lid on it. Terry's dinner steaming on the kitchen table was too much for any dog to resist. Twice it happened. The first time it was four sausages and a pile of mash. Daisy Higgins had queued up for those sausages, and was nearly as cross as Terry. The second time it was macaroni cheese, and Terry came down to find his plate licked clean. His roars for Bert sent the three smaller children scuttling out into the street.

Bert cuffed Wat and dragged him outside, and Daisy dished up more macaroni for Terry.

With his mouth full, Terry said, 'That dog will have to go.'

Bert had just come back from scolding Wat and chaining him up at the back door, and heard. He stood in the doorway and said, 'Go? Where's he s'posed to go to, then?'

Daisy made a flustered movement with her hands.

'There are dogs' homes. There's one in Battersea, I've heard tell.'

Bert knew about the Battersea Dogs' Home. Abby had told him about it, because the schoolroom dachshund had come from there, rescued years ago by Johnnie Cary. 'I'm not taking Wat there to be murdered. They put them down after a week if nobody claims them.'

'I don't care where you take him so long as the brute is out of the house when I get back tomorrow morning. It'll be the worse for both of you if he's still here.'

'Who are you to talk?' said Bert hotly. 'This is my home, and the only person who decides who stays in it is my mum.'

'Bert . . .' said Daisy imploringly. 'Mind your manners, do.'

'Mum! I'll make sure he doesn't take any more food. I'll take him to school with me when I start tomorrow. They won't mind if I keep him tied to the railings. Mum, he's not even mine! I said I'd take care of him. I promised Abby.'

'Promised who?' demanded Terry, scraping the last of the macaroni out of the pan.

'Abigail Cary. A friend of mine.'

'Then tell her to come and take her flaming dog away.'

'She can't. She's in America.' Bert turned again towards his mother, saying urgently, 'Mum, please . . .'

She glanced from Terry to Bert and back again, finding no comfort in either of their unyielding faces. She clasped her hands together in her lap, and said, 'I could go to the police station tomorrow, Terry. The sergeant might know of someone who needs a watchdog. A caretaker, or a night watchman, maybe.'

'See here, Daisy,' Terry said flatly. 'Either that dog is out by tomorrow, or I walk out for good myself. I've been thinking of joining the army for some time, anyway. It's entirely up to you.'

Bert felt like telling Terry O'Rourke that he could walk out and keep walking, but he managed to restrain himself. His mum had never let him down yet, and he saw no reason to think she ever would. But she did not speak, and when Bert looked at her he realised with a sinking feeling that she was going to give in to Terry.

Daisy had one more try. 'Please, Terry. Give us a day to work out what's best to do.'

'You heard what I said, and it's my last word. I'll be late for work if I stay here arguing any longer.' Terry stood up, took his jacket from a hook on the door, and stumped out of the kitchen. The street door creaked and slammed.

Daisy looked at Bert. 'Try to understand.'

Bert looked back at her, and said bitterly, 'I should never have come home. Wat and me are obviously not wanted.'

'It's not like that. It's just . . .' Daisy hesitated, seeking words to convey to her son something of the aching loneliness of widowhood – of being without a man in her bed for so long. But she knew that there were no such words, and for the first time she was even relieved to hear the all too familiar wailing of the air raid sirens.

'Bother it,' she said wearily. 'Well, I'm not trailing down to the shelters tonight with all you kids. Too much trouble. We'll have to sleep downstairs. Help me to bring the bedding down, will you, Bert? We'll do it before we have tea, and the little ones can go to bed under the stairs. You and me'll have to go under the kitchen table.' She smiled into her son's frowning face, thinking to placate him with a mild joke. 'It'll be a bit of a squash, won't it, now you've grown so tall.'

He did not smile back. 'I'm not staying. I'll take Wat to the shelter under the church. They don't mind dogs there. I asked.'

She sighed. 'Don't be like that, son. It's not Terry's fault that he doesn't like dogs.'

'It's not my fault that you like Terry.' The words 'better than me' hung between them unspoken. Mother and son glared at each other. But Bert could never stay in a temper for long, so he shrugged his shoulders. 'Let's get those mattresses down before I go.'

'Don't go. I wish I could think of someone who wants a dog as a pet.'

'Don't bother. Wat and me are staying together.'

She sighed. 'Stay and have tea, anyway.'

Bert smiled at her for the first time since Terry had slammed out of the house. 'OK, Mum. I might, at that.'

'Nothing but bread and scrape,' said Daisy. 'And we know who's fault that is.'

'I tell you what, Mum. I'll bring some fish pieces from the stall for a pie,' said Bert. 'And some spuds as well.' Mum suffered cruel from varicose veins, which were made worse by so much queueing for food. 'The market is next door to the church shelter, and me and Wat can get there early.'

Her eyes mocked him. 'What's this? A minute ago you were leaving for good.'

'I'll come back afternoons while he's sleeping. I could take the kids out. Give you a chance to put your feet up.'

She gave his arm a squeeze, and led the way up the stairs to get the bedding. There was a distant crump of bombs, and then, for the first time, they heard a sinister thrumming drone, which grew louder and louder every minute. The three children came running in, half excited, half scared. 'Planes, Mum! Loads of 'em, all bunched together!' Then their voices were drowned by a howling sound followed by a much louder, nearer explosion. The whole house shook.

Bert never went to the shelter that night. Up until then, Daisy had found air raids to be tiresome, sleep-disrupting affairs, but this one was something else. Stepney was right in the middle of it, and she begged Bert not to go out in all that din, with bombs falling, houses collapsing, glass and slates showering all over. 'Wait until the raid is over, do.' She told him she needed him.

So the Higginses and Wat huddled together all that evening and night, lying on two mattresses under the stairs in a swathe of blankets. Just as it was growing dark, another whine and violent explosion shook the house, and the lights went out. Joe started to whimper, but Daisy took him in her arms and soothed him back to sleep. The girls slept fitfully, waking sometimes when a bomb fell deafeningly near, or when the crash of splintering glass and falling slates from upstairs frightened them into wakefulness.

Bert and his mother talked a lot as the hours dragged by, dozed occasionally, woke again and sipped tea from a thermos flask, before talking some more. Bert talked the most, for with Terry in the house and all the fuss about the dog, it was the first time he had had his mum to himself. Lying in the dark made it easier to find the words.

He tried to give her a picture of what Dulcimer had been like, told her about Abby, and how all the Cary children had been sent away to America. It helped to talk, even though they had to break off when it grew too rowdy outside. His mum really seemed to want to know about the Dulcimer people, and he felt warmed by her interest and answered her as best he could – not all at once, but in snatches throughout that endless, frightening, sometimes deafening night. He wanted to share these fragments of that other life with her, for he did not think that he would ever go back to Dulcimer. It might not fade so fast, if Mum and he could talk about it sometimes.

The All Clear sirens came with the first light of dawn, clear and steady, unlike the banshee swooping of the warnings. Stiffly, careful not to wake the children, Bert and his mother went into the kitchen. It was all over plaster dust and broken glass, and there was no gas when they tried to light the stove, and no electrics either. They cleared the glass and grime from the table and sat down companionably to eat a slice of bread and drink some cold water. The night and all that talking had made it all right between them. Presently Bert stood up to go. Wat was already by the door, plumed tail waving, eager for an outing.

Bert gave his mother a quick hug

She saw that he was serious about leaving. 'How will you manage?'

'I've got my harvest money.' She had refused to take his money when he came home.

She said, 'It won't last long if you have yourself and that great dog to feed.'

'I'll get jobs. There's always jobs going in the market. There's sometimes soup kitchens at the church, too, and during the week I'll get my dinners at school.'

'Please yourself,' she said, sounding as though her throat hurt. She went to the dresser. 'You'd better take your ration book and identity card. You might need them.'

126

'Thanks, Mum,' he said awkwardly. He knew she was upset, but there was nothing to say, really.

'Look after yourself, son.'

'I'll bring the fish on Thursday, if they've got some.'

'Come anyway, fish or no fish. Come in the afternoon.' They did not speak of Terry. She opened the door for him, and watched the boy and dog picking their way down Cotton Street, skirting the scatter of fallen slates and rubble on the road, Bert's boots scrunching on broken glass. She had an impulse to call him back, but did not. They turned the corner, and were gone from her sight.

Old Aggie Bream came out from over the way, wearing curlers and a bath cap on her head. 'Lotta noise last night, Daisy. Jerry busy down at the docks, from the sound of it. Your Terry back yet?'

'It's still too early,' said Daisy, trying to ignore a qualm of anxiety. 'Worst of it is, he'll be wanting his tea, and I've no gas.'

'Bring your kettle in to me. I've dug out my old Primus and it works lovely.'

Abby wrote to Nanny, asking for news of Bert. Also, she was curious to know what had made Madame Odette change her mind about allowing Josef and Marie to come to America. Miss Brimley and Mamzelle had been no help. Either they had decided not to say, or they simply did not know. After Abby had driven the governess half distracted with her questions, Miss Brimley just said that Madame Odette had decided against sending them. Marie had had a nightmare about drowning, and was terrified of crossing the sea.

'Such an upset for the Vorst family at the last minute!' the governess said. 'The trouble with foreigners is that they are so emotional. Your dear mother was quite indignant on Mr David's behalf, after he had taken so much trouble.'

'I bet Josef was sorry not to be coming with us,' said Abby. 'He was looking forward to it.'

'I dare say he was,' said Miss Brimley, pursing her lips, 'but it's no bad thing. They wouldn't have fitted in. I wouldn't have known how to manage them. They made absolutely no effort to speak English when they were in London.'

'Maggie and Mamzelle know French, Brimmy, and Maggie would have looked after them.'

Miss Brimley sniffed and dabbed her nose with a crumpled handkerchief. 'Maggie is finding it difficult enough fitting in herself.'

'She wouldn't if you and Mamzelle and the others were nicer to her. Why isn't she allowed to eat with us? She always used to.'

'I told you. Mrs Sandridge and I agreed that it would be best. Some of the smaller children might have asked questions about her face, or passed remarks about her bruises. Maggie would not have liked that.'

'But her bruises have practically gone now. I bet she hates being treated as a leper. I know what it is. You're jealous of her.'

'Now, Abby,' said Miss Brimley, her neck reddening. 'How many times must I tell you not to be rude?'

'It's not rude to tell the truth.'

But Miss Brimley had turned away, for Miss Fortescue had arrived in the playroom with a daily paper. Eagerly both women bent to look at the front page. The headline screamed: 'Bomb terror over London. Fires in the docks. Hundreds feared dead.'

The governess sucked her top teeth, a habit she had when she was disturbed or excited. 'Dear me! Those poor people!' She looked over her rimless spectacles at Abby. 'Madame Odette must be feeling sorry now that she didn't send those children. I don't see the Vorst family taking so much trouble a second time.'

Miss Brimley sighed after Abby had stamped out. Truth to tell, the governess was out of her depth and deeply unhappy. She was not blessed with a sanguine disposition. There had been an early sadness in her life, when a young curate to whom she had given her heart had been killed at the battle of Mafeking. They had never been betrothed, and after his death she had nothing but fading memories to remember him by, and a locket containing some rather dusty looking hair which she wore all the time. With no hope of marriage, she had entered the scholastic profession, working in other people's houses as a governess to their little boys.

It was not an ideal life for a timid woman with fragile self-esteem and feelings that were very easily wounded, but until lately Miss Brimley had thought herself content. She read her Bible daily, and derived satisfaction from her Scripture Union notes, and also from knowing that her little boys would go on to their preparatory schools able to read and write and recite their arithmetic tables. A good grounding, that was what she gave them. She grew fond of many of her charges, and would shed tears when she had to move on to another family.

When John Cary was killed and his widow and children came to Dulcimer, she had been asked to postpone her retirement to teach his son and daughter. She had been staying with her married sister in Dulcimer village when Lady Dulcimer called to see her.

From the first she had been doubtful about taking on a girl. Boys were Miss Brimley's speciality. But Lady Dulcimer had clasped her hand so warmly and simply begged her, so she had given in, and had been happy giving the Cary children their lessons at Dulcimer Hall. She had even thought, when Lady Dulcimer and Antonia implored her to go to America in Nanny's place, that it would be all right, and safer than staying in England.

It was not all right. She had never been in sole charge of her pupils

128

before. She discovered that it was one thing to give morning lessons, and to hand her pupils back when the lessons were over. She used to enjoy walking home to Dulcimer village afterwards. She had been terrified of Lady Dulcimer's dogs, of course, and sometimes felt slighted by the upper servants, but there had been few worries and no need to think about the children out of schoolroom hours.

It was very different now that she was in America. From Maple Valley, Miss Brimley looked back at her life at Dulcimer as a lost heaven. If she had known what it would be like in the New World, the governess would have chosen to stay and brave the bombing and an invasion by the Germans.

But there was no going back. She had set her hand to this strange and alien plough. She was not going to give up, whatever the cost! It was hard. Pangs of homesickness would gnaw at her innards, worse than any nausea experienced on that dreadful voyage across the Atlantic. Whenever she allowed herself to think of England, of Marmite or Cooper's Oxford marmalade, or remembered how she used to sip Earl Grey tea by her sister's cosy fire at the end of the day, she felt ill with longing. And when Abby was particularly impossible, wilfully refusing to understand, or to do what she was told, she would shed tears of despair in the privacy of her bedroom.

But she was a parson's daughter, and had been brought up to know that despair was a sin. She knew her duty, and would do it, come what may. Those fatherless children were her responsibility, and she had resolved when leaving English shores that she would protect them from harm, and guide them kindly but firmly in the way they should go. And as far as possible, she meant to see that they returned home a credit to her, as all her previous charges had been.

The trouble was that Abby refused to be guided, and made it plain that she had no wish to be a credit. Such a fuss over a few sums!

'It's the summer holidays, Brimmy. It's not your business to give me lessons anyway. I'll do sums when I get to my new school.'

'They won't teach you English money sums, dear. Pounds, shillings and pence are much more difficult than dollars and cents, and it won't do for you to fall behind. How do you expect to get on at an English school if you can't do money sums or recite the kings of England?'

'When I need to know those things, I'll learn them.'

'I should be failing your dear mother if I did not make you keep up your English history and money sums.'

'Mummy wouldn't give a damn about money sums. She says the only thing to do with money is to spend and enjoy it.'

With matters slipping out of control, Miss Brimley had said severely, 'That will be five cents in the box for swearing, Abigail. And if you settled down to your sums instead of arguing, you could finish them and be down at the swimming pool in fifteen minutes.'

It was not only lessons. They argued about everything. Miss Brimley insisted on sun hats for fear of heatstroke, would not let the children play barefoot for fear of thorns or splinters, forbade reading in bed for fear of eye strain. So it went on, a tiresome and nerve-fraying little war of attrition, with both the contestants exasperated almost beyond bearing. And if, as sometimes happened, Abby was sent to bed for some misdemeanour, Miss Brimley suspected that Maggie made matters worse by sympathising with the child. Certainly, Abby was for ever to be found in Maggie's company. Miss Brimley found this annoying, but could scarcely forbid it.

There were blessings, of course, and Miss Brimley did her best to count them. Miles was a dear, easy little boy who was good at sums and liked listening to *Our Island Story*, and even Jamie was not so daunting now that he was out of nappies. But Abby was a dreadful worry. What with this, and the latest state of the war, Miss Brimley sometimes tossed and turned half the night.

Abby was growing more rebellious with every day that passed. It would be even harder to control the child, the governess feared, once she had started at an American day school. At one time the governess thought of appealing to Mrs Vorst, but had not done so. Their hostess was invariably charming and friendly, with a way of coming into the playroom to chat and ask them all for news of their day. She took an interest in everything they did and said, and might have listened to Miss Brimley's troubles with sympathy. But could she be relied upon to take a firm line with Abby? Recalling the outrageously spoiled Kim, and how she managed to twist her grandmother round her little finger, Miss Brimley feared not.

Instead she confided her troubles to her fellow governess over a cup of tea. Miss Fortescue was a stern disciplinarian who kept a slipper in her bedside drawer with which she spanked the little lordlings if they got out of line. She privately thought Miss Brimley a poor thing, but told her that she was quite right not to ask Mrs Vorst for help at this stage.

'You never know with these Americans. They bring their children up so differently. I'd get rid of your nursery maid, if I were you, Miss Brimley.'

Miss Brimley looked flustered. 'I don't know. What reason could I give? The girl hasn't done anything wrong.'

'That's as may be,' said Miss Fortescue obscurely. 'If Abby is being tiresome and rude, you can be sure that someone is stirring her up. Why does she spend so much time with Maggie?'

Miss Brimley said rather helplessly, 'Abby seems to like her.'

Miss Fortescue frowned. 'There's no accounting for tastes. My little Anthony was quite frightened by the sight of her at first. Even

130

now he runs to me when Maggie comes near, and buries his head in my lap until she has moved away.'

They agreed that little boys were more sensitive than girls. Then Miss Brimley said in an aggrieved voice, 'I was trying to explain to Abby that Maggie is only taking her meals with the American staff as a protection from the children passing remarks. Abby says I'm pushing her out of the way.'

Miss Fortescue frowned and stirred her tea. The nursery maid's bruised face was better – you would hardly notice anything wrong these days. When she smiled, some people might even think her pretty. All the same, Miss Fortescue did not think she was suitable company for her charges.

She leaned forward and asked quietly, 'Tell me, Miss Brimley. Between you and me, what exactly happened to her before she joined the ship?'

'A family argument, she says.'

Miss Fortescue clicked her tongue disapprovingly. 'More like a drunken brawl, if you ask me. The stewardess on the ship told me that there were bruises all over her body and on her arms, too. Shocking. What sort of background did she come from, I ask myself?'

Miss Brimley was affronted. This criticism seemed to reflect upon her employers. She said defensively, 'Maggie's father is head keeper at Glen Cary – Lord Dulcimer's place in Scotland, you know. A most respectable man, from all accounts. He was the one who beat her like that. I never found out what she had done, and I don't think Mrs John knew either.' After another sip of her tea, she went on, 'Perhaps Mrs John – Mrs David Vorst, as she now is – did not care to ask. They were still only newly married then, and it was Mr David who was set on sending Maggie to America with the children. I'm not quite sure why.'

'Her husband? The one who is in the RAF?'

'Yes. A most brave and charming young man. Years younger than Mrs John, of course . . .'

'I see. Well, all the more reason for us to watch that schoolroom maid of yours, if she is keen on the men. I expect she's behind this Abby nonsense. What with that Kim behaving like a little savage too, it's a wonder that all our children aren't getting out of hand.'

They exchanged glances. Kim was a caution, but they felt unable to do anything about her. After Mrs Sandridge's little talk, it would not do to make a complaint.

'There is one comfort,' said Miss Brimley. 'Abby and Kim don't get on.'

Abby went upstairs fuming. 'Brimstone is an utter beast! I'd like to kill her.'

'No you wouldn't! There's enough on the wireless and in the papers about killing, so don't you start,' said Maggie. It was Monday, and she and a pretty housemaid called Mary-Jo were changing sheets on the attic beds – a weekly task that took up half the morning. 'Here,' said Maggie, tossing some pillowcases in Abby's direction. 'Since you're here, you might as well fold these up and put them in that basket.'

Abby folded a pillowcase, and said in depressed tones, 'I hate dirty sheets.'

'Think yourself lucky you don't have to wash and iron them, then,' retorted Maggie, going past her to strip the third bed.

Abby said morosely, 'Brimstone is such a gloomy old thing! Do you think if the Germans bomb London a few more times, Madame Odette might send Marie and Josef after all?'

Maggie said nothing. She had been asking herself the same thing.

News from England was sparse and erratic, and when it did come it brought little comfort. Letters from Britain were few, and although anxiously awaited by the refugees, often the British censor had been so busy cutting out place names or anything that might be construed as helpful to the enemy that they were reduced to tatters, and unreadable.

Over the last weeks of August, the undercurrent of worry had been growing stronger. The British visitors were not the only ones to feel the tension. David Vorst was a favourite with the Maple Valley household, and even though he had been away in Europe for a long time, everyone from Mrs Sandridge to the newest kitchen maid was concerned for his safety. Maggie supposed it was only natural, for with Mr David flying Spitfires in the battle against the Germans, he was everybody's hero.

'I told Brimstone that you ought to eat with us,' said Abby, when Mary-Jo had gone off with a preliminary load of sheets. 'She is so mean to you, never letting you come to the beach with us, or on picnics.'

'I've no time for picnics,' said Maggie shortly. 'Miss B and I would get on better if you minded your own business. She's finding everything strange and new here. Why must you make things more difficult for her?'

But before Abby could answer, Mary-Jo came back, and between them they bumped the basket of laundry down the curving turret stairs.

Maggie watched Abby go through a door into the front hall, and sighed.

She felt sorry for Miss Brimley. The governess had been so ill on the ship, and when she surfaced once more she could not have enjoyed being told by Lady Adele that Maggie had coped very well with the children during the storm. Maggie was aware that Miss Fortescue did not approve of her either. She was not dismayed. People either liked you, or they didn't – and if they didn't you just had to put up with it.

She would have been astonished to know that several people at Maple Valley House had formed a good opinion of her.

At first, going into the servants' dining room had been an ordeal – worse even than those early days at Dulcimer Hall. She would sit at the long table, her head lowered over her plate and hardly eating a thing, because a cut on the side of her mouth still made chewing a problem. One of her eyelids still drooped, however hard she tried to open it properly, and she was miserably certain that all these American strangers must think her a freak.

Offered more to eat, she would shake her head and murmur thanks. She was not very hungry in the summer heat, but most of all she did not want to expose her hands. Her hands and arms had been badly marked by her father's flailing crook. Ian Dunlop had lost all control in the end and had aimed at her face and head, and she had partially avoided the blows by ducking under her bound arms.

They were kind, these people, even if some of them were uncomfortably curious. The first day, one of the young men smiled at her across the table and asked if she had met Mr David Vorst over there in England. The chatter at the long table lulled to a murmur as everyone waited to hear her answer, but it was a full minute before she could manage to speak, remembering all too vividly how she had last seen Mr David. He and the minister had stood over her as she lay on Gran's bed, lying there in filth and blood. What happened after that was a blur in her mind, but she learned later that they had taken her off to the manse, and that when her father tried to stand in their way, Mr David had knocked him down. But this could not be told, and there were twenty pairs of eyes upon her, and everyone was waiting for an answer.

Her voice came out in a sort of croak. 'Aye. I saw him. Just on two weeks ago.'

They asked her countless questions. What was the new bride like? Was she pretty? Was it true that she was years older than Mr David, and would she stay to face the bombing with him? How did the children get on with their new stepfather? Maggie had no idea, afterwards, what sort of answers she had given, but she was sure they must have thought her half-witted or just plain odd.

'We sure enough wondered about you,' said Mary-Jo later when they worked together and were getting on well. 'You looked scared to death that first day.'

'Well, so I was.'

'You can't blame folks for being curious,' said Mary-Jo, looking at

Maggie a shade reproachfully. 'Mr David getting married all of a sudden like that was romantic enough to be on the movies! And now with those cute kids of his here, we're just dying to hear more. I never saw Mr David myself, but the girls who knew him thought he was just a doll.'

Thinking of Joan and Betty Munnings and the vacant-eyed dolls which they were for ever dressing and undressing, Maggie gave a small choke of laughter. 'He's like no doll I've ever seen.' Then she added seriously, 'But he's kind ...'

Mary-Jo looked at the Scots girl, and wished she would be more forthcoming. What had happened to her to give her those terrible bruises? Why was she embarrassed to speak about Mr David? Mary-Jo would have given much to know. Still, with Mr James telling them all that Maggie was not to be questioned about her face and her bruises, it was generally thought wiser not. You did what Mr James said at Maple Valley House, if you knew what was good for you.

Maggie's first encounter with Mr James was when she had only been at Maple Valley House for one night. She was trying to find her way to the staff dining room when she was approached by a slight man in a dark suit. 'Good morning. I think you must be Maggie Dunlop?'

She looked down at her feet, not wanting him to be revolted by her bruised face. 'Yes, sir. That's me.'

He eyed her with concern, 'You look as if you've been in the wars. Are you feeling all right?'

Her head sank lower. 'I'm fine, sir.'

'No need to call me sir. I should have introduced myself. I'm John James. Tell me. How is your mother these days?'

Her head jerked up and she looked at him in sheer astonishment. He added quickly, 'Didn't she tell you about me?' And as she continued to gape at him, he added, 'I'm surely right in thinking that you are Mary Dunlop's daughter?'

'Well y ... yes,' she stammered and in her agitation added baldly, 'at least, I was, but my mother is dead.'

He stood very still, and she sensed that she had dealt him a blow by answering him so brutally. But he brushed away her half uttered apology. 'Dead? You say Mary Devlin is dead?' And when she looked blank at his use of her mother's maiden name, he added, 'I knew her long before she married your father.'

Maggie said nothing, merely nodded.

He shook his own head as though to clear it. 'I never knew. I wish someone had told me. When did she die, Maggie?'

'Soon after I was born, I think. She was run over in Glasgow. I didn't mean to give you a shock, sir. Did you know her well?'

'Very well.'

She would have asked him more, but a breakfast bell rang and the moment was lost. He nodded, and went away, and she gazed at his retreating back almost hungrily. He had known her mother and, unlike most people, he did not seem reluctant to speak about her.

But by the time Mary-Jo had finished telling her who Mr James was, and impressing upon her what an exalted position he held in the hierarchy, she lacked the courage to approach him again.

People were sometimes curious about James and his position at Maple Valley House. Anyone who asked would be given a variety of answers, but went away no wiser. Mrs Vorst would say simply that he was James, and she did not know what they would do without him. She meant what she said. He was the chauffeur, but more than that. There were two other chauffeurs at Maple Valley, who washed the cars and drove the family and staff about, so how did James fit in? Others spoke of James as a sort of butler, but there was already a stately individual called Wilding who fulfilled this role. The family called James: the Oracle; a joke name invented by David when he was still at school. The name was apt enough to stick, and over the years James had indeed become a sort of family oracle, to be consulted and confided in from time to time.

He was not very tall, a wiry man with a mild manner and un-assuming ways, always formally dressed in a suit and collar and tie. When he drove Mr or Mrs Vorst about, he wore a peaked cap and gloves. He did not say much, but when he spoke – in a voice which still held faint traces of a Yorkshire upbringing – people tended to listen. Mrs Sandridge was different. She was never still, a small powerhouse of energy, and her clear decisive tones could be heard from afar. James was not often heard and was seldom in a hurry, but he was usually there when he was needed. Between them Mrs Sandridge and Mr James ensured that the house and estate ran on oiled wheels. Hand in glove, they were, those two. They saw to everything, took charge of everything, and did their best to shield Mr and Mrs Vorst from day to day worries.

But much as they wished to do it, they failed to save Comelius and Chrissie Vorst from worrying over their younger son, David.

'He must be too busy to write,' said Chrissie forlornly. 'If only he or Antonia would send a cable now and then. Not hearing anything makes me imagine such horrors. How can we tell which of the newspaper reports are true?'

Comelius grunted. He was quite as worried as his wife, but he tried to persuade her that radio and newspaper reports were bound to be highly coloured and exaggerated.

Chapter 11

David had indeed been too busy to write. It was even difficult for him to find the time to keep Antonia happy.

After leaving St Andrews and being posted south, they had been determined to stay together and had booked a room in a pub near the airfield. It was not a success. Antonia was very soon bored and longing to be almost anywhere else. It was both uncomfortable and lonely in the Wheatsheaf, for with David's squadron flying several sorties a day, she saw very little of him. And none of David's fellow pilot officers had leisure to amuse her either.

At length she rang her friend Marjorie in London and asked her to lunch at the Vorst. Marjorie accepted with alacrity, and Antonia told David that she might stay on in the flat for a few nights. She could go shopping. She might even go to some shows.

David drove his wife to the railway station, and installed her in a first class carriage. They kissed and clung until the whistles started to blow. David looked bleak as he stepped back and closed the door. Antonia was in tears.

'Ring me after six, darling,' she said. 'I'll be waiting in every evening until I hear from you.'

'I'll try to, honey. Remember that I love you, and come back soon.'

He watched the train out of sight, knowing that he had failed her. He did not think she would be back soon, and in his secret heart he was just a little relieved. He moved out of the pub within an hour. It was much easier living-in at the airfield.

He tried to call Antonia every day, but it was almost impossible to get through. Everyone wanted to use the one mess telephone at the same time, and often the operator would only allow three minutes for each caller. Unable to have a proper talk, with the others impatiently waiting for their turn, he went to the Wheatsheaf in a lull between sorties, and rang Antonia from there. It was more private, but not more satisfactory. When he told Antonia that he would not be able to join her in London that weekend, she had been at first hurt, and then irate. The operator cut them off while he was trying to explain. Since then, there had been no time to ring at all.

* * *

It had been David's intention to visit the Vorst Hotel every week. He had so far failed to do so even once. He wanted to see Odette Steiner. The Frenchwoman had filled in for him as hotel manager, and he wanted go over the accounts with her, and to discuss problems that had arisen. He had pretty well thrown Odette in at the deep end when he joined the RAF, and felt she might need support.

He did not doubt that she would do well, for she had taken charge of the Paris Vorst for six whole months when Michel was ill, and had more than proved her capabilities. The trouble was that not everyone shared David's confidence. David's brother Conway had cabled from New York to say that he and the other directors were not pleased that he had appointed a woman to manage the London 'house'. The board had voted unanimously in favour of replacing Madame Steiner without delay, and Conway instructed David to find someone.

David had been sufficiently tired and strained to feel extraordinarily nettled by Conway's cable – embarrassed, too, for Odette had been obliged to read it to him over the telephone. His first impulse was to tell his brother to go to hell. Conway might be his boss, but his cable had been a damned insult, not only to his judgement but also to Odette. However, Odette prevailed upon him to take a more conciliatory line, and a cable was despatched, assuring Conway that Odette's appointment was temporary but that she was doing well.

As August drew to a close and the Luftwaffe grew more active, he had had to call off so many visits that it was becoming a real worry. So Odette came down to visit him in the country, with a suitcase full of account books and letters. She brought a scrawl from Antonia, in which she sent her love, but said nothing about coming back.

Odette brought Josef and Marie with her, and the children had a lovely time being entertained by three off-duty WAAFs. After lunch, Josef wandered off and found two mechanics repairing a Hurricane which had been damaged in a dogfight. He enjoyed this so much that he had to be dragged away at the end of the afternoon.

David felt better after Odette's visit. All was going very well at the London Vorst. Odette had engaged a new chef, a young Jewish refugee from Paris who had been turned down by the armed forces because of a crippled leg. A sous-chef at the Crillon before making his escape, the boy had a miraculous way with sauces, and even with unpredictable wartime ingredients had greatly improved the standard of cuisine. By the end of August the restaurant had become so popular that people had to telephone a week ahead to be sure of getting a table.

Odette had boosted the hotel profits in other areas, and the hotel rooms had been booked solid for nearly two months. They drafted another cable to New York in David's name, blandly announcing these outstanding results.

'One in the eye for Conway,' said David before his visitors left. 'He thinks nobody knows a thing about the hotel trade except himself. I wrote and told him that you were good. But words don't cut ice with Conway. He's a numbers man, and he'll be mighty impressed by those August figures, Odette. If you go on as you are, he'll be trying to lure you over to America.'

Odette's visit had taken place on a quiet day, the best they had enjoyed for weeks, with low cloud, and not a single call to action stations. Miraculously, he and Odette had concluded their business without any interruption. It was a day to remember in the hectic weeks ahead, particularly after what happened the following day – a day that came to be called Black Wednesday.

The squadrons were scrambled twice, but had made no contact with the enemy. They flew back to base in good spirits, chatting on the R/T and barely hiding their feelings of relief. Their cheerfulness was short-lived. They came back to a scene of carnage.

The Luftwaffe had come to call, screaming out of nowhere and straf-ing the field with gunfire, dropping their bombs and roaring away again. Two large craters pitted the runway, and there were fires and smoking ruins all around the perimeter of the field. The final bomb had scored a direct hit on the WAAF sleeping quarters, flattening it completely. Sixteen night duty girls had been sleeping in there when the bomb hit, and for many hours all available hands were busy moving rubble and heaving carefully at twisted metal and broken concrete in hopes of finding survivors. Two WAAFs were brought out badly wounded, and were rushed to hospital. The other fourteen girls were dead.

Joe Burgess was the best mechanic on the station. A little man with a face like a walnut, he often worked right through the night, patching up damaged planes, making them fit to fly again. But he was always there to greet the returning squadrons, his face inscrutable, his bright little eyes searching for signs of damage. Joe was shot through the head while walking back to the repair sheds. It seemed incredible to David that he would not be there any more. Somehow Joe's death hit him harder than any so far.

He chose not to tell Odette about Black Wednesday. Those three pretty WAAFs had given the children such a happy day. Best for the children to remember them that way.

He had not seen Antonia for two weeks. He resolved to go to London – driving there and back in a night. If he could only see her, hold her, he could make her understand. Telephoning was hopeless.

He should have known better than to count on a meeting. Next day the Luftwaffe turned its full attention on London, and the first of countless big raids began. For several days David's constant flying duties were made extra hideous by his fear for Antonia's safety in London. Reports from the capital were appalling, and there was no getting through by telephone – no way of reaching her.

A letter came from Lord Dulcimer. Antonia had arrived at the Hall. She was well although tired, and the earl wondered if Antonia and David would like to borrow a house on the estate. Antonia had seen it, and seemed to like it. To David it seemed like a lifeline, and he accepted his uncle's offer with alacrity.

David had not expected Odette to keep her next appointment. But she arrived on the agreed day, and was waiting for him in the officers' mess when he came in. Inwardly he groaned. He had no wish to pore over columns of figures. His head ached, and more than anything he yearned to sleep. However, he summoned up a smile, and said it was good to see her.

'Did you bring the kids?'

Odette was so shocked by David's appearance that it took her a few moments to find words to answer him. His eyes were red-rimmed and bloodshot, and he looked grey with fatigue. His normally charming smile was no more than a grimace. She shook her head in answer to his question. 'No children. I have to talk to you, David. I have been offered another chance to send them to America. Some people had cabins booked on a liner but now they cannot go.'

Almost squinting in his efforts to keep Odette in focus, he said, 'What do you feel? I still think it would be sensible to send them.'

'I think so also.' She laid a hand on his wrist, and he saw that her eyes were shining with unshed tears. 'If I do send them, could they still go to your parents at Maple Valley?'

'Of course they can, Odette. You will miss them like hell, but do send them. It's the only sensible thing to do!'

'Thank you.' She did her best to smile. 'Now, go and get some sleep. You look as if you need it.'

The squadrons were scrambled again at sunset – the fourth time that day. Men rolled fully dressed out of bunks, coffee cups were pushed aside and playing cards thrown down, and there was a general stampede through the doors of the assembly hut. There had been a heavy shower of rain, and as David and the other pilots ran to their respective aircraft, the red evening sky was reflected in the puddles on the rain-wet tarmac. It was like running through a shallow sea of blood.

He exchanged a few words with the new flight mechanic before climbing into the cockpit, switching on the engine, running the usual checks. Within fifteen minutes all five squadrons were airborne and climbing steadily.

David's nerves tightened and the usual cramp of fear gripped his entrails. He forced himself to concentrate on what he was doing, watching the dials, flying with practised precision, commanding himself not to think ahead to what might happen, even less to think back.

Forget yesterday when Jack Sibley 'copped it', his engine on fire, his screams coming over the radio as he went plunging down, trapped in his flaming Spitfire. Don't think of the poor little WAAFs dying when their dormitory hut was hit. Don't think of Antonia's complaints . . .

The flight controller's calm voice came over the radio. 'Bandits at six o'clock.'

They saw the enemy almost at once, black specks on the horizon, a swarm of deadly flies heading for London – Dorniers with fighter escort. As habit and necessity dictated, David pulled a visor over his mind, both fear and recollection put on hold. The job took over.

The British squadrons had the advantage of altitude, and with the setting sun at their back, could hope to surprise the enemy. The radar boys were warning them sooner these days.

It was a savage fight, just another of many. The order to attack, the screaming dive towards the bomber formation to break it up, fingers on the firing button, the rattle of his own guns. Was that a wisp of smoke trailing from a Dornier's port engine? No time to be sure. The yellow nose of an enemy fighter appeared in his mirror. Pull over and roll to evade. Below, he saw another Jerry on the tail of a Spitfire, and put his aircraft nose down to dive in pursuit. As the enemy aircraft went spiralling away towards the ground, he heard someone laughing madly, to find that the laughter was his own. In the whirling chaos of the battle, there was no time for fear. Hot, primitive rage possessed him. It was a strange chemistry, but useful. The enemy had been wreaking havoc in London for over a week. All that mattered was to intercept, to harry, cripple or destroy some of the seemingly endless stream of enemy bombers heading for the British capital. It was the only thing that existed while the battle was going on.

It had been the same from the beginning. It seemed years ago that David had flown south with some others to join the squadron. At that time the Germans had been busily attacking British convoys in the Channel, or bombing the Channel ports. More recently, as on Black Wednesday, they had strafed and bombed airfields, aiming for planes on the ground, destroying at least one large aircraft factory, knocking out vital radar stations. Now it was London's turn.

In David's mind, these individual fights and phases had fused together, blurred into an eternity of scrambles, take-offs and landings, dogfights, the death of friends and constant grinding and growing exhaustion. Now and again, he was visited by a sense of amazed gratitude that he was still alive and fit to fly, when so many of his mates were wounded or dead.

The latest fight ended as suddenly as it had begun. He found himself flying alone above a mottled fleece of pink clouds, with no other aircraft in sight. Below, it would be almost dark, but up here the sky was still blue. As the fury of battle drained away, David found that he was bathed in sweat and beginning to shake – an all too familiar reaction after a fight.

Reality broke in with the flight controller's voice ordering the squadrons back to base. He landed presently without incident and climbed stiffly out of the cockpit and walked over to attend a debriefing. He learned that his friend Peter Faulkes had collided in mid-air with a German fighter. Both planes had been seen plunging to earth locked in a flaming embrace. Neither pilot had baled out.

By supper time, two more of their number were unaccounted for. One of them presently rang in from Kent, to say that he had baled out and was making his way back by train. They never heard from Toddy Paul, a sergeant-pilot with a young wife and a small child back in Birmingham. He had been telling David only days ago that he wanted her to take the child into the country. Toddy's body was picked up next day, floating face down in the sea.

This daily waiting for the tally of survivors was one of the worst things, and like other bad things, the seasoned pilots had learned to nurse their grief or anger in silence – at least while on the station compound. No good dwelling on what had happened when within hours you would be off on another sortie, with all to do again.

It was harder for the newly trained pilots, some barely old enough to be out of school. These boys were often acutely affected by the death or injury of their fellow pilots. There were some wan faces at the breakfast table next day.

One boy had the shakes. Like others who had come to replace those lost or wounded, this boy had only recently won his wings, and when the squadron leader took him up that morning for a flying session, David knew that the shaking hands on the coffee pot had not escaped notice. Douglas believed passionately that no pilot could survive without having complete control of his own aircraft, and insisted on constant practice in formation flying and some pretty hair-raising aerial acrobatics. The aim was to make each pilot come to feel that his aircraft was as much a part of him as his hands or his feet. Weary as they were, people grumbled about these compulsory training sessions, but they took place whenever there was a lull in enemy activity.

David and others were detailed to take more youngsters up, and when they congregated later, the boy with the shakes was being commended for his efforts and was looking rather pleased with himself. Douglas's breezy cheerfulness was good medicine for them all.

Bert Higgins, meanwhile, was living a strange nomadic existence. It rather suited him. He came and went between the shelter and his mother's house in Cotton Street. Rita or Ivy would meet him at the street corner to let him know if the coast was clear. When it was, he slept under the stairs with his mum and the others. Otherwise he and Wat bedded down in St Ronan's shelter.

He found a new world in the crypt under the church. Several families had moved in for keeps until things got better. It was too much trouble lugging kids to the shelter every time the sirens went, and at least you were never lonely in the shelter. There was a communal stove at one end of the long, arched crypt, a chipped sink for washing up in, and the small children had others to play with all day while their older siblings were at school.

Towards evening the shelters began to fill up with schoolchildren, day workers and old people. Bert saw his mum's neighbour Aggie Bream come in as regular as clockwork, shuffling in on her swollen legs, with a string bag full of food and the usual bath cap over her curlers. Along with some of the older regulars, she had a special place at one side of the crypt. Bert kept his head down whenever Aggie went by, because she must not know that he was living out. His mum said that Aggie was a kind soul, but a gossip.

It had been growing dark that first time Bert had seen the bulk of St Ronan's Church looming ahead. He was feeling exhausted. He and Wat had walked all day since leaving Cotton Street, and he was carrying a parcel of chips and a bag of buns from the baker's, which he planned to share with the dog.

The sirens started wailing. People walked faster all around him, laden with bags and baskets. One woman was carrying a loaf, another was pushing a pram with two howling toddlers in it, their wails half muffled by a heap of blankets and a large cardboard box. Their harassed mother suddenly stopped pushing, delved in the box and handed each child a jam sandwich.

Food! There was danger here. Bert clipped Wat's lead to his collar, and held him tight. The district was still without power, and two flickering candles on the stairs into the church crypt did little to dispel the gloom. Bert groped his way from step to step, wondering how in the world he was going to cure Wat of stealing, or manage to feed him. There had been a heap of raw offal at the butcher's labelled 'dog food', but how would he cook it in the shelter?

Afterwards Bert wondered what he would have done if he had not met up with Sam. It was smoky and dim in the low crypt, and while Bert was peering in, a man with a face like a monkey came and laid a hand on Wat's woolly head.

'Nice dog you have here.'

'Yeah.' Bert tried to sound noncommittal. 'A mongrel.'

The little man bent down to get a closer look 'Mongrels are often the brightest,' he said. 'They have to be. Why not bring him over by me, unless you've got a place already?'

'Thanks,' said Bert gruffly.

142

Sam found a straw-filled mattress for Bert and a blanket, and the two of them shared the first of many meals with the ravenous Wat. While they ate and drank, Bert told his new friend that he had just left home, and why.

'Steals food, does he? Well, that's only natural.' Sam took a cold greasy chip from the spread out paper and held it out to the dog. 'You'll have to train him. Give him something else to think about.'

'I've tried,' Bert said wearily. 'But it's not a bit of use. He doesn't understand.'

But Sam had worked in a circus, and knew a bit about training performing dogs.

'You start by showing him that you're the boss. After that, it'll be easy with that one. He's young enough to learn tricks, and bright enough to know which side his bread is buttered.'

There was a lot of singing in the shelter while the raids were going on, often led by the vicar himself. Anyone who had a story to tell, or could do some sort of turn, was much in demand. And once Sam and Bert had convinced Wat that there were better things to do than steal people's food, the whole St Ronan's community adopted the dog as a sort of mascot.

School was definitely not a success. Wat objected to being chained to the school railings and howled dismally, so after two days of this, Bert went to the market instead of to school.

The boy and his dog got on well in the market. The itinerant stallholders liked them. Nobody could suspect Bert and his dog of being government inspectors, and they found him useful. He was strong, for all his skinny frame, and a good worker. And the dog was a right comedian, too, keeping the customers laughing while they queued for food. With his work in the market, Wat's education, and his visits to Cotton Street, Bert was both busy and content. It was not until the sixteenth of September that he was reminded of Abby.

There had been a bad raid in the night. An incendiary bomb had exploded on the vicarage roof, but two voluntary fire watchers had managed to put it out before it did much damage. The stationer's shop near St Ronan's was not so lucky. It had been blasted to bits and the proprietor killed outright. The building was still smouldering when Bert picked his way past it, his hand over his face to muffle some of the choking reek of smoke and cordite. Wat trotted at his heels. Among the debris which had spilled out onto the pock-marked pavement Bert suddenly saw postcards.

Most of them had been ruined by the firemen's hoses, but one looked fairly all right. Bert picked it up. It was a picture postcard of Westminster Abbey. It was then that he remembered. He did not expect to see Abby again, but he had promised to write. He wondered how she was getting on in America. Likely she had forgotten all about him by now.

Abby had not forgotten about Bert, but her life was busy and full of surprises and new things. She had been chosen for the hockey team and had come home from school in a high state of excitement. She came upstairs and flung her arms round Maggie's neck. Her fingers felt something unexpected.

'What's this round your neck?'

Maggie pulled at a thin gold chain and lifted something which winked and flashed – three strands of gold, cunningly woven together to form a ring. The jewel lay on Maggie's work roughened palm, glinting in the evening sunshine.

Abby was charmed. 'How pretty! Did someone give it to you as a present? Is it new?'

'As a matter of fact, it's very old,' replied Maggie seriously. 'More than a hundred years old, so Mistress Fraser thought.' She looked down at the ring, smiling a little. Abby had an idea that there was something not quite happy about Maggie's smile. She wondered why. But before she could ask, Maggie was saying cheerfully, 'It was my mother's. Mistress Fraser gave it to me from my gran. Gran was too poorly to come to the manse before I left.'

'Why do you keep it hidden? If it was mine, I would wear it all the time.'

Maggie slipped the ring back into its hiding place between her breasts, and laughed. 'What? Wear it while I'm bathing the boys or washing dishes? And with hands looking like mine do just now?' She spread them out, palms down. Two of the nails were still split and distorted. 'That ring belonged to my mother, and to her mother and grandmother before that. I shall wait until my hands are better before I wear it. My mother had pretty hands, so Mistress Fraser said.'

Abby knew that Maggie's mother had died when Maggie was a baby, so that explained why she had been looking sad.

What Abby did not know was that Maggie had found a letter from Mrs Fraser and was struggling to come to terms with the news it contained.

If Mary-Jo had not asked to borrow a case to go to a wedding, there was no knowing how long the letter would have stayed undiscovered. Mary-Jo found it lurking under a copy of *The People's Friend*, with which Gran had lined the bottom.

'Thanks for the loan of your bag,' she said cheerfully, returning it. Then she remembered, and groped in her pocket for a crumpled envelope. 'Guess what? I found this in the bottom. It's got your name on it. A letter from a boyfriend, do you think, vowing to love you for ever?'

'Not likely,' said Maggie, taking it. She recognised Mrs Fraser's handwriting, and went quite pink with pleasure. 'Thanks, Mary-Jo.

144

This is better than a love letter. It's from a lady who has always been good to me.'

Mary-Jo laughed, and advised Maggie to tell that to the marines. Why was Maggie blushing, if it wasn't from a boyfriend? Then she relented and went to the door, saying, 'OK. I'll leave you to read it in peace. But mind you tell me the juicy bits later.'

'Get away with you, Mary-Jo,' said Maggie, smiling. When the girl had gone, she slit open the envelope. The letter was several pages long.

'My Dear Maggie,' the minister's wife had written. 'Mrs Dunlop wanted you to have your mother's ring, and I will give it to you before we get to the ship. Mr Fraser remembers seeing your mother wearing it on her pretty hand. Mrs Dunlop also asked me to tell you something which should wait until you are feeling better. Your grandmother thinks it is time you were told the truth about your parents . . .'

Maggie read the letter many times, until the paper was limp and the ink blurred in places where tears had fallen on it. She felt lost, overwhelmed. She did not think that she would ever be able to tell anyone what was in that letter. Not now, not ever.

In her bed, the only place where there was time to think, she would lie in the dark and think about it, her fingers clutching the little gold ring. In the turmoil of her thoughts, the ring was something to hold onto, one point of certainty in the maelstrom of her bewildered mind. The ring had belonged to her mother, and she clung to it. It was the first and only thing of Mary Dunlop's that she had ever owned.

All her life, Maggie had woven fantasies about her dead mother. She longed to know what sort of person Mary had been, and what she looked like.

Tom said he remembered their mother as pretty, always singing about the house – which they would not have dared to do themselves Growing up in the belief that Ian Dunlop had been totally devastated by Mary's death, the young Dunlops also knew that any reminder of her was sure to bring on one of his black moods. Her grandmother had said bleakly that they were not to talk of her. Mary had gone to heaven, and that was that.

But since reading Mrs Fraser's letter, Maggie knew that her mother had not gone to heaven. She had gone to America, had run away from Glen Cary with a cousin called Jack, never to be heard of again.

Mrs Fraser told her more. 'Your mother was loved by everyone who knew her – and your father once loved her more than anyone. She sang in the choir at the kirk, so my husband knew her well. He never understood what happened to make her leave home. Jack, her cousin, was a sponsor at your baptism. He told my husband that he was going to seek his fortune in America. Women are sometimes given to doing irrational things after the birth of a baby. Your mother may have suffered some sort of crisis in her mind.

'She left a letter for your father, but he burned it without letting anyone else read it. He was nearly out of his mind, and he made your grandmother tell the boys that their mother was dead. The neighbours were told the same story, and the very few people who knew the truth were sworn to secrecy. But your grandmother asked me to tell you all this, now that you are also going to America.'

The minister had written a brief postscript in his spidery hand. 'Enjoy Mary's ring, my dear, and never doubt that your mother truly loved you – her little baby daughter. You will grieve, I know, but do not allow yourself to grow bitter.'

These few lines upset Maggie more than the rest. She did feel bitter. She could not help it.

Up and down went her spirits, round and round went her thoughts. She did not have to wonder what had made her mother run away. She had done the same herself, and hoped never to see her father again. But to leave them all behind!

But then another thought dawned. Ian Dunlop would have certainly gone in pursuit of Mary if she had taken the boys. The thought made Maggie shudder. She did not blame her mother for leaving, but an aching sense of loss stayed with her for a long time.

Unable to sleep for thinking of Mrs Fraser's revelations, Maggie went around in a daze all next day. But the following morning she woke to a guilty realisation that she was being selfish. There were other people to be thought of, and things she must do. She owed Mrs Fraser a letter of thanks and an explanation of how the letter had only just been found. More urgently still, and far more difficult, she ought to beard the great Mr James and tell him that Mary Dunlop had not died all those years ago, but had deserted her husband and children and run away to America with a lover.

The more she thought about it, the more she dreaded telling him. Over the past weeks he had been so kind, never too grand or too busy to smile or nod when they passed in the house, and she knew from Mary-Jo that he had forbidden the other servants to question her about her injuries. These had now largely faded, but she was grateful to him, even if she held him in considerable awe. Mary-Jo assured her that after Mr and Mrs Vorst, Mr James was the most important person in the house. But in an odd way she had come to feel that he was on her side. It was a wonderful feeling.

But it was only because he had once liked her mother that he had been so kind. She knew that. So what would he think when she gave him Mrs Fraser's letter to read? It seemed the only thing to do, even though its contents would probably shock him and destroy his illusions. Yet she had to use that letter as a means of telling him. Her emotions were still in a perilous turmoil, the mere thought of her mother immediately bringing a lump to her throat and tears to her eyes. She would be undone if she tried to tell the story in her own words: and Mr James, that most controlled and undemonstrative man, would certainly despise her if she started weeping like a waterspout. Showing him Mrs Fraser's letter felt like betraying her mother, but she could not think of any other way.

She dealt with the easier task first, and wrote to Mr and Mrs Fraser, assuring them that she was not feeling bitter, which was at least partially true. At the end she added, 'I hope my mother is happy in America, and that by some miracle I shall one day find her. This is a lovely place. Everyone is so good to us, and they don't seem to mind us being foreigners and different. I have a friend called Mary-Jo who lives in the town. I have been twice to her house, and she has the nicest parents and a brother and two sisters and a much older step-brother who is coming from New York today. On my last half-day we all went to the movies. Imagine! I have a half-day once a week.'

At first she had been dismayed about the half-day. Days off had never figured in Maggie's life. She had never wanted time off at the manse. True, she had spent some afternoons studying French, but they called it work in case her father should hear of it.

'It is very kind of you, Mrs Sandridge,' said Maggie, bewildered. 'But I really don't need a half-day.' She could not imagine what she would do with it. She would be too shy to venture into the servants' sitting room, or to walk in the gardens by herself. 'Truly I don't need it. Besides, who would bath the children, or help with their tea or put them to bed?'

'We can find someone to help with that,' said the secretary, smiling. 'One of the other maids would help out, I believe. Leave it to me, dear. Shall we say every Wednesday afternoon?'

So Maggie thanked the secretary and went away feeling bemused. In the event, she had no difficulty in using up this daunting gift of spare time. Mary-Jo and her family were wonderfully hospitable and urged her to come over any time. And James's sister invited her to tea on another Wednesday.

Miss Gladys, Mr James's sister, was another new friend and was, in her way, almost as indispensable to Mrs Vorst as her brother. When Mr James had been at Maple Valley for a few years, the Vorsts had built him a house, and he had invited his sister Gladys to come from England to live with him. Before she emigrated, Gladys had worked for a leading London dress designer, and for some years now she had designed and made the softly pleated dresses which were Mrs Vorst's invariable day wear at Maple Valley: flowered silk in summer and gossamer-fine wool in winter. Miss Gladys also made the long tea gowns which Mrs Vorst donned on informal evenings.

She had a workroom in her own house, but for mending and alterations and things that were needed quickly she sometimes worked in the sewing room beside the basement laundry. Finding her there one evening, bent over one of Mrs Vorst's dresses that had got snagged on a rose bush, Maggie had shyly offered to help. There seemed quite a pile of garments awaiting Miss Gladys's attention, and unsure of herself though she was, Maggie was confident about her sewing.

Her offer was accepted.

'Who taught you to darn like this, and to hem so beautifully?'

'My gran did. She was a terror for making clothes last.'

'She taught you well. If you're not too tired, I would like you to help me some evenings.' And when Maggie looked at her, hesitating, she added, 'Mr James and I live just behind the stable yard. The little house with the green door.'

'I'd like to come if Miss Brimley can spare me, Miss Gladys.'

'She won't need you after the children are in bed.'

'She likes me to stay upstairs and listen. Jamie sometimes wakes up and cries.'

'Well, come when you can.'

Since that first meeting, Maggie had several times gone to help Miss Gladys, and they would sit sewing together and chatting. Once Mr James joined them, but mostly he was away at the big house in the evenings.

On one occasion Miss Gladys gave her a photograph to look at. Maggie stared at the faded sepia snapshot in its old-fashioned frame. It showed a very young looking Mr James dressed in army uniform standing beside a smiling young woman. Maggie knew that Mr James had served in the trenches in the Great War because Miss Gladys liked to reminisce about those days, but she asked her hostess who his young lady was.

Miss Gladys looked startled. 'I thought you'd know. It's the only one we've got of your mother, dear. That snap was taken in 1916, just before Jay went off to France. Your mother was in Leeds for a family funeral.'

Maggie looked excited again now, for she had never before seen a photograph of Mary. As Tom said, their mother had been pretty. She turned a radiant face on Miss Gladys and thanked her for letting her see it. She told this new friend a little of how it had been at home, how any mention of her mother was forbidden for fear of upsetting her father. There had been no photographs. Mary might never have existed.

By the time her letter to the Frasers was finished Maggie had made up her mind what she would do. She would give Miss Gladys the letter about her mother on her way to Mary-Jo's house, and ask her to pass it on to Mr James when he came in. It was a coward's way out, but Maggie was accustomed to thinking of herself as a coward.

* * *

Mr James was a man of even temperament, with a reputation for staying calm through all manner of tempests and frenzied situations. Yet, on more than one occasion since the arrival of the British refugees, he had been a prey to uncertainty. He could not make up his mind what to say to Maggie Dunlop.

Orphaned at six years old, he had been brought up by Mary's parents, and looked on Mary Dunlop as a sister. When Maggie told him that she had died so long ago, it had been a severe shock: though it did explain another mystery. She had never answered the letters he wrote to her from America.

His first thought had been that Ian Dunlop might have had the decency to let him know. But on reflection this lack of communication did not surprise him. Mary's husband had been a jealous creature, and would have been devastated by Mary's death. Neither he nor Mary had troubled to hide their joy at being together, and Ian had sat glowering at them from a corner of the room. And as for young Maggie, plainly she had never been told about him, and still less did she know that he had been a sponsor at her baptism.

She had shown amazement when he told her that he knew her mother, and he had expected questions from her. None came. He saw her most days, of course, and was pleased to observe that she no longer looked so ill or so scared; now that her bruises had faded she was starting to look quite pretty. But whenever he greeted her, she only smiled shyly and hurried on by. A man of few words himself, he respected reticence in others. But he was left in a quandary. How much should he tell her? Would Maggie be pleased or embarrassed to learn that she had a godfather here in America?

But when he had digested Mrs Fraser's letter, he knew that he could never tell her. His thoughts took another direction. Where was Mary?

Miss Gladys carried a tea tray into the sitting room, and found James standing where she had left him half an hour earlier. He was looking into the fire, deep in thought and probably still struggling to come to terms with the contents of that letter.

'Drink your tea while it's hot, Jay.'

He sat down on the other side of the hearth and they drank in silence. The fire crackled. There was an excellent central heating system in their cottage and no need for a fire, but Miss Gladys had decided to light one that evening.

Breaking the silence, James heaved a sigh and said, 'I just don't know what to think, Gladys. One thing I am sure of: Mary would never have walked out on those children. Never!'

'Might she have tried to follow you to America?'

'No. Anyway, why should she?'

She said helplessly, 'How should I know? I saw very little of you or

Mary. I was in London serving my apprenticeship while you were both growing up, and then Mary married young and went to live in Scotland. But I always knew you were fond of each other.'

'We were. I looked up to Mary. She was four years older than me: a lovely girl, sensible, wise and loyal. And as for surly old Ian with his possessive ways and jealousy, she assured me that she loved him and was happy in her marriage, and I believed her.'

'So,' said Miss Gladys slowly, 'we're told she was never run over and killed by a car. You and I clearly know that you never eloped together, so just what *did* happen to Mary after you left?'

James looked at her and said gravely, 'God knows. Old Mr Fraser would not have written what he did to Maggie unless he believed she'd run away. It's no use writing to him. One day I shall go back to Glen Cary and see him, but we'll have to wait until the war is over for that. And if Mary hasn't been seen for seventeen years, we may never know what happened.' He got to his feet. 'What matters now is Maggie. At least I have had time to think. If she'd come herself and told me that farrago, I might have given myself away.'

'She's still your god-daughter. You'll have to tell her.'

His smile was twisted and his eyes sombre, 'You think so? With Maggie believing that her godfather is the man who ran off with her mother? Am I to declare myself as the wrecker of her entire family?'

'You could tell her that Mrs Fraser got it wrong.'

'Would she believe me? And even if she did, how would I explain her mother's disappearance? We have no way of knowing if Mary is dead or alive. At present Maggie thinks her mother is somewhere in America with a fictional character called Jack. ...' He fell silent again, and finally he sighed and said, 'She knows me now as Mr James, a middle-aged employee of the Vorsts who once knew and liked her mother. That's true enough. We'd better not elaborate on that.'

James and Maggie met next morning. She glanced at him apprehensively before her eyes fell away. He said quietly, 'Thank you for letting me read Mrs Fraser's letter. A bit of a bombshell for both of us, I'm afraid.'

She looked at him then, the embarrassed colour flooding her face. 'You'll be shocked and wishing you hadn't been so good to me, Mr James.'

'Why would I wish that?'

She looked at him sadly, 'You must think of my mother as a bad woman. But if you knew what my father was like, you'd understand why she had to go away.'

'Nothing would ever make me think ill of your mother, Maggie,' he assured her quietly. She was so surprised and relieved by his words that she walked on air for the rest of her busy day.

* * *

150

James knew that Mrs Vorst had not been sleeping well at night, for she told him so. For years he had driven her about, and sometimes she would ask him to stop the car and would climb into the front beside him. Mostly she just sat there quietly, but sometimes she liked to talk. Lately, she had talked to him about her son David, reminiscing about his boyhood days, remembering how James had rescued her son from the consequences of some prank. She said nothing about her present anxieties. She had no need.

Looking ahead through the windscreen one afternoon, he ventured to say quietly, 'David will be all right this time too, ma'am. I am sure of it.'

She did not answer, and he was pretty sure that she was close to tears. A very private lady, Mrs Vorst, not given to showing her feelings. She thanked him later, and said that it had helped, being able to talk about David.

He wanted to believe her. Maybe it had helped. Cornelius Vorst was just as consumed with worry, and furious with David for upsetting his mother. They probably found it hard to speak of him together. But Cornelius could at least distract himself from his worry with work. The hotel business was never far from his thoughts, and although he did not go to his office every day now, he kept a firm hand on what went on in the numerous Vorst houses. When speaking of one of their hotels, the Vorst family invariably used this modest word 'house', even when the hotel in question was more like a palace.

Cornelius went about more than Chrissie, and had more people to talk to. Like Chrissie, he had confidence in James's discretion, and used him as a sounding board from time to time. He could thrash over both his business problems and his private worries with his lawyer and a Harvard classmate who was his banker. And he worked closely with his elder son, Conway.

Conway was thirty-four years old, a well set up young man with a serious, blunt-featured face and an air of dependability. Since joining the family hotel business, which he did straight after graduating from Harvard, he had little thought for anything else, and over the years had taken on a great many of his father's responsibilities. The Great Depression had come and gone, with some casualties among the smaller establishments in the Vorst chain. But on the whole they had weathered it better than many, and in the past decade the company had expanded and flourished. Cornelius would tell people that this recovery was to a great degree due to Conway's foresight and zeal.

Father and son saw eye to eye over many things, and where they did not, Conway generally thought it best to bow to the older man's wishes. They were both dedicated to improving standards of service, food and comfort in the hotels. They agreed about a need for publicity – although not always about what was the right sort. At all events,

Cornelius was pleased when Conway was seen from time to time in the right places and with the right people. He was photographed escorting beautiful society ladies to the races, or squiring a new movie star to the opera, and dining with her at some fashionable night spot. In summer he made a point of accepting a few invitations to debutante parties, and was frequently mentioned and photographed in the society journals. C. C. Vorst, Junior, heir to the worldwide chain of Vorst hotels, had become quite a well-known figure on the social scene. People would recognise his face and his well-dressed figure when he passed through the lobbies of the Vorst houses, and would feel themselves complimented when he paused to greet them.

Chrissie had not liked it when Conway first became a public figure. She had been raised in the belief that it was vulgar to have one's name in gossip columns. But when Cornelius teased her for being old-fashioned, and explained that she must try to move with the times, she deferred to his judgement. She knew very little about commerce, and had always welcomed her husband's efficient handling of her own considerable fortune. Nor did she mind that he thought her old-fashioned. Cornelius preferred her that way. And she was also truly glad that Cornelius and Conway got on so well these days.

It had not always been so. Cornelius, tough businessman though he was, was also a lifelong lover and collector of beautiful things. He enjoyed music and poetry and pictures, and read widely. It had been a disappointment to find that his elder son took little interest in any of these passions. Conway had always been a sensible boy, a hard-working student, and had never given either of his parents the least trouble. But for years Cornelius had found few things to talk about with his firstborn, and the relationship between father and son had been no better than tepid until they suddenly discovered a shared enthusiasm for making money and running the family hotels.

For her part, Chrissie had always been a loving mother to her two sons and to her pretty daughter Tina, wholeheartedly admiring even their smallest achievements, indulgent of their foibles, and cherishing a strong conviction that no woman in the world had a better husband or more handsome and gifted children. When people praised one or other of them, their eulogies always seemed natural and justified.

And she felt the same about Kim.

'Brimstone says we've got to be nicer to Kim,' said Abby, after Miss Brimley had first told her about Mrs Sandridge's carefully phrased fiat. 'But how can we, when she never comes near us?'

She soon found out. The next day, Kim and her two brothers started coming near them too often for everyone's comfort. Every day since then they had arrived for lunch in the children's dining room –

part of a campaign to prevent Kim and her brothers from feeling excluded. The little brothers were harmless enough, and their nurse a pleasant young woman. But Kim, in Maggie's words, was a right wee besom.

The British children, fairly ordered to be nice to her, were stunned and rather admiring. Kim got away with murder. She was outrageous, played tricks on everyone, was rude to Miss Brimley, put a frog in Miss Fortescue's bed, and a nest of ants in Nanny Munnings's bathroom, tried to trip Maggie up when she came in with a laden tray. When Aunt Chrissie or Uncle Cornelius or her own parents were around, she behaved prettily, curtseyed demurely when shaking hands, smiled and chatted to whoever was sitting near her. But Abby told Maggie that it wasn't a bit of good. Kim rebuffed all friendly overtures except when an American grown-up was looking her way.

As for the British nannies and governesses, she teased them and mocked their odd ways. She kept the English children in agonies of suppressed giggles with her imitation of Miss Brimley trying to eat toast with her badly-fitting false teeth. She took off Nanny Munnings' bustling waddle and Mamzelle's way of flapping her fingers when she was upset. She drew a crude caricature of Miss Fortescue on the playroom blackboard, portraying her as a Roman emperor with a crown of laurels on her head. The British children hooted with nervous laughter before they wiped it off.

The nannies bore it as best they could but got increasingly ratty, and scolded their own children when they caught them sniggering at Kim's pranks. Miss Brimley took to wondering aloud why Abby made no attempt to play with her American cousin.

'Mrs Sandridge tells me that Quentin and Kim were the best of friends this last summer.'

'Quentin is welcome to her, Brimmy.'

Abby was tired of hearing about her cousin Quentin. Kim took a tiresome delight in boasting to Abby about her stay at Seagrass Island. She and Quentin had gone sailing, lobster potting and aquaplaning. And to put the lid on, Kim had added loftily, 'You wouldn't have enjoyed it. None of you Limeys can swim a yard.'

'Who says I can't swim?'

'I only have to look at you, and Quentin says it too. And he says you can't play tennis.'

This was true, for with the Dulcimer grass court turned over to croquet, Abby had never learned to play tennis at all. To have Kim and Quentin discussing her made her feel ready to explode. Condescending beasts! And as for swimming, she might not swim like a seal as Kim did, but she could do breast-stroke pretty well. Haughtily, she said so.

'Oh, yeah? Only old ladies do breast-stroke.'

Abby was still trying to muster a suitably crushing retort when Kim walked off with her nose in the air.

There were several ornamental lakes in the Maple Valley gardens, with rowboats moored on the biggest one and a punt on the smaller pond below the house. None of the nannies could swim, and accordingly they would not allow their charges to go out on the boats. This was a great score for Kim, who spent hours rowing herself about among the lily pads, skimming in and out under the overhanging trees on the largest lake, or punting herself skilfully on the smaller one below the west wing of the house. The British children could only watch enviously from the shore while Kim disported herself and occasionally threw them a pitying look.

One day while punting on the small lake, Kim saw Mamzelle walking with Joan and Betty, and could not resist offering to take them aboard. Pleased and flattered, the two little girls and the Frenchwoman hurried down the grassy bank. Kim waited until they were nearly installed among the cushions at the far end, and then turned around and gave the flat-bottomed craft a tremendous shove with the punt pole. Shrieking with dismay, Mamzelle staggered and fell on top of Joan, who roared. Chuckling, Kim went off, carrying the punt pole over one shoulder, and the laden, lurching punt drifted slowly into the middle of the pond.

Convinced that they would drown, Mamzelle lost the last shreds of her sang-froid as Betty leaned over and tried to paddle with her hands. Mamzelle slapped her hard and forbade either child to move, and the unhappy trio spent half an hour circling among the lily pads and shouting for help. At length one of the gardeners heard their cries and came to investigate. He lost no time in wading into the water and pulling them ashore. But he was impatient with Mamzelle's voluble and somewhat tearful French, and relieved when the French governess chivvied her charges away.

'That Kim again, I suppose?' he said to James, meeting him on the drive. 'She's worse than ever this summer. Can't say that I blame the kid, though. That Frenchwoman was squawking away like a pea-hen, while all she had do was take her shoes off and wade ashore. The little lake's no more than two feet deep at this time of year.'

James grunted. He was entertained by Kim's latest start, and no more inclined to interfere than before. Abby laughed too when she heard about Joan and Betty's plight on the lily pond.

Chapter 12

James collected the mail in the mornings and brought it to Mrs Sandridge's office where they opened it together. They were aware that if anything dire happened to David Vorst, the family would be informed by cable. They had tried to figure out which one of them would break the news to Mr and Mrs Vorst, without reaching any conclusion. One September day there was a Western Union envelope among the letters

For the space of several heartbeats neither of them moved or spoke. James said, 'Hadn't you better open it, May?'

She nodded her neat head but made no move to touch the cable. James took up a paper knife and slit it open. He sighed, and something inside her shrank.

But James was smiling as he passed the paper over. 'David wants his mother to take two more kids – the French ones who didn't come last month. How many more is he going to land us with, I wonder?'

She felt almost weak with relief. 'So long as he's all right himself, he can send us as many war waifs as he likes. Mrs Vorst will be pleased. There is so little she can do for David, she'll give him anything he asks for.'

'Big brother won't be so pleased,' remarked James as he sorted the rest of the mail. 'He's been keeping well away these past weeks.'

'Oh, I forgot to tell you. Mr Conway called up last night,' said Mrs Sandridge. 'He plans to come down next weekend and is bringing four people to lunch on Sunday.'

'The September board meeting is on Tuesday,' said James drily. 'No doubt Conway plans to bend Mr Vorst's ear.'

Conway Vorst owned a house at Maple Valley, but unlike his sister Tina and her fanatical golf-playing husband Bill Faber who lived in theirs all the time, he went there rarely. Most of the time he lived at the New York Vorst Hotel, and if he felt like getting away from work, he would retire to his service apartment, two blocks away. He also belonged to a country club in Connecticut where he played golf.

But as James and Mrs Sandridge were aware, he made a point of staying at the Maple Valley house at least once a month, usually before the monthly board meeting when there would be matters to discuss with Cornelius. He often invited people for the weekend, taking care to choose guests who would be acceptable to his parents, for there was no getting out of Sunday lunch at the big house.

Cornelius Vorst loved his wife, and had taught his sons to treat her with indulgence bordering on reverence. The two boys learned early on that the only capital crime in their father's eyes was to do something to offend or worry their mother. So as Chrissie liked having her loved ones around her, and regarded Sunday lunch as a celebration of their identity as a family, Cornelius insisted that everyone should come to this weekly feast.

Conway brought two couples from Philadelphia to stay for the weekend. One of the men was a fellow hotelier and the other a state senator with a very pretty wife. Saturday had been pleasant and relaxed, with the gentlemen playing golf at nearby Piping Rock Club, and their wives meeting up with them for lunch. In the afternoon they lazed about on Conway's terrace overlooking one of the smaller lakes, and that evening Tina and Bill Faber brought their own house guests to dine, and they danced and chatted until the small hours.

Conway went to bed, satisfied with the day. He had given them a good time, and in the course of the evening had learned some interesting things about property opportunities in Philadelphia.

There was still Sunday to be endured. Chrissie never served wine with lunch at Maple Valley, so Conway prudently fortified his visitors with strong martinis before driving them to the big house, taking them through the wrought-iron gates and up the magnificent beech-lined avenue. They were impressed, as he knew they would be, and he explained that his mother had a 'thing' about Sunday lunch.

'The old lady sets great store by having us there. We think she must have been a mother hen in another life. It's no good calling up to find out who is coming, because Mother has a way of inviting several extra strays at the last minute.'

'Your sister and brother-in-law said they would be going,' said the senator's wife.

'Oh, sure,' said Conway. 'And they will be bringing their children. My mother adores children.'

Conway had in fact called up Mrs Sandridge to tell her to arrange for the lordlings to be present. He had not, so far, seen the three little British boys, except in a crowd of children and adults at Grand Central Station when the British refugees first arrived. He thought he ought to speak to them before he cabled their parents to say that they were well. England sounded to be in a bad way, and British dukes on the way out, but you never knew. He had also asked for the senator's wife to be placed beside him at table. She was pretty enough to take Cornelius's fancy, and he did not want to risk his father getting fresh with her. Chrissie never seemed to mind when her husband flirted with younger women, but Conway minded very much.

He ushered his guests into the white parlour, to find Tina and her party there already, talking stiltedly with a couple of very dull neighbours and to a young Austrian violinist, another refugee from Europe. He had been loaned a cottage in the grounds, and Chrissie thought he looked hungry and had asked him to lunch. Another lame duck, Conway thought resignedly. At that moment Lady Adele and his father came in from the conservatory. Cornelius had been showing her his much prized orchids.

There was another round of introductions. Conway had met Adele Devenish briefly in New York, and had not liked her. She was a tall woman, very thin, with a high bridged nose and an infuriating air of assurance. Her clothes were uninspiring enough to be termed dowdy, but he suspected that this was not due to reasons of economy but because she felt no need to embellish her angular person. She certainly made no effort to charm him, but shook his hand briefly before turning to greet the senator's wife. He wished all the more that he had gone back to New York that morning. The senator had been buttonholed by the dull neighbour and was being told in detail about a local flower show. He looked as if he needed rescuing.

He was about to go to him when he caught sight of his mother, looking more like a mother hen than usual, surrounded by a brood of quaintly dressed children of all shapes and sizes. He cast his sister Tina a look of horror.

'Don't tell me that mob is joining us for lunch? Not all of them, surely?'

Tina laughed at his expression. 'What did you expect, Con? Mother looks on them as family, and you know what that means. Anyhow,' she added, a shade maliciously, 'she knew that you would be dying to meet David's stepchildren.'

Brother and sister regarded each other. Then Conway turned to take a second glass of dry sherry – the only alcoholic beverage offered on these occasions – and drained it in one gulp.

Tina watched him, and then winked at James who was holding the silver tray. 'Thank you, James. I guess I'll take a second one too. No more letters from David, I suppose?'

'Just a few lines on a postcard for Mrs Vorst, Miss Tina, but it was mailed over two weeks ago . . .'

Tina bit her lip, saw Kim watching her anxiously, and said with determined good cheer, 'Well, that's natural enough. European mails are taking ages. And David's no letter writer.'

Conway was not listening. His mother was smiling at him and was coming over, leading a small boy by the hand, and followed by a thin little girl with freckles and straight, mousey hair. Chrissie reached up to

157

kiss her son. 'Good morning, Conway. I want you to meet Abigail and Miles Cary – David's new stepchildren. Children, this is your Uncle Conway, another member of the family whom you won't have met.'

Abby, shaking hands with him politely, tried to ignore Kim's mocking grin.

Sunday lunch was the only meal that the British refugees took in the dining room. At other times they were served in a room beside the inner hall. Abby dreaded Sunday lunch.

The food was gorgeous, of course, always ending up with a dreamy homemade ice cream. But there was a price to pay – a barrage of admonition from Miss Brimley and the other nannies as to how they must mind their table manners, wait to eat until the grown-ups did, only speak when they were spoken to. They had to wear their best clothes, too, and Abby knew very well what Kim thought of her party dress. It was made of blue frilled organdie, and prickled, and Abby had hated it from the first day it came from Hayfords. It seemed wholly unsuitable to wear in the country. But Miss Brimley said that she must wear it, and Maggie had prevailed on her to give in.

'Nobody will notice what you wear,' the nursery maid assured her. 'The grown-ups will be talking to each other. And if Kim says your dress makes you look like a baby, just ignore her. She only does it to tease.'

The dining room was lofty, darkly panelled and shadowy, the windows curtained in some rich crimson fabric, and the huge fireplace topped with an antique mirror framed by wood carvings of fruit and flowers reaching almost to the ceiling. There were many portraits on the walls. But on Sundays, all eyes were drawn to the long mahogany dining table, which gleamed and winked with highly polished silver, cut-glass goblets filled with iced water, the whole room fragrant with a long, low centrepiece of Aunt Chrissie's favourite roses. Every place was laid with the finest linen and lace napery. It was all wonderfully pretty, but daunting, and Abby found herself envying little Jamie and the very small children who sat with the nannies at the far end of the room. And of all the unlucky chances, she found herself seated next to Kim. On her left was a pretty lady who wore a white silk dress.

Cornelius never sat at the head of his own table when they had company at Maple Valley, preferring to put himself beside Chrissie. The truth was that he was easily bored by small talk, and Chrissie was never offended if he decided not to talk at all, or if he suddenly remembered something he wanted to do, and walked out. It was therefore Conway who presided at the head, facing his mother who was seated between her husband and the senator at the opposite end. The senator's wife was on Conway's right hand, and Lady Adele on his left.

It was inevitable, Conway supposed, that the talk should turn to the war in Europe, and from there to the bombing of London, and of Winston Churchill's latest stirring speech. Inevitable, too, that this should lead to further talk of the battle for air supremacy over England, and of his brother David's exploits as a fighter pilot. Conway contributed little to the conversation. He nodded from time to time, his square-jawed face showing nothing at all of his inner, growing irritation. He was, in fact, sick of all this war talk and adulation of his younger brother.

'You must be so anxious for him,' said the senator's wife. 'Does he get time to write?'

'My mother had a card from him but I don't believe it said much.'

'Amazing that he found time to write at all,' put in Adele in her rather mannish voice. 'I like that brother of yours, Conway.'

He was not obliged to say anything because his pretty neighbour was claiming his attention. 'I think your mother is just wonderful. How does she manage to look so serene?'

'Aunt Chrissie is an amazing lady,' said Adele, smiling. 'We are living at Bellefield, and believe me, everything has been thought of, even flowers in the rooms when we first arrived. Some clever person left us a most useful list of telephone numbers, too. I wish I knew how to repay your parents' kindness, Conway.'

'It gives my mother pleasure to help people,' said Conway. His own opinion was that his parents had gone off their heads loading themselves with all these children and charmless grown-ups for an indefinite period, but he was not in the habit of airing his opinions within the family circle. Instead, he looked down the long table and exchanged a warm smile with his mother. 'She is unique and wonderful, and we all love her.'

'Tell me,' said Adele, switching to another subject in her abrupt way, 'is Wendell Wilkie going to be your next President?'

'I believe and hope so,' he replied seriously. 'The campaign is going well. I want to see a new man in the White House.'

'What's wrong with President Roosevelt?' demanded Adele. 'He's a splendid person.'

'You think so?' murmured Conway. He exchanged a fleeting look with the senator's wife who, like himself, was a staunch Republican. 'And just how long have you been in our country, Adele?'

'You know perfectly well,' she retorted. 'Four weeks ago you met us at Grand Central Station, and bundled us aboard those cars to Long Island.'

'I have not forgotten,' Conway said drily. She had irritated the hell out of him then, and was doing it again. 'So after four weeks you have decided who should be our next President? Would it surprise you to know that some people would disagree with you?'

Adele looked at Conway curiously. She had found him abrupt at their first meeting, and difficult to read. However she received his acid words with a good-humoured shrug of her shoulders and said, 'I dare say my opinions must seem very one-sided. But your President and our Prime Minister have come to know and trust each other, and we greatly value Mr Roosevelt's support and friendship. It takes time and care to build up that sort of relationship, and I dread it coming to an end. Such a waste . . .'

'Some Americans are pretty scared of Winston Churchill dragging us into your war, Adele. If that happened, it would be more than a waste.'

'That,' she began, 'is a matter of opinion—'

'It would be a disaster.'

They glared at each other, and then second thoughts and self-interest took hold, reining them back. Adele remembered just in time that she was a guest of this boorish man's parents. Besides, she wanted to use the Vorst Hotel as a base for a project. She had already cleared it with Cornelius, but it would not do to antagonise Conway.

Conway realised to his dismay that he had very nearly lost his temper with this arrogant British female. He prided himself on being in command of himself at all times, of never showing his emotions; he despised those who lacked his iron self-control. Setting his teeth, he stifled his annoyance and turned his attention to the dessert, which was being handed around in elegant silver and crystal dishes.

The dessert proved to be coffee ice cream with hot chocolate sauce. Abby caught the oldest lordling's eye across the table and they grinned at each other. To children who had suffered from years of indifferent milk puddings and over-stewed fruit, Maple Valley ice creams were total heaven.

Lunch, Abby began to feel, might be going worse. Lady Adele's sixteen-year-old son was sitting on the far side of Kim, her two younger daughters and a couple of other quasi-Devenishes were across the table, talking in their cheerful, assured way, and joking about what fools they had looked in a Garden City store, buying gym shoes for school.

'Luckily we spotted what we wanted, and pointed at them. Sneakers on the sidewalk are more fun than gym shoes on the pavement. What other new words can you teach us, Kim? Charles is making a Limey/Yank dictionary, and we are all going to be millionaires.'

So Kim, apart from one taunting, whispered 'Hi, frilly baby!' as she slipped into her seat at the beginning of lunch, had been fully occupied and entertained by the larking Devenishes. The fair-haired lady in the white dress was busy talking to Kim's Uncle Conway and the other grown-ups at her end of the table – another mercy. True, she had asked questions. Did Abby feel homesick? What was it like on the boat coming out? What was her favourite American food?

Abby said truthfully that the ice cream was the best in the world, and that she liked being in America. That way, people smiled and left you alone. Better not to talk about the things you did not care for, like the different taste of the bread, sweet potatoes, or poison ivy. Better still not to mention the occasional pangs of longing for home things. These were for night time, and private – and Maggie was right. Miseries usually felt better by morning.

'Coffee ice cream for dessert, Abby,' said the senator's lady to Abby with a smile. 'That will please you, I hope.'

Abby smiled back. She liked the look of her neighbour. She was reminded of her mother, a little, for the lady's hair was golden and her eyes very blue. Being a grown-up and a guest, she had been served first, as had the adults at either end of the table. Abby was in starvation corner, being the last on the children's circuit, but Kim's turn came, and then it would be hers. She watched Kim take some ice cream from the crystal dish. Then she ladled chocolate sauce lavishly over it.

Helping oneself to food like this was one of the things that made Sunday lunch unnerving. The ice cream was easy, for it had been shaped into neat blobs. The chocolate sauce was handed to Abby next – a silver sauceboat with clawed feet standing on an octagonal silver salver. The parlour maid held it low at Abby's left side, so that she could fill the ladle, and carry it to her plate.

Kim put out a hand and pinched Abby's leg under the table. It was a hard pinch, and Abby jumped and her hand shook on the ladle. It was odd, really, how disaster could happen simultaneously at different speeds – slow motion and instant. She watched the sauceboat skating sideways on its little ice rink. She grabbed for it, as did the parlour maid, but the jug tipped over with a clatter, splurting chocolate sauce in all directions before rolling out of sight under the table.

The senator's wife tried to get out of the way, but was too late. When she stood up, there were splashes and rivulets of chocolate oozing down the front of her dress. Abby was starting to gasp an apology when her shoulders were seized, and Conway shook her violently, his hard fingers digging into her thin shoulders.

His irritation had been seething inside him all through lunch. When the English child splashed chocolate all over his guest, it erupted.

'Little vandal! Look at you, throwing your food at a lady! For heaven's sake, Mother! Put these English children to eat someplace else until someone teaches them manners!'

Conway's fury went from boiling to cold within seconds. He released Abby, and she staggered and fell against the table. Grimly, he stared down into the frightened, freckled face of David's stepchild, seeing in his mind's eye not Abby but his younger brother. Thanks to the English child's clumsiness, he had lost his temper and made a public exhibition of himself.

He said in a quiet, bitter voice, 'Just get out, little girl.'

161

He turned away, felt the senator's wife's hand on his shoulder, and turned to look at her. 'God, Barbara. I'm so sorry. I should never have brought you to this zoo.'

Aunt Chrissie, at her end of the table, was momentarily frozen with dismay at Conway's sudden outburst. She started to rise from her chair, only to find that both the senator and Cornelius were trying to restrain her.

'But Corney!' she said in distress. 'We must do something . . .' She broke off, however, for Conway was no longer shaking Abby, and James had come to the rescue and was already halfway to the door, with a hand under Abby's elbow.

'Nothing to worry about, dearest,' said Cornelius. 'It was just an accident.'

'Leave it to me, sir,' said the senator, getting to his feet. He joined the group at the far end of the table. His wife was laughing helplessly, while Adele and Tina dabbed at her with their lace-edged napkins and Conway stood by frowning.

'Tell them it's all right, Charlie,' Barbara implored him. 'Conway, it was just an accident. My dress will clean up fine.'

'Barbara is an old campaigner,' said the senator. 'As a politician's wife she has had worse things thrown at her than chocolate sauce.'

Everybody laughed, and the feeling of tension eased. Even Conway managed a brief smile, but he shook his head. 'I'd have given anything not to have had this happen. Anything!'

'It doesn't matter. But Conway, that poor little girl was so mortified. Maybe you ought to go comfort her.'

'James will do that,' said Tina quickly. 'Barbara, you and I are much the same size, so why don't I lend you a dress? I keep several upstairs, for when Mother springs a party on us without warning.'

James took Abby out of the dining room, pushing through a swing door that led into a pantry. Maggie had been helping behind the scenes, and the first she knew of any drama was when a parlour maid came rushing in with chocolate dripping from her hands and her white frilled apron. She was saying something to a footman about 'All hell let loose' when James came in with Abby. At the sight of Abby's face, Maggie started forward.

'Maggie, there's someone here who needs you,' said James, making it sound as if it was no big deal. But as Abby ran to the safety of the nursery maid's arms, he added quietly, 'You know where the office is. Take the kid in there until I come.'

It took a while for Abby to stop shaking, and Maggie did not try to speak, or to ask what had happened. She just held her.

The first thing Abby said was, 'I can't stay here.' And while Maggie was still trying to think what to say, she added in muted desperation,

'I want to go home, Maggie. I *must*. He thinks I did it on purpose. He really hates me. I can't stay . . .'

'I don't believe a word of it. Who is this person that is supposed to hate you?'

'They all do. Uncle Conway and the lady I threw chocolate onto . . .'

'You did what?' Maggie held Abby away from her, saw the wreck of the blue organdie, and the smears of chocolate that had now attached themselves to her apron, and said with a smile, 'Yes, I see. And now you've thrown chocolate onto me, too, but I don't hate you.'

Abby choked on a shake of unwilling laughter.

'That's better.'

'It's not better. And it's no joke,' said Abby crossly. 'The lady was wearing a *white* dress, Maggie, and now it's all dripping and disgusting. And you should have seen how Uncle Conway looked.' She shivered, and finished drearily, 'Kim hates me too.'

'Well, you aren't silly enough to listen to anything that one says, I should hope,' said Maggie bluntly. 'Did you say you were sorry to the lady in the white dress?'

'Well, I tried to, but Uncle Conway started shaking me and scolding.'

There was a knock at the office door, and Mary-Jo came in with a bowl of water and a towel, and one of Abby's cotton dresses under her arm. She also brought a pair of sandals. She said that James had sent her to get them, and between them the two girls lifted Abby's frilly dress and petticoat over her head, and washed her face and hands and her chocolate-streaked legs.

'You've done a thorough job, right enough,' said Maggie, tossing brown smeared silk socks onto the discard heap on the office floor. 'Hand me that dress, would you, Mary Jo?'

James ushered Miss Brimley into the office. The little governess was out of breath and distraught, her hair wisping out of its net and pins, and two spots of colour on her wrinkled cheeks. At the sight of Abby, damp from recent washing, skinny and barefoot in vest and knickers, she said distressfully, 'There you are! Abigail, I did not know where to look back there in the dining room. I did warn you to mind your manners!'

Abby looked at her coldly. 'I didn't do it on purpose, Brimmy.'

'I dare say not.' The governess seem to be on the verge of tears. Then she said sharply to Maggie, 'You should have taken Abby upstairs. This is no place for her to be standing about half naked. Get her dressed, do. She must come and apologise to Mrs Vorst and that other lady.'

'I rather think,' said James, 'that Mrs Vorst has gone for her afternoon rest, Miss Brimley, and Mr Conway has taken his house guests away. Why don't you lie down yourself? I'll get some tea sent up . . .'

He led Miss Brimley to the small elevator which was generally kept for the exclusive use of Mr and Mrs Vorst, and took her upstairs.

163

Tina and Bill, who good-naturedly gave up his second round of Sunday golf, invited Conway and his friends over to their place. It seemed a good idea. Everyone made an effort to please and to be pleased, and indeed the Fabers' pretty creeper-hung white house was delightful, and they admired the delicately muted mural that had just been painted in the dining room. Later they sipped iced tea in Tina's conservatory, taking care to include Conway in their light-hearted but desultory talk.

He scarcely took in what they were saying, for he was wondering glumly what had come over him. In his mind he saw his mother's imploring eyes, and the look his father had given him. The old man's craggy, high-coloured face had later worn a closed-in look. Trouble brewing there, without a doubt.

He mentally shrugged these thoughts aside, but he was relieved when the senator got up and said they ought to be heading back to New York.

When Tina and Bill took the others away, Kim had been missing. Tina had shrugged and had said a word to James. Kim often stayed on at the big house, and James would bring her home when she was ready. Tina did not know that her daughter had gone into hiding.

Ever since she had pinched Abby's leg, Kim had been riding a switchback of bewildering emotions. Gleeful at first, she was dismayed by the scale of the mess – and the sight of her uncle grabbing Abby had shocked her. Almost, she wished she had never played that trick.

They all left the dining room. The smaller children were sent upstairs for afternoon rests, and the older ones drifted into the playroom, or wandered aimlessly about the front hall.

Feeling at a loss, Kim peered through the office door, and saw Abby with her face pressed against the nursery maid's shoulder. She started to go in. But Maggie gave her a very cool look, and a dismissive shake of the head. Nettled, Kim went away.

She came face to face with Edward Devenish. She rather liked this older English boy. During lunch he had asked about the lake and the rowboats, and she smiled, thinking to take him for a row.

But he was as bad as that nursery maid. Before she could speak he said flatly, 'That was your fault, Kim. Why did you do it?'

'Do what?'

'Whatever you did to make Abby jump like that – pinched her, or stuck her with a pin. A rotten trick, whatever it was.'

Kim said furiously, 'I can do what I like in my grandma's house.'

But she only spoke to his back, for he had turned and walked away.

That did it. Stirrings of remorse were swept away, overtaken by a renewed hatred of English interlopers, shame, and a determination that she would show them!

She stalked into the playroom. Joan and the eldest lordling were playing a game called 'hangman' on the blackboard. She pushed them out of the way and wiped their game off. Then she took coloured chalks from a jar and started to draw, slashing at the board with vengeful strokes.

'There!' she said, when she had drawn a portrait of Maggie. She stood back. Joan and the lordling watched round-eyed. 'And if either of you wipe that off, I'll kill you!' said Kim. She stalked into her grandfather's study and hid herself behind the heavy brocade curtains.

She went there instinctively, for she needed a respite, some place to sort out the turmoil of her thoughts and feelings. She had forgotten that it was Sunday, and only remembered her mistake when she heard her grandfather come in.

Cornelius always retired to his study after Sunday lunch. He would put a favourite record on his Victrola and turn it up full blast, before sinking into an armchair for a nap. Until he rang his bell or came out, no one ventured to disturb him. On this particular day, though, he called up James on the house telephone and said he wanted him.

James found Cornelius sitting at his leather-topped desk, his hands clasped before him, and his bushy white eyebrows drawn together in a frown. He did not look at all sleepy.

James paused in the doorway. 'Yes, sir?'

'Shut the door, James, and come and sit down.'

James complied, and waited.

'Did you see what happened at lunch? You usually see what goes on.'

'I saw some of it, sir.'

Cornelius looked at him. 'So? How did it happen?'

'It was an unlucky accident, Mr Vorst. Little Abby was pretty upset, but that Scottish girl will sort her out. Nothing to worry about.'

'Fine. But it is my own family that I'm asking you about.'

'Mr Conway was taken by surprise, sir. No doubt he has a lot on his mind.'

'And Kim? What about her?'

For a long moment James did not answer. Kim had looked far too angelic at the time, certainly. But what had Cornelius seen?

'Come on, James,' said Cornelius irascibly, 'Answer me. Was Kim to blame for that upset?'

'I think she must have played some trick, sir. But I didn't see her do it.'

'Well, of course you didn't. It happened under the table, but I saw her look at Abby and saw her arm move as she pinched her. The little demon . . .' Cornelius's eyes twinkled for a moment, but he said quite seriously, 'It won't do, James. Mrs Vorst would be

165

horrified. You see, she truly believes that Kim can do no wrong.'

'Yes, sir.'

'My wife and Miss Tina took a notion into their heads that the British children weren't being kind to Kim. I wondered about that. Kim may look like an angel, but there's a lot of Vorst devilry in her, and she isn't that easily upset. What did you think?'

James grinned. 'The same as you, sir. She has had a great time playing tricks on them all these past couple of weeks.'

'What sort of tricks?'

James told him what he knew. Once or twice Cornelius permitted himself an appreciative grin, but he listened in silence. When James had finished, Cornelius looked at his servant grimly. 'You should have told me.'

James returned his look, but said nothing.

'So why in hell didn't you?'

James smiled. 'Kids are better left to sort themselves out without interference.' And when Cornelius just frowned at him, he added, 'Kim could do with a friend of her own age who would stand up to her.'

Cornelius shrugged. 'Maybe so. Pinching Abby was a spiteful, lowdown trick, though, and I mean to have it out with her. Where is Kim right now?'

'She must be somewhere about. Will I fetch her to you?'

'No,' said Cornelius, rising to his feet. 'We will find her together.' And as they crossed the inner hall, he said decisively, 'I want to get this over before my wife gets up from her afternoon nap. I won't have her plagued with it.'

The study door closed. Crouched in the window embrasure, Kim let out a shaky breath. Then she slipped to the floor and went through the tall screen doors to the terrace. Crouching down and hugging the wall of the house, she reached the top of the terrace steps and sped down them. Once on the lawn below, she looked quickly to left and right, and began to run.

Maggie went off to change her apron. Abby made sure that the hall was clear and crossed it. She was still feeling shaky and unwilling to face people. She went into the red drawing room and saw a group of children playing cards within a few yards of Kim's cruel caricature of Maggie. There it was, showing the nursery maid as she had once looked, with purple bruising and a drooping eyelid. At the sight of it, a flush of rage reddened Abby's freckled cheeks.

'You might have wiped it off, damn you!' she scolded, seizing a duster and doing so.

'Kim said not to.'

'She said she'd kill anyone who did.'

'She did, did she?' said Abby, throwing the duster down. 'Well, she won't, because I'm going to kill her myself. Where is Kim now?'

One of the smaller children piped up, 'Kim went past the window just now. I saw her starting down the steps.'

'Right.' Abby sped out of the screen door. It fell shut behind her with a whine and a bang, and she plunged down the terrace steps.

She caught sight of her quarry running ahead between the trees and shouted to her to stop. But after a quick glance over her shoulder, Kim ran faster. Both of them were swift runners; Abby might not have caught up but for the fact that Kim checked on a plank bridge. She had to climb a gate.

By this time both of them were gasping for breath, and scarlet with exertion – and in Abby's case with rage. She yanked at Kim's leg as she straddled the gate, tumbling her down on the wooden planks then falling on top her. Kim yelped. Abby had just time to notice that her cousin had been crying, when Kim rolled sideways and kicked her painfully on the leg.

It was a disgraceful fight, hair-pulling, slapping and scratching, with Abby gasping with fury, and Kim uttering every rude word in her vocabulary. But it did not last long. Grappling and kicking, they rolled to the edge of the little bridge, and toppled over, splashing into a shallow reeded brook in a tangle of legs and arms and curses.

The shock of the water sobered them, and they sat up, waist deep in mud and reeds. They looked at each other. Abby spat out a mouthful of muddy water, and watched Kim trying to blink mud and green stuff out of her eyes. Her cousin was a sight, with a bleeding scratch on one cheek, and brown slime oozing out of her hair.

It looked like chocolate sauce, and at the thought of the disaster at lunch, Abby began to laugh. A glowering moment later, Kim started laughing too. They tried to get to their feet, but Kim fell back. Abby offered her a hand, and together they crawled and scrambled up the bank and lay gasping and laughing on the rough grass.

'I don't mind you playing tricks on me,' said Abby a good deal later. 'But that drawing of Maggie was just horrible.'

'I meant it,' said Kim simply. 'I saw you in the office, and I was about to say I was sorry but Maggie shook her head at me. She doesn't like me.'

Abby said indignantly, 'Why on earth *should* she? You've been an absolute beast to her from the start.'

'You Limeys can't take a joke. What's so special about Maggie? She's only your maid, isn't she? You laugh when I play tricks on Miss Brimley or that other tubby nanny.'

'You can do what you like to Brimmy and the others, but not to Maggie. If you do anything horrid to her again, I'll fix you, even if it means Aunt Chrissie and Uncle Cornelius sending me away. Anyway, if I had known how to get back to England, I'd have run away after lunch.'

Kim looked at Abby as though seeing her anew. 'You mean that? Don't you like it here?' And when Abby shrugged her thin shoulders and said it was all right most of the time, Kim said peevishly, 'That's not very nice. Grandma' has worked all summer long making the place pretty for you. She didn't talk of anything else for weeks. What's wrong with being here?'

Abby said hastily, 'Nothing. Nothing at all. Aunt Chrissie is lovely, and so is the house. I didn't mean to sound ungrateful.'

'What did you mean, then?'

Kim was still sounding affronted, and Abby was in no mood to put up with it. 'I don't like living with people who hate me. I know about you. And now there's your uncle hating me too.'

Kim said nothing at all for a long moment, confronted with the surprising knowledge that she did not hate Abby. Not any more. The fight and their fall in the brook had changed things. Along with this discovery came the memory of something she had heard James say back there in her grandfather's study. Something about her needing a friend.

But there was no time to examine this, for she was visited by a less agreeable thought that both her grandfather and James were on her trail. She, too, had been running away when Abby came after her. That was another thing they shared. And, like Abby, she had nowhere to run to.

She said soberly, 'We'll have to clean up before we go back. Maybe I'll run over to my house and change into shorts.'

'And what am I supposed to do?' demanded Abby crossly, thinking that even Maggie would be fed up with her for wrecking two dresses in one day. Besides, she was supposed to apologise to Aunt Chrissie.

'Let's go to the yard,' suggested Kim. 'There is a faucet there, and a hose with a spray. We can wash this goo off, and I'll lend you something to wear.'

But they never managed to reach Kim's house. They came into the yard where all the automobiles were kept, and stopped short. Cornelius was there with James, and Maggie was with them.

Cornelius surveyed them – two bedraggled little girls, both filthy, both wearing expressions of shocked guilt on their scratched faces. He did not ask them where they had been, or what had happened. In a voice of ice, and a look on his face that had caused hardened businessmen to shake in their shoes, he said, 'You had better get cleaned up. James will take you to his house. After that, I have something to say to both of you.'

Kim started to speak, but before her first stammered words were uttered, her grandfather had turned his back and left them.

Chapter 13

Abby lay on top of her bed, peering through puffy eyelids at the windows of her attic bedroom where the wire mesh flyscreens were partly hidden by frilled white muslin curtains. Her eyes were swollen and her arms and legs itching and on fire with poison ivy, so she was an outcast from the herd during this sunlit weekend towards the end of September. Indian Summer, Aunt Chrissie called it. It was as warm as midsummer in England.

At first being up here on her own had been a pleasure, for solitude was a rare luxury in Maple Valley House. So many people, always, and constant chat and clamour and footsteps. Eleven other children and five adults slept up here, and they were planning to bring a fourth bed into the large room which Abby shared with Joan and Betty. Marie would sleep in it soon, for the French children were already on their way.

Presently Abby dozed off. She woke to see Maggie standing by her bed.

'A pretty sight, you are,' said Maggie, looking down at her. She touched the side of her own mouth with one finger, feeling the raised scar which was barely visible now. She shook a bottle of calamine lotion. 'Still, you should be all right for school by Monday if you don't scratch too much.'

Abby did not answer. She gripped her hands together to stop them straying to her worst itches. She did not want to miss school. It was fun there, and Miss Brimley could not get at her.

But when Maggie began dabbing calamine on her itches, she grumbled about her headache and how she was missing the fun at the swimming pool. She got no sympathy.

'Serves you right.' Maggie knew fine that Abby had run off into the woods after school. 'Poor Miss Brimley was mortified when Mrs Vorst wanted to know where you were and she could not say.'

'Brimmy fusses so.'

'Miss Brimley can't help worrying. It's her nature. Besides, she feels responsible for you.'

'We were only climbing trees. What did she think would happen to us?'

Maggie was by then dabbing lotion on the angry red rashes that had erupted on Abby's legs and arms. Some of them had ripened into yellow blisters, which in turn broke and dried into scabs. 'Happen to you?' she echoed, taking a fresh piece of cotton wool and anointing the side of Abby's mouth. 'Isn't this enough?'

Abby shrugged bony shoulders. 'The woods are so pretty. All red and purple and gold, and Aunt Chrissie never said we weren't to play there.'

'Your Aunt Chrissie likes to know where you are, and that you are safe. Imagine what it would be like for her if she had to write to your mother and tell her that you had been badly hurt or something?'

'Kidnapped, you mean?'

Maggie looked at Abby. Mrs Vorst's fear of kidnapping was well known, but all the household had been told not to speak of it to the children. It was due to Mrs Vorst's fear of kidnapping that all the indoor staff were recruited from distant places, their references subjected to intense scrutiny before they were taken on. Kim said that Mary-Jo was a rare exception. She lived three miles away in Maple Valley village, but was acceptable because her father was a policeman. Kim was always finding out things.

'For goodness' sake,' said Maggie. 'Don't start talking about kidnapping, specially not to Miles. We don't want him having nightmares again.'

Abby started to grin, knowing that she had scored. But the grin was lopsided due to a poison ivy crust at one corner of her mouth. She lay back against the pillows, and sighed. Perhaps Maggie was right, and she should avoid the woods if this was going to happen every time. But Kim had persuaded her to go over and climb the trees in her garden, and saying no to Kim was not easy.

Maggie had been working it out. She said suddenly, accusingly, 'So! It was Kim who told you about the kidnapping, wasn't it?' And when Abby merely shrugged, she said, 'Kim is too knowing for her own good. Right spoiled, she is, too. Gets her own way with everyone.'

Abby did not trouble to deny it. They got on quite well these days, but Kim was still a force to be reckoned with. Maggie had hit on the right word. Kim was indeed 'knowing', and being her chosen friend was sometimes fun, and sometimes hazardous.

Maggie went away, and Abby lay back on her pillows. She tried stretching her lips into a cautious smile, but it was too uncomfortable. She shut her eyes, and thought about school, and being in the fifth grade, and playing hockey, and what fun it all was. Never having been to school before, Abby had no way of comparing Greenacres School with any other. But Laura, another English girl in the fifth grade, said it was miles nicer than the boarding school she had left

170

behind in Hampshire. The teachers were so friendly, and so were the other children.

'It's super not having to wear uniform, too,' Laura added.

Having never worn school uniform in her life, Abby had been secretly disappointed about this. Still, they wore a kind of uniform for games, blue shorts and yellow shirts and sweatshirts.

Remembering how Bert and his sisters had been persecuted and made mock of at Dulcimer village school for their cockney accents and their ignorance of country ways, Abby had resolved to open her mouth as little as possible to begin with. But at Greenacres it was apparently not a crime to be different, and the other children seemed on the whole more interested than despising of the British visitors. Nobody at school teased her for talking in a funny English voice, and anyway, unkind teasing was generally looked down on in the fifth grade.

Kim, who had no scruples about teasing, thought the fifth grade girls a dull lot. 'You would have much more fun if you were in the fourth grade with me,' she told Abby jealously. 'Why don't you ask them to move you down?'

'Certainly not. I'm happy where I am.'

This was true. Abby was in high fettle, enjoying school, even enjoying lessons for the first time in her life, for it was all new and interesting, and the teacher never treated her pupils as underlings.

More than anything, Abby was counting the days until Josef and Marie arrived. Kim was scornful about the French newcomers, and teased Abby about her Frog Prince. She did not expect to like Josef, and said so.

People were either in or out with Kim. If you were out, she would ignore you or torment you. But if you were in, she was hard to resist.

Abby discussed this muddling situation with Maggie after school one day. Maggie was in the laundry room next to the kitchens, ironing.

'And the silly thing is,' Abby concluded, 'at times I don't like Kim any more than you do.'

'Who says I don't like her?'

'Anyone can see you don't.'

Maggie folded away a pair of Miss Brimley's long fawn knickers, and added them to the growing pile of ironed clothes in her basket. 'Kim's all right. If she had been skelped once or twice in her life she'd be even better.'

'Nobody would dare to smack her.'

'They tell me there's only two people she's a mite feared of,' said Maggie thoughtfully. 'One of them is Mr Vorst, of course.'

Abby thought about this, remembering how she and Kim had been summoned by Uncle Cornelius after the fight. Abby had been shaking at the knees when James ushered them into the library.

In the event, it had not been so terrible, only embarrassing. Uncle Cornelius asked them questions, aiming most of them at Kim, and requiring answers. He seemed to know that Kim had caused the chocolate disaster, and when she started to deny it he had just looked at her. Kim must have hated that interview, and at the end he had banished her from the big house. 'I don't want your grandma to see you in this shameful state. She would be upset, and I won't have that. And Abby had better go with you, for the same reason. Come back when you both look like nice little girls again.'

They had gone to Kim's house, feeling remarkably foolish.

Abby said to Maggie, frowning, 'I don't think Kim is scared of Uncle Comelius, exactly. She just doesn't like him thinking badly of her.'

'That's better than being feared.'

'Mm. So, who is the second person she minds about?'

'Her uncle over in England. Mr David Vorst.'

Abby was surprised and rather intrigued. 'David? But he's so quiet and . . . not at all frightening. Maggie, who told you all this?'

'Never you mind who told me,' said Maggie. 'I'll say this for your new school, they don't expect a lot of starch and braid and redding up like our schools at home. Sensible, I call it, the way you go to school in ordinary home clothes.'

They both turned as the door opened. It was Miss Gladys. She smiled at Abby, and nodded at the nursery maid. 'You coming down this evening, Maggie?'

Maggie said doubtfully, 'I've some mending to do for Miss Brimley.'

'Then bring it with you.'

'I'll need to ask. I will come down if I can get away. Thank you, Miss Gladys.'

When James's sister had gone, Abby looked at Maggie and smirked. 'So that is how you know all that stuff about David. Kim says that that Miss Gladys is making you a dress.'

'Better than that. She's showing me how to make one for myself.'

She did not tell Abby that Mr James was teaching her to drive a car, though. She had not told anyone about that. She had been out with him twice already, and had a feeling that Miss Brimley and the others would try to stop her when they heard about it.

Mary-Jo hurried in late the next morning, grabbed a drying-up cloth and came to stand beside Maggie who had nearly finished washing up the children's breakfast. 'Sorry,' she said. 'My pa had a flat tyre this morning, which made us both late. Can you meet me at the back door after you have put the kids on the school bus. I have something exciting to tell you.'

Maggie wondered what Mary-Jo wanted. She was inclined to be

172

wary of Mary-Jo when her voice took on that excited, 'just for your ears alone' tone. It usually had something to do with her stepbrother Cagney, whom Maggie was trying to avoid.

She was right. It was about Cagney. 'Come down to our place next Saturday evening,' Mary-Jo said when Maggie arrived, pink-faced and tousled from walking up the avenue against a blustery wind. 'Cagney and his New York crowd are coming, and guess what? He's asked you and me to go out with them. You can change your day off to Saturday, if you ask now.'

'I'm sorry, Mary-Jo. I said I would go with Miss Gladys to her church social that day,' said Maggie.

Mary-Jo laughed incredulously. 'A stuffy old church social compared to a night out with Cagney and his friends? You must be crazy.'

'I told Miss Gladys that I'd go.'

Mary-Jo did not heed this. She went on. 'We're going to the James Hamilton Roadhouse, a real snazzy place. Tell Miss Gladys that you would rather be with folks your own age.'

Cagney, Mrs Morgan's son by her first marriage, was at least thirty, hardly Maggie's age. Maggie was aware that Mary-Jo thought him a figure of fascination and mystery. He drove fast cars, wore natty clothes and usually had a sexy-looking girl or two in tow.

'I'm so sorry, Mary Jo,' Maggie said awkwardly. 'It was kind of you to invite me.'

'It wasn't me that thought of it,' said the other girl archly. 'It was Cagney. He wants to get to know you better, Maggie.'

'Does he?' said Maggie, not at all flattered. She had met Cagney when Mary-Jo had invited her home one evening to meet her family – which included three younger sisters and an elder brother. They had all played cards and cooked hot dogs and marshmallows over a fire in the garden. 'You know fine that Cagney looks on me as a Scots oddity, and laughs at the way I talk.'

'You don't want to mind Cagney's teasing. He thinks you're a real cute kid.' In fact, he had described Maggie as that 'luscious little Limey broad', and ordered his sister to bring her along, but Mary-Jo was not sure that Maggie would care for the description, so she did not repeat it. 'Oh, do come with us, Maggie! You'll love it.'

'I've already told you I can't. Thank your brother, please, and tell him that I have another date.' She saw that Mary-Jo looked crestfallen, and added, 'If you want someone to go with, why not ask one of the other girls? Dessie or Jess would go, if you asked them.'

'I might do that,' said Mary-Jo pettishly. 'And when they tell you what fun it was, you'll be sorry.'

Mary-Jo was more than crestfallen, she was worried. She so wanted to go dancing with that sophisticated New York crowd, and was afraid that Cagney might refuse to take her along unless Maggie

173

came. And her mother might try to stop her going if she found that Maggie had refused.

In the event, the promised treat never materialised, so she was glad she had not asked one of the other girls. Cagney was like that, changing his plans at a moment's notice because some deal was on the boil. She did not think that Maggie's tiresome refusal had anything to do with him changing his plans this time. But it was a letdown, and Mary-Jo blamed Maggie. Next day, she refused to speak to her, and it was almost a week before she started talking, and longer still before she invited Maggie home again.

Maggie was sorry about the coolness, for she had enjoyed her visit to the happy-go-lucky Morgan household. When Mary-Jo at last came out of her sulks and asked her over for supper and a movie, she was pleased – but Cagney was there, and her pleasure turned to dismay. He had a way of sitting in a corner of the room, stroking his moustache and watching her – which made her feel profoundly uncomfortable.

The Morgan family teased her, and said she had made a conquest, but if being friends with Mary-Jo meant that she must pretend to like Cagney, Maggie did not think she could. She was finding it increasingly difficult to respond suitably when his doting sister sang his praises. Mary-Jo could not seem to keep off the subject.

'Don't you like Cagney?'

'I . . . I hardly know him, Mary-Jo. I've only met him twice. Your brother Ed is the one for me. Ed and I get on fine.'

'Oh, Ed's just a kid. No more'n two years older than us. Ed hasn't been anywhere or done anything, and probably never will. Cagney is different. He's a man of the world.'

'I feel more comfortable with Ed.'

'No good getting romantic ideas about Ed. He won't marry until he's worked his way through college, and he has more time for books than girls.'

Maggie laughed. Mary-Jo was marriage and romance mad, always trying to set people to partners. 'That makes two of us. That may be why Ed and I get on.'

Mary-Jo looked at Maggie curiously. It was true that Maggie read a lot, and she and Ed would sometimes argue quite fiercely about some dead and gone character in a novel or a history book, as though they were real and alive and actually mattered. Mary-Jo had for some time decided that quiet, bespectacled Ed's lack of interest in girls and romance was a sign of his being undersexed. It certainly made him stuffy. Could the same be true about Maggie, or had that bad experience with a man before she sailed for America turned her off? Someone had certainly given her a terrible going-over. It was all very interesting, all the more so because Cagney still seemed to have quite a yen for the Scots girl.

Ever since she started work at Maple Valley House, Mary-Jo had been in the habit of meeting her stepbrother to talk 'business'. These meetings had all the trappings of an intrigue, which delighted her, all the more so because she knew that her parents would not approve. Cagney drove into the area every so often, always in a different automobile, telling her where she must come at the last minute. At their next rendezvous she voiced her newly formed theories about Maggie, but only succeeded in making Cagney laugh. Undersexed? Nothing of the sort, he said. Maggie was just playing hard to get.

'I know her kind,' he told his sister, taking a comb from his pocket and running it through his mirror-smooth black hair. 'All cool and collected on the surface, but yearning for it underneath. You must have seen her the other evening, pretending that she hadn't seen me, but going as pink as a rose and sitting down sudden as though she wanted to still the ants in her pants. You'll see, Sis. We'll take it easy for a while. Just call me when she comes to the house. I'll have that little broad burning and begging for it before I'm done. And if she likes being beaten up – they say the Brits like that sort of treatment – I'll give her a taste of that for dessert.'

Mary-Jo giggled. Cagney said such awful things! Then she said a little anxiously, 'You won't hurt her, will you? Maggie is my friend.'

He smiled and stroked his thin black moustache. 'I'll give your friend Maggie exactly what she wants, don't you worry. In a little while she'll be wetting herself with excitement at the sight of me.'

She giggled again, but added, 'For heaven's sakes don't talk vulgar like that at home – specially not in front of Pa.'

Cagney gave her arm a squeeze. 'Do you think I would? You're my best pal, and I can say what I like to you. And mind, Sis, not one word to anyone about our other little arrangements.'

Mary-Jo bit her lip. 'I don't know, Cagney. It may not be as easy as you think. Even lifting money is getting harder. Those Englishwomen have begun squawking about coins missing from their purses or dressing tables, and one or two of the kids too. They don't leave money around any more, and the children's money boxes get locked up. And get this, Cagney,' she added with a grin, 'I heard one of those Englishwomen say she thought Maggie might be the thief. I nearly split myself when I heard. Maggie, of all people!'

'What's so funny?'

Mary-Jo shrugged. 'That shows how little you know her. She's worse than Pa about borrowing things.'

He turned on her sharply. 'How do you know that?'

She looked down at her hands, and said nervously, 'It's just the way she talks sometimes.'

'Don't give me that crap. What're you hiding?'

She went on studying her hands, wishing that she had not given herself away. He would be angry, she knew. Reluctantly, she said, 'Well, Maggie saw me put a silver thimble in my apron pocket yesterday, and she made me put it back.'

'Like hell she did! I might have known you would bungle it.' Cagney pulled his sister round and glared down at her, his hands like steel pincers on her upper arms. 'What did you tell her?'

'Cagney, that hurts!'

'Answer me, damn you! Did you tell her it was for me?'

'No! As if I would! Anyway, Maggie promised tell not to anyone, so long as I don't do it again.'

He let her go, and sat frowning out through the windscreen. Then to Mary-Jo's relief, his expression changed and he smiled as though something pleased him.

'We shall have to find a way of fixing that little Limey bitch . . .'

Conway had given orders that he must not be disturbed. The clerks at the front desk thought they knew why. Wednesday was the British women's day at the New York Vorst Hotel.

They had only been meeting there for a couple of weeks, but already their numbers had more than doubled and they needed more space. They had also asked for a place to store the gifts of clothes and tinned food which had started to pour in. The tall woman who was their spokesman had also asked for tables on which to sort and pack the 'Bundles for Britain'.

Conway looked irritated when they passed this request on to him. 'Oh, give them whatever they want. Otherwise they'll give us no peace.'

But when Wednesday came round again, none of the clerks was surprised to be told that no calls were to be put through, nor any visitors admitted. The youngest girl at the front desk opined that Mr Conway was in hiding from the Limey ladies. In fact, Conway had hardly given the British women a thought; he needed solitude for other reasons.

Over the past ten years Vorst Hotels Inc. had been gradually and prudently expanding, buying up small city hotels – some whose owners were growing old, others that had declined for lack of capital input. These investments had prospered, and to Conway went much of the credit. Cornelius boasted that there was nobody better at driving a hard bargain than his elder son.

Now Conway, on the lookout for further avenues for expansion, had found something different. Up to this time, Vorst houses had been in city locations, never far from places where wealthy and discerning travellers wished to be. But Conway wanted to break the mould and move in a new direction.

He had found a seaside property south of San Francisco, and had made up his mind to have it. It was a place in a million. If he moved

176

fast, he could buy all the land as a single lot.

They wanted a lot of money for it. The development of his dream could wait. There would one day be a luxury hotel, golf courses, holiday homes – but not yet. It was finding funds for the initial purchase that kept him awake at night, and was making him jumpy during the day.

The door of his office opened, and he looked up sharply, about to blast the intruder. It was only a waiter with a sandwich and coffee. The man set the tray down and went out without a word, wondering what was eating the young boss today. He looked ready to kill.

As Conway drank his coffee, and peered inside the sandwich to check that it was exactly what he had ordered, he tried think of a way out of his difficulty.

He had had to go down to Maple Valley three times before he got Cornelius to listen. When he had finished his spiel, the old man had looked at him as though he had grown a second head.

'How much did you say they wanted?' And when Conway told him again, Cornelius had shaken his head emphatically. 'It's a crazy scheme, Con. Forget it. It would be a hell of a risk at this time.'

'Sir, the site is truly exceptional.'

'It's not our sort of thing. We know about city hotels, and how to manage them. Anyhow, we can't take on more commitments. The Lord alone knows what sort of bills will come in once this damned war is over.'

'But that may be years, Father.' Conway kept his voice even and reasonable with an effort. 'We could lose the European houses for good, and would then have to find other ways to go.'

'There's no spare cash right now.'

'We could raise a loan.'

'Loans have to be paid back with interest, and usually at the worst possible moment. We came through the Depression because we were cautious and refused to borrow beyond our means.'

'Yes, sir. But times are changing.'

'They certainly are. We may be on the brink of war ourselves.'

'God forbid,' said Conway. 'I'm not going to war for a parcel of Limeys.'

Conway made no secret of the fact that he disliked most things British, and had no liking for the London house in particular. He was less forthcoming about the underlying reasons for this enduring prejudice.

He had been nine years old when his whole world had gone awry. His adored mother had deserted him. She had stayed away for almost two years, and he remembered those bleak months as the unhappiest and angriest time of his life – and the wounds and an abiding sense of injury had never wholly left him.

The events which had caused such anguish to the young Conway had long since been hallowed by time and become part of family legend.

Near the end of the Great War, Cornelius had sailed to Europe as part of the American relieving force. Chrissie missed him dreadfully, and when Cornelius wrote to say that he felt just as miserable, she decided to act. She left Conway and little Tina in charge of a cousin and a host of reliable attendants, and resolutely travelled to London to be near him.

She put up at a respectable family hotel just off St James's Street, with only her personal maid for company. Cornelius visited her whenever he got leave, and their reunions were blissful. Chrissie was fond of saying that those months in London were the happiest in her entire life. And, wonder of wonders, she found that she was going to have a child.

This second son was special to both of them. They called him David. They also liked the location of the hotel where the baby was born, so Cornelius bought it while property prices were still depressed in the aftermath of the war. The purchase of that modest establishment started Cornelius upon what was to become a lifelong obsession. He made up his mind then that the American-based chain of Vorst hotels would one day become truly international. From then on he laboured tirelessly to promote and fulfil this vision.

Conway shared his father's vision for the hotels. But he never shared his parents' conviction that young David's birth was a miracle. When they came back from Europe in the spring of 1919, the Great War was over and the family was once more united. Only Conway felt shut out, unable to share the general jubilation. He pretended to, because it was expected of him, but he wished that the baby had never been born.

Chrissie Vorst had always seen her family through rose-coloured spectacles, and this somehow made it necessary for them to live up to her illusions. And because of this need to please his mother, it had become a lifelong habit for Conway to stifle his dislike, and go along with the general view that David was pretty special. He managed it by avoiding his young brother, taking up golf and skiing in the vacations, and retreating in relief to Groton and later to university at the start of each semester.

It made it no easier that David became in due course an outstanding athlete and student, excelling easily in all the things that Conway worked so hard at. The boy won a place at Harvard at a preposterously young age, graduated amid general acclaim, and duly joined the family business.

Most of the time Conway's early, painfully acquired habit of concealment held good. Very few people had any idea of his seething inner feelings. His jealousy grew within him, a cancer that gave him little ease.

Wanting his brother out of the way, it had seemed good to send David to Paris to train, and Conway had lent support to David's subsequent request that he should be allowed to work in the London Vorst. Some time after this, Conway came up with the suggestion that David should take charge of Vorst Hotels, UK. There were three British houses – in London, Edinburgh and Bath.

Conway was wryly amused when a letter of thanks came from David. He felt like a spider being thanked by a fly. Conway had once worked at the London Vorst himself, and had found the English clients tiresome, and the staff stubborn and opposed to new ideas. Even five years ago the place had felt seedy and in decline. It would not break his heart if the London house was destroyed by a bomb or had to be sold. And if the golden boy's wings got singed, as seemed likely, it might do him good.

Conway pushed his half-eaten sandwich away. David. No doubt a shrink would have a great time analysing the sibling jealousy that had darkened his formative years.

The boy had such outrageous luck. It was over a year since his promotion in London, and the downturn in profits at the London Vorst had not yet taken place. Rather the reverse. And who could have foretold that Odette Steiner from Paris would be on the spot, available to stand in when wonder boy needed her. She would very likely do great things for the London house, and David would get the credit for it. It was a pity, but Madame Steiner would have to go. He had cabled David to that effect, but the wretched boy had done nothing so far.

He would have to wait before taking a strong line. David had dashed off and joined the Royal Air Force, and was now looked on by everybody as a hero. Cornelius was both worried sick and ecstatic about him, and had wasted a good ten minutes of boardroom time in telling them that David had been promoted from pilot officer to flight lieutenant in record time.

Conway picked up the telephone, and asked his secretary to put him through to his attorney.

'I'm sorry, ma'am,' said the spruce young lady at the front desk. 'Mr Conway is not available. Can I help you in any way?'

'You can help me by telling me where Mr Conway is,' said Adele Devenish, drumming her fingers impatiently on the counter top. 'I really must speak to him.'

'But Mr Conway said—'

'Ah! So he told you to say that he wasn't available. Is he in his office?'

The girl looked helplessly at her tall interrogator, wondering how to hold this woman at bay. 'I cannot say, ma'am.'

'Won't say, you mean? Please call Mr Conway on the telephone, then, and tell him that Adele Devenish needs to speak to him. It is important or I would not ask.'

'Ma'am, I'd be fired if I did that.'

Then she sighed with relief. Mrs Post was crossing the lobby. Mrs Post would know how to deal with this insistent Englishwoman.

'Having trouble, Miss Janice?' the older woman inquired unnecessarily. The child behind the desk looked to be close to tears. 'Oh, good afternoon, Lady Adele. Can I help you?'

'You can indeed, Mrs Post.' Adele never forgot a name or a face. 'I must speak to Mr Conway. I asked this young lady to call him on the telephone, but she says she dares not.'

Mrs Post considered. 'I'm not sure that I would dare myself, Lady Adele. He really does dislike being intruded upon, and I just don't know . . .' She looked at the tall English lady, knowing pretty much how Mr Conway felt about her, and said, 'Mr Conway did ask to be left alone this afternoon.'

'Very well,' said Adele, seeing that Mrs Post was perfectly serious. 'I'll tell him that you tried to stop me.' She lifted the wooden flap beside the front desk counter, and passed them before either of the two women had guessed at her intention. They started after her, but she was through Mr Conway's door by then and had shut it on their flustered protestations.

Conway was at his desk, speaking into the mouthpiece of his telephone. He heard someone come in, and looked up. He said sharply, 'Adele! What are you doing here?' Then into the telephone he said curtly, 'Something has come up. I'll call you back.'

He glared at her. She was leaning against the closed door, looking down her large nose at him.

'Can't you see that I'm busy?'

'I'll wait,' she said. 'Call that man back, Conway, and then I must talk to you.'

'No, Adele. If you want more tables or some fancy kind of tea, tell them at the front desk.'

'It's not that. I've just heard some terrible news, and I don't know how to tell your parents. I hoped you could advise me, or even come to Maple Valley and help break it to them.'

Conway sat very still. In a carefully even voice, he uttered one word. 'David?'

She shook her head. She was pale. 'Not that, thank God. But frightful, all the same. The British Consul just called me to the telephone . . .'

It was indeed terrible news. The British ship, the *City of Benares*, had been sunk by a German U-boat on 17 September, four days out from Liverpool. The vessel had been crowded with refugees from England, many of them children and young mothers. The consulate had been awaiting word about the scale of the disaster, and this had just come. Knowing Adele and her affection for the Vorsts, the consul had called her. Among the list of passengers who had lost their lives were the names of two small protegés of the Vorst family: Josef and Marie Steiner.

At about the time that Conway Vorst and Adele Devenish were driving out to Maple Valley, David was with his wing leader, applying for leave to go to London.

Douglas was sympathetic, but adamant. The squadrons under his command were stretched to the limit, having lost five pilots in the past two days – two of them experienced leaders, three of them new boys. David could not be spared until the squadrons were back to strength. 'And God knows when that will be.'

'I ought to go to Odette. I told her to send the children on that ship. I said they would be safer out of England . . .'

'And now you feel as guilty as hell. Aren't you being a little dramatic?'

'Those kids were all she had, Douglas! Her husband is a Jew, and is either dead or in Gestapo hands. I advised her to get the children to America, and now this happens.'

'You couldn't know that the ship would be torpedoed.'

'There was always a risk.'

'We are all at risk in wartime. Get your wife to visit Mrs Steiner. Use my telephone, if you like.'

Antonia was not well enough to come to the telephone. She was in bed with a bad dose of flu, so Lord Dulcimer travelled to London to see Odette. He arrived just as the All Clear was sounding, and walked to the Vorst from Victoria Station. At the palace end of St James's Street he was stopped by a policeman.

'There's no way through to Piccadilly, sir.'

'I need to get to the Vorst Hotel, officer. Any hope?'

'The Vorst is still standing. Some of the windows blew in last night, but that's all.' The policeman thought the elderly gentleman in the bowler hat and tweed suit looked a bit out of place in war-torn London. He was wearing a black tie. 'I tell you what, sir, I'll come with you. Some of the wardens might try to stop you. Authority goes to their heads now and again.'

The man in the bowler hat smiled. 'That's very good of you, officer. I should be grateful.'

In the dimly lit lobby of the Vorst, Lord Dulcimer was astonished to find Dart. For a moment he peered at his son in disbelief.

'What's this, Edward? You rang from Wales yesterday.' There was a throat-catching smell of smoke and dust in the hotel lobby. An elderly man was sweeping glass into a shovel, and they were hammering boards over a broken glass door. 'What on earth brings you to London?'

Even in the semi-darkness Lord Dulcimer could see that his son's expression was tight-lipped and unusually grave. 'I heard about that ship going down, and knew Odette's children were on it. I felt I must come.'

'I didn't know you knew her.'

Dart's tight mouth twisted. 'Everyone knows Madame Odette of the Vorst, Father. I come here when I can. It's the best place to eat in London. I suppose you're here on David's behalf?'

'That's right. He can't get away, so I said I would come. A bad business.'

'Unspeakable.'

'Well,' said Lord Dulcimer heavily, 'we had better see her.'

'She's not here.'

The elderly man put his shovel and bucket in a corner and came towards them, stripping off a pair of workmanlike gloves. He wore a striped waistcoat and looked shrunken.

Dart said, 'This is my father, Stebbings. I told him that Madame Odette had gone out.'

Lord Dulcimer shook Stebbings by the hand. 'I've heard of you from Mr David. He asked me to come. Where is that poor woman? Do you know?'

Stebbings shook his sparsely furnished head in bewilderment. 'She just walked out through that door in the middle of the raid, milord. I saw her go but was too late to stop her. Mrs Cornberg had been with her in the shelter. We did not think Madame should be left alone, her being so shocked.'

'Quite right.'

They saw a tear trickle down the old man's withered face. 'I saw Madame come up from below, just as she was in her thin dress and no hat or gloves. I'd no notion what she meant to do until she was out of the door.' He twisted his gnarled fingers together, and his voice was strangled by a sob as he added, 'There was a terrible din going on, fires starting up all over, and shrapnel falling. For all I know, Madame may be dead by now.'

There was the sound of a door opening. They turned. Odette stood just inside the closed door, a grey lady, a ghost of her usual self, her hair and her once black dress and shoes coated with dust, face streaked with smoke and grime.

In a thread of a voice she said, 'As you see, I am not dead. They did not get me this time.'

Lord Dulcimer went over and took her hands. Her fingers were freezing. 'David sent me, my dear. He wanted to come himself, of course . . .'

Lord Dulcimer got home very late, and went at once to find his wife. She thought he looked unutterably weary. She kissed him, and finding that his face was cold, said, 'Come to the fire, Bernard. Did you see Vestry as you came in? I thought you might like to dine in here tonight.'

He did not seem to hear her. He stood, holding cold hands to the blazing logs, his shoulders bent. He was shivering. She hoped that he was not going down with Antonia's flu.

Vestry came in with the whisky decanter and a couple of glasses. He put it down and went out, saying that he would bring dinner.

'Thank you,' said Lord Dulcimer, without turning round.

'Was it so very bad, dearest? I've been thinking of you and that poor woman all day.'

He turned round then, and she could see that his mouth was trembling. She put her arms round him, and they stood there together without speaking for some time.

'This damned war, Effie,' he said at last. 'This bloody, hellish war . . .'

'I know. How is Madame Steiner?'

He looked at her, frowning, as though he did not quite understand. 'I don't really know. She did not want to talk about it. She gave us coffee, and then she said she had work to do, and sent us away. She's got guts, that woman, I will say.'

It was Lady Dulcimer's turn to feel bewildered. 'So why were you so long? Was the train late?'

Vestry came in, followed by Trumpet. They were both carrying trays which they set up on a table by the fire. They were about to leave, when Lord Dulcimer seemed to come to himself.

'Wait a minute,' he said. He bit his lip and added abruptly, 'I'll tell you now. You will have to know sooner or later. Perhaps you would tell the rest of the staff for me.'

After a pause, the earl went on, 'I thought I would look up Bert Higgins and his mother. I had a note of their address in my diary. Number Twenty Cotton Street, it was. It was difficult getting through. The docks were blazing, and there were no taxis. Then I had a stroke of luck. You know that friend of Antonia's, the one Dart calls the Bad Fairy?'

'Marjorie? Yes, dearest. What about her?'

'She recognised me when I was arguing with a warden, and shouted to me to get in her van. She drives a mobile canteen, and they let her through, of course. We found Cotton Street after a bit . . .' He looked at his feet and said curtly, 'Or what was left of it.'

Then he told them what they were already beginning to fear. There were three gaps in the row of Cotton Street houses, and a gang of demolition men were busy shoring up the wall of a fourth one. When they asked for Number Twenty, the men had shaken their tin-hatted heads.

Number Twenty had been flattened by a direct hit three days ago. A neighbour was able to tell them about it – an old woman with bandaged legs and a bath cap over her curlers. She seemed more angry than distressed.

'You askin' for Daisy Higgins, mister? That's bad. I told 'er to come down to the shelter but she wouldn't never take a telling. Not Daisy. They brought 'em all out dead, Daisy and all her kids – and that fancy man she had with 'er. Time and time again I told 'er...'

Chapter 14

'I had a Hallowe'en card from darling Quentin this morning,' said Kim as the school bus started on its wheezing way. She patted her schoolbag. 'Would you like to see it?'

'No thanks,' said Abby.

'I'd like to.' Joan's round eyes peered at them over the top of the seat ahead. 'Let's have a look, Kim.'

Kim said coolly, 'Certainly not. Abby and I were talking privately.' She sighed theatrically, and twisted sideways to look at Abby. 'It's getting to be pretty dire, travelling on the bus with all these prying kids. I guess I'll have to get Grandma to send me to school in her car.'

Joan was impressed. 'Goodness! D'you think Aunt Chrissie would?'

'Sure. Why not?'

By this time, Betty had risen up beside her older sister. She stood on the seat to get a better view of Kim. 'With one of the chauffeurs, you mean? Truly?'

'More likely with James. I'll just tell her that one of you Limeys has been unkind to me on the bus. She knows I'm easily upset.'

Both round-eyed faces registered shock. Just like a couple of Hallowe'en lanterns, thought Abby, repressing an unwilling quiver of laughter.

'But none of us have been in the least unkind.'

'It's wrong to tell lies, Kimmy.'

'Not if it gets me what I want,' retorted Kim sweetly. 'And if you go on calling me Kimmy, I'll push you both in the lake on a really cold day when you're not looking.'

The bus driver had been glancing irritably in his mirror, and he suddenly roared at Joan and Betty to sit down. The lanterns disappeared from view.

Kim turned to Abby, her dark eyes glowing with mischief, and whispered, 'Aren't they just too cute? Bet they don't dare walk near the lake for ages, just in case I do push them. They would believe anything.'

'I wouldn't put it past you,' said Abby.

'A swim in the lake wouldn't make them any wetter.' She was

185

about to say that with any luck they might drown, and remembered just in time not to.

Abby did not answer. She was looking out of the bus window, her mind gone away somewhere else. She had a way of doing that, these days, and Kim wished she would not.

She nudged her. 'How can you bear to share a bedroom with those two drips?'

'They aren't so bad.' Abby was silent for a further minute or two, thinking how her likes and dislikes had shifted lately. Was it just living near people, or terrible things happening to people in the war, or what? Even Miss Brimley's tiresomeness had dimmed a little, for to go on hating her seemed petty beside the stark horror of Josef and Marie being torpedoed in the terrifying Atlantic. 'I quite like that Mamzelle of theirs. She's started giving Maggie French lessons, and they yatter together when nobody is listening.'

'Maggie's got a new boyfriend,' said Kim two days later.

Abby stopped still in the middle of the driveway, her arms full of schoolbooks. 'Who says so?'

'I heard the Fortress and the Brimstone talking together.'

'You shouldn't listen in.'

Kim grinned unrepentantly. 'They shouldn't talk so loud. How else can I find out what's going on?'

'There's nothing new about Mary-Jo's brother Ed asking her to go to the movies.'

'It wasn't Ed they were talking about. It sounded like someone older. They were really mad at Maggie, said that she was giving you Limeys a bad name. They were just like a couple of Hallowe'en witches.'

'When was this?' Abby was disbelieving. Kim told such outrageous lies. 'You're making it all up. I bet you never heard them talking at all.'

'I did *so* hear them! They're probably jealous of Maggie having two boyfriends while they haven't any.'

'They're both too old to want boyfriends, silly.'

'Not too old to be jealous. Uncle Conway is pretty old, and he's jealous of my Uncle David.'

'How do you know that?'

'I just do.'

'What else did you hear, then?'

'Well,' said Kim slowly, looking at Abby sideways. 'I'll tell you if you promise not to get mad at me.'

'Fire away.'

'Listen to this, then. Miss Fortescue said they ought to tell Grandma, and have Maggie sent back to England.'

* * *

As soon as Abby got Maggie alone, she asked her what it was all about.

'Goodness knows,' said Maggie, without looking up from her sewing. 'Just Kim and her havers, I expect.'

'But *have* you got a new boyfriend?'

'If I had, do you think I would tell you about it?'

'That's not much of an answer,' said Abby crossly.

'It's all the answer you're going to get. Pass me my scissors, please.'

Abby went off, her mind relieved of care. Maggie would surely not be so calm if Kim's story were true.

Maggie was wondering what to do? Miss Fortescue had seen her sitting in James's car and Miss Brimley had tackled her about it. With extreme reluctance, Maggie had confessed to the driving lessons.

'Driving lessons, indeed!' said Miss Fortescue with a sniff that verged on a snort. 'I can think of another name for it.'

A brief glimpse was all she had been afforded before her bus moved on, but Miss Fortescue could have sworn that the man in the car had an arm round the girl's shoulders. Miss Fortescue knew what James's car looked like – and that Wednesday was Maggie's half day.

Titillated, consumed with curiosity, Miss Fortescue got off the bus and walked back along the tree-lined sidewalk. She was rewarded by the sight of James's car coming slowly out of the side road where it had so lately been parked. She turned away to gaze at a leafless tree – but not before she had recognised both occupants of the car.

'The effrontery of it!' she said to Miss Brimley. 'Well, I've had my doubts about that girl all along. What was that you once told me about Mr David Vorst taking a fancy to her? Did that start with driving lessons too?'

Miss Brimley was not always comfortable with her friend's habit of innuendo. 'Oh no, Maud,' she said earnestly. 'There was never enough petrol for driving lessons in wartime. And besides, Nanny kept Maggie very busy.'

Miss Fortescue did not seem to be listening. 'Disgusting! Mr James is old enough to be Maggie's father. But of course that sort of girl will run after anything in trousers.'

Miss Brimley wanted to change the subject. She was pretty sure that driving lessons was all it was. It occurred to her that James might have been trying to take Maggie's mind off the loss of those poor little French children.

'I expect James only meant to be kind,' she ventured feebly.

Miss Fortescue undoubtedly snorted this time. 'What made them so secretive, then? Tell me that.'

Miss Brimley tried to explain. 'Maggie was afraid that I would not like her learning to drive. I must say, I was rather taken aback. Whoever heard of a nursery maid driving a car?'

'That's why I don't believe a word of it. She probably made up the driving lessons as a cover for what they were doing.'

Miss Brimley sighed. 'I'll talk to her again,' she said reluctantly.

Miss Brimley hated every minute of the second little talk. At the end of it, she said, 'It's for you own good, dear. You wouldn't want people to talk about you, now would you?'

'No, Miss Brimley.' Maggie spoke meekly, but inside she was fuming, hating Miss Fortescue for making up such a salacious farrago. She supposed that the beastly woman must have seen James with his arm round her shoulders. If only she had been able to control her tears, none of it would have happened!

On Wednesday morning a letter had come from Nanny at Dulcimer, with news that the entire Higgins family had been killed when a bomb fell on their house. She had been busy with housework that morning, so with Mary-Jo chattering on and herself feeling numb and stupid, she had had little time for thought. It was only when she was driving through the town with James that the numbness wore off, and the misery and impossibility of the whole thing threatened to overwhelm her. Before she knew it, tears were spilling over and running down her cheeks.

James told her to stop the car and asked her what was the matter. She told him about Bert and his family, clutching the steering wheel and gazing blindly ahead as she told him. She tried to explain how impossible it was. How in the world was she to tell Abby that Bert Higgins was dead? The child had barely come to terms with the horror of Josef and Marie's ship going down. For nearly a week now, she had managed to sleep through the night without waking up, terrified and weeping. She had lost her haunted look. And now this!

'Here.' James detached Maggie's rigid fingers from the steering wheel and pushed a handkerchief into her hand. He put an arm round her shaking shoulders, and held her.

Presently Maggie said, sniffing, 'Bert was such a nice, funny boy. Clever, too. It's such a waste. But most of all I can't bear it for Abby. Bert was her very first friend, and they did everything together at Dulcimer. She has had one card from him, and is expecting and hoping for a letter. I'm afraid that her dog must be dead too. Nanny said that Bert had taken Wat to London . . .' Tears welled up again.

Presently she blew her nose, and said wretchedly, 'How can I break Abby's heart with this, Mr James? She's only just starting to feel happy again – she's happy at school, anyway.'

'Who else knows about it?'

Maggie raised tear-suffused eyes and looked at him in a bewildered way. 'I don't think anyone does. I mean, I haven't told Miss Brimley yet. I just could not bear to talk of it.'

'If I were you,' said James slowly, 'I would burn that letter and try to forget you ever had it.'

'But ... but Abby is bound to hear sooner or later.'

'Maybe so. But does she have to be told right now? Anyway, you certainly shouldn't be the one to tell her.'

'Better me than Miss Brimley, Mr James. Miss B never really approved of Bert.'

'I was thinking that Mr or Mrs Vorst might do it. Anyway, why not leave it alone for a couple of days? You may feel better about it yourself, by then.' Then he added briskly, 'Now we'll go home. Gladys has made a cake. And this time I'm doing the driving.'

James had been so kind. Maggie thought dolefully that she would miss seeing him, more even than having to give up learning to drive. But she had promised Miss Brimley. She went in search of him, determined not to say a word about Miss Fortescue and her embarrassing insinuations.

She found him with Mrs Sandridge.

'Hello there,' said the secretary. 'Which of us have you come to find?'

'I ... I came to see Mr James, really, Mrs Sandridge.'

'Would you like me to go away?'

'No, please ...' Maggie took a deep breath. She looked at James, and said gravely, as though she was reciting a lesson, 'I want to thank you for all you have done for me, Mr James, teaching me to drive, and that.'

'It has been a pleasure, Maggie,' said James, with equal gravity. 'We'll make a good driver of you one of these days.'

She looked at him unhappily. 'No. That's what I came to say. I cannot come driving with you any more.'

'Why ever not, Maggie?'

'I can't say why not.' They saw that her face had gone red, and her lowered eyes seemed to be studying an ashtray on Mrs Sandridge's desk. In a choked sort of a voice, she added, 'That's all. I am just so sorry, and ... and thank you ...' She turned to go.

'Hey, wait a minute!' said James. 'What's been going on?'

She shook her head, beyond speech.

'Did Miss Brimley talk you into this nonsense?' He read an answer in her startled eyes. 'I thought so.'

'Please ...' she began, wondering how she could stop him talking to Miss Brimley and making everything worse. 'Please don't say anything to Miss B about it.'

He looked keenly at her for a moment, and then said slowly, 'Very well. I won't question Miss Brimley if you don't want me to.'

Maggie thanked him, and hurried away. When she had gone, James turned to Mrs Sandridge. 'That will be a nice job for you, May.'

189

All that he could see of the secretary at that moment was her neat head, as shiny as a new conker. Her hands were busy aligning some writing pads on her desk top. 'You want me to talk with Miss Brimley?'

'Please. Try to find out what this is about.'

She said without looking at him, 'I had Miss Fortescue in here just now.'

James made an exasperated sound. 'So that's it. She saw me driving with Maggie. And so what?'

Mrs Sandridge's smile was wry. 'A most unpleasant woman. She assured me that you were parked up a side street, necking.'

He stared at her. 'She can't have thought that! For one thing, I'm twenty-five years older than Maggie!'

'I told her that she was talking nonsense, of course. But James, what did she see to make her dream up such a thing?'

'She should have brought her spyglass with her,' retorted James drily. 'Maggie was in tears over some friends who had been killed in the Blitz, and I put my arm round her shoulders. Just that.'

Mrs Sandridge sighed. 'You know, you might be wise to skip the driving lessons. That woman is going around saying that Maggie is man mad, crazy for anything in trousers.' She paused as James swore softly and incredulously. 'She used those very words, I promise you. Maggie has volunteered to give the lessons up, so why not leave it at that? After all, she's not yet eighteen. There's time enough.'

He looked at her. 'You made me learn to drive an automobile when I was not much older. Remember?'

She looked up, laughing at him. 'James! You were at least twenty-four when you came to Maple Valley.'

'A scrawny, homesick immigrant boy, all the same. You told me then,' he went on, 'that this was the United States of America where all men are free and equal. You said that opportunities would come my way, but advised me never to pass up a chance of learning a new skill. I haven't forgotten what you said, May, or how greatly you helped me. I want Maggie to have the same chances. Call it the repayment of a debt, if you like . . .'

There was silence in the office for a full minute, and then James said briskly, 'I'm not going to give up teaching that child to drive – not without a fight. I'll speak to Mr Vorst in the morning.'

Two days later Mrs Sandridge asked Miss Brimley if she could spare her a few minutes.

'It's about Maggie Dunlop,' the secretary said when they were alone in her office. 'Mr and Mrs Vorst have heard that Mr James has been teaching her to drive an automobile, and they think it's a wonderful chance for her. But James is afraid that you may not approve, and of course he wouldn't care to do anything against your wishes. What do you think, Miss Brimley?'

Miss Fortescue was indignant with her friend for caving in. Did she want Maggie to disgrace them all?

Miss Brimley said weakly, 'What else could I do but agree, Maud? It seemed so unkind not to allow it.'

Miss Fortescue sniffed, and walked out of the room.

Maggie knew nothing of this, but she was pleased when Miss Brimley told her that her driving lessons were on again. At the time it seemed worth a few frowns from Miss Fortescue and some sly comments from Mary-Jo about people with friends in high places. It did not occur to her, then, that she had made an enemy.

In New York City a charity dinner and dance was to be held at Vorst Hotel in aid of British bombed-out families. Four hundred highly priced tickets sold out within weeks, and there was a waiting list of people still wanting tickets.

Time magazine sent a reporter to talk to Conway. Conway was good with the press. On this occasion his manner was friendly and confiding, and he spoke of the forthcoming party as though he really wanted everyone to share his excitement. The ball was going to be a highlight of the Thanksgiving weekend, something special and unforgettable. A gourmet dinner, pretty girls in ball gowns selling tickets for the prize draw. Jimmy Dorsey and his band would play throughout the evening, and the winner of the star prize – a holiday for two at a Vorst hotel of their choice – would be announced by a mystery Personality. The reporter went away warmed by Conway Vorst's friendly manner and impressed by his enthusiasm for the Bundles for Britain Ball. The editor called up next day to ask for a photograph to accompany the article.

Lady Adele Devenish was chairman of the organising committee, and she gave interviews to the *Herald Tribune* and the *New York Times*. She ended by saying how grateful she was for the friendliness and support given by Americans both in and around New York. Such overwhelming kindness and generosity had left her speechless.

Conway smiled when he read his paper next morning. He heard Adele's voice fully a minute before she came in, and stood up with the *Herald Tribune* in his hand. 'Good morning, Adele. So your loss of speech is not permanent? I'm relieved to hear it.'

'You should be,' she retorted with an answering smile. 'It would have been awkward at tonight's meeting if I could only whisper. That young reporter gave our party quite a good boost, don't you think? They want a photograph of both of us in the ballroom. Must we?'

'We'll talk about it over at lunch. I hope you like steaks.'

191

'I certainly do. The thought of a steak reminds me that I had no breakfast.'

'Then don't unbutton your coat. We will go out right away.'

He ushered her into the street, putting a hand under her elbow to steer her in the direction of the park. She wondered what this was all about.

When a secretary had called up to say that Mr Conway wished to give her lunch, issuing the summons like a royal command, she had been tempted to refuse. She was due in New York at eight that evening to chair a meeting of the dance committee. If she had lunch with Conway, it would mean hanging around in the city all afternoon – not her idea of fun. But she was curious, and found herself accepting without really wanting to go.

She also felt beholden to Conway Vorst. She knew him to be anti-British and a confirmed isolationist, but he had been surprisingly helpful over the dance. He had come in person to each of the committee meetings, when he could quite well have sent an underling. And she would never forget that terrible September day when she had burst into his office. He had not wanted to come with her to Maple Valley, and told her to go away. Yet in the end he had driven her to Long Island, and they had broken the news to Cornelius and Chrissie together.

Why had he done it? Conway was a such an unaccountable man. There was no making him out. She had found him hard to read from the start, sensing antagonism and an undercurrent of anger in him. Even after two months and several encounters, she was still asking herself what made him behave as he did. Why had he agreed to come on the dance committee? Why should he bother, and indeed take so much trouble to be helpful – to the frankly expressed astonishment of his secretaries and others who knew him? And why, more immediately, had he invited her to lunch?'

Conway was aware that she was curious. It amused him to see the masterful Adele for once thrown a little off her balance. He had, indeed, a purpose in inviting her to have lunch with him, and thought that if she could be kept in a state of uncertainty he would have a better chance of winning his point.

All the same, if she had asked him to explain his motives and his attitude towards her, he might have found it hard to do so.

He took her to his apartment. She went past him into an enormous open-plan space and stood gazing out at a stunning view of Central Park, bare treetops and misty skyscrapers beyond.

'Good gracious, Conway!' she said, stripping off her gloves and unbuttoning her coat. She made no attempt to remove her hat. It was the one that Abby had likened to a teapot. 'Who does this wonderful place belong to?'

'It belongs to me.'

'What a mysterious man you are! I thought you lived at the Vorst.'

'Sure I do. I come here when I want to get away.'

She laughed, still with her back to him because she was admiring the view. 'Quite a convenient love nest. Gerald would love to have something like this.'

'Who is Gerald?'

'He's my husband, of course. He's with his regiment in North Africa.'

She came away from the window and loped in her long-legged way across the expanse of carpet to where another huge window looked out the other way. A table was laid for two, with matching dark blue linen napkins and tablecloth. Adele watched as Conway opened a huge icebox and took out a bottle of wine.

She said in surprise, 'Are we going to have lunch here?'

'Where else?' He poured her a glass of iced hock, and added, 'Does it make you nervous, being alone with me in my love nest, Adele?'

'Not in the least,' she retorted, a shade too quickly. 'But it makes me wonder what in the world you want.'

He laughed. It occurred to her that Conway did not often laugh. He said, 'Let's attend to your wants first. I thought you said you were hungry.'

'So that's it. You asked me here to cook your steak for you. You have a nerve, I must say.'

'Certainly not. I wouldn't trust you not to wreck it.'

'I am not a bad cook,' she protested.

'Maybe so. I, on the other hand, am a very good cook.'

'You're changing the subject again. I want to know what this is all about. What do you want?'

'Drink your wine, Adele. I'll tell you what I want when I'm good and ready.' He looked at her, and added gravely, 'May I ask you to do me one great favour?'

'What sort of favour?' she asked suspiciously.

'Please take your hat off.'

She had to admit that the steak and the burgundy that he served with it were utterly delectable, and despite of her now rampant curiosity she enjoyed both the food and his company. He asked about her marriage, and about her life as a soldier's wife before the war. Later he talked about the hotel business, and the financial difficulties caused by the war in Europe, and finally about the California project which he had been forced to abandon. He sounded quite calm about it, but she was not deceived.

'Difficult for you, working with family,' she said thoughtfully. 'If I had not married Gerald and got away from home, I might easily have murdered both my parents. And yet I love them dearly – most of the time.'

He was making coffee as she spoke. His back was turned to her. Adele had been looking round his kitchen area. She was thinking how streamlined and well-organised it was – but suddenly became aware of a lack. There was no kitchen sink. Merely a tiny thing with taps in the corner.

She said suddenly, 'Where do you wash up, Conway?'

'I don't.'

'No doubt you have slaves who come in from the hotel.'

'Not from the hotel. This is a service apartment.'

'Well, someone must look after all this glory. And don't ask me to believe that even the most devoted slave could wash up in that silly round thing.'

He had finished making the coffee. 'Come over here and I'll show you.'

She walked over to him, pushing hairpins into the heavy bun at the nape of her neck. They had a tiresome way of escaping. He slid a door sideways and showed her the little elevator which took all the dishes down to the basement – and a chute where the garbage went straight down into bins at the back of the building. She was admiring and envious. The slaves, it seemed, came and went, and he seldom even saw them to speak to.

'So nice for you to be a millionaire,' she said.

'It has its advantages,' he agreed. He took the coffee tray across the room and put it down on a low table.

'Now tell me,' he asked her while she was pouring coffee, 'what do you plan to wear at the ball?'

She looked at him in surprise. She had not so far given the subject any thought. 'Probably my old black velvet.'

Conway had seen the black velvet. He leaned back in his low armchair and said, 'You can do better than that. There is plenty of time for you to get something made.'

She shook her head, and a hairpin clattered and bounced on the glass table. She retrieved it, and put it back where it belonged. 'As long as I look respectable, I can't see that it matters.'

'Appearances always matter.'

She looked at him. Conway had taken his jacket off while he cooked, but his shirt and tie were crisp and immaculate, and she thought he probably had his hands professionally manicured. 'I think,' she said slowly, 'that men set more store by appearances than women. Gerald certainly had to look just right, and my son Edward is nearly as fussy. My daughters are like me. I have to bully them even to brush their hair.'

'It's obvious you don't give a damn what you look like,' he said, frowning at her.

'What's the matter, Conway? Are you afraid of being ashamed of me?'

194

He did not answer her at once. He thought about her, and how outraged he had been that she had persuaded Cornelius to let her hold a ball at the New York Vorst. He had started coming to the meetings in a spirit of considerable irritation, determined to allow no sloppy standards to prevail. Trust Adele Devenish to trample over other more promising candidates, annexing the position of chairman!

She had fulfilled his worst prognostications when she came to the first committee meeting, looking like a rag bag in her drooping tweed suit, wearing that deplorable hat with a handle that wagged as she spoke. He thought she would never manage to control the large committee – a mixed bunch of English do-gooders and wealthy American socialites – and foresaw that he might have to take charge. There had been some stifled sniggers from the far end of the conference table, where the younger, more fashionable married women were congregated.

But Adele had been a remarkably effective chairman. Before long, her committee had stopped making jokes about Boadicea and were eating out of her hand. She had a way of getting people to do what she wanted, without seeming to push them around. He was not sure if it was her air of utter assurance that impressed them, but impressed they certainly were. And whatever she looked like, she was as much of a perfectionist about the arrangements as he was himself.

She was saying in her downright way, 'My work will be done by the night of the party, Conway. If you think I'll let the side down by the way I look, I'm quite prepared to stay away.'

'That won't do, Adele, and you know it. You need a new dress, and you are going to have one.'

She sighed. 'Look, Conway. I am not a debutante. I'm fast approaching forty, if you want to know, and it would be just a waste of money trying to doll me up.'

His only reaction was to look at his watch. 'I'll get your coat, Adele. It's time we went.'

'Time we went where?'

'We're going shopping, and after that I'm going to take you to a good hairdresser. I can't dance with you with pins pinging around my feet.'

She looked flustered for the first time. 'You don't have to dance with me. This is ridiculous. Even if I wanted a new dress, I really cannot afford one at present.'

'One of the advantages of being a millionaire,' he said drily, 'is that I can afford to buy things for people. You are having a new dress, whether you like it or not.'

'You cannot buy me clothes. It would be most improper.'

'Don't be commonplace, Adele. It doesn't suit you. If it bothers you, I'll put it down as expenses for the ball.'

She bit her lip. 'I've had dresses made for me before but they never look right. And I don't want a haircut. I've always worn my hair this way.'

'It's time for a change,' said Conway.

He picked up her hat, and she held out her hand for it. But he turned away from her and before she realised his intention he had opened the hatch and tossed it down the chute. 'That's the place for garbage. I'll buy you a new one, I promise. Let's go.'

'Mrs David Vorst was on the telephone while you were out, milady,' said Vestry, coming into the little hall where Lady Dulcimer and Trumpet were drying the dogs. 'She would like to come to luncheon after all.'

'I hope you told her to come at one o'clock.'

'I suggested a quarter to one, milady. As we know, Mrs David sometimes forgets the time.'

Lady Dulcimer wished that Antonia could have telephoned sooner. Bernard had invited her at least five days ago, and she had promised to let them know. 'I can't remember what Cook and I planned for lunch. I hope it's something that will stretch.'

'I ascertained that we shall be serving rabbit stew today, milady. Cook assured me that there would be plenty to go round.'

'There always is,' said her ladyship in a depressed voice. 'Antonia will probably refuse to touch it, and she doesn't eat much at the best of times.'

'Perhaps his lordship might wish me to open a bottle of wine today.'

Lady Dulcimer stared at the butler. She and her husband had been worried about the young Vorsts lately, and Bernard was hoping to have a word with Antonia after lunch. But neither of them had said anything to Vestry.

He was right, of course. If Antonia was in a mellow mood, there was just a chance that she would listen to Bernard. A bottle of wine might help – though Lady Dulcimer doubted it.

Antonia was now living in the dower house nearby, with Nanny as a daily housekeeper and cook. The Dulcimers had offered it to the young Vorsts because they believed that newly married people should have their own space, and London was no place to be at present. Now, they wished they had never given them this refuge. It was too close to home.

'We could do with a bit of space ourselves,' said the earl that evening. 'At least while Antonia was staying at the Vorst we weren't obliged to suffer a daily bulletin of her complaints about David. Worse than the BBC, and every bit as depressing. Will she ever grow up?'

'Some people never do,' said Lady Dulcimer. 'Dogs are so much easier, aren't they my darlings . . .'

'Antonia is a spoilt child,' said his lordship crossly. His attempts to persuade Antonia that she should stop grumbling and consider David's point of view had not been well received.

'Two of his closest friends were killed last week,' he had told her. 'When he comes home you should give him a chance to sleep and eat and unwind. Think yourself lucky that your husband is alive, and that he visits you as often as he can.'

'But he's always ringing up to say he can't make it. And when he does come, he might just as well not bother,' she answered fretfully. 'He is not in the least interested in anything I have to say. He lives and breathes that wretched Air Force – tells me silly jokes about Johnny and Douglas, uses Air Force slang until I could scream. When his pet mechanic was killed in a raid, he was far more upset than he would be if I dropped dead tomorrow.'

'Nonsense, Antonia. David adores you. Think how worried he was when you were stuck in London during the first big raid.'

She lifted a shoulder, looking sulky. 'He has a strange way of showing his adoration these days.'

Lord Dulcimer wanted to slap her, but he said evenly, 'David is risking his life day after day. He must be under huge mental and physical strain. Try to be patient with him, my dear.'

But he had said too much, and knew it. Antonia did not come near them at the Hall for several weeks, and was broadcasting her discontent around the village. In a way it was a relief to be rid of her moans, but he felt uneasy.

Dart came to stay, and after listening to his father, rather reluctantly walked up the path to the dower house. He had been avoiding Antonia for nearly six weeks.

He found her alone in her pretty drawing room, nursing a half-empty glass of whisky and water. She was surprised to see him, and very pleased. She had been missing Dart.

Before long she was telling him what she could never have told her father-in-law. On David's last leave – arriving one evening and dashing away the next morning – he had embraced her with desperate urgency, but when they made love, he could not manage it.

'He used to be great in bed, especially when he was feeling jealous of you, Dart darling. But last time he could do nothing but say he was sorry before he went limp and fell asleep. I tried to wake him, but he was like a dead man . . .' She started to cry, both hands nursing her empty glass. 'You were perfectly right. I should never have married him. He's far too young for me.'

Dart looked at her. Antonia was thinner, and seemed to have lost her ability to shed tears without spoiling her complexion. He felt a sudden acute sympathy for the absent David.

She held out her glass to him, demanding a refill.

After a swig at it, she stopped crying and went on, 'He is absolutely obsessed by this flying business.'

'Of course he is, Tonia. He wouldn't be any good at it if it wasn't the most important thing. He has to get up there every day, to shoot or be shot down by the enemy, to hide his fear...'

'David never said anything about being frightened.'

'Well, he wouldn't, would he?' Then, before she could argue, he went on, 'This flying business, as you call it, may very well have staved off a German invasion – for a time, at least. And now they're trying to stop the bombers reaching London and other cities. From all accounts it's not easy, now that so many raids are taking place at night.'

'Marjorie told me that there was no sign of our fighters over London in the first big raids. Nothing but barrage balloons, and anti-aircraft guns that never shoot anything down.'

'The fighter squadrons try to intercept them before they get to London. Anyway, much Marjorie knows about it!'

'She knows all about it. She works for the WVS in London. Frightfully brave of her! She drives a mobile canteen, and hardly ever gets time off. She has been here only once in the past six weeks.'

'I hope she chose a time when David was away.'

'He was here, as it happened, but had to go back after a few hours.'

'I'm surprised he lingered so long with that woman in the house.'

'Don't be catty, Dart. You and David may call her the bad fairy but she's a good friend to me.'

'Does she tell you how hard done by you are?'

She lifted her chin. 'She's a good deal more sympathetic than you are, certainly.'

'That was what I was afraid of.' There was a silence between them.

Then Antonia put her glass down on a small table and smiled at him. 'We're wasting time. It's absolutely ages since we were alone together, and Nanny's out for the day. We could go upstairs...'

He stared at her, feeling distaste and not a feather of desire. 'Behave yourself,' he advised her curtly. 'I only came over because Father asked me to come and cheer you up.'

'Funny, that,' she said, once more sounding peevish. 'I've never known you to be more depressing.'

He was tempted to return the compliment but did not. Instead, he said perfectly seriously, 'Snap out of it, Antonia. You're only feeling miserable because you haven't got enough to do. Instead of drinking and complaining to everyone about David, why don't you get out there and do something useful. Train to be a cook, a secretary, or join one of the services. Anything. You might even consider joining your friend Marjorie in her canteen.'

'David wouldn't hear of me being in London. And my doctor told me not to get tired.'

Dart sighed. 'In that case, you might as well take yourself off to America, which David wanted you to do. It would probably be a weight off his mind to know that you were safe and cared for at Maple Valley.'

'You're remarkably full of concern for David today.'

'I feel for him, poor fellow. You aren't exactly a bundle of joy, if this morning is anything to go by. Take care that you don't drive him away altogether.' He got up to go. He was lunching with his parents.

At the front door, she decided to ignore his rudeness. She kissed him and said, 'You'll come to my birthday party, won't you?'

'I might if I haven't been sent abroad.'

'Please try to come. David says I can choose all the people I most want. Dinner, and dancing after. You'll know most of them. No Air Force bores at all.'

'Oh? Has Flight Lieutenant Vorst been invited? Or is he banned as an Air Force bore?'

'Don't be silly, darling. Of course David is coming. How could I have a birthday party without my husband?'

In the event, on the eve of the party, Dart rang up. It was no good. The regiment were on standby with all leave cancelled, and he could not come to her party. He was sorry, but there it was.

David did not get there either. He did not even telephone. He eventually showed up when the party was all over.

On the morning after Antonia's birthday, David woke in the cold dawn to the sound of rain battering on the bedroom window panes. There was a gale blowing outside, and he lay still, thankful that yesterday had been calmer. Not a good day, yesterday.

Antonia lay asleep beside him, sprawled sideways over the top of the bed, her face streaked with last night's make-up, her hair in a tangle. She looked as if she had fallen asleep in mid-tirade. Careful not to wake her, he eased his way out of bed and covered her with a bedspread before making his way to the bathroom.

Downstairs, he was welcomed ecstatically by Benjie the dachshund, and by Nanny, who looked at him over the top of her glasses, and said, 'Well, sir? So you came after all?'

'Not well at all, Nanny. I arrived as they were all leaving. What's more, I must go back, as soon as I can get myself to Haywards Heath Station.'

'What a pity Madam's car is away for repair. Otherwise she could have taken you to the station.'

He shook his head. 'I don't want to wake her. We were pretty late, and of course she was upset . . .'

Nanny surveyed him. 'You don't look up to much yourself, sir. Sit down and I'll make you some breakfast.'

'I'd kill for some coffee, Nanny, but first I must telephone—'

'Not from here, you won't. Not from the Hall, either,' said Nanny in the satisfied tone of one imparting bad tidings. She reached for the coffee, which she had ground freshly a short time ago. 'The lines are dead this morning. One of those pesky bombs dropped on the exchange, so Mr Vestry thinks.'

'Then it looks as if I will have to walk to my train,' he said resignedly. He looked down at his salt-stained and still sodden flying boots. Fur-lined, and good for warmth at high altitudes, they were not the greatest footwear for walking. He already had a blister on one heel. 'I can't ask Uncle Bernard for a lift. He so hates to use his petrol ration, except for emergencies.'

Even as he spoke, there was the sound of the front door opening, a scamper of canine feet, and two of the Boys pushed their way into the kitchen. They were followed by Lord Dulcimer, wearing a dripping mackintosh and a tweed cap.

'Good morning!' he said cheerfully. 'Do I smell coffee? You make better stuff here than ever I get at home. Making coffee is one of the things you Yanks do well.'

David smiled, and shook his uncle's rain-wet hand. 'Nanny won't like you calling her a Yankee, and she's the one who makes it around here.'

'I wish you would show my people how to make it, Nanny.' And then, remembering the purpose of his visit, he added, 'They rang up from your squadron last night, David, just before the line went off altogether. Somebody called Douglas, I think, though I couldn't make head or tail of what he said with the line crackling so badly. He said something about lucky you had your water wings with you, and that you were to enjoy the party. He wants you to ring him this morning.'

'Nanny says the telephone is dead. After I've drunk her coffee, I'll need to go find one that works.' He looked around him rather helplessly, and said to Nanny, 'I gave Vestry a sort of basket when I arrived last night. Have you seen it? It's got my flying clothes in it, and I'll need to take it with me.'

'You'll go nowhere until you've had some breakfast, Mr David. Just you take his lordship and the coffee tray into the morning room, and I'll bring toast and porridge. And take those dratted dogs with you as well.'

'No toast for me, Nanny,' said the earl. 'Why don't we have our coffee in here?'

'Because I want you out from under my feet, milord. Off you go, the pair of you.'

Lord Dulcimer winked at David, and they made their way past signs of party devastation to the morning room, where a newly lit fire was crackling cheerfully.

'Best room in the house, this,' said the earl. He sat down, and took an appreciative sip. 'So what kept you yesterday? Couldn't you have telephoned? We didn't lose our lines until after nine.'

'No telephones my end,' said David briefly.

Nanny came in with porridge, toast and a volley of scolds about the contents of David's rush basket. She had tracked it down to the larder, and it smelled strongly of fish. 'If you'd only thought to hang your clothes up, I might have been able to make them fit to wear this morning. Mr Vestry would have done it for you if you'd asked him.'

'There wasn't much time to tell Vestry anything,' said David, wincing at the memory of last night's scene. 'Don't worry, Nanny. The basket will do as it is.'

'You'll never travel in a first-class carriage with that thing! And you an officer in His Majesty's Air Force! It reeks of fish!'

'That figures. The guy who loaned it to me was a fisherman.' He smiled at Nanny. 'This porridge is the best thing I've ever tasted.'

'Did you have nothing to eat last night?'

'Dinner was over. What with Antonia being upset, and the bad fairy swooping on me, I kinda forgot about food . . .'

The earl had been putting things together – water wings and wet clothes smelling of fish. 'So you were shot down, were you?'

'Mm.' David had finished the porridge, and his mouth was full of toast. He had only just realised that he was starving. Already he was feeling decidedly better, and glad to be alive. 'Baled out, and splashed into the sea off Portsmouth. If that sharp-eyed guy hadn't spotted me, I might still be floating about this morning. Or frozen to death. My God, it was cold!'

'Did Antonia realise what had happened?' demanded Lord Dulcimer, frowning.

'I told you. No telephones. And it was so late by the time I got here, that it did not seem worth trying to explain.'

'You should have told her.'

His uncle was right, of course. But yesterday had been a long day. When they were scrambled, it was the third time since dawn.

They had spotted the enemy and were climbing to gain height when the leader's cheerful tones came over the air. 'We'll need to knock this lot off quickly, David, old boy. I promised that pretty wife of yours that I'd get you to her party, even if I had to drop you by parachute . . .'

'OK by me, Douglas.'

He shot down a 109. One of its wings fell off, and he saw it spiralling out of sight, and was immediately jumped by another enemy aircraft. The first he knew of it was a stream of tracer ripping into his port wing. Jerry had got him. Something spun and clattered over the perspex hood, possibly one of his own propeller blades. He struggled with controls that did not respond, and knew that he was for it, even before the nose of the Spitfire dropped. This was the third time he had been forced to bale out, so he knew the drill. Any second the plane would go into a spin. He reached for the hood, and to his relief it slid back at once. Last time, it had stuck stubbornly for agonising moments. With the second downward spiral he was thrown out head first, simultaneously pulling the ripcord and hurtling down into thick wet cloud. A spine-wrenching jolt and jerk told him that his parachute had opened, and as the cloud thinned he looked up to see it flowering wondrously above him.

His relief was short-lived. Instead of a patchwork of fields and woods, he looked down to see a misty coastline and an expanse of grey sea. There was an offshore breeze, and as he floated lower, bracing himself for the inevitable freezing splash, it looked cold and choppy. No sign of the coast now. He hoped fervently that one of the squadron had seen him bale out and had alerted the Air Sea Rescue boys. The only other time he had baled out into the sea – in early October – it had been achingly cold. Now it was November. Just before he hit the water, he remembered Antonia's birthday party.

The fishermen had seen the parachute, and he was barely twenty minutes in the water before being hauled aboard a shabby wooden boat. Even so, his brain had gone numb and stupid, and he lay face down on a pile of fishing nets, so frozen and bemused that it was minutes before he could unclench his teeth to gasp out thanks to his rescuers.

When he finally arrived at the dower house, it was all too apparent that the party was over. He heard voices and car doors slamming, and watched the dim, shaded lights of cars nosing down the short drive. He decided to go in by the back door. Vestry and one of the landgirls were sitting at the kitchen table with coats on, evidently on the point of leaving.

As he came out of the back premises into the hall, four people converged on it from the drawing room – Antonia, a couple he knew as Bill and Heather, and the inevitable Marjorie. There was a moment of startled silence.

He was still cold to the marrow and close to collapse after the events of the day, but it needed no more than a glance to show him that Antonia was both furious and drunk. She stood there swaying, wearing her new silver dress and positively glittering with rage.

'Well! Look who's here!'

He went quickly forward. 'I am sorry, honey! I couldn't make it sooner, believe me. How did the party go?'

She struck his hands away. 'Don't touch me. You and that Douglas planned this, specially to humiliate me! So don't even try to say you are sorry!' Then she seemed to take in his strange attire – a fisherman's jersey and trousers that barely reached the top of his flying boots. 'Why are you dressed like that?'

He ventured a feeble joke. 'You never like me in uniform. This is a bit different.'

This seemed to be the last straw. Antonia turned from him and started running up the stairs, but she was wearing high-heeled sandals and she tripped and missed the second step and clutched at the banister, staggering. She was sobbing angrily when he reached her and helped her to her feet. 'Come to bed, Antonia. You'll feel better if you lie down.'

He half supported, half carried her upstairs, and came down to find the others still standing in the hall. They looked guiltily at him, and then Bill said rather too heartily, 'It's past my bedtime too, I reckon. Come on, darling.'

Heather, smiling but not really looking at him, said, 'Goodnight, David. It was a good party. Such a pity you had to miss it.'

When they had gone, Marjorie said coldly, 'Did you let her down on purpose?'

He sighed. 'Not really. I'll turn the lights out if you're ready to go upstairs.' Marjorie always stayed the night when she visited.

'I'm not going anywhere until I've had my say. Antonia has been on pins and needles all day. How could you treat her like this?'

He did not answer. He did not feel up to a scene with the bad fairy.

She was incensed by his silence, and said angrily, 'Well, if you want to know what I think, David, you're a complete and utter bastard!'

He left her standing in the hall. She could turn out the lights, or leave them burning. He was past caring.

When he went into the bedroom after a quick shower, he found that his long day was not yet over. Antonia was pacing up and down, barefoot, but still wearing the silver dress, and railing. Her pent-up emotions broke over his weary head. He was selfish, dishonest, and had spoiled her party. He had promised to come in time. Why hadn't he rung her? Even Dart had been decent enough to telephone and say he was sorry!

'Antonia, please. Let's talk about it in the morning. Just now I really need to sleep.'

'Sleep? That's all you ever want! You leave me alone for weeks on end . . .' Her voice was shrill and a little slurred. 'How do you think I felt, with everyone wanting to know where you were? How could I tell them anything? You hadn't even bothered to ring up. I tell you, I was utterly mortified . . .'

He lay down, almost fell on the bed, and closed his eyes. He felt swamped by tiredness, too weary to explain, or to take her in his arms and make love – which might have mollified her. He fell asleep while she was still scolding, and was dimly aware of her fists pummelling his slumped shoulders before sleep overcame him.

Lord Dulcimer and the dogs went away, but not before the earl had made David promise to tell Antonia what had kept him away from her party. Accordingly, David went upstairs, but she was still out for the count. He came down again, to find the bad fairy standing in the front hall.

Brick-red in the face and sounding as if it was the last thing she wanted to do, Marjorie offered to drive him back to the airfield. He was tempted to tell her to go to hell. The thought of being imprisoned in a car with Marjorie for seventy miles was not alluring.

Still, her offer was too good to refuse. He had to get back, and the sooner the better. He thanked her, salved his pride by promising to put petrol in her car when they reach the airfield, and climbed in beside her. He had to fold his long legs almost double to fit in the passenger seat of her Austin Seven. The malodorous basket reposed on the back seat.

For the first ten miles, neither of them spoke. Then David said, 'Did my Uncle Bernard twist your arm?'

'You could say so,' she replied, keeping her eyes on the road. 'He told me that you were anxious to get back and would prefer a lift from me to an apology.'

'There was no need for either, Marjorie. Last night you were angry on Antonia's behalf, and I don't blame you.'

'I should never have said what I did. I knew the moment I said it. And when your uncle told me what had happened, I felt every sort of beast.'

'Forget it,' he said, looking out of the window. He wanted to change the subject and asked politely about her work with the WVS. Marjorie was a great talker and an enthusiast about her voluntary work, and with a nudge or two would probably hold forth for the rest of the journey. 'You must have had a hell of a time. Do you take your mobile canteen to the shelters?'

She said that they went wherever they were sent, and then confounded him by saying abruptly, 'You look as if you could sleep for a month. Why not shut your eyes and make the best of the next couple of hours – if you can manage to drop off in my little tin can of a car, that is.'

David smiled at her with sudden humour and warmth. 'I can drop off anywhere, Marjorie. If you're sure you don't mind.'

'I'll wake you when we get there.'

Chapter 15

Christmas came and went at Maple Valley House. It was a time of great beauty and blazing fires, of whispers, secrets, rustling presents and carols. The great house was filled with the scent of evergreens from several large Christmas trees – and with a rising crescendo of excitement and expectation among the children.

Abby had lost her faith in Father Christmas long ago at Dulcimer, when Quentin burst into her room and dumped a bulging Christmas stocking on her feet. Kim had known for years that it was her mother. However, they went along with the Santa Claus myth, partly because it was fun, and rather more because Maggie threatened them with awful consequences if they spoiled it for the others. Joan and Betty were firm believers.

'The poor dopes,' said Kim. 'They would believe anything.'

'I don't know,' said Abby. 'When Quentin gave it away, it spoiled things.'

They were playing cards in Kim's pretty bedroom, having gone there to get away from the latest upset. Everything was in an uproar because Miss Fortescue's watch had been stolen.

'The Fortress wants Mrs Sandridge to call the police,' Kim said. 'But she won't. She asked the Fortress why nobody had mentioned the poltergeist before.'

With hindsight, it seemed odd that they had not reported the earlier thefts, but when the trouble started months earlier, none of them wanted to kick up a fuss about a small outbreak of pilfering – particularly as it seemed to be confined to their British occupied attic. 'Better to keep it to ourselves,' said Miss Fortescue firmly. 'We can't have these Americans thinking that one of us is a thief.'

At first they were not even sure that there really was a thief. Money went missing from money boxes and schoolbags, certainly, but everyone knew how careless children could be. Maggie found money gone from her purse, and said so. But the others said that she had got her sums wrong, and next time she did not bother to tell them and decided to take her own precautions. Mamzelle complained about being robbed once, although when pressed she admitted that she could have mistaken a five dollar bill for a single dollar. But when Miss Brimley's gold-topped fountain pen went missing, Miss Fortescue, not for the first time, confided her suspicions to her fellow governess. 'If you want your pen back,' she said, 'you should help me search Maggie's room while she's out.'

'No, Maud.' Miss Brimley was a malleable little person, but she refused to budge on this. 'It would be dishonest and unfair. Why are you so sure that it must be Maggie?'

'Because her work takes her in and out of all our rooms every day.'

'No more so than the American girl, and Nanny Munnings' nursery maid. And there are others who come upstairs from time to time.'

They kept their handbags with them, hid their valued possessions and watched each other. Miss Fortescue locked the lordlings' money boxes in her trunk. As a result of these precautions, there was a lull in the poltergeist's activities. Everyone was relieved – Maggie more than any, for she was aware that Miss Fortescue disliked and mistrusted her.

But at the end of November, just when everyone had put the matter to the back of their minds, Miss Brimley's locket vanished, and a more than usually horrid storm blew up, with Miss Fortescue appointing herself as chief interrogator. Two unpleasant days followed, with the Munnings' nursery maid and Maggie and Mary-Jo being rigorously questioned, their movements inquired into and checked on. Nothing was achieved except a general feeling of suspicion and mistrust.

But next day, Maggie found the locket. She was turning Miss Brimley's mattress when her attention was caught by a glint of gold near the bedhead. She reached down, her breath quickening, and there it was.

Miss Brimley was thrown into a dither. She said reproachfully, 'Maggie, how is this possible? You told me that you had looked under the mattress yesterday and the day before. I particularly asked you.'

'I did,' said Maggie grimly. She was about to say that the locket had not been there then but she thought better of it. She needed time to find out what Mary-Jo was playing at.

She said awkwardly, her colour rising, 'I suppose I must have been blind. I am sorry.'

Miss Brimley said distractedly, 'I don't know how to explain this to Miss Fortescue. Really I don't.'

'At least you've got your locket back,' said Nanny Munnings consolingly. 'And it will do Maggie no harm to be caught out skimping her work. Girls get lazy unless one keeps on at them.'

'Maggie is not lazy. She had all the rooms to do today,' said

Mamzelle. 'Mary-Jo stayed at home with a cold.'

'A bit of extra work won't hurt Maggie,' said Miss Fortescue sourly. 'She's far too full of herself.' It seemed to her that Maggie's discovery was too neat to be believable and she could not resist voicing her incredulity. 'Quite a coincidence, wouldn't you say, that she *happened* to find the locket? She also *happened* to be working alone when it reappeared. What fools she must think us! The truth is that she lost her nerve when I questioned her and talked of calling in the police.'

The other women stared. They knew that Maud Fortescue did not like Maggie, but this was going a bit far.

'You are saying,' said Mamzelle in a bewildered voice, 'that Maggie took the locket and afterwards put it back?'

'It would not surprise me.'

'Why should she do so?'

Miss Fortescue sniffed. She never wasted time explaining things to the Frenchwoman. She cast an expressive glance at Nanny Munnings, but she was frowning down at her knitting.

Annoyed, she turned to Miss Brimley. 'The girl went bright red when I questioned her, a picture of guilt.'

'Maggie blushes easily, Maud.'

Nanny Munnings suddenly spoke up. 'This is ridiculous. We ought to speak to Mrs Sandridge and place the matter in her hands.'

'We've already decided,' said Miss Fortescue in her royal way, 'that this is a private problem. When I have caught that girl red-handed, we can send her away quietly. No need to bring outsiders—' She broke off. Mary-Jo had come in to pull the curtains.

As she turned to go, Miss Fortescue said sharply, 'Mary-Jo! Did you hear that Miss Brimley's locket has come back to us?'

Mary-Jo stopped and turned round, her eyes wide with surprise. 'Is that so? Where was it?'

'Under Miss Brimley's mattress – dangling from the bed springs.'

'But that . . . that's not possible!' exclaimed Mary-Jo. 'Maggie and I pretty well pulled the bed to pieces.'

'It was your friend Maggie who found it nevertheless,' said Miss Fortescue, with a glint in her eye.

'Oh!' Mary-Jo started to speak, then looked confused. 'Well, I don't understand it . . .'

Mary-Jo went through the door to the servants' part of the house, outwardly demure but inwardly elated. Cagney was right! His plan to 'fix' Maggie was starting to work, as he had assured her it would.

When he had told her to put the locket back, she had been indignant. It was too bad of him, particularly after it had been so difficult to lift. Miss Brimley always secreted the locket in her bedroom when she went out. It should have been easy to finger, but on the morning before Mary-Jo's meeting with Cagney, she could not get a moment to herself. Maggie stuck to her like glue until she was half afraid that she would join her brother empty-handed. Luckily one of the downstairs maids called up the stairwell to ask Maggie something, and she got her chance.

She told Cagney that he was a genius and he accepted the compliment as his due. He smiled, his eyes narrowed against the low evening sun. 'What did I tell you, Sis? Those old women won't know what to think now that the piece has shown up again. So that snooty little broad found it and took it to them, did she? I hope they gave her a hard time.'

Cagney was angry with Maggie because not only was she still refusing to go out with him but she had recently sent an early Christmas present back unopened. Mary-Jo was cross with Maggie too. The rhinestone necklace he had got for her was a beaut, far too good for Maggie in Mary-Jo's opinion.

'It's something real pretty, Maggie. Unwrap it and you won't be able to resist.'

'I can't take presents from him, Mary-Jo. Please make him understand.'

'Cagney's feelings will be hurt.'

'How else can I make your brother believe that I don't want him to give me things, or to go out with him? Tell him that it's no good. You must see that I am not his sort of person. Cagney is wasting his time.'

'How can you be so hard-hearted, Maggie? And so ungrateful. You were pleased enough to come around to our place when you didn't know anyone else. What's happened to you, that you've grown so uppity? Mother keeps asking for you.'

Maggie had no wish to offend Mary-Jo or her mother, but she shook her head. There was no way of explaining the revulsion that Cagney aroused in her. Ed had an inkling of it, and when Maggie felt obliged to tell him that she would not be coming to the Morgan house any more, he said, 'It's Cagney, isn't it? Does he scare you?'

She nodded uncomfortably.

'I thought so. You're right to stop coming. Cagney seems to get a kick out of scaring people, particularly when they show it as you do.'

She was a little put out. 'Was I so obvious?'

He smiled at her. 'Only to me. I used to have problems with Cagney myself. One day Pa came in while he was twisting my arm and punching me about the head. I don't know what happened, because Pa sent me away, but since then Cagney has mostly left me alone. He's careful if Pa is around, anyhow, and I keep out of his way.' Ed fumbled in his jacket pocket, and pushed something small into Maggie's hand, saying in a muffled tone, 'Here. This is something I'd gotten you for Christmas. I guess you'd better have it now, in case I don't see you. So long, Maggie.'

That was the last she saw of Ed. She missed him, for with their shared interest in books and movies there was always plenty to talk about. If it had not been for Cagney, Maggie would have liked to have kept up with him.

As the weeks drew on towards Christmas, Miss Fortescue's sense of frustration mounted. She was convinced that Maggie was to blame for the outbreaks of pilfering, but she needed irrefutable evidence to convince the others. Without saying anything, she tried searching Maggie's bedroom but found nothing to support her suspicions – less than three dollars in money and little else. She was holding out against the suggestion that they should consult Mrs Sandridge. Miss Fortescue did not like the secretary. She had not forgotten how she had taken Maggie's part over the driving lessons. But when her own watch was stolen two days after Christmas, that was a different matter. It was her most prized possession – a circular gold brooch with a watch face in the centre. Miss Fortescue wore it pinned to her formidable bosom like a badge of office.

How it came to be left on her bedside table was never clear, but by the time she went upstairs after breakfast, the watch had gone. It was a valuable ornament, and after the first unavailing search, Miss Fortescue stormed into the secretary's office to complain of her loss.

Mrs Sandridge expressed sympathy, and listened in silence while Miss Fortescue told her how items had been going missing in the attic for months. But she refused to involve the police. 'I realise it is distressing for you, Miss Fortescue, but we like to handle these things ourselves. There are some unfortunate people who cannot resist taking things. But if one can avoid alarming them, they often give themselves away.'

'Give themselves away? How?'

'It varies. Sometimes they boast of their cleverness, or cannot resist wearing a new, pretty piece of finery. A boy who worked in the pantry took some silver spoons and sold them in the town. It was sad, really. He wanted to win favour with his girlfriend by buying her something pretty.'

'Surely you sent for the police then.'

Mrs Sandridge shook her head. 'We gave the boy another chance. He went to work in the garden. There was less temptation there.'

Miss Fortescue thought this quite extraordinary, and demanded to know what steps were going to be taken to retrieve her watch. She said acidly, 'Are you suggesting that we should wait until I meet someone wearing it?'

'It's more likely that the thief will sell it.' And before Miss Fortescue could object, she added that she would speak to the local police chief, who would circulate a description of the missing object. 'But I won't bring the police into the house. It would worry Mrs Vorst and be upsetting for all of us.'

'Upsetting!' echoed the governess hotly, 'I'll have you know that the Duchess, the boys' mother, pinned that watch on my coat with tears in her eyes. She said she wanted me to have it because I was the only one she could entrust with her boys.'

Mrs Sandridge, unable to imagine how anyone could leave their children in this woman's care, said soothingly, 'I understand your being upset. Let us try to think how best to find the culprit, shall we?'

'It's my watch I want to find.'

'Finding one will lead to recovering the other, I hope. We must be on the alert for signs. If anyone appears to be richer than usual, or boasts of being given expensive presents, please come and tell me.'

The New Year staff party at Maple Valley House was a highlight of the year, at least for the younger people. All the indoor and outdoor staff and their wives were invited, and it took place in the covered tennis court, the only building large enough to contain such a numerous company. Dinner came first, with everyone seated at long tables. After dinner the tables would be removed and there would be dancing to a live band. Mr and Mrs Vorst and the family came along at this stage, and usually stayed for the first few dances.

Mary-Jo was in a high state of excitement. She and the younger girls had been planning what to wear for weeks. Bets were laid about who would be first to be kissed under the mistletoe.

On the day of the party, everyone helped to decorate the tennis court. By the time Maggie left, anything less like a tennis court could hardly be imagined. Long tables were covered with scarlet cloths, candles and greenery, and twin Christmas trees winked and sparkled on either side of a stage.

Abby and Kim went with her to Miss Gladys's house to see Maggie's new dress. Even choosy Kim approved of it. It made Maggie look taller and very slender.

'Just like Cinderella,' Abby told Maggie. 'A handsome prince will sweep you into his arms and dance you away.'

'And the other girls will be sick with jealousy,' put in Kim, grinning.

Miss Gladys gave the hem of Maggie's dress a tweak, and got off her knees. 'She looks nice, doesn't she? You've made a good job there, Maggie. See you enjoy yourself tonight.'

'I mean to, Miss Gladys. And thanks.'

'Come down and change after the kids' supper, and we can walk to the party together. If it rains, Jay said he would collect us.'

So Maggie showered quickly and made herself as nearly ready as she could before seeing to the children's final meal. She wore her working dress, but under it were the silk stockings given her by Mr and Mrs Vorst on Christmas Day. With lipstick and Abby's scent on, and wearing her few pieces of jewellery, she ran downstairs feeling festive and excited. Quite a few of the men had already asked her for a dance, and she was looking forward to the evening.

All but the smallest children were going to the party with the Vorsts. Fizzing with excitement in their party clothes, they capered around the front hall as soon as their supper was over. Mrs Sandridge was dressed for the party too, and she smiled on them as she went to find if there were any messages in the office. She was not pleased to find that Miss Fortescue had followed her in. She was even less pleased when she heard what the governess had to say.

'Miss Fortescue, this will have to wait.'

'You told me to keep my eyes open, Mrs Sandridge. And now you don't want to know.'

'The staff party starts in half an hour. Why risk spoiling the evening when this matter can be dealt with in the morning?'

'The morning may be too late. You said yourself that these people take sudden urges to show off. Such effrontery! I could hardly believe my eyes. A ring on her hand, a chain with a pendant round her neck, gold earrings – all good stuff, and none of them ever seen by any of us until tonight.'

'They may be Christmas presents. Now, Miss Fortescue, if you will excuse me.'

'So you don't mean to do anything about it, Mrs Sandridge?'

'No, Miss Fortescue. I do not.'

The secretary nearly added something about it being the season of goodwill, but decided not to waste her breath. She doubted if goodwill figured in the woman's vocabulary.

Maggie and the other maids cleared up at speed. At last they were done, with only coffee and tea to be taken to the red drawing room. As she crossed the hall, she was halted by Kim and Abby.

Kim looked agog and Abby worried. 'What's going on in there, Maggie?' she demanded. 'Miss Fortescue came in and turfed us out, and Brimstone looks as if she might cry. Have they heard about someone being killed, do you think?'

Maggie felt a jolt in the pit of her stomach. Bert, she thought. They must have heard about Bert. She shook her head at the children. Ed's earrings swung about her face, reminding her that she had a party to go to. Please God, not Bert! Not tonight. 'Stop imagining horrors, you two. If you let me by, I'll try to find out. I might even tell you.'

The British women were seated in a circle about the drawing-room fireplace. Maggie glanced at them as she served their chosen evening

211

beverages. None of them spoke. Abby was right. Something was wrong. Nanny Munnings and Mamzelle took coffee without looking at her. Miss Brimley took her cup of tea in a tremulous hand, glanced at Maggie's face, and then away as though she found the sight distressing. If it was about Bert's death, surely Miss B would not look at her that way.

Maggie served Miss Fortescue last, because the lordlings' governess liked her tea strong, and the tray containing the teapot, milk and sugar had to be left beside her so that she could help herself when she judged the brew to be just so. She was sitting, chin on hand, in a wing chair by the fire, her eyes on the flames. Maggie put the tray down and straightened up.

'I will clear away first thing in the morning, Miss Brimley. I said I would go to the party with Miss Gladys—'

'Not so fast,' said Miss Fortescue. 'You will go to no party until you tell us what we want to know. In the first place, where did you get that ring? Here, girl. Hand it over. I want to look at it.'

Maggie backed away, covering her mother's ring with her other hand. 'It's mine. You'll not touch it!'

'Where did you get it?'

'It's my mother's. Why do you want to know?'

'Your mother's, you say?' Miss Fortescue turned to Miss Brimley. 'I thought you said that her mother was dead.' And when Miss Brimley corroborated this, she turned back to Maggie. 'You had better think of a better story to tell us than that.'

'It's no story. It used to be my mother's before sh-she died.' Maggie was shaking all over by this time, and her voice shook too. She looked imploringly at Miss Brimley, 'My gran sent it to me.'

'Let's have a look.' Miss Fortescue was not going to be deterred. 'While I'm at it, I'll want to see what's on that chain round your neck, and those earrings.'

Maggie backed further away, determined that this dreadful woman should not lay a finger on her precious ring. 'Leave me alone. It's none of your business what I wear to the party. It just shows that I was right to hide my things until now!'

'So that's your story. Why don't you admit that you have just bought that ring, and paid a pretty penny for it, if I'm not mistaken. How much did you get for my watch when you sold that?'

Maggie felt as though she had been punched in the stomach, and for several moments could only stare at Miss Fortescue's high-nosed, flushed, triumphant face. She felt her own face growing hot with shame and anger. The others were all staring at her with bemused expressions on their faces. No help there, Maggie thought bleakly.

The shock had its uses, for it steadied her and wiped out her sense of panic. She found that she was no longer shaking, and took several deep, deliberate breaths. This was a fight, and she was alone. She would need all her resources.

Miss Fortescue took Maggie's sudden stillness for an admission of guilt. 'I thought so! You had better cooperate with us, young lady. We none of us want a scandal. Get my watch back for me, and we may decide not to give you away to the police when they come.'

Miss Brimley said suddenly, 'Maggie, I find this all very difficult to understand.' She turned to Miss Fortescue and added, 'Maud, let me take Maggie upstairs and talk to her.'

'And give the girl time to concoct some glib story? No thank you. You saw her face when I demanded my watch. Of course she took it. And your locket, I dare say. She has guilt written all over her. She took them, all right.'

'I don't believe that Maggie would do such a thing.'

'Thank you, Miss Brimley,' said Maggie. Her voice wobbled, for she was utterly astonished at this unexpected support. She said earnestly, 'I certainly did not take Miss Fortescue's watch. Nor did I sell it, as she seems to think.'

Hands fastened on her shoulders and swung her round. 'Now then, young woman, you won't help yourself by telling lies.'

Maggie wrenched herself away from those fiercely retaining hands, but stood her ground just out of reach. 'I do not tell lies, Miss Fortescue. What makes you so sure that I am a thief?'

The other nannies and Mamzelle sat frozen in their chairs. They watched Maggie standing there, refuting Miss Fortescue's accusations, her manner calm and coldly polite. It was a revelation. Mamzelle gave voice to some of their thoughts later, when she declared that never again would she look on Maggie as a child.

'I only had to look at your face,' Miss Fortescue answered haughtily. 'A picture of guilt, you were.'

'Not guilt, Miss Fortescue. You startled me.'

'That's one way of putting it. You thought you'd got away with it, I suppose. You were even bold enough to flaunt your new finery in public. I've had my eye on you for some time, but when I saw you dolled up tonight, I knew.'

'No. I have already told you about my mother's ring. The chain was given me by the minister's wife at home. The earrings and the St Christopher charm are Christmas presents from friends.'

'So why have none of us seen these things until tonight? Explain that away, if you can.'

'I could explain,' said Maggie, although they sensed a sudden reluctance in her. 'But I don't know that I shall. What I wear and who gives me presents is my affair. I put my ring and chain in a safe place some weeks ago. Why should I tell you anything more?'

'Insolent girl! How dare you defy me!'

'Miss Fortescue, you give me no choice. I am not a thief. I never took your watch or any of the other things. I have a right to defend myself.'

'We'll see about rights! You may say what you like about possessing your ring and chain for so long, but nobody will believe you. Not when I tell the police what I know.'

'Oh? And what is that?'

Miss Fortescue's fierce gaze flickered. It was her turn to look hesitant. But only for an instant. She said with renewed firmness, 'Very well. I was certain that you were the cause of all the trouble, and I decided to search your room. There was no sign of that ring three weeks ago, and nothing but small change in your purse. I suppose you'd already spent the proceeds of your thefts.'

Maggie stared. She said bleakly, 'I wondered who had been poking about among my things. I was thankful then that I had asked a friend to keep my ring and chain. How disappointed you must have been!' She glanced briefly at Miss Brimley, then back to her tormentor. 'Was it all of you, or just yourself, Miss Fortescue?'

'None of your business,' snapped Miss Fortescue, ignoring a protesting twitter of 'Maud, dear . . . ' from Miss Brimley. 'You realise, don't you, that the police will require proof that your ring and chain actually came from Scotland, as you claim? They will want to know who gave you the other presents, too – names and addresses that will have to be checked. How will you feel when they discover that there are no such people, that you bought the jewels yourself? Ungrateful girl! We are only trying to save you. None of us want to bring the police into it.'

'Very good of you,' said Maggie drily. 'Given a choice, I'd rather talk to the police. They may have heard about people being innocent until proved guilty. What proof have *you* got, Miss Fortescue? If I stole Miss Brimley's locket, then why did I find it again and give it back to her?'

'You know very well why. I threatened to call the police, and you lost your nerve.'

'Is that it?' said Maggie tightly. 'You know, Miss Fortescue, if anyone has a nerve, it's you, saying such things.'

Miss Gladys came into the room at this point, carrying a dress box. Abby and Kim followed her. Miss Gladys was just starting to say, 'Oh, there you are, Maggie . . .' when Miss Fortescue gave way to her rising temper and frustration, and slapped Maggie's face hard. The sound was like a pistol shot in the large room.

There was a short, stunned silence. Maggie turned away blindly with a hand to her face, her eyes watering from the blow, and Abby came running. She demanded to know what was going on.

Looking past Abby, Maggie pulled her ring off and held it out to

214

Miss Gladys. 'Take it back to Mr James, please. He will explain that he had been keeping it safe won't he?'

'Yes, dear, if you want him to.' Miss Gladys took the ring, and stared at it. But she was a single-minded woman, and had come for an urgent purpose. 'Let's talk about it later. I've brought your dress, and you'd better change quickly. We're late for the dinner already...'

Maggie had forgotten the party. She felt weak and shivery, awash with shame and humiliation, and an urgent need to hide, to go somewhere where she could be alone and weep. She just managed to say, 'Go on without me, Miss Gladys. I just can't ... can't seem to fancy eating or dancing tonight....'

She turned and stumbled out of the room, reaching the attic floor just in time to be violently sick in the nearest lavatory.

Recriminations were inevitable. Everyone wished that Miss Fortescue had not been so hasty. It seemed that Maggie had asked Mr James to keep her ring and chain some weeks before. There was no doubt about that.

'If only she had told me,' said Miss Brimley, distressfully. 'I would have kept her treasures for her, and could have put you right, Maud. Why should she run to Mr James, I wonder?'

'I dare say Mr James would do anything to please the hussy – even lie for her, if need be.'

'Abby says that Maggie has worn the ring on a chain under her clothes since September.'

'Abby is equally under the girl's thumb. Most undesirable. If you had sent the girl back to England when I told you to, we would have been spared a lot of trouble.'

Mamzelle weighed in. 'The way you speak of Maggie is not at all gentille.'

Nanny Munnings just got on with her knitting, and did not look up when Miss Fortescue sniffed audibly and walked out of the room.

James was outraged when he heard what had happened. 'That damned woman!' he growled.

Mrs Sandridge looked at him. James very rarely swore. 'We have known for a long time that Miss Fortescue is unpleasant,' she remarked. 'It now appears that she is remarkably stupid as well. Thank the Lord she is not coming to Palm Beach.'

Chapter 16

It was Mr and Mrs Vorst's custom to go to Florida every winter, leaving after the New Year and returning north at the beginning of April. The British children went to join them a few days later.

When they left Maple Valley House, the gardens lay muffled under snow, lawns white-blanketed, hedges and shrubs snow-laden. A black tracery of avenue trees glinted silver-threaded beneath a lowering sky. Looking back from the hindmost car, Maggie fancied that the great turreted mansion wore a melancholy, deserted air, despite the fact that Mr Wilding the butler and most of the household staff were still there. A black butler and some other servants lived in the Florida house all year round, so the first three months of the year were vacation time for the Maple Valley crowd.

A smiling Mr James met them at Palm Beach station and drove them to the Spanish-style house beside the ocean. Chrissie came out to greet them, the dachshunds swarming and feathering around her elegantly shod feet. She was dressed for summer and held a posy of waxen gardenias, and Mrs Sandridge looked as cool as an ice cream in a short-sleeved linen dress. They at least were comfortably familiar, while everything else about the Florida house was different.

It was charming in a rambling way, honey-coloured, with wide arched colonnades shading it all around. Purple bougainvillea swung from the arches, roses bloomed on the walls, passion flowers and stephanotis twined green tendrils here and there. The terracotta tiles on the roofs had long since faded to a soft shade of coral, in contrast to the garden which was a riot of vibrant colour.

Within the house, all was dimness and shaded calm. Ceramic tiles gleamed on the floors – cool to the children's feet when they padded in barefoot from the sun-drenched gardens. Later, when Florida was just a happy memory, Maggie had the impression that they had lived in the garden and by the swimming pool nearly all the time.

'Such a waste of all this, having to go to school,' said Abby on the first morning of term. 'Kim says we won't learn anything, because southern schools are miles behind Greenacres. I wish I had stayed with her in Long Island. She wanted me to.'

'Thank goodness you did not,' said Maggie, who was leaning out over the broad upstairs balcony which ran the whole length of the house. 'I would likely have had to stay behind too. I never thought to have a grapefruit tree under my bedroom window.'

'You're lucky. You don't have to go to a horrible new school.'

Miss Brimley feared that Palm Beach was not going to agree with her. She went to her bed as soon as they arrived. For three days she lay with the shades pulled across the windows, waited on by a worried Maggie. The little governess did not fancy anything to eat, and felt dizzy when she went to the bathroom. Nanny Munnings and Mamzelle went to see her, and later Mrs Sandridge. A doctor was called in.

The doctor was not able to find much wrong with Miss Brimley. He gave her something to soothe her stomach, and told Mrs Sandridge that the English lady seemed depressed. Was she grieving or worried about something?

Mrs Sandridge looked at Maggie. 'What do you think?'

Maggie might have told them that the governess worried about everything all the time, and if homesickness counted as grief, she was suffering from that, too. But she did not think that Miss Brimley would like her to say it. She said slowly, 'She gets tired in the heat, and journeys upset her. Likely she'll be better when she has had a chance to rest up.'

The children and their attendants spent a lot of time in and around the pool. Even in the evenings the air and water were blissfully warm. A wide, shaded veranda overlooked the pool, and here they enjoyed barbecue meals at weekends.

'Aunt Chrissie says we will need more than one bathing suit because we swim several times a day,' said Abby while she was getting dried after a weekday evening swim. She had become reconciled to the new school, finding it small and friendly, with marvellously easy lessons and no homework. 'She's getting us new clothes, too. I wish I could have a playsuit like the one she gave Kim in the summer. Do you think I could ask Aunt Chrissie?'

'Abigail!' Miss Brimley's voice quavered from the shade of the veranda. 'You will do no such thing. On no account must you ask for anything. I just hope Mrs Vorst does not tire herself, shopping in this heat.'

Miss Brimley need not have worried. Mrs Vorst's idea of shopping was not quite in the common way. Mrs Sandridge called up Lord and Taylor and another large store, and boxes full of children's clothes were sent round. On Saturday, the children trooped along to the spacious hall to find clothes laid out all around: dresses, playsuits, hats, shoes, bathing suits. Abby looked at this amazing impromptu bazaar, and drew a shuddering breath.

Aunt Chrissie was as excited as anyone. She would pick a dress and hold it up against Abby or one of the other girls, to see if the colour suited them. They would need something tidy for Sunday school, she said. There was one dress she liked, and when the girls said they liked it too, she told Mrs Sandridge to order one for each of them. Abby did not much want to be dressed exactly like Joan and Betty and the little Munnings twins, but she had been given a playsuit and a new bathing suit and was, for the moment, in a state of uncomplaining bliss.

Abby could not recall that anyone had ever sought her opinion on what she wore. At home her garments had been bought by Nanny, and occasionally by Antonia, and Abby had to wear them whether she liked them or not. Aunt Chrissie expected them to choose and decide for themselves.

Nor were the boys forgotten. Mrs Sandridge's list grew longer and longer. It took up half the morning, and by the time Edward, the Palm Beach butler, came to tell his mistress that her luncheon was served in the east porch, they were all feeling tired and even a little dazed.

At the poolside, James was cooking hot dogs and hamburgers on a charcoal brazier, and maids were flitting about with jugs and bowls of salad. The children were served first, and later took their ice-cream cones into the garden to eat.

Taking his place between Mamzelle and Miss Brimley, James smiled at Maggie. He looked different in Palm Beach, cool and neat in cream-coloured clothes and a straw hat. Maggie thought he looked fit and well – more relaxed than at Maple Valley. She no longer felt in awe of him. She had confided in him often in the course of her driving lessons. He was never critical, totally unshockable; the perfect listener.

The special thing about James, Maggie reflected, was that he was the same with everybody, friendly and humorous, without a trace of unkindness. He had been like that when he took her driving in Maple Valley. He was the same with Miss Brimley and the other women. He was no different with Mr and Mrs Vorst. No wonder they liked him so much. People seemed to brighten up when James was there.

Maggie had seen comparatively little of Mr or Mrs Vorst at Maple Valley House. In this smaller establishment, with Miss Brimley unable to do more than sit writing letters in the shade, she saw them all the time, and they treated her as just another member of their large wartime family.

And Miss Brimley and the nannies, taking their cue from the Vorsts and James, were suddenly much more friendly. Miss Brimley clasped her hand, and said tearfully that she did not know what she would have done without her dear Maggie. Basking in warmth and this unexpected general approval, Maggie felt that the sun had come out for her.

A college student came on Friday afternoons and held a swimming class for the British children. His name was Bill, and he had the face and figure of a Greek god and skin like polished mahogany. The youngest children were soon dog-paddling about and learning to put their faces in the water. The older ones were to learn the crawl. Bill was a slave-driver, and had them holding boards at arm's length and kicking up and down the pool for ages.

Watching them on the following Friday, Chrissie asked Maggie why she had not joined in the lesson. 'Everybody ought to learn to swim, my dear.'

Tom had taught Maggie to swim at an early age, and she longed to try swimming in the beautiful garden pool. But Miss Brimley and the nannies did not swim, and neither did any of the maids. Only James – and he was, after all, a privileged person – swam a dozen lengths of the pool every day, and that was before anyone was up in the morning. But with Mrs Vorst saying that she should join Bill's class, she boldly wore her new Palm Beach bathing suit next day and swam with the children.

'What did I tell you?' said Abby, when nobody disapproved.

Maggie felt a surge of pleasure, and for the hundredth time thanked heaven that Miss Fortescue had not come with them to Florida. The lordlings' ducal parents had arranged for the boys and their governess to stay with friends in Tucson all winter. To be free of Miss Fortescue was an extra special pleasure.

Maggie had not realised, until then, just how much the other British women had followed Miss Fortescue's lead. She found herself treasuring this new and happy state of affairs, and hoped it would last. So when Bill teased and flirted with her during the next swimming lesson, and complimented her on her stylish crawl, she wished he would not.

But the nannies only laughed. They even approved when Bill asked her to go with him to his college dance.

'They may not let me,' she told him. 'Besides, I don't know how to dance foxtrots and things.'

'Phooey,' said Bill cheerfully. 'I'll show you. And if it's Miss Brimley you're worried about, I'll fix her.'

And fix her he did, and when he came to collect her in his old jalopy of a car, a crowd of nannies and children swarmed to the door to wave her off. James gave Bill a clap on the shoulder, and told him to behave himself, winking at Maggie.

'Have a great time, Cinderella.'

Far from leaving at midnight, she came home just before breakfast, footsore from dancing all night. The dance floor had been in a garden under the stars. A group of them went down to the beach, and Bill had taken her behind a tree fern and kissed her. Afterwards they danced some more, but were never more than halfway round the floor before one of the others cut in, leaving Bill watching ruefully as Maggie was whirled away.

Often he danced with other girls, but was soon back to claim her, spinning her into a foxtrot or a waltz. When dawn was breaking he suddenly seized her hand and pulled her off the floor before any more of his mates could get to her.

'You're much too pretty, Maggie,' he told her. 'I wanted to dance with you all night, but I keep losing you to my friends who want to know my English girlfriend.'

'Havers,' said Maggie. 'Who are you calling English? I'm a Scot.'

It was heady stuff. Never in Maggie's life had so many people wanted her to have a good time. Still less had anyone told her that she was pretty. She wished that Tom could have seen her. How he would have laughed!

She joined in on expeditions to faraway beaches, and a trip to the Everglades. Mr Vorst and James took her deep-sea fishing, saying that she was needed to keep the children in order. But it was Maggie who reeled in a large swordfish, heaving and struggling in the swivelling chair, to a chorus of admonition and encouragement from the others. James gave her a photograph of herself and Mr Vorst with her catch. Again she wished that Tom could have seen it, but the anguish of missing Tom had receded a little in her present state of happiness. She could think of him almost without pain.

Her driving lessons were not neglected. She had at last learned to relax behind the wheel, and everyone was pleased when she passed her driving test in Palm Beach. All the same, when Mrs Vorst asked her to drive the children to school, Maggie was momentarily deprived of speech. She looked round for James, expecting him to say that she was not ready.

He smiled. 'What's the matter? You know how to get to the school.'

'Yes, but . . .' She found that she was stammering. 'D-do you think I could do it on my own?'

'Why ever not?' James sounded surprised. 'I must be a pretty poor teacher if you can't.'

So she gulped and agreed, and most mornings she left Jamie with Miss Brimley and drove the big station wagon to the small Palm Beach school. She felt full of new confidence – not a child any more but a grown-up person.

Adele Devenish had reluctantly agreed to fly to Florida with Conway. 'Won't your mother think it odd? She knows that we don't get on. It used to worry her.'

'It would. Mother expects all her loved ones to love one another.

She will be pleased to find that we're getting on better.'

Adele looked doubtful. 'I wouldn't want her to think that there was anything going on between us.'

'Certainly not, Adele. Why should she think anything of the kind?' He laid his hand on her knee, and felt the tremor that went through her. 'You're being ridiculous, you know. I often bring friends to stay in Palm Beach, so why not you?'

'So I qualify as a friend, do I? That *will* surprise your mother.' She put his hand firmly back on his own knee. 'You promised to keep your hands to yourself.' Then, after a pause, she added rather wistfully, 'I won't deny that I'm tempted.'

'Then quit behaving like a shrinking maiden.'

'I meant,' she said severely, 'that the thought of *sunshine* is a lure. This New York winter would make anyone yearn for warmth.'

'Come to Florida, then. You can soak up the sun by the pool while Father and I go to work in Miami.'

'I will if you make at least a pretence of behaving like a gentleman.'

'I can pretend to be anything, Adele. If you're quite sure that's what you want?'

'I'm perfectly sure.'

'It's a pity you make such a lousy liar.'

Conway and Cornelius went off to Miami, and Adele swam and lazed beside the pool until the sun grew too hot for comfort. Then she found a long chair in the shade and dozed, watching idly as people came and went between the house and the pavilion. The sun glinted through the leaves above her, the sky was postcard blue above the rustling palms. She lay there, thinking about Conway. He was intruding in her thoughts a lot these days – too often for her peace of mind.

She had seen a fair amount of him since the night of the ball. He had chosen to take an increasing interest in her work for British charities, which made fundraising much easier. He seemed to know everyone in New York, and money and clothes and food came pouring in. Conway's support was invaluable. Several times he invited her out to dinner or luncheon in the city – occasionally they went with business friends, but more often they were on their own. She had enjoyed these excursions, and although she did not tell him so, she liked having her hair well cut and knew she was looking better and smarter than she would have thought possible. Living as she did in a largely female environment at Bellefield, these visits to New York had been stimulating and a welcome change.

All the same, she found it surprising that Conway continued to seek her out. She could not discover a single thought or sentiment that they possessed in common. They saw things differently, argued

221

briskly about everything from politics to religion and morals, and if the price of peanuts had come up, they would have taken opposite sides about that. He bullied her about her clothes, occasionally presenting her with a dress or coat or a hat and prevailing upon her to wear it. If she tried to refuse, he accused her of idleness and arrogance. Did she think that being a British aristocrat excused her from taking trouble with her appearance? It was an insult to her friends, going about looking like a down-and-out.

Once he had refused to take her out to lunch unless she came with him to buy a less shabby pair of shoes – and she had gone home hungry. But one day he took her to his apartment, and told her his reason for seeking her out. He wanted to take her to bed.

She hid her astonishment quite well, and told him that it was out of the question. 'I'm a married woman, Conway, with a nearly grown-up family. I have no intention of sleeping with you.'

He smiled crookedly. 'I was not planning to sleep – unless you bore me. Somehow,' he added, looking her over thoughtfully, 'I don't think either of us will be bored.'

'We're not going to find out. Try someone else, Conway.' She got up to go. She added awkwardly, 'I've enjoyed these past months so much. Believe me, I'm grateful. But I never dreamed that you wanted . . . that you would want to have an affair with me.'

'You can't be that dumb, Adele. What else did you suppose I wanted?'

'But Conway, I am not that sort of person. It must be obvious, even to you. You say I look dowdy, and I am plain and too tall. I'm thirty-seven, older than you, and the very few men that have made passes at me were drunk at the time.'

'That,' said Conway, still lying back on the sofa surveying her, 'was before I made you over, Adele.'

She flushed and said angrily, 'And you dare to call *me* arrogant! I'm off, Conway, and I suppose we had better not meet any more, except at Maple Valley House. Do you want me to move my Bundles to another hotel?'

He got up and stood beside her. They were much of a height, but he was broader and stronger by far. She felt helpless even before he put both arms round her and said, 'Suppose I decide not to let you go? What are you going to do about it?'

She wondered whether he would take her by force. There would be little she could do to prevent it, if that was what he intended. She made herself stand still and said coolly, 'You know, I had hoped that we might, in time, have become friends. Don't spoil it, Conway.'

After what seemed an age, he said, 'All right, Adele. I can wait for what I want. When you change your mind, just tell me.'

Watching drowsily from her shady refuge, Adele saw a long-legged girl carrying little Jamie Cary to the pool. They sat on the shallow steps, splashing with their feet and chatting, and presently the girl slipped into the water, and turned to hold out her arms. The little boy barely hesitated before plunging in towards her, and she caught him. She was laughing, and Jamie squealed with pleasure. He was soon paddling about like a happy dog, and the girl trod water, keeping an eye on him.

Later the Munnings nanny arrived with her four-year-old twins. After a while the little girls were coaxed into the pool, too, while their nanny kept an eye on them.

Adele watched from under lowered lids, finding it delightful to see them bobbing about the pool – a charming, animated frieze. It was all the more delightful because they were nothing to do with her. This chance to be idle was bliss. No worries, no irksome responsibilities, no teenage moods to cope with. Edward and her two daughters, much as she loved them, were at an awkward age, not to mention her nephews and nieces and the other families with young children who lived under the broad Bellefield roof. She would gladly have lain in this warm dappled shade for the rest of her life.

The frieze grew more animated. People came and went with trays and armfuls of linen, and others started laying tables under the pavilion porch. Chrissie Vorst appeared between the gardenia bushes, with her usual escort of yapping dogs. Mrs Sandridge was with her, and they stopped to watch the children in the water. With an inward sigh, Adele bestirred herself and moved towards them, tying the belt of her bathing wrap about her waist.

Chrissie suggested to Adele that, with Conway and Cornelius in Miami, they should eat beside the pool. Adele had another leisurely swim. When she went into the pavilion to shower and change her wet bathing suit for a dry one, she made a discovery.

A voice beside her said, 'I'll get you another towel, milady.'

The pavilion seemed dark after the sunshine outside, but she knew the voice. 'Maggie?' she said uncertainly, peering. 'Is that you?'

'That's right, milady.'

Adele's eyes were adjusting, and she stared. The tall slim girl with the brown curls and golden tan was Maggie, a totally transformed Maggie. 'I didn't realise who you were out there. How are you, my dear?'

'I'm fine. It's nice to see you here, milady.'

'I've never seen you look better.'

'Thank you,' said Maggie, bending down to straighten a lock of Jamie's sun-bleached hair. She was still not good at dealing with compliments.

223

For Maggie these months in Florida were a time of healing and joyful surprises. There was so much to be thankful for. Her new-found happiness was a suit of armour which nothing could pierce. She felt freed from care, and even when Mr James came to tell her that her brother Alistair had died in a bombing raid near Glasgow, she was ashamed to find how little grief she felt. She was saddened, certainly, and concerned for Glynis and her grandmother, but it all felt rather far away: a shadow of the prolonged and grinding misery she had suffered after Tom was killed. She wondered whether her present good fortune was making her callous and uncaring.

She posted her letters of condolence later, reflecting as she did so that if her father ordered her home after this second family bereavement, she would need all the callousness she could muster to refuse him. But even this worry soon drifted to the back of her mind. She would think about it when she was back in Maple Valley.

Only when Abby talked about Bert Higgins did she suffer a real pang of misery and guilt. She had never yet summoned up the courage to tell Abby about the death of the boy from Stepney. Some day she would have to do it, but she kept putting it off.

At Dulcimer, when the news of the Higgins tragedy spread, everyone went around in a state of shock and mourning. They felt haunted. Such a wicked waste. If only the children had not run back to London.

The death of the children hit Nanny like a hammer blow. She felt really angry with Bert for going off. She went about her work at the dower house feeling saddened and very old.

After the initial shock, Lord Dulcimer managed to keep cheerful and busy. He disapproved of funeral faces. All the same, Bert kept on popping into his thoughts during those first weeks. There were so many things that brought the boy to mind. He had been so curious and interested in everything, had learned to milk the cows, to change the plugs in the motor car, and could fix the tractor better than most of the farm workers. Even necessary things like going to the downstairs cloakroom brought memory flooding back.

That cloakroom was Lord Dulcimer's special sanctum. None of the staff went in for fear of being roared at, but the earl had come upon Bert there one day. The boy had been gazing spellbound at the large mahogany throne with its decorated enamel pan. He was so admiring and interested, even rhapsodising about the dark Victorian wall tiles which Effie was always wanting to remove, so instead of blasting him, Lord Dulcimer had laughed. The boy wanted to know how the lavatory worked, and where the water came from. Unable to explain these mysteries, Lord Dulcimer sent for the estate handyman.

But life had to go on, and it was no use wringing one's hands. There were other things to worry about, like the lack of proper weapons for the Home Guard. Lord Dulcimer had written to demand rifles for his men. Did they expect them to hold off the Germans with a few shotguns, some pitchforks, homemade catapults and one bow and arrow? Repeated requests yielded five pre-war rifles and a small amount of ammunition. Not enough, but better than nothing, the earl supposed.

There were domestic worries, too. After Christmas, the Dalmatian Walls had been run over by the village bus, and Lady Dulcimer was broken-hearted. Lord Dulcimer even considered getting a puppy to console her, but did not. Feeding even three dogs was a problem in wartime. They did not need a fourth.

Both Dulcimers worried a good deal about Antonia and David. Antonia still felt neglected, and David looked more weary every time they saw him. As the dreary winter dragged on, Antonia suffered two more bouts of influenza which left her thin and more depressed than ever. David came over whenever he could, but he made no secret of wanting to send his wife to America. Antonia was adamant. She would only go to America if David went with her. If he loved her, he would leave the Air Force and take her there.

And now David was in trouble on his own account. Lord Dulcimer listened to what his nephew had to say, and recommended him to go to a Harley Street specialist in London.

'A good man, Daniel Bruce,' he said. 'I was up at Oxford with his elder brother. Come to think of it, I read in *The Times* that he is now some sort of consultant physician to the Royal Air Force. Just the man for you, my boy. Shall I give him a ring and ask him to see you?'

There was a certain bitter irony, David thought, that he had been taken off flying duties only days after he had been awarded a bar to his DFC.

Suffering two blackouts within a week was worrying enough, but when he passed out at fifteen thousand feet he knew that he could no longer keep his condition a secret. He had lost consciousness while piloting a two-seater Beaufighter in the dark, trying to intercept the German bombers that poured across the Channel every night. He had come to himself with the sound of his radar operator yelling over the radio, and the aircraft plunging earthwards. Somehow he managed to pull the machine out of its screaming dive, but he had frightened himself badly – though probably not quite as badly as his radar man. He went to see the station medical officer, and was afterwards sent for by his commanding officer.

He wished that it could have been Douglas, but Douglas had been promoted to wing commander and posted south. In the general shuffle that took place after the Battle of Britain, David had been sent to join a newly formed Beaufighter unit, where the planes had recently been equipped with a not very effective radar system. His new CO was a competent, precise man, who had been in the Air Force since before the war. He had been at staff headquarters at Bentley Priory during the Battle of Britain, and to hear him talk you would think that he had won it single-handed. He was known to have a poor opinion of pilots who regarded themselves as aces. Nor did he care for Americans.

He did not ask David to sit down. 'Well, Vorst,' he said with a tight smile. 'I hear that you nearly lost an aircraft and killed your radar operator yesterday. You seem to have convinced the MO that you had a blackout.'

'Yes, sir. I blacked out completely.'

'Have you sought any other medical advice about these blackouts?'

'So far only the MO.'

'Very well, Vorst. I obviously have no choice but to pass on his report to headquarters. I should tell you, however, that I intend to express my own view about this sudden ailment of yours. In my day your condition would have been diagnosed as a lack of moral fibre.'

David was thunderstruck. LMF was forces jargon for cowardice. He said stiffly, 'Is that so, sir? You are entitled to tell them what you think, of course. Why am I supposed to have invented these black-outs?'

'Do you deny, Vorst, that you told the MO that you were scared stiff, and felt that you needed a break from flying?'

'I was scared all right. Why not? Parker and I were both lucky not to be killed.'

'Quite so. I shall tell headquarters that in my opinion you risked a skilled radar operator and a valuable aircraft in order to make your point. I do not doubt that he will deplore it as much as I do.'

'You may tell him what you damned well like, sir. I shall deny it.'

David left the CO's office fuming, and poured out some of his pent-up wrath to a friend in the mess. Afterwards, he wished he had not, for the members of his squadron were so angry on his behalf that the moderate part of David's nature rose up in alarm. He tried to damp the flames he had kindled, telling them that it was pointless to march in to the CO and protest. It would do more harm than good.

Next day, David was sent on leave – indefinite leave, until a decision was made about what to do with him. The CO was probably anxious to get him out of the way. The squadrons were up on a training flight when he drove away from the airfield. He felt lonely and humiliated, as though his world had come to an end.

'Squadron Leader Vorst, Sir Daniel.'

The eminent physician looked with interest at the thin young man who had just been ushered in. He got up and they shook hands. 'Please sit down, Squadron Leader. Lord Dulcimer rang me, as you know, but he did not tell me much. What can I do for you?'

David sat back in a wide, padded chair and tried to think what to say. He looked up, met the older man's calm eyes, and said baldly, 'I'm in trouble, sir.'

'What sort of trouble?'

'I keep passing out without warning. My commanding officer thinks I have invented or imagined these blackouts because I'm afraid of flying ...' He paused, looking down at his hands. He was mildly pleased to see that they were not shaking. It had cost him something to say all that.

'And are you afraid of flying, Squadron Leader?'

'Why yes, sir. Very much afraid, sometimes, but in a crazy way I love it.' He added with a bleak smile, 'I tried to ignore the way I passed out the first two times, but I nearly killed my radar operator a week ago, so that was that. Now they want to ground me for good.'

'Who wants to?'

'My commanding officer. He thinks I lack moral fibre.'

'Does he indeed?' Sir Daniel pointed to the ribbons adorning David's uniform and said quietly, 'A strange accusation to make to a man with your war record, I should say.'

David shrugged. 'He probably believes it. I'm just as much a coward as anyone, really. It's all a matter of adrenaline.'

'Mm. Is it possible that this man is jealous of your achievements?'

'I don't see why he should be. He just doesn't like Americans, and I don't blame him for that. All the same,' he added, his voice growing clipped and his dark eyes narrowing, 'unless you can prove to me that I'm a nutcase, or find something incurable going on in my head, I mean to fight him. I'll take on the whole Royal Air Force hierarchy if I have to because I sure as hell mean to get flying again.'

'In that case,' said Sir Daniel, 'we'd better not waste time. Tell me about yourself.'

David looked up in surprise. He had never been ill in his life, so he knew nothing of the ways of doctors. He had expected a simple X-ray, or to have his reflexes tested, or for the doctor to take a torch and look into his eyes. He could not imagine how talking about himself was going to get them anywhere.

'What do you want to know?'

'Anything you can think of to tell me.'

'All right, sir. Where do you want me to start?'

'Start at the beginning.'

He had not wanted to go into hospital for tests, but he had gone all the same. He had slept a lot in the quiet annexe beside the Air Force hospital. He and Daniel were now on first name terms, and the specialist visited him every day. At one point David had declared, rather irritably, that Daniel was like a vacuum cleaner, for his mind seemed to have been turned inside out and upside down and shaken, information sucked out of him without him knowing it had been there. He had found himself speaking of things that he had vowed never to tell anyone, and instead of feeling mortified he was conscious of a staggering sense of relief.

It was not all talk. There were X-rays and countless other tests. They were thorough in that Air Force hospital. He saw a neuro-surgeon, a consultant eye man, and other medical gurus. He was subjected to strenuous fitness tests, too. It was tiring, but at the end of each day he just went back to sleep, which after months of inadequate rest was the ultimate luxury. After four days at the hospital, his enforced leave no longer felt like quite such a disaster.

When he got home, Nanny appeared at the door and told him that Antonia was in bed and running yet another temperature. 'I don't like the look of her, Mr David. She never picked up after that last dose of flu, and she won't eat a thing, try as I might to tempt her appetite.'

He went up the stairs two at a time, and found Antonia lying in semi-darkness with the curtains drawn. He knelt down and kissed her, and she put her thin arms round his neck and clung like a frightened child. She felt very hot, and as thin as a baby bird.

'David, what is the matter with me? I think I'm better, then down I go again. Sometimes I wonder if I'm dying.'

'Then stop wondering, honey. You know that doctor I've been to, Sir Daniel Bruce? I told him about you, and he's coming down to look at you on Saturday.'

She said despondently, 'He'll be just like Dr Grundy.'

'He is not the least like Dr Grundy. He's very good-looking, for one thing. I shall be surprised if you don't like him quite a lot, Antonia.'

For a full week David worked tirelessly in the dower house garden, cutting back shrubs, sawing logs, digging. There were signs of spring everywhere. Lord Dulcimer came upon him holding a single wild violet to his nose.

'What did Bruce have to say about you?'

'He's coming to see Antonia. He's staying the night, and will tell me my fate at the same time.'

'Did you like him?'

'More than I expected.'

'That's not saying much. You went off looking as glum as a pig.'

David laughed. 'I was scared, I admit. But Daniel is a good guy. I feel better just for seeing him. With luck, he'll be able to help Antonia too. She thinks he'll just give her another bottle of medicine, but at least she's gone off to have her hair done in his honour.'

'A good sign.'

There was a pause. David got to his feet, and looked at his uncle. The earl looked hesitant, an unusual state for him, and David wondered what was up.

'Is anything the matter, Uncle Bernard?'

'Mm. Two things. Ian Dunlop's other son has been killed. He and his wife were working in a food office in Glasgow, living in Clydebank. It seems that there were hundreds killed in a night. Poor old Dunlop. Rotten luck, really. He set great store by those boys of his. Now he wants me to get Maggie back from America. I had a letter from him yesterday, and he wants me to forward another to Maggie. She is to come home and keep house for him and his mother.'

David wiped his soil-covered hands on the seat of his dungarees and frowned. 'Tell him there's no way of getting her back. You heard what he did to her before she went away. Lucky for him that we rescued the poor kid before he killed her.'

Lord Dulcimer nodded. 'I know it was bad, but the daughter-in-law refuses to come back. Maggie is his daughter, and old Mrs Dunlop is not so strong these days. I cannot understand what came over him. He is so good and gentle with dogs. He must have suffered a brainstorm.'

'You think so? According to the Frasers, Dunlop has bullied Maggie all her life. You ought to have a word with the minister before you do anything, Uncle.'

'He came on the telephone this morning. He feels the same as you do.'

'There you are. Tell Dunlop that you can see no way of getting her back.'

Lord Dulcimer sighed, and said testily, 'Oh, very well. I'll think about it.' There was a pause, and then the earl said abruptly, 'Dart rang up just now. He was at the Vorst Hotel. I gathered that much, at least, but he sounded odd.'

'What sort of odd?'

'Gabbling about Bert and his dog being buried under rubble. Well, I ought to know. I saw the house.'

'But that was in October, Uncle Bernard. Nearly six months ago.'

'That's what I told him, and then the damned telephone went dead. I did wonder whether Dart had been drinking.'

'What else did he tell you?'

'Nothing that I could make head or tail of. I don't want to bother Effie until I find out more. David, do you think Dart could be going off his head?'

'More likely he'd been drowning himself in the Vorst gin.'

Chapter 17

In April 1941, Dart was sent for by the War Office. He hoped that this summons would lead to something new and interesting, and took a train to London on the day before his appointment. Wartime trains were unreliable, particularly when it mattered. Months ago he had left a case full of clothes at the Vorst Hotel, and decided to stay there and ask Odette to dine with him in the restaurant.

He was lucky, for the train steamed into Euston Station no more than thirty minutes late. With only a leather briefcase, it seemed a good idea to walk to Savile Row and visit his tailor. If the regiment were to be sent to North Africa soon, which was highly likely, he would need lightweight uniforms.

He was looking forward eagerly to going abroad. Almost any sort of change would be welcome after spending so many months in Yorkshire. The winter seemed to have gone on for ever, with the discomforts of snow, slush and rain, dreary army quarters and interminable grey skies. The regiment had lost all its tanks and essential equipment in France, and the dreary winter weather and general lack of action had undermined the men's morale. It was the same in the officers' mess. Tempers and nerves became frayed, and quarrels had broken out over the most trivial things. But in the past month matters had got better. Supplies started arriving in more satisfactory quantities, and there was a general bustle and a feeling of hope.

The tailor assured Dart that his uniforms would be ready for a first fitting within a week. He apologised for the dust everywhere. There had been a raid during the night, and the charwoman had not come in. A most reliable woman. She lived in Balham, and he only hoped that she was all right after the raid. They had cleared up as best they could, but with so many gentlemen needing lightweight uniforms in a hurry this past week, he and his two elderly assistants had been too busy to do a thorough job.

Dart commiserated, thanked him, and escaped down the street. He had not visited London since Christmas, and noticed many new signs of bomb damage. One building in Piccadilly was still smouldering from last night's attack, and a pall of smoke hung over the rooftops. The air was thick with dust and a throat-catching smell of burning.

When he was halfway down St James's Street, a demolitions lorry went by, with three tin-hatted men standing in the back.

The lorry slowed down and turned in towards the Vorst Hotel, and Dart followed it a few minutes later. For a moment he thought that the hotel must have been hit, but peering through a dust cloud at the end of the street, he found that he was mistaken. The demolitions lorry had drawn up beyond the Vorst, and the dust was thickest where there had once been a boarded-up bomb site. He thought it odd that a second bomb should hit the very same place. Talk about lightning striking twice! Rubble and broken boards were strewn all over the road, and a knot of people had assembled to see what was going on.

'The back wall collapsed in the night,' said one of them. 'It was the blast from that one in the park what did it. They should never've left that wall standing. I told them over and over.'

'What are they trying to do?'

'Clearing the road, most likely.'

Another woman, nearer the front of the crowd, said. 'The warden thinks there's somebody trapped under there.'

Two wardens came forward dragging a makeshift barrier of trestles, and the crowd were told to stand back. Reluctantly they began to withdraw, but Dart wanted to get to his hotel, and went up to the warden who seemed to be in charge.

'Let me past please, warden. I have an appointment at the Vorst Hotel which I cannot afford to miss.'

The warden looked at Dart, and for a moment seemed about to refuse, but a fierce altercation between the demolition crew and another air raid warden took his attention and made him change his mind.

'Get on with you, then, but don't hang about. There might be another collapse.'

Dart went as far as the hotel door, but paused there without going in, curious to watch the sideshow.

One of the demolition crew was talking loudly. He sounded weary and disgruntled. 'Look, mate, six major emergency calls have come in during the past hour. This 'ere building was bombed more'n four months ago. You say the remaining wall fell down. D'you expect us to prop it up for you? Is that what you call an emergency?'

'There may be somebody alive under there,' said the warden. 'That's why we sent for you.'

'After four months? Come off it.'

Another of the demolition crew said urgently, 'Come on, Bill, we're wasting our time here. Let's get on.'

A tin-hatted policeman joined the group. 'Now then. What's the trouble?'

'There's someone under there, officer. I'm sure of it. There's a dog sniffing and whining. He'd not do that if there wasn't something there.'

'The remains of a jam sandwich, most like,' said someone else. 'The dog will be a bombed-out stray.'

Dart had by this time come up to them, and peered past at the scene of the collapse. Where the dust was thickest he saw movement, and made out the form of a large dog. The animal was digging furiously, and as Dart watched, it threw back its head and emitted a howl. He went forward to look more closely.

There was a shout behind him. 'Don't go in there, you fool! It's not safe.'

Dart took no notice, for there was something familiar about the dog, grey with dust though it was. He clambered over a high stone block to get a closer look, oblivious of the shouts behind him.

'Wat?' he called on a sharply questioning note. 'Wat, come here, boy!'

For an instant the dog turned his head. He gave a small wag of his tail, before resuming his frantic scrabbling.

The policeman picked his way over a mound of rubble and joined him. 'Now, sir, just come out of there, if you please. You heard what the warden said.'

Dart seized the policeman's arm and shook it. 'I know that dog, officer. He wouldn't dig for nothing. Tell them they've got to make sure there's nobody alive under there. If they won't, I'll start digging myself.'

Bert Higgins awoke to find himself in the dark. Something heavy was holding him down. He had dreamed that they had got him out from under that wall, so it was a crushing disappointment to know that he was still buried. For a moment panic made it hard to breathe – or was it the heavy thing on top of him? He wanted to shout, but lacked the strength to do it.

Then whatever was squashing him moved, and something rough and wet was licking his face. Wat? So Wat had not after all darted out of the way when the wall started to collapse. He ought to be sorry, but it was a comfort to have the dog there with him after all they had gone through together. He opened one eye, and saw the dog's woolly face very close to his own. For some reason he could not raise his arms to hug him, but this did not matter because he was suddenly, gloriously aware of his mistake. He was no longer buried. He was lying in a proper bed, and although his head ached horribly, he was no longer cold. Turning his head painfully, he could make out the outline of a door, and a dim glow of light beyond it. He was in a proper house for the first time for months, with tall curtained windows, and Wat was sprawling on top of him, a ton weight, very much alive.

Bert turned his face into Wat's furry neck, and wept with relief. It was the first time he had allowed himself to cry unrestrainedly since the October day when he had walked away from Cotton Street for the last time.

It was daylight when he next awoke. The tall curtains had been drawn back, and a pale April sun projected a magic lantern reflection of window panes and bare branches upon the bedroom wall. He still felt too weak to worry about where he was or how he had come there. He was safe and warm, and Wat lay quiet with his shaggy head on the pillow beside him. It was an odd sensation, this drifting and letting go after months of being on the run from school inspectors and policemen, of trying to keep warm and finding safe places to sleep. For what seemed half a lifetime he had been scrounging food for Wat and himself, keeping just one step ahead of the busybodies who wanted to take him into care and send Wat away. Soon, he supposed, he would have to move again. But not yet. Not just yet. Despite his many aches and pains, Bert slept.

He woke later, conscious that people were in the room. He kept still, feigning sleep. It seemed best.

Lord Dartmore's voice spoke somewhere above his head. Bert would have known that voice anywhere. 'I must get back, Odette. I can only spare a few minutes, and then I won't be returning for several weeks. I'm damned sorry to have brought this on you without warning. I've been kicking myself. When I carried the boy in last night, I was afraid you were going to pass out.'

'It was nothing. Just a passing foolishness.'

'I should have rung to warn you from the hospital, but there was no time. The matron refused to keep the dog in the hospital overnight, so as soon as Bert's leg and arm had been set, I decided to snatch both boy and dog. If I had not been so angry, it might have been funny. A doctor and the witch of a matron chased me down the hall, the doctor shouting that Bert's plaster was still wet and that I couldn't take him away, and the matron threatening to send for the police. Two nurses came out of a doorway and twittered, and Matron told the hospital porter to stop me going out of the door.

'I was sorry for that porter. He started towards me with his arms outstretched, but Wat snarled at him, and he backed off smartly. The poor chap had to decide whether to obey the dog or the matron. In the end he just goggled at us as we went out. This dog saved Bert's life, you know. Not a doubt of it. I couldn't let them send him off to the dog pound. So you see . . .'

'Do not concern yourself, Lord Dartmore. We will manage. Mrs Cornberg will help me to nurse the boy, and the hall porter likes dogs. He will take it out in the park. But please do not leave the boy with us long.'

'Only for a day or so, I promise. As soon as Bert is well enough to be moved, he can go to Dulcimer. Father will fetch them. I tried to ring home to tell him Bert was found, but we were cut off. It always happens when I really need to get through . . .'

The voices faded. Bert lay there, his eyes still closed. He knew that he must pull himself together and work out what to do. But he was no nearer to doing so when another wave of sleep washed him under.

Odette saw Dart off, and went back to her office. Work was always the best therapy for her, and she was not sorry to learn that three key members of the hotel staff had failed to come in that morning. This meant working in the kitchens until noon, and then she had to supervise the restaurant throughout an extended luncheon hour. As the day wore on she felt like dropping with fatigue, for she was not sleeping well, but at least there was no time to think. It was not until early evening that she was once more reminded of Bert Higgins.

Stebbings was crossing the lobby with Bert's dog at his heels. She frowned and said sharply, 'I told you to keep that dog on a lead.'

'I know you did, madame. But he won't let me.'

'I cannot allow a dog to run loose around the hotel.'

'That's as may be, madame. When I tried to put the lead on him he growled something horrible. Lucky for me the boy woke up before I had me arm bitten off.'

'If the dog is savage, it will have to be shut up.'

'He was no trouble after the boy told 'im to go with me.'

Odette looked at the dog, who looked back, panting slightly. She said wearily, 'We will talk of this later, Stebbings. Next time, be sure to take the dog out by the staff door.'

She sat in an armchair in her sitting room, trying to put her thoughts and emotions in order. She decided that coffee might help. It was utterly foolish to be so deeply disturbed by the arrival of the Higgins boy and his dog.

Mrs Cornberg brought coffee, and she sipped it gratefully. She was less grateful for the housekeeper's rambling dissertation about Bert. It went on until she felt like screaming. Mrs Cornberg thought he must have been starved before his accident, and embarked on a catalogue of the food she had given him during the day. Odette sat through this recital, willing Mrs Cornberg to go away.

'The poor lad lost his whole family in an air raid back in the autumn, madame. No wonder he sets store by that dog. It's the only family he's got left.'

Odette said evenly, 'So Lord Dartmore told me.'

'It will be nice to have a youngster among us, won't it?' Odette looked up sharply, and at the sight of the Frenchwoman's face the housekeeper broke off. Her highly coloured face flushed, and she said rather huffily, 'Oh well, I'd better get on, madame. I've still the bedrooms to check before I can put my feet up. I'm all behind, with having to look after the boy all day. You won't forget to give him his next lot of pills, will you?'

'I will not forget, Mrs Cornberg.'

Odette sat still, trying to be calm and reasonable, ashamed of betraying her rage at the housekeeper's tactless remark. She was ashamed, too, of the feeling of revulsion that assailed her at the mere mention of Bert Higgins's name. It was ridiculous. She had offended both Stebbings and Mrs Cornberg. She would normally have thanked them warmly for helping her with Lord Dartmore's strays, but she had not, and they had been affronted. Actually, she had wanted to murder them, just as she had wanted to shout and rail at Lord Dartmore when he asked her to take charge of a strange injured boy.

They would never understand. Why should they? She did not understand it herself. All she knew was that ever since they told her that Josef and Marie were dead, lost at sea when their ship was torpedoed, Odette had dreaded being with children. To her tormented mind, every little girl was Marie, and she saw Josef in all skinny, dark-haired boys. She wondered if losing the children and grieving for them for so many months had finally unbalanced her mind. Some part of her brain had never accepted that they were dead. When Lord Dartmore came in with an unconscious boy in his arms, she had believed for one mad moment that he was bringing Josef to her.

Darting forward, she had recoiled almost as rapidly. It was not Josef. She had, as Dart had seen, been close to passing out. The feeling of faintness soon passed, to be replaced by raw pain and an irrational and savage resentment that this injured boy looked enough like Josef to have deceived her. She did not want to look at him, or keep him in the hotel. Still less did she want to nurse him.

She reached for the telephone, and after at least a dozen rings Stebbings answered. The switchboard woman had gone home, he said. He sounded put upon. She asked him to put through a call to David Vorst's number at the dower house, for David was the one person who might be able help her. A few minutes later the telephone bell rang shrilly. It was Stebbings again, announcing in a voice of gloomy triumph that there was no reply from the dower house.

Sir Daniel Bruce arrived in Sussex on Saturday morning, and David left him alone with Antonia. Coming in from the garden later, he found that his wife had mislaid the idea that she hated all doctors. David was relieved that they got on so well, and sat contentedly watching his wife smile and laugh and chatter to the eminent physician throughout luncheon. Antonia was much too thin, of course, but today she had lost the look of drooping exhaustion which he had found alarming. True, she had swayed a little and had to be supported by the doctor's arm when they made their way to the dining room, but her blue eyes were bright and alert. There was even a little colour in her cheeks, and not all of it due to a skilful application of rouge.

Nanny came in and plonked a rhubarb tart in front of Antonia, saying, 'I can see Lord Dartmore coming up the path, madam. Shall I tell him to come back when you have finished talking with Sir Daniel?'

But Antonia was over at the window in a flash, waving and beckoning. 'Goodness! What a day of surprises!' She explained to the doctor that Dart was David's cousin, and that she had not seen him for weeks. 'You won't mind if he joins us, will you, Daniel?'

'Not at all. Lord Dartmore can keep you happy while I talk to David.'

They left Dart and Antonia drinking coffee, and went along the hall. All too familiar wires of tension pulled at David's nerves as he ushered his guest into the fire-lit morning room. This was like the start of a sortie, only worse. Was this the end? Was he about to be told that he would never fly a plane again? It had happened to others. How would he handle it? It would be death to all his hopes and ambitions. The carriage clock on the mantel shelf struck the half hour. It sounded like a miniature knell of doom.

The two men disposed themselves in armchairs beside the fire, and David said with a quick, tight smile, 'Tell me first what you make of Antonia. It seems to have done her good to meet you.'

'We will talk about you first,' said Sir Daniel firmly. 'I had a conference with my colleagues at the hospital, and to tell you the truth, we don't think there is much wrong with you. Nothing that cannot be cured by a month free of strain, and lots of fresh air and exercise. You've been pushing yourself beyond tolerable limits for months, that's all.'

David stared at him and said with a touch of impatience, 'Well, sure I pushed myself. Everybody has to, and we all get tired. But that doesn't explain why I started blacking out.'

'That's where you are wrong. The human brain has a built-in warning system, and was plainly telling you to call a halt.'

'Call a halt? It damned nearly bumped us both off! Now stop filibustering, Daniel. Are you trying to break it to me that I won't be able to fly again?'

'Unless I am much mistaken, you will be flying again by midsummer. Go away for six weeks, and then come back and see me. I wish I could send you somewhere warm like the south of France, but failing that, don't the Dulcimers have a place in Scotland? You could fish, shoot a few rabbits for the pot, and walk on the moors. Why not take Antonia with you and have the honeymoon you never managed to have?'

David shook his head. Not Glen Cary, he thought. He had a sudden recollection of himself and Mr Fraser labouring to carry big Maggie Dunlop out of her father's house, and of the burly head keeper barring their way. He had thrust Maggie at the sister-in-law, and knocked the man down with a straight left to his jaw. It had cleared their path and had been satisfying, but it would be awkward going back.

He said, 'That won't do. Antonia would be bored out of her mind at Glen Cary.' Then he added, 'How is she, Daniel? We're all very worried about her.'

'Nothing that a holiday and a bit of cosseting won't cure. I get a lot of patients these days in the same state of war weariness.'

'I want to send her to my mother in Maple Valley but she won't go.'

The doctor looked at David thoughtfully. 'She might go if you went with her . . .'

Nanny went into the dining room. She found Dart and Antonia smoking companionably at the disordered table, and neither of them showing any inclination to leave.

'Why not take madam out into the garden, milord,' she said, clearing a space for her tray. 'It's a lovely day, and she could do with some fresh air.'

'It's freezing out, Nanny,' Antonia protested. 'You know I can't afford to catch another cold.'

'Then take his lordship into the morning room. I need to clear up in here. It's past three o'clock, and I've to go down to the Hall later.'

'That's no good. Sir Daniel and David are talking secrets in the morning room.'

'Not any more. They've gone out through the French windows. Don't you want to join them and find out what Sir Daniel had to say? If you wrap up warm and keep moving, a little walk in the sun won't hurt you.'

'Oh, Nanny . . .'

Dart smiled at Nanny and stood up. 'Better do as we're told. Come on, Tonia. Where's your coat? I must say,' he added presently, as he wound a warm muffler round her neck, 'your session with that good-looking doctor has done you good. I hope Daniel Bruce's verdict on David is favourable, because I've come to ask his help. How does he seem to you?'

'He was never really ill, or so he says,' she replied, as they headed outside. 'He just had these frightening blackouts, and they took him off flying. Long may they continue to do so!'

'I wonder . . .' Dart looked thoughtfully towards David and Daniel Bruce who were strolling back in their direction. He turned to Antonia. 'I saw a man in the War Office this week. They are sending me to

Washington. I can't go into details, but in general my visit will be to drum up support and supplies from the Americans, and afterwards to visit some Canadian Air Force training schools. If David is well enough, he could be a great help in Canada. What would you say to a few weeks' holiday in Long Island with David?'

'At Maple Valley, you mean? Will you be there?'

'I'll probably manage to get away at weekends.'

'It sounds like heaven to me,' said Antonia.

It was the middle of April before the British children returned to Long Island. They came back to a changed world. No longer were there bare trees and frost. The dogwoods were flowering in the gardens and the woods – bursts of magic here and there, rivers and drifts of blossom, snow white, palest pink and vivid carmine. Maggie liked the white dogwoods best. There were carpets of daffodils, too, and washes of bluebells and pale windflowers under the trees. Birds were nesting, making a racket overhead.

Maggie set off through the gardens on her way to take tea with Miss Gladys, singing softly as she went along. Two gardeners were scything grass beside the lily pond, and she waved and smiled at them out of sheer happiness.

She remembered arriving at Maple Valley, way back last August. Then she had been an overweight frightened child, bruised in body and spirit, totally lacking assurance. Since that time, she had grown up and changed – and was as much transformed as the Maple Valley gardens.

It was not wholly clear to her how this change had come about. Physically she was slender and fit, and the Florida sun had given her skin and hair a golden glow. She no longer shunned mirrors. Last year she would never have smiled and waved at those gardeners. She would have slunk past them with eyes lowered, hoping not to be noticed.

This growing up had crept up on her, but she knew one thing for certain. The real start and cause of her present happiness was her good fortune in coming to America. Unlike poor Miss Brimley, who was more homesick than ever, she had no yearning to return to Britain. One day, perhaps, she would find the courage to go home and face her father – but not yet.

Miss Gladys was waiting for her, and Maggie ran up the path and was in her friend's arms. Maggie did so love James's sister. She never changed. It was thanks to Miss Gladys that Maggie was now a competent dressmaker, so she had put on a dress that she had made while in Florida, hoping that her tutor would approve.

Miss Gladys smiled. 'I like it, my dear, and by the look of you, Florida must have suited you very well. Come right in. James is having his tea early because he has to drive Mr and Mrs Vorst to Bellefield. You and I can enjoy a gossip together while he's away.'

James was on the telephone. 'All right, May. At a quarter to five, you say? No. I won't say a word, if that's the way he wants it. I'll ask Maggie.' He put a hand over the telephone mouthpiece and said, 'Maggie. May Sandridge wants you to meet some people at the airport. I know it's your day off, but would you mind?'

'I would love to, Mr James,' said Maggie, beaming. She had not expected to be given driving jobs now that she was back at Maple Valley. There were others whose responsibility it was to ferry people about.

James nodded, and said into the mouthpiece, 'She says she will. I'll tell her to call by your office in good time.'

He put the telephone back on its hook, and passed his cup to Miss Gladys for a refill. Miss Gladys scolded him for making Maggie work on her day off. 'Besides, I want to hear what she's been getting up to in Florida.'

'She can come another day,' said James, gulping his tea and getting to his feet. He picked up his peaked cap and driving gloves. 'You'll take the new Cadillac convertible, Maggie. Jason is filling it with gasoline and washing it, and will bring it round. He will follow in the station wagon and bring the bags. That way you can bring your passengers straight back.'

Maggie stared. 'You w-want me to drive the new car, Mr James? I thought it was only delivered yesterday.'

'That's right. It's a beauty. I had it out this morning.'

'But how shall I know these people, Mr James?' asked Maggie, rather anxiously.

'You'll know them all right, Maggie.'

And then he relented, and told her who it was she was being sent to meet.

Maggie got to the airport in good time, left Jason in charge of both automobiles, and went to engage a porter with a large wagon. Then she stood on the balcony overlooking the water and watched as a small dot on the horizon grew larger, and the drone of engines swelled from a murmur to a roar. Knowing nothing about sea planes, she watched in some trepidation as the aircraft circled, straightened out, and landed on the water, throwing up twin wings of surging spray. For a moment it looked as if it had sunk, but it reappeared, turned slowly and headed briskly towards two US Army motor launches which were waiting to meet it. Maggie watched, fascinated, as the first launch guided the plane to a large buoy. Within minutes a larger launch had nosed its way forward.

It was a slick operation. An officer ran up steps into the plane, and after a pause re-emerged with three passengers. These were deftly handed into the launch. Maggie turned from the balcony rail and went quickly down the staircase to join the porter. Her heart was thumping as loud as a drum.

'They said we would be met,' said David Vorst, striding in ahead of the others. He was wearing civilian clothes, and he looked about him with a frown. He wanted to get Antonia home and into bed without delay. She was close to exhaustion.

He was looking for James, or for May Sandridge, but could see neither. A tall brown-haired girl smiled at him. He nodded at her absently and let his gaze move on past.

'Good evening, Mr David,' the girl said. 'Mrs Sandridge sent me.'

David stared in mingled surprise and relief. He shook the girl's hand and said, 'Thank you. My wife is not well, so they're bringing her in a wheelchair. Have you got another car for the bags? Good. I want to get Antonia to Maple Valley and into bed. That's why I cabled Mrs Sandridge and asked her not even to tell my parents that we were coming. She needs quiet and rest. Lord Dartmore is flying straight on to Washington, but we won't wait to see him off.'

'Whatever you say, sir. Jason is waiting outside and will follow with the bags when they're ready.'

They turned to see a drooping and very frail Antonia being pushed in a wheelchair, and Lord Dartmore looking impossibly healthy and handsome in the uniform of a British Army major. Maggie was used to going weak at the knees at the sight of her childhood hero, and she still thought him the epitome of glamour. Her knees, however, gave her no trouble.

She said with outward composure. 'Good evening, madam. Good evening, my lord.' She looked at David. 'If everybody is ready, shall we go?'

'Fine,' he said. 'Lead on and we'll follow.'

Mrs Sandridge met them at the front door of Maple Valley House, her face illumined by a warm smile. She took one look at the sleeping Antonia and said quietly, 'I am sorry she has been ill, but all the same, David, this is a wonderful surprise! We've put you in the Chinese wing. You can be as quiet as you like there. Will you go up right away? Take your mother's elevator.'

'No need,' said David. 'Antonia weighs next to nothing these days and won't wake if I carry her.' He eased his frail burden out of the car, settled Antonia more comfortably in his arms, and set off up the steps of the house.

Some time later he left Antonia sleeping under the watchful eye of a white-clad nurse and went to shower and change in the adjoining dressing room. Once changed, he decided to go downstairs, but found someone waiting for him in the passage. It was the girl who had driven them from the airport.

'May I speak with you, Mr David?'

'Fine,' he said, wondering what she could want. 'How can I help you?'

'It's about Abby,' Maggie said tensely. Her voice was shaking, and she blushed in her agitation. 'She still doesn't know about Bert Higgins and Wat being killed last winter. I . . . I never told her, because I knew she would be upset. I should have told her, of course . . .'

David did not speak. He was looking at her intently, his dark brows drawn together.

The frown was unnerving, and Maggie faltered, 'I am very sorry, sir. I should have told her but I kept putting it off. I wanted to warn you though, because she is bound to ask for news of Bert . . .'

All at once he knew her. She looked quite different, but her soft Scots voice was uniquely her own and had not changed. 'Maggie? It *is* Maggie, isn't it? I'm sorry, I was only thinking of Antonia back at the airport. I didn't realise it was you.'

She merely nodded, and said impatiently, 'It's no matter. I just came to warn you that the children may come back any minute. Mr David, how are we going to break it to her about Bert?'

He smiled at her. 'No need to break it. There's wonderful news. Bert and Wat were found only last week. They've been living rough all winter, running away from the authorities who wanted to separate them. Right now they're together at Dulcimer.'

He saw that she had gone pale, her grey eyes suddenly dark with shock. 'Alive? That can't be right. Nanny wrote months ago to say that their house had been bombed . . .' She rocked back on her heels, blindly putting out a hand for something to hold onto.

He took her groping hand, turned her about and pushed her into his dressing room and into a chair. 'Here. Put your head down on your knees.'

She resisted the pressure of his hand behind her head. 'It's all right. I'm not the fainting type. Tell me again, please. Was Nanny wrong? You say they are alive? Truly?'

He said soberly, 'She was right about the rest of Bert's family. We thought Bert and Wat had bought it too, but he's fine – except for a broken arm and leg. That dog of Abby's saved his life. Get Dart to tell you about it when he comes back from Washington. It's quite a story.' He saw that she still did not believe him, so he smiled at her encouragingly and gave her hand a shake. Her fingers felt icy within his grasp. 'Bert's fine, Maggie, no kidding! You don't have to worry any more about telling Abby.'

241

'Oh, thank God! Thank God!' said Maggie, and this time she did put her head down and burst into a torrent of tears.

The lordlings were back, brown and healthy, and full of their winter holiday adventures. Miss Fortescue was back too, gracious and condescending to all, particularly to Miss Brimley and the others – a queen returning to greet her less fortunate subjects. She treated them to glowing accounts of the wealth and the charm of their hosts in Tucson who – as she informed them – were well-known leaders of society in Washington DC, on intimate terms with all the best people, from the President and Mrs Roosevelt down. Many important guests had come to stay at their vacation home during the winter, and she and her boys had been introduced to them. If Miss Fortescue was to be believed, the three lordlings had been a bit of a showpiece.

'Having no aristocracy of their own,' their governess announced to the room at large, 'they were very interested to hear about the duke and duchess and their way of life. They wanted to know all about the castle, too, with its moat and eighty bedrooms . . .'

Presently she added, 'Ever so many people remarked on how well-behaved my boys were, and asked me how I did it. I told them that it was a matter of training and discipline. But of course it won't do any good for them to know that. You know how these Americans spoil their children . . .' She paused, her attention diverted by an irregularity at the far end of the red drawing room. In her parade ground voice she commanded, 'Alfred! Come back at once! Just where do you think you are going?'

But she was too late. The door had closed behind a trampling bevy of children who had just fled from the room – the only sound coming from an incensed Kim, who was dragged out forcibly by the others.

'If I'd stayed any longer I'd have been sick,' said Abby after they had retreated to the relative safety of one of the hall window embrasures.

'That ghastly old snob!' said Kim, rubbing her arm crossly. 'Why did you grab me like that? I only wanted to ask her why she didn't stay away if she found it so wonderful. What harm in that?'

Abby and a still scarlet-faced lordling exchanged glances. 'No harm to you, you spoiled Yankee darling, but plenty for us,' Abby retorted.

After a short, offended pause, Kim joined in the laughter. 'What was it like out there?' she asked the number one lordling curiously. 'Was it fun?'

'It was all right,' said Alfred, with his usual caution. 'But we had to keep changing our clothes. I like it better here.'

After two days, it was decided that the nurse was no longer needed. Antonia lay back against her lace-trimmed pillows and watched under lowered lids while Maggie the nursery maid moved quietly about the room. David was right. The girl had changed since coming to America. She must have lost stones in weight, and it was no wonder David had not recognised her at the airport. As he said himself, his only thought had been how best to get her, Antonia, safely into bed.

Dear David. He could not do enough for her now that he was away from England and the everlasting RAF duties that had turned him from being a delightful companion into really rather a bore. He was almost like his old self again, the doting young man that she had married – and after last night she no longer feared that the war had made her husband impotent. Rather the reverse, she reflected, with a delighted wriggle of pleasure. It had been ages before she had been allowed to go to sleep.

Dr Daniel had told her that a change of scene would restore him. He also said that David would be well enough to fly again in six weeks, but Antonia had made up her mind that it was going to be a great deal longer than that.

There was a knock at the bedroom door. Maggie went to open it, and Antonia saw her children grouped there, peering at her a little anxiously, in case she was asleep. She smiled and held out her arms to them, and within moments they were all ensconced on her silk-hung four-poster bed. She found it delightful to have her children about her again. She had not realised how much she had been missing them. Little Jamie was delicious, nearly as beautiful as Miles, with an enchanting lisp, and both boys were golden-skinned and with hair bleached almost white by Florida sun. Even Abby, though covered with freckles, was full of smiles and affectionate in her manner.

David came in and kissed her. 'You ought to be painted together like that. Shall we keep your mother in bed up here for ever?' he asked the children. He added, 'Don't be in too much of a hurry to get better, my darling. We like having you to ourselves.'

'What about Aunt Chrissie coming to visit you here, Mummy?' suggested Abby, who never remembered her mother looking so lovely or so happy. She had not scolded any of them even once.

'My mother will have to wait,' said David firmly. 'Aunt Chrissie quite understands, Abby, that Antonia has been ill and needs time to regain her strength. It was a long, tiring flight for her. I was pretty tired myself.'

'But that was the day before yesterday,' said Abby. 'You look quite all right to me, Mum.'

'Abby darling, if you argue, you will have to go away,' said Antonia in a faint voice. 'I was hoping that you had grown out of the habit.'

Abby might have retorted in kind, but was diverted by the arrival of Mary-Jo and Maggie with two luncheon trays. David preferred to eat upstairs with his wife whenever she was awake. Maggie took the children away.

As the bedroom door closed, David said, 'We must do something about that girl. The letter from Dunlop is ticking away like a time bomb in my briefcase.'

'What's the hurry? You've evidently made up your mind that she ought not to go back to Scotland.'

'True. All the same, her only remaining brother has been killed in the Clydebank blitz, and I don't even know if she's been told.'

'Tell her yourself then,' said Antonia impatiently, putting down her fork and lying back against the pillows, 'and have done with it.'

'I'll probably ask James's advice,' said David, deciding to do just that. This was the third time that he had broached the subject of Maggie with his wife. He sighed. Better not to pursue the subject. She never encouraged him to talk about other women – certainly not if he happened to admire them – and on the whole he was careful not to do so. He had blundered over Maggie. Had it been naive of him to expect Antonia to share his pleasure in the way the Scots girl looked after nine months in Maple Valley? Even when plump, the child had been charmingly soft-spoken, with a nice smile and good grey eyes, but these days she was truly lovely and carried herself with an air of smiling assurance.

He stifled another sigh. Antonia was lying back, watching him from under her preposterously long lashes, doubtless waiting for him to suggest that she should eat her salmon soufflé. Coaxing Antonia to eat had become a bit of a chore.

How would she react if he told her that for all he cared she could starve? It would not have been true, of course, but Antonia had used her lack of appetite as a weapon for months now – ever since her first bout of flu – and he was tired of being solicitous. His tenderness and concern seemed only to bore her. Dart would have known how to handle her. If Dart had married Antonia, she would never have carried on like this.

'Eat your soufflé, Antonia,' he said with unusual curtness. 'Otherwise you won't be well enough to dine downstairs when Dart comes back from Washington.'

Cornelius and Chrissie Vorst grew daily more nervous at the prospect of meeting Antonia. Every day they braced themselves to meet her, and still she remained upstairs. Cornelius watched Chrissie fretting, and grew angry.

Nobody but Cornelius knew just how upset Chrissie had been when they learned of David's marriage to Antonia Cary. For several nights in a row, Chrissie had been unable to sleep. She kept saying that someone

244

should have stopped the marriage. Effie must have seen what was coming.

Cornelius had pointed out that they had little choice but to accept the situation, and Chrissie had reluctantly agreed. Still, Cornelius was aware that the meeting between Chrissie and Antonia was likely to be precarious. He was beginning to think that only a miracle would save it from disaster.

It had been a week of miracles, beginning with the heart-stopping moment when they came home and saw their younger son waiting at the door. The Cary children had been ecstatic to learn that their mother had come to Maple Valley and would have rushed upstairs, but David told them that they must wait until morning to see her.

Chrissie wept for joy on David's chest. It was too good to be true. Only later did she have a chance to look at him properly, and suffered an acute spasm of alarm at the change in his appearance.

'I hardly recognised him, except for his likeness to my father. He looks so much older, Corney!'

'Naturally. It's three years since he went to Europe. He *is* older. He is a grown man with a wife and three stepchildren. He certainly seems very worried about Antonia.'

Chrissie sighed. 'Oh dear. This suspense is dreadful. What if I dislike her on sight? Effie found her very tiresome when she was married to Johnnie.'

'Forget Effie and her letters, dearest. Even Effie would admit that Johnnie Cary was not perfect. What matters now is that Antonia is married to David, and for his sake we must give her our support and love.'

'You cannot switch love on and off like a light.'

'You can try, dearest. Antonia may be just as scared of meeting you.'

'Scared? I doubt it. Antonia was after Dart in the first place, and only grabbed our son because Dart wouldn't have her. She must be pretty tough to have carried that off.'

It was another day before Antonia felt ready to face the world. She came into the orangerie where Chrissie and Cornelius were drinking tea. David gave her hand a squeeze, before releasing it.

She paused for a moment in the doorway. Her pallor and evident fragility were as startling as her silvery beauty, but it was her air of wide-eyed apprehension that went to Chrissie's tender heart. Corney was right. The child looked frightened to death, as though expecting to meet with rejection, or worse.

'My dear! Are you feeling rested?'

'Oh yes!' said Antonia, moving forward with eager graceful steps. 'Thank you for letting me sleep so long.' Then she went down on her knees beside Chrissie's chair and held out both hands in a supplicating gesture, 'Aunt Chrissie, you must hate me for marrying your David, but he's such a darling and I love him so much. Please try to forgive me.'

David had never doubted that his parents would welcome Antonia with warmth and kindness. As it was, within a few days they were completely captivated by their new daughter-in-law. Dart arrived in Maple Valley for the weekend, and stood watching Antonia and Cornelius laughing and flirting together on a sofa at the other end of the room. Cornelius loved pretty young women. They made him feel young again.

'A remarkable recovery,' Dart said with a twisted grin. 'It seems that your little cat thrives on Maple Valley cream. I rather thought she would. Antonia has always craved adulation.'

David handed Dart his drink, and picked up his own. 'She looks more like herself. How was your visit to Washington?'

'Interesting. Just now I'm feeling my way. Washington is unknown territory to me.'

'How come? Was there nobody at the British Embassy to give you the gen? I had visions of the diplomatic world turning out in force.'

'Oh, I was wined and dined, and had a half-hour with Mr Roosevelt, but it's not going to be easy.' He studied David's uncommunicative profile. His cousin's face was all angles and shadows these days, and he looked older than his twenty-four years. Dart had not been ten minutes in the house before his Aunt Chrissie had taken him aside to tell him she was worried about David's health. He glanced at her. 'I might need your help when you're feeling better.'

'I'm fine now. What sort of help do you think I can give you?'

There was a diversion. Tina and Bill Faber came in, and there was a rush of barking dachshunds and noisy family embraces. Wilding and one of the footmen came in too, so David was no longer needed as a dispenser of drinks. He went to join Dart and the Fabers.

'You started to tell me that you wanted help. What sort of help?'

'Would you come with me to Washington? You could open some doors there, I believe.'

David shook his dark head. 'I'm no politician, and I don't know any influential people. Conway's your man for that.'

Dart looked doubtful. He and his cousin Conway had never got on. 'You think he would? David, could you ask him for me?'

'Not a hope. Con would never lift a finger for my asking. But Tina might help you, if you're nice to her.'

Dart put an arm round Tina's trim waist. 'Tina! Admit! I have always been nice to you.'

'So I recall. You were always charming when you wanted something, Dart darling. Even the stage leer is the same.'

David laughed. 'He wants inside gen about Washington. He's come to charm the birds out of the trees on Capitol Hill. His problem is, which birds out of which trees? We think Conway might advise if you could ask him.'

Tina's brows drew together. 'He might. I wonder, Dart, do you know someone called Adele Devenish? You do? Well, you should talk to her about getting Conway's help. They've been seeing a lot of each other. He even brought her to Florida.'

Dart and David burst out laughing. Dart said incredulously, 'That beanpole? You don't say.'

Tina smiled back. 'I do say! It's true.'

'Conway could never stand British people or British voices,' said David, stating a fact. 'Tina, you're making this up!'

She shook her head. 'I didn't believe it myself until I saw them together. Beanpole or not, Adele looks different. Her hair is nicely cut, and she dresses better. Conway told me that it was all his doing.'

'Incredible!'

'So Adele is the one to ask. It's worth a try.'

David chuckled. 'Well worth it. I can't wait to see Adele succumbing to the Dartmore charm . . .'

'Damn you, David!'

'. . . And if you end up with a crick in your neck from looking up at her, Mother will fix you up with her masseuse.'

Tina told them that they were both abominable and that Adele was no taller than Dart. 'You'll see what I mean when they come over for the polo match,' she assured them.

'Yeah,' said David. 'Meadowbrook against Maple Valley – the first match of the season, and especially for us. Dart, has Father told you that you are a key member of the family team?'

Dart shrugged. 'He has. I told him to get someone else. I've not played since the war started. But he didn't listen.'

'He's remarkably deaf when it suits him. You and I had better put in a bit of practice if we're not to make fools of ourselves. Do you mind coming down to the stables early? I told them eight a.m.'

Dart was surprised. 'Are you up to playing polo? I thought you'd been told to take fresh air and gentle exercise.'

'I'd rather play polo than sit about socialising and watching others. Mother has started clucking, of course.'

'She doesn't think you look well,' murmured Dart, glancing once more at his aunt. 'Something tells me she won't like you going to Canada either.'

'She certainly won't. Why do you need to go to Canada?' demanded Tina curiously. 'Are you going fishing?'

Dart smiled at her. 'Fishing of a sort. A lot of Americans have gone north to volunteer for the Canadian Air Force and the RAF, and are being trained there as pilots. David and I are going to look at the training schools.'

'That is what I'm here for,' David explained. 'I wanted to bring Antonia to Maple Valley, and when Dart asked me to help with this job when he went to Canada, I said I would if he could wangle it for Antonia to come too.'

'Why can't Dart go to Canada by himself?'

'We'll do better together.'

It was Dart's turn to cast David a look of mock concern. 'These Vorst women! Take care, or they'll have you locked up in a convalescent home for the rest of the war.'

'I'll take care.'

Tina could tell from David's closed-in look that he was getting annoyed. She turned to Dart. 'Give me one good reason why you cannot handle this Canada trip on your own?'

'Easy, my dear. David is essential to its success. I shall be mainly an observer on this leg of the trip.'

'It won't help if David passes out in the middle of it.'

'We're not going for at least four weeks. I shall be busy in Washington until then. Your little brother is tougher than he looks.'

'Thanks,' said David, still tight-lipped.

Dart said seriously, 'Try to make your mother understand, Tina, that without David we will get nowhere. We need trained pilots in Britain, and if things go right for us in Canada, we may get them sooner rather than later. The Canadians expect Squadron Leader Vorst, a real live Battle of Britain pilot complete with medals. They will listen to him, and David will know the right questions to ask. If I turned up on my own, I would be fobbed off with the flannel they reserve for military nosy-parkers.'

David's dark eyes had narrowed with laughter, but before Tina could start to argue, dinner had been announced, and Chrissie and Antonia were moving in their direction. Dart shook his head warningly at Tina.

'Leave it for now. I want to take Aunt Chrissie in to dinner.'

On their way to bed at the end of the first weekend, Chrissie took Antonia's hand in a warm clasp, 'Bless you for bringing David safely back to us, my dear. I'm relying on you to keep him here. If anyone can persuade him to stay home, it will be you.'

Antonia returned the pressure of Chrissie's fingers. 'If I have my way, he will stay in America until the war is over.'

Cornelius smiled benignly upon the two women. It rather looked as if he had been granted his miracle.

Chapter 18

Antonia blossomed in her new surroundings. She lost her look of drooping exhaustion, and every day she felt better and looked prettier. She had a winning way with people, enthused about the house and the gardens, and never failed to give smiling thanks for even the smallest service. Her palpable delight in her children and her air of affectionate deference to the old Vorsts won her many friends. The general opinion in the house was that David Vorst's new wife was an absolute honey.

There were two people at Maple Valley House who took another view. One was Maggie. The other was Kim, who thought nobody good enough for her favourite uncle.

'Dearest child,' said Aunt Chrissie, after twice hearing Kim address David's wife with scant courtesy. 'It would be more polite to call David's new wife "Aunt", don't you think?'

'I'm sorry, Grandma. I just couldn't.'

'Why not?'

'Ant Antonia! So stupid! As though I had a stutter.'

David lowered the *Herald Tribune* and advised Kim to solve the problem by saying 'aunt' in her mock English accent. 'Sounding stupid doesn't bother you when you talk like that, I notice.'

'Antonia might think I was making fun of her.'

David looked at his niece and asked blandly, 'Now, why should she think that?'

He went back to his newspaper and said no more, for he had overheard Antonia's children discussing Kim's nickname for Antonia, and had been amused. For as long as he could remember Kim had thought up names for people. Maybe he would tell Antonia of it when she knew Kim better.

Abby was curious. 'Cotton candy? Why do you call Mum that?'

'I don't. I just think of her that way.'

'Why?'

They were climbing a large beech tree, and Kim was hanging upside down with her legs hooked round a branch above. 'I guess I'd better not tell you.'

Abby thought Kim's face looked very odd when she grinned upside

249

down like that. 'Oh, come on! I won't tell Mum. I just want to know,'

'OK. Your mother is so sticky sweet that she gets in my hair.'

'Huh! Mum thinks you're spoiled. As you jolly well are.'

'I jolly well am, aren't I?' said Kim in her English voice. She sounded satisfied, as though she had been paid a compliment. 'I like to be spoiled by people. You should try it.'

Abby laughed, though she had not meant to.

Cagney had been away, and had only lately been in touch. He was avoiding Long Island, so sent for Mary-Jo to come to New York City, swearing her to secrecy. He told her to say that he was still in Mexico. He asked her a lot of questions, wanting details about Maple Valley House and the people in it. He seemed particularly interested in the David Vorsts, and even asked about the children. He wrote down her answers in a notebook.

Mary-Jo wished that Cagney had not come back. Life was simpler without him, particularly as Maggie was being difficult.

'Cagney, I can't do any more commissions. Maggie knew that it was me the last time.'

'Hell! Don't tell me you admitted it?'

'Of course not! But she watches, and says she won't keep quiet if anything else goes missing.'

'Relax, Sis. That stuff was peanuts. This year I'm playing in a different league.'

'What does that mean?' she demanded uneasily.

He eyed her, and decided not to say. 'Just do as I tell you when the time comes, and we can kiss goodbye to Long Island. I've a yen to visit South America. Or maybe Canada.'

Mary-Jo had no intention of leaving her staid but loving family, but did not say so. She tried to make sense of what he had said. 'When the time comes for what, Cagney?'

'You'll know soon enough. And forget about lifting stuff just now. Although if something comes up that's worth a lot of dough, it might be different . . .' He fingered his moustache thoughtfully. 'What about this Limey bride? Has she got any good stuff?'

'The old Vorsts have just given her some stunning pearls. They were a birthday present.'

'Pearls.' Cagney was disparaging. 'Now, if it was diamonds, good ones – then you'd be talking!' He was silent again, and said suddenly, 'You know, sis, Maggie could be a real menace with her prying ways. You say the new wife doesn't like her? Any chance that Maggie might get fired?'

'Not really. Someone has to look after the kids.'

'If Maggie got fired, it could be an opening for you.'

'Maybe,' said Mary-Jo without enthusiasm. The bride was as sweet as honey to herself and the other maids, but overhearing her speak to Maggie, Mary-Jo was not so sure that she wanted to work for her.

Maggie had not expected to be appointed as Antonia's personal maid, and tried to get out of it. 'I would not know what to do,' she told Mrs Sandridge. 'Surely Mrs David would be better being looked after by Miss Roscoe.'

Mrs Vorst's personal maid had offered her services, a mark of great condescension, but David said that Antonia would prefer Maggie. Mary-Jo would help out with the housework in the Chinese wing. Mrs Sandridge wondered why Maggie did not jump at the chance.

She said, directing a searching look at the nursery maid, 'What's worrying you? Is it something to do with the things that went missing at Christmas?' And when Maggie looked startled and even a little alarmed, she added, 'I don't see you as our poltergeist, so there is really only one other person who fits, isn't there?'

Maggie looked gravely back at the secretary, and waited.

Mrs Sandridge said after a pause, 'Would you feel happier about working for Mrs David if Mary-Jo was not involved?'

Maggie took her time to answer. At last she said, with a rather stubborn set to her mouth, 'Mary-Jo and I work fine together. What exactly do you mean, Mrs Sandridge?'

'I think you know what I mean.' There was a pause, and when Maggie showed no inclination to speak, the secretary smiled slightly, before saying, 'If Mary-Jo is not your reason for being scared of this new job, can you tell me what it is?'

Maggie's eyes dropped to her hands, and her colour rose uncomfortably. 'I just don't think I could do it properly.'

'David told me that you used to wait on her in England. She hasn't been well and would find a new person tiring.'

Maggie said more lamely still, 'I wouldn't know how to be a proper lady's maid.'

'But Maggie, you already look after the children's clothes—' The door opened and David came in. 'David, I need your help. This silly girl doesn't believe that she is capable of looking after Antonia.'

David smiled at Maggie. 'What's this? Antonia and I are hoping to see more of you and the children now the nurse is going. What's the problem?'

'I'm no lady's maid, Mr David. I don't know how to do massage, or manicures, or hairdressing.'

'What makes you think Antonia would want that?'

'Won't she?' Maggie asked doubtfully. Then before he could answer, she said earnestly, 'I thought Mrs John ... Mrs David would be happier with somebody experienced like Miss Roscoe.'

David smiled warmly at her. 'Maggie, it's you we want. Please. In our eyes you are one of the family.' And when Maggie said nothing but looked rather hunted, he added, 'But if you don't want to take us on, you don't have to. I'll fix it with Antonia.'

Maggie looked up, and said ruefully, 'Now you've made me feel ungrateful. If you want me to give it a try, Mr David, then of course I will.'

But she came back into the office later, looking determined. Mrs Sandridge looked up impatiently, hands poised over the typewriter keys. It had been a tiresome morning. 'Well, Maggie? What now?'

Maggie plunged into her carefully rehearsed speech. 'About Mary-Jo,' she said. 'There won't be any more things missing from now on . . .' She added rather breathlessly, 'That's all I have to say, Mrs Sandridge, and I'm sorry to have bothered you.' She turned and almost ran out of the office, leaving the secretary staring.

So Mary-Jo and Maggie started work in the Chinese wing next day – Mary-Jo visibly thrilled, and Maggie outwardly serene but inwardly apprehensive. However hard she tried to blot them out, memories from Dulcimer came back to oppress her. She recalled Antonia's impatience with Abby, and other occasions when barbed words and small cruelties to herself had reduced her to a state of wordless misery. She was not so vulnerable these days, or so she hoped, but she was not looking forward to being Antonia's handmaid.

Her fears were soon realised. When the children or David were there, it was not too bad, but when they were not it was very different. There was no pleasing Antonia, and Maggie came to dread her duties in the Chinese wing. She had been braced to bear a chilling air of boredom, and some irritable or capricious demands. But it was worse than that. She came to the conclusion that what Antonia felt for her this time was neither boredom nor indifference, but positive dislike. She would have liked to ask what she had done to earn this antipathy, but never found the words to do so. It would not have occurred to Maggie that Antonia was jealous.

But so it was. Antonia had taken it for granted that Maggie would wait upon her. The girl was part of her entourage, and might as well make herself useful. When David suggested that she would find Maggie more to her liking than his mother's maid, she had shrugged and told him to arrange what he liked.

Maggie was obliging and polite, but she was not what Antonia had expected. The Maggie of Dulcimer days had been a big clumsy child, easily cowed by a raised eyebrow or a mocking word, and firmly under Nanny's thumb. Dulcimer Maggie had been painfully anxious to please.

These days she showed no sign of anxiety at all. Rather the reverse, Antonia told herself sourly. She moved about her tasks with insolent poise, and if scolded for being late or stupid or otherwise taken to task would apologise with outward meekness but with a thoughtful look in her grey eyes that made you wonder what was going through her mind.

But it was David's attitude that irritated Antonia beyond bearing. He had started off badly, of course, by boring on about the letter from Maggie's father. Before long Antonia noticed other things. It seemed to her that the nursery maid had only to come in with her breakfast tray or to start tidying up for this to be David's cue to wander through from the dressing room next door. He would smile and chat with Maggie with every appearance of enjoyment, behaving as though he had known and liked her for ever. Equally tiresome was the way Abby and the boys followed her about. When Maggie left the room, they all too often dashed out in pursuit of her, instead of staying affectionately by Antonia's side.

Dart was no help. He expressed his amazement at Maggie's changed looks.

'A miracle!' he remarked, watching Maggie's retreating back view appreciatively as she carried Jamie away to bed. 'To think dour old Dunlop actually fathered that delectable little creature!'

'Not so little,' said Antonia, veiling her annoyance with a mocking smile. 'Maggie has lost a mountain of weight but by any standards she is still a big girl.'

'I love big girls – more to get hold of. Your Maggie must look sumptuous in a bathing suit! With those legs, she could get a job with the Rockettes.'

'She may need to. I've heard things which have made me wonder if Maggie Dunlop is a suitable person to look after my children. Not quite so demure and innocent as she appears, is Dunlop's daughter, and I've heard other things about her that I don't like.'

Dart grinned, and would have demanded details if Cornelius and Chrissie had not just then come through the garden gate.

He had not missed the resentful note in Antonia's voice. So Antonia was jealous of pretty Maggie, was she? She could never abide a rival. He remembered a good-looking parlour maid whom he and Johnnie had rather fancied, and who had departed from Dulcimer under a cloud. Antonia had always sworn that she had nothing to do with this, but Dart had wondered.

Meanwhile, David consulted James and found that Maggie knew about her brother's death. Lord Dulcimer had cabled Cornelius telling him about it, and Cornelius asked James to break the news to Maggie.

'Both brothers killed within the year; that's pretty tough on the whole family,' James said soberly. After a pause, he added, 'Maggie was shocked, of course, but she is not one for tears or dramatics. Her main concern was for his widow. She went to school with her. The brother she was close to was the sailor, Tom. He was killed last summer.'

'I know,' said David, recalling how Antonia had not told him about Tom's funeral. Had she resented his interest in Maggie even then? He pushed the thought aside. 'So what shall I do with

Dunlop's letter? Won't it distress her to get it?'

'Very likely, but it won't come as a shock. She's been expecting to be summoned back.'

'Will she go?'

'Who knows? She suffers from an exaggerated sense of duty. She might decide to go for the old lady's sake.'

'Not if I can help it,' said David flatly. 'After the way they used her, she owes her family nothing. The minister's wife at Glen Cary has offered to find a housekeeper for Mrs Dunlop, and if nurses are needed, that can be arranged, too.'

'No doubt,' said James. 'But Maggie might not like that. She has a mind of her own, that girl. You'll need to watch your step, David. If we take the children to the beach tomorrow, you could talk to her then.'

Maggie was about to take Antonia's breakfast tray downstairs when she was called back.

'Wait. I want to talk to you.'

Antonia invariably needed a rest after the exertions of her morning bath, and she was in bed, studying her reflection in a small hand mirror. But as Maggie hovered in the doorway, she looked up and added sharply, 'Put that tray down, girl, and come over here. I can't be expected to shout at you across the room.'

Maggie obeyed, and after a pause the older woman put the looking glass down and surveyed the nursery maid with eyes that were coldly appraising. Maggie said nothing. She found it best to say as little as possible when alone with Antonia.

Antonia felt a surge of annoyance. The girl was so maddeningly composed. She said, 'You seem very pleased with yourself these days, Maggie. I wonder why that should be.' And when, once again, Maggie said nothing, she added on a more incisive note, 'Just how long is it that have you been working for me?'

Maggie wrinkled her brow, and said slowly, 'It will be nigh on two and a half years. It was in September nineteen thirty-eight that I first came to Dulcimer—'

'Quite so,' Antonia cut in coldly. 'When you came to us, you were engaged as nursery maid to my children, were you not?'

'Yes, ma'am.'

'And what were your duties when you were first engaged?' Maggie did not answer immediately, so Antonia said silkily, 'Why do you hesitate? Surely you cannot have forgotten what Nanny taught you?'

Maggie could not imagine what this was leading up to, except that the situation bore all the signs of an imminent dressing-down. With an inward tremor of dread, but with face and voice expressionless, she replied, 'I looked after the children's clothes, cleaned the nurseries

254

and brought their food up from the kitchens. Sometimes I helped to bath the older children.'

'And when you came here, did anyone tell you that your duties would be different?'

'No. I still do those things. I'm afraid I don't understand. Have I done something wrong, Mrs David?'

Antonia sighed in a rather exaggerated way. 'You know, Maggie, if you were just a little more intelligent or even normally sensitive like most people, I would not have to speak to you like this. Unfortunately, someone has to give you a hint . . .'

Past experience of being scolded – by her father, her grandmother, teachers at school, by Cook at the manse or by Nanny – had brought Maggie to certain conclusions. Best to take what was being said to you without comment. It was no good trying to defend yourself, because the minds of people in mid-harangue are rarely in receiving mode. If you could switch your own mind off what they were saying, so much the better.

But she found no way of switching off as Antonia's well-aimed barbs took their hurtful toll. She felt herself to be in a pillory, tied down while the sweet, contemptuous, rather high-pitched voice rehearsed her many shortcomings. She had lost a great deal of blubber, Antonia said disparagingly, but it was a pity that she had not tried change herself in other ways. She was still clumsy and tactless, never knowing her place, or able to tell when she was not wanted. She talked too much, and showed off when there was absolutely no occasion to do so. 'I have been very much embarrassed by what people say of you, Maggie.'

She spoiled the children, in particular Abby, currying favour, and from all accounts encouraging her to be rude and disobedient to other grown-ups. Antonia said contemptuously, 'There is no need for you to hang around Abby, you know. There are better qualified people to care for her and the boys, so from now on you had better confine your duties to looking after their clothes and cleaning their rooms.'

Maggie waited, hoping that Antonia had finished. She had not.

'Another thing. My husband and I came to Maple Valley for privacy and a chance to be together on our own. I may tell you that Mr David has several times asked me why you are always hanging around up here, chattering and trying to draw attention to yourself. He finds it intensely irritating. In future, when my husband comes in, you will take yourself off until he has gone.'

Maggie went away inwardly shredded by Antonia's malice. More than anything, she found herself seething with resentment at David Vorst's perfidy. She had come to think of him as a friend. He had been so understanding when she had wept over Bert Higgins. He had encouraged her to tell him what she thought of Maple Valley and being in America. Worse still, he had cajoled her into waiting on Antonia. He was double-faced, always greeting her with a smile or some silly joke when they met – and all the while he had been grumbling to his wife about how she disturbed his privacy and got in his way. From now on Maggie resolved to avoid David Vorst like the plague.

Miserable and humiliated, she was easy prey to temptation when Abby came looking for her, wanting her to go to Jones Beach for the day. It soothed her wounded feelings to know that Abby wanted her, whoever else did not. It would be wiser not to go; Antonia would be cross if she found out. But Maggie's rebellious feelings were smouldering, and the thought of escape to sand and sea and fresh air was impossible to resist. She would go, and for this one day would forget about wisdom – and even try to forget about Antonia. David would be safely out of the way too, dancing attendance on his wife while she shopped in New York – and serve him right! Miss Brimley made no objection, so she ran upstairs to grab a towel and sneakers.

It was too late to back out when she discovered that David had not gone to New York. She jolted to a standstill at the sight of him, and then dived into the back of James's car, wishing that she had never agreed to come. How would she manage to avoid him on the beach?

They came to the ocean before she had reached a solution, and David confounded her by coming straight over and helping her out of the car as if she was the only person in it. Still holding her arm, he eyed her narrowly. 'Are you feeling all right today, Maggie?'

'I . . . I'm fine, sir,' she assured him breathlessly, trying to pull away, and refusing to look at him.

He released her and said quietly, 'Then why did you look so horrified when you saw me this morning? Have I done something to offend you?'

She looked up into his thin, dark face, and was sufficiently reassured by what she saw in it to smile at him waveringly. 'Offend me? N-no. I thought you'd gone to New York with Mrs David, and was surprised to see you. That's all.'

'I see.'

He did not believe her, but was relieved to see the colour and life come back into her face. As they all carried picnic baskets, buckets and spades, baseball bats and rugs down to the sand, he reflected that 'surprise' was not what he had seen in her face when she came out of the house and saw him. She had shied like a terrified horse. He wondered why.

The late spring weather was fine but chilly. It was too cold to swim, so they ran relay races and played softball barefoot on the sands, with David and James picking the teams. Maggie had never before seen baseball played, and looked forward with interest to being a spectator.

But this was not allowed. They made her join in, and her inept efforts started everybody laughing. After dropping two easy catches, she hit a passable shot and ran to first base, only to find that Betty was still there. Again they fell about laughing at the pile-up. When their picnic had been disposed of and they were roasting marshmallows over a driftwood fire, Abby and Kim tried to explain some of the niceties of the game.

It was a good morning, and after lunch James took the children along the beach to look for shells. Kim did not want to go, but David sent her off, saying that he wanted to talk to Maggie. When they were gone, he took Ian Dunlop's letter from his pocket and gave it to her.

He walked down to the edge of the sea so that she could read it alone. She joined him, and he stood looking down at her bent head. She seemed quite composed.

He said, 'Well? Have you been ordered home?'

'Yes.'

'Do you want to go?'

'No. I'd like to stay. But it's true enough what my dad says. Gran is not getting any younger. I'll have to think about it.'

'Will you be offended if I tell you what *I* think?'

She raised her head to look at him. Her grey eyes met his dark ones. She said simply, 'I'm not easily offended. Tell me what I ought to do, Mr David.'

He smiled at her. 'Advice is easy to give. Not so easy to take.'

'Well, I don't have to take it, do I?'

His smile deepened, but when he launched into his spiel, his manner became wholly serious. He really seemed to care. He told her that she should feel no obligation to go back but should think of her own future. She heard him out, as though listening to a sermon. Only when he suggested paying for domestic help for her grandmother did she raise her chin and say firmly that it would not do.

'Gran wouldn't hear of it. She likes to keep things in the family.'

'You don't need to tell her where the money comes from.'

Maggie shook her head. 'It's good of you, sir, but neither my gran nor I would feel comfortable taking your money.'

'Maggie, this is absolute nonsense! Your grandmother is a courageous old lady and I want to help her. But most of all I hate to think of you to being a drudge in your father's house again. How long will it be before he treats you as he did last year?'

She sighed and smiled faintly. 'Perhaps not at all. Maybe now that I'm older I can deal with him better. I don't want to go back, of course, because I'm feared to, and I like it in America.'

'So why not stay? Do let us help. What is money, after all? You've given Antonia's children so much love, and they truly need you – Abby even more than the boys. James has told me how you cared and

257

comforted her after the Steiner children were lost at sea. Give us a chance to pay back a little of what you have given our children. Antonia wishes it as much as I do.'

'I'm paid every week by your parents, Mr David,' she said, accepting his kindly lie without a blink. No way could she tell him what Antonia had said to her. Her face grew hot at the memory. She pushed the thought of Antonia away, and said doggedly, 'Truly, Mr David, money doesn't come into it. I enjoy looking after the children, and will stay on if I can.'

'Mrs Fraser has offered to find a housekeeper for your grandmother, you know.'

But Maggie said again that it would not do, and when he tried to argue, she grew agitated and begged him to drop the subject. He did as she asked but could have shaken her for being so obdurate. It seemed incredible to him that she could contemplate going back to Scotland out of a mistaken sense of family duty. She must know what going back would mean.

He wondered fleetingly why he felt so strongly protective of the Scots girl. She seemed very sure of herself these days, and appeared to know what she wanted. In fact her air of sturdy independence delighted him, even though he wished she would take his help. She bore little resemblance to the soft-spoken child from Dulcimer, and none at all to the groaning, inert creature that he and Mr Fraser had carried from her father's house all those months ago.

David did not know it, but Maggie had had to fight off tears when he had shown concern about her problems. She had misjudged him. She knew, without knowing how, that David Vorst would never deal in deliberate unkindness or deceit.

When it was time to leave the beach, Kim, Abby and the eldest lordling were nowhere to be seen. This was not the first time that they had teased Maggie by hiding. She walked along the beach, calling their names. She got no answer but the cry of gulls and the sound of the wind.

She began to be annoyed and even a little worried. Walking back higher up, she caught sight of them in one of the car parks. They were talking with animation to some people in a car. As Maggie shouted into the wind and went towards them, the car began to move off, but not before she had recognised its occupants. It picked up speed, and accelerated away towards the highway. She watched it go, feeling startled and uneasy. As always, she had only to catch sight of Cagney for her feelings of dislike and distrust to come flooding back.

She told herself that Cagney had as much right to visit a public beach as anyone. She turned to the children. 'Who was that? Mrs Vorst does not like you to talk to strangers.'

'Just some men we met,' said Abby, looking guilty 'They wanted to know if we had been swimming.'

'Didn't you hear me calling?'

'Sure we heard you,' retorted Kim with smiling insolence. 'We heard you mooing and roaring like an old cow after a lost calf.'

'Then why didn't you answer? I was beginning to get worried.'

'We were having a private conversation.'

'Well, please come now. Your uncle wants to go home. We'll have to run or he'll start getting worried too.'

'Uncle David has more sense,' said Kim haughtily. 'He doesn't fuss about every little thing like you and Grandma.'

Kim loved her Uncle David, and disliked sharing him with so many others. From time to time during the day she had felt scratchy, and had not liked it when David shooed her off, saying that he wanted to talk to Maggie. It had been a fun day in its way but she wished Maggie had never come to the beach. However, she broke into a reluctant jog-trot in the wake of the other children. She was given no choice, really, with Maggie chivvying them on from behind.

The light was starting to fade by the time they reached the cars, and James's vehicle was already on the move with its complement of children, the headlight beams sweeping palely over the beach grasses. David waited by the second one. He did not smile or speak and his thin dark face gave nothing away. Abby and Alfred climbed hurriedly into the back seat of the station wagon, feeling chastened. Kim and Maggie were the last to come up from the shore, and Kim went, as of right, to her place in the front seat. She was checked by a hand on her shoulder.

'Not this time, Kim. You will sit in back with the others,' said David. 'Maggie will sit with me.'

'That's no fair,' Kim protested. 'You promised I could sit with you all day.'

'And you promised to be back here on time. You've kept us waiting, and given Maggie the trouble of chasing down the beach to find you. How's that for playing fair?'

Maggie had regained her breath. She said quickly, 'That's all right, Mr David. I'll be fine in the back seat. I usually sit there.'

'I am sure you do, so for a change I would like you to sit in the front with me.' He was holding the car door open. 'Please get in. If we don't go soon, my mother will be sending out search parties.' He added in a different tone, 'Kim! What are you waiting for?'

Maggie and David talked about the worrying war news from North Africa, and David told her that he was going to Canada. He hoped to be back in England and passed fit to fly by midsummer. After that, quite long stretches of the journey passed in silence. It occurred to David that Maggie was a restful person to be with, and supposing she wanted to think about her father's letter, he concentrated on his driving.

259

He could not know that Maggie was wondering what Antonia would say about her spending a whole day at the beach.

Kim was in a black sulk on the way home. She sat fuming beside Abby, straining jealous ears to hear what David and Maggie were saying to each other. With the engine noise and the other children chatting around her, she could make out very little, which made her more resentful still. What right had the nursery maid to usurp her appointed place? It was bad enough having to share David with other children. That Maggie should push her way in was really too much!

Chrissie Vorst wanted to give Antonia something new and pretty to wear, for they had been allowed very little luggage on their military plane. Accordingly, Mrs Sandridge was asked to take Antonia shopping in New York. They enjoyed a successful and expensive morning, and afterwards Mrs Sandridge dropped Antonia off at the Vorst Hotel.

It occurred to Conway, as he sat between Antonia and Adele in the restaurant, that no two women could have had less in common – except that each regarded the other with disdain. Adele had once described Antonia as a simpering little moron – not good enough for his intelligent brother. To punish her for daring to praise David, Conway had been particularly attentive to Antonia after the polo match. He had found her decorative and amusing, if rather bird-brained, and thought it might be a good plan to get to know her better. Adele was still holding out against him. If she saw him enjoying himself with Antonia, it might help to focus her mind.

During lunch he therefore gave Antonia all his attention, and at one point raised one of her slender hands and brushed her fingers briefly with his lips. Adele did not seem to notice any of this. Her own attention was directed at her food – a starter of soft-shelled crab, and then Maine lobster with mayonnaise.

Antonia enjoyed Conway's homage, unaware that she was taking part in his mating dance. She ignored Adele, and set herself to amuse and entertain her host. She complimented him on the New York Vorst, assuring him that the London house was utterly dreary in these days of blitz and shortages. She also told him about her morning in the shops, confiding that Mrs Sandridge had encouraged her in the most wicked extravagance. Imagine! They had bought two dresses that morning, and a dream of a hat!

'Mrs Sandridge said that Aunt Chrissie would want me to have both dresses, but I don't know. What do you think? Should I take one of them back this afternoon?'

'Maybe you should. Get Adele to go with you. She loves shopping for clothes.'

Antonia opened her blue eyes wide and looked at the other woman.

260

'Goodness! I didn't think you'd be interested.'

'Conway is trying to bait me. He knows I loathe shopping,' said Adele cheerfully. 'Nothing fits me, and he despises me because I'm too lazy to get things made.'

'You could buy ready-made things and get them altered surely?'

'I'm over six feet tall. Nobody makes clothes for giraffes.'

'Oh, I see! Actually, I have the same problem. Only in my case I need to get things shortened or taken in at the waist.' She cast a limpid look at Conway. 'You can have no idea how tiresome it is to be so tiny! However, my nursery maid will alter my new dresses. It will give her something to do while the children are at school.'

'Maggie?' Adele smiled at Antonia with real warmth for the first time. 'What a nice girl she is – so enterprising, driving a car and speaking French and making her own clothes. She is so much improved in looks that I hardly knew her in Palm Beach. Such a sea change . . .'

But Antonia had turned back to Conway. 'I wonder. Would you have time to show me round the hotel after lunch? I would truly love that.'

'My mother said that you might wish to lie down after lunch,' he replied, with a glint in his eye. 'You are not to get too tired.'

Antonia's silvery laughter rang out. 'Somehow I don't feel tired in your company, Conway.'

'What a pity, then, that you won't have much longer to enjoy it,' said Adele drily. She was dealing with her last lobster claw. It yielded with a subdued crack, and Conway wondered if it was his neck or Antonia's that had just been ritually broken. 'Not if you still want Monsieur Gaston to cut your hair. He is expecting you at three o'clock. We ought to leave here in five minutes.'

'How competent you are, Adele darling! I had almost forgotten!'

After a belated tea with Chrissie and Cornelius, Antonia went upstairs to her bedroom, and rang the bell for Maggie. No one came, so she went to look for her, and presently found Miss Fortescue in the red drawing room. Antonia had met the lordlings' parents in England, and since coming to Maple Valley House had enjoyed several talks with the governess. She thought well of her. Unlike Miss Brimley, Miss Fortescue never had the least trouble controlling her charges. She exacted instant obedience from all three boys, had trained them to be polite to adults, to stand up when spoken to, and to hold doors open for them. Not only that. The governess's opinion of Maggie Dunlop coincided with Antonia's. They were agreed that the girl needed to be put in her place, and Miss Fortescue, speaking in the strictest confidence, had confided some other things about her.

'I'm looking for Maggie,' Antonia said. 'Have you seen her?'

'She went off to the beach this morning, Mrs David. That one never misses a chance to go gadding.'

Antonia frowned. 'How tiresome . . .' She broke off as Miss Brimley came into the room, carrying her everlasting writing case and knitting bag, and blinking in her nervous, pink-lidded way.

Antonia pounced. 'Brimmy! Why has Maggie gone to the beach? Nobody bothered to ask me. I need a dress shortened before dinner, and if they're late back, it won't be done in time.'

Miss Brimley was full of apologies. Maggie had been roped in at the last minute. Mr James had wanted help with the children, and Abby had begged for Maggie to be allowed to go.

These explanations did nothing to mollify Antonia, for she resented Abby's habit of chasing after Maggie. Annoyed, she began to sweep from the room, colliding with an equally bad-tempered Kim in the doorway.

'Clumsy child! Look where you're going!' said Antonia sharply.

'Look out yourself! It was as much your fault as mine,' retorted Kim. She had kept her bad temper battened down in the car and needed to spew it over someone.

Abby said, 'Don't take any notice of Kim, Mum. She's in a filthy temper but it won't last. Did she hurt you?' she added belatedly, seeing that Antonia looked anything but benign herself. 'I'm sure she didn't mean to.'

Antonia rubbed her elbow and looked at Kim. Kim in her turn was glaring reproachfully at Abby. Antonia demanded, 'Whatever is the matter with her?'

'David wouldn't let her sit beside him in the front of the car and she's been in a rage ever since.'

A contemptuous smile curled Antonia's lips. 'What a silly little girl. What does it matter which part of a car you sit in? Only spoilt babies mind about that sort of thing.'

Kim flushed. 'I wonder how much you would like it if Uncle David made you sit in back with a bunch of kids while he chatted and laughed with Maggie in the front. You'd hate it, I bet.'

Antonia's lips went on smiling, but her eyes had narrowed. Abby stood on Kim's foot, and said curtly, 'Shut up, idiot. Mum, Kim's making that up. David and Maggie hardly spoke to each other all the way home.'

'Don't interrupt. I want to hear what Kim has to say.'

Kim's rage had subsided but she was still feeling aggrieved. 'Nothing much,' she said crossly. 'Only that it was s'posed to be a fun day for us and Maggie ruined it by fooling about in our baseball game and kept Uncle David to herself for hours on the beach. I wish she wouldn't push her way into everything.'

For once, Antonia found herself in accord with David's spoiled little niece. It was in that moment, too, that she made up her mind that Maggie would have to go.

Chapter 19

David was at first delighted to be home. He was even a little surprised by the intensity of his own pleasure. Vividly as he remembered the joys of returning from boarding school, this time it seemed like Christmas, Easter and the Fourth of July all rolled into one, and when Cornelius and Chrissie fell so quickly under Antonia's spell, this added another dimension to his mood of euphoria.

But moods, like the weather, are subject to change. At first he felt only occasional pinpricks of irritation: at Antonia's refusal to discuss Maggie's affairs, and her reversion to semi-invalidism when something did not please her. He could have done without his mother fussing so much and for ever imploring him to rest. And almost as soon as they arrived, Antonia started urging him to extend his leave. Six weeks was not enough, she said, after all they had been through.

He told her that no extension was possible, and after a few more tries, she said no more. But he had begun to feel stifled, not least by the relentless succession of social events which had been laid on to celebrate his marriage and homecoming. Family and friends all wanted to meet Antonia. When yet another gushing matron implored him to bring his lovely little English wife to a cocktail party, he found himself wishing he was back in uniform and doing a job of work. Even if the RAF rejected him as a pilot, he told himself, he would fly a desk for them rather than continue on this futile social round.

Life was not easy for Maggie either. Expecting trouble after her stolen day at the beach, she had been surprised and more than a little relieved when Antonia said nothing about it for over a week. Her relief was tinged with unease, however, for she did not think that the matter would end there. Even so, the manner and ruthlessness of Antonia's reprisal took her by surprise.

'Maggie, dear,' said Mrs Sandridge, 'I have something rather embarrassing to tell you. Mrs Vorst does not wish you to drive the children any more.'

Maggie experienced a sinking feeling, and knew at once what this meant. Antonia usually took care to hit where it hurt. With an effort she made herself say mildly, 'Mrs David did not say anything to me while I was driving her, Mrs Sandridge.'

Mrs Sandridge was taken aback, for Chrissie Vorst had not wanted Antonia's name mentioned. She said reprovingly, as though Maggie had said something she ought not, 'I was speaking of Mrs *Cornelius* Vorst, Maggie. There have been complaints about you driving too fast and scaring your passengers. Naturally she became worried for the children's safety.'

'Oh,' said Maggie, rather blankly. Then after another short pause, she added in a subdued voice, 'Very well, Mrs Sandridge. If Mrs Vorst does not wish me to drive them, there is no more to be said.'

She turned and walked out of the room, leaving Mrs Sandridge to her puzzled thoughts. She had expected the girl to protest, but instead Maggie had accepted the ban without demur.

James heard about it, and asked to know the reason. Mrs Sandridge told him.

James stood looking at the secretary, his thin face thoughtful.

Sensing criticism, she said, 'You cannot blame David's wife. Her nerves are still in a bad way after the London bombing and all the worry about David. And she was ill so many times last winter. She came to me and apologised, and said she had never meant to make trouble. And as I said, Mrs Vorst asked me not to mention her part in it.'

James grunted.

'The odd thing was that Maggie seemed to expect it. She must have done something careless, don't you think? If not, why would she take it so meekly?'

James said, 'I have never known Maggie to drive too fast. Never once, and certainly never dangerously.'

Mrs Sandridge smiled at him a little wryly. 'We all know that Maggie can do no wrong in your eyes, James.'

James was taken aback. He said, frowning at her, 'Now, May. Do you seriously imagine that I would recommend her to drive those kids about if I had doubts about her driving?'

'Of course I don't think it, but even the best drivers can make mistakes.'

'Meaning?'

She met his frowning gaze squarely, and said, 'New drivers can grow over-confident. Perhaps Maggie will be more careful from now on.'

Antonia revelled in the sybaritic ease of life at Maple Valley House. She adored being indulged by both Chrissie and Cornelius, who vied with each other to give her pleasure, buying her presents and planning treats for herself and David. She had been made welcome, too, by the rest of the Vorst clan and their friends, and never doubted that David enjoyed it as much as she did herself.

264

Since she had trained Maggie to vanish whenever David was about, he seemed to have forgotten about her. Out of sight, out of mind, she thought with satisfaction. He was back to being his old agreeable self, happy to enter into whatever enterprise took her fancy. They dined several times with Tina and Bill. David escorted her to lunch and dinner at the Country Club several times, and even agreed to attend an occasional cocktail party, just to please her.

Conway invited them to dinner and a theatre in New York. They were royally entertained, taken to see *Arsenic and Old Lace*, and on a subsequent occasion they dined with Conway and a group of his close friends at the Vorst, ending up in a dark and very exclusive nightclub where they danced until the small hours. Conway, for all his stolid appearance, was an excellent dancer, never forgot to send Antonia flowers next day, and was smoothly polite and complimentary whenever they met.

She thought that it would take only a little encouragement from her to make Conway fall for her in a big way. She told David, laughing, that if she had met them both at the same time, she would have found it difficult to choose between them. David had merely smiled and gone back to reading his Neville Shute, but then, he rarely gratified her by showing signs of jealousy.

So their holiday sped by, full of fun and laughter, and no work or worries to plague them. Antonia gave herself wholeheartedly to life with the Vorst family, choosing not to think of the future. Last winter she had felt wretched all the time. The Sussex countryside had been dank and dreary, with wartime food and fuel shortages, news bulletins telling of one disaster after another, constant rain and cold and the blackout. This sojourn in Maple Valley House was total bliss.

Dart came to Maple Valley every weekend, which added another dimension to her happiness. She never doubted that he came expressly to see her.

David did not seem to mind Dart being around. He took his cousin's arrival as a cue to go off with James and the children, leaving Antonia to enjoy whatever social entertainments were on offer. Dart was always more than willing to escort her, and his good looks and his title made him an acceptable substitute for David. More than one Long Island beauty had fallen a victim to his charm.

'So, Tonia?' said Dart, on his next visit. 'You seem to have swept all Maple Valley before you. Clever little thing, aren't you?'

'Everyone is sweet to me here,' she said sunnily, stretching up with one slender arm up to lay hold of an overhanging branch of magnolia. Conway had remarked last week that her white skin reminded him of magnolia petals, and she had taken this as further confirmation that Conway fancied her. She looked at Dart from under her long, dark lashes. 'It's so comfortable here, and even if the Americans complain

265

that it is too cold for May, there is none of our constant English rain. I feel that I have been miraculously transported to heaven.'

'You certainly look better, Tonia,' he said, aware of what was expected of him. It was indeed a pretty sight to see her surrounded by sun-dappled leaves and flowers. 'In positively rude health, I might say. David looks better too.'

'Don't tell Aunt Chrissie that,' she said quickly. 'She is still dreadfully worried, and is on the trail of some learned Austrian professor to come and check him over. But don't mention it to David. He hates a fuss.'

Dart laughed. 'David may have already smelled a rat, Tonia. He told me that you and his mother were as thick as thieves.'

'Aunt Chrissie is just divine to me,' said Antonia rather smugly, fingering the triple string of pearls which her doting in-laws had given her for her birthday. 'She is not at all like Mother Dulcimer. She is so interested in nice clothes, and really quite sentimental. I keep on having to remind myself that the two of them are twin sisters.'

Dart considered Antonia. This did not match his own view of his mother and his aunt. Twin tigresses would be nearer the mark if their loved ones were threatened. However, he saw no occasion to share this passing thought with Antonia. Instead, he said with genuine admiration, 'Even Uncle Cornelius seems smitten. He's usually a shrewd old bird. But when he told me what a remarkably well-read young woman you are, Antonia, I could hardly keep from laughing. Where in the world did he get that idea?'

She showed him a mischievous face. 'David told me that his father was mad about poetry, and I happened to come up with a quotation. He pays the children to learn reams of it, you know. Abby recited something called "An Ode to a Nightingale", and he paid her ten dollars. I didn't approve of that, and told Uncle Cornelius that Abby ought not to be bribed.'

'Spoilsport!' Dart laughed at her, flipping the new pearls with a careless finger. 'You should try to practise what you preach, Tonia.'

'Nonsense, Dart! This is a birthday present.'

'A rose by any other name . . .' he murmured softly. 'I can roll out a few quotations too when I feel like it.'

'I don't know what you're talking about,' she retorted. 'Let's go in. It's starting to get cold.'

'You have been given some truly beautiful things, Mrs David,' said Miss Fortescue when she and the other nannies had been shown Antonia's pearls, and David's birthday offering of pearl and diamond earrings. 'Don't think me impertinent, but may I suggest that you hide them, or better still get Mrs Sandridge to lock your jewel case in the safe. You've heard about the outbreak of petty thieving last autumn.

There has been no trouble for months, but you never know. We were never able to prove who had taken our things.'

Antonia looked at Miss Fortescue. They had discussed those winter disappearances in private. She said slowly, 'Who do you think did it, Miss Fortescue?'

'I have a pretty good idea, Mrs David, but I have yet to catch her at it.'

'Aren't you going to give us a name?'

There was a stir among the other women. Miss Brimley said, 'Really, Maud, I don't think—'

'Brimmy,' Antonia cut in, 'if Miss Fortescue knows who was guilty last time, she ought at least to warn us who to watch. What are you so anxious to keep from me?' She looked around the circle of worried faces. Then she said to Miss Fortescue, 'If it is Maggie that you suspect, I ought to be told.'

Miss Brimley gave vent to a mewing protest, and Miss Fortescue uttered a short bark of laughter. 'I admit, Mrs David, that I would dearly like to catch that young woman red-handed.'

Maggie would have needed to be blind and deaf not to know what was being said about her, and it made her feel both angry and desperate.

Nobody actually accused her. It might have been better if they had. And when Antonia found that her pearls were missing from their leather case one morning, she eyed Maggie ominously and said that it was a lady's maid's prime responsibility to look after her mistress's jewels. She told Maggie and Mary-Jo that she would be out all morning and was planning to have lunch at the Country Club. When she got back, she would expect the necklace to be returned to its proper place. Before she left, she spoke to the housekeeper about her loss.

Maggie and Mary-Jo and the housekeeper pretty well turned the Chinese room and the dressing room upside down but did not find the necklace. Later Maggie cornered Mary-Jo in the laundry.

'I meant what I said. I'm not going to sit quiet while everyone thinks it was me. Did you take it, or are you playing the hiding-finding game again?'

Mary-Jo looked ready to burst into tears. 'Cross my heart, Maggie! I never touched them! Besides, Cagney says—' She stopped, for she had been about to say that he was only interested in diamonds.

'Yes?' said Maggie, in an interested voice. 'What does Cagney say?'

Mary-Jo hunched a sulky shoulder. 'Nothing. He's in New Mexico, so how can I tell what he might be saying?'

'You're quite sure about that?'

'I had a postcard from him yesterday,' said the other girl, looking Maggie straight in the eye, a habit she had when things got difficult. 'Of course I'm sure.'

'I just wondered . . .' said Maggie vaguely. Her thoughts were racing.

She had seen Cagney at the beach, so Mary-Jo's tale about Mexico was an obvious lie. Had Cagney been at the back of those other disappearances? She added more quietly, 'Well, Mary-Jo, I suggest that you leave Mrs David's jewels alone – and anything else of value. You know what Miss Fortescue is saying about me, and I simply refuse to be a meek scapegoat a second time.'

'I swear to God I didn't touch those pearls, Maggie,' said Mary-Jo, dissolving into tears. 'Go find someone else to bully.'

Maggie said nothing for a full minute, and then she walked out of the laundry and went to look for Mrs Sandridge.

David paid a visit to Conway in his New York office, and came away in a flaming temper. Despite rising profits in the London house, Conway was still opposed to Odette Steiner running the UK operation. He had arranged to replace her with a man called Hudson from Cleveland who had managed the Vorst Hotel in that city for some years. He paid no heed to David's arguments and objections.

Returning to Maple Valley, David decided to do some telephone research before tackling his father – and walked in on another kind of storm. He saw Antonia and Miss Fortescue heading for Mrs Sandridge's office. He followed them to the door. The secretary and Maggie were waiting inside.

Antonia said, in a voice he barely recognised, 'So, Maggie? Have you put them back as I told you to?'

Maggie was facing the door, and was immediately aware of David; she felt his presence to be the worst blow of all. Her face grew hot, but she looked resolutely at Antonia, and said, 'No, ma'am. Mary-Jo and I have looked everywhere. I wonder whether you could be mistaken. Are . . . are you quite sure that you put them away when you came in last night?'

Miss Fortescue and Antonia exchanged glances. 'There you are, Mrs David!' said the governess, grimly triumphant. 'That was what the girl asked Miss Brimley before. The barefaced cheek of her!'

Maggie did not even glance at Miss Fortescue. She said, in a voice that shook only slightly, 'Mrs David. Whatever Miss Fortescue may think, I did not steal her watch last winter. Nor did I take Miss Brimley's locket and pretend to find it afterwards. And I have certainly *not* removed your pearls. Please believe me. I last saw them when I fastened them round your neck last night, before you went to dinner with Mr Conway.' With a flash of spirit, she added, 'If they were in your jewel case overnight and missing first thing this morning, when exactly am I supposed to have taken them?'

Antonia seemed to hesitate, and Miss Fortescue said impatiently, 'Take my advice, Mrs David, and get Mrs Sandridge to ring the police. She might do it for *you*. They'll know how to get the truth out of her.'

David, who had been watching and listening, suddenly came to his senses. He went forward and cupped a hand under his wife's elbow. Antonia jumped, looking up in wide-eyed surprise.

'Goodness, darling! Back already? How did your meeting go?'

He looked down at her and said drily, 'I'll tell you about it later. What's this about your pearls?'

'They've gone, and Miss Fortescue thinks Maggie has taken them. Other things went missing last winter . . .'

David looked at the Fortress for a long moment, and then said in a chill voice, 'I'm not greatly interested in what happened last winter, Miss Fortescue, or what made you think Maggie is a thief. You should be careful about accusing people, you know. My wife's pearls are perfectly safe, so we really don't need you here any more. Please leave us.'

Mrs Sandridge bowed her head to hide a smile. The governess made a gobbling noise in her throat, and after a brief hesitation marched red-faced out of the room.

David shut the door, saw Maggie at bay beside the secretary's desk, and then looked at his wife. Antonia was staring up at him in speechless indignation.

He said gently, 'Honey, remember how hot it was last night? You gave me your pearls before we swam in Conway's pool. I put them in my jacket pocket and forgot to give them back.' Antonia blinked and gave a little gasp. He nodded. 'We owe Maggie an apology.'

Antonia said nothing at all. Her memories of the impromptu midnight bathing party were distinctly hazy, but if anyone was to blame, it was David. If he had given the necklace back to her, this would never have happened. She said in a stifled voice, 'Trust you to be so careless!'

David looked at Maggie and smiled. They were both well-acquainted with Antonia's habit of leaving her possessions scattered around – rings, bracelets and watch in the bathroom, clothes on the floor. He said ruefully, 'I must have drunk too much of Conway's wine last night. Please forgive us, Maggie.' And after a pause, when Antonia said nothing, he added, 'You'll find that tiresome necklace in the pocket of my linen jacket. I hung it in the dressing-room closet after we came in.'

Mrs Sandridge said, 'Maggie thinks that Antonia's jewels might be better in my safe from now on.'

'Good idea,' said David, before Antonia could voice her indignation. She had a good deal to say later, but that was a private matter between the two of them.

After an informative session on the telephone, David marched in on Cornelius and accused him of plotting with Conway. 'Conway says you knew about this new manager, Father. How come you never spoke to me about it?'

269

'We thought it best not to bother you, Dave.'

'Not *bother* me!' David echoed furiously. 'Hudson sailed for England almost a week ago. Did you know that?'

Cornelius said gruffly, 'I only learned of it yesterday.' And when David glared at him, he said defensively, 'No need to look like that. As senior vice-president of the company, Con had to appoint someone. The London house is too important to be left drifting.'

'If either you or Conway had bothered to read my reports,' said David, biting out words as though spitting out teeth, 'you would know that Odette Steiner is running the UK operation better than I ever did. The profits speak for themselves, which is something of a miracle, considering the bombing and the impossible conditions last winter. There is no question of things drifting, as Conway very well knows.'

'Hudson is said to be a reliable manager.'

'A has-been who was due to be fired until Conway decided to foist him onto London. I know. I've been asking around.'

An indignant spark kindled in Cornelius's blue eyes. 'Who said that? All right, don't bother to tell me. If Conway has confidence in this man, that's enough for me. He has always been an excellent judge of people.'

'I'm not criticising Conway's judgement but I have my doubts about his motives,' said David grimly. 'Odette has had enough to bear without being treated shabbily by us, Father.'

Cornelius sighed. 'If I had been at the May meeting, I would have spoken up for her. No news of Michel yet, I suppose?'

'None,' said David. 'We don't talk about Michel these days – or of her children.'

'Now, boy, don't go thinking that Conway is heartless. He knows what she has been through. When she's free, he means to offer her a really good job over here.'

David did see, and was bitterly aware that he should have seen it sooner. Before coming over, he had warned Antonia that things had never been easy between his brother and himself, and that she might not find him too friendly. So when Conway had gone out of his way to charm her, David had been surprised and relieved.

Fool that he was, he had allowed himself to believe that Adele Devenish was the cause of this new mellowing, forgetting that Conway was a master of camouflage. He and his father had been successfully diverted, had seen only what they were meant to see – until it was too late.

He thought about the morning's interview with Conway. He should never have let his temper ride him. Conway had been maddeningly cool, even contemptuous, and when David stormed at him for interference, had said, 'If you had not been so busy playing war games, I wouldn't have needed to take a hand.'

David had walked out. But he was not finished with Conway. He would take a lesson from his brother, and play it cool and friendly from now on. His experience of 'war games' might yet prove useful, if it came to a tactical battle. War games indeed! The insult rankled.

He said curtly to Cornelius, 'If Odette goes because of this, I shall quit with her. Somebody else can pick up the mess after Hudson has undone all her good work.'

'For Pete's sake cool down, Dave, and don't make such a drama of it,' said his father irritably. 'We can work something out.'

All the same, the old man was sufficiently alarmed by his younger son's threat to warn Conway about it when next they met.

Conway expressed concern, but ventured to say that if David's bluff were called, they might be doing him a favour. 'No wonder he started having blackouts. He was trying to do two difficult jobs at once, and probably did both less than well. If it had been anyone but David, Father, you would admit that he has not been worth his salary this year.'

'Dave is family, and he's threatening to quit. I won't have it. Be careful how you handle this, Con. I am not so sure that he *is* bluffing.'

Conway agreed to handle the situation gently, but reflected that it would do the boy wonder no harm to live on his Air Force pay. He might start to find out what real life was about.

To Cornelius he said soothingly, 'If David walks out, he can always come back when he's got this flying nonsense out of his system.'

'He may not be passed fit to fly again,' said Cornelius hopefully. 'Have you tracked down Professor Zimmerman?'

'I'm working on it,' Conway assured him.

In the following days, David became almost sure that Maggie was avoiding him. She had thanked him briefly and warmly for making it right about the pearls, but next day her attitude had changed again. She no longer smiled at him when they met, but avoided his eyes and hurried on by. This capricious behaviour annoyed him a bit, and he considered tackling her about it. Nobody had any right to be so natural and charming one day, and turn into an iceberg the next.

He did not dwell on the matter, however, until one day Abby and Kim waylaid him.

'We want to know what's going on, David,' said Abby. She looked worried. 'Maggie has gone all boring and queer. She doesn't do things with us any more. Mary-Jo walks us to the school bus, and meets us in the evening. Maggie does things for Mum and for Wilding in the pantry, but the rest of the time she just sits in her room with the door locked. She's different, David, and we want to know why.'

'She told you why,' put in Kim, mocking as usual. 'She said that she was tired of children.'

'It's not true! Maggie doesn't get tired of us, like . . .' She glanced at David and said lamely, 'Like some people.'

Kim was impatient with all this dodging. 'Abby thinks that Antonia and the Fortress have told Maggie to keep out of our way. The Fortress hates Maggie.'

Abby looked at her feet, and said nothing.

'Neither of them likes Maggie,' Kim added. 'Not a suitable person to care for children, they say.'

David looked at Kim. 'How come you know they said it?'

'I just happened to hear them.'

'I thought I had cured you of prying when you were just a little girl.'

'I don't often listen in. Only when I need to know things.'

He laughed, and said that he would speak to Maggie.

'There you are, Maggie!' said David, meeting her next day. She was carrying a stack of clean sheets and pillowcases, balancing them under her chin. She paused with obvious reluctance, her eyes downcast. 'James and I are taking the children to the zoo this afternoon. Will you come with us?'

'Thank you, Mr David.' She kept her eyes lowered, 'I'm sorry but I can't. I've too much to do.'

'Again? What makes you so much busier all of a sudden?'

A tide of colour rose in her cheeks but she would not look at him.

'Just the usual house things, Mr David. Excuse me, please, I must not stay. Mary-Jo is waiting for me.'

She made as if to dodge past him, but he side-stepped and took the stack of sheets from her. He dumped them on a chest and turned to take her gently by the shoulders. 'Maggie, what's wrong? Even Abby complains that you're boring these days, with no time to talk or play, and we all want to know why. If you're really so over-worked, you need more help. But I get the impression that you're deliberately avoiding me – and probably Abby as well. She's really quite upset about it, you know.'

He thought she winced, but she merely said steadily, 'I'm sorry to be boring, but I can't do anything about it, Mr David. Please let me by.'

Antonia emerged from her bedroom and saw them standing there, oblivious of her presence. David was holding the girl by the shoulders and his dark head was inclined towards hers. She was invaded by such a savage qualm of jealousy that it almost took her breath away. She had to steady herself before going forward.

The sound of light steps upon the parquet floor alerted Maggie – these days she could sense Antonia's presence before she heard or saw her. Momentarily she closed her eyes, and stood very still.

'Good morning, Maggie,' Antonia said in the honeyed tone she used in front of others. David had lowered his arms and she took hold of one of his lean brown hands, and smiled fondly up at him. 'Darling, Maggie's got work to do. It's not kind of you to hold her back. Mary-Jo has been waiting for her for ages.'

If possible, Maggie's cheeks burned more hotly than ever. She murmured an apology and grabbed her now dishevelled burden of sheets. David watched her go without speaking.

He was rather silent that morning. Maggie's frozen expression and the way her shoulder jerked and stiffened under his fingers had left him prey to some unwelcome thoughts.

They were changing for dinner that evening when David came into Antonia's bedroom. He was still in shirtsleeves, knotting his tie, his dark hair wet from a shower. He said, 'What's the matter with Maggie? She doesn't look happy. Even Abby has noticed it.'

'Oh,' said Antonia, speaking stiffly because she was putting the final touch to her lips. When she had finished this delicate task she said, 'I'm sorry to say that Maggie is in a bit of a sulk. She blames me for that muddle over my pearls, for one thing. Honestly, darling, she's barely civil when we're alone. And another thing, she had grown stupidly possessive of my children, and feels that her nose has been put out of joint since our arrival.'

'I asked her to come with me and the kids this afternoon, and she turned me down flat.'

'Well, there you are.'

He looked down at Antonia's delicately tinted, flawless face and said quietly, 'Have you told Maggie to keep out of my way, Antonia?'

'Now why,' she demanded, her blue eyes very wide, 'should I do that?'

'You haven't answered my question.'

She stood up suddenly. 'Did Maggie say so?' He just went on looking at her thoughtfully, and she added, with a mirthless little trill of laughter, 'What other confidences did she murmur into your ear on the beach that day? Or in the car on the way back?'

'None at all,' he said gently. 'There's really no need for you to be worried about Maggie, you know. She's a hard-working, rather serious-minded young woman who has had a tough time, and is finding friends and happiness here for the first time in her life. That pleases me, I admit, but otherwise my interest in her is not very great.'

'Yet when she complained of me, you believed her.'

'Maggie did not complain of you, Antonia.'

'But you just accused me . . .'

He sighed. 'We seem to be going round in circles. I had an odd notion that you might have told her to keep out of my way, and merely asked you if it was so.' He seemed to ponder for a moment, and then said gravely, 'I have never discussed you with Maggie, and don't intend to. You have all my love and loyalty, Antonia.'

She went on looking at him in stony silence, and he sighed, and turned to go back into the dressing room. He had almost reached the door when she spoke his name. He turned his head.

'David! Oh, David!' She came rustling over to him, almost running on her preposterously high heels and holding out both her ringed hands. 'Darling, forgive me,' she said, the painted flower of her mouth suddenly tremulous. 'I can't help it if people tell me things, and it's common knowledge that she likes men, and some of them seem to find her attractive. I was afraid that you would be smitten. Maggie is nearer your age than mine, and seeing you together makes me feel middle-aged and unloved.'

This confession disarmed him completely, and his anger melted in a sudden warm rush of tenderness. He caught her up into his arms, and careless of her *maquillage* and the fragile lace of her dress, lost no time in reassuring her. He loved her, she was the most desirable, beautiful, darling girl. How could she think he would look at anyone else when she was around?

They hurried in late for dinner that evening, and so loving and intimate was their manner to each other that they might as well have been alone in a private world. Dart drew certain conclusions.

'A lover's tiff, Tonia?'

'No such thing,' she replied with a toss of her silvery curls. 'We just got carried away and forgot the time.'

A friend loaned David his sailboat for a day, and he and James took the older children sailing on Long Island Sound. They came back sun- and wind-burned, and pleased with themselves. One small thing only had marred the day for David. Something Miss Brimley had said that morning had taken up residence at the back of his mind, sticking there like an invisible burr.

The governess had been on her way to the children's breakfast, and he had wished her good morning. 'I hear that you are leaving us, Brimmy. The children will miss you.'

The little governess was about to return to England. After months of homesickness, she had at first been ecstatic to know that her exile was at an end. But no sooner was it settled than she began to remember that last sea voyage, and her waking thoughts were haunted by visions of giant waves and circling U-boats. She could not sleep at night for worry. Antonia had been irritated. David felt rather sorry for her.

'You mustn't worry about the journey, you know,' he told her. 'The seas are a lot safer than they were a year ago.'

She smiled at him waveringly. 'It's foolish of me, I know. But I feel ever so much easier in my mind now that Maggie is coming with me.

But someone ought to tell Abby soon . . .'

David frowned and would have asked more, but the breakfast gong drowned both speech and hearing for nearly a minute. Wilding came to say that his own breakfast was ready, and a crowd of children trooped by. So David smiled vaguely and went on his way.

He emerged from the bathroom that evening, shaved for dinner and washed free of salt and sand. He went next door to talk to Antonia about Maggie.

He had let the subject drop for nearly two weeks, telling himself that Antonia needed space and time to adjust. It was not his wife's fault that she was inclined towards jealousy and needed constant reassurance. He blamed himself for being naive and clumsy, never thinking that she would feel threatened by the nursery maid's changed looks. If he kept out of it, Antonia's good sense and kindly nature would surely re-assert themselves. But his encounter with Miss Brimley had made him think again. If her rather rambling words meant what he thought they did, he could no longer evade the issue.

He found Antonia in front of a long triple mirror. He crossed the room and stood behind her, bending down to plant a kiss on one bare shoulder. 'Hello there,' he said. 'How was your day?'

'Less energetic than yours, darling, from what the children told me. Miles is burned as red as a beetroot. You should have made him wear a sun hat.'

'He did wear it, but it blew off.'

'I only hope he doesn't get sunstroke.'

'I doubt it. They are all pretty much used to the sun, after Florida.' He walked across the carpeted floor and sat on an upright chair by the window. 'Antonia, Miss Brimley said something this morning about Maggie. What did she mean? It sounded as though you had arranged to send them to England together.'

'Adele Devenish is arranging it, if you must know. She's a bore, but she has her uses, and is trying to get them a double cabin.' She moved towards the door. 'It's time we went down. I want a drink before dinner.'

'Wait, Antonia.' Something peremptory in his tone made her pause and turn to face him. He said evenly, 'Let me understand this. You are actually proposing to send Maggie back to her father, knowing quite well how he treated her last year?'

'She doesn't need to go home. Where Maggie goes after she gets to England will be entirely her affair. She is a free agent.'

'Where else could she go but to Glen Cary? Antonia, Maggie is not even nineteen yet – too young to be pushed out into the world.'

'I was married to Johnnie when I was not much older,' said Antonia. She came towards him, smiling into his dark, serious face. 'Don't be cross with me, darling. I only wish you could have seen Brimmy's expression when I told her that I was sending Maggie to hold her hand on the journey. The poor little thing almost wept for joy.'

'Miss Brimley,' said David unsmiling, 'seems to have a higher opinion of Maggie than you do. Have you told the children that they are going to lose her?'

'Not yet. It may be weeks or months before they sail. No need to tell them yet.'

'You are aware, of course, that Abby and the boys absolutely adore her?'

'Children have no way of judging character in adults. They like Maggie because she spoils them.'

'Listen, Antonia,' said David in a tone that he tried to keep reasonable. 'If Miss Brimley goes away, Maggie will be needed here more than ever. Someone has to mind the children and do the chores.'

'Mary-Jo can do all that. In fact she has started already, and Miss Fortescue will keep an eye on things.'

'Good Lord! You can't mean to leave our kids to that woman's mercies.'

'May I remind you, David,' said Antonia beginning to lose her temper, 'that they are not *your* kids but very much mine. And Maggie is not your employee. If I choose to send her back with Brimmy, I shall do so.'

'Does my mother know what you mean to do?' he inquired. 'She has a high opinion of Maggie, I know, and the same goes for Father and James. They all like her.'

'I don't deny,' said Antonia, her tone waspish, 'that Maggie has ingratiated herself most cleverly with your parents. But Abby and Miles are my children. I want them to learn to do things for themselves from now on. Maggie waits on them hand and foot, and it is not good for them.'

'Is that so, Antonia?' He had too often overheard Antonia ordering the nursery maid about, and it was an effort to hold back an acid comment.

'Now that they are both at school all day,' Antonia was saying, 'they don't need a governess, and still less a nursery maid. Maggie must do her duty by her grandmother, and go home. She is not needed here.'

'Have you forgotten that the summer vacation is three months long?' His mouth twisted. 'Will you enjoy bathing Jamie every day, taking him to the john when he needs it, changing and washing his wet pants when you don't get there in time? I wonder if your pretty motherly affection for him will survive under those conditions.'

She flushed angrily, nettled by his derisive tone, but before she could utter a heated reply, he got up from his chair, and said in sudden remorse, 'Forgive me, honey. That was a horrible thing to say.' And when she did not answer him, he added, 'We have so little time left. Less than a week. I hate to quarrel with you like this.'

'Then stop interfering between me and my nursery maid.'

'I wish I had never taken charge of that damned letter, or asked you what to do about it, or spoken to Maggie,' he said discontentedly. 'I seem only to have made matters worse.'

'I could not agree more. Of all the boring things to quarrel about!'

He looked at her and said slowly, 'Promise to treat Maggie fairly, Antonia, and I'll leave it to you.'

'What do you take me for? I see nothing unfair about paying her passage back to England, not to mention double wages for looking after Brimmy.'

'Miss Brimley is worried about how Abby will feel about Maggie going. She thinks we ought to warn her.'

'Brimmy worries about everything, the silly old thing. I shall tell Abby when the time comes. And don't you go upsetting her, David,' she added rather sharply. 'Leave me to deal with Abby in my own way.'

'Have you warned Maggie not to tell her? You ought to, if you don't want her to know.'

'Maggie doesn't yet know herself.'

'Doesn't know . . . Antonia, do you mean to tell me,' he said slowly and incredulously, 'that you have never consulted Maggie or asked her what she wants? She may prefer to stay in America.'

Antonia flushed angrily, but before she could say anything the booming sound of the dinner gong came to their ears. 'Damn you, David,' she said, hurrying to the door. 'I shall miss my evening cocktail, all because of that girl. The sooner she sails for England, the happier we shall all be.'

David followed her more slowly, and Antonia had closed the elevator and gone down before he reached it. He decided as he trod down the stairs that there was nothing for it but to speak to Maggie himself. If she wanted to stay in the United States, he would encourage her to do so.

But he never got to speak to Maggie because when he looked for her after dinner, they told him that she had already gone to bed.

Frustrated, David retired to bed himself. Antonia twined white arms round his neck and said in a concerned tone, 'You said something about only having a few days left, darling. It's been worrying me. Whatever did you mean?'

'You know what I meant. I have to be back in England by mid-June. Before that, Dart and I have a job to do in Canada.'

'Surely not so soon. We've only just come.'

'Six weeks' leave was what they gave me.'

'You could stay on longer if you wanted to. David, won't you even

277

consider leaving the Air Force? You've more than done your bit. It's time you thought of Aunt Chrissie's happiness, and mine.'

'Antonia, I have no intention of leaving the Air Force. It's my job. Don't go on about it or we'll start fighting again.'

'What if they don't want you? They may tell you that you aren't fit to fly.'

'I'll face that when the time comes.' He pulled away from her, kissed her briefly, before rolling over and lying with his back to her. 'Let's go to sleep. I'm pooped after all that sun and sea air.'

Antonia lay beside him in the dark, pondering how to change his mind. He was in no mood tonight, and for this she blamed Maggie. Tiresome girl. Happily, she would not be around much longer.

So, how to delay David's going? If only he would stay until he had been seen by Aunt Chrissie's professor. A thought dawned in her mind and, made her smile in the darkness. The visit to Washington! Conway had laid on a weekend of meetings and entertainment, all aimed at helping Dart to make contact with influential Washington people. She and David were going along too. It might be just the chance she needed.

She thought drowsily of those blissful honeymoon days at the London Vorst, when David's only wish had been to please her and give her anything she asked for. She would ring the Washington hotel in the morning and ask for a suite well away from Dart or Conway. She would order flowers and have champagne on ice. Even if it meant neglecting the others, she would soon have David eating out of her hand. On this heartening reflection, Antonia turned over and was soon asleep.

Miss Fortescue was not so fortunate. She had been suffering from insomnia for almost a week, and all on account of Maggie Dunlop and what was fast becoming an obsessive need to get even with the girl. Time after time she relived her moment of humiliation in the secretary's office, when David Vorst had looked at her with such contempt and ordered her out. Not only that, but the story of the missing pearls had reached Miss Brimley's ears, and the little governess had upbraided her for being unjust to Maggie. Her reproaches should have been laughable, really, as though a timid mouse had suddenly grown claws and fangs. But Miss Fortescue had not felt like laughing.

It had been a setback for Mrs David, too, for all that she tried to laugh it off and pretend that her husband's forgetfulness was to blame. Miss Fortescue was not deceived. Antonia Vorst had it in for Maggie Dunlop, not a doubt of it. She had almost jumped at the chance to discredit the girl over the pearl necklace. She would doubtless welcome another chance – if it were offered to her on a plate. And the next time they would make sure.

Chapter 20

The black Buick was screened from the road by overhanging trees. They had hired it for the morning only, for Cagney had persuaded Bones that it would not do to use the same automobile too often, in case someone remembered the number plate or the make. The transit van with the souped-up engine was being kept in reserve.

Fifty yards from the highway, they watched the children filtering between the tall wrought-iron gates of Maple Valley House, holding schoolbags and chatting, dancing and fidgeting about while they waited for the school bus. The men knew who these children were and which ones to watch for. Kim and Abby had caught the current yo-yo craze and were challenging each other to do triple round-the-worlds with variable success and some laughter. They had to scramble to collect their belongings when the bus wheezed to a stop beside them. Mary-Jo waved a relieved hand and turned to walk back up the avenue.

'So that's the kid sister? How much does she know, Cag?'

'Better than to ask questions.'

'Maybe so, but she must wonder. What if she starts singing after we've done the job?'

'She won't. I've got all I need from Sis now, and I told her I was taking the train to Chicago tomorrow night.'

'And she believed you?'

'Sure she did. My little sister believes everything I tell her,' said Cagney smugly. 'Quit worrying, Bones. Everything's fine. You're all set up in the Long Beach apartment, and I'm lined up this end. All we have to do is decide on the time and the place, and press the button. The Fourth of July will be nothing to it.'

Both men laughed, and were still chuckling at their joke when Cagney turned the Buick out onto the highway and stepped on the gas. The tension was building. They had taken much time and care over their plans, but hiring cars and buying and testing out fireworks had pretty well cleaned them out. Cagney said vehemently that they could not fail. They told each other this several times a day, even managing to believe it when they had downed a beer or two, but as the day drew nearer, their nerves were strung tighter than wires. Of the two, Bones had a more cautious nature. He was younger than

279

Cagney, and at first had wanted to bring one of his older cousins into it, but Cagney had not wanted to share the loot.

Bones said, 'How about checking out the school again? It's a shorter getaway from there.'

'Maybe you're right.' Cagney was in two minds. He had first of all pressed for Maple Valley as the best place, assuring Bones that very few people knew his face in this neck of the woods, and anyway they would be masked on the day. But from time to time he thought uneasily about Ed. It would be just like his brother Ed to come along and spoil things.

He decided that they should spend a couple of days in the school area, trying out the side roads, working on timing. No harm in having a second plan, anyway, and Bones's constant doubts were getting on his nerves. He said, 'We'll case the school again next week. Right now let's get the hell out. Nobody saw us this morning, but I don't like to stick around so close to where my folks live.'

Cagney was right. Nobody had seen them that morning. But Maggie had spotted them twice during the past week.

'So what could Cagney be up to?' Maggie asked Ed Morgan.

She saw Mary-Jo's student brother quite often these days, for he had an evening job in the Maple Valley gardens. He seemed to be the right person to tell about Cagney.

'Your mother and Mary-Jo had postcards from him in New Mexico. That's what she told me, but actually he's here on Long Island. I've seen him three times – once on Jones Beach some weeks ago, and twice this week at different places on the property. As you know, I'm silly about Cagney. He gives me the creeps.'

She had half-expected Ed to laugh at her, but he did not. He was adjusting his bicycle seat with a small spanner, and when it was tightened to his satisfaction, he said soberly, 'I'd be willing to bet that Mary-Jo has been seeing Cagney someplace. She avoids me, and has that look about her . . .'

Maggie had no difficulty in understanding what Ed meant. Mary-Jo had been avoiding her, too, and there was something excited and furtive about her which reminded Maggie of the time when she had lifted Miss Brimley's locket and then put it back.

'No good asking her, though,' said Ed. 'If Cagney told her to say he was sitting on the North Pole, that's what she would swear to. Where was he when you saw him yesterday, Maggie?'

'Not far from the front gates. I'd missed the bus from town and was walking home and saw their car parked in the lane near Mr Conway's place. I ran back through the trees because I didn't want Cagney to see me. What do you suppose they were doing there?'

'They?'

'There was another man with him, possibly the one he was with on the beach when they got talking to the children. I don't like it, Ed. I don't want to make trouble for your family but I ought to tell someone.'

'Who would you tell?'

'I thought of saying something to Mr James or Mrs Sandridge. They like to know who comes and goes.'

'I wish you wouldn't,' said Ed alarmed at where this might lead. 'You'll get me fired – and M-J as well. Cagney's a pain in the neck but why shouldn't he sit in an automobile and talk to someone?'

'No reason, but I wish he would do it somewhere else,' said Maggie with feeling.

When Ed had ridden off, she thought sadly that she would absolutely have to speak to James. If Ed lost his job, he would blame her and not want to see her any more. She liked Ed and would miss their chats in the garden, but she did not see what else she could do.

She also knew that there could be no talking to James until after the weekend. He was away with the David Vorsts. They had departed for Washington DC that morning. Antonia had been particularly capricious and demanding, changing her mind several times about what clothes to take for the visit, trying on first this and then that dress, and complaining that Maggie had failed to wash and iron her favourite nightgown.

Conway had arranged for them to stay at the Washington Vorst. Dart was waiting in the lobby, and Antonia was surprised and rather put out to find that Adele Devenish was with him. The tall Englishwoman greeted Antonia affably, as though she was a hostess and this was her house party. Conway had been held up, she said, but would join them as soon as he could.

'What's that woman doing here?' Antonia asked Dart fretfully. She was cross, because David had as good as dumped her in the hotel lobby and driven away with James to some place outside the city. There had been no time to protest. He had kissed her on the mouth, said something about talking to her later and was gone.

She looked around her flower decorated suite while Dart was tipping the bellboy, and demanded, 'Has Conway taken Adele Devenish on as a housekeeper or something?'

Dart looked at Antonia with amusement. 'Conway would like to take her on all right, but as something more intimate than a housekeeper. He's been stalking La Devenish for quite some time, but with what success I don't know.'

Antonia was incredulous. 'That ugly woman? Surely you're making that up!'

Dart looked at her in amusement. 'Did you have designs on Conway yourself?'

'Certainly not! As if I would!' She felt rather dashed down, however, and said in an aggrieved tone, 'Do you mean to say that David knew about Adele and never warned me?'

'Perhaps he did not want to spoil your fun, Tonia. Or maybe he was supporting Conway in his little game of bluff.'

'Whatever do you mean?'

Dart looked at her, and wondered whether it had yet dawned on David that his wife was in some ways a rather stupid woman. 'If you don't know, it's not for me to tell you. I'll give you some advice instead. David sees more than you think. If you are wise, you won't try to cheat on him.'

'I'd never cheat on him. Not really.'

She expected him to laugh at that, but he did not. He merely reminded her that they were due to meet Conway and Adele downstairs in an hour's time, and went away.

Worse was to come. David called up to say that he would not be returning. There was a lot of work to be done, he said, tests and essential check-ups. He would have to stay where he was until they were completed. He would join her in Maple Valley on Monday, and asked her to relay his apologies to the others.

So much for her second honeymoon! She had planned it so carefully. 'You can't do this to me, David. I wouldn't have come to Washington if I'd known you were going to stand me up!'

'I'm truly sorry, darling but this project has come up, and I can't miss it. I warned Dart, though, and he promised to amuse you.'

'What *is* this thing? Are you testing some new sort of plane?'

'You know I can't answer that, Antonia.'

'Well, is it to do with the Air Force?'

There was a short pause before he said, 'You could say so.'

'And what am I to tell people when they ask for you at this big dinner tonight? They'll probably think you're tired of me and are cavorting in some brothel with a floosie.'

'Tell them her name is Mata Hari, honey. They'll enjoy that.'

'Very funny.'

'Just a minute,' he said. She heard a confused murmur of voices, and David's voice saying something that she did not catch. Finally, his voice came to her loud and cheerful. 'I have to go, Antonia. Someone is waiting to see me. Be sure to enjoy yourself in Washington. And tell James to take you to Mount Vernon if Dart is too busy.'

'James is to stay with you. Aunt Chrissie told him to make sure that you didn't get too tired.'

David laughed. 'Mother never stops trying, does she! I've sent him back to you. Enjoy your weekend, Antonia.'

'Oh, go to hell!' She slammed the telephone down in a fury, and only later remembered that she had wanted to ask him about Conway and Adele.

* * *

She did her best, during that surprisingly enjoyable weekend, to find out what stage the romance between Conway and Adele had reached – if romance it was. Such an unlikely pair! If it was a love match, it was like no other she had known. A succession of sparring bouts was more like it, for they never stopped arguing and contradicting each other all weekend long. All the same, she once or twice surprised a look in Conway's eyes as he watched La Devenish, which made her think that Dart could be right.

It was bizarre and interesting. Adele was cheerful, loud-voiced, laughed even louder than she spoke, and loped around like an off duty lacrosse player. Antonia watched her with growing fascination, and even chuckled to herself when Dart got up to his tricks, joining in the running arguments and trying to draw Adele out.

Antonia was forced to admit that despite her unfortunate looks, Adele contributed her fair share to a harmonious and enjoyable weekend. She was interested in a wide range of subjects, could talk knowledgeably about books and politics and the progress of the war, and had them laughing about the oddities of people she worked with in New York. She seemed to know a lot of well-known persons on both sides of the Atlantic. In spite of herself, Antonia was impressed, and thought that it might be worth enlisting Adele as an ally.

One of Adele's 'causes' was to encourage British people – particularly those with skills – to go home and join in the war effort. She had already prevailed on several British ex-patriots to do so, using her many contacts with the Royal Navy and the British Consulate to get them across the Atlantic.

'American friendship and support is vital to us,' she said. 'We need money and aircraft and ships, and trained people to man them. But to have any hope of winning this total war, British people here – all the able-bodied ones – must understand that they are needed back home. They should go and do their bit.'

'If that is what you believe, Adele, why are you here?' inquired Conway, running a ruminative eye over her silken-clad form and smiling slightly. 'Your body looks able enough to me.'

'I mean to go home as soon as my sister arrives to take my place,' retorted Adele calmly. 'She is waiting for her visa to come through.'

Dart raised his brows. 'Thus exchanging one able British body for another?'

'No. My sister has been invalided out of the ATS. She commanded a gun battery all through the Blitz in the hairiest of conditions, and then, of all things, succumbed to a bad bout of food poisoning and strained her heart. Someone has to take charge of our young people at Bellefield, and it seems best for us to swap over. Jennifer's eldest girl will be going home with me. She's nearly eighteen, and

283

desperate to join one of the women's services.'

'Tell her to chose the Wrens,' advised Dart, rising to his feet with a yawn. 'The uniform is more becoming than the others, particularly on girls with good legs. I'm for bed. It's been a good day, Conway. Thanks to you, I believe I'm getting somewhere at last.'

There were more meetings for Dart and Conway next day, so the two women explored the sights with James as their guide and chauffeur. Adele found Antonia both friendly and confiding – which was something altogether new. She was amused, and perfectly willing to encourage these overtures. She listened to Antonia's confidences, parried certain probing questions with perfect good humour – and gave nothing away.

She had earlier thought Antonia rather stupid, a lovely little fool with an eye to the main chance. Back in New York, she confessed to Conway that she had wronged her. 'You know, I think she could be dangerous. However, we have one thing in common. We both love James. That man is a wonderful guide, and evidently a great admirer of George Washington. He made both the man and the history of Mount Vernon come alive.'

Adele paused, remembering that she had promised to do Antonia a favour – and other things. She said thoughtfully, 'I understand, now, why so many people rave about David's wife. When she turned that searchlight charm upon me, I veered towards liking her myself. She had me believing that black was white, at least while I was with her.'

Conway lay in bed and watched Adele. She was seated at the dressing table, clad in one of his silk dressing gowns. He was not much interested in what she was saying. He wanted her back beside him in the bed, but was at the same time conscious of a rumbling tummy. They had eaten nothing since leaving Washington. A cheese sandwich would fill the gap. He said drowsily, 'I'm glad you two girls had a fun day.'

Adele's boisterous laugh rang out suddenly. 'Antonia had less fun than I did. She tried not to show it but she was desperate to find out the truth about you and me, Conway.'

'And what did you tell her?'

'I hope I left her guessing.'

'You're good at that, you bad girl. You kept me guessing for months, and for God's sake don't ever ask me to go through another weekend like this last one.' He added curtly, 'I could do with a sandwich or something. Adele, why do you have to swathe yourself in that silk thing? If I didn't know you better, I would think you were ashamed of your body.'

'I used to be,' she admitted, coming over and sitting on the bed. 'Being with you has changed me, Conway. You've made all things new for me, even my lanky body. But I don't have to tell you that . . .'

He pulled her down beside him and tweaked at the ties of the dressing gown, and with one thing and another, the bread and cheese lay undisturbed in the icebox. It was almost dawn before they fell into a more prolonged and exhausted sleep.

They had made it a rule never to have sex in any of the Vorst houses – Adele refused to call it 'making love', saying that it was no such thing – so the enforced abstinence of the past three days and nights had tried Conway almost beyond bearing. So urgent was his hunger for her that he had angrily insisted on flying back to New York on Sunday evening, even refusing to sit anywhere near her in the plane.

By the time they made it by taxi to Conway's New York apartment, he had been practically growling with his pent-up need, and had dragged her towards the largest sofa, pulling her clothes off as they wrestled crablike across the floor. She had been doing the same for him, and they had not quite finished their double striptease when he had taken her brutally and without finesse. Adele had responded joyously, and with a lust that matched his own.

Presently they ended up in his huge bed next door, slept for a while, woke and started all over again in a more leisurely fashion. This time he took care to fondle and caress this newly aroused and extraordinary woman. He was not a humble man, but he was conscious of a sort of amazed appreciation of the pleasure they had shared since her capitulation a week ago. During the eternity of frustration while she had held him off, he had been aware that she wanted him but had never suspected just how much. Having once decided to give way to her desires, her generosity and the molten heat of her ardour had delighted him. She was a veritable human volcano, like no woman he had ever known, full of contradictions, all shuddering surrender one minute and shouting with ribald laughter the next.

They breakfasted late and substantially, and ended up drinking coffee and reading the morning papers like any married couple. With a stab of jealousy, Conway remembered Gerald Devenish.

'Adele,' he said suddenly. 'Don't go back to England.'

She smiled at him. She was fully dressed, and almost on the point of leaving for the Long Island railroad. 'I won't be going this week, I promise, and probably not for several months. You'll be glad to see me go in a week or so – or a month.'

'I doubt that. I'm not so changeable.'

'From what I hear, you change your girlfriends as often as most people change their socks.'

'That's untrue, Adele, and I don't think of you as a girlfriend. You told me I made you feel wonderful, and you do the same for me.'

'Thank you.'

She might have been thanking him for passing the butter. He

suppressed a hot retort, and said, 'Promise me, at least, that you won't leave until the summer's over.'

She shook her head. 'No promises, Conway. We agreed to enjoy a temporary affair while it still works for both of us – to live for each moment as it comes. Let's stick to that. I must go, or I shall miss my train.'

She gave him a brisk peck on the cheek, before picking up her suitcase and going out.

'Brimmy, do you know where Maggie is?' demanded Abby, coming into the bathroom with Kim at her side. Abby was out of breath and looking worried. 'I can't find her, and her brush and comb have gone, and some of her clothes.'

'She's been sent to work at Bellefield for a few days,' said the governess, who was leaning over the bath and dabbing tentatively at Jamie's face with a face cloth. 'They're short-handed there, it seems. Lady Adele rang Mrs Sandridge this morning and asked if she could be spared.'

'Why didn't they send Mary-Jo or one of the others?'

'I've no idea. Oh, dear! Where has Jamie's towel got to? Ah, there it is! Now, Jamie, be a good boy and don't *wriggle* so! It seems,' the governess added rather breathlessly, 'that your dear mother saw no objection to Maggie going, so Mrs Sandridge drove her over while you were at school.'

'Your dear mother,' said Kim when they were out of the bathroom, 'spent all last weekend in Washington with that Adele woman. She probably told her to ask for Maggie specially.'

'Why should Mum keep wanting to send Maggie off?'

Kim shrugged her thin shoulders. 'I s'pose she wants her out of the way. You shouldn't make it so obvious that you like Maggie best.'

'I don't do anything of the sort.'

'You do so!'

They came to the top of the back stairs and clattered down it with accustomed breakneck speed. It was a matter of pride among the older children to get down the eighty-four spiral stairs in less than a minute. When they got to the bottom and were standing panting in the passage which led from the servants' quarters to the front of the house, James came by. He smiled at them.

'How did the track trials go today, girls?'

'Fine,' said Kim. 'I was chosen for the fourth grade relay and the fifty-yard dash, and Abby is in the fifth grade ditto and the high jump.'

'So when is sports day?'

'Thursday after next, and graduation the day after that. Grandma says that she's coming to watch our races.'

'You know fine that Mrs Vorst would never miss your sports day, nor Miss Tina either. Abby will have her own mother to root for her this year. That will be nice.'

Abby agreed that it would be nice. Then, on an impulse, she asked, 'Mr James, how long is Maggie going to be away?'

'Is she away?'

'She's gone to Bellefield to work. Mrs Sandridge drove her there this morning.'

'Is that so?' James smiled at Abby. 'Then Mrs Sandridge will know how long Maggie means to stay. I'll find out and let you know.'

He went into the office, and was greeted by May's usual cheerful smile. 'So how was Washington DC? Antonia seems to have just loved her weekend.'

'She seemed happy. They all did.'

'Oh? Did the brothers Vorst have fun together? That would be something new.'

'Not they. David played hookey. Something top secret. He asked to be dropped off outside a military compound, and whatever they were doing behind those gates went on all weekend. He never came back to join the others.'

'Antonia must have been pretty mad at him for running out on her.'

'Not noticeably.'

'Not many wives would tolerate that sort of treatment,' said Mrs Sandridge, shaking her head. 'That wife of David's is as good-natured as she is pretty.'

James grunted. 'I've just brought David back from the airport. He seems mighty pleased with himself. He doesn't give much away, but you know the way his eyes used to glow when he was happy?'

'I remember well.'

'I hear Maggie has been sent to Bellefield to work.'

'She has indeed. You know, at first I thought she was going to refuse. And she hardly spoke to me all the way over.'

'Any particular reason for this sudden banishment?'

'Bellefield are short-staffed, and Antonia did not object to her going. I wondered whether she had grown tired of looking at Maggie's sulky face.' Mrs Sandridge was silent for a little while. Then she said with a frown, 'You know, I had a high opinion of that girl but she's been behaving oddly these last weeks. Do you think Mr and Mrs Vorst spoiled her while she was down south?'

Maggie's silence on the way to Bellefield had not been caused by sulks but by something very different. True, she had not wanted to go to Bellefield, for she saw her banishment as another move in Antonia's campaign to remove her. But when she arrived at her bedroom on the attic floor and found both Antonia and Miss Fortescue standing in it, she was filled with foreboding.

She paused in the doorway.

'Have you come to do your packing, Maggie?' inquired Antonia in a cooing voice. 'What time are you going to Bellefield?'

Maggie looked at first one and then the other, knowing them for her enemies, and wondering what they were up to. Nothing good, she was sure. She answered mechanically, 'In half an hour, ma'am. Was there something you wanted?'

'I do have something to say to you before you go. But finish your packing first.'

So with both of them eyeing her – Antonia seated on the only chair, and Miss Fortescue by the door – Maggie set about packing clothes for Bellefield. She went to get her washing things from the adjacent shower room but could not find her sponge bag. She came into the bedroom holding her face cloth, toothbrush and paste, and stopped short. Antonia was on her feet, the missing bag in her hand.

'You'll be wanting this,' she said. 'But if it's all right with you, Maggie, I'll keep my earrings. My husband gave them to me, and I value them.' She held out a hand, and the twin jewels lay on her upturned palm. She added, in the sweet voice that never failed to make Maggie cringe, 'It's just as well you're going to Bellefield today, Maggie. Otherwise I should feel obliged to tell Mr and Mrs Vorst about this unfortunate habit of yours, as well as my husband and the children . . .'

Maggie sat hunched beside Mrs Sandridge in the car, struggling with a sense of outrage and incredulity and remembering their looks of triumph and malice. She recalled her stuttering denials to which they paid no notice at all.

Some part of her brain was wondering which of them had planted the earrings. Or had they done it together? It did not matter. The thing that mattered was that Antonia had won and that she had been defeated.

She had known all along, really, that she would lose. In the past weeks Antonia and Miss Fortescue had been moving in on her. One by one, she had been stripped of her more enjoyable duties. Branded as too dangerous a driver to take the children about and her veracity doubted, nobody invited her to ferry the servants about or to run errands. She never got near the children or joined in their expeditions, for Miss Fortescue knew of Antonia's embargo and made sure that it was enforced.

Antonia had kept her busy. There was underwear to be washed and ironed every day, new clothes to be altered. Sometimes she made Maggie work on a garment twice or three times before saying that she supposed that it would do. It was remarkable how each day filled up with new, irritating and time-consuming tasks. She could no longer count on her half-day off, and had not seen Miss Gladys for weeks.

Today was just a culmination, a climax to their campaign. She was being sent away to be forgotten and finally eliminated – and if she tried to protest her innocence it would be their word against hers.

She arrived at Bellefield in a mood verging on despair, but it did not last. Almost at once she felt her spirits rising. A teeming, haphazard community lived together in the big echoing mansion, not only a multitude of Devenishes, with Adele very much in command, but three other families with small children. There was so much going on that she had no time and certainly no solitude to dwell upon her troubles.

She was welcomed briskly by Lady Adele, and everybody went into lunch. When the meal was over and cleared away, Maggie was taken upstairs by a yellow-haired slip of a girl called Sophy whose room she was to share. Maggie had seen her on the boat, and once or twice since, but never to speak to until now. Sophy promptly lit two cigarettes and handed one to Maggie.

'Now tell me all,' demanded this young woman, dropping onto the second bed and tucking thin brown legs under her. 'I'm dying to know what you've done to be sent away from Maple Valley House.'

Maggie squinted at her through the smoke, sucked at her cigarette tentatively, and choked. When she had recovered she said, 'I don't know what I'm supposed to have done. They said you were short of servants here, so I'm on loan for a while.'

Sophy laughed. 'A long, long while, if Antonia Vorst has her way. The shortage of servants thing was only Aunt Addie's excuse for sending for you. Antonia made her promise to, you see, because she doesn't want you near her children any more. Now what I want to know is, what dreadful deed have you committed to be sent away?'

Maggie stared at the vivid, excited little face before her, and said slowly, 'I'd like fine to know myself. What did Lady Adele tell you?'

'Oh her,' said Sophy dismissively. 'The poor thing is too old-fashioned to know about any really exotic vices, and she wouldn't sully my ears with them anyway, more's the pity. She just knows that Antonia wants rid of you.'

'That's true enough,' said Maggie, taking another puff at her cigarette. It was not so disastrous, only plain nasty. She swallowed, for she was beginning to feel rather sick.

'Look, Maggie. You don't have to smoke that if you don't like it.' Sophy reached over. 'Give it to me and I'll finish it.'

'Thanks,' said Maggie with real gratitude.

'So stop stalling, for heaven's sake, and tell me all.'

Maggie was silent for nearly a minute, trying to think how best to answer. Laying aside the affair of the earrings – and she could not yet bear to think of it, let alone speak of it – what was there to say?

'The trouble is,' she said apologetically, 'that I haven't the least idea what you're hinting at. Mrs David doesn't like me, of course. Also, she says I spoil her children and thinks I drive dangerously. At least, she told Mrs Vorst so, a while back . . .' She looked up, and saw that Sophy was looking crestfallen, and added with a tremor of laughter, 'I can see that I'm a dreadful disappointment to you.'

'I'll say you are! I counted on you being truly steeped in evil, and you are no different to all the other dullards here.' Then with just a flickering ember of hope in her eyes, she ventured, 'Maggie? I suppose you couldn't by any chance be pregnant?'

'Certainly not!' retorted Maggie, trying to look shocked but unable to help laughing. 'Sophy, do you always talk like this to people you've met five minutes ago?'

'Only when I think they are involved in a juicy scandal,' retorted Sophy. 'I haven't given up yet. There must be *something* . . .'

'Maggie, there you are!' cried Abby, plunging down the bank and flinging her arms round the nursery maid's waist. The child's freckled face was flushed and beaded with sweat, for she had just walked three miles along the road. She came upon Maggie and Sophy sitting on a low wall. Maggie was shelling peas, and her companion had a book open on her lap. 'I've come to make sure you're all right. Are they cruel to you here?'

Maggie returned Abby's hug, and said darkly, 'Torture chambers on every floor. It's great to see you, but shouldn't you be at school?'

'I am at school. I mean, I'm supposed to be,' she amended, as Maggie looked at her. 'We had a graduation practice this morning, and it was so hot marching that Mary-Lou Forster fainted and the rest of us were sent to rest in the library. As long as I get back before the school bus, nobody will know.'

They revived her with a glass of lemonade, and Maggie said that she would walk her back to school. Sophy, who had been ploughing through a battle scene in *War and Peace*, decided to come with them.

'Good practice for square-bashing,' she said cheerfully when they had marched along the hot highway for nearly an hour and were in sight of their goal. 'I'll have six weeks of it when I first join the Wrens. After that it ought to get interesting, with lots of dashing officers lining up to take me dancing.'

'Oh?' Abby had been so pleased to see Maggie that she had barely noticed her companion. 'You must be something to do with Harriet Ducane. She's in my class, and when we had speech making, she talked about the Wrens. Actually, it was quite interesting.'

'Fascinating would be a more civil word to use!' retorted Sophy with a snort. 'If it was only "quite interesting" Harriet must have made a muck of it. I wrote the speech for her.'

'So you're one of those Devenishes?'

'Part of the clan,' Sophy admitted. 'Same clan, different name. There are fourteen of us in all.'

'Harriet says that you're going back to England.'

'Sooner rather than later, I hope,' said Sophy with a grimace. 'It's taking simply ages to find a boat to go on. I've been trying to persuade Maggie to come with me.' She did not notice Abby's look of dismay, for they had reached the roadside store that stood beside the school gates. 'Walk on while I buy some ciggies. I'll catch you up.'

Abby's freckles stood out on her shocked face. She stared wide-eyed at Maggie. 'You wouldn't, Maggie?'

'Wouldn't what?' said Maggie, to give herself time.

'Go back to England with that girl.'

'I might have to, Abby. Nursery maids never stay for ever, you know. That's probably why I was sent here, to help you get used to being without me.'

'So Mum *did* send you away.'

'I didn't say that, Abby.'

'And I'm not getting used to it at all.' Abby's voice started to wobble. 'I miss you all the time.'

Sophy came back, so there was no time to say more. They took Abby as far as the school gates and watched her walk rather forlornly away.

'Sorry, Mags,' said Sophy. 'Did I put my foot in it, telling her you might be going home?'

Maggie did not answer, for she was peering towards a clump of nearby trees. She grasped Sophy's arm and said in an odd voice, 'Start back, will you? There's something over there I want to look at. I'll catch you up.'

Sophy peered in her turn, noticed a glint of metal between the lower branches, and said, 'Some guy waiting for you in his car?'

'Not for me. But I need to see who it is.'

'Some necking couple?'

'I hope it may be that,' said Maggie, tight-lipped with sudden unease.

It was no necking couple. As she feared, it was Cagney and that other man again, only in a different car. Sitting behind tightly closed windows in the afternoon heat, the men were watching through binoculars as the school buses drove in, one by one.

Sophy, who had insisted on coming along, whispered, 'What are they doing, Mags?'

'I wish I knew,' said Maggie with feeling.

Chapter 21

'Damned fool boy!' said Cornelius when David told of his second visit to Conway's office, and what had happened there. 'So the Steiner woman sent a cable to say that she's leaving? So what? That doesn't mean you have to do the same.'

'Father, I warned you that I wouldn't stay on if Odette was forced out.'

'Nobody forced Madame Steiner to do anything. You young people are so hasty. Give yourself a week, and when you've cooled down I'll send for Conway and we'll talk this over quietly.'

'Dart and I leave for Canada tomorrow. Don't tell me you have forgotten. I told you at least a week ago.'

Cornelius flushed angrily, for he had indeed forgotten. He said, 'You are in no fit state to be haring off to Canada, and you know it!'

'There's nothing the matter with me, Father.'

'Your mother thinks you look ill, and so does Antonia. Everybody knows that British medicine is still in the dark ages, so at least get yourself checked out properly while you are in America. Professor Max Zimmerman is coming to New York next week to address a medical symposium. He is *the* authority on your sort of problems, Dave. Stay home and let him look at you, and if he says you are wholly recovered, your mother and I will be satisfied with his verdict.'

'As it happens,' said David, taking an envelope from his jacket pocket, 'I saw Professor Zimmerman last weekend in Washington. He ran every test he knew, and gave me the all clear. I even made him put it in writing, Father, since I knew you would not believe it otherwise.'

Bereft of speech, Cornelius took the proffered letter. But after reading it once and then again, he was shaken by a sudden gust of rage. 'Damn you, David! What the hell do you mean by going behind my back like that?'

'I wanted to know the score before bringing all the rest of you into it.'

'Did you cheat on Antonia too?'

'I did not tell her I was seeing Zimmerman, if that's what you mean.' David did not add that he and Antonia had barely been on speaking terms since coming back from Washington. She had not forgiven him for running out on her there. 'I told her just now, and reminded her that I won't be coming back after the Canada trip. She's upset, but I'm due to face a medical board in London in two weeks' time and don't intend to miss it.'

'What?' Cornelius's high coloured face had darkened to an alarming shade of purple. A vein bulged beside his temple. He banged a freckled fist on his desk top and said. 'You don't deserve that wife of yours! The poor girl positively dotes on you for some reason, and when I think of all the things we've been doing to smooth your path – Conway trying to track Zimmerman down, your mother and Antonia starting to fix up Pond Cottage as a surprise for you . . .'

'If Mother had asked me,' David said coldly, 'she could have saved herself a lot of trouble. I have no intention of living in Long Island again until the war is over and maybe not even then.'

'But Antonia said—'

'I am not speaking for Antonia. She loves it here, and doesn't want to come back to Britain with me. Even if she changes her mind, transport will take time to arrange, so I would be grateful if you would look after her and the children for the present.'

'You've an odd way of showing your gratitude,' said Cornelius sourly.

He got up stiffly, working his shoulders to loosen the feeling of tension that had built up. He was assailed by an urgent need for fresh air, and for Chrissie's company. They would go into the garden and look at her newest roses, and perhaps in the rose garden he would find the resolution to break the news that David would not be coming back after Canada. In her present state, Chrissie could hardly bear to let her darling out of her sight for so much as a day, and had been counting on the professor's verdict going the other way. Telling her was not going to be easy, but even balked and infuriated as he was, Cornelius did appreciate that the boy had to fulfil his commitment to the Royal Air Force. No son of his could go back on his word, and so he would tell Chrissie.

He was aware that David had neither moved nor spoken for several minutes. He said heavily, 'I guess I lost my temper, Dave. If only we had more time. I shall tell Conway that I won't agree to your leaving the company. Once this damned war is over, there will be a lot of rebuilding to do, and you will be needed.'

'Speak to Conway by all means,' said David. 'But he's not likely to feel the same way. He had a letter of resignation ready for my signature.'

'Don't tell me you were fool enough to sign it?'

'As a matter of fact,' said David, 'I did not. I brought the paper away with me, and John Graham will check it out this afternoon.'

'Why not Van Dusen? He's our company lawyer.'

'Exactly. Conway even suggested bringing him in, which left me in no doubt that he had him squared. From now on I shall fight my own corner and I've appointed John Graham as my New York attorney.'

'Dave, this is a family matter. No need to bring others into it.'

David looked at his father. The old man's angry colour had receded, and he looked blotched and somehow diminished. He said more mildly, 'Graham won't talk. Conway thinks me too busy playing war games to be worth my salary. If he gets his way, I shall be living on my Air Force pay and the interest from Grandmother Kimberley's legacy, and I need someone to get the best deal from Conway and the company. When I'm back on full-time ops, I won't have time to deal with those things myself.'

He turned to go, but Cornelius called him back. 'Dave, I implore you. Don't do anything drastic before you get back to England. Madame Steiner may have resigned for some quite other reason. It's worth taking time over decisions which may be hard to reverse.'

'I shall wait to make my mind up after I get to London and have seen Odette. That's what John Graham said I should do.'

'Sensible man. Listen to him, then, if you won't listen to me.' Cornelius added in an almost pleading tone, 'And for the Lord's sake, please don't talk to your mother about leaving the company. As it is I don't know how I am to tell her that you aren't coming back from Canada.'

Antonia felt cheated. David was going away. Neither smiles nor wiles, nor her final burst of temper had made the slightest difference. Worse than that, he was talking of leaving the hotel business and living at the dower house on the tuppence a year the RAF paid him.

She found Dart in the white parlour and poured out the gist of this.

Dart watched her. There was a degree of sympathy in his eyes.

She met his gaze and felt better. No wonder Dart felt sorry for her. David had treated her disgracefully, acting as though he had not a care in the world, fooling around with the children. He was deceitful and devious, getting Daniel Bruce to track down Professor Zimmerman and sneaking off to see him. No doubt he bribed the man to give him a clean bill of health.

'I doubt if the professor could be bribed,' said Dart judicially. 'Besides, why would David want a false diagnosis?'

'He's desperate to get back to flying.'

'But not daft enough to do so if Zimmerman thought he was not fit. That would be suicidal madness.'

'I wonder. Sometimes I suspect that all that flying at high altitudes has turned David's brain. To think of walking out of a well-paid job at the Vorst, throwing away our lovely top-floor flat and the only comfortable place to stay and eat in London – all because of that ugly

Jewish woman he likes so much. If that's not crazy behaviour, I don't know what is.'

'Ugly? Odette is a damned attractive woman and a first-class hotel manager. I often look her up when I'm in London.'

'No accounting for taste. Well, you won't find her at the Vorst after this.'

'Don't sound so pleased about it. Have you managed to get rid of the Dunlop girl yet?'

Antonia's lips tightened, and she sat up straight in her chair. 'Adele Devenish needed help at Bellefield so I sent her to work there.'

'So you fixed Adele, did you? What excuse did you give her for wanting rid of Maggie?'

'I told her the truth. I don't like the way she spoils my children, and I don't trust her. She will stay at Bellefield until the children have gone to Seagrass Island, and I shall send her home with Brimmy later.'

She looked up and saw David, swallowed and smiled at him rather nervously. He did not return her smile.

David was seeing his beautiful wife in a new remorseless light these days. This was his Antonia, whom he had once loved almost to distraction. They had been married for very nearly a year, and he wondered if he had ever known her at all. He felt very little liking for her at present, and when she had screamed at him that she was damned if she would go back to England, that he could go alone and lump it, his uppermost feeling had been one of relief.

He said bleakly, 'You're needed upstairs, Antonia. Abby has locked herself into the bathroom and Brimmy can't get her to come out. Apparently she's breaking her heart over your plan to get rid of Maggie.'

'How did she find out?' demanded Antonia sharply. 'I told Brimmy to keep it to herself.'

'You can't expect to keep secrets in a place like this,' he said coolly. 'Take my advice and tell Abby the truth. She may not like it, but plain speaking is often best.' He turned away from her, and began to talk to Dart about the Canada trip.

At Bellefield next morning, Adele asked Maggie what was going on. She said, 'Sophy thinks that you have been having a difficult time with Antonia Vorst.'

Maggie blinked, and then said wryly, 'It hasn't always been easy, milady.'

'Why does she dislike you, Maggie?'

Maggie had asked herself this question often enough but had not expected to be asked it by anyone else. She said slowly, 'There's never been any reason for Mrs David to *like* me. I mean, people like you or they don't. At Dulcimer Hall she used to pick on me sometimes. But it's only since she came to America that she has taken a real scunner to me. I've thought and thought, but I still don't understand why.'

'Have you tried asking her?'

Maggie tried to imagine herself doing so, failed, and said with a rueful smile, 'Asking her would be a waste of time. She would just think me impertinent.'

'Has she ever accused you of impertinence?'

Maggie thought, and shook her head. 'No. Just other things . . .'

'Such as?'

Maggie looked down at her hands, and said lamely, 'She thinks I spoil the children, and talk too much, and annoy Mr David by chattering and showing off when he's around . . .' She felt her face growing hot as she remembered that blighting lecture in Antonia's bedroom. 'She even accused me of stealing her pearls once, but luckily Mr David had them in his pocket. And yesterday—' She broke off, and said apologetically, 'I shouldn't talk about it, and mostly I don't. Nobody wants to hear a chapter of grumbles.'

'Did something happen yesterday to upset you? Why not tell me? Nothing shocks me, whatever Sophy may say. And talking about it might help to clear your mind – and mine, for that matter. Try me.'

'There are no two ways about it,' said Adele when Maggie had poured out the unspeakable business of the earrings. 'You simply mustn't go back. Why wait for Antonia to nail you on some other trumped-up charge before she sends you away with Miss Brimley?' And when Maggie looked startled, she added, 'Didn't you know she means to do that?'

Maggie shook her head. 'I would like to stay for the sake of the children, particularly for Abby. She came here yesterday, and I hate to desert her.'

'So I heard. Sophy told me that, too. But as for your feeling guilty, that's just silly. It's high time you started to put yourself first. You don't want to waste your life washing clothes and listening to children's prattle. Go back to Britain and start afresh. You could join the Wrens like Sophy, or some other branch of the forces.'

'If I go home my dad will expect me to look after Gran, milady. It's not what I want, but I probably ought to do it.'

'Nonsense. Why should you? From what David told me, they didn't treat you too well at home.' She eyed Maggie's flushed face thoughtfully, and changed tack. 'Now what's this about strange men outside the school?'

'Oh!' Maggie's hand went to her mouth, for she had forgotten to tell Mr James about Cagney. She got to her feet hastily. 'Milady, I've remembered something. Do you think I could ring Mr James? I'll pay for the call, of course.'

'Why not drive over and see him? I don't need the station wagon this morning.'

'I'd rather telephone, milady.' She was not going back to Maple Valley while David Vorst was there. Antonia would have told him that she was a thief and he would believe whatever told Antonia told him. Of course he would. David Vorst worshipped the ground his wife walked on.

David drove himself to Bellefield. He had always hated going there. He remembered being taken to visit his great-aunt as a small boy, and having to kiss her bristly cheek. He felt as reluctant this time, but with Antonia flatly refusing to discuss Maggie's affairs, he felt impelled to talk to her before he went away. He had rung Adele to tell her that he wanted to see her.

Adele met him in the hall. 'I should have checked with Maggie before I said you could come over. She says she won't see you.'

'Why not? I only want to tell her that she doesn't need to go back to Scotland unless she wants to. Something else can be arranged.'

'All right. I'll tell her that, but personally I think she ought to get away.'

He said, frowning, 'Adele, please ask her to see me. I have to know if she's OK.'

'She's quite all right, but you'll have to take my word for it,' said Adele. 'Come into the drawing room. I'll give you a cup of tea.'

'No thanks,' he said mechanically. 'I never drink tea. I don't get this. Why won't she see me?' He looked vaguely round the hall which seemed full of bicycles, pushchairs and other children's possessions. 'Have you any idea why?'

Adele had, in fact, a pretty good idea. She said merely, 'Things have not been easy for her, as I think you know, and she wants to put it behind her and start afresh.'

He stood perfectly still, his face devoid of expression. 'I still don't get it. Did Antonia do something to offend her?'

'Surely she would have told you if she had.'

'Not necessarily,' he said bleakly. 'Very well, so Maggie doesn't want to see me. Tell her, will you, that they are sending Kim and Abby up to Seagrass Island immediately after graduation.'

'That seems like a good idea.'

'Will Maggie go back to Glen Cary?'

'I have really no idea.' She thought he flinched, though she could not be sure. She felt sorry for him.

'Will you let me know what she decides?'

'Not if Maggie doesn't want it.'

His lips twisted. 'A dead end is what you both want, is it? I suppose that's what I'll have to accept. Thanks, Adele. Dart and I are off this

297

evening, so I'd better get going. Maybe I'll see you sometime when you get to England.'

A moment later he was out of the door and halfway to his car.

Maggie stood at an upstairs window, and saw him get into his car and slam the door. The engine roared into life, and gravel spurted from under the tyres as he shot down the drive.

There had been more than impatience in his abrupt departure. As well as despising her, he must have been angry because she would not see him. She heard rather than saw David Vorst driving out of her life, for tears had blurred her vision.

She told herself sternly, as she had told Abby so many times, that things would look better by next morning. It occurred to her that people really did say the most fatuous things to children.

Three days later Maggie sat in the lakeside temple at Maple Valley, surveying the expanse of dimpling water, bird life and surrounding trees. At the far end of the lake the turrets and rooftops of Maple Valley House shimmered in an afternoon heat haze. A small suitcase lay at her feet. She was leaving America for good, and this was her way of saying goodbye to a place where she had once been happy.

Adele had persuaded her not to wait for Miss Brimley, but to sail for Britain with Sophy in two days' time. 'I can't leave just yet, and I don't want to send Sophy on her own. Take this chance, Maggie, and get away. You should write to Antonia, giving her formal notice. I will hand it to her on Sunday after lunch.' Adele added, 'You may wish to write to Mrs Vorst, too. She will be sorry to lose you.'

So the letters were written, and Adele kept her lunch date at Maple Valley House. Against her better judgement, she took Maggie with her. Maggie insisted on saying goodbye to James and Miss Gladys. 'They have been so good to me since I came, milady. I could not go off without a word.'

Adele did not think it wise. Maggie ought not to risk another unpleasant meeting with Antonia or Miss Fortescue. 'Why don't we ask Miss Gladys and James to come here, Maggie? Miss Gladys would pack your remaining belongings and bring them over, if you asked her.'

Maggie said stubbornly, 'I couldn't ask her, milady. Please drop me at their cottage, and I'll run in and collect my things while you are all at lunch. Mr James will likely be working, but sometimes he comes home on Sunday afternoons.'

When she reached the cottage, however, she learned that James was away in Canada. He had driven Dart and David to Toronto, but was returning straightaway. Miss Gladys exclaimed at Maggie's tidings, and repeated in dismay, 'Leaving so soon? What has happened to make you decide so suddenly?' She looked at Maggie's downcast face and added shrewdly, 'Trouble with Mrs David and that Miss Fortescue? Is that it?'

Maggie said nothing, but nodded.

'Ah! James thought so.'

'Did he?' said Maggie, momentarily surprised out of her gloomy thoughts. 'How did he know?'

Miss Gladys said vaguely that James tended to know things, and then became very brisk and told Maggie to come into the kitchen.

'If you are set on going back to food rationing and wartime hardships, you might at least eat a good lunch today.'

Miss Gladys did not ask questions. In fact, they talked very little. Maggie said presently, 'I'll run over and get my things together. With luck everyone will be in the dining room.'

'No need to gobble your dessert, dear. I'll come over and give you a hand.'

Maggie was carrying her case down the winding back stairway, Miss Gladys ahead of her to keep a lookout, when halfway down they heard footsteps and women's voices behind a door.

One voice Maggie would always know. With a little shiver, she eased the door open a crack, and saw Antonia walking swiftly towards the Chinese wing. She was alone. Her companion must have gone another way.

On impulse, Maggie whispered to Miss Gladys to meet her in the sewing room, and followed. She found Antonia seated at her dressing table. Maggie's letter of resignation lay propped in front of her.

She looked up, startled. Her lips tightened. 'I thought I told you to keep away from this house.'

Maggie clasped her hands together, and said, 'I see you have my letter, madam. I've come to say goodbye.'

'You will have to work out your notice. As soon as the children are away, you may come back and make yourself useful until you take Miss Brimley to England.'

'No, madam. I'm leaving on Wednesday. Isn't that what you wanted – to be rid of me?'

'You can't walk out on me like that. What will everybody say?'

'You will think of something, madam. Between you and Miss Fortescue, inventing things has never been a problem. I've been wondering which of you planted those earrings in my room.'

'Don't speak to me like that! You were caught stealing, and if Miss Fortescue had her way, you would go to prison for it. You ought to thank me for talking her out of that.' Maggie just looked at Antonia, and after a pause the older woman looked down at her hands, saying peevishly, 'If you are so innocent, why are you running away?'

'Because Lady Adele advised me to go. She knows I am not a thief, even though I cannot prove it.'

Antonia looked taken aback.

'Please give the children my love,' Maggie added, her voice suddenly husky. 'I don't suppose I shall see any of them again . . .'

She turned and went out. She had faced Antonia, and felt better for doing so.

She sat for a long while in the temple. She ought to go. It would not do for Lady Adele to call at the cottage and find her missing. But as she got up, she heard voices and laughter in the woods. Somewhere children were counting in ragged unison, and running footsteps sounded close by. Kim and Abby dashed along the lake path.

She nearly shouted to Abby to watch out for poison ivy. She smiled inwardly. It was no longer her business. Besides, if they had stopped, they would have been delayed in their search for a hiding place. Garden Sardines had been all the rage this summer, since Maggie had persuaded them that an outdoor variety was as good as the one they played indoors in winter. With two walled gardens, a thatched playhouse, several summerhouses and countless garden sheds and dense shrubs and woods to hide in, Maple Valley gardens might have been designed especially for the purpose.

Maggie frowned. Kim and Abby were naughty to run near the lake. This part of the property was strictly out of bounds, and unless Mary-Jo had let things get out of hand, the other children would not look in this direction. The largest lake was deep and dangerous, and too close to the main highway at the far end. Trust Kim to play a trick on the others!

Suddenly, Maggie remembered Cagney. She had told Mr James about his lurking habits, and he had promised to deal with the matter. But James was not due back until tonight. Maggie picked up her suitcase and hurried after Abby and Kim.

'Not this way!' panted Abby for the third time. She caught up with her cousin. Kim was pushing past some bushes, and Abby said breathlessly, 'This end of the lake is off limits. The others will never look for us here.'

'Mary-Jo is going to give them a clue. She told me about an old quarry and cave at the end of the woods. She says it's a great new place to hide in.'

'They will take for ever to find us there,' said Abby sceptically. 'If you want to share a damp cave with spiders and beetles all afternoon, I don't. I can think of better things – and better hiding places.'

'Where then?'

'What about the treehouse, or the loft above the stables.'

'We've used them before! This place is new.'

'Huh. Have you seen it?'

Kim said irritably. 'Of course not. Mary-Jo only told me about it last night when she was taking me home.'

'How did Mary-Jo find this blessed cave? Don't tell me she went exploring in the woods herself?'

Neither of them spoke for a few moments, for Mary-Jo feared the deep woods, hated walking in the summer heat, and seldom left the garden paths for fear of getting mud on her shoes. The older children teased her about it, but liked her because she left them to their own devices. Abby felt differently. She blamed Mary-Jo for usurping Maggie's place, and when the girl became suddenly very friendly with Kim, said darkly that she was up to something.

Kim was remembering things. There was Mary-Jo's insistence on walking her home at the end of each day. For someone who hated walking, it did seem odd. Also, before James went to Canada, he had come into the red drawing room and warned the older children against talking to strangers in the gardens or the woods, adding that on no account must they approach anyone sitting in a car. They had promised not to do so. She said suddenly, 'Why don't we take a look at this quarry from up above? If we don't like the look of it, we can go someplace else.'

It took them a little time to reach the high wall that encircled the property, and even longer to clamber up the steep wooded slope beside it and reach their goal. They grinned at each other, and wormed their way through the undergrowth to peer over the little escarpment. Kim thought that Mary-Jo had described the place well. There it all was – a grass path coming out from the woods, a stony track crossing it, and the disused quarry below. In its neglected state it was little more than a shallow basin of weed and ivy-covered stones. The cave, Kim realised, must be out of sight underneath where they were lying. She pointed downwards and Abby nodded.

They were wriggling back through the bushes when the sound of a car door closing quietly made them freeze where they lay. They heard footsteps coming up the hill, and waited with held breath. A man came in sight. He came towards them up the slope, bent double as though unwilling to be seen. He wore a dark sweater and a broad-brimmed hat and had a bag on his shoulder. They buried their faces into the turf and lay still.

The footsteps ceased only yards away. Abby raised her head cautiously, and saw the man rolling a broad log to one side. He then bent over some sort of hole. He groped inside the bag, with his back turned to them. He seemed to be waiting for something to happen. For a terrible moment he turned his head their way. Abby buried her face into the ground to stifle a shriek of horror. Kim quivered beside her.

301

The man had no face. When they looked again, he was peering into the hole again. A match scraped and flared.

Nobody saw Maggie walk purposefully into the clearing and pick her way over the quarry stones and into the cave. Quietly, she called Abby's name; getting no answer, she called again more insistently.

The man above heard the indistinct sound. It was what he had been waiting for. He bent towards the hole and dropped something down it, then crawled away. Abby and Kim watched him go, hearts thudding with relief.

After the bright sunlight, the cave was totally dark. Maggie wished she had a torch. What were they playing at? She was just beginning to wonder if they were there at all when something clattered at the back of the cave, and a flicker of flame answered her silent prayer for light. There were no children there, just a shallow oblong of damp rock and something hissing and sparkling on the ground at the back. Then she was knocked sideways by a deafening explosion, and the world was a welter of noise and sparks and choking smoke.

At the sound of the explosion, Bones brought the transit van smoothly out onto the track and drew up at the edge of the quarry. Cagney slid down the last few yards and landed with a thud on the grass. They did not speak, but each took a chloroform soaked towel in their gloved hands, and moved purposefully towards the cave. They waited for the children to emerge.

Smoke was billowing out beautifully now, and at first there was no sound from within. Then they heard coughing and choking noises, and somebody crawled out amid the smoke. The two men gaped at the gasping, black-faced apparition that staggered to its feet. Even Bones could see that this was no child. He heard Cagney cursing, and moved forward, trying to peer into the smoking cave mouth.

Even choking and half blinded by smoke, there was no mistaking Cagney's voice. Maggie managed to focus her streaming eyes, and at the sight of the mask and an outstretched towel in gloved hands, she dodged sideways and started to run. She was pierced by an even more savage stab of terror when she heard Abby and Kim's voices calling her name from somewhere up above.

Still running, she yelled hoarsely, 'Abby! Kim! Go away! Run! Do as I say! Run and get help . . . Don't come near. . .'

Cagney was close behind her, his breath rasping, his hands grabbing at her skirt, then her sleeve. Then his hands were on her and round her, and a stinking cloth was stuffed over her face before she could manage another warning yell. She was stifling, dying, but before she went down into darkness she heard Cagney saying, 'I'll get you for this, you Limey bitch . . .'

302

Maggie came to her senses in a misery of hurtling darkness, for they had pulled something hot and stifling over her head. She felt deathly sick, but was so afraid of puking into her gag that somehow she managed not to. She heard the panicking shouts of her captors above the roar and rattle of the speeding van, and once the wail of a siren. There was a chase going on, and at one point a rush of air and the sound of a gunshot assailed her ears. The van swerved and turned this way and that with shrieking tyres, and each time Maggie was thrown slithering across the floor of the vehicle. They had tied her hands together in front, and thrown her forward to pin them under her body. But with every swerve she rolled this way and that, and suddenly one of her fingers encountered something sharp. The vehicle steadied for a blessed instant, and despite the pain and her blindness, she knew what it was. A knife

She was aware of cutting herself as she strove to fray the rope round her wrists against the serrated blade. After what seemed an age, her bonds began to slacken. Moments later her hands were free, and she started to fumble towards her muffled face.

With the malodorous sack off her head, she lay weakly where another swerve had thrown her, bruised, hands slippery with blood, but almost light-headed with relief. Then, and only then, did she indulge herself by being horribly sick.

'The bitch is throwing up,' said Cagney with savage satisfaction. 'I thought she would when she came round. She'll have worse to suffer before I've finished with her.'

Bones was tired and scared, and was heartily wishing he had never got involved with Cagney. Everything had gone wrong. The children had run off into the woods, and after they had bundled the unwanted and unconscious girl into the van and driven off, they had hardly gone a hundred yards before they saw the first police roadblock. That was more than an hour ago, and Bones had no idea which way to turn. They had halted for a while in a wooded side road, but another siren sounded and sent them off again. It seemed that the entire Long Island police force was after them. They would never reach the apartment in Long Beach, so what now? Cagney was no help, for he could do nothing but rage and swear and talk about what he would do to the puking girl who had overset their plans.

Suddenly Bones remembered his uncle's boat. If they could reach it, they could sail across Long Island Sound and up the coast. He knew the man who kept the spare keys. His uncle would half murder him for taking the boat out, but it seemed the only hope.

He broke into Cagney's tirade, and won his grumbling assent. Like

Bones, Cagney could see no way out. It was all Maggie's fault for interfering.

It was raining. They headed cautiously towards their goal, travelling by small back roads, and passing through a large private property to avoid a main highway. It seemed that luck was going with them at last. No gates barred their way, they met no police cars, and no heart-stopping sirens pursued them as they drove quietly towards the little harbour.

'Would the Vorsts pay to get that English broad back?' Bones asked, wagging his head towards the inert figure behind them.

'Not a chance. She's a maid who is being sent away in disgrace. Besides, by the time I've done with Maggie, nobody will know her.'

'Stow that, Cag,' advised Bones sharply. He parked the van in a side road with a view of the harbour. 'We've no time to waste. Give me exactly six minutes to get the keys and open the gates. Then drive to the end of the second jetty. You can see the entrance from here, the one by the flagpole. I'll be waiting for you, and if anyone tries to stop you, run them over.'

He opened the driver's door and vanished into the sheeting rain.

The six minutes dragged. The rain drummed on the roof of the van and streamed down the windscreen. Cagney turned his head to look at Maggie, but she had been thrown sideways and all he could see were her legs and one bare foot. An all-pervading smell of vomit made him retch. Four minutes. He moved over into the driver's seat, and started the engine.

Time to go. Cagney drove the van onto the harbour road, unlatching the door to ensure a quick exit. Past the flagpole he swung down the narrow jetty, heard sirens behind him and caught a glimpse of fast approaching car lights behind curtains of driving rain. He stepped on the gas, desperate now.

Everything happened at once. Bones stepped out suddenly, danger-ously close. Cagney braked, and Maggie crawled up behind him and clasped one of the towels over his eyes and mouth. He screamed and tried to shake her off, and his foot hit the accelerator. Bones went under the front wheels. The van bumped and careered on and slewed to the side of the jetty, somersaulting onto the deck of a moored sailboat. Cagney was hurled out of the unlatched door, before the van tipped over the edge and slapped into the water. Cagney lay groaning on the foredeck of the damaged sailboat.

Maggie tried to hold onto the doorframe as water surged past her. A policeman's flashlight lit on her groping hands, and he jumped into the water and put brawny arms round her upper body. He held her fast until more help arrived, and she was pulled free only seconds before the van sank. They told her she was lucky to be alive.

* * *

304

James came back from Canada to find everything in a state of uproar, and most of the household assembled in the front hall. The news of Maggie's safe release had just been brought to Maple Valley House, and Kim and Abby were in Chrissie Vorst's arms, sobbing and laughing with relief. There was a clamour of relieved voices. Even the normally imperturbable May Sandridge shed a neat tear. Maggie had been taken to hospital but was going to be all right.

It had been a tense and anxious two hours. In fact, if felt like several lifetimes since Abby and Kim had gasped out their terrified account of Maggie being bundled into a van and driven off by faceless men.

The news of her release was given to Mary-Jo in the town. She had run off home when she heard what had happened, and was still being interrogated at the station in the presence of her grim-faced father. When they told her that Maggie had been rescued, Mary-Jo gave vent to a squawk of relief and lapsed into hysterics. She had been frightened enough for herself and had been protesting her innocence for hours. But she had been far more terrified of what Cagney would do to Maggie. Maggie was her friend. She had never meant to do her harm.

In the end they let her go home. The girl had been punished for her deceit and folly, for she would certainly lose her job at Maple Valley House. The old Vorsts would never let her come within a mile of the children again.

'So all's well that ends well,' said Adele to Conway the following evening. 'But the sooner I get Maggie out of the country, the better.'

The FBI chief who had taken Maggie's evidence recommended that the Vorst family should send the girl away. She could be in danger.

Cagney was recovering from his injuries in a prison hospital. He would later be tried for attempted abduction and possibly for the death of his accomplice. Cagney was only a small-time criminal, but Bonaparte Lupino, the youth who had been killed by Cagney's speeding van, was a member of a powerful Mafia family. None of his family had been involved in the bungled kidnap, but Cagney was claiming that Maggie had caused the boy's death and the police were concerned for her safety. The Lupinos were a ruthless bunch, and would not hesitate to exact vengeance on anyone who had harmed one of their own. Miss Dunlop had given her evidence and had acted with presence of mind and courage. She should be sent back to Britain without delay.

Conway had temporarily forgotten about the girl who had saved the children and been abducted in their place. 'Isn't she still in hospital?'

Adele nodded. 'Until tomorrow. I'd like to get her on that boat with Sophy tomorrow night. We don't want any more trouble.'

'I'll say we don't,' said Conway with feeling.

It had been a long and troublesome day. Conway had been in Chicago when he heard, and had travelled all night to get home. Since his early-morning arrival, he had dealt with everything, the police, the press, traumatised staff, and finally with his mother who had had a dizzy turn and scared Cornelius into something near a heart attack of his own. The old man had been in a panic, ordering Conway to send for a heart specialist, and despatching James into the town to collect their own doctor and bring him to the house.

Though haunted for years by a dread of kidnappers, Chrissie had at first failed to understand that Abby and her beloved Kim had been the intended victims. So when a quietly triumphant Federal agent arrived from Cagney's Long Beach hideaway and showed the old Vorsts a prepared ransom note, along with a photograph depicting two iron bedsteads complete with leg and arm shackles, the shock to Chrissie had been severe. However, her dizziness and lack of breath had been of short duration. She had recovered before James came back with the local doctor. A heart specialist came and went, and now Chrissie was tucked in her own bed, mildly sedated, with Cornelius dozing in a chair at her side.

'So after all their preparations, the children won't be able give a party for Maggie,' said Antonia, still rather tight-lipped after a brush with Adele Devenish. She sat down beside Miss Fortescue on a shaded bench. The swimming pool was swarming with children, and a noisy game of water polo was going on at the far end.

Miss Brimley, withdrawn even further into the shade, was writing a letter to her sister. She looked up, wondering what had upset Mrs David.

Antonia said indignantly, 'That Devenish woman told me she's putting Maggie Dunlop on a boat this evening. She wants her to go home as company for her niece. A pretty good cheek, I told her, stealing my nursery maid away without asking me if I minded.'

'As for stealing,' said Miss Fortescue, 'I hope you warned Lady Adele to search the girl's luggage before she sails, and particularly to look in her sponge bag,' she added rather archly.

'I did warn her,' said Antonia peevishly. 'And she more or less accused me of lying.'

'No!'

'She did. I asked her to tell me how else my earrings could have got into Maggie's room if she hadn't put them there herself.' Antonia drew a breath, trying to contain her simmering sense of outrage. Adele had been remarkably offensive. She had actually dared to suggest that she or Miss Fortescue had done it.

'Excuse me, Mrs David,' said Miss Brimley's voice from the

shadows. 'Did I hear you say that Maggie was going home?'

'That's right. Rotten of her to desert us, I think. And particularly rotten for you, considering how often you have tried to defend her.'

'Perhaps you ought to tell Deirdre what we now know, Mrs David.'

Antonia threw up her hands in mock horror. 'Are you asking me to speak ill of our heroine? Shame on you, Miss Fortescue.'

'Deirdre ought to be told.'

Miss Brimley had laid aside her letter and emerged blinking out of her retreat.

'Brimmy,' Antonia said, sounding apologetic, 'I am afraid that you have been mistaken in Maggie. She did her best to steal my earrings. Miss Fortescue found them in her sponge bag and told me.'

Miss Brimley's lips moved but she made no sound.

'I always said she was a thief,' said Miss Fortescue sententiously. 'The trouble with you, Deirdre, is that you are too trusting by far.'

Miss Brimley began to tremble. 'Trusting? Oh Maud. Maud, how could you? I saw you pick the earrings off the table after Mrs David left them behind. I assumed that you had gone to give them back to her – only Mary-Jo said she saw you coming out of Maggie's room and wondered what you had wanted in there.'

They stared at her. She turned to Antonia. 'Maggie is a good, truthful girl, Mrs David. And she saved Abby from those wicked men. It is very wrong to bear false witness.'

On this biblical but slightly ambiguous note – for it was not clear to which of them her final remark had been addressed – Miss Brimley walked unsteadily away. So great was her inner turmoil that she left her writing case behind and did not notice her loss until the evening.

Later that night, a blacked out merchant ship weighed anchor and set out to join a convoy bound for Europe. Maggie Dunlop and Sophy Ducane were going home.

Adele drove back into the city. Conway was waiting for her. It had been an arduous few days, and they were looking forward to some peace and relaxation.

Part Three

September 1943
to
September 1945

Chapter 22

Bert Higgins lay on his stomach in the heather, watching a pair of buzzards through the minister's field glasses. The birds with their broad wing span were circling lazily some way below, for his chosen lookout was on the highest moor, with the ground sheering off only yards from where he lay. He felt safe and rather superior at the top of this rock-faced eyrie, poised between sky and earth. All Glen Cary lay spread out below – and nobody, not even Mr Dunlop, knew where he was.

It was just as well. The bearded head keeper's word was law, and by coming to Jock's Crag, Bert was flouting his authority. The thought of Mr Dunlop gave him a momentary qualm, but he dismissed it. The man was away. Bert turned his head and looked at a row of jagged rocks and a solitary aircraft wing piercing the skyline like giant teeth. Bert was afraid of Mr Dunlop, but he had waited two years to visit this place.

A German bomber had crashed here in the summer of 1941. Parachutes popped out of the clouds, so many aerial mushrooms, and six German airmen landed safely on the Glen Cary moors. It had been a thrilling episode. The Home Guard and the army came, eagerly joined by others from the glen, and there was a grand chase up and down the heather-covered slopes.

It was dark before the last German airman had been rounded up, but earlier, soon after they had baled out, the stricken bomber had crashed and exploded on the high moor. It broke up on the rearing rocks of Jock's Crag, showering metal fragments around the deep peat hags.

The plane had never been salvaged. The prisoners said there had been bombs on board, and despite a mighty explosion which rattled the teacups on cottage tables for miles, there was the danger of more bombs lurking in the peat hags. Experts from the Air Ministry came and sweated up the hill. They looked and went away, as did a carload of police and bomb disposal men, and government officials wearing bowler hats and carrying briefcases. But in the end it was agreed that the difficulty and expense of salvaging a wreck from such an inaccessible place could not be justified. Bomb disposal squads were

311

stretched to the limit in the summer of 1941.

Jock's Crag was declared out of bounds. Grouse shooting was in abeyance, so there was no reason for anyone to go there. Even so, warning notices were posted at intervals along the glen road, and beside the sheep track leading to the crag. Mr Dunlop erected a fence of tangled barbed wire around the forbidden summit, and discouraged curious visitors when they came to peer at the Dornier wing through field glasses.

But this was in the past. No trippers came to look any more, but to the glen people the single wing had become a symbol of hope – their hilltop cenotaph. When the war news was bad, they would glance up the hill, and pray that one day the fighting would be over and men could live in peace.

But the high moor and the remains of the Luftwaffe bomber meant something different to Bert Higgins. They had become his private Bluebeard's chamber. He had arrived too late for the great chase, but he wanted to learn all about it, and his relentless questions nearly drove his victims mad. Still, the London boy had lost all his kin in the Blitz, and had an arm and a leg in plaster. People felt sorry for him, and told him what they knew – and from then on Bert decided that, ban or no ban, he would one day visit Jock's Crag and see what was there for himself.

But the minister put a stopper on that. He made Bert promise not to go there.

'Not while you're staying with us,' he said, looking unusually stern. 'I need your promise, Bert. You know the dangers. One of these days the army will deal with it, but until then the sensible thing to do is to keep out.'

'There may be nothing there but broken bits of plane, Mr Fraser,' said Bert. 'Nobody knows for sure that there are bombs.'

However, he gave his grudging promise, and kept it for more than two years. Now, in the summer of 1943, he had his chance. Mrs Fraser had been summoned to Edinburgh for an operation, and the minister planned to go with her – and Bert would lodge with the head keeper.

He had wanted to stay at the manse, and offered to look after it while Cook took her annual holiday. He was much offended when his offer was rejected. Did they think he was a child, not to let him stay on his own? But then he recalled the minister's words – 'While you are staying with us'. If he stayed with Mr Dunlop, he would be released from his tiresome promise.

But there was a difficulty. Bert's mongrel dog Wat had lately taken against Ian Dunlop, growling at him and raising his hackles when he appeared. Bert said Mr Dunlop must have kicked Wat or hit him when nobody was looking, and said so to Maggie when she came on

312

leave. 'He never growls at people, only at other dogs if there's a bitch around.'

Maggie frowned, and absently ran a floury hand through her hair. She was cutting out scones in her grandmother's kitchen. 'That's strange. Dogs usually like Dad. His sheepdogs and the labradors never leave his side.'

'Wat wouldn't growl and shiver like that for nothing.'

Maggie did not speak. As she carried the scones to the stove, she wondered if Bert's dog could sense the pent-up violence in her father. She used to shiver as a child, sensing the onset of another black mood. She went to wash her hands at the scullery sink.

'Try to keep Wat out of Dad's way,' she advised the boy. 'I mind the time when our collie puppy bit him on the hand and he took it out and shot it. He told Gran that it would likely turn on us children once it had gone savage. Tom and I cried, because he was our puppy, and we loved him.' She smiled at Bert, and went into the garden to join her grandmother.

Bert looked after her without speaking. He was shocked by the grisly tale, but more shocked still by Maggie's matter-of-fact manner. This, and some other glimpses of her life as a child, caused him to ask Mr Fraser how Maggie had grown up to be such a happy person.

'Maggie happy? Do you think so, Bert? We certainly find her a joy to have around.' The minister rubbed his chin thoughtfully. 'She told me once that she found happiness in America for the first time in her life, and I believed her. It has never been easy for her at home. Still, she has a loving nature and a capacity for laughing at herself. She will never lose that, whatever happens.'

The minister had solved Bert's quandary about Wat by taking him to Edinburgh. 'He has lived in a city before. He should be all right.'

'He'll be fine,' said Bert with relief. 'He'll be company for you, Mr Fraser. Just make him walk to heel.'

Mr Dunlop expected obedience, and generally got it. He did not bother with promises. Jock's Crag was out of bounds, and that was that.

The first week at Dunlop's cottage passed peacefully, for everyone was bringing in the harvest and went to bed tired out. Stuart, an evacuee from Glasgow, was pleased to share his room with Bert, for he lived in fear of his host and seldom spoke in his presence. The strapping landgirl who occupied the larger attic did not talk much either. She was a quiet creature, except at night when she snored fit to wake the dead. The boys would snigger into their pillows when they heard her thundering away behind the bedroom wall.

Mr Dunlop was civil to Bert at first, pleased to be paid for the boy's bed and board. Old Mrs Dunlop liked the money too, and she also liked the London boy. She had met him several times with Maggie, but nobody spoke of Maggie in front of Mr Dunlop.

The peace might have continued if Ian Dunlop had not happened to overhear Bert and Stuart discussing ways of reaching the high moor unseen? He slammed his stick down on the kitchen table. 'You'll go nowhere near that place, do you hear me?' He made as if to swing the stick at Bert's head, but instead brought it down on the table top with a second resounding thwack. 'Can you not read! The signs say KEEP OUT, and keep out is what you'll do if you know what's good for you.'

This outburst was so sudden that the boys gaped at him, and were still doing so when Mrs Dunlop hurried in and begged her son to mind what he was about. After that it was words, torrents of them, and he threatened to flog the boys if they went near the high moor. Then he flung out of the cottage and was gone. That evening the boys went to bed early, hoping that the storm was over.

It was not quite over. They were awakened in the night by the sound of a bellowing voice. Further sounds of disturbance came to their ears – a door opening, shuffling footsteps, and voices. They could not make out the words, but the old lady seemed to be reasoning with her son. After a while they heard a door close, and there was peace. In the morning Mrs Dunlop remarked, casually, that her son sometimes suffered from bad dreams. She hoped the boys had not been disturbed.

The Glasgow boy took Ian Dunlop's words to heart, vowing never to so much as glance at Jock's Crag in future. It was different with Bert. He was all the more determined to visit the place, and began to wonder about the head keeper. Wat did not like him, and Maggie admitted to being scared of her father.

'Why does Maggie hide upstairs when Mr Dunlop comes to the manse?' he asked Mrs Fraser.

'It's a long story, Bert, and not a happy one.'

He asked Maggie for a reason, but she was not forthcoming. 'My dad and I don't get on,' she said as she boarded the train after another short leave. 'He knows I come to visit Gran, but he doesn't want to set eyes on me himself. Nor I him,' she added, smiling down at the boy as he stood on the platform. 'To tell the truth, even the sound of his voice frightens me as much as ever. Silly, isn't it?'

He shook his head and smiled back at her, finding it hard to believe that Maggie could be frightened of anyone. She looked so smart in her WAAF uniform. She had just been made a Section Officer, and he had felt shy of her when she first arrived at the manse. However, once in ordinary clothes she was herself again. They spent a morning at the cottage, and afterwards went out on the moor.

He loved being with Maggie. She made him laugh with tales of Air

Force life. She was blithe and lissom and never seemed to tire, walking the moor with her slow hill walker's stride, and teaching him about birds and their habits. She took him to her brother Tom's favourite fishing haunts, and on her last day they went with Mr Fraser and fished on a hill loch. They came home to the manse with six trout in their creel.

Bert watched the train pull away, and wished that Maggie's brief leave could have lasted longer. Maggie was the most beautiful, wonderful girl. He remembered with astonishment how he had recently looked on Veronica Lake as the perfect woman, and wished that he could perform some noble act to earn Maggie's gratitude and admiration. If only he had been older, larger, he could have started by telling her father what he thought of him! But he was only fifteen and skinny – no fit adversary for the burly head keeper.

The only thing he could do, Bert decided, was to keep an eye on Ian Dunlop. He was a bully, and must have been horrible to Maggie to frighten her so much. A man like that would be capable of anything. So he started to watch him.

In January 1944, David Vorst emerged from an interview with the supreme commander of the allied forces and other top brass persons. He was assailed by conflicting feelings. The new assignment would mean promotion, of course. He ought to feel flattered, but after more than three years in the Royal Air Force, he had come to feel a part of it. It would be a wrench to work outside that now familiar orbit.

His Royal Air Force colleagues were startled when he said he was leaving them. They felt betrayed. They had confidence in their successful wing commander, and did not want to lose him.

David's second-in-command had to be told more than the rest, and when he heard what the job would entail, he told David bluntly that he was crazy. 'An impossible task. You should have turned it down. The Americans have their way of doing things and won't want you sticking your nose in. Just imagine what we would feel here if some blasted Yank came along and started telling us what to do!'

'You've survived it pretty well for the past year and a half,' retorted David drily.

The other man looked at him, startled. 'You know, I'd quite forgotten that you were a Yank.'

'Is that meant as a compliment?'

'It's the only one you'll get from me, old boy, and if you take this job, I can only call you a fool. Our gallant allies will either ignore you or tear you to pieces when you start throwing your weight about.'

Since this was what David also thought, he merely grinned. His second-in-command sighed and shrugged. Experience had taught him that Vorst's air of quiet reserve masked an iron determination. If he had made up his mind to tackle this hornet's nest of a job, there was no future in trying to stop him.

He could not resist saying, though, with a touch of malice, 'You know what this promotion will mean? You'll be saying goodbye to active flying. Group captains are much too valuable to be put at risk.'

David just laughed. He had his own ideas about that.

When Air Marshal Tedder first told him what was wanted, he had replied quite bluntly that what the commanders needed was a diplomat, not a mere pilot. They wanted David to form a team which would visit the various Allied air forces – British, Canadian, Polish, Free French, above all American. Their task would be to assess the strengths and weaknesses of each sector. At the end of this research, they were to submit a report of their findings, with recommendations as to how these forces should be deployed and coordinated before the forthcoming invasion of Europe. It took the supreme commander himself to talk David into it. Ike could usually persuade anyone to do anything.

David had made stipulations and gained some concessions along the way. He would be free to choose and co-opt people to his team, and would be given access to classified information and to visit wherever he thought fit. To his relief they also agreed that he could continue to fly when he judged it to be expedient. Observers, he told them bluntly, were rarely welcomed by crews on active missions. Only if he could fly with them and prove his own ability and experience as a pilot would he gain their confidence and find out what he needed to know.

He foresaw that it was not going to be easy. His first port of call was a large American base in East Anglia, from where heavy bombers and medium fighter-bombers had already given a good account of themselves against the enemy. He was aware that they would be just waiting for him to make a fool of himself.

They were. When it was learned that an RAF group captain was coming to teach them British ways, there was a heavy groundswell of resentment. Since coming to Britain these young men had too often felt themselves patronised by veteran members of the RAF, who regarded them as ignorant rookies. And now they were expected to welcome a pompous British officer on their home ground!

But when the interloper came, he was not what they had expected. For one thing, he was American, and he seemed keener to learn than to instruct. He spoke quietly but incisively about the difficulties of his allotted task, remarking that dovetailing so many separate air forces into a cohesive whole would take something of a miracle to achieve.

'So? What are you doing here, sir?' demanded one of them, who was lounging at the back with his feet on a table. 'Do you see yourself as a magician or a Messiah?'

Laughter spread around the room. David looked at the man, waiting for the chuckles to die, and then said coolly, 'I see myself as a student and I want to learn how you do things. Your commanding officer has agreed to let me come with you on your next few missions. Already the United States forces here outnumber the other allies. You are better equipped in nearly every way than the RAF and the French, and from what little I know of your activities since coming to Europe, the RAF may have to adjust some of their thinking to fit in with yours.'

'That'll be the day,' said another voice.

'Why start on us, then? Go change those Limeys first.'

This time there was a burst of general laughter and a cheer or two. Again David waited impassively for the noise to subside.

Then he said seriously, 'I'm not in the business of changing anything. You could say that this is a reconnaissance mission – and only the very start of it.' And he added more briskly, with a wry grin, 'And if you guys think to give me a hard time, I can assure you that there are just as many pigheaded bastards among the Brits who can't wait to do the same.'

They laughed with him for the first time. It could not be said that he managed to win them over, but by the end of an hour there was a general feeling that they ought to give this Vorst guy a chance to prove what he was made of.

The leading doubter returned from furlough later, and was sent for by his commanding officer. He came out fuming, having had his objections overruled. As the most experienced pilot on the station, he had been chosen to take this interloper with him as an observer on the next mission over Germany. He had protested, and fully intended to protest again. He was damned if he would welcome an English spy on his aircraft. He had better things to think about when he was working.

'He's not that bad, Ben,' one of his fellow pilots told him. 'And get this. He's clean-shaven – not a handlebar moustache in sight. And he's an American.'

'If he's American,' growled Ben, stomping off to change for the evening, 'what the hell's he doing in a clapped-out outfit like the RAF?'

The mess was full that evening, for with varying degrees of glee or apprehension, everyone expected fireworks. Ben Horowitz had installed himself in his usual corner and was drinking beer with his cronies when he became aware that the commanding officer had come in. He did not turn round but winked at one of his companions.

'Ben.' The commander was all at once in the centre of the dissident group. 'I believe you have not yet been introduced to our visitor from the Royal Air Force.'

317

'No, sir. I have not,' Ben began grimly, but whatever he meant to say next was suspended. He stood up slowly, his eyes widening. The two men were much the same height, taller than many of those around. For a long moment they eyed each other. David's thin, dark face gave nothing away.

He said quietly, 'Hello there, Ben.'

'My God!' Horowitz turned on his boss. 'Is this the guy you were talking about, sir? You don't want to let him in here! Dave Vorst is dynamite. He damn nearly got me thrown out of law school years ago!'

'Is that so?'

'I'll say it was! So don't blame me if something goes wrong when I take him up tomorrow. Something bad is bound to happen with Crazy Dave aboard.' He turned then and held out a strong, freckled hand, grinning. 'David, you old son of a gun! So you've joined the Brylcreem boys? Your hair need's cutting, as always, but it's sure good to see you!'

That was the start of it. They had been good friends at Harvard, lost touch for years, but almost immediately it was as though they had never been apart. They still argued about everything, examined and discussed matters of interest with fire and fervour. At college it had been girls, football, automobiles and sometimes politics. This time they wrangled over ways of waging war from the air.

Their mutual liking and trust never faltered during those months before D-Day, but they occasionally surprised each other, for the crucible of war had changed them.

For David the war was no longer a passionate affair. When he remembered his youthful Battle of Britain self he thought he must have been half demented in those days. A combination of high altitude, lack of sleep and the adrenaline caused by the rage and terror of battle had acted on him as a thrilling intoxicant. It was different now. Each operation was just a job to be done. Fear was never wholly absent, but he had learned to disarm it by concentrating utterly on his work. He had taught himself to plan deliberately, to focus the cold light of logic on each problem or plan, reviewing past pitfalls and seeking ways to avoid them. War was certainly not the great adventure that it had started out to be. Those careless days were long gone, and too many good friends were dead or lay maimed or hideously burned in hospital. He was thankful to have survived. He wanted to finish the business and be allowed to get on with his life.

Ben had entered the Army Air Force in a very different spirit. For years he had hated the Nazis and all they stood for. He hated them still. He rarely spoke of the Viennese sister and brother-in-law who had been taken away by the Gestapo. Only once, when David told him that Odette Steiner had been dropped in France and was working for the French underground, did Ben speak of the tragedy that had blasted his family apart.

David was upset that Odette had gone without warning him. 'She left the Vorst Hotel to work for the Free French,' he told Ben. 'She wanted to take a more active hand in the war. I never dreamed that she would volunteer for something as dangerous as that!'

Ben looked at him. 'She would be driven to it. You and your kind will never know what it is to hate as we do. Every time I fire a rocket or give the order for bombs away, I do it for Sylvie and Bruno and their kids, and Bruno's family. I want to kill every Nazi down there! Your girlfriend has lost her family too and will feel as I do.'

'She's no girlfriend,' said David sadly, remembering how Odette had once spoken to him with equal bitterness but other words. 'Just a very brave and talented woman bent on throwing herself away.'

The visit to East Anglia was over sooner than David expected. When he moved on, he had recruited Ben to his team.

Despite a difference in outlook and experience – or perhaps because of it – they made a good partnership. Sometimes they worked together, but more often separately, comparing findings later. As the winter of 1944 blustered its way into spring, the urgency and pressure of work increased. They travelled all over the British Isles in their unceasing search for information.

At the start of their mission, they regarded the precision bombing of key targets – the work they had previously been doing – as the most important thing. Air supremacy was a first essential if an invasion was to succeed, and hammering the enemy's rail and road networks a vital preliminary.

But as time went by, a less simplistic pattern began to form in their minds. There were so many factors to be considered and woven into the fabric of the grand design. As they compiled their reports, met weather experts, designers of floating harbours and other innovations, and occasionally sat in on meetings with those who were in charge of Operation Overlord, there grew in them a sense of the awesome scale and intricacy of the whole enterprise.

Even Ben, who had initially scoffed at David's liking for boffins and code experts, came to see that in the game of bluff and counter-bluff, these people played an essential part. Reading the mind of the enemy and feeding them false information was no less important than the destruction of rail and road systems between Germany and the western coast of Europe. They travelled to radar stations and top security units where reconnaissance photographs were developed and assessed by teams of WAAF and RAF experts.

They were shown films of German coastal defences in France and

Belgium. They read reports of enemy troop movements and rocket sites sent by secret agents in France and the Netherlands. They were for ever on the move, driven from place to place by their discreet WAAF driver, constantly learning and comparing notes with each other and with the French Canadian and a young New Zealander who had more recently joined their team.

Everywhere they went they passed troops: troops marching, troops training, tanks, guns and armoured cars lined up under trees, and acres of camouflage netting everywhere, hiding all this from enemy snooper planes. They went to heavily guarded coastal regions where every harbour was thronged with seagoing craft – awaiting orders to join the latter-day armada which was soon to set sail. Air bases were loud with the roar of departing and returning aircraft, and the relentless pounding of the enemy went on. Fat wooden gliders crouched in rows on the perimeter of airfields.

Ben's impatience was growing unbearable. Surely it would not be long now. The build-up and the mock build-up – which was aimed at keeping the enemy guessing – had been going on for months. Security was tighter than ever.

It was no longer a question of whether there would be an invasion. It was now a question of when, and where.

A blustery April day in 1944 saw David at the Vorst Hotel. He had never fulfilled his threat to resign from the company because Odette had talked him out of it. He collected his mail, and found a letter from Antonia. Letters from his wife were a rarity, and the sight of her sprawling writing on the red, white and blue air letter gave him a slight shock. He wondered what she wanted. He slit it open and presently put it away in his breast pocket. Antonia had written to say that she had decided to come home.

It was almost three years since he had left her in Maple Valley, and there were times when he did not think of her for weeks on end. He thought of her now with reluctance and some surprise, quite unable to believe that she had been missing him and longing for them to be together again. He looked at his watch. It was getting late, so he decided that he had better go to work, and wait until later to read her letter again. It would take time to puzzle out why Antonia had suddenly grown so affectionate.

He spent an hour with Hudson, the Vorst manager, who was in fact doing surprisingly well. He then met two new members of staff, and left by a side door. He joined Ben in the back of the Air Ministry car. Jean-Louis sat in front with the WAAF driver, his head turned towards her as she steered the large vehicle through the war-scarred London streets. The French Canadian was talking volubly, but with a glass partition in between, the others could hear no words.

Ben chuckled. 'Jean-Louis turning on the Gallic charm, eh? D'you think she'll fall for it?'

'Why not? Jean-Louis is a good-looking boy.'

'Boy?' echoed Ben. 'He's the same age as us, and you know it.'

'Sometimes,' said David heavily, 'I feel old enough to be my own grandfather.'

Ben glanced at him, saw the corner of an air letter sticking out of his pocket, and said, 'What's wrong? Bad news?'

David pushed the letter out of sight. 'A letter from my wife. She's thinking of coming back.'

'After all this time? Does she say why?'

David laughed, and said more amiably, 'None of your business. Let's get on with our report, or it won't be finished in time.'

'Thank God it's the last,' said Ben, with feeling. Weeks of tearing all over the country had left him feeling jaundiced. Today they would hand their findings over to others. At times it had seemed like vital work, and at others just a lot of hot air and reams of paper.

It would be good to get back and start hammering the enemy. One good thing. He had persuaded the powers that be that David should fly with his outfit in the run-up to D-Day.

Ben wondered, too, as they returned the WAAF driver's smart salute and strode to this final meeting, what that exceedingly discreet young woman was thinking. Knowing Dave Vorst well, he sensed that he had an interest there – which might explain why this news from his absent wife had disturbed his equilibrium.

But Section-Officer Dunlop was an enigma. He wondered if she played poker in her spare time. She ought to.

Chapter 23

Section Officer Dunlop sat in the canteen on that last day and thought about David Vorst. She had promised herself, after leaving America, that she would never have any dealings with that family again. Adele Devenish had told her bluntly that she ought to get away and make a life for herself. Had Adele seen that she had fallen more than half in love with David Vorst?

Maggie smiled wryly. She had not expected to see him again. He was an attractive man who had been kind to her, and if her subconscious mind teased her with recollections of his voice or his smiling dark eyes, it would do her no good to heed these tricks of memory. She was resolved to put all thoughts of David Vorst out of her mind for good.

It had not been so very hard. When she first volunteered for the Women's Auxiliary Air Force and was going through an arduous mill of basic training and square-bashing, there had been no time to think of anything but the exhausting present. There had certainly been no time to dwell upon the traumatic events of her departure from Maple Valley.

In common with the twenty-odd girls in her squad, all her waking thoughts and efforts had to be focused on learning Air Force ways – how and whom to salute, remembering to call officers 'sir' or 'ma'am', and mastering a whole new language and way of life. In the Air Force you ate with 'irons', washed yourself at 'ablutions', wore blackouts instead of knickers, and slept at night on 'biscuits', three rock-hard squares of mattress which had to be stacked up every morning in proper Air Force fashion. What with all this and being chivvied and shouted at on the parade ground, surviving kit inspections and trying to keep out of trouble with the uniformed tyrants who ruled over you, other matters faded into the background.

Those first months had been hectic, in some ways reminding Maggie of being trained by Nanny, only far less lonely. It had certainly not been lonely, for there was no privacy, and always the other girls to laugh or grumble with. It had been the same in Harrogate where she trained to be a Motor Transport driver, and later working at a large Lincolnshire airfield where the men outnumbered the girls by roughly ten to one. There had been safety in numbers there, too, for if you agreed to go out alone with one of the men, it caused a buzz of jealousy and gossip. It was safer to stay in, or go out in a group.

Loneliness had come later, when she passed out of officer training school and was sent to a small east coast radar station where the only two other WAAF officers were considerably older, and looked down on her because of her youth and her Scots accent. She sometimes wondered why she had been sent there, for there was very little for an MT officer to do, except for driving the station personnel into the local town on Friday and Saturday nights in the only available lorry. Precluded by her officer status from joining the other men and girls in the pub, she would sit in the lorry and wait for the minutes to crawl by until closing time.

Her other duties consisted of organising physical jerks for the aircraftwomen – an unpopular activity which they evaded whenever possible – overseeing their chores, typing letters and filling in forms, and occasionally meeting a visitor at the railway station. Her leisure hours were divided between walking in the freezing east coast wind, bird-watching or sitting in her Nissen hut bedroom writing letters to Sophy Ducane, to Mrs Fraser or her grandmother, reading or teaching herself shorthand out of an instruction book from the library. It was a dismal time. The six months she spent there gave her plenty of time for thinking of the past.

Sophy, enjoying life as a Wren, had a habit of ringing up from time to time. She advised Maggie to ask for a transfer. But it was a chance remark made by a visitor that encouraged her to change direction. This official – she never saw him again – climbed up beside her in the front of the lorry, and retrieving a French history book from the floor, asked her if she spoke that language, and if so why did she not make use of this skill? Thus it was that she applied to be re-mustered and was eventually posted to a basement 'somewhere in southern England'.

In this high-security posting, she became part of a team receiving and decoding radio messages from members of the French and Belgian underground. Sometimes when their cover was blown, these agents had to be taken out, and Maggie would help to debrief them. At other times she took verbatim reports from servicemen who had taken part in raids across the Channel. It was top secret work, and stressful, particularly when one of the contacts was captured or a raid went wrong, but it was nearly always interesting.

They were warned at the outset against becoming emotionally involved with the 'clients'. But Section Officer Dunlop was twenty years old, curious about this sex thing which the other girls never stopped talking about, and ready for love. She met Paul. He had been sent to the unit to be debriefed between raids. He was half French and spoke both French and English with a stutter.

Paul found Maggie less daunting than the other officers, so he asked her timidly to have supper with him. Fraternising was frowned on, but Paul looked so unsure of himself, and his French accent was so appealing that she agreed to go. They had two weeks together, snatching meetings whenever they could, and Paul said he loved her and wanted to marry her after the war. They made love just once in a rather damp field, a painful and enlightening experience. Paul seemed to like it, but privately Maggie decided that sex was something she could do without.

A week later Paul was killed in action. Maggie was one of the officers detailed to debrief the survivors of that disastrous raid, and had to listen and type out details of how it had gone wrong. Paul and two others had been blown to pieces by a land mine, thereby alerting the defenders of the gun emplacement which they had been sent to destroy.

She did her best to hide her shock and distress, and presently handed her typed report to the officer in charge. It was like that in the basement. You just had to get on with the work. All the same, life became something to be endured from that day on.

Possibly Section Officer Dunlop's white face and lack of appetite had been noticed by those in authority, or one of the other girls may have let on that Dunlop and the dead boy had been friends. Whatever the reason, Maggie was sent for and informed that the Air Ministry was looking for a discreet WAAF to act as driver and secretary to a newly formed top brass team. They were thinking of recommending her. What did Dunlop think?

This was the first time since joining the WAAFs that anyone had asked Maggie what she wanted. She was feeling too low to be gratified, for they had lost two more 'clients' in the past weeks. But she asked them to put her name forward. The thought of getting out of the basement was a lure. When she was eventually chosen for this new job, she was even quite pleased. Driving brass hats about would be a holiday after the stress and unhappiness of the basement.

It had been no holiday. It had been three months of arduous work and bitter-sweet torment, and now it was over. She wondered, as she had done many times, what she would have done if she had been told that her new boss was to be David Vorst. Not normally given to self-deception, Maggie thought that she would have been unable to resist a chance of seeing him again.

Ben Horowitz was in charge when she first reported for duty. The Group Captain was away up north. She took over from a temporary WAAF who said she was glad to be leaving. The Group Captain arrived at Euston Station three days later, and he barely glanced at the girl in Air Force uniform who was holding the car door. He had been away for nearly a week, and his mind was on questioning Ben and comparing notes. He returned her salute mechanically and, still talking, folded himself and his briefcase into the back of the staff car. Ben climbed in beside him with his own folder of maps and papers, and they were deep in an exchange of information and opinions for over an hour.

They were driving through the New Forest when Ben tapped on the glass partition and told Maggie that they would stop for lunch. She spread a rug and left them to their sandwiches, and David paused in mid-sentence to watch her walk back to the car.

Ben followed David's gaze. 'Good legs, eh?'

'Trust you to notice, you old lecher,' said David. 'So we've got our new driver, have we? They promised to send one who knows how to keep her mouth shut.'

'This one looks buttoned up mighty tight. Want a beer?'

'Just coffee, I think,' said David, reaching for the vacuum flask.

Later David emerged from the woods and found the new driver stowing remnants of their lunch into a basket. She did not raise her eyes, and her hands were neat and deft. But a rush of rosy colour betrayed her confusion, and he knew her in an instant, for sure.

He felt a warm glow of pleasure, and would have uttered a pleased exclamation, only Ben's voice behind him made him hesitate, and he decided to wait. Within minutes they were in the car and heading for Dover, planning the next week's schedule.

But when the journey was over, Ben and the newly recruited Jean-Louis went off, and David stayed behind. Maggie was about to drive the car away when he spoke behind her.

'Maggie. Since when have you been a WAAF, and why didn't I know it?'

She turned, looking at him nervously. 'I joined up as soon as I got home. You see, Gran didn't need me . . .'

'Well, that was good. You know what I thought about you going back there. Maggie, it's great to see you again.' He laughed suddenly, an unexpectedly joyous sound. 'So you're our honest, competent and wholly discreet WAAF driver. Your last boss gave you a glowing telephone reference, you know. But I was dumb enough not to realise that Section Officer Margaret Dunlop was none other than our Maggie.'

Once more her face suffused with colour, and she said hesitantly, 'I never realised either, sir. I nearly fell down when Major Horowitz mentioned your name. I just hope it's all right, my being here.'

He smiled at her. 'If you are half as good as they say, I'll be deeply thankful. Your predecessor was practically a moron.' He paused, 'Tell me, does Ben know that we've met already?'

She shook her head. 'I thought I'd better not say, sir.'

He laughed again. 'As promised – the very soul of discretion. Then

325

we'll keep it to ourselves. But, believe me, Maggie, it'll be good to have you with us. It's made my day.'

Maggie watched him walk away, and drew a shuddering breath. What had she just let herself in for?

She discovered almost immediately that she had let herself in for a lot of work. In less than an hour she was sent for to take dictation, and it was late before the Group Captain's extensive report had been typed, signed and put in the appropriate file. She had been driving all day, and within minutes of climbing into bed she fell into a dark well of sleep.

David was weary too, but sleep eluded him that night. His brain was behaving inconveniently, with thoughts and memories jostling each other for position. Unable to banish this tiresome bout of mental indigestion, he got up and stood looking out of the window.

It was Maggie, of course. He had been delighted by her sudden reappearance in his life – quite extraordinarily pleased, which was odd because during the past three years he had scarcely given her a thought. He remembered liking her, of course, and when his mother wrote to say how her prompt action had saved Kim and Abby, he had been impressed and grateful. But he had not written to Maggie. For one thing he did not know where she was. Besides, he remembered Antonia, and how he had resolved on leaving America to steer clear of women.

Antonia and Maggie. He had been angry with both of them on the day he left Maple Valley. Yet today he had been overjoyed to see Maggie. He sighed. He rather thought he had given himself away. Had she noticed? He hoped not. She was here to do a job, and so was he – and he would not wish her to get ideas about him.

He went to sleep, resolving to treat his new secretary/chauffeur exactly like any other WAAF who happened to work for the team. He would lose no more sleep over her. He was married to Antonia, even though she was still in America. Maggie was not for him.

They worked in the south coast prohibited areas that week, and David watched Section Officer Dunlop dealing with checkpoints, and presenting priority passes with practised composure. When nobody was looking he studied her half-averted profile. She was no longer the suntanned golden girl of Maple Valley. Her skin was pale and clear and her face thinner than he remembered.

They were treating each other with distant formality, with David saying little more than 'Good morning, Miss Dunlop', giving her his notes to type, and thanking her politely at the end of each day. It took a brush with the Luftwaffe to bring them closer.

Ben went off to the Midlands, driven by David's batman. Maggie was to take the group captain to a meeting in Lewes, and to bring him back afterwards. She loaded all the suitcases into the car. Orders were to take everything with them at all times. Plans had been known to change from hour to hour.

The meeting took all day, and it was late afternoon before they headed towards the coast – the Group Captain writing notes in the back, and his driver driving smoothly and carefully. Then they heard the sirens, and soon realised that there was a raid going on over Dover town.

David tapped on the glass, and for ten minutes they stood together on the clifftop road, watching the raid. Puffs of ack-ack punctuated the evening sky, and streaks of pink-tinged smoke and vapour trails of wheeling aircraft traced crazy patterns above the town. There was a distant sound of gunfire, and black burgeoning smoke gave witness to direct hits in the docks. Presently the marauders drew off out to sea, with RAF fighters in pursuit.

'German spy planes,' said David, passing his binoculars over for Maggie to take a last look. 'They come in under the radar, take pictures and fire a rocket or two before heading for home. Not much harm done—'

He stopped speaking abruptly, and they heard it coming before they saw the dark shape of an aircraft silhouetted against the setting sun. One look was enough for David. He seized Maggie's wrist in a painful grip, reached for his briefcase with the other hand, and said briefly, 'A Jerry. He may have spotted us and go for the car. Run up the road and get under the hedge! Get going! Run!'

Maggie tried to shrug him off, saying something about suitcases and her bag, but he cut her short.

'Leave them. Do as I say, Maggie!'

'Sir! I can't leave my bag.'

'Yes you can. Come on, you stupid girl!'

He dragged her with him, urging her to run faster as the tearing scream of a diving aircraft rent the air. Maggie lost a shoe and would have paused to retrieve it but was dragged on. She thought her lungs would burst from the effort of running uphill, but bullets spattering on the road gave her the impetus to put on another spurt. Suddenly she was hurled to the ground and rolled face down under the hedge, with David on top of her. A deafening blast and an explosion assaulted their senses and left them shocked and flattened where they lay.

In a little while he lifted himself off, still with a hand between her shoulder blades holding her down. She tried to struggle free, for her face was pressed into some thorns that lined the muddy roadside ditch.

'Keep still. He got the car, but he may come back to look.'

At last he let her sit up. The sharp breeze was acrid with smoke and a smell of burning, and they both ducked involuntarily as the petrol tank of their Air Ministry car exploded. Side by side in the ditch, they watched in stunned silence until the leaping flames began to die down.

Maggie found that her whole body was shaking. She said crossly, 'You might have let me bring my bag.'

He was shaken too, for it had been a close shave, but he laughed at her scolding tone. 'Don't worry, Miss Dunlop. I'll buy you another when we get to London.'

'It's not that. It's Air Force property. Our documents and passes are in it, and I'm responsible for keeping them safe.'

He started to say that he was responsible for keeping them both alive, but saw the blood running down her face, and said with sudden concern, 'Maggie. Your face is bleeding.'

'So would yours be if you'd been squashed half to death and rubbed into a thorn hedge,' she said, starting to crawl painfully out of the ditch on scratched knees, and scolding because she was in danger of bursting into tears. 'We'll need to walk, by the look of things, and I don't know how I'll manage with only one shoe.'

'Where is it?'

'It fell off while you were dragging me along.'

'OK. Stay there, and I'll go find it.'

They spent the night at Dulcimer Hall, arriving by taxi without clothes or luggage, Maggie with her scratched face, torn stockings and muddied uniform. Maggie supposed that she must be suffering from delayed shock, for it did not seem at all strange to be in the panelled morning room with Lord and Lady Dulcimer, gulping down an enormous glass of sherry and vying with the dogs for a place by the fire. Later she was chivvied upstairs by Nanny to have a bath and be tucked into bed in the night nursery.

'Best place for you, my girl. Mr David wanted me to find you something to wear for dinner downstairs, but I told him you would have it in bed. I'm going to scramble you some eggs. I look after the hens these days, and they've started laying again.'

'I'm really not very hungry, Nanny. Just a cup of tea would be lovely.'

'You'll eat what you're given and like it, young lady. You've grown so skinny I scarcely knew you. Don't they feed you properly in the Air Force?'

Maggie laughed sleepily. Really, the sherry was making her feel very strange.

'That's right, Nanny,' said David from the doorway. 'You keep my insubordinate section officer in order.'

'And what's a section officer when it's at home?' demanded Nanny. 'I never can get my tongue around those newfangled Air Force titles.'

'I'm the lowest kind of officer, Nanny, a sort of nursery maid in Air Force blue.'

Nanny picked up Maggie's muddied tunic. 'Not much blue about it. What have you been doing? Rolling in a ditch?'

'Under a hedge actually,' said David. 'I pushed her there because a nasty German was firing rockets us.'

Nanny clicked her tongue in disapproval. For all the world, Maggie thought, as though the nappies had not been aired properly. She began to giggle and found it difficult to stop.

'Now, that's enough, Maggie,' said Nanny sharply. 'There's nothing to laugh at. You're both lucky to be alive, I fancy.' So saying, she scooped Maggie's uniform into her arms and headed for the door. 'Don't keep Maggie talking too long, Mr David. She's had a shock, and as soon as I've given her some supper, she must go to sleep.'

'It's nothing to do with shock,' Maggie protested with a hiccup. 'It's all that sherry his lordship gave me downstairs.'

Ignoring her, Nanny looked at David over her spectacles, and said, 'You'd best bring me your trousers to brush, Mr David. The turn-ups were all over mud, I noticed.'

'Vestry noticed too and took them away, Nanny,' said David meekly. The butler had fitted him out with a pair of Dart's corduroy trousers and a sweater. 'But it would be great if you could do something about Maggie's uniform.'

Maggie roused herself to sit up. 'No such thing! Please leave it, Nanny. I'll brush it myself in the morning. What time do you want to start, sir?'

'Not before midday. Major Horowitz is collecting another car and bringing it down from London, but I've asked him to call at the Vorst to collect some clothes for me. He could do the same for you if you'll tell me where you keep your spare uniforms?'

Maggie looked at David and said simply, 'I've only got the one, sir. It'll brush up all right in the morning. But I'm afraid my cap was in the car . . .'

He smiled at her. So she only possessed one uniform? Yet she still managed to look neat and trim whenever she was on duty. At this moment she might have been about twelve years old, propped up against pillows, wearing one of Nanny's high-necked nightgowns, her hair tied off her scratched face by a red ribbon. She was smiling at him muzzily. Nanny had painted her scratches with some bright red potion to match the ribbon.

He wanted very badly to kiss her, as he had been wanting to do ever since she had crawled so crossly out of that muddy ditch, fighting tears and grumbling to keep them at bay.

He touched her hand with one finger. 'See you in the morning, Maggie. Sleep well.' He smiled at Nanny, and went out.

Ben Horowitz arrived at Dulcimer with a new Air Ministry car, bringing security passes and a new bag to keep them in. He had also scrounged a complete book of clothing coupons, and a section officer in Adastral House had been cajoled by him into parting with her hat. It was too big for Maggie, but it seemed churlish to say so. She stuffed it with strips of newspaper, which at least stopped it falling over her eyes every time she bent her head.

They left Dulcimer in the afternoon, meeting up with Jean-Louis who had already been some hours at their next port of call: a newly built radar station with underground offices and sleeping quarters. It was dark before the men finished their investigations. They decided to set off at once. Maggie disliked driving at night, for the car's blacked out headlights were reduced to two narrow slits, and she had to drive along slowly by their feeble beams, peering anxiously ahead into the gloom. It was nearly midnight before they drew up at the door of a New Forest guest house. David's batman, Bill, came out to meet them, his broad face creasing into a relieved smile.

Bill had also done some successful scrounging, and proudly displayed a replacement typewriter and other office equipment all set up and ready for Maggie. He exclaimed volubly about their lucky escape, and said what a good thing it was that he had taken the Group Captain's files with him in the jeep that day. She smiled, said yes it was lucky and the new typewriter looked better than the old, and went to wash her hands in her small bedroom. With a brief yearning look at the bed, she went downstairs again, drank a strong cup of tea to keep herself awake and started typing up the day's notes. It was business as usual.

Informed of the loss of the Air Force car and its contents, an official had sent a sheaf of buff forms which had to be filled in. Maggie sighed. It seemed that they required exact descriptions of all the lost items, information as to where and when each object had been acquired, its colour, shape and value, and a good deal else. Inured to Air Force red tape Maggie started making lists next morning. She found that even her own modest case had actually contained a bewildering number of things.

But the forms were never filled in, for David came into the makeshift office and told her to throw them away.

'There'll be trouble if we don't answer their questions, sir.'

'Forget it. Forms are a waste of time.'

'I don't mind filling them in. It's my job.'

'Your job is to do as I say,' he retorted, and though his face was serious she had an odd notion that his dark eyes were lit from within. He added abruptly, 'Did you have anything to eat last evening?'

'I had a cup of tea and some biscuits, sir.'

'You can't live on tea and biscuits.'

'Stop bullying the poor kid,' said Ben from the doorway. 'Isn't it enough that you've rubbed her pretty face in a thorn bush? And why the red war paint?'

Maggie laughed, and said that Nanny had been responsible for the war paint. It was her preferred antiseptic to the more painful iodine. But she put the hated forms in the nearest bin with alacrity, relieved to be rid of them, happy indeed to do whatever David Vorst wanted. She even tried eating more sensibly, although she felt little need for food. Her whole being was suffused with a quite unreasoning happiness. It was no longer a matter of being half in love with David Vorst. She was wholly and shamefully nutty about him. It was hard to know why, especially when she knew that he was not hers – and never would be. His manner was polite but generally rather distant. He seldom spoke to her except to say good morning or to thank her at the end of the day, and she was pretty sure that most of the time he had no idea that she was actually there. But her light-hearted mood refused to go away. David Vorst was there, somewhere within her orbit. She could see him, watch him in the rear mirror of the car, listen to his slow deep voice when he talked with the others, take dictation from him in the evenings and bring him his notes to be checked and signed. Although reason told her that he belonged to Antonia – and that pain must be the inevitable outcome – it did not seem to matter.

One thing that certainly worried Maggie was the loss of her clothes. Despite constant travelling and a mountain of work at the end of each day, the problem nagged at her. It was all too much like the time when she had been at the officer training college and had been dismayed to find that, once a WAAF officer, she would have to buy her own uniform. She had been wonderfully lucky in her friends on that occasion. They knew that Dunlop had no money except her meagre Air Force pay, and promptly rallied round. One of them discovered a girl who was about to discard her uniform tunic and skirt in favour of a new outfit, and another heard of a married officer who was pregnant and leaving the service, and was only too happy to sell her kit. Thanks to her hard bargaining friends and some hasty alterations to these purchases, Maggie had been suitably attired when she took part in the final passing out parade. From time to time she had acquired other garments, and had accumulated a passable wardrobe.

But yesterday the Luftwaffe rocket had sent all her possessions to blazes, and now she had next to nothing. Nanny had been sympathetic and helpful, for she had not only brushed and pressed Maggie's muddied uniform, but washed her shirt and underwear and had insisted on giving her the voluminous nightdress and two pairs of well·darned lisle stockings to take away. Maggie was touched and very grateful, but there were still difficulties. Ben Horowitz had handed her a wad of clothing coupons, telling her with a wink that she was not to ask where they came from. But coupons were no solution in themselves. Unless she sold half of them on the illegal black market to raise funds, she lacked the money to buy even a fraction of what she needed. Apart from shoes, she must have gloves, at least one more shirt, some stockings and a good many other garments which were considered essential accoutrements for a WAAF officer. She was in urgent need of new black regulation shoes, too, for one had been damaged in the desperate uphill run to safety, and needed to go to the menders.

She drove the Group Captain to work in Southampton next day, and while idly watching a group of Wrens passing down the street, a possible solution popped into her mind. Sophy Ducane! Sophy might help her. They took the same size in shoes and Sophy, with her spendthrift ways and her wonderful generosity, might have a pair to spare.

Maggie laughed to herself as she polished the windows of the Group Captain's camouflage painted vehicle. The thought of Sophy was always heartening; Sophy with her unending supply of gossip and silly stories and her willingness to share her clothes. She was a passionate collector of both new and second-hand things to wear, and boasted that she never threw anything away. On leaving America she had arrived at the dockside with a gigantic cabin trunk with a domed lid, despite her Aunt Adele telling her that she was only allowed one suitcase. And Sophy managed, by smiling engagingly at a bemused crew member and enlisting Maggie's help, to fit the trunk into their tiny double cabin. It took up all the floor space and they barked their shins or fell over the monster every time they got in or out of their bunks.

The two girls had become friendly during the slow, remarkably tedious journey home, and had promised to keep in touch. All the same, Maggie had not really expected to hear from Sophy, supposing that she would quickly find new friends and new interests in the Wrens. But Sophy, for all her scatty ways, did not forget her promise. Her first WRNS job had been as a despatch rider, roaring about from place to place on a motor bike, collecting and delivering Naval messages. From time to time she rang Maggie up to ask how she was getting on, and then they would talk and talk.

Sophy never bothered about pips or having to put more coins into the slot, and often she managed to use a telephone belonging to one of her numerous relations. Her telephone calls were a source of comfort and entertainment to Maggie. Sophy's life in the WRNS sounded so utterly different to her own in the Air Force, like a film, enviably full of excitements and changes of scene. Sophy switched merrily from one job to another, and changed her most favoured admirers almost as frequently. There had never been any lack of good-looking Naval officers for her to choose from, and no telephone call to Maggie was complete without an update on Sophy's love life. A few months ago, Sophy had started a secretarial job at the Admiralty in London and had moved into a dungeon belonging to one of her aunts. Sophy had more aunts even than clothes, or so it seemed to Maggie.

She had, in fact, spoken with Sophy only a week ago, and on her way to look for a call box she wondered if Sophy would be bored by yet another call so soon. But Sophy answered at the second ring, and gave a whoop of delight when she heard Maggie's voice, saying that she had been dying for someone to talk to. And when Maggie confessed that she had lost all her clothes, she was even more pleased. On the sea voyage from America it had always been Maggie who had everything under control, and she who kept losing and forgetting things.

'What? All of them? Were you drunk, Mags? Have you broken out at last?'

'Sorry to disappoint you, but no.' Maggie smiled at the grubby wall of the call box. 'It was an accident. My boss and I lost our things yesterday. Sophy, have you got a spare pair of regulation black shoes you could lend me? I've no time to go shopping, and the heel of one of mine has worked loose.'

'Sure. I'll hunt out a pair for you. What else do you need, Mags?'

There were a good many things, but since Sophy was six inches shorter than Maggie, it was hard to believe that many of her clothes would do. She said, after some thought, that she would be glad of a pair of pyjamas and some underwear, and perhaps some gloves and a handkerchief or two. And at the end, she asked if she might borrow an old cardigan. It was sometimes cold sitting over the typewriter at night.

'And what about your boss? Is he going around half naked too, the poor old buffer?'

Maggie replied sedately that her boss possessed other uniforms, adding with truth that he had decided to replenish his store of socks and underpants and had asked her to collect these from Harrods when they visited London at the end of the week. 'I'm to drive him to London for a meeting.'

'Why can't his wife go to Harrods and collect his undies for him?'

'She's with the children in the country,' said Maggie, blithely presenting the Group Captain's fictitious wife with some offspring. Always rampantly curious as well as being dangerously indiscreet, Sophy must on no account be allowed to suspect the true identity of Maggie's boss, and a week ago she had kicked off her campaign of deception by adding twenty years to his age.

'Gracious! Isn't he a bit long in the tooth to have kids?'

'Their eldest boy is in his teens,' said Maggie firmly, and it was presently arranged that Sophy would leave a bag containing shoes and other necessities in the Harrods parcels office on her way to work.

'Why don't we meet for lunch while your boss is at his meeting?'

'Sorry, I can't,' said Maggie. She wasn't going to risk Sophy setting eyes on David. 'He expects me to wait for him in the car. We'll leave for the country straight after the meeting.'

Maggie had driven David to London for his meeting at the Air Ministry and, following his earlier instructions, she turned right along the Embankment after crossing the river. It was blowing a gale and raining hard, and the river looked grey and choppy through the streaming windows of the car. They were nearing Chelsea Bridge when David raised his head from his notes and pulled the partition glass aside. He told Maggie to drive to Savile Row.

Outside a military tailoring establishment which was so famous that even Maggie had heard of it, she stopped the car and got out, meaning to hold the rear door for him. But he was already out on the streaming pavement, handing her his briefcase and telling her to come along. They charged through the downpour with lowered heads, Maggie clutching her over-large hat with one hand and carrying the Group Captain's briefcase in the other. Inside the shop it was blessedly warm and dry.

They were expected. Two elderly and soberly clad gentlemen greeted David with deference, and a black-clad woman of severe aspect beckoned Maggie into a spacious panelled fitting room. When she saw what was hanging there, Maggie turned right round and went back into the main shop.

David was sitting with his briefcase open on his knees. Maggie went up to him and said in an anguished whisper, 'Sir! They've got two uniforms in there, half made. The woman says they're for me, and I'm to try them on.'

He looked at her, his dark brows raised. He looked displeased by this interruption. 'So? Hadn't you better do as she asks?'

'Sir! It won't do. I couldn't possibly afford one from a place like this. I mean to find something second-hand when there's time to ask around.'

'And just when do you propose to find time, Miss Dunlop?'

He had never spoken to her so coldly or looked at her with such evident disdain, and she found herself stammering. 'I . . . I thought on my day off, sir . . .'

He said curtly, 'While you are working for me, Miss Dunlop, there will be no days off. No time to waste on foolish argument, either. Go and ·get done with your fitting, or you'll make me late for my appointment.'

Maggie turned without a word, and went back into the spacious fitting room and let the elderly female assistant help her into the first of two blue skirts, before summoning the tailor. She stood mutely while they pinned and twisted and turned her this way and that. Only when she was buttoning up her own well-worn tunic did the woman unbend rather surprisingly.

She patted Maggie's arm. 'Don't be upset, dear. These high-up officers get to think they own the world. We see a lot of it in here. What rank is that one of yours? A wing commander?'

'Higher than that. He's recently been promoted to group captain.'

'That would account for it, and I dare say all the medal ribbons on his chest make him even more big-headed. What is it that you do for him?'

'I drive him about – him and some other people.'

'Then take my advice, dear, and re-muster as a cook.' And when Maggie opened her eyes at this surprising knowledge of Air Force jargon, the woman added confidentially, 'I've a niece in the WAAF who used to be a batwoman. Now she's a cook in a canteen, and she says that life is ever so much better. None of them act tyrannical to you if you're a cook. They talk nice, hoping to get second helpings or the best bit of stew – and one of the greedy ones even took her to the pictures.'

Maggie laughed, and was still laughing when she was ushered out of the fitting room.

'Ah,' said David, watching with regret as the amusement faded from her face. 'If we go now, Miss Dunlop, we may even be on time.'

They did not speak on the way to the Air Ministry. David vanished into the building, telling her that he would be at least an hour and suggesting that after she had collected his parcels from Harrods she should look for some sandwiches for their lunch. She collected Sophy's promised zip bag and his parcels, but sandwiches were hard to come by that day. She dashed three times through the rain into likely shops without success, and eventually tracked down what appeared to be the last three sandwiches in London. She bought them quickly, not because they looked appetising, but because she did not want to keep David waiting outside the Air Ministry.

She saw him as soon as she drove up. He had just ushered another high-ranking officer out of the sandbagged entrance, and she was out of the car and ready with deadpan face and her smartest salute, but only just in time. The two men returned her salute and got hurriedly into the car to escape the relentlessly driving rain. She shut them in together and presently drove the elderly Air Commodore to his Hertfordshire home. Here David declined the offer of a drink, and they once more headed north. The rain ceased, and the sun came out, turning the wet country road to a silver ribbon before them.

They had gone about ten miles when he told her to stop the car. She did so, and he came to sit beside her in the front. She was briefly pleased to have him there, but her pleasure was short-lived, for he did not speak and his face wore a brooding, sombre expression. Maggie felt little urge to talk after his quelling behaviour in the tailor's shop. Instead, as she drove on she thought glumly about re-mustering. Doubtless he would speak when he wanted something.

She was right. He said suddenly, 'Any luck with sandwiches, Maggie?'

'They're in the boot, sir. I'll stop and get them out, if you like.'

'Well, aren't you starving? I certainly am.'

They were passing through a Hertfordshire village, and she drew up beside the village green. There were ducks on the pond, and willows trailed bare winter branches at the water's edge, and the wind-rippled surface of the pond showed distorted reflections of the church and the pub with its inn sign which was wagging noisily in the strong breeze. It was all very neat and English and picturesque, thought Maggie sadly. She felt a sudden pang of yearning for the rough rocks and heather of Glen Cary.

She decided that it was hunger that was making her feel so low, and got out of the car. It was a struggle to close the heavy door again with the wind blowing so strongly. Suddenly a swirling gust lifted the uniform cap off her head and sent it bowling along the gutter towards the duck pond, scattering its newspaper stuffing into puddles as it went. Maggie gave a cry of dismay, and started in pursuit.

But David was already out of the car and running on his longer legs. He stamped on the errant cap just before it reached the water. He bent to pick it up, gave it a shake, and began gathering up the sodden newspaper. He turned back to Maggie, his face alight with laughter. 'What's this? I once knew a man who kept a kipper in his hat in case he got hungry. But why the *Daily Telegraph*, Maggie?'

She took the cap from him, blushing hotly. 'Nanny takes the *Telegraph*. It was to stop my cap falling over my eyes. You see, it's too big for me.'

He shouted with laughter, and she couldn't help laughing with him.

'Now,' said David, getting down to things that mattered. 'Let's have those sandwiches before we both starve to death.'

Maggie fetched them, and they sat in the front of the car and eyed them rather dubiously as they lay on their bed of greaseproof paper. The last sandwiches in London had a weary streetwise expression, both inside and out. She said apologetically, 'They were the only ones I could find.'

'What's in them?'

'Fish paste the man said, but he didn't seem to know what kind of fish.'

David picked one up and examined it cautiously. 'Very old fish, I guess. Did you get it in an antique shop?'

She laughed.

'Maggie,' he said suddenly, watching her. 'What were you laughing about in the tailor's shop?'

She looked back at him, her grey eyes suddenly bright and angry, and another tiresome blush beginning to warm her cheeks. 'It was just something that the sales lady said to me in the fitting room.'

'Come on. Tell me.'

Maggie knew she ought to feel indignant. He had been horrible to her in that shop, and now he was smiling at her in a destructive and unfair way. She said crossly, 'We were laughing about you, sir, if you really want to know.'

'Well, what about me?'

'The sales lady said not to be upset, as lots of high-up officers get to think they own the world. She told me I ought to re-muster as a cook.'

'Why a cook, for Pete's sake?'

'She said nobody acts tyrannical to cooks, even in the forces.'

He laughed. She began to join in his laughter, but he suddenly grew serious. 'You know, Maggie, that woman had a point. You ought not to be doing this job.'

For the second time that day, he seemed to be trying to hurt her. It was so unlike him. She looked at him in silent reproach.

'Don't look at me like that,' he said, and his voice sounded rough. 'I didn't mean to hurt your feelings, but we need to talk things out before this goes any further.'

'What sort of things, Mr David?'

He looked at her. He seemed to hesitate, and then he said, 'I'm going to send you away. I thought I could do it without telling you my reasons, but when you looked at me so accusingly just now, I knew that nothing but the truth would do.'

They fed the sandwiches to the ducks, and he took her arm and led her to the pub, deaf to her protests. They were no longer serving lunch in the dining room, but the landlord smiled on them and said he would rustle up some bread and cheese in the bar, and what would they like to drink?

'What have you got?' asked David. 'Any beer left in the barrel?'

The landlord brought a pint for the Group Captain and a half pint of cider for his driver, and went away through some swing doors.

Maggie said in a furious whisper, 'You don't have to feed me, just because you're meaning to sack me. Anyway, I'm not hungry.'

'Well, I am. Drink your cider. It'll make you feel better.'

'Drink it yourself.' She pushed the glass towards him, spilling some of its contents on the varnished table. 'I didn't ask for cider. I'll go to sleep at the wheel after lunch if I drink it.'

'Don't worry,' he said calmly. 'I'll drive the rest of the way.'

She felt like hitting him. He had no right to sit there looking so smug and taking no notice of anything she said. But violence was not a practical option because the landlord reappeared with the bread and cheese: and at the sight of the feast that lay on the wooden platter, her tummy gave a disloyal lurch of longing. If she had to face disaster it might be sensible to mollify her traitorous tummy first. So she took the cheese and pickle sandwich that David presently put on her plate, and rather sulkily began to eat it. She sipped at her cider, too, and looked up to find him watching her.

'Better?'

'A bit,' she conceded. 'But why are you planning to sack me?'

'I'm not.'

'But you said you were sending me away. Is my work not good enough?'

'Your work is everything I hoped it would be.'

'Well then. Why?'

It was a while before he answered, and when he did it was almost as though he had forgotten her question. They had moved to a squashy sofa at the far end of the lounge bar, and the landlord had brought a pot of coffee and some cups. She was about to press him again for a reason for wanting rid of her, when David asked abruptly, 'How long have you been in the WAAFs, Maggie?'

She told him that she had joined up more than three years ago.

'More than three years? Then many men will have told you you're lovely and paid you other compliments, and some will have tried to make passes. Do you have what my mother calls a "special beau" right now?'

This second question seemed as irrelevant as the first, so she answered it with stark truth. 'I did have one, I think, but Paul was killed in an MTB raid on the Brittany coast.'

'Maggie! I'm so sorry. How long ago was this?'

'Over two months now.'

'Just two months? You poor child. I suppose you took this job for a change of scene. Do you want to talk about him?'

She tried to think about Paul, and how to describe him, but with David Vorst sitting beside her on the old leather sofa speaking with such heart-shaking gentleness, she found it hard to remember Paul's face, or very much about him. She said hesitantly, 'There isn't a lot to say. We knew each other for a very short time. But you're right. I did take this job to get away.'

She turned to look at him, and saw that he was staring at her with the strangest expression on his thin, dark face: a mixture of concern and indecision. She put out a hand and laid it over his. 'What is it, Mr

338

David? If it's not my work, please tell me why you want to get rid of me. Don't worry about my feelings. They don't matter, and I'm sensible, really, and pretty tough.'

He took her hand in both of his and smiled at her, a warm teasing smile that made her heart begin to pound. 'Oh Maggie, I'm sure you're as tough as old boots, and very much more sensible than I am. That wouldn't be difficult. If I'd had any sense at all, I'd have sent you away that first day, because even then I knew what was likely to happen. But I was so overjoyed to see you that I just couldn't bring myself to do it, and now the damage is done. I've fallen dreadfully and unforgivably in love with you, and half of me wants to believe you feel the same. I thought, when you were a little tipsy with Uncle Bernard's sherry, that it might be so . . .'

She gazed at him as though she had never seen him before.

'Maggie. Am I crazy to think you love me?'

Her voice was barely audible, but her dawning smile reflected his. 'It looks as if we're both crazy. I've tried to hide it, and I've been that ashamed of myself for being so soppy. I'm worse than any teenager with a crush on the teacher. But I never thought that you . . .' She broke off, and said suspiciously, 'Are you having me on?'

'I wouldn't do that, Maggie. I love you very much.' He lifted her hand to his lips, kissed it and felt it tremble. Suddenly serious again, he said, 'I shouldn't have told you, because it's only going to make things even harder for you. We'd better start thinking about what sort of job you would enjoy after you leave us.'

'But why must I leave?'

He frowned at her, suddenly looking irritated. 'Surely you must see. The work we are doing is the only thing that matters. There are other teams involved in research of equal importance, and it will be for the commanders to decide how to fit the puzzle together. But they must be given the data they need, and it must be right and they must have it on time. Until our mission is completed we shall be working to relentless deadlines day after day. There will be no time for anything else, and as for our private feelings, or any other diversion, they must be put out of the way. I wasn't joking when I said there would be no days off, you know.'

She said wryly, remembering how he had slapped her down, 'I never thought you were joking.'

He waited for her to say more, and when she did not, he said quietly, 'I am sending you away for another good reason, Maggie. I'm married to Antonia, and you know what she's like. Even the children liking you best was more than she could take. There can be no future for you and me together, even as the most platonic of friends, and I'll not insult you by suggesting a casual affair.'

She said nothing, recognising this as a painful truth she'd known all along. Her grey eyes rested steadily on him as he went on speaking.

'I worshipped Antonia when I first knew her, and positively badgered her to marry me. She doesn't want to leave America at present, but wherever she is, she is still my wife. When the war is over, I shall go back.'

'Of course. The children will need you for one thing.'

His burning look made her tremble again. 'Those children! Don't you ever think of yourself, Maggie?'

She said faintly, 'Go on.'

'This job may last a long time, for months most likely. Of course I don't want to send you away. I want to see you every day as I have done lately, to hear you speaking, even very occasionally to talk to you alone. I want to be driven about by you, to have you type our reports and smooth our way in the wonderfully competent manner you have. Ben says that you're a honey, and I'm an ungrateful bastard to treat you so casually. He tells me that since coming to live in Britain I've become a real stuffed shirt.'

'He's been telling me that, too. So why have you?'

'Because if anyone suspects how I feel about you, there'll be gossip. You know the Air Force grapevine.'

'I'm not afraid of a bit of gossip.'

'Then you ought to be,' he said severely. 'I won't have you talked about. That's why I'm going to send you away.'

'Why spoil people's fun? There's nothing they enjoy more than a juicy bit of scandal.'

He ignored this frivolity. 'If there is even a whisper about us, you may be sure that Antonia will hear of it.'

She took her hand out of his and looked down at it. 'Do you think it likely that she will come home while the war's still on?'

'Maybe, or she may decide to stay in America. I never know what to expect from Antonia, but I doubt if she'll want to come back and face an English winter at Dulcimer. She's too comfortable where she is. I'll tell you one thing, though. If Antonia gets even a whiff of gossip about you and me being together, she'll be on her way back in a trice. Do you see?'

'Oh,' said Maggie blankly. 'Yes. I see.'

She turned to face him, 'I've listened to your plans for me. When are you going to ask me what I want for myself?'

He chuckled. 'I'm asking you now. What do you want?'

'I want to go on working for you and your team, David. You say that I do my job all right. I find it hard work and very interesting. I like Major Horowitz and Jean-Louis and Pete, and Bill is as besotted about you as I am. You say it may take months to finish, and I want very much to see it through. Why must I be sent away? I can be as stuffy as you can, and hide my feelings just as well. What are you afraid of?'

He did not speak for quite some time. Then he said, with hope giving an edge to his voice, 'You think you could do it? It won't be easy. We shall need to be careful, and I shall treat you with deadly formality. Not much fun for either of us. You could help by grumbling about me to the others.'

Her grey eyes sparkled. 'That won't be difficult.'

'I ought to send you off. Some people are far too noticing. Keeping you on as a member of the team will put you at risk.'

'We are all at risk in wartime,' she said with a smile that made his heart turn over. 'We may be killed tomorrow. We very nearly were the other day.'

'So we were.' David felt his spirits rising. They could do it. They would make it work. They would be tied to a hectic schedule, working against the clock, with little time for anything but work and sleep and moving on. But Maggie would be there. He felt suddenly exalted. Amazingly, Maggie had told him that she loved him, and she would be there.

'All right,' he said quietly. 'If you are willing, we'll give it a try. Is that a deal?'

Her voice was hardly above a whisper. 'It's a deal.'

He went through to the public bar to thank the landlord and settle their bill. This done, they went out together, but he drew her back into the shadow of the porch and held her for a moment in his arms. He felt her tremble, and said remorsefully, 'I should be shot for doing this to you. It would have been better for you if we'd never met again.'

'That was what I told myself when I joined the WAAF,' she agreed with a smile. 'No more thinking about America, or remembering picnics on the sands with Mr James and Mr David. But things don't always work out as you think. One thing, I shall always be thankful that I was sent to America. It has changed me, changed my life.'

'Yes,' he agreed soberly. 'Despite everything, I'm happy to know that you were at Maple Valley and met my family. Talking of family, Maggie, there's been no time to ask why you weren't needed at home. Last time I saw you, you saw no way out.'

'It was a miracle,' she said. 'My father did not want me home, after all. When I get leave, I spend time with Gran, but sleep at the manse. There's no room for me at home, anyway, because there are lodgers in the attic rooms, and the rent money pays for Gran to have help. So you see, I was free, free to join the WAAF. I told you. It really did feel like a miracle.'

He smiled down at her. It was time to go. He pulled her closer, bent his head and kissed her for the first and last time that winter. 'One for the road, Maggie. When we do this again, our work will be finished. That's our deal, and we'll keep it.'

He strode ahead of her into the early February sunshine. As they crossed the village green, Maggie said peremptorily. 'Sir! Just a moment, please.'

He turned and replied in kind. 'What is it, Miss Dunlop?'

'Why were you so horrible to me in the tailor's shop?'

'Tyranny seemed the best policy. I was afraid that you were about to reject your new uniforms and make a scene.'

'Well, I was. I was going to ask what they charged in that place but then you bit my head off and I forgot.'

'It won't cost you a cent. The insurance will pick it up.'

She eyed him. 'I'm not sure that I believe that.'

'That's no way to speak to your superior officer, Miss Dunlop. Get in the car. It's time we were going.'

As promised, David drove all the way to the RAF bomber base where the rest of the team were assembled. Again, Bill came out to greet them wheeling a sturdy trolley for the Group Captain's luggage

'What's this?' David asked, when a strange zip bag emerged from the capacious boot. 'Something of yours, Miss Dunlop?'

'I've borrowed some clothes from a friend, sir. I told her that I had lost my luggage and was short of things to wear, so she left this at Harrods for me.'

'A useful friend.'

'Yes, sir. Sophy's wonderfully generous.'

'Did you tell her how you managed to lose all your luggage?'

'No, sir,' said Maggie primly, suddenly thankful that she had not.

'You don't need to worry about Miss Dunlop talking out of turn, sir,' said Bill soothingly. With the rest of the team, Bill felt that the Group Captain did not value his secretary/driver as highly as he should. 'Leave it to me, miss,' he added as Maggie started to pick the bag up. 'I'll see it gets to your billet with the rest of your stuff. They've put you to sleep over in the WAAF officers' quarters, but you'll maybe want to collect Major Horowitz's notes before you go over.'

He trundled away with his trolley.

David said thoughtfully, 'Sophy? Not by any chance that niece of Adele Devenish?'

'Well, yes,' she admitted. 'She's in the Wrens and works at the Admiralty, but we still talk on the telephone regularly.'

'Where does she live in London?'

'In a basement flat in Cheyne Place. I haven't seen it yet.'

'You could do with a base in London,' he said thoughtfully. 'Somewhere to keep your things, and to stay the odd night in. I can't take you to the Vorst with the others, and I hate to think of you trekking out to Lambeth to that WAAF hostel. Would she rent you a corner of her flat?'

Maggie was shocked. 'She would, I think, but it'd be much too expensive. Two pounds a week was what she charged her last lodger. And actually, I haven't many things to leave. That hostel's not bad, when there's room in it. Are we likely to be in London often?'

'From time to time we will be, and you'll be no use to me if you have to sleep in the car because there's no room in the hostel,' he said. Ben Horowitz was coming across the tarmac, so David added with finality, 'Offer your friend whatever she asks, Maggie, and don't be silly.'

Three months as part of the team brought them all very close. Ben Horowitz treated Maggie like a kid sister and teased her unmercifully. He called her Miss Prim when she blushed at his more outrageous sallies, and taught her to play backgammon. Jean-Louis was frankly admiring and corrected her French pronunciation, and Pete Smith from New Zealand followed the French Canadian's lead in flirting with her when they were off duty. Alone with her, Pete was rather tongue-tied. She found his shyness touching.

Only the Group Captain was cool and sometimes peremptory, at all times keeping his Section Officer at a proper distance. He held himself aloof from the joking and fun when she was there, and she was just as formal in her manner to him. They kept to their bargain, but when Maggie learned that Antonia was coming back from America, she wished that she had never agreed to David's deal.

It had been the minister's idea that Bert Higgins should sit for a bursary at a well-known Scottish public school. Bert, at fifteen, had wanted to serve an apprenticeship with a garage owner in the town. As soon as he had turned seventeen he was determined to join the army.

But the minister, who had tutored him since his arrival from London – they did a correspondence course together – thought he should continue his education. He wrote to his old school in Perthshire, and eventually persuaded Bert to give their scholarship exam a try. Both teacher and pupil enjoyed the challenge more than they expected. It was good to have a target to work for, and when Bert won the school's top scholarship, a great many people were pleased and impressed.

The MacDuff Scholarship was a handsome award. Except for clothes, everything would be paid for by the school, and Lord Dulcimer sent money to cover clothes and certain extras. Miss Trumpet looked out a passable kilt and tweed jacket that had been made for Dart when he was in his teens, and Mrs Fraser's deft fingers altered the jacket and moved the kilt straps to fit Bert's skinny form.

'That kilt!' Dart exclaimed, when the Frasers told him. He had come unexpectedly to Glen Cary for a single day, and called in at the manse with a purpose. 'I remember fighting tooth and nail against having to wear it.' He looked at Bert, who had just come in. 'I heard that you were here. Are they letting you out for long?'

'I go back on Sunday evening, milord,' said Bert formally. At a glance from Mrs Fraser he added, 'I have to thank you for letting me borrow your kilt. They wear the kilt for best there.'

Dart nodded, and then came to the point. 'Bert, would you help with the heather burning tomorrow? Donald finds the walking hard enough, and carrying the kit too much – though he won't admit it.'

'I'd like that fine.'

Dart nodded. 'If this fine spell holds, we'll start early. I've only got one day, and mean to make the most of it.'

'So where will Wat go if the Frasers need to go away?' inquired Dart after a flurry of snow had whitened the heather and no more fires could be lit. Dart had a soft spot for Bert's dog, feeling an almost proprietory interest in him. 'Why not ask Dunlop to keep him? He's good with dogs, and there's plenty of room in his kennels.'

'That won't do,' said Bert. 'Mr Dunlop and Wat don't get on.'

'Why ever not?'

Bert shrugged. 'They just don't, but Cook will be happy to keep him. Wat will be fine at the manse.'

Next day, Dart went to re-join his regiment and on Sunday Bert went back to boarding school.

'So this is your dower house,' Maggie said unsteadily. It was their last day. It was over. 'Thank you for letting me see it. Could I come in for a cup of coffee before I take the car back to London?'

David did not answer. Like Maggie, he was gazing unseeingly through the windscreen. He did not look at her. There was no need. He knew her every feature by heart, was conscious of her every movement at his side.

They had dined on the way, but conversation had been sticky. There were too many things they wanted to say but must not. Neither of them had done justice to the food. They sat on, reluctant to move although the bill had been paid long since.

Maggie had said into the silence, 'Major Horowitz tells me that you will be joining him on Monday.'

'That's right. What will you do, Maggie?'

'Glen Cary for a week's leave. After that, back to my work in the basement.'

He said, 'Must you go back? It caused you such unhappiness last time.'

'This time will be different. I won't fall in love with any of the "clients".'

'Does losing your Paul still hurt so much?'

She shook her head, pressing her lips together to stop them trembling. Paul was no more than a dim memory. David probably knew what was causing her present hurt, but he would not speak of it. What would be the point, with Antonia and the children returning to England any day now. 'Hardly at all these days.'

He smiled at her. 'You'll never make a good liar, Maggie.' He added seriously, 'Why go back to a place where you'll be reminded of him? There are other things you do so well. Did you go to see the air commodore I told you about? I gave you a glowing reference, with never a mention of how often you put us in the ditch.'

'That's not fair! It only happened once when it was snowing! The other time it wasn't my fault. A front tyre burst. You know it did!'

'I was writing notes at the time, so I never noticed.'

'You were always writing notes.'

They laughed together, suddenly more at ease. 'So what about the air commodore? He seemed a nice old guy.'

'I never saw him. I rang his secretary to say that I had been posted elsewhere. I'm finished with driving officers about.'

He smiled at her. 'As bad as that, Maggie?'

She looked into his glowing dark eyes. 'There were some interesting moments. But we kept our bargain well, don't you think? Group Captain Vorst and his meek secretary/chauffeur. Nothing for anyone to talk about.'

'You look anything but meek from where I sit, Miss Dunlop. I have an odd feeling that you are up to something. Your eyes are full of light and mischief.'

She shook her head. A hovering waiter came to look at them, and went away. Maggie stood up. 'It's late. I think they want rid of us.'

David drove the last lap to Dulcimer. Maggie was grateful, for she had still to take herself back to London. She was bone weary. It was all over – three months of hard work and excitement, of pushing herself beyond reasonable limits of exhaustion. She had trained herself to do with little sleep. Now it was over, and she had ventured to ask David for this one last evening together.

She planned to ask him a favour before they parted.

'A favour, Maggie? May I buy you some little thing, after all?'

She shook her head. He had wanted to give her a memento. 'You know I don't want that.'

'What then?'

It was Maggie's turn to take her time to answer. He had invited her in, made coffee, and carried it to the morning room where chintz

345

curtains had been drawn and a fire burned in the grate. Nanny's work, he told her.

They sat sedately on either side of the fire. Another first and last time, Maggie thought, looking round the room as though trying to imprint it on her memory. Her eyes turned to David. He was in a deep armchair watching her, long legs stretched out and feet propped on a shallow brass fender. He raised a questioning eyebrow, wordlessly requiring an answer to his question.

She got to her feet and laid her empty cup on the mantel shelf. She was pleased to find that it did not rattle in the saucer. She tried to breathe deeply, to still the panic racing of her heart. At officer training school they said that deep breathing helped to calm the nerves.

She said in a low voice, looking down into the fire, 'You said once that you would not offer me a casual affair. I wouldn't want that either, but would you take me to bed with you just once, tonight?' He said nothing, and she did not dare to look. She began to speak more rapidly, for fear that her courage would drain away before she had done. 'You offered to give me a memento – something to remember . . .'

His feet in their highly polished shoes were just within her line of vision, unmoving. She said weakly, 'That is what I would like. But of course if you don't want to . . .'

She got no further, for he was on his feet and looking at her, a hand on the mantel shelf. He said, 'Maggie, it's nothing to do with what I want. You know very well that I would like nothing better than to take you to bed. But it won't do. I have a wife, and you are young and good and I love you . . .'

She moved towards him then, hot with embarrassment and almost faint with relief. His silence and stillness had unnerved her utterly.

He held her at arm's length, and said seriously, 'Maggie, listen to me. You may not be able to believe it right now, but one day you will find someone else to replace your first love – someone young like Paul who will want to marry you and give you children. I can offer you none of those things. You deserve better than a sordid affair with a married man.'

'David.' Her eyes were luminous and full of hope, 'You've got me all wrong. My father calls me a whore, and I have been called other things, but I am not a child who needs protecting from harm. Why would it be sordid for us go to bed on this one night if we love one another? I shall be gone first thing in the morning, so we won't harm anyone at all.'

'Maggie . . .'

She put up a hand, and said firmly, 'It's your turn to listen. I'm going to tell you about Paul.'

'No need for you to tell me anything, Maggie.'

'Please listen! Paul was a nice boy, and I was sorry for him because he was lonely and in dread of going back on active service, and I was very upset when he was killed. But as for being my first love, I doubt if we were in love at all. We had sex together once. He wanted it, and I was curious to find out what it was like.'

'And what was it like, Maggie?'

Her lips quivered. 'Paul liked it more than I did. The only place we could find was a soggy field, and a thistle kept popping up and scratching me.' She could not contain her laughter any longer. It bubbled up irresistibly, almost strangling her attempts to speak. 'There was a cow looking over the fence, and she put me off by mooing . . .'

They were both suddenly convulsed with laughter, and she was in his arms being kissed very roughly indeed. 'Maggie darling, you're hopeless. Why did you have to make me laugh?'

At Glen Cary and in the glen to the west of it, there had been several incidents of sheep worrying. The keepers from both glens and aggrieved shepherds had been keeping watch for marauders – and two dogs were caught in the act, and shot. One of them was Wat.

'The bloody murderer!' said Bert through set teeth. 'If I'd been there I'd have taken his gun and shot him myself.'

'Just as well you were away at school, in that case,' said the minister. 'And I wouldn't go around calling Ian Dunlop a murderer, if I were you. You know as well as I do that any dog caught chasing sheep is liable to be shot, particularly at this time of year when the ewes have lambs at foot.'

'Wat wouldn't chase sheep. He never has . . .'

The minister looked thoughtfully at Bert from under his bushy grey brows.

'Well, all right then,' Bert conceded reluctantly, his face going red under this mild scrutiny. 'But he only did it twice, when we first came.' For the first time since hearing that Wat was dead, he no longer sounded quite so distraught. He said imploringly, 'Mr Fraser, ever since you made me put him in a pen with that black-faced tupp, Wat has been afraid of sheep. You know that.'

The minister agreed that he did know it, but he also knew something of the unpredictable ways of dogs – and men. Bert held to it that the head keeper had shot his mongrel friend on purpose, and Mr Fraser wondered about it but said nothing. The head keeper was a stark and unforgiving man, and Mr Fraser had come lately to wonder if he might also be disturbed in his mind. Old Mrs Dunlop would never have mentioned to him the fact that her son talked so wildly and strangely in his sleep, unless she had been deeply worried.

Still, the fact remained that Wat and another dog had been seen chasing a flock of ewes with lambs at foot and Wat had taken one ewe by the throat – a capital crime in the glen. Both dogs were dead. He told Bert that no amount of argument or recrimination was going to bring his mongrel back to life.

Bert knew this to be true but he was too miserable and angry to leave the subject alone. 'Mr Dunlop shot a dog of Maggie's once because it bit him. With a temper like his, he ought not to be allowed to carry a gun.'

And with this bitter parting shot, Bert flung out of the manse and was not seen again until he came in, wet and cold, well after dark. They fed him hot soup and shooed him upstairs to a hot bath. Neither then, nor for some time afterwards, did Bert allude to Wat or to the manner of his death at the hands of Maggie's father.

But he had not forgotten. Nor had he forgiven. Bert had always been a solitary boy, spending whole days on the moor with just his dog for company. With no Wat to go with him, he still went off for hours and sometimes for whole days alone. The Frasers worried, but thought it best to leave him be. In another fortnight he would be back at school.

They could not know that Bert had come to see that the unbearable loss of Wat had bestowed two benefits upon him. Happy and busy though he was at his new posh school, Bert was determined to join the forces as soon as he was seventeen – in just over a year. Two schoolfriends with birthdays in August were planning to do the same, but Bert had been worried about what would happen to Wat. That, at least, was no longer a problem.

And there was a second advantage. Without a dog at his side, it was easier to stalk the head keeper – which he took to doing in grim earnest during that Easter holiday. And he had found out things about Ian Dunlop that both surprised and mystified him.

The head keeper was a regular visitor to the forbidden Jock's Crag, going there always by night. He went alone, without his dogs, and by the light of a small torch moved freely among the peat hags on the summit – a place which he had declared to be riddled with unexploded bombs. He kept a spade and a crowbar on the summit, and one windy night Bert could have sworn that he had been talking to someone. What was he about? Did he also have a radio transmitter hidden among the crags? Everyone knew that the invasion of Europe would start soon, and that the enemy needed to know about troop movements.

Bert returned to school with reluctance at the start of the summer term. A notion had come to him that Mr Dunlop might be a German spy.

Chapter 24

Maggie woke to find the spare room awash with milky pre-dawn light, and turned to look at her lover's sleeping face. She was familiar with David's ability to focus his attention wholly upon whatever he was doing. He slept with the same look of concentration, his dark head turned sideways on the pillow, his breathing deep and slow, and eyes tightly closed in a face that was now entirely dedicated to the business of sleeping.

It had been the same last night. Once he had given way to her request, he had been just as single-minded in his lovemaking. It occurred to Maggie that every poetical and biblical cliché had been coined afresh for her since yesterday. Going away was going to hurt damnably. She would only be able to bear it because she must.

She lay there trying to fix every small detail in her mind. She had been doing it for weeks, storing up small jokes and remembered pleasures like precious stones to be put away and looked at later. They had been few enough, these moments, for David had seldom lowered his guard where she was concerned – just the momentary meeting of eyes or exchange of smiles at some private joke, and a few occasions when they had been alone together and could talk without fear of being overheard.

For the most part she had been obliged to content herself with watching him, hearing his voice, listening to him arguing or sharing a joke with Ben Horowitz. The members of the team talked shop all the time, discussed new findings. David encouraged the others to talk, listening to what they had to say, occasionally putting a question or making a comment – but sparing with words.

Maggie had thought herself content with her few treasures. Now that David had given her this night of love, this revelation of anguish and ecstasy, she wondered if she would ever be content again. She lay there, remembering it, a kaleidescope of foolish fears and growing passion and joy almost beyond bearing.

They had abandoned the morning-room fire and gone upstairs together, flushed and dishevelled, hand in hand. David carried Maggie's small canvas grip. As of habit, he opened the door of the master bedroom, and Maggie balked on the threshold in sudden dismay. Antonia's room. It could only belong to Antonia. Maggie's shrinking gaze took in the frilled dressing table, the lace bedspread over a pink satin coverlet, the bottle of Chanel No. 5.

'Not here,' she whispered imploringly. 'Is there somewhere else?'

The little case tumbled to the floor as he put his arms round her. 'Darling Maggie, how dumb can I be!' He added in half-laughing contrition, 'There's a promising field with cows outside, but come and take a look at the spare bedroom before you decide.'

The spare room was spacious and pleasantly furnished. All the same, it had been a mistake to leave the morning-room fire, for by the time Maggie had bathed and put on the nightdress she had bought in Harrods 'just in case', she was in a high state of nerves. David came in and found her standing by the empty fireplace, shaking with cold and apprehension. He took one look at her and said, 'What's the matter?'

'David, I don't think I can. I was like this with Paul, and when I told my friend Sophy that I hadn't much use for sex, she said I must be frigid.' She was close to tears. 'I . . . I'm most terribly sorry.'

He held her to him, and said gently, 'We won't do anything you don't want, my darling. But come to bed and get warm. You're all goose pimples in that fetching gown.'

She shook her head. 'It wouldn't be fair to you.'

'I'll be the judge of that. Come on, before we both catch cold.'

The bed was huge and soft as a cloud. David switched the lights off, pulled back the window curtains, and the room was filled with the faint light of a waning moon. Then he slipped in beside her and held her close. They lay still in the transparent darkness, and he made her laugh by reminding her of their first real talk together, years ago in the kitchen garden at Dulcimer.

As his body warmed her, so her panic subsided. After a little while he began to touch her, gentling and stroking until she began to gasp and stir in his arms. He pushed down the straps of her satin gown, bending his dark head to kiss her breasts, cupping them warmly and laying his lips on first one nipple and then the other. A rush of inward burning made her utter an agonised moan.

'Don't you like that?'

'Yes. No. Yes. Don't stop . . . Now! Take me now, please.'

'There's no hurry, my love. Hours left until morning, and you're so beautiful . . .'

When at last he relented and the climax had flared and flowered and died, they lay panting and spent upon the tumbled sheets. Maggie was suddenly overcome by the wonder and beauty of it all. Tears welled up and she began to sob as though her heart would break. David held and kissed her, murmuring endearments and tasting the salt wetness of her tears. When her sobs had changed to an occasional unromantic hiccup, she raised her head to look at him, and saw with surprise that there were tears in his own dark eyes.

But before she could speak he was smiling. 'One thing is sure, Miss Dunlop,' he said. 'Your good friend Sophy Ducane is even more foolish than she is pretty.'

'How do you know she's pretty? You've never met her.'

'That's all you know. I was dining with a Navy friend of mine in Portsmouth the other night, and Sophy walked in with a crowd of adoring swains. She came to say hello, reminding me that she had met me in Maple Valley. She even told me about a flatmate – someone who used to be Antonia's nursery maid. She invited me to dine with you both in Cheyne Place.'

Maggie said wistfully, 'How I wish we could. Although I don't think I'd enjoy watching Sophy trying to vamp you.'

'Would she try?'

'Oh, yes,' said Maggie, who was recovering fast. 'Sophy finds older men irresistible, you know, particularly when they are ten feet high and covered with medals and gold braid.'

Maggie was due to return the staff car to the London depot in the morning. They overslept, and the first thing they knew, it was seven thirty and someone was banging on the front door and leaning on the electric bell.

David remembered just in time to rush through to Antonia's room before he opened a window. Lord Dulcimer's rubicund face looked up at him. He seemed to be out of breath. 'Let me in, David. I've got something to tell you.'

'Uncle Bernard. It's not even eight o'clock.'

'I know what time it is.'

'Has somebody died?'

'For God's sake get some clothes on, boy, and let me in.'

David realised with a tremor of laughter he was stark naked and already chilled from hanging out of the window. He rooted in his dressing-room cupboard for trousers and a sweater, pulled them on, shoved bare feet into a pair of slippers and ran out to the stairs.

Maggie was standing in the spare room doorway, clutching a sheet around her nakedness. Her eyes were wide and startled. He shook a tousled head at her and ran on down.

Lord Dulcimer almost charged through the front door, a key dangling in his hand. 'What the hell did you put the chain on for? You never normally bother to lock.'

David smiled crookedly. 'I got in late and hoped not to be disturbed. I'm not as lively as you in the mornings, Uncle.'

Lord Dulcimer looked at him. 'You were driven down, I gather. I saw that hearse of a staff car from my dressing-room window. Did your WAAF driver bring you?'

351

'She did.'

'The same girl who drove you last January?'

'That's right, Uncle.'

'Dunlop's daughter. I like her. But you'll have to get rid of her, you know.'

David said with barely suppressed exasperation, 'Uncle, if you had waited until a more reasonable hour, there would have been no staff car and no Maggie. Last night she was more weary than I was. She'd spent the day delivering my team to their quarters, and I offered her a bed. Against the rules, I know. The WAAF authorities are always braying about the good repute of their girls but I saw no reason why they should know.'

'You don't imagine that I will tell them, do you?'

David's smile was wry. 'You have not yet told me the reason for this dawn raid. Is it to tell me to get rid of one of my staff? If so, I have to say that it's none of your business. What's this about, Uncle B?'

'I've come to warn you, David.'

'Warn me about what?'

Lord Dulcimer said in a little embarrassment, 'Not warn exactly. No doubt you will be delighted. Antonia arrived last night.'

'What? Who . . .'

'Antonia. Your wife,' said his lordship. 'She and the children arrived after midnight, wanting the dower house keys. But they seemed exhausted and we persuaded them to stay with us. Just as well, eh?'

David stood very still.

'So get rid of that damned car and its driver,' said his lordship curtly, turning to the door. 'See you later, my boy.'

David followed him out, demanding to know what reason Antonia had given for arriving so much sooner than expected. Lord Dulcimer did not seem to know. They parted at the end of the dower house garden, and David walked back slowly to the open front door.

He closed the door behind him, and saw Maggie standing at the top of the stairs. She was fully dressed, her uniform as spruce as ever. Her face was white and set.

'I heard,' she said bleakly. 'I'd better tidy up the bedroom, and then I'll go. How long have we got?'

'You're not going without breakfast.'

'I'm not hungry,' she said, coming down the stairs towards him. He clasped her trembling body in his arms for a moment, and said, 'I'm not hungry either. Come into the kitchen. I'll put the kettle on.'

Coffee warmed them, but they barely touched the toast. Maggie said in a low voice, 'I thought she wasn't due for another week.'

'That's what I thought too.'

'If I'd known she was even in the country, I wouldn't have come here. David, I'm sorry. I behaved like a tart, and now I've made trouble for you.'

He looked at her and said almost fiercely, 'Don't say that, Maggie! I ought to apologise to you, but I won't. We've known all along that today must be the end. Antonia coming so suddenly is a shock but it makes no difference. Nothing can take away what we shared last night – not unless we let it.'

'We ought to think it funny, me hiding upstairs like someone in a bedroom farce. His lordship knew I was here, didn't he? What must he think of us?'

'He won't say anything.'

Maggie sat gripping and ungripping her hands in her lap, and looking down at her uneaten toast.

He got up suddenly. 'If you sit there looking tragic, Maggie, I shall do something foolish. We'd better go upstairs and clean up the scene of the crime.'

Antonia's inopportune arrival in Britain had not been in accordance with her own wishes. She was enjoying her life at Maple Valley far too much to think of leaving – until driven to it by circumstances.

She and her three children had been living in Pond Cottage for over two years. It was a charming, creeper-covered house with lawns sloping down to one of the smaller lakes. Cornelius had given her a car and a generous allowance, and with a Dutch housekeeper to see to the children and two cheerful maids to cook and clean, Antonia had no domestic worries. And she had freedom to come and go as she wished. Adele Devenish went back to England before Christmas 1943, and Antonia was not sorry about that, either.

Conway, on the other hand, felt angry and betrayed by Adele's departure. He had come to rely on her, and had assumed that Adele felt the same. But as soon as the fourth successive 'Bundles for Britain Ball' was over, Adele arranged her departure. He argued and even pleaded, but it made no difference. With her son Edward she boarded a Portuguese ship bound for Lisbon, and was gone.

Conway was not only furious. He felt oddly bereft and lonely, unable to sleep, and such was his habit of reticence that he was unable to share these unfamiliar pangs with anyone. He arrived for the obligatory Christmas lunch in Maple Valley House in a very bad temper. All those scampering, laughing children with his smiling mother under the Christmas tree made him angrier than ever, and when Antonia touched his arm and said why didn't they go somewhere quieter, he followed her into the orangerie, and allowed her to charm him out of his crossness. She was pretty and silly, everything that Adele was not, but at least she shared his dislike of massed kids.

Cornelius and Chrissie left for Florida in January 1944, but this time Antonia stayed north. Her two boys went to Florida with the others, and Abby went to stay with Kim. Work in the Greenacres eighth grade was getting serious, and Abby did not want to miss out. It seemed a natural arrangement, for she often stayed with Kim for days on end.

So when Conway called in at Pond Cottage one evening, he found Antonia alone, prettier than ever in a velvet tea gown, and ready with sympathy and a perfectly chilled martini. Antonia had not been married to a Vorst for three years without learning that particular skill. Conway stayed to dinner.

She had other skills, too, and the winter passed pleasantly for them, and Conway was once more able to sleep at night. They were seen dining together in New York, and in late March he took her once to his apartment overlooking Central Park. He had avoided this rooftop retreat for months, and had taken Antonia there in the hope that her presence would exorcise the ghost of Adele Devenish. It did not. Adele seemed to be very much there. He could almost hear her laughing at his infatuation for Antonia.

He began to compare one with the other. Antonia was exquisitely pretty, but she lacked Adele's style and honesty. And she was expensive. She had none of Adele's dislike of shopping. He took her once or twice to dress shops, but soon found reasons to send her alone, telling her to charge things to his account. Once he gave her a diamond brooch from Tiffany's, but when she raved about a ring that had been designed to go with it, he did not seem to be attending. He began to think of the brooch as a parting present. Enough was enough. The family were due back from Florida within the week. Their little affair had been fun, and had helped to readjust his sleep patterns, but Antonia was his brother's wife. They had never mentioned David during the past months.

This decision made, Conway called up a flowershop and told them to send three dozen red roses to Pond Cottage. He would visit her, and they would part with outward affection and unspoken relief. She would know the score.

It was a pity, really, that some trouble with the San Francisco house made it necessary for him to fly out west for nearly a week. By the time he came back, the massed red roses were still blazing all over Pond Cottage, the children were back home, and Cornelius and Chrissie had also returned to Maple Valley House.

Antonia had indeed calculated the score. Conway had been confident that she would, but he could not know that she would arrive at an entirely different total. It was a huge relief to her when the roses arrived, because before that she had been in a state of panic.

'Darling!' she cried when the housekeeper ushered him into the drawing room. He had armed himself with more flowers, white violets

354

this time, and she buried her face into their velvet sweetness and breathed in the faint, flowershop fragrance. 'Too, too kind, Conway. You spoil me. After all those wonderful red roses, too.'

The smiling housekeeper took the flowers away to put in a vase. The Dutchwoman had been in Florida with Antonia's children since January, and Antonia was amused by Conway's faintly apprehensive expression. 'Don't look like that, angel,' she chided him. 'All my noisy darlings have gone to the movies with the herd, and will spend tonight at the big house. Come on in. There's a bottle of Krug waiting for you to open. No children underfoot this evening, I promise you.'

'Good,' said Conway. 'I meant to visit you a week ago. There are things we need to talk about, and I wouldn't want to be interrupted.'

'I always like it best when we are alone, darling,' she said. 'I've given the servants a night off. There's a lobster salad and some lemon soufflé over there, and we can eat whenever we want.'

A round table near the window was laid with silver-covered dishes and more glasses, but she led him to where a gold-topped bottle was embedded in crushed ice. He opened it with his accustomed finesse, and when he had poured foaming wine into two glasses, she raised hers in mock salute.

'Let's drink to us, shall we? I've missed you so much this week, Conway, but your wonderful red roses told me everything I wanted to know.'

He looked at her, taking in her delicately flushed cheeks and shining eyes, and a rather disturbing air of suppressed excitement. He might have asked her what she meant about the roses, but her expression suddenly changed, silken lashes swooping over her eyes.

Looking down at her glass, and running a red-painted fingertip delicately round its edge, she said, 'I want you to know, Conway, that I have finally decided to ask David for a divorce.'

He was astounded. 'Divorce David? Why?'

'What a silly question, Conway,' she said in the prettily teasing voice which had rasped his nerves lately. 'Surely you must know the reason.'

He said curtly, 'It sounds like madness. We don't have divorces in the Vorst family. The parents would never stand for it.'

She stared up at him. He realised that he had shocked her. Two patches of rouge showed clearly on her blanched cheeks. She tried to speak, but the words did not come. Finally, she stammered, 'You said we had something to discuss. When your roses came, I . . . I thought I knew what you wanted to say – and that it would be easier for you if I told you that David and I were washed up.'

'Easier for me?' He was staring at her with narrowed, incredulous eyes. 'What has your crazy notion to divorce David got to do with me?'

She was not a perceptive woman, but there was no way of mistaking the meaning of his look or his words. All the same, she persevered. Things being how they were, she had to. She said helplessly, 'I thought the flowers were your way of saying you loved me, and that you wanted us to get married . . .'

'Certainly not,' he said brutally. 'I am not a marrying man.' He added with careful restraint, 'I sent those flowers to thank you, Antonia, and came here to bring our enjoyable affair to an end. I thought, perhaps mistakenly, that you would like us to part in a civilised way.'

She turned her head away, biting her lower lip. She had not meant to tell him why it was imperative for them to marry. Now she would have to. She said, 'It's too late for that, Conway. You see, I'm going to have a baby.'

He said coolly, 'Careless of you, Antonia. Who's the happy father?'

Once more he had shocked her. 'Conway! How can you ask that? I didn't mean it to happen but how could it be anyone's but yours?'

He laughed, and the jeering sound struck her like a blow. 'A pretty trap. I don't fall into traps, or respond to blackmail. Take my advice and go to England and jump into bed with David. Unlike me, he might fall for it, or at least pretend to do so.'

So there was nothing for Antonia to do but to take Conway's ungentlemanly and unwelcome advice. Next day she went to the big house to talk to Chrissie Vorst.

Chrissie was relieved when Antonia said that she wanted to go home to Britain. She had not liked it when David had gone alone. A wife's place, in Chrissie's opinion, was by her husband's side, and she had regretfully come to realise that she had been mistaken in her daughter-in-law. Antonia was a beautiful woman, but Chrissie wondered sometimes if she was capable of feeling love for anyone but herself.

But now she wondered all over again. Had she been unfair? Antonia was looking pale and upset, less well-groomed than usual, her fingers twitching nervously as she talked. She said that she had been pining for David all winter. Giving her the benefit of a still lurking doubt, Chrissie kissed her and said that she quite understood. They would speak to Cornelius about how best to get her back to England.

Cornelius, better informed about the comings and goings at Pond Cottage, wondered what had caused Antonia's sudden flight. All the same, he gave her the help she needed. They also arranged a small farewell party on the terrace, and Cornelius made a little speech about her courage in going back to war-torn England.

Conway was absent from this gathering. It was Conway, however, who contrived to get Antonia and the children flown home in a converted bomber full of generals and senior service personnel. If he had known of David's consternation when they arrived at Dulcimer, he would have been delighted and amused.

David arrived at Dulcimer Hall in time for lunch, to find Abby and the boys with their grandparents, but no sign of Antonia. They said she was sleeping. The children were very full of their flight in the Liberator bomber. Evidently they had been made much of by the crew and the other passengers. Somebody had given them each a dollar bill, and everyone on the plane had signed their names on them.

'Look, David,' said Miles, proudly holding out his bank note. 'It makes me a member of the Short Snorter Club. We're some of the first civilians to fly the Atlantic.'

'David! David!' Jamie tugged at David's arm. 'I saw an iceberg out of the window.'

'And we stopped at places called Goose and Gander.'

'The captain let me steer the plane all by myself.'

'You don't say,' said David. He looked up and smiled at Abby, grown tall and leggy since he had last seen her. 'So how was everybody at Maple Valley?'

'Fine,' said Abby, smiling back at him. 'Aunt Chrissie gave me a letter. Shall I go upstairs and get it?'

'Give it to him after lunch,' advised Lord Dulcimer, who hated waiting for his meals. 'If Antonia isn't coming down, we'll go in. Vestry has already looked in twice.'

'I don't think Mum wants lunch,' said Abby. 'She was sick after breakfast, and went back to sleep.'

'Trumpet will take her something light when she rings,' said Lady Dulcimer, taking David by the arm and following her dogs through the door. Dulcimer canines always dashed first into the dining room. The family had be quick, for sometimes Vestry was not there to defend the food. 'Poor Antonia. The long flight must have upset her. What about you, my dear?' she added to Jamie, looking down at him. 'Did they give you anything to eat on your bomber?'

'Just sandwiches,' said Miles behind her. He often spoke for his younger brother.

After lunch the dogs needed a walk, so they went to look at the dower house. Antonia had told the children that they would live there, and that they could each choose a room for their own. Antonia had not rung her bell for Miss Trumpet because she had been waiting for David. She watched them go from her window, feeling annoyed that he should be so offhand.

Her very necessary reconciliation with her husband seemed fated to be becalmed by events. All set to welcome him into her bed with open arms, he was somehow never there. He left Dulcimer after dinner on that first evening, for he was about to start a new tour of duty and

357

wanted to get on with it. It was almost a month before she saw him again. She tried contacting him on the telephone, but all she got was an American male voice telling her that Group Captain Vorst was not available.

One day, after another abortive telephone call, she heard on the news that the long delayed Operation Overlord had started.

Abby could have told her about it a day earlier. She had started at a boarding school in Dorset, and one June night the girls were woken by a loud roar of aircraft in the night sky. As it grew light, they craned out of the windows and saw a weird sight. Wave after wave of planes trailing fat camouflaged gliders filled the sky. Like a swarm of thunderous flies, they went by with scarcely a break all day and all the next night, carrying parachute troops and guns and ammunition over the sea to France. Meanwhile, on the grey choppy sea, the first vessels of a vast armada of ships were approaching the Normandy beaches.

The headmistress urged them to say extra special prayers for the brave soldiers and airmen who were on their way to drive the Germans back where they belonged. They sang 'God Save the King' with shrill fervour, and filed excitedly to their classes.

The headmistress, a nervous woman, rendered up a second prayer of thanks to the Almighty. She had suffered great anxiety since the start of the summer term, daily expecting to be told that one or other of her precious pupils had been leapt upon and raped by a helmeted GI from the camp in the woods. But in a single night, the American soldiers had vanished as suddenly as they had come. For the moment, at least, it seemed that this particular hazard of war had passed by on the other side.

'Take my advice, and have an abortion,' said Marjorie, to whom Antonia had confided her predicament. They had gone up to the Vorst rooftop apartment where they could talk without interruption.

'I wouldn't know how to go about it. Besides, David likes children.'

'He's a seriously nice man, Antonia. You are not being fair to him, foisting this little bastard on him.'

'Don't call it that, Marjorie. It will be no such thing, if David would stop playing war games and come home.' Sometimes Antonia slipped into Conway's patterns of speech. 'But I can't ever get through to him.'

'Possibly,' said Marjorie drily, standing up and pulling on her gloves, 'David is busy. The invasion is still in its early stages, and now these new pilotless planes have started dropping on us. I hear that one of them fell near Dulcimer the other day. Where is David stationed?'

'He gave me nothing but a telephone number, the bastard, and that never works.'

Marjorie looked at Antonia, who was lolling back, dressed in one of her many elegant American outfits. 'If I were you,' she said coldly, 'I wouldn't talk quite so freely about bastards. Anyway, what do you expect? You've stayed away for three years. He's probably got a girl in tow. Men were never meant to be celibate, you know.'

When she had gone, Antonia lit another cigarette, and decided that Marjorie had become very tiresome and spiteful. To cheer herself up, she picked up the telephone and rang her new admirer, Aylwin Peabody. They had met on the plane coming across the Atlantic, and at the end of a refreshing little talk with him, she invited him over to dine.

One of the new flying bombs had indeed fallen in a field halfway between the Hall and the village. Windows had been blown out at the home farm, and two at the Hall itself, and a bullock had been killed. David and Antonia looked down into the charred and blackened crater. He had arrived unannounced before breakfast, and it was the first time Antonia had seen him for weeks.

She said nothing about this, but greeted him with her prettiest smile, and when he wanted to see where the bomb had fallen, she borrowed a pair of Abby's gumboots and went with him. It was rough crossing the field, so she had to steady herself by holding his arm. At the edge of the crater, he removed her clinging hand and moved away. She felt an inward qualm which had nothing to do with morning sickness.

'How long can you stay, angel?'

'Just tonight. I must be back by midday tomorrow.'

'You never told me where you are stationed.'

'No.'

The quiet negative was spoken calmly, but she felt her temper beginning to rise. It was an effort to speak calmly. 'David, it worries me not knowing where you are. I might need to contact you, or you might be killed . . .'

'If I'm killed, the Air Ministry will get in touch with you, Antonia. Shall we go back? Uncle Bernard will be fussing about lunch.'

'Bother Uncle Bernard! David, I have a right to know where to find you. I'm your wife, remember?'

'I remember. I've been rather wondering,' he said, looking down at her thoughtfully, 'what has happened to make you recollect it so suddenly. Why did you decide to come home?'

'I wanted to be with you. I want to start again where we left off. I've missed you so very much this winter. I became positively ill with misery.'

He said nothing, but his glance was disbelieving, and she felt suddenly unable to go on. They walked down the hill to the Hall in silence. David wondered what could have gone wrong for her, to send her scurrying back to find him.

Antonia was recalling Marjorie's ill-natured parting shot about celibate men, and wondered if David had indeed taken up with some woman. She was handed a clue at lunch. Miles, home for half term, suddenly turned to David and asked after Maggie.

'Vestry says that she's your Air Force driver, and that you brought her here after Christmas.'

'That was some time ago, Miles,' said David with a calm he did not feel. Inwardly cursing Vestry, he said aloud, 'Maggie has left. I don't know where she is now.'

'Oh?' Miles looked crestfallen. 'I wanted to tell her about us coming home in a bomber.'

'Eat your dinner, Miles, and don't talk so much,' said Lord Dulcimer. 'Antonia, I want to show you something. Effie has found a nice watercolour of Johnnie, painted when he was eighteen. We think you ought to have it.'

'So why won't you make love to me? You were never so reluctant in America.'

'I'm not in the mood tonight, Antonia.' She had drunk more than she should, and was all too clearly in a dangerously emotional state. 'I need to catch up on sleep, and you look pretty tired yourself.'

She managed to smile at him archly. 'How unflattering of you to say so, darling. For my part, seeing you again has reminded me what a preposterously handsome man I'm married to.'

He laughed shortly. 'Thanks, Antonia. Will you turn the light off, or shall I?'

'Kiss me goodnight.'

He came over and kissed her so perfunctorily that her precarious control snapped. She said waspishly, 'I bet you can do better than that with your WAAF driver.'

He straightened up, seeming to tower over her. 'What did you say, Antonia?' His voice was quiet, but she wished she had not spoken. For a moment something had flared in his dark eyes. More quietly still he repeated his question. 'What did you just say?'

She looked away, and shrugged a lace-clad shoulder. 'You heard what I said. I can't say that I admire your taste.'

No longer thinking very clearly, she had entertained some wine-inspired hope of provoking him into argument, and even into striking her. This always worked well with Conway, who used to make furious and satisfactory love after an argument.

It was different with his brother. David turned and walked wordlessly into the adjoining dressing room, shut the door and turned the key. She tried knocking and calling his name, but got no response.

Finally she retired to bed, and burst into angry, frustrated tears.

Early the next morning, she woke to find him standing over her, dressed in his Air Force uniform. She blinked at him.

'Get dressed,' he told her, pulling the bedclothes away. 'We have to talk, and as you may not like what I have to say, we will go outside. I don't want to wake up the whole house if you start having a tantrum.'

He looked so daunting that after a brief protest about the ungodliness of the hour, she allowed him to pull her to her feet. 'I'll give you five minutes,' he said crisply. 'Get a move on.'

'David, I drank too much wine last night. I'm sorry for what I said.'

'Five minutes, Antonia,' he said, going back into the dressing room but leaving the door ajar.

He took her to the summerhouse, where in the old days Nanny used to sit and knit. Antonia sank into a cane chair. The cushion had been left out all night and struck cold through her thin slacks, but she did not feel equal to making a complaint. Her head throbbed, and she was beginning to feel queasy.

'Now,' he said, propping himself on a sturdy wooden table and speaking in a tone she had never heard before. 'There are things we ought to get straight before I go back to work.' Erring subordinates in the Air Force could have told her that when the group captain spoke like that, it meant trouble. 'You say that you want to mend things and get our marriage back together. It may not be as easy as you seem to think. Three years is a long time, and we parted on bad terms even then.'

She started to say something about bygones, but he checked her with an upraised hand.

'I haven't got long, so please keep quiet and listen. I don't know why you have suddenly chosen to come back to me, though I might hazard a guess.'

She was assailed by a sudden feeling of alarm. Guess? What had he guessed? Had Marjorie told him?

He was speaking again. 'We must work out what to do, if only for your children. They tell me that you plan to live at the dower house. You had better move there at once, and since I shall not be here, you will have to make the arrangements yourself. I will open a bank account for you in East Grinstead, and you may draw on it for your needs – housekeeping, car expenses and so on. But there will be no arrangements for an overdraft. Don't blow a whole month's allowance and then expect to be given more. My secretary at the Vorst will take care of the children's school fees, uniforms and their travel. When I get leave, I will come and see you. To outward appearances we will try to act like any married couple.'

She put out a hand and would have thanked him, but his next words drove the impulse away. 'You were staying at the Vorst last week, I hear, but I'm afraid I must ask you to make it the last time. From now on the flat will be taken on as part of the hotel. We could have booked every room twice over last winter. It's a waste leaving it empty.'

She found her voice. 'Our lovely flat? You can't expect me to stagnate in the country, David. I need to go to the hairdresser, and . . . and other things.'

'You could go up for the day, or join a London club,' he suggested coolly. 'Or book a room at the Vorst if you want to, but don't charge it up to me. Get your current admirer to foot your bills. What's the latest one called? Aylwin something or other, the children said.'

She said weakly, 'I never thought you could be so mean.'

'No? I'm no longer a besotted boy, Antonia.' He paused, and said more gently, 'One thing more. If you really want us to make a go of our marriage, you will have to try to control your jealousy. I see no hope for us unless you do. About Maggie Dunlop. At Maple Valley you resented her because the children loved her. And when you heard that she had been my WAAF driver, you leapt to the conclusion that she must also be my mistress.'

He leaned towards her, and she shrank back in alarm, but he merely said quietly, 'Maggie has done well in the Women's Air Force. She's a section officer, and was driver and secretary to my unit for a while. I did bring her here just once, after we had lost our things in an accident. We borrowed clothes, and Nanny put Maggie to bed in the old night nursery. You may ask her if you don't believe me.

'I will tell you what happened, and then we won't mention her again. Maggie worked for my team. She shared the driving with my batman, typed our reports, took her meals separately because I liked to talk shop with my colleagues while we ate. For the duration of the job I seldom spoke to her, except to give orders and dictate reports. We were all too busy. The unit has now dispersed, and I don't know where she is.'

'You will meet her when you go to Glen Cary, or you could find out through the Air Force,' she said sulkily.

'Don't worry,' he said. 'I shall not be seeing her again.' He left the summerhouse and walked back to the house, where a new driver was awaiting him.

Chapter 25

At the end of July, Ben Horowitz was killed. Flying above and behind the main flight, David saw all too clearly when a single shell blew Ben's plane to smithereens.

They had been returning, tired but exultant, after a successful pinpoint raid on railway workshops. It had been planned, like all Ben's operations, to the last detail. The system was essentially the same, but they took care to vary the direction and style of their attacks. As Ben never tired of saying, it did not do to be predictable.

David's squadron reached the target area first. They went in low and fast, spearheading the attack with rockets and dropping the marker flares. The gun crews below, alerted, would be making ready to receive more marauders on the same flight path, but Ben brought the main force in from another direction. They plastered the target with everything they had, and the two forces joined up on the way home. The rockets must have hit something pretty big, for there had been a massive explosion down below.

'What d'you reckon, Dave? A trainload of rockets, maybe?'

'Looked like it. Well done.'

Ben's laugh came over the R/T, loud and raucous over the distorting air waves. 'That'll teach the Nazi bastards . . .'

That was the last time David heard his friend's voice. Ben and his co-pilot must have been killed instantly. He was still craning his head backwards and down, in the vain hope of seeing a parachute open, when a random shell tore a hole in his own fuselage, and from then on he was fully occupied on his own account.

His co-pilot was wounded in the leg and the steering mechanism damaged. To the accompaniment of the wounded man's occasional groan of pain and his own vigorous swearing, David managed to nurse the rocking, yawing, meandering aircraft over the Channel, but failed to make it to Lydd airport where they were expected. He finally lost control and crash-landed in a field only a mile from the air strip. David was trapped for two hours in the wreck, fully expecting the damaged plane to catch fire before they got him out.

By some miracle, the plane did not burst into flames at all. David's colleague, a young man from Wisconsin, was taken out and driven away in an ambulance. The medic told David that his colleague had lost a lot of blood, but from what he could tell he was not seriously hurt.

This was a consolation, for the boy was young and only newly arrived from home. David needed some small comfort, for he was in considerable pain, unable to move because one of his feet was trapped amid a tangle of staved-in metal, and the other leg was lying at a very odd angle. The rescue men went off to look for metal-cutting equipment and were away for what seemed a very long time. He passed some of it conversing with two Red Cross women who insisted on staying with him, despite his warning about the danger of fire. The effort of making small talk tired him, so presently he started reciting poetry. He had not been raised by Cornelius for nothing. He tried not to think of Ben, or of Maggie. Waiting in pain is a lonely business. No point in courting another sort of anguish.

Two days after leaving Dulcimer, Maggie stepped off the train at Glen Cary Halt to find Bert Higgins waiting for her in a pony and trap. By this time she had herself in hand.

Bert seized her suitcase and presently they clip-clopped away, watched by the stationmaster and a couple of sheep in a crate. It was Bert's last day before returning to school, and the minister had gone to see a hill shepherd in the cottage hospital. The pony and trap belonged to Mrs Fraser, who found walking tiring these days.

It took a while to trot down the long glen to the manse, and by the time they arrived there, Maggie had heard all about the tragedy of Wat's death and her father's part in it. Bert also told her about the head keeper's odd nocturnal habits and his recently formed suspicions.

Maggie laughed. 'A spy? Dad? That's wishful thinking, Bert, and you know it.'

He said rather huffily, 'What else would he be doing on Jock's Crag at night?'

She shook her head, 'Dear knows, but a spy for the Germans he would never be. Not in a thousand years.'

Bert grunted. He was disappointed in her. Up to this moment he had respected her judgement. Now he wasn't so sure. He decided not to tell her what else he had found buried under the peat hags. It would serve her right if he never told her about the cave and his treasure trove.

He left her at the manse door, and drove off without a word to turn the pony out to grass. Mrs Fraser and Cook drew Maggie in and gave her a belated breakfast of tea and scones still warm from the girdle. She thanked them, and smiled and ate and drank her tea – and managed to give no sign of the anguished sense of loss which she must at all costs keep hidden from this time forward.

***

Walking down the glen to visit her grandmother one Sunday afternoon, Maggie saw her father coming towards her on the narrow sheep path. There was plenty of time for her to move off into the heather and allow him pass as was her habit, but this time she stood her ground and waited for him. So much had happened to her lately that she felt no fear. She even managed to smile at him.

The head keeper saw a slender tweed-clad woman standing in his way, and raised his deerstalker hat with a dour 'Good day, ma'am', and made to step aside. Then something about the carriage of her head and the fact that she was smiling made him pause and look at her more closely.

For one aghast moment he believed he was seeing a ghost. It was Mary, standing there and smiling at him. Mary to the life! But even as his stiff lips tried to utter her name, he realised his mistake.

'Dad,' said Maggie, seeing that he had suffered a shock at the sight of her. His swarthy face had gone grey and pinched under his grizzled beard. 'Dad, are you feeling all right?'

He raised his horn-handled stick, and for a moment she thought he was going to attack her. But instead he shook it as though to ward her off, turned on his heel, and walked down the hill very fast, with his dogs at his heels.

She gazed after him in dismay, and for the very first time in her life felt rather sorry for him. She knew that she resembled her mother, for several of the older glen people had remarked on the likeness. Gran, waking up in confusion after a nap, had more than once called her Mary. She judged that Ian Dunlop had seen the resemblance, too. It was, after all, the first time that he had been close enough to see her properly. She had kept out of his way so far and, wherever possible, out of sight.

She went on her way, considering Mary Dunlop's flight to America from another angle – that of her bereft father. Striving to come to terms with losing David, she acknowledged a fellow feeling.

The two cases were different, of course. David was not for her, and never could be. She had known this from the beginning and, loving him, had asked for a night of love. Now she was paying the price. It must have been worse, far worse, for her violently jealous father to have been married for years and be suddenly deserted. Mary must have dealt a hideous blow to his pride by going off with another man. No wonder he was bitter and had chosen to tell everyone that she was dead.

'Gran,' she said that same evening when she had helped the old lady into bed. 'Tell me about my mother. I know that she left, and I have the ring you sent me, but other than that I know so little.'

365

'There's little enough to tell,' said Mrs Dunlop, pursing her lips and stirring her evening cocoa. 'Mary packed all her clothes late at night, and by morning she was gone. She must have been in a hurry, for I found the ring under her pillow next day, and one of her silver hairbrushes under the bed. She set store by her few pretty things, did Mary, and I wondered at her leaving one of those brushes behind.'

'I set store by her ring myself, Gran. It was good of you to send it. But I don't remember seeing a hairbrush.'

'You won't have. I put it away in the attic, for fear that it would upset your dad to see it. He's never got over Mary's going, and I doubt he ever will.'

'No,' said Maggie soberly, looking down at the gold ring which she always wore, except when she was in uniform. 'Gran, I must tell you that I gave him a bit of a shock today. He saw me close up for the first time, and for just one moment I'm afraid he took me for my mother.'

'I told you to keep out of his way, lassie. What did he say?'

'Nothing at all. He just looked at me as if I was a ghost, and walked away towards the burn.'

'You shouldn't have let him see you. He can't do with being put in mind of Mary. Meeting you like that will have been enough to start him shouting in his sleep again. And next thing he'll take to the whisky and start ranting,' said the old lady, obviously much disturbed. 'It all happened after of your baptism, all those years ago, and he took to blaming you as well as Mary. Just keep out of his way, next time.'

'Gran,' said Maggie seriously, taking the cup and saucer out of her grandmother's trembling hand. 'Are you sure that Dad wouldn't be better off trying to talk it out with someone – the minister, perhaps? There are doctors who specialise in helping people.'

'My Ian won't speak of Mary. Not to me, nor to anyone in all these years,' said Mrs Dunlop, a tear trickling down a wrinkled cheek. She wiped it away with the back of her hand and became brisk. 'It's time you were going, lassie. Ian will be back, for he never misses the nine o'clock news on the wireless. Before you go, take a look in the attic and see if you can find that hairbrush. I've a notion I wrapped it in newspaper and put it at the far end behind the last rafter.'

'Pretty!' exclaimed Sophy Ducane, who had arrived in their basement flat to find Maggie polishing a silver-backed hairbrush. 'Where did you get it?'

'My gran told me I could have it.'

'Mm. So she should. It has your initials on it.'

'It was my mother's. Her name was Mary, so our initials are the same.'

'That's convenient,' said Sophy, stripping off her black tie and casting her uniform jacket onto the pine dresser in the corner. She bent to untie her sturdy black uniform shoes and kicked them away into a corner 'Any bathwater left?'

'I left it for you. I thought you would be going out.'

'You're a saint. Come with us, Maggie. There's a gang going to a play and dancing afterwards.'

Maggie laughed and shook her head. 'Thanks, but your beautiful naval types scare me stiff. I don't think I will.'

'What you mean is, all men terrify you. It must be something to do with being bullied by your father. Honestly, Mags, you'll never get over your hang-up unless you make an effort to meet some fellows.'

'I need to pack. I'm being posted to Norfolk tomorrow.'

'What? Two weeks ago you were returning to where lover Paul rolled you in the cowpats.'

'That was two weeks ago. Just like the Air Ministry to change its mind. Now I'm being re-mustered as mess officer to a large bomber station – a sort of glorified housekeeper and general dogsbody.'

Sophy said crossly, 'What a bore. I suppose that means I shall never see you. Norfolk is the absolute back of beyond.'

'That won't bother me. I grew up in another back of beyond. All the same, Sophy, you should get someone else. I won't need a London billet now.'

'You might as well keep it. The Air Ministry has paid your rent to the end of the year, so it's yours until then. I may lend your room to people I like, but it will be here whenever you want it.' She saw Maggie's look of embarrassed surprise. 'Didn't you know? They paid me a whole year in advance. I wish the Admiralty would splash out like that.'

'It must be a mistake,' said Maggie, well aware who must have paid it. 'I'd better write to them.'

'Don't look a gift horse in the mouth,' advised Sophy. 'I never do.'

Antonia peered out of the hospital window to where her good friend Aylwin stood beside a Jeep, smoking one of his pungent cheroots. He waved at her, and she fluttered fingers at him in greeting. Dear Aylwin, such a perfect gentleman and so useful, with his never failing supplies of cigarettes and American petrol. When she spoke of travelling to Oxford by train, he had exclaimed that she would find it tiring, and insisted on collecting her at the dower house and driving her all the way to Oxford. They would stay one night at the Randolph – in separate rooms, of course. Since discovering her condition, he had become extremely solicitous, treating her with slightly apprehensive respect.

David's left leg was no longer in traction, but visiting him was a bore, for he had little to say for himself and kept falling asleep when she was in the middle of telling her own news. She had come, really, because the Dulcimers had started making pointed remarks, and even Abby had asked her when she planned to visit David in the Oxford hospital. So when Aylwin made his obliging offer, she decided that she would go. It would silence the criticisms, at least for a time, and one had to try to keep up appearances.

David was not asleep. He only slept in snatches these days, because the pain from his crushed foot kept waking him up. Giving him their verdict after nearly six weeks in traction, the doctors at his first hospital had expressed themselves pleased with his progress, but the head consultant told David that he was not happy about the damaged foot. David had been pretty severely mauled during their lengthy examination, and could not resist saying acidly, 'You're not happy? How happy do you think I feel, Mr Gordon? But you can forget about taking it off. I'll risk dying of gangrene rather than that.'

They had not liked being talked back to in that military hospital. Patients were supposed to lie still and do as they were told. No doubt they had been relieved when their dissident patient had been loaded into an ambulance and moved to Headington near Oxford for a second opinion and possible further treatment.

He had not expected to see Antonia so soon. Her infrequent visits in Sussex had encouraged him to hope that she would find Oxford too far afield. When she came fluttering into his private room, reeking of Chanel No. 5 and embracing him fondly under the indulgent eye of his special nurse, he was tempted to tell her to go away.

Instead, he said, 'Nice to see you, Antonia,' and wondered how long she would stay.

He felt so weak and ill, listening to her prattle, that he had taken refuge in feigned sleep. He might even have dropped off properly for a few minutes, though he could not be sure. He was not at all sure of anything. He wondered how long he would go on feeling so totally feeble, hardly able to think coherently, with neither the will nor the energy to read or even to listen to the war news on the radio. That morning there had been a further ordeal when the Oxford professor and his cohorts examined him all over, took swabs and blood samples and sent him for new X-rays. Once back in his room, he had been too exhausted to eat any lunch.

He opened his eyes with caution, in time to see the discreet flutter of Antonia's fingers. It barely interested him to know that she had come with a companion, but he did see something else which captured his attention. The odd notion that had been lurking, a vague surmise in his mind, hardened suddenly into certainty. The September sun had come out, its rays lighting Antonia's pale gold hair and shining through the flimsy material of her dress. Under this loose-fitting garment he could see the outline of her lower body, and an unmistakably pregnant bulge.

Antonia did not stay long. They exchanged relieved farewell pecks, and she went away, leaving him in a thoughtful mood.

So Antonia was expecting a baby, and had been expecting it for some time by the look of things. No need to puzzle, now, over why she had come home in such haste and had been so desperate to get him into her bed! And what a dilemma for the poor silly woman when he had not obliged her.

He understood, also, why Antonia had been so angry with him after the crash, finding him all strung up and surrounded by drips and drains. She seemed to think that he had reduced himself to that sorry state only to annoy her, and told him in a voice of bitter loathing that he had better get well soon, or else! In the light of what he now knew, he realised that her fury had been rooted in panic.

He wondered who the father was, but after a period of reflection decided that it would be wiser not to ask. Antonia would lie to him if it suited her, and on the whole it might be better not to open that particular Pandora's box. What if he found that it was someone that he knew well, and liked? The thought came to him that it might be Dart. Had Dart told her to get lost, as he had done before? Dart could be ruthless when defending his freedom. For all her beauty and sex appeal, Antonia had never had much luck with the men in her life.

It took only a short calculation to realise that Dart could not possibly have been responsible for this poor little bastard. Antonia had been in Long Island until the end of April, and Dart had certainly not been back to America for well over a year. Throughout the spring he had been stationed with his regiment on Salisbury Plain, and had sailed with them to Normandy on D-Day plus four. David was truly glad to know that it could not be Dart. What a complication that would have been, with everyone at Dulcimer cooing over Antonia's new baby, and Dart looking on and laughing up his sleeve!

The thought of this bizarre scenario was enough to start David laughing weakly. He was still laughing when the nurses came to tidy him up. His special nurse, Susan, was glad to see the Group Captain looking so much more cheerful. She thought he was a lovely man. He was still in a lot of pain, she knew, but he seldom complained, and gave her very little trouble.

The doctors at the Wingfield Morris Hospital were more sanguine than their Sussex counterparts. The head pundit came to see David, showed him X-rays, and pointed out the extensive damage to the foot that had been crushed and was still giving trouble. After some professional flannel about respect for his Sussex colleagues, he relieved his patient's mind by saying that he was not in favour of amputation

– certainly not at present. He would in due course wish to operate upon the mangled foot. He warned David against expecting an instant cure, saying that it might be necessary to operate more than once. In any case, he refused to contemplate surgery until the present inflammation and infection had been dealt with, and David's general health had improved. He was rundown and severely anaemic. As for the infected foot, there was a new drug coming on-stream, and he intended to try what it could do to improve matters.

In time David began to feel better, and was allowed out of bed. They brought him a pair of crutches – horrible wooden things – but after some practice he grew quite handy with them. He still tired easily, but was determined to get fit again. All the lying in bed had left him weak as water.

Nurse Susan told him not to run before he could walk, and he laughed, and said, 'That's your third cliché of the day. Your full quota.'

He had rationed her to three only. She stared at him, putting her head on one side like a spaniel he used to own called Bonnie. Susan always looked like that when he teased her. She looked the same when he called her Bonnie, for that matter. 'No chance of running yet awhile. But I'm getting better with them. Look!'

She smiled indulgently and followed as he swung himself out into the passage. She was a pretty young woman, an agency nurse who had been sent from London to look after the Group Captain, and she liked him very much indeed. Hearing that he was to go home for ten days before the operation, she asked how he would manage. She knew that his wife was pregnant and not strong. Patients told you all sorts of things when they were wakeful at night, and the Group Captain was no exception. He had even asked her to call him David, which she tried to do.

'Who will look after you and give you your pills?'

'Bill will do all that's needed,' he said carelessly. 'But I'm capable of taking a few pills myself, you know. I may be a cripple, but I can still read a label and a clock and count up to five, Bonnie.'

Susan made a clucking sound, a habit she had when he shocked her. She knew Bill, for David's recently retired batman lived in north Oxford and brought him clean pyjamas twice a week, and took away others for washing. She and Bill were both concerned about what would happen at the dower house after the operation. He would be in no condition to climb stairs for some weeks. Susan broached the subject.

'Oh, that,' said David. 'I'm going to make our dining room into a bedroom for me. There's a cloakroom next door, so we can get a door knocked through. That way I won't be a bother to anyone.'

'You will need careful nursing after the operation, David.'

'Are you offering to come with me, Bonnie dear?'

'I would have to consult my agency before deciding that,' she said, trying not to look too pleased. 'My controller would have to know all about where I was going before she permitted it.'

But she called up the agency that very day. It would be a pleasure to nurse the Group Captain. He was a model patient.

Only on the last day at the Wingfield Morris did the Group Captain prove recalcitrant. A porter had come for his case, and he had consumed an early lunch. Bill was waiting in the car. A porter came in and parked a wheelchair near the door.

'What's that for?' demanded David. 'I'm perfectly capable of walking to the car.'

'Matron's orders.'

'Really? She can order what she likes, but I'm walking.'

Susan looked flustered. 'You really mustn't. I promised Matron that you would go in a wheelchair.'

'You may tell Matron, if she asks,' said David pleasantly, 'that you did your best but that I flatly refused to get into the damned thing. I climbed out of my baby carriage at the age of two and they never got me back into it again.' He reached for his crutches. 'Let's get going.'

Susan followed him out, looking as if it was all too much for her.

Bill drove David home, and Antonia came running out of the house to greet him. The children were away at school, she told him. Even Jamie lived away during the week, and the Dulcimers were staying with friends for the weekend.

'What heaven, darling,' said Antonia. 'I hardly remember when we were last alone together. I've had a fire lit in the spare room, and Bill says he'll bring us supper after he has helped you into bed. Then we can have a cosy talk.'

By the time Bill had half-carried, half-boosted him up the stairs and got him into bed David did not feel like talking. So Antonia held forth, interspersing her fevered small talk with periods of silence during which he was aware of being watched apprehensively. Despite his exhaustion, David felt sorry for her.

Bill removed their supper trays, and when the man had gone David said wearily, 'Antonia, if you're wondering how to tell me about the baby, there's no need.'

She gaped at him, her delicately painted lips forming an O, her eyes staring. 'Who told you? Surely not Marjorie?'

He smiled at her wryly, feeling something like affection for her for the first time in ages. 'Honey, I've got eyes.'

She said on a small gasp, 'I'll tell you how it happened, David.' She searched his face with another speculative look. 'I was lonely for you in America, as you know . . .'

He stopped her, reluctant to listen to lies and wanting to be left alone. 'Don't, Antonia. What matters is the present, and the future of this child. You hoped I would think it was mine, did you?'

She said sulkily, 'Of course. But you were cold and cruel to me when I first came back, and then there was that wretched accident. I couldn't think what to do.'

'You could have told me the truth. Did you think I would disown it?'

She stared at him. 'You mean you don't mind?'

If he had not been sinking with exhaustion he might have laughed at this ingenuous question. He shook his head and tried to smile at her.

She said softly, 'You mean you won't try to divorce me?'

'Not unless you want me to, Antonia. Better to give this baby of ours a welcome, don't you think?'

She came over and flung herself on his neck and burst into noisy tears of relief.

For two whole days, Antonia was sweet and remorseful, and exhaustively assiduous in her efforts to minister to her invalid husband. They made plans to tell the children and the Dulcimers about the baby's coming, and with Bill and a sturdy landgirl dealing with the cooking and the housework, all was peaceful at the dower house.

After that things started to go wrong. David broached the subject of making himself a temporary bedroom downstairs and Bill was summoned home to Oxford in a hurry. His wife had broken a leg and needed him. He was full of apologies, and wanted David to contact Nurse Susan, but David assured him that he could manage. The landgirl came in to clean anyway, and would very likely do some cooking if they asked her.

'Off you go,' David told Bill. 'I'll see you in Oxford when I come for my operation. I'll really need you then. Tell your wife I was asking after her . . .'

'Make my lovely dining room into a sick room? Don't you dare!' Antonia was outraged by David's plan. 'You will ruin the feel of the whole house. The hall will reek of Jeyes Fluid and other hospital smells.'

'It's only for a couple of months, Antonia,' he replied, looking about him critically. The house would have been better for a good clean, he thought, but since he did not want to escalate the fight, he only said, 'It's just until I can get up and down stairs on my own again.'

'And when will that be if this operation doesn't work? This year, next year, or never? Am I expected to wait years before I invite anyone to dine?'

'We can eat in the kitchen. It's much the warmest place.' He found himself wishing that he had not given her such an easy ride over the baby. Her initial relief and gratitude had worn remarkably thin during the past twenty-four hours.

'And what about the baby's christening party?'

'We can have it at Dulcimer. How many people are you planning to invite?'

'I don't know. It's unlucky to make plans before the baby is born.'

'And when will that be? I don't mean the January date we have agreed to tell people. I'd like to get a fix on when it's actually going to arrive.'

Antonia reached for the bourbon, another gift from Aylwin, and drained the last of it into her glass, spilling some on the kitchen table. 'How can I possibly tell when it will arrive?'

He raised his dark brows. 'If you can't, Antonia, nobody else can – except the mystery father, and we've decided to leave him out of it.'

'It's not fair of you to taunt me, David. When we were first married I thought of you as the perfect gentleman.'

'Did you, Antonia?' he said rather wearily, levering himself up from the kitchen table and reaching for his crutches. 'I fear that we are none of us quite as gullible as we used to be.'

'Just what's that dirty crack supposed to mean?' she demanded belligerently.

'It means,' said David, settling his second crutch under his arm and starting on his laborious and painful way to the hall and the staircase, 'that I am about to haul myself upstairs to bed. Goodnight, Antonia. Sleep well.'

He was almost at the top of the stairs, having hitched himself backwards a step at a time on his bottom, with the heavy wooden crutches attached to his belt, when Antonia's voice sounded shrilly from below.

'All this nonsense about needing to live on the ground floor! You manage to crawl up and downstairs perfectly well now, and you can go on doing so after your operation. I'll be damned if I'll have my house ruined. Over my dead body! If you send builders along to start knocking through to the cloakroom, I'll just send them away again.'

'You do that, Antonia. Goodnight.'

This time he did not tell her to sleep well. She almost certainly slept better than he did. Her heard her stumbling up the stairs and going into her room. After a little while all was quiet.

David lay wakeful for a very long time. He had been exhausted by the altercation about the dining room, and after the painful struggle up the stairs could barely find strength to reach the broad spare-room bed. He lay there inert, still wearing all his clothes. Even so, the winter cold soon made his bones ache, and presently he started to shiver. The windows were open behind the black-lined curtains, but he lacked the strength to close them. He managed to ease the large eiderdown from under his body, and huddled it round him.

There was no easy refuge in sleep for David that night. His body ached, his bandaged foot throbbed, for he had knocked it on a banister during his climb. His thoughts were all of Maggie, of Maggie in this room where they had made love so rapturously. He could have cried out with his longing for her. She had asked him to do her a favour that evening. It had taken courage, for she had more than half expected him to turn her down, and he saw in his mind how she looked as she turned towards him in dawning relief, her eyes luminous with love. Maggie later, a frightened doll in satin and lace, and the softness and warmth of her in his arms when he had taken her to bed.

He wanted and needed sleep, but he could only remember and yearn for Maggie, her silken skin, the glory of her breasts, and her joyous astonishment and triumph when they finally came together. She had wept afterwards. Lying in the cold dark after all these months, David felt like weeping himself.

Dart flew back to England on a forty-eight-hour pass, and hearing that David was home from hospital, walked through the rain to visit the Vorsts. He found the front door unlocked and, following the sound of David's voice, strolled into the spare room brandishing a pair of dripping wooden crutches.

'Found one of these in the bushes, and the other dangling from the ivy,' he said. 'Don't you need them any more?'

As he spoke he was noticing other things – David's unshaven chin and hollow eyes, his crumpled clothes and one heavily swathed foot. Dart's eyes measured the distance between the bed and the open window.

'You look pretty rough, David. Where's Antonia got to?'

'Gone to East Grinstead for the day.'

'Have you had breakfast?'

'No such luck. The landgirl doesn't come in today.'

'I'll go down and bring you something. First things first.'

'No. Hand me those crutches and I'll come down with you.'

Dart told him that there was no need, but David had already struggled onto his one fairly stable leg. Once upright, he scrubbed exploratory fingers over his bristly chin. 'I ought to shave.'

'Breakfast first,' said Dart firmly. 'I'll bring your razor and stuff downstairs. You know, David, you ought to sleep on the ground floor. It would save a lot of trouble.'

David gave vent to a short laugh, and manoeuvred himself to the top of the stairs.

Dart watched his cousin's practised but ungainly descent of the stairs in silence, but when they reached the kitchen he said, 'So Antonia threw your crutches out of the window. Why ever?'

'I had annoyed her.'

'You mean she left you stranded upstairs and waltzed off for the day? The little bitch.'

'Pregnant women have their foibles,' said David drily.

'You ought to beat her. I would if she was my wife.'

David, who had insisted on making the coffee without help and was now waiting for the toast, said even more drily, 'At present I haven't the strength to beat up a baby mouse. Certainly I'm no match for Antonia in a temper.'

'So what was the fight about?'

'I want to turn the dining room into a bedroom, and knock a door through into the cloakroom. Just temporarily, but she won't hear of it. Of course the sensible thing would be to go to a convalescent home after the operation. I would be no bother to anyone there, but with the baby coming, I don't like not to be around. Not that I will be much use, either upstairs or down, but I could reach for the telephone if it starts to come.'

'Mother told me that the child wasn't expected until mid-January.'

'Babies have been known to arrive early.'

'David,' said Dart after a moment's thoughtful silence, 'is this baby yours?'

There was a rather longer silence. Then David said in a distant tone, 'Naturally, any child that Antonia has will bear my name.'

'Even,' said Dart with equal coolness, 'if someone else is its father?'

'Even then.'

The cousins eyed each other, before David added, 'Which is an absurd and offensive suggestion, if I may say so, Dartmore. I hope you don't mean to repeat it.'

'No. I won't repeat it,' said Dart, and abruptly changed the subject. 'I flew home with Odette Steiner. She was caught and questioned by the Gestapo just after D-Day and is in a bad way. They broke all the fingers in one hand. Luckily the brutes had to leave in a hurry before they had finished with the other. So as I was flying home for a couple of days, I offered to bring her back to see what can be done for her crippled hand. She's in hospital.'

'I'd like to see her,' said David. 'But I guess I'll need to finish with my own hospital before I visit hers.'

'I shall see her tomorrow and give her your love,' Dart promised, and when his cousin merely nodded, he added seriously, 'I was damned sorry to hear about Ben Horowitz. You must miss him.'

'Sure, I miss him. We had some great times together.'

Dart nodded, and stirred his lukewarm coffee. He looked about him, noticing the heaped plates near the sink and the general air of squalor. 'Nanny would have a fit if she saw this place. She used to keep it gleaming. Why does she no longer come to help?'

'Antonia took against her.' David's tired eyes lit with sudden mischief. 'I rather think,' he said gravely, 'that Nanny spoke her mind once too often. She kept looking at Antonia, and saying, "Mark my words, madam, you must have got your dates wrong. That baby of yours will be here long before Christmas." Not,' David added blandly, 'a popular suggestion.'

Once again the cousins eyed each other. This time they both burst out laughing.

'Oh, and by the way,' Dart said before walking back to the Hall, 'don't worry about the dining room. I'll talk to Father about that.'

Chapter 26

In November, the manager and staff of the London Vorst Hotel were thrown into a flurry by a cable from head office. They were told to expect a visit from the senior vice-president of the company, Mr Conway Vorst. A distant and powerful figure, none but the most elderly staff had ever set eyes on him. They wondered what was bringing him to England. Then it dawned on them that he would be visiting his brother who was recovering from a serious operation at the Wingfield Morris Hospital.

Conway arrived in London, also wondering why he had come. He had offered to visit David on impulse, and was wishing he had not.

At Sunday lunch with his parents, Conway had found Cornelius and Chrissie in a grand fuss over a letter from Adele Devenish. On her return to London she had started an agency for hiring out medical staff, and as one of her nurses had been looking after David, Adele had written to give his parents a report on his injuries and his current progress. Cornelius and Chrissie were appalled. Their only previous source of information had been one of David's more enigmatic postcards, which told them only that he had broken a leg in an accident. When Conway arrived for lunch, they had already decided to send James to England at once. Conway, unravelling the mysteries of Adele's looping handwriting, surprised himself and his parents by offering to go to London himself.

The first three days of his visit were spent investigating the affairs of the London house, but to the relief of all he left for Oxford on the fourth day. At the Wingfield Morris, mindful that he would have to give a full account to Cornelius and Chrissie, he spoke for a long time with the professor. It was too early to be certain, the pundit said, but he hoped that a second operation would not be necessary. At present the patient was pressing to be allowed to go home to his pregnant wife, and the professor was inclined to allow it.

Conway spent rather less time with David, and found his younger brother looking so much changed that he did not, for once, needle him about his prolonged absence from the London house. David thanked him for coming, but was much preoccupied with the question of when he would be allowed home. Conway told him what the

377

professor had said, and for the first time, David's thin face lit up with relief. Privately, Conway was shocked by his brother's appearance. Something stirred in him, which might have been compassion, but he chided himself for foolishness later. People who tried to be heroes were bound to get hurt sometimes.

Conway did not ask David how Antonia was keeping. Somehow he could not bring himself to do so. As for the London Vorst, it was doing well. True, there had been a downturn in profits since the onset of the flying bombs and the new rockets, but with the Allies advancing fast, it was hoped they would soon overrun the launching sites, and the tiresome bombardment would end.

Conway headed back to London. He was looking forward to tomorrow at all events, for Adele had invited him to lunch

Conway walked along Wilton Crescent and rang the bell of Adele's house.

He had considered taking flowers, but upon reflection thought it better to send some the following day. That way, she would be sure to call him up and thank him, and they could take it from there. He had given himself a gap of three days, mentally earmarking them for Adele. After that he would inspect the Bath and Edinburgh houses before heading back to New York. The fact that she had invited him to her home was encouraging.

When the door opened, however, it was not Adele but a very tall, thin man in a grey flannel suit, who introduced himself as Gerald, Adele's husband. 'Come in, Mr Vorst,' he said, opening the door wide. 'We haven't met but I've heard all about you.' Conway must have looked blank, for he added, 'Adele's on the phone to one of her blasted nurses but she won't be long.'

Silently thanking heaven that he was not clutching a posy, Conway went in.

'How nice of you to look us up, Conway,' Adele said, coming into the drawing room with her habitual loping stride. 'Have you been to see David?'

'I came over to see him. You certainly caused a storm of alarm at Maple Valley with that flimsy letter of yours.'

'I thought it was time your parents were told. Tell me, how was he?'

'He looked and sounded pretty feeble – mainly interested in getting back to the little wife. He hopes to go home next week.'

'Of course he'll want to. He worries about Antonia being on her own, and she refuses to move to the Hall. And as for being feeble, he has had weeks of pain and it was a tricky operation. They are still saying no visitors – with the exception of his loving brother, it seems.' She broke off then, and smiled at him for the first time. 'Conway, my dear, I am so glad that you took the trouble to visit him. It must have meant a lot to your parents. Tell me, how are Uncle Cornelius and Aunt Chrissie?'

'Apart from worrying about their pet lamb, they're fine. You know what they're like about David.'

She looked at him in silence for a moment, and then said in a different tone, 'It's time we ate. Fish pie, I'm afraid. Still, Gerald has found some quite nice wine in the cellar . . .'

He went back to the Vorst in a rage. Adele had spent a good part of lunch talking on the telephone, leaving him with Gerald. How dared she treat him like that!

He was thoroughly put out, and was curt with Hudson who was hovering in the lobby of the Vorst to greet him. There were more things to annoy him in Bath, and matters were not much better in Edinburgh. In fact, it was more than ten days before he found himself back in London. By this time he had made up his mind to leave Adele severely alone, and to fly home at the earliest possible moment.

Despite warnings from the staff, Conway had installed himself in the top-floor apartment, refusing even to look at the downstairs suite that they had prepared for him. The Vorst family, he told the housekeeper and the manager coldly, always stayed up there. He was not going to be chased downstairs by buzz bombs, doodlebugs or V-2 rockets.

About midnight on his second night, a particularly loud crump made him start up in his bed. He had heard one of the new rockets exploding before, and there was no mistaking the sound. He reckoned that tonight's one must have fallen quite near. He got up and, feeling wakeful, poured himself a large brandy, shrugged himself into his camel hair overcoat and went outside.

With the apartment lights extinguished, he stood in the roof garden to watch. There was plenty to see and hear – guns firing, ambulance bells ringing in the street below. It was quite a display, really, and he thought with satisfaction of how he would recount his experiences at the next board meeting.

The V-2 had started a fire, and above the leafless trees of Green Park the night sky glowed red, and smoke billowed between the rooftops. More gunfire from the park, and then a doodlebug and another went by in quick succession. Fiery-tailed in the darkness, these unmanned aircraft sounded different from normal airplanes. They emitted a rough growling sound – until the moment when they cut out and slanted downwards.

Two more buzz bombs passed along the distant skyline, and subsequent explosions told of some faraway destruction. Then a third appeared overhead, and a sudden cessation of sound made him recall the housekeeper's warning.

He retired quickly, closing the windows and blackout curtains. He had just switched on a lamp when a shattering explosion made him fling himself headlong onto the floor. It had sounded alarmingly near, and the lamp went out. But although the windows rattled, there was no sound of splintering glass. Feeling rather foolish, Conway reached for his bedside torch, switched it on and climbed into bed. Thank God he was going back to America tomorrow. It was some minutes before his heartbeat steadied. He drifted back to sleep.

The next day he decided to go for a walk before he left to catch his plane home. They told him that the buzz bomb had fallen at the far end of Green Park.

He never got to see the damage. The sound of an opening door made him look up. Antonia stood smiling at him. She was wearing a tiny hat with a veil on her upswept curls.

Conway stood up, and only then saw her changed shape. Even knowing what he knew, it was a shock to see her like that, and not a welcome one. 'Antonia! Where have you sprung from?'

'I came to see you, darling. They told me that you'd come for a flying visit and could not resist. Say that you're pleased to see me.'

He was anything but pleased, but he took her gloved hand and kissed it. He wondered as he led her to a chair whether the gloves had been charged to his account last spring. He clearly remembered paying for the hat.

The sweet high voice which he had once found so charming said, 'I came up from Dulcimer especially to see you, darling. Are you going to give me lunch? I had no breakfast, so I'm starving.'

'Antonia, I can't give you lunch. I'm flying home this afternoon. The embassy car is picking me up in under an hour.'

'But Conway—'

'Look, Antonia,' he said, 'I'll order you a quick sandwich in here. How about that?'

She said mutinously, 'Why can't we eat in the restaurant? It's not at all full. I looked.' And when Conway looked disconcerted, she said, mocking him, 'Are you ashamed to be seen with me in my . . . my condition?'

He said, 'You should not have come.'

She twisted her gloved hands together, and said forlornly, 'I suppose not. I thought . . . I hoped you would be pleased to see me.'

'Does David know that you're here?' He saw her blue eyes widen in surprise, and added, 'I understand that he's back home now. When I visited him in hospital he was desperate to get back to you, the poor dope. Or maybe it would be more accurate to call him a poor dupe?'

Antonia stared at Conway, and said baldly, 'You hate David, don't you? Well, I'll tell you this. Your brother is no dope and no dupe. He knows.'

He stood very still. 'What exactly does he know?'

'He knows that the baby isn't his, of course. It couldn't be, and he knows it, damn him! He started by refusing to touch me, and then had this plane crash. He has never once asked me who the father is. I don't think he wants to know. As far as the world is concerned, the baby is his and mine.'

After a moment's astonished silence, Conway began to laugh. She watched him in speechless indignation. The train journey from Haywards Heath had been an ordeal, even though a polite sailor had given up his seat. Conway laughing like this was too bad. She pulled herself to her feet with an effort and said, 'I'm not staying to hear you gloat. Get me a taxi, will you?'

'I'll do better than that. Where do you want to go?'

'Victoria Station.'

'I'll get Hudson to drive you to your train, Antonia.'

David and Susan ate their supper at the usual time. They wondered aloud about what could have delayed Antonia. David did not seem unduly worried. She was often late, he said.

In her first five days at the dower house, Susan had come to dislike David Vorst's wife almost as much as she liked and admired her patient. Instead of welcoming her husband with joy, Antonia appeared to be suffering from a strong sense of grievance, and offered him a coldly averted face to kiss. It was almost as if she had not wanted him to come back.

She certainly gave every sign of resenting his nurse, for she hardly spoke to Susan. And in five days she had never once entered the converted dining room where David spent most of his time. She complained that the alterations offended her eye and gave her a headache.

Though heavily pregnant, she was always going off somewhere without telling anyone where, and the landgirl who came in to clean told Susan that Mrs David kept a vodka bottle in her bedside cupboard. Susan thought privately that it would be a good thing if Antonia stayed with her friend Marjorie for several days.

'One thing,' said David, looking at his watch for the third time. 'Marjorie will send us a message if Antonia decides to stay the night. It has happened before.'

They switched on the radio and listened to the evening news. The King and Queen had attended a church service in the ruins of Coventry Cathedral. American troops under General Bradley were advancing towards the River Roer. Joint American and British air forces had carried out yet another bombing raid on German repair yards and transport systems. The incident of a flying bomb falling on a railway line outside Croydon, killing a train driver and injuring several passengers, was not reported. Details of the daily toll of buzz bombs and V-2 rockets were seldom mentioned on the BBC. Such reports were judged to be bad for public morale.

David looked yet again at the telephone, and wondered whether he ought to call Marjorie.

Susan took their supper dishes away. She wished savagely that Antonia would stay in London for good. The Group Captain was looking totally exhausted this evening. In the scullery she turned the taps full on, and started washing up with vigour. Thus it was that she did not hear a car driving up to the door.

David heard it, and made his way into the hall, to find a small man in an ARP tin hat almost carrying a drooping Antonia over the threshold.

He greeted David with every appearance of relief. 'You the husband? Take her, mate. She's had a shock. There now, missis, you'll be all right now.'

A thud of the front door slamming and a subsequent unidentifiable clatter brought Susan running into the hall. She found David teetering on one leg, trying to steady himself against a table while holding a sobbing Antonia in his arms. His crutches had slithered away across the parquet floor. Susan went at once to his rescue.

Even when Antonia had been wheeled into David's bedroom-cum-dining room, she refused to relinquish her frantic hold on his arm. She wanted to touch him, to feel the wiry strength of him under the cloth of his jacket. She sat pressed up against him on the sofa, wept on his shoulder, and implored him not to leave her, never to leave her again. David sat beside her, mute and still, arms round her trembling body. From time to time, he patted her shoulder, and wished his head did not ache so badly. He had suspected all day he was going down with flu.

It took time to find out what had happened. A buzz bomb had fallen on the railway line, killing several people and wounding others. Antonia had been hurled to the floor of the carriage, with people screaming all around her in the darkness. She had seen a man lying dead on the railway embankment.

Susan said practically, 'Mrs Vorst, you've had a tiring day and a bad shock, but you'll feel better after a hot bath. If you'll come upstairs, I'll help you.'

'I don't want your help. I want my husband.'

'That won't do, Mrs Vorst.' Susan and David exchanged glances over Antonia's head. 'Your husband cannot manage the stairs yet.'

'He could if he wanted to. He managed fine before.'

'No, Mrs Vorst. I'm sorry, but I cannot allow the Group Captain to exert himself so soon after his operation.'

'It's a bit late for you to call him Group Captain. I've heard you talking to him when I'm not around.'

Susan looked helplessly at David, and he jerked his head towards the door without speaking. She went out

'Come with me, darling,' Antonia whispered, nestling under his chin as though wanting to share his warmth. 'I'll be afraid of having nightmares upstairs on my own. You can't imagine how terrified I was in that train. I thought I was going to die alone among strangers, and my baby would die too. Come up with me.'

'I can't, honey, but you could have my bed in here. I'll sleep on the drawing-room sofa.'

She looked at the high hospital bed and made a face. 'I wouldn't sleep a wink in that ugly iron thing.'

David felt that even a spiked iron grid would have made a welcome couch, but said with arduous patience, 'How about Susan sleeping upstairs? You could shout or ring the bell for her if you're lonely, or if you need something.'

'I'm not having your wretched nurse upstairs. It's you I want, David. I never thought you could be so heartless.'

'Antonia, I doubt if I could make it up the stairs tonight.'

'And he is certainly not going to make the attempt,' said Susan firmly from the doorway. 'I've just put a hot bottle in your bed, so come along, Mrs Vorst, and no more nonsense.'

When Susan had gone, Antonia lay between smooth linen sheets and looked dreamily about her pretty bedroom. The rose chintz curtains with their swagged pelmets, the frilled organdie dressing table and the pink-shaded lamps had a calming effect upon her spirits, and there was a steaming cup of Ovaltine on the bedside table. The nurse, having got her way, had been competent and gentle, and to soak in a scented bath and then to be wrapped in a warm towel had been pleasant and reviving. Susan had brushed Antonia's hair, promising to wash and set it tomorrow, if Antonia so wished.

She rather thought she did wish it. The nurse had taken away her dust-soiled clothes. It was ages since anyone had waited on her like this, and the girl might yet be turned to good account. After all, David did not need much nursing any more. He was tiresomely independent, adamantly refusing to use his wheelchair, and impatient for the moment when they would give him a walking plaster. No need for the nurse to wait on him hand on foot. Tomorrow she would let the girl wash and set her hair. It would give her something to do.

Some time after midnight she felt a hot gush of liquid between her legs. She cursed inwardly. So the waters had broken, as they had done before Jamie's birth. Why did these things always happen in the middle of the night? She lay for a while, remembering all too clearly how the doctor had insisted on her going to the nursing home straightaway, and how she had waited hours before the contractions started. She wasn't going to let that happen again. She would wait until morning, and with luck might even get back to sleep.

Presently, feeling shivery, she felt for the bedside light switch, and encountered instead the dinner bell and the cup and saucer, which crashed to the floor in the dark. She managed to get the light on, and it was then that she saw the blood. There was blood on her hand, blood in a great pool in the bed, blood on the carpet, and she was bleeding still. She began to panic. She tried to shout, but her voice was hardly more than a croak. The room seemed to be going round. Then everything went black.

Nurse Susan never knew what made her wake. David had asked her to sleep in the spare room, despite Antonia's objections, and she lay for a while thinking of how weary her patient had looked by the time she had got him to bed.

She thought about Antonia too, and presently decided to go across the landing and make sure that her temporary patient was all right. Better to make sure. She opened the door, and gave a gasp.

The doctor and the ambulance seemed to be a long time in coming. Waiting below, David felt that another age had gone by before the stretcher bearers reappeared at the head of the stairs.

When they reached floor level, he hobbled forward and peered anxiously at his wife's bleached face and closed eyes. He looked up at the doctor, who was holding her wrist, and asked a wordless question.

The doctor shook his head. 'Too early to say. Do you mean to come with us?'

David did not answer, for Antonia had uttered a fluttering sigh and was looking at him with anguished eyes.

Her lips moved, but although he leaned closer, he could not make out the words. He took her clammy hand, and squeezed it.

'Hi, honey. The baby's started, and we're off to hospital.'

'Lonely . . .' The gossamer thread of sound was clearly audible now. 'Up . . . there . . .'

'Were you, honey?' He looked up, and in answer to the doctor's urgent signal, added, 'I'm coming with you now anyway. Let's not keep them waiting.'

He was wheeled up a ramp into the ambulance only seconds after the stretcher, but she was already in distress, groping for his hand. Even barely conscious, the clutch of her fingers was convulsive as she tried to speak again.

He leaned close; his face was touching hers. 'Don't try to talk,' he said gently, planting a kiss on her damp, cold forehead. 'I'm here. Nothing to be afraid of. You're going to be all right.'

But he was wrong. Antonia died with her hand still clutching his, and he knew she had gone even before the doctor straightened up in the swerving, bell-ringing ambulance and shook his head.

They found the big brass bell where it had rolled under the bed, and shards of bone china on the carpet. The post-mortem verdict was that Mrs Vorst and her unborn child had died from a haemorrhage caused by placenta previa. At the inquest the verdict was given as death by misadventure. It was nobody's fault. A sympathetic coroner offered Group Captain Vorst his most sincere condolences.

Grim-faced and outwardly calm, David picked up his crutches, and hobbled out of the church hall where the inquest had taken place. He refused an invitation to stay at Dulcimer Hall, and Susan drove him back to the dower house. He wanted nothing, he told her with a bleak smile, only to be alone. Still in that deadly polite tone, he also suggested that his nurse should take the rest of the day off. Then he went into the morning room and firmly shut the door in her face. Accordingly she went into the scullery and wept copiously into a roller towel on the wall. She had been rigorously questioned about the dinner bell. Had she perhaps forgotten to leave it on the bedside table? The more she insisted that it had been placed there, the more feeble her protestations began to sound, even to her own ears. In the end they had accepted her story, but it had been a dreadful week for everyone.

They buried Antonia at Dulcimer beside her first husband Johnnie. This time David was to all appearances himself again, chatting politely to fellow mourners over sherry and sandwiches, and later playing card games with the children who had been brought home from school for the funeral. Making the effort to deal with the children helped a little. When Adele Devenish came on the telephone later, an anxiously hovering Susan actually heard him laugh for the first time since the day of the tragedy.

But though outwardly much as usual, David was haunted for a long time by Antonia's death, gnawed by the certainty of his own guilt. Antonia had begged him not to leave her. But he had been weak and self-indulgent, and had fallen asleep within minutes of Susan taking her away. The nurse had been obliged to shake him quite hard before she could rouse him and make him ready for bed.

He had slept soundly in the downstairs room that Antonia disliked so much – and while he slept on, she had been bleeding upstairs, lonely, frightened and unloved. 'Over my dead body' had been her very words when he had suggested sleeping downstairs. The coroner might say what he liked, but David blamed himself.

Chapter 27

Adele was pleased when Nurse Susan came to see her at the agency. The girl was a shade simple-minded but was good at her job. It seemed that she was looking for another post.

'This is an unexpected bonus, my dear. I didn't expect to see you again. It seemed likely that you would be swept to America as part of the Vorst menage. Cornelius and Chrissie Vorst have a way of carrying all before them.'

'They did ask me to go with them, Lady Adele. You see, when they go, they want to take David with them.'

'And what does David have to say?'

'He wasn't saying much, but he advised me to come to see you. I think he may be thinking of remaining in England. He doesn't seem to know what he wants – but that is only natural, after being so ill. One night, when he was delirious with pneumonia, we were afraid we were going to lose him.'

'I heard that he was pretty bad,' said Adele.

'Indeed he was. It poured with rain on the day of the funeral, and he got soaked to the skin in the churchyard. The next thing was, he was down with pneumonia. He was very ill, and several times the district nurse and I had to hold him down, for fear that he damaged his foot. He kept thrashing around and calling out.'

When Susan left, Adele sat still, thinking over what she had just heard. She found it hard to imagine David unable to make up his mind. But one thing which had mystified Susan, she understood with no difficulty. If what the nurse said was true, David needed help.

Adele believed that if you wanted something, it was best to go to the top to get it. She had met Air Chief Marshal Sir Arthur Tedder several times. She rang up one of his aides, and was lucky enough to secure an appointment to see him.

'How would I go about finding out,' she said, going straight to the point, 'where a certain serving officer in the WAAF was stationed?'

Sir Arthur Tedder looked at her. 'I'll tell you just how to go about it, Lady Adele. Give the girl's name and number to my secretary, and she will do her best to find out what you want to know.'

Adele beamed at him approvingly. 'Dear Sir Arthur,' she said. 'I was very much hoping you would say that.'

Within a week, the Air Chief Marshal's secretary was on the telephone. She had some news to impart about Section Officer Dunlop's latest movements.

'Wonderful, Miss Allardyce! Sir Arthur told me that you would find her, but I didn't dare to hope that you would be so quick.'

Coming into the Vorsts' suite unannounced, Adele saw David before he became aware of her. He sat unmoving in the sun-filled room, his dark head bent and hands hanging down. He looked like a man who had given up hope.

He looked up, and at once smiled a welcome, and reached for his crutches. She went over quickly. 'Stay put. Tell me, how's the foot?'

'A lot better, thanks, Adele. It's going on fine.'

Nurse Susan had said that he always gave the same answer. 'Tell me what the doctors say.'

'The usual. That it will take time, and that I must be patient.' He smiled in the bleak way that had become habitual to him during the weeks following Antonia's death and his illness. 'I'm having a special shoe made, so hopefully I shall be able to walk about normally soon.'

'That's good.' They sat without speaking. Adele drew a breath and said abruptly, 'I expect you know that Effie Dulcimer has been trying to contact Maggie Dunlop, the girl who once looked after your children. She wants her to leave the WAAFs and come back to them.'

David looked at her as if she was a stranger. He said evenly, 'The children's plans are under control, Adele. They are at Dulcimer for the holidays, and my parents and I will join them for Christmas. Apart from the grandparents, there's their old nanny and a landgirl to look after them, and in another few weeks they will be going back to school.'

His expression was so forbidding that she nearly went away without saying anything. Then she remembered what Susan had said about him calling out for 'Maggie', and made herself go on.

'David, there is something you ought to know. I have made inquiries, and it seems that Maggie is to be posted overseas in less than a fortnight.'

There was no doubt of his antagonism now. His eyes were twin spears. However she went on doggedly, 'If we want her back, we must act quickly. It would not be easy later. The RAF are sending her to India.'

'Why are you telling me this, Adele?'

Adele stared at him.

He said with quiet violence, 'God save me from yet another interfering woman! I've stopped my mother and Aunt Effie from

387

meddling, and now there's you. My affairs and those of my stepchildren are none of your concern, Adele.'

'David, I was trying to help.'

'Then please don't. Well-meaning interference is the last thing anyone needs, least of all Maggie. I know that she's about to go overseas. You told me once that she should get away and make a life for herself. I told her the same myself, more recently.' He moved his injured foot and his face twisted in a momentary grimace. 'So now that she has decided, the best thing we can do is to let her go.' He looked down at his hands and said almost inaudibly, 'She has a happy and resilient nature, and India is a wonderful country.'

Adele sat facing him, bereft of speech. She did not remember ever being so sharply put in her place. She was relieved by the arrival of Chrissie Vorst, who came in and greeted her with delight.

'Adele my dear, what a lovely surprise! Thank you for keeping David amused while I was out.' She did not wait for Adele to answer, but turned to the doorway. 'Look who has come to see us, dearest. It must have been telepathy. We were saying only yesterday how we wished we had seen you. Bless you for sending for us when David was ill.'

Chrissie and Cornelius were feeling jubilant. After stalling for weeks, David had agreed to go home with them. They hoped to travel immediately after Christmas if David was well enough.

Adele took her leave before long. David shook her hand and bade her goodbye, but with eyes as wintry as the weather outside in the street. Cornelius put her into a taxi.

Before he shut the door and stepped back, he said apologetically, 'David was in a mood today. Don't heed him. Once we get him home he'll begin to feel human again. He's had a bad time, with Antonia dying in that appalling way and being so ill, but he's young and resilient. Give him three months, and he'll be a new man. As soon as the war is over, why not come to Maple Valley?' He added, 'Come next spring when the dogwoods are flowering. By then, I promise you, David will be recovered, and I'll make sure he stays home this time. Chrissie, of course, hopes that he will fall in love and marry again.'

'You truly think the war will be over by then? As soon as next spring?'

'Sure it will. Just one more push, and our armies will be over the Rhine. My guess is that there'll be victory in Europe around eight weeks from now. After that, it will take us a while to deal with the Japs . . .'

As her taxi drove away, Adele reflected that Cornelius was a master of wishful thinking. His prediction that the war would end in a matter of weeks she regarded as extremely unlikely

She considered, too, that Cornelius was over-optimistic about

David. He and Chrissie had talked about him as if he was not there, turning to smile indulgently at him from time to time. David had not spoken a word.

Adele felt sorry for the old Vorsts, for surely they were courting disappointment. There had been something unnerving about David's brooding, inimical silence, and the dark look he gave her as she left. She was reminded of a caged eagle she had once seen. The great raptor's plumage had been bedraggled and moulting, but the eyes had told another story as the captive bird stared menacingly through the bars of his prison.

David would go with them to America, and they would wrap him round with their love and solicitude. He would stay until he had regained his strength – and what then? She did not think he would stay very long in their gilded cage. David Vorst, in her judgement, was quite as ruthless in his own way as his elder brother.

She was eventually proved doubly right. In late March Group Captain Vorst returned to Europe and witnessed at first hand the crossing of the Rhine and the advance of the Allied forces into Germany. Cornelius's conviction that the war would end within weeks was proved wrong very much sooner. Within two days of Adele's visit to the London Vorst Hotel, news came that German Panzer divisions under Von Runstedt had pierced the Allied lines in several places, and that a desperate battle was being fought in the deeply ridged and forested area of the Ardennes.

The Germans had moved fast, taking their adversaries by surprise. For several weeks the Allied armies were plunged into the gravest crisis they had known since 1940.

When Major Lord Dartmore arrived back in Holland in the autumn of 1944, even the most cynical veterans in his squadron admitted that it was good to see him back.

They knew Major Dart's ways. He had a temper, and when roused, his command of invective was as fluent as it was colourful, but he was one of the lucky ones, having fought from Normandy to their present position with never a scratch on him. They told the new boys that his coming was a good omen.

There were many newcomers to the regiment that autumn. So many junior officers had been killed or badly wounded in France that experienced leaders were thin on the ground. Very often tanks were commanded by NCOs who knew the ropes better than many an untried subaltern.

The same applied to other ranks fresh out from England. Some of them had been at school less than a year ago. They were taken in hand and 'broken in' to the realities of tank life by the regimental sergeants and other NCOs. There had been sporadic fighting throughout the autumn, with both sides probing for advantage, but no large-scale assault. The squadrons were constantly on the move, ever watchful for signs of the enemy. Inevitably a good proportion of a recruit's time was spent in being educated by his more experienced colleagues – seasoned veterans not much older than themselves, who had survived Normandy and fought their way north through France.

The weather was miserable all through October and November, with freezing fog, cold, rain, and roads often a sea of glutinous mud. People grumbled, of course, and pitied the poor foot-slogging infantry who had to force their way through the mire, eyes on the ground, on the watch for the deadly schu-mines which could blow your feet and legs off in an instant. Newcomers to the infantry envied the tank boys, and cursed them when they charged by high and dry in their tanks, spraying them with mud and filth.

It took a first sight of a Sherman tank being blasted by an enemy shell to adjust their thinking. The tank commander was killed outright, and his slumped body lay spouting blood over the rest of the crew, who were vainly trying to escape through the shattered turret. None of them got out. Peering from a ditch, the shocked infantrymen saw a tree-high sheet of flame, and heard muffled screams and cries from the trapped crew inside as the Sherman 'brewed up'. Tommy cookers, the Germans called them.

After that, there was less talk about tank toffs. Better to suffer miseries of cold and wet and blistered feet. You had at least some chance of plunging into a ditch when an enemy gun or tank opened up. Better anything than ending like those poor roasted blighters. And as for grousing about the weather, the older ones told them that they ought to have been with Monty in Africa. Heat was worse than cold any day, they said. They did not know, then, of the snow and savage cold which was about to turn the Ardennes battlefield into a frozen hell that Christmas.

The blizzard came fast on the heels of the German advance, deep snow blanketing the woods and ravines, obscuring tracks and roads and contorting familiar landmarks. Communication between head-quarters and the battlefield was disrupted by enemy saboteurs – but even more by the atrocious weather. Nobody seemed to know for certain how far the German advance had penetrated. Several times a squadron of tanks and supporting infantry found themselves alone in the snow-distorted woods at twilight, and had to wait until dawn to get their bearings, hungry, cold and unable to light fires for fear of betraying their presence to the enemy. Worst of all, with low cloud and blizzard conditions, the Allied air forces were grounded and impotent for nearly a week.

In the snow-laden woods and valleys, men strained to pull

armoured cars out of ditches and hidden streams, engineers had their numbed hands cut and abraded by frozen metal as they struggled to start engines that were out of action. These were, by comparison, the lucky ones. At least they were able to move about.

The men in the tanks were in a worse case. Binoculars iced over and lenses blurred. Commanders peered ahead for signs of the enemy through watering eyes, hoping yet fearing to see an unusual shape among the trees before they were spotted and fired on by the enemy. Inside the tanks the crews crouched frozen for hour after hour in their cramped seats, buffeted and bruised as the tank laboured and swerved up each snowy ridge. Once over the ridge, the driver would yell a warning and they clung for dear life as the vehicle plunged down the next slope. Tank tracks were rendered largely ineffectual in deep snow and ice, and drivers could do nothing but struggle and swear as thirty tons of iron careered and smashed into the next ravine, a monstrous self-willed toboggan. There was little chance of manoeuvring, of outflanking the enemy in these conditions, or of trying to evade anti-tank shots by deliberate and skilful handling. Exposed at the top of each ridge, it was a temptation to fire into the next group of trees, only to find that the odd snow-muffled shape was nothing more menacing than a ruined hut.

By the start of the second week the weather improved slightly, although it was still bitterly cold. Dart's squadron moved into easier terrain, and arrived at a small town at nightfall, with orders to stay until further notice. Artillery fire had reduced the town to little more than a heap of rubble, and there was no sign of the Belgian inhabitants.

Dart and a sergeant climbed over the first heap of rubble, looking for some form of shelter for the night. They had paused at the edge of the village square when an enemy sniper opened up from a ruined building beside the church. The sergeant was killed, and Dart was wounded; he keeled over, bleeding on the pavement.

It seemed that Major Dart's luck had run out at last. They told him later that the battle news was good. The Panzer divisions were in full retreat along the wooded roads, and what proved to be Hitler's last grand offensive had failed. He grunted with satisfaction, and closed his eyes. Even in pain and being jolted towards the nearest dressing station, he could appreciate being warm for the first time in almost a week.

Maggie arrived at Glen Cary two days after Christmas. Her colleagues in Norfolk had given her a hectic send-off, and she was hoping to have a quiet New Year. As for the rest of her embarkation leave, she was not sure what to do with it.

When she had asked for transfer, she had hoped to be on a troopship and far away before Christmas. The administrative wheels of the

Royal Air Force had revolved speedily at first, and she travelled on a conveyer belt of training sessions, briefing, lectures about India and the Far East, health checks and some remarkably painful injections. They even gave her an allowance to pay for hot weather uniforms. By December she was kitted out, braced and ready to take off to the other side of the world.

She was running away and she knew it, but the thought of another month of hoping for some word from David had been too much to bear. She knew about Antonia's death. She had written him a letter, but had torn it up. He knew how she felt about his wife, and her trite words of sympathy would ring false – and might even be unwelcome. If David wanted her, he would come to her, or write.

She also shied away from contacting anyone at Dulcimer. If any of them needed her – and she would have liked to help with Abby and the boys – they knew where to find her. She rang up Sophy to ask if a letter had come to the flat. She rang several times, but it was never any good.

'Oh, it's you again. Hang on. I'll take a look.'

Maggie waited, picturing her friend scrabbling through heaps of papers and letters. Sophy had a habit of leaving obvious bills and boring letters unopened. The pips went, and Maggie put more coins in to keep the call alive.

Sophy's voice came on the line. 'No, sorry. Not a sausage. Is it important, Mags?'

'Not really. I just thought there might be bills. I don't want to go off without getting myself straight.'

'Bills for what?' And when Maggie hesitated, Sophy said accusingly, 'You never have bills. You always pay on the nail. Admit it, Maggie. You're hoping for a letter from a chap. Have you fallen for someone at last?'

'You know that's not likely.'

'More's the pity. Did I tell you about Albert? Such a dish . . .'

She was halfway through Albert when the pips went again. Maggie was still digging vainly in her pocket for more pennies when they were cut off.

The weeks wore on and by Christmas week Maggie's last hopes had dwindled and died – and still she had no orders to embark. She got practised at smiling and saying goodbye and thanking people for complimenting her on her recent promotion to flight officer. At times her face felt quite stiff with smiling. Then she was given three weeks' embarkation leave.

Three weeks! The train ground to a stop at Glen Cary Halt. She reached for her luggage and opened the door. The prospect of her unwanted leave stretched ahead – a weary road. Sophy had asked her to stay in Cheyne Place, but she did not think she would. Better to make a clean break there, too.

But she was pleased to be back at the manse, and relieved to hear that the minister and his wife were planning to celebrate New Year at their own fireside. Mrs Fraser was not feeling up to the Hogmanay ceilidh, where the neighbours would dance and sing the New Year in. Maggie would not have gone anyway, for her father would surely be there.

Mrs Fraser appeared in the open doorway of Maggie's room. 'Maggie dear, this is such a treat for us. It seems ages since you were here.'

'I've had no leave since May, Mrs Fraser.'

'Then you will be needing a rest,' said the minister's wife. She went to the dressing table where four wrapped parcels lay. 'These look exciting. We've saved our presents for Hogmanay. Bert has to play his fiddle in the band but will eat with us beforehand. He has something special for you this year. He's been very secretive about it, but I think he's excited. Be prepared to make all the right noises . . .'

Maggie laughed, remembering other presents from Bert. 'Another jar of tadpoles? Or shaving soap from the jumble sale?'

'Something small, anyway. He begged some of my red crêpe paper to wrap it in but only needed about ten inches square. My dear, what a pretty hairbrush! Have I seen it before?'

'It belonged to my mother. Gran gave it to me.'

'So now you've got this as well as your ring. How nice.'

'You know, Mrs Fraser,' said Maggie soberly, 'now that I'm older and not so very afraid of Dad, I feel sorry for him. How terrible to be deserted by someone you . . . you once loved and trusted . . .' Maggie picked up her uniform tunic and turned to hang it in the wardrobe, but not before Mrs Fraser had seen the look on her face.

She wondered, as she and the minister had wondered last May, whether Maggie's cheerful demeanour did not hide some secret anguish. Perhaps one day she would tell them about it.

On New Year's Eve they all gathered in the warm parlour to give each other presents. These were often homemade, and always inexpensive. Mrs Fraser had knitted socks for Bert and a woollen muffler for the minister, and had found a china thimble with roses on it for Maggie. Maggie had hemmed handkerchiefs for the Frasers, and gave Bert a second-hand compass.

Bert's giving came last.

'Whatever can it be?' Maggie smiled at him as her careful fingers undid his parcel. But despite Mrs Fraser's warning, and Bert's tense air of nonchalance, at first she could not utter a word. Maggie sat and stared at the silver-topped jar with its engraved initals.

Mrs Fraser put out a hand, concerned at Maggie's sudden loss of colour. Bert said in a cross voice, 'It's a bit battered and the glass is chipped – but if you don't like it I'll get you something else.'

Maggie pulled herself together and said with truth, 'Bert, it's lovely. So much so that it took my breath away.' She got up and hugged him. 'Thank you. Where did you find anything so perfect?'

'Never mind where I found it. As long as you like it.'

'I shall take it with me when I go abroad.'

'All right. I'll get off to the hall then.'

In the firelit parlour, three puzzled people stared at Bert's present to Maggie. The engraved letters matched those on her silver hairbrush, which Maggie had fetched from her bedroom. M and D entwined. Maggie's initials, but also those of her mother.

Maggie asked the question which was in all their minds. 'Where did Bert find it?'

'I didn't steal it, if that's what you mean, Mr Fraser,' Bert said belligerently when the minister asked him about it. He was looking remarkably guilty. 'I found it.'

'Found it where?'

Bert said sulkily, 'On the moor. Buried in the peat. There were other things as well.'

'Could you show me the place? There might be more things to find.'

Bert hunched a sulky shoulder. Then he muttered, 'There aren't any more. I went and looked.'

'Went where exactly?'

Bert sighed and capitulated. 'I found them on Jock's Crag.'

For a long moment there was no sound in the minister's study but the ticking of a clock on the overmantel. Then Mr Fraser spoke. 'I seem to remember that you promised not to go there.'

'That was years ago.'

'Book tokens and cheques go out of date, I know. But not promises, once given.'

Bert said defensively, 'They ought to when they don't make sense any more, Mr Fraser. You thought it wasn't safe for me on Jock's Crag, but Mr Dunlop goes there and prods about with a crowbar and a spade. He wouldn't if he really thought there were bombs.'

The minister frowned, and said slowly, 'How do you know?'

Bert said simply, 'After he killed Wat last spring, I followed him. At first I thought he might be a German spy . . .'

So it all came out, and when Bert had finished his tale and brought his other treasures to be inspected, he and the minister sat in silence. The clock whirred and struck eleven times. It was New Year's morning of 1945. When the tinny chimes had finished, Mr Fraser asked Bert if anyone else knew what he had found.

'No. Not even Maggie, so far.'

'Could you keep it to yourself a little longer?'

'What if Maggie asks me about the jar?'

'She won't. You can leave Maggie to me.'

Bert frowned. 'I knew there was something wrong the minute I saw her face. Why did she look like that, Mr Fraser?'

The minister stared down at the little heap of objects that made up the rest of Bert's treasure trove. There was a comb, a discoloured clock face, a buckle with a rotting strap. He sighed. 'I don't know, Bert. I don't yet know what to think.'

Maggie had been unusually silent over the holiday week, visiting her grandmother every day, and tramping the moors afterwards. She was trying to think out what to do. On Sunday she went to morning service with Mrs Fraser.

Until this January day Maggie had always tucked herself away in a back pew, out of sight of her father who had his place on the balcony. But this time she asked Mrs Fraser if she could sit with her at the front, and told her why, *this* time, she wanted her father to know she was there. She wanted to speak with him.

'My dear, is that wise?'

Maggie's smile was twisted. 'I don't know. In the past when I wanted to say things to Dad I could never get the words out. But I'm older now and I must try. And I may be a little tougher than I used to be. I nearly dressed in my uniform to impress him.'

'You look very nice in your pretty tweed. Is it new?'

'One of Sophy's mother's cast-offs. I liked the tweed, so I altered it to fit me.'

'One day I'd like to meet Sophy.'

'When I come back I'll bring her to see you.'

They pulled on gloves, picked up prayer books, and started on the short walk to the kirk. Passing out of the manse gate, they exchanged greetings with neighbours going the same way. These people well remembered Maggie Dunlop from when she was a large and awkward child, and knew that the head keeper and his daughter were not speaking.

When the service was over, the congregation stood chatting in the pale winter sunshine. The minister and the elders came out last, and Maggie moved towards them.

'Dad,' she said quietly. 'I'd like a word with you.'

Ian Dunlop stared at his daughter, and for a moment his eyes flickered with some emotion which Maggie could not read. He said roughly, 'What is there to talk about?'

She looked at him squarely. 'Can we go back into the kirk? I won't keep you long.'

'I've nothing at all to say to you, Maggie, and you know it.'

'That's as may be. But I have something to say to you, and something to ask. Must it be here, or will you come where we can be private?'

'Come up to the manse, Ian,' suggested the minister, laying a hand on the head keeper's arm and finding it as rigid as a tweed-clad iron bar. 'There's a fire in my study.' And before Ian could speak, he added almost sternly, 'Your daughter is about to go abroad, perhaps for the rest of the war. You owe her the courtesy of a few words before she leaves.'

As the study door closed behind the departing minister, father and daughter faced each other. It occurred to Maggie that his skin was a bad colour and he had lost a lot of weight. She might have asked him if he was feeling all right, but his first words drove the impulse from her mind.

He said in a biting tone, 'Off whoring again, are you? Never still. Just like your mother.'

'People tell me that I look like her,' Maggie said calmly as she laid her hat and gloves beside her prayer book. 'You noticed a likeness, didn't you, when we met last summer? But nobody who knew her has ever hinted at her being what you say.'

'You'll keep your mother's name out of this. I'll not have it spoken, do you hear?'

'No need to shout, Dad. Very well, let's not talk about her. I'll tell you about myself, instead.'

'I've no time to listen to your blether.'

'I won't take long. You should know a few facts about me, Dad. When I sail for the Far East, I shall be in charge of a group of aircraftwomen and non-commissioned officers. I joined the WAAFs as an aircraftwoman myself, and since then I have worked and studied hard to get where I am. The Air Force is particular about their officers and how they behave. Do you really think they would have promoted me to flight officer if I had ever carried on as you say?'

Ian glared at her. 'Is that all you have to say to me?'

'No. Mainly it's about Gran I want to talk. She's not getting any younger.' She ignored her father's acid comment that he did not need to be told his mother's age, and went on resolutely, 'And she sometimes gets confused and anxious.'

'Why not just say your grandmother is senile, and that's all about it? If she were a bitch, I'd say it would be a kindness to put her down.'

'If you're saying that to shock me, Dad, don't bother. I'm only interested in Gran's welfare, as you should be. She's your mother, and she's slaved for you lifelong, and that woman who keeps house for you now is not treating her right.'

'Who says so?'

'I say so.'

'I'll thank you to keep your nose out of my affairs, Maggie. When you walked out and went to America, deserting your grandmother and myself, you lost all rights as a daughter under my roof.'

Maggie said quietly, 'I don't recall having rights, Dad, and I certainly never walked out. I was carried out unconscious because you had beaten me so badly and were threatening to do it again. Without Gran's intervention and some help from Glynis, you might have killed me. For that rescue alone I owe it to Gran to help her. She is too confused and frightened to help herself.'

'Meg Hurley does her best,' said Ian, sounding suddenly less sure of himself. 'It's not just so easy to get help these days, and your grandmother took against the last woman. Did she complain to you of Meg?'

'No. She did not.'

'Well then.'

Maggie looked at her father, and said, 'I think she may be afraid to say anything.'

'Havers! My mother has never been afraid to speak her mind. Never in all her life, and you know that as well as I do, Maggie.'

'I thought I knew it, but she's afraid to now. Mrs Hurley handles her roughly, and shouts and scolds when nobody is about. I've heard her at it before she knew I was there. And I suspect her of threatening Gran with being sent to the Sanctuary if she gives trouble or complains. Gran thinks you mean to put her there if Mrs Hurley decides to leave. Is that true?'

There was a long silence, and then Ian said grudgingly, 'It's not called the Sanctuary these days.'

'I know. They call it an eventide home, don't they, but it's the same grim building with old people sitting in rows staring at nothing. So it's true? You're actually thinking of putting her away?'

'I didn't say that. And I've never once discussed it with my mother. But I'm not made of money. Why should anyone want to look after a half-senile and incontinent old woman when they can earn good money making munitions or joining the forces?'

'How much do you pay Mrs Hurley, Dad?'

'That's my business.'

'If I'm to help you, you'd better tell me. Or would you rather I asked Mrs Hurley herself?'

He swore at her for an interfering besom, but when Maggie repeated her question, he reluctantly named a sum. It was almost double what she would earn as a flight officer. Looking more shame-faced than angry, her father muttered, 'What else could I do? Meg threatened to pack her bags if I refused to give her a rise. The harvest was just starting, and there wasn't anyone I could turn to and no time to look about.' And when Maggie looked at him without speaking, he added angrily, 'Easy for you to come here and carp about Meg Hurley. If you cared you would stay home and do the work yourself, instead of dashing off to enjoy yourself at the other end of the world.'

'It won't be a holiday, Dad. There's still a war on out there.'

But even as she spoke, she knew that this time there could be no escape for her.

Next morning Maggie and Mr Fraser went to see the head keeper. The minister had insisted on coming, and Maggie was grateful. On the way, they worked out what to say.

Mrs Hurley opened the door. She was a large-breasted woman, and she wore curlers and a pink flannel dressing gown. She seemed reluctant to let them in, and said to Maggie, 'Come to make more trouble, have you? You're too early to see your granny. She's still asleep.'

'Then I won't wake her. I've come to see my father,' said Maggie. 'Please let us in, Mrs Hurley.'

The woman hesitated, but finally she sniffed and stood aside. The head keeper was sitting at the kitchen table. He looked at Maggie and at the minister standing at her back, and said curtly, 'Well? What now?'

'Could we go into the front room, Dad? If Gran's asleep, I don't want to disturb her.'

'What you mean,' said Mrs Hurley, wrapping her flannel gown more firmly round her stout form as if girding herself for battle, 'is you don't want me there when you tell your next pack of lies. Ian told me what you said about me. The ingratitude of it is what gets me. When I think of all I have to do for your granny, all I have had to put up with—'

'For the Lord's sake, Meg,' said Ian, 'go and get dressed.'

When the door closed with a defiant slam, he glowered at Maggie, and said baldly, 'What do you want? Is that lass of mine leading you by the nose again, minister?'

Mr Fraser pulled out a chair for Maggie, and sat down beside her. 'Maggie has decided to leave the Air Force, Ian.'

'That's right, Dad. I want to come home.'

For a moment Ian looked perfectly astounded. Then he asked his daughter sceptically, 'What's come over you that you suddenly decided that?'

'Finding Gran the way she is now. That, and what you said to me yesterday – that I should come home and do the work, instead of carping about it.'

'What makes you so sure I want you here?'

Maggie smiled faintly. 'I won't cost you as much as Mrs Hurley.'

He smiled unpleasantly. 'So you expect to be paid, do you? Any decent daughter would do the work for love.'

'I shall take care of Gran for love. But there has never been any love between you and me, so a business arrangement would be best – a verbal agreement which the minister has kindly come to witness. I shall want regular housekeeping money, and we should get some hens. In return I shall act as housekeeper and try to keep out of your way.'

'You've a nerve, Maggie, coming in here and laying down the law. I know you. As soon as I send Meg Hurley packing, you'll go off and leave us in the lurch.'

'No. I won't do that. But if you raise a hand to me, I may not be able to stay. If I have to leave, Dad, I shall take Gran with me.'

Ian blustered and swore at his daughter, assuring her that he was master in his own house, and that Meg Hurley suited him fine. But in the end the thought of saving so much money won him over, as Maggie had known it would. Grudging to the last, he agreed to her terms.

Next day she contacted her station commander by telephone, and within weeks she had left the Air Force.

Chapter 28

Ian Dunlop had never liked his daughter, for he had never been able to forget that it was after her birth that everything had gone so horribly wrong.

As a child and in her teens, she had irritated him beyond bearing, and he had come to think of her as his evil genius. The mere sight of her stirred his sleeping devils, and often he would end up hating not only Maggie but despising himself as well. She had a way of staring at him with her grey eyes so uncomfortably like his Mary's, an unwelcome reminder of so much that he wanted to forget.

'Get on with your work and keep your eyes to yourself,' he would growl when she was younger and the lump of a girl would turn away but not before he had seen the fear in her eyes. 'If the lass showed a bit of spirit I would be better able to live with her,' he once told his mother when Mrs Dunlop had tried to put in a word for her granddaughter.

And here she was again, back in his house and showing all too much spirit for his liking. A graceful young woman she was now, who took charge, getting rid of Meg Hurley, dictating terms to him and bamboozling the minister into taking her part. That she had gone whining to Mr Fraser had been an act of disloyalty.

'Don't dare to go behind my back again, Maggie. If you've a complaint to make, you may make it to me.'

She just looked at him, and said nothing – and the old anger stirred. 'I'll tell you this much,' he said belligerently. 'Meg Hurley may have been a bit rough and ready, but she meant well.'

'Let's not talk about her, Dad,' said Maggie. She put the tea tray down beside him, and went quietly out of the room.

He glared at the closed door. He had taken up residence in the front room on the day that Maggie came back. It would do her no harm to carry trays in and out.

There were many things to rile him that winter, not least the fact that his mother made a good recovery in both health and spirits. Neighbours began to call, and she attended the kirk on Sundays and an afternoon whist drive in the village hall. It was good to know that his mother was better, of course, but he could have done without people saying how lucky it was that Maggie had come home.

Mrs Dunlop's recovery brought another disadvantage. She had started speaking her mind again. He blamed Maggie for that, sure that she had prompted her grandmother to lecture him about his health.

'You're not looking well, son,' she told him. 'Shall I ask Dr Mac to leave you a tonic?'

'There is nothing the matter with me bar a touch of indigestion, Mother. If Maggie was half as good a cook as yourself or Meg Hurley . . .'

'There is nothing wrong with Maggie's cooking that a bit of practice won't put right.'

Maggie turned from the stove, her face alight with laughter. 'Gran, try sticking to one story at a time. Remember what you said about my pastry?'

Mrs Dunlop's pale lips tightened, a sure sign that she was determined not to smile. Ian took himself off to the front room. He felt excluded. Maggie had never smiled or looked at him like that. A sudden thought mocked him. What had he ever done to make her smile? Perhaps he should not have tried to bully her at the outset.

He had been determined to make his daughter wish that she had never come home. Like his mother, she was far too noticing. She had chosen to push her way in and must be kept in her place. But Maggie went about her work with cheerful competence and did not seem to notice that she was being got at. She was either very stupid or she had grown tough during her time in the WAAF. Balked, he redoubled his efforts to subdue her.

Maggie had not expected to enjoy her homecoming. The first month was the worst. Her grandmother was in low spirits and could not bear to be alone. For that reason, the outside work had to be done in a series of short rushes, or after the old lady was asleep at night. There was the weekly penance of getting housekeeping money out of her father. He haggled over it every week, and grudged every penny. And she could sense that his anger was simmering perilously near the surface.

She had threatened to go away and take her grandmother with her if he beat her up. But where would they go and what would they live on? The manse was too close to home, and the Frasers had done enough for her already. And more than likely her grandmother would refuse to be taken away, for fear of what the neighbours would say. Dunlop troubles had always to be dealt with at home – and never confided to outsiders. Then one March evening the storm broke, and her father came at her with his horn-handled stick.

Something bad had been brewing all day. Her father looked exceedingly unwell, and sent his womenfolk off to the morning service without him. He ate his midday dinner in the front room, and stayed there all afternoon. Maggie went in with his tea. The room reeked of whisky. Neither she nor her father spoke, but she could feel his eyes on her.

'Leave him be, Maggie,' said her grandmother. 'Best not go in to your father tonight. You know how he can be when something has upset him.'

'So what is his trouble this time?'

'It's a bad time of year, lassie. I'll be glad for him when March is by.'

'The Ides of March?' said Maggie sceptically. 'I thought you said he was worst in January on the anniversary of my baptism?'

'Ian and Mary were married on the fifteenth of March, so it's another one.'

'He ought to throw away his calendar,' said Maggie crossly. 'Don't worry, Gran. I'll clear away his tray in the morning. Hopefully he will have sobered up by then.'

She was tiptoeing past the front room door on her way to bed when an agonised groan from within made her pause. A second groan took her to the door, and she went in. Ian was doubled over in his chair, and she asked him what was the matter.

It might have been worse. She had time to seize a chair and use it as a shield, backing out of the room while he was still gasping for breath. Whatever ailed him certainly helped her to escape with only minor injuries, and she reach the kitchen and barricaded herself in for the night.

Next day neither of them spoke of the rumpus, but she noticed him glancing at her bruised cheek and swollen fingers, and he lit his own fire that evening. He even shut up the hens. She wondered if these unusual actions were his idea of an apology. She remained on her guard but he did not hit her again. All the same, he found plenty of mental sticks to beat her with, and seldom let a chance go by.

Maggie got on with the work and said very little. It seemed best to avoid confrontation. She cooked and cleaned, got her grandmother up in the mornings and put her to bed at night, carried trays to her father, washed up, washed and darned his clothes. She chopped firewood into manageable logs and lugged them indoors, skinned rabbits and hares and dealt with any game birds that Ian had tossed into the outside larder.

She had once thought her work in the Air Force tiring, but keeping house for Ian was more draining than anything she had known. She was grateful for one thing. She had no time to look back – no time for anything but getting through each day. If she had a moment to spare, she spent it with her grandmother, reading aloud, playing cards, and regaling her with tales about her life in America.

It was a measure of her isolation that she looked forward to a weekly visit from a grocer's van from the town. The driver was an ex-soldier with a ready tongue and a liking for gossip. Mrs Dunlop enjoyed his chatter too, and would put the kettle on when she heard the merry jingle of his bell – until one day Ian joined Maggie at the van door and started tossing her purchases out of the basket.

'A shilling for that totty bag of oatmeal? You never gave that! I can get oats and flour in the market, and far cheaper. And what's this? I never touch jam, as you well know.'

'Dad, please! Gran likes something sweet on her bread. The doctor says it's good for her.'

'Then buy sugar, and make jam at home. Shop jam is rubbish – a sheer waste of money.'

'All right. So where I would get fresh fruit in April?'

But he had turned out her second basket. 'You'll surely never be buying toilet paper? What is wrong with the *Daily Record*? Are you too niffy-naffy to use it these days, or too lazy to cut it up? That'll be it, no doubt.'

Bert laughed when he found Maggie threading squares of news-paper on a length of string. She laughed with him, for he was home for Easter and his company was a refreshing change, and she laughed again when he gave her a packet of Bronco for Easter.

But she hated her father. He had been in his glory that day, tormenting her, carping and penny pinching – an orgy of his favourite pastimes. She stamped off raging through the rain to collect the milk. Ian had been looking like death all the week, and she knew he was in pain. But that afternoon, Maggie felt that a bit of suffering was just what he deserved.

From then on she walked to the manse on Thursdays and did her shopping from the van anyway. It was a small thing, but it gave her pleasure to outwit him.

Mr and Mrs Fraser were worried about Maggie but could do little to help. The minister had seen her bruised face and her swollen knuckles. She told him airily that she had tripped and fallen.

'So I pretended to believe her. What else could I do?'

'Nothing, unless she asks for help.'

'I don't see her doing that.'

Mrs Fraser asked curiously, 'What did Mrs Dunlop say about Maggie's bruises?'

The minister shook his shaggy head. 'Never a word. You know her way.'

Maggie would have been astonished to learn that they felt helpless. Without their friendship during that long winter, she could never have stuck it out. Just to see them from time to time was a tonic to her spirits. And Cook came sometimes, and would sit drinking tea and gossiping with the old lady. This left Maggie free to go out. She got the vegetable patch dug over, and seed potatoes planted.

April was bitterly cold, but despite the weather the first daffodils glowed yellow in the grass. The young hens started laying their half-sized eggs, and the head keeper's strength ebbed. By mid-April he no longer had the strength to walk uphill, and the high ground was taken over by the hill shepherds.

Ian had known for some time that he was dying. He had fainted in a train in the autumn, and landed in hospital. The surgeon had told him the score. He had wanted to operate, but Ian would have none of it.

'I've no time to be ill, doctor. I've a job to do, running the farm with nobbut a boy to help me, helping the shepherds and managing the moor. And I've an old mother to care for. Just give me a line for painkillers, if you would. I'll manage fine.'

So they gave him the prescription he asked for, and some advice and warnings that he did not heed. They also gave him a letter for Dr Mac, which Ian read and put onto the fire.

He went on with his work, and told nobody about his illness. He had always believed that trouble was best dealt with alone, and he felt no differently now.

But it was growing daily more difficult. The painkillers were not working any more, and whisky made him feel ill. As for taking them both together, he was wary of that after the other time. He had come to his senses in the small hours, with a throbbing head and no clear recollection of what had happened, but the broken china in the front room and Maggie's bruises told an unwelcome tale next morning. She had ignored his lapse and the bruises had faded, but his sense of shame lingered. Now and again he was forced to acknowledge a feeling of pride in his daughter.

The pains were worst at night. This monstrous thing that was gnawing and growing inside him gave him no peace. And when he woke to physical pain in the small hours, there was no escape from the old torments. They crowded into his mind like jackals to a kill. He would not be able to hold out much longer. The Perth doctor had warned him. 'When these don't work any more, Mr Dunlop, we can give you morphine.' Morphine, Ian knew, would be the beginning of the end.

'When that happens, I'll give you leave to cut me up,' he told the doctor with a grim smile.

He would have to tell someone soon. He had always sworn that he would never give in, never admit to pain and beg for help. Not yet, he told himself, as visions of the indignities of illness came to dismay him. His mind sheered away. He would manage. Another notion came, only to be put firmly away. Sick people were visited by irrational thoughts, he told himself. The thought came again, this time more like a yearning. He wanted to confide in Maggie.

It was a long time since he had regarded his daughter as a mocking shadow of his lost wife. Somewhere between her homecoming and the present time, the illusion had faded. There was nothing shadowy about Maggie. She was herself, determined, unique – a young woman with strength and courage and a steadfastness about her which he had been far too late in seeing. He saw it now. It would have been good to have Maggie to lean on.

But those wistful thoughts were for the night time. And when Mr Fraser showed him Bert's treasure trove, he felt utterly betrayed by both his mother and his daughter. Alarm made him feel stronger and angrier than he had been for months.

'Come and see what's here, Ian.' The minister uncovered a tray containing Bert's finds – with the engraved lid of Maggie's jar shining brightly among the shabbier objects.

Ian put his spectacles on his beak of a nose, jutting more prominently now that his face had lost flesh. He stared. The silence lengthened. He continued to stare.

He looked up. 'What is this, Mr Fraser?'

'I hoped you could tell me.'

'Rubbish best put on the tip, I'd say.'

'Look again. I think you must recognise that jar. Mrs Dunlop says that it was part of a set belonging to your wife, Mary. And she knew the little clock face. Mary took a travelling clock with her when she left.'

He said in a husky voice, 'Mother gets confused.'

'I don't think she was confused,' said the minister quietly. 'I was happy to find your mother so clear in her mind.' He did not add that Mrs Dunlop had closed her wrinkled eyelids tight at the sight of Bert's treasures, as though trying to shut them out. She had seemed ready to faint, but recovered almost at once, demanding to know where they had come from.

Ian Dunlop had no colour left to lose. His face remained grey and still, but unlike Mrs Dunlop he did not ask where these things had been found. He knows, the minister thought. After a further silence, he added, 'Your mother was in better spirits than I have seen her. No doubt having Maggie at home is a comfort.'

'You'd not say that, minister, if you heard her telling the lass off!'

'That's exactly what I mean. She was in her element yesterday, giving orders and scolding. The tea wasn't right, and Maggie should have·used the best spoons. Later she sent her upstairs to fetch something. Your Mary left other things behind. Maggie has Mary's

405

ring, now, and a hairbrush that matches that lid. You will remember both, I feel sure.'

Ian said tersely, 'Mother never told me.'

'Perhaps she did not want to upset you. You don't like her speaking of Mary.'

'True enough. And I'll thank you not to speak of her either, minister.'

'It's sometimes better to speak. Troubles fester in the dark. You've been in trouble for a long time, have you not?'

Ian got to his feet, his face livid. 'I'm not staying to listen to this. I'll tell you one thing. Maggie knows nothing of her mother except that she is dead. And Mary is dead to me, and has been ever since she went off. If that cursed bairn had never been born, none of it would have happened.'

'That cursed bairn, as you call her,' said Mr Fraser drily, 'gave up a promising career in the Air Force to come home. It's time you came out of the past, Ian. It's well over twenty years since Mary went away.'

'Do you think I don't know it? I live with it night and day.'

The minister sighed after the head keeper had gone, and thought how ill and wretched he looked. Even in the past week, he seemed to have shrunk. His clothes hung on him, and the skin under his grizzled beard was the colour of putty and thin to emaciation. He had seen other men look like that, and wondered how long he would hold out in his solitary martyrdom.

Ian drove home with rage-engendered speed, cursing and burning with anger and hurt. His mother had gone behind his back, betrayed him. It was as if the bottom had fallen out of his world. The old woman was getting past it, unable to keep things to herself. He hurled himself out of the car, leaving his dogs inside. They would have to wait for their dinners this night.

A spasm of pain seized him, and it was several moments before he could straighten up and draw breath enough to move. Well, pain or no pain, he would have it out with them. He flung open the kitchen door, and stopped on the threshold.

'Where's Maggie?'

'Gone to fetch the milk, son. She'll not be long.'

He flung his hat and stick on the table, and stood glaring down at her. 'Mother! You might have warned me before you took the minister into your confidence.'

She did not pretend to misunderstand him. She said, 'Ian, if I had known where they were found, I'd never have said they were Mary's. But how was I to know?'

'What did you tell him?'

'Nothing! Nothing that mattered, son.'

'You're lying! You swore on the Good Book that you would never say a word. And the next thing, out it all comes. And what about giving Mary's ring to that troublemaking bitch? You'd no right, as you well know – and to have gone behind my back like that . . .'

'Will you stop your bellowing, son. I'll explain.'

'You'll explain nothing. Tell me what you said to Mr Fraser. Tell me, you daft old woman. I need to know.'

She stood there, a little bent, backed against the stove and shaking her head. Beside himself between mounting pain and frustration, he leaned forward and slapped her cheek. 'Come on, Mother! Let's have it.' His mother's knees buckled under her.

Maggie heard the bellowing voice and the smack of flesh on flesh. She hurried in to find her grandmother on the floor – a black-clad rag doll propped against the stove, both hands over her face. Ian was bending over her.

Maggie dumped the milk can on the table with a deliberately loud clank.

'What's all the shouting, Dad? I could hear you a mile off.' She pushed past him, and knelt beside the old woman, gently parting the trembling hands. There was a reddening mark on the soft, wrinkled skin of her cheek.

Maggie got to her feet and faced her father, so angry that she never thought of what he might do. He had moved over by the dresser, his head bent, with clenched hands pressed against his too large waistcoat. He was breathing fast, gasping as though he had been running.

'You hit her, Dad! Shame on you!'

He raised his head, and said hoarsely, almost in a whisper, 'She brought it on herself. She went behind my back . . .'

'One of these days,' said Maggie contemptuously, 'you will kill someone in one of your rages. It's just as well I came in when I did.'

She saw his colour rise as he started towards her, but she seized the kitchen poker in one hand and the tongs in the other, saying fiercely, 'Stay where you are! I've had just as much as I can take from you, Dad, and you'll listen to me.'

He stood still, and said, 'Calm yourself, lassie. I can explain.'

'Don't bother! Get out of the house, and leave me to deal with Gran. I warn you! They taught us self-defence in the Air Force. Come one step closer and I'll hit you where it hurts most.'

To her astonished indignation, he chuckled. 'Ay, and I believe you would, lass!' He looked past her to his mother, who was watching him dazedly. He hesitated. 'Will she do? Should I fetch Dr Mac?'

'Come back in half an hour and I'll tell you.'

'I'll be in the yard if you need me,' he said, and went out.

Spring came late that year, with squalls of rain and battering April showers. Bert came to say goodbye to Maggie before he went back to

407

school. He bounced into the kitchen, and found her on her knees washing the linoleum.

'Back to prison today,' he said cheerfully, squatting down beside her and giving her a quick hug.

'Prison, indeed! You know you love it there,' she said as she got to her feet. She did not tell him how things were in her own self-inflicted prison – or of her latest quandary. She would have to work it out for herself, but with Gran still keeping to her bed there was little time to think.

'This term will be my last. As soon as I leave I shall join the army.'

'The war may be over by then. They may not need you,' said Maggie practically.

'They'll need the army to keep the Germans in order. Maggie . . .' Bert's bony face was suddenly sober. 'Maggie, did you see the newsreel about the concentration camp at Belsen? I went with the Frasers, and they showed it.'

'Mr Fraser's *Picture Post* was more than enough for me,' said Maggie with an inward shiver. She took the bucket outside to pour water down a drain. Nobody who had seen the photographs could fail to be haunted – men, women and even children with faces like living skulls, the piled up bodies. She came back into the kitchen. 'And some of us thought we had a hard time during the war! It made me think we had very little to grumble about.'

David Vorst was one of those present on Luneberg Heath when the German generals came to Field Marshal Montgomery's headquarters. After much coming and going, they signed the unconditional surrender of the German forces in the British sector. It was a grim little ceremony.

There would doubtless be celebrations later, but David felt only thankful that this would mean an end to the killing. He had recently visited the death camp at Bergen-Belsen, looking for some trace or news of Michel Steiner.

On his way through London he went to see Odette.

She knew where he had been. The sight of his face was enough to tell her that he had nothing good to tell. She drew him into the sitting room of her tiny flat, and turned to face him. 'So? Tell me, David?'

He noted the dark shadows under her eyes and her lined and ravaged face. He spoke with reluctance. 'It is not what you want to hear.'

'Tell me anyway.'

'Michel was there at Belsen, Odette.'

She said on an indrawn breath, 'Was?'

He went on, his face grim but his voice without expression. 'Yes. I took your photograph with me, and showed it around. There was a Frenchman in hospital who recognised it, and even knew his name. They had been together in Auschwitz, and were brought later to

Belsen. Michel had been good to him, the Frenchman told me.'

She did not speak. Her eyes were fastened with painful intensity upon his face.

David went on, because there was no help for it. 'Michel's friend was in a fever, and weak. But one thing he said several times. In the last days, the camp guards had rounded up the stronger prisoners and forced them to carry the dead bodies out of sight. He said that Michel had been part of that working party.'

David had seen sweating, dishevelled SS guards doing the same grisly work at gunpoint, watched by a jeering crowd of former inmates. He pushed the memory aside and said bleakly, 'The others came back, but Michel did not.'

She bowed her head.

'That man was pretty confused, Odette. He said once that the guards had fired on the prisoners for going near the wire, and that others had collapsed out of weakness and lay where they fell. I went back next day to see if he remembered anything else, but he had died in the night . . .' His voice trailed away.

She looked at him, dry-eyed. 'If Michel is dead, at least I shall not have to tell him about Josef and Marie. That is what I fear most, to have to kill him all over again with that. He would be better dead.'

Again he could think of nothing to say. He took her undamaged hand, and held it. She had spoken before of this dread of telling her husband that the children had been lost at sea.

After a moment, she withdrew her hand. She said in a calmer tone, 'I read in the paper that before the British came, the guards drove off and left the gates open.'

He nodded. She would, of course, have read every horrific report and seen the pictures that had appalled the world. He wondered, not for the first time, at her extraordinary composure – and still could think of nothing to say.

He watched her walk to the window. She wore a fine leather glove over her mutilated hand, and had trained herself to manage with the other. This was not the moment to tell her about the groups of tattered scarecrows that he had encountered on the roads in Germany. Not all of them had been in the Nazi death camps. Others had been made homeless by the relentless Allied bombing. Hundreds more had been foreign workers, brought into Germany to work in the factories of the Ruhr, and thousand upon thousand of ordinary German people had trekked west to escape the advancing Russians. A million or more homeless persons were on the move in war-ravaged Germany, seeking lost relatives, trying to get back to where they belonged, scavenging for food, stealing, crowding onto goods trains when there were any running.

There had grown in David, more than ever in the past difficult months, a fuller understanding of the dehumanising effects of total war, a chain reaction of hatred and despair. They were planning bonfires and street parties in Britain to celebrate the end of the war. Everyone would be talking of peace and prosperity, but true peace, he feared, would be a long time in coming for many.

When Odette eventually spoke, her voice was stronger, almost brisk. Turning from the window, she said, 'I shall go to the Mas. If Michel is still alive, it is to Normandy that he will go.'

One sunny morning in May, on the day which had been Antonia's birthday, Nanny took Miles and Jamie to put bunches of tulips and narcissi on their mother's grave. Abby refused to join them. She found it hateful to think of Mum lying under a slab in the churchyard. They had buried the poor little baby with her, and sometimes you would think that Nanny minded more about that baby dying than the rest. If only Mum had not been having David's baby, she would be alive still, and Christmas would not have been so wretched, with David angry with her, and Miles crying every night, and the other grown-ups trying to be jolly to make up.

Abby still did not know why asking about Maggie had made David so cross. She had only said it would be good if Maggie could come and look after them.

He had turned on her, and said, 'Maggie isn't your slave. She wants to go to India, so do her a favour and don't bother her with what *you* want.'

True, he had said he was sorry and had been kind when he found her crying in the dustsheeted ballroom – she went there sometimes to get away. He had mopped up her tears, and said in his deep, tired voice that paying someone's wages didn't mean that you owned them. 'We all took Maggie too much for granted. I did myself. This time we must think of her, and let her get away.'

Abby had asked what made him so sure that Maggie wanted that, but he just said that he did know it. He did not seem to want to discuss Maggie, or even to see her. It was a pity. In America they had always got on so well.

Abby sighed. David was coming to Dulcimer soon. He was going to take them to London.

David turned up in the middle of a street party in Dulcimer village, and afterwards drove Abby and her brothers to London. At the Vorst they left the car in the underground garage, which had only recently been reinstated after serving as an air raid shelter for most of the war. In the hotel lobby, Abby was surprised to see her Uncle Dart emerging from some revolving doors.

'So you made it? Good,' said David, who had been expecting his

410

cousin. 'I didn't tell them you might come, in case there was a last minute hitch. I know what hospitals can be like.'

'No hitches,' said Dart, releasing Abby after hugging her tight with his only serviceable arm. The other was in a sling, and they had done their best to immobilise his shoulder with a lot of strapping. Abby had not expected to see him at all, so it was a lovely surprise. He had been in hospital for ages having his shoulder put together.

The street doors revolved again, and a tall thin boy appeared with some luggage, which he put down as David came to greet him. Abby looked at this newcomer, and wondered why he looked familiar. Suddenly he turned his head and grinned at her.

The grin gave him away. It was Bert, who always turned from an ugly boy into a wicked gnome when something amused him. Bert Higgins, the Stepney boy whom she used to like so much. He had changed, of course, and had grown tall and lanky with hands that looked too big for his skinny wrists. Nanny had once told Abby that Bert had been sent to live at Glen Cary after his family were killed in the London Blitz.

'Hello, Westy,' he said in his deep, young man's voice.

'Bert.' Abby smiled back at him, suddenly shy and very conscious of the braces on her teeth. But before either of them could think what to say next, David declared that they had better get going if they didn't want to miss all the fun on the river.

Dart had already said that he hated public jollifications, and preferred to do his own private celebrating in the Vorst bar. Bailing himself out of hospital and going to London to meet Bert had left him feeling extraordinarily limp, and he wished he had never telephoned Bert's housemaster in Perthshire. It had been an act born of a sudden impulse, and as he now believed, an act of folly. He had felt then that the London boy ought to be invited to share in his native city's victory celebrations. And he thought Abby would like to see Bert again. But now all he wanted, most urgently, was for David to take the crowd of young people away, so that he could swallow some painkillers and lie down.

David directed a thoughtful glance at him, and promptly took Jamie by the hand and told the others to follow. They went out into the street and mingled with many more excited, elated people who were streaming towards the Embankment to watch the victory procession of boats.

They saw Winston Churchill's car go by, the Prime Minister sitting in the back with a hand upraised in one of his well know V for Victory signs. Later, swept along by the jostling mob, they landed up in front of Buckingham Palace, and climbed the steps below a statue of Queen Victoria. David lifted Jamie onto his shoulders to give him a better view, and Bert and a friendly stranger boosted Miles and

411

Abby onto a ledge. Presently, Bert climbed up after them, and stood with an arm round Abby's shoulders to keep himself from toppling off.

Everyone chanted and laughed and sang, and at long last the royal family came out. Five tiny figures on a distant balcony could be seen: King George, Queen Elizabeth and the two princesses and the Prime Minister, all of them waving to the shouting, cheering and rejoicing people, a great sea of faces that stretched as far as the eye could see.

Dart had gone to bed by the time they got back to the hotel, but the rest of them dined late in the Vorst restaurant, with candles on the table and waiters hovering. Bert sat between David and Abby, and since they had got over their shyness, they talked of all manner of things, ending up reminiscing about Wat who had been Abby's dog before she went to America. Bert told her how he had trained Wat to do tricks, and how the dog used to entertain the people in the shelter while the bombing was going on. Bert was planning to enlist in August. Jamie, very tired by now, fell asleep into his bowl of ice cream and David had to wipe his face before finally carrying him to bed.

Next morning they went their separate ways; Bert by train to Scotland and Dart back to his hospital, sleeping most of the way in his taxi and relieved that the excursion was safely over. The surgeons had not wanted him to go, for they were planning to do yet another operation on his shoulder very soon. Abby's brothers were taken to Sussex by a secretary from the hotel, and David would put Abby on her school train later in the morning.

Abby was hugging a secret. Before they said goodnight, Bert had asked her to write to him at school. Taking care to copy his offhand manner, she conceded that she might find time to write, but not unless he wrote to her first. On these terms they had exchanged addresses.

Abby had occasionally envied girls who were able to boast about the boys they knew, dashing downstairs when the post came, in hopes of finding a letter. Now she would have a letter from Bert to look out for.

David presently took her to her school train, looking very distinguished in his uniform, and a senior girl asked who the tall Air Force officer was. Abby felt proud of him.

But even though he had been super all weekend, and had given them a good time, she was careful not to remind him of Maggie. He could change all too quickly into a daunting stranger, and she did not want to risk that a second time.

Things had changed between Maggie and her father since the day he lost his temper and slapped his mother. Still silent and morose, he suddenly elected to eat in the kitchen. A week or so later, she was clearing away the breakfast dishes when at long last he emerged from behind his wall of reserve.

'I'm on my way out, Maggie,' he said suddenly.

She paused, and turned to stare at him.

'That's right,' he said, answering her unspoken question. 'You heard what I said. It's the cancer, and there's nowt they can do. But that's between you and me. No bleating to the doctor, mind.'

'Dad, you'll need help.'

'I'm not going near any hospital. I'd rather shoot myself.'

Maggie looked at him, and said in what she hoped was a confident tone, 'You'll never do that. You have too much courage. And too much consideration for Gran, I should hope.'

After a pause, he said, 'Maggie. You'll look after your grandmother?'

She looked at him. 'Did you think I would not?'

He looked at her, and there was a spark of something that might have been admiration in his sunken eyes. 'I counted on you keeping her safe. That's why I let you come. I never wanted you – could never bear the sight of you from a child. If it hadn't been for Mother I'd have told you to stay away.'

'Thanks, Dad,' she said drily. She was inwardly amazed that he should talk to her so frankly about dying. She stacked the plates and said with outward composure, 'Tell me if you change your mind about asking Dr Mac for help, won't you? If that's all for now, I'll take Gran her breakfast.'

'Ay, do that,' he said. 'But when you've seen to Mother, there's more I want to say.'

'I've the outside work to see to.'

'Do as I tell you, Maggie. The work can wait.'

When she came back into the kitchen, he was standing, breathing in a quick shallow way that told her that he was dealing with another bout of pain. He put an arm round her shoulder and drew her close.

He smelled of tweed and sweat and illness. His bearded face was wet with sweat, but his hands when they trailed a path down her face were cold. He cupped her chin for a moment, and all at once his fingers were round her throat, caressing her skin. Her flesh crawled, but she forced herself to stand still.

'Ay, my lass,' he said in a voice that was hardly more than a grating whisper. 'Your neck wouldn't break so easy, I'm thinking. You said I would do murder some day, Maggie. Did you know, when they found those things of hers, that I'd killed your mother?'

Oddly enough, she felt as if she had known all along. She managed to say, 'I wondered, Dad.'

'God forgive me,' said Ian Dunlop. 'Mary was but a dainty wee thing, and I broke her neck after she kissed that cousin of hers goodbye. I called her a whore and shook her, and before I knew it she was gone . . .'

413

*   *   *

Once the dam of his long reticence had broken, there was no stopping him. Maggie sat stunned and silent, while her father's story poured out like pulsing blood from a wound. The guilty secret had burned in his brain for over twenty years, and he recited it like some terrible catechism.

He had cradled Mary in his arms, weeping and calling her name. Only after it grew dark did the reality dawn. She was dead and no amount of calling and praying could bring her back. And he was a murderer, and would hang for his crime if they knew.

He needed a scapegoat, and the cousin who had stood sponsor for the baby was the obvious choice. Jack was emigrating to America. He devised a story of how Jack and Mary had run away together, and told it to his mother and the minister. Other than that, the rest of the world and his sons were told that Mary was dead.

Grief-crazed, he had buried Mary and her belongings in the peat hags of Jock's Crag. He had thought himself safe. But when the German bomber crashed on Mary's burial place, he had regarded it as a judgement from on high.

He himself had started the whisper about unexploded bombs, and like all rumours it had taken on a life of its own. Only later did he see the trap that he had made for himself. They would send bomb-disposal men to comb the peat hags one day, and they must not find her. He went to retrieve Mary's bones and bury them where no one would find them. But dig and probe though he did, he had found no trace of her.

Maggie found the minister picking raspberries in the manse garden. After only a little hesitation, she said, 'Mr Fraser, if I told you something in confidence, and it was something ... something unlawful, would you keep it to yourself?'

'I wouldn't be much good at my job if I could not.' He looked over the top of the raspberry canes, and considered her pale face and shadowed eyes. 'Has your father been talking?'

Her eyes widened. She nodded wordlessly.

'I have been praying that he would. He has needed to tell someone for a long time. Your mother never left the glen, I think?'

'So you knew?' She gave a great sigh, as if laying down a load. The minister led her to a wooden bench at the end of the garden, and in a little while she had told him all of it.

She looked at him sombrely. 'Mr Fraser, what am I to do? He wants me to go up there and find her, before they come looking for bombs, now that the war's over.'

He said sternly, 'I trust you said you wouldn't.'

She shook her head, unable to explain why she could not refuse Ian's request. 'I said that I would see what could be done. I thought,'

414

she added, eyeing Mr Fraser warily, 'that Bert might tell me where to look.'

'He would revel in it,' said the minister with a grim smile. 'So let me implore you, Maggie, not to tell him.' He saw she was about to protest. 'Now, Maggie. Bert is no more the person to deal with this than you are. Leave it to me. I'll work something out.'

To Bob McGill and the doctor, he said bitterly, 'What a man! For years he treated her like an unwanted dog. But to ask the child to dig up her mother's bones, that's worse than anything.'

The doctor, apparently asleep with a pipe between his teeth, said indistinctly, 'Well, Angus. I assume that we have been summoned here for a purpose.'

'We'll have to try to find her, of course. Bob says he'll help.'

'All very fine. What will you do when you *have* found her?'

There was a silence, and Bob McGill said seriously, 'Have you thought, minister? There may be nothing left to find. There was a grand explosion when the German plane blew up, remember?'

'I remember well,' said the minister wearily. 'But we cannot be sure unless we look.'

So they looked. They dug up the bones of small animals, the skeleton of a deer, shards of metal, but nothing at all that resembled human bones.

Mrs Fraser, who had disapproved of the whole business, implored them to call a halt. 'You'll kill yourself at this rate, Angus.'

'Bob thinks we should have one more try, my dear.'

'Bob's another silly old fool. Well, if you must go again, take Bert with you. He knows the place and could do the heavy digging.'

'I cannot involve the boy in this.'

'If Bert is old enough to join the army, he's no longer a boy. Let him help.'

'It would be asking him to break the law.'

'There's no law against digging.'

'True, but if we find Mary's bones and try to move them . . .'

'Tell Bert what you're looking for, Angus. Let him decide for himself.'

The minister sighed. 'What time did you say he's arriving?'

Bert had come to Glen Cary to say goodbye to the Frasers and Maggie. He had expected to be bored. Maggie, he knew, was tied to her invalids in the cottage, and much as he loved the Frasers, there would be little for him to do.

But Bert was not bored. He went with the minister and Bob McGill to the high moor and was able to tell them that they had been digging in quite the wrong place. He led them to where he had found his

415

treasure. Between the rearing, rusted plane wing and the precipice he led them to two tall rocks and parted the heather to show them the deep funnel which went down between them. The older men followed Bert down this crevice. On a rock floor, ten feet below the plateau, they saw the mouth of a cave. Here Bert had found his treasure. Here, if anywhere, Mary Dunlop's bones must lie buried.

It was slow work, chopping away the peat at the back of the cave. Bob took charge. They probed the hard-packed peat before slicing it out in sections, and at last their patience was rewarded.

Bert did not think he would ever forget the sight of old Bob's gnarled fingers as they stroked the last crumbling peat aside. The unmistakable shape of a human skull was laid bare in the yellow glow of the lanterns.

'Here she is, Mr Fraser. What now?'

'She's safe enough here for the moment, God bless her,' said the minister. 'Put the peat back, Bob, and then we'd best be going.'

Mary Dunlop had lain undisturbed for years, pressed far down into the peat, and guarded from above by the base of the German aircraft wing.

Mrs Dunlop died in her sleep at the end of July. It was ironic that Ian, who had been given three weeks to live in May, still lingered on.

'Come away in, Maggie,' Cook said when Maggie came knocking at the back door of the manse after the funeral. She added, in what Maggie thought of as her 'illness and death' voice, 'You gave Mrs Dunlop a lovely send-off, dearie. She would have liked it fine. Such a crowd of folks that came to the house after!'

'It was good of you to help with the tea, Cook.'

'What news of your dad?'

'He's keeping his bed. He's like that. Up one day and down the next.'

'What a mercy you found him and they got him to hospital in time!'

Maggie smiled at Cook. People kept saying that it had been a mercy. She could not agree. She had found him lying unconscious by the river bank, but he had regained consciousness and begged her to leave him be.

But it had been too late. The ambulance had arrived within minutes.

'Once you had found him, you had no choice,' the minister assured her. But Maggie still wished that her father had died that night. He truly wanted to die, and kept on saying so. But at least she had been allowed to bring him home.

She gave herself a mental shake. If only something cheerful would happen! Just one ray of light among the gloom.

The minister watched her. She had lost weight. Her eyes were enormous and dark-circled. She needed a break, of course, but while Ian was still living and clinging to her, she was unlikely to get one.

Then he remembered why she had come to see him, and added, 'You wanted to see the register of your baptism? Well, come along.'

Maggie had long ago hoped to meet her mother in America. But lately, having learned that Mary had not gone away at all, she had started to wonder about the godfather who had been falsely accused of eloping with her.

The minister had marked the leatherbound register at the right page. Maggie looked down at it, and stared and stared.

In January 1923, after her baptism, her godfather had signed the register with his full name – John Geoffrey James. When signing for letters or parcels at Maple Valley House, Mr James had always used his initials – J.G.J.

She had many times thought of Mr James as a substitute father. He had been so unfailingly kind, had taught her to drive, had supported her and given her almost her first taste of being loved and valued. But a godfather, and a kinsman to her mother? He had never told her that. It was unbelievable, but the minister assured her that Jack James was indeed the man.

That night Maggie wrote Mr James a letter. Even if others had chosen to put her out of their minds, Mr James would never do so. The letter took her half the night to write, but weary though she was, she did not grudge the effort. Mr James was her loving godfather, her good friend and her longed-for ray of light.

Odette Steiner, too, had reached low ebb. All summer long she had clung to her preposterous belief that Michel was alive somewhere and would come to the Mas. In her imagination, she saw him walking up the path from the farm, and she would clasp both hands together above her head and wave to him, as she had done so often in the happy days before the war.

But the summer was nearly over, and he had not come. Her belief was beginning to fade like an old watercolour exposed to sunlight. Soon there would be nothing left, and what then?

Dart, convalescing after months in hospital, came to stay with her in late August. He told her bluntly that she ought to move to Paris, or perhaps to London, where she had friends. It was not good for anyone to live alone in this primitive shack, with nobody but the dour old couple at the farm for neighbours, and the nearest town five miles away.

'You'll mope to death here in the winter,' he told her. 'Why not come to Glen Cary with me in September? It will be a change of scene for you, and company for me. I mean to take Antonia's children with me.'

She shook her head. 'Dart, I must stay here, at least a little while longer.'

He looked at her. This was the first time he had heard her express even the smallest doubt. 'Send me a telegram if you change your mind,' he said, and left it at that.

Next day he scored a minor triumph by persuading Odette to let him give her lunch in the town before he boarded his train. She usually refused to leave the Mas for more than the short time it took to drop her visitors at the station and rush back.

It was late before she turned off the high hedged road onto the farm track. She and Michel had always parked their ancient Renault in the farmyard. The Mas lay high on a clifftop beyond the farm, the only approach being a narrow stone track. In pre-war days they had chosen to have it that way, primitive, even without a telephone, though the chimneys drew well, and the plumbing worked. The Mas had been their escape from the pressures and luxury of the Paris Vorst, and since coming back, Odette had neither the heart nor the will to make changes.

She drove into the yard, saw a dark blue saloon car parked there, and was tempted to drive away again. She knew that vehicle. It belonged to the new manager of the Paris house, a kindly young man who had been trying to persuade her to give up her irrational vigil and move back to Paris. But she was in no mood for visitors – especially not Pierre.

She sighed. He would be waiting for her with more solicitude and well-meant advice. She would have to make him welcome. He had done so much to help her in her fruitless search for news or some trace of Michel. It would be churlish to tell him to go away.

She kicked off her tidy shoes and put them in the car. Then she slipped bare feet into an old pair of espadrilles, and set off up the stony path.

She never knew what made her look up. The Mas was a low, stone built building, crouching on the brow of the hill, with shoreside windows facing over the stony beach and the sea. A figure came round the side of the building, and paused there, outlined against the sky. Too far away to see clearly, she narrowed her eyes and wondered who it was. A man, certainly, but not Pierre. Even so far away, she could see that this one was tall and thin, a little bent. Then who? As she stared at him, the man started to move down the track towards her. Then he paused, raised both arms and waved with hands that were clasped together.

She stood rooted, her handbag in her one functional hand. The man waved again in just the same way. Letting the handbag fall, Odette returned the salute. Then gasping out Michel's name, she began to run.

Chapter 29

James got back from Seagrass Island earlier than anyone at Maple Valley had expected. Later the same day, David brought his parents back in the company plane. 'Why didn't they stay the full week?' asked May Sandridge. 'What went wrong?'

James took a moment to think about it. 'Possibly Mrs Vorst found it quiet without any kids. With Miss Tina out west with Kim and the boys, it was a mite peaceful even for me.'

'And to think how we used to long for a nice orderly life!' said Mrs Sandridge. She fell silent. She had been getting the house back to normal all summer. The red drawing room was once more restored to its former elegance, and the decorators had been busy in other parts of the house. She had even managed to take her mother away for a proper vacation, but had been feeling strangely flat since coming home.

It did not make sense. Like everyone else she was deeply thankful that the war with the Japanese was over, and glad for the young men and women who had already started to arrive home. The second chauffeur's brother had returned only a few weeks back, but Jason was worried about him. The young man wanted to do nothing but lie in bed, or sit by himself in the garden. David, who had also been in the Far East recently suggested acidly that they should quit fussing and leave him alone.

Mrs Sandridge said with a frown, 'How is David?'

James was beginning to glance through his mail, but he looked up and said without enthusiasm, 'As usual he says he's fine, just fine.'

'I know what he *says*,' she retorted.

James was an American citizen and proud of it, but he had never thrown off his native English need for an occasional long hot soak in a bathtub. Showers were fine when you were in a hurry, but a bath gave you time to think.

He lay back in the steam and thought about David. To anyone but his parents and the few who knew him well, he was his old self again. His foot was badly scarred, but he walked without a limp these days and had played a couple of energetic games of tennis during his stay on Seagrass Island. All the same, there was something missing. David said he was fine, but Chrissie and Cornelius were worried about him. To James, equally concerned, David was like a man at the end of a journey to nowhere.

'Leave him be, dearest,' said Cornelius. 'Dave has always needed to work things out for himself.'

'If only he would stop being so horribly polite and obliging.'

He tried to laugh her out of her worry. 'Chrissie, you're the one who taught him manners.'

'What nonsense! It was you!'

'One thing,' said Cornelius with satisfaction. 'He was all lit up last week about Michel Steiner getting back. I think, like the rest of us, Dave never expected to see him alive again.'

David came in, a letter in his hand. 'Odette was the one who was convinced he was still alive. She would never allow herself to doubt it, and never gave up hope. I thought she was just whistling in the dark, but maybe she really did know.' He tapped the letter with a finger. 'I must go to them, Mother. I'll arrange to fly to France next week. Neither of them can think of leaving the Mas at the moment. And you know how Odette was dreading having to tell him about the children.'

'Poor woman, it must have totally spoiled things for her.'

David smiled at his mother, for he was feeling relieved and happy for his old friends. 'There was no need. Michel already knew – he's known for nearly five years. He and their old Rabbi were together in his first prison camp, and the old man told him.'

'If you plan to go to Europe anyway, why not change your mind about going to London?' suggested Cornelius, who had been impressed when David had been invited to take part in a victory fly-past on what was now to be called Battle of Britain Day. 'You could travel on the same plane as James.'

'Trying to arrange a wet-nurse for me again, Father?'

'I merely thought that James would appreciate your company, you dope. He's taking a month's vacation, and plans to go to Europe.'

'Oh, so I'm to be the nurse this time? I'll think about it.'

'So what is this?' David said next day when he and James were walking down the avenue. 'A subtle ruse to keep an eye on me, or are you really going on vacation? I never heard of you going away for a whole month before.'

'I've got business to see to, and as it's more than twenty years since I've been over there, I want to give myself time to look around. Don't worry. I doubt if I'll have time to keep an eye on you – not unless you plan to visit Glen Cary.'

'I thought your cousins lived in Yorkshire.'

'Sure they do. And I mean to look them up.'

'So why Glen Cary? You can hardly have business there.'

'Unfinished business, you might call it. I had a letter from my goddaughter. She's been having a rough time, and now that her father is dying, she may need a helping hand. Not that she said so. Maggie was never one to complain.'

David stopped in his tracks, and said quietly, 'Say that again.'

James stopped too, and they faced each other.

'What did you just say?' David repeated with barely suppressed urgency. 'This goddaughter. . . .'

James smiled. 'There were reasons why I could not tell her who I was. But I really am her godfather, and now Maggie knows it. And there's the other matter—'

'*Maggie?*'

One look at David's expression, and James drew a careful breath. For some reason this seemed to matter. He said evenly, 'Maggie Dunlop. You remember her?'

'*Remember* her?' David's voice shook, and he uttered a strange little laugh. 'What in hell's name do you think I have been doing these past months?'

'I never asked you, and you never said. What *were* you doing?'

'Looking for Maggie, of course. I've been all over India and Burma and other hellish hot places trying to find her, pulling strings, getting people to look up records, searching for anyone who knew her. But she seemed to have vanished into thin air. I let her go when I was sick and stupid last winter, but I need to see her again. I just have to see her . . .' He turned on James with sudden painful anxiety. 'You're not kidding me, are you? Do you actually know that she's alive?'

'You'd better read her letter,' said James prosaically. 'Come down to my house, and I'll give it to you.'

'Guess what?' said Harriet Ducane when Abby arrived to stay with her schoolfriend in Hampshire. 'Sophy is getting married in October, and I'm to be her bridesmaid. I've got to go to London to get a dress made. I hope you don't mind coming too.'

Abby said she would love to visit London. They were going to stay a night with Harriet's sister. Abby had once seen Sophy Ducane when she had come roaring up the school drive in a Jeep. Sophy had been dressed in her Wren uniform, squashed in between two burly American Marines. The girls had been playing a lackadaisical game of rounders on the front lawn, and they watched round-eyed as Sophy climbed down, pounced on the startled headmistress, kissed her warmly and told her that she had come to take Harriet out to tea. Minutes later, the Jeep roared away, with Harriet, still in her games clothes, waving from a back window.

Abby wondered what Granny Dulcimer would say if she knew about London. She had made enough fuss about her travelling alone to Hampshire, wanting to put her in the charge of the train guard, or sending her personal maid Trumpet with her to make sure she was safe.

'You may think me an old fusspot, darling. I don't like you going all that way alone.'

Luckily Grandpa D intervened. 'Give the girl a chance to stand on her own feet, Effie. She's nearly fifteen and not wholly half-witted. If she gets lost, she can ring us up, can't she?'

So, with multiple admonitions about holding onto her ticket, not speaking to strange men, and to be sure to ring up when she got to Hampshire, they allowed her to go alone.

'Such a hoo-ha,' she complained to Harriet. Harriet assured Abby that her own family were just as bad, and they shook their heads over the folly of old people.

'A day over twenty,' said Harriet, 'and they start going downhill. Even Sophy's gone stuffy since she decided to marry Sebastian. I wanted us to go to the Bag o' Nails or the Four Hundred after the theatre, but she says it's dinner at the Savoy or nothing. Aunt Addie is paying,' she added ingenuously. 'Sophy is saving up for her trousseau.'

Abby had somehow expected the dashing and beautiful Sophy's flat to be like one of the grander rooms at the Vorst. In fact it was like a large underground mouse's nest, with so many things strewn about and spewing out of cupboards and drawers that their diminutive hostess was at first nowhere to be seen. A rustling from a dark hole under the stairs gave them a clue, and Sophy backed out of it, dressed in a torn shirt and dusty bell bottoms. She flung her arms round Harriet with a gasping shriek of pleasure.

'And this is Abby,' said Harriet when the Devenish transports were over. 'She was at school with me in America, too.'

'You came to Bellefield and we walked you back to school!' said Sophy with a friendly grin. 'Maggie's Abby. She made you out to be a cross between Mary in the Secret Garden and one of those tiresome children in Arthur Ransome.' She saw the expression on Abby's freckled face, and added, 'Didn't you know that Maggie had a room here before she went to India?'

Abby had not known it. She wondered if Sophy knew Maggie's address, but Sophy was already telling Harriet about their sleeping arrangements.

'You're both sleeping in Maggie's room, but there's only one bed. You'll have to toss for which of you sleeps on the floor. It's all in a bit of a mess because the removers are coming, and I've got to get everything into boxes.' She looked at her watch, and gave a gasp.

'Damn! I said we'd meet Sebastian at seven. I'm filthy. Make yourselves at home while I have a quick bath.'

A bit of a mess was putting it mildly. It was worse than the sitting room. They stood in the doorway in momentary astonishment. By the looks of it, the room had been used as a depot for broken and unwanted objects for centuries.

'Let's change first and think about clearing a space later,' said Harriet practically. 'Sophy never waits. If we aren't ready by the time she's dressed up, she'll dash off to find Sebastian and leave us behind.'

'When did you say the movers' van was coming?' demanded Lady Adele when she came to collect them next morning.

Abby and Harriet were ready and dressed, but Sophy was still in pyjamas when her tall aunt arrived to take them to Fulham. Adele had discovered a 'little woman' who did dressmaking for next to nothing.

'Tomorrow? Gracious, child! You will never be ready for them at this rate. Hurry up and get dressed, and when we've fixed up your wedding dress, I'll come and give you a hand. You two girls won't mind helping, will you?'

Harriet made a glum face at Abby, for there had been talk of going to the movies. However, they said they didn't mind.

'Where is Sebastian?' demanded Adele, looking about as though Sophy's fiancé might be lurking under one of the heaps of clothes.

Sebastian, it seemed, was on duty at the Admiralty and would not be available.

'Wise man. Starting as he means to go on, no doubt,' said Adele drily. 'But we'll need a strong man or two to help with this lot.'

When Sophy returned from what she described as darkest Fulham, with the problems of wedding garments solved, the flat looked worse than ever. However, at two o'clock two brawny subalterns arrived from Chelsea barracks. Adele said they had come to help.

The young men eyed Adele warily. She had invited them to dine and dance at Quaglinos that evening, but they wished they had not fallen for this bribe. They looked even more apprehensive when they saw the interior of the flat. But Sophy smiled at them and thanked them enthusiastically for coming to her rescue, and by the time they had swigged down a tankard of beer apiece and eaten some cheese sandwiches, they were feeling more cheerful.

Adele took charge, and within hours the flat was transformed. Clothes had been sorted, resident china stacked, kitchen equipment washed and put back in the cupboard. The landlady-aunt's glassware was lined up sparkling on a table, and Sophy's belongings were ready for the removal men.

Adele had been ruthless about keeping them all to the task in hand. All the same, delightful discoveries had been made in the course of the afternoon. Objects turned up that Sophy had not seen for ages. Harriet fell upon a teddy bear with a cry of delight. 'I can take him home, can't I?' She had already annexed a moth-eaten fox fur tippet with a malevolent face, and was wearing it round her neck.

Sophy's school trunk had served as a coffee table. Adele eyed it.

'You could start packing your shoes into that,' she said, but it was found to be full of papers. 'Sophy! Don't you ever open letters or pay your bills?'

'Only letters when they look interesting. And what's the point of opening bills if I'm broke?' Sophy looked at the other accumulation of old magazines, letters and bills on the table, and said, 'Let's chuck this lot out.'

'You can't do that,' said Adele. 'Harriet and Abby can start sorting.'

At six o'clock, she called a halt. The strong men were sent off to change for dinner. Harriet and Abby went off to a newsreel cinema in the King's Road, with instructions to get themselves to Quaglinos by eight. The charlady from upstairs, who had agreed to help, went away saying that it would be easier to clear up after the removal men had been.

'Some more things under here,' said Sophy in a muffled voice. Adele was washing her hands at the kitchen sink. Sophy groped deeper behind a heavy oak chest which the young men had recently pulled from the wall, and came out with both hands full of objects which had slipped down behind it.

She dropped a single glove, letters and magazines and a pair of scissors on the top of the chest. There was a good deal of fluff and dust too. She looked down, and said in an odd voice, 'Oh, Lord!'

Adele came through the door. 'What now?'

'It's a letter addressed to Maggie. She rang at least four times before last Christmas, asking if a letter had come. It must have been here all the time.'

Adele reached for it. It was addressed to Section Officer M. Dunlop. For Adele, there was no mistaking the handwriting on the envelope. She saw in her mind a vivid picture of David Vorst as she had last seen him, and an echo of a voice full of bitterness and pain. 'Maggie wants to get away, and we must let her go . . .'

Sophy was almost in tears with remorse. 'It's been lying there for almost a year. Shall I open it and see what it says? The trouble is, I haven't got her address. She never wrote . . .'

'You had better leave it to me,' said Adele. 'I will see what I can do.'

'How can you do anything, Aunt Addie? We don't know where she is! Maggie never gives much away, but I had a feeling that she was rather desperate about that letter. Truly, I could shoot myself.'

'That wouldn't do your friend Maggie any good,' said Adele bracingly, putting the grubby letter into her handbag. 'Besides being messy and inconsiderate. You'd better get washed and changed for dinner instead.'

There was a subdued bustle in the lobby of the Vorst Hotel when Adele walked in next morning. She felt unusually apprehensive. Her first objective was to find out David Vorst's whereabouts. After that, she would need to play it by ear. She had not forgotten the stinging rebuff he had dealt her last winter.

Some new guests had recently arrived. There were three separate piles of luggage by the porter's cubbyhole, and people were waiting their turn at the front desk. The manager had come out from his office at the back and was talking to a thin man in a dark suit.

They turned to look at her. Adele blinked, and then went forward with her hands held out. 'James! What a bit of luck! How is it that you always turn up when you're needed?'

James smiled, and said that he had only just come in from Northolt. 'You're looking well, ma'am. What can I do for you?'

'You can tell me . . .' Then she stopped. 'Mr Hudson, could we use your office? Just for a few minutes, if you don't mind.'

'You see,' Adele said, when she and James were alone, 'my niece found this yesterday.' She laid the letter on the desk between them. 'It was written by David and posted in November of last year. I need to know where he is, James.'

James picked up the letter and studied it for a brief moment. Then he drew a breath, and said as though to himself, 'So that's why she never answered his letter.'

'Is he still in the Far East, or at home in Maple Valley, or what?' Adele asked, sounding irritable. 'I feel badly about that letter. I've got to tell him, or cable him with the gist of it.'

James smiled at her reassuringly. 'Don't worry, ma'am. He had business at the Air Ministry but he should be here any minute.'

Maggie did not like leaving her father alone in the house. The doctor thought that he would not last out the week. He was very weak and fretting anew, because the bomb disposal people were coming to clean up Jock's Crag.

The minister, coming in, thought that Maggie looked tired to death. He said, 'I'll sit with him for an hour. Go and lie down. You look as if you could do with a sleep.'

She smiled. 'I don't seem to be able to sleep in the day, Mr Fraser. But if you could stay with him, I might get a breath of fresh air outside.'

'Why not take Tom's rod and fish the Lodge pool? The water is perfect after last night's rain.'

Half an hour later she came over the brae with Tom's rod in her hand, and a net slung on her shoulder. She stopped short. Somebody was already fishing the Lodge pool. She felt an irrational sense of disappointment, and glared at the interloper's back.

There was a swirl and a splash. The tip of the rod bent. The scream of the reel came to her ears as the fish tore away, appearing as a brief flash of silver above the rough water downstream.

She realised almost at once that it was Lord Dartmore fishing down there. Everyone in the glen knew that he had been wounded – a shattered shoulder, which had been operated on twice. Maggie was surprised to see him, and more surprised that he was able to wield a fishing rod. She walked down to the water, and later netted the fish for him, because when he needed it, his own net was fifty yards upstream.

His eyes widened as he recognised her. 'It's Maggie, isn't it? Maggie Dunlop? They said you were in India.'

'I meant to go, but my grandmother needed me. So I came home.'

He frowned. 'I'm sorry I couldn't get to her funeral, Maggie. I was in and out of hospital until a few weeks ago . . .' And then, as though following on from this, he added, 'How is your father?'

'Not well, milord. The doctor says he hasn't long. He would like fine to see you, if you could spare the time.'

'Of course I'll come. We're old friends, your father and I.'

She said a little anxiously, 'You'll find him changed. His speech gets a wee bit slurred when he's tiring.'

Dart nodded, finished reeling in his dripping line and reached up for the cast which was flirting in the breeze. Securing it, he said, 'I'll try not to tire him. When shall I come? Not tomorrow. I have to be in Edinburgh all day. How about Friday?'

Maggie agreed to Friday. 'Could you come in the forenoon? Dad is at his best in the mornings.'

'I'll be with you at twelve o'clock. Will that do?'

Maggie agreed to twelve o'clock. She walked with Dart as far as the road, and there they parted.

Ian did not say much when he learned that he was to have a visit from the young laird – but she knew that he was anxious. She, too, had been worrying.

She knelt to tie his shoelaces on Friday morning – he had insisted on getting up and dressed to receive his visitor. Above her head he said suddenly, 'Likely his lordship will say they are needing the house.'

She tied the second lace slowly. Her father was probably right. The cottage went with the job of head keeper, and the factor was rumoured to have engaged Ian's successor.

'I could ask his lordship to give us more time.'

'You'll do no such thing! You'll ...' Ian struggled to get the words out, and as often happened when he was angry or anxious, his throat and lips worked, but no words came.

'All right, Dad,' Maggie said, getting to her feet. 'I won't ask if you don't want me to.'

She did not tell him that she had thought of something better. The caretaker at the Lodge had recently retired, and it seemed to Maggie that the new head keeper and his family could quite well live in the spacious back part of the Lodge. She had made up her mind to suggest it to Dart.

When Bob McGill brought the milk, she begged him to sit in the kitchen while she ran to the Lodge. The old joiner told her placidly to take her time. He was fond of Maggie. He had known her all her life.

Almost running down the road, she wondered with amusement how Dart would manage for two weeks without a housekeeper. He liked his comforts, did Lord Dartmore.

After knocking at the back door and getting no answer, Maggie pushed past an assortment of raincoats and gumboots, and entered the cavernous kitchen. At the same moment, Abby walked in at the other end, wearing a man's sweater over pyjamas and no shoes. She was reading a book and munching on a piece of toast.

'Oh!' The toast dropped to the floor and the book flopped with flailing pages onto a dresser. Abby swallowed a mouthful of toast, and looked guilty, as though caught out or unsure of herself. She stammered, 'M-maggie!'

'Abby!'

They moved together, and kissed awkwardly. Then Maggie held Abby away, and said with a shaken laugh, 'My! You've grown nearly as tall as me. I never thought to see you here of all places!'

'I came with Uncle Dart the day before yesterday, and the boys are arriving tomorrow. Maggie, Uncle Dart said that you weren't in India at all but are living here. I wanted to go down to see you but then I remembered ... I thought you might not feel like seeing me.'

This time, Maggie hugged Abby as though she meant it, and said, 'I'll feel like seeing you any time ...' She broke off, and said in a different tone, 'You're never going to eat that toast, not after it's been on the dirty floor.' Looking down as she spoke, she saw that the floor was indeed dirty.

'It's the last bit of bread. I ate the rest yesterday,' protested Abby, resisting when Maggie tried to wrest the toast out of her hand. When Maggie had thrown it into a bucket full of ashes, she said crossly, 'That was the last crust and I'm starving. There isn't anything else left.'

Maggie stared, then looked around the kitchen. It certainly looked bare.

'Where's your uncle? Is he still in bed?'

'No. In Edinburgh. He said he might stay another night if he met someone he liked. That's why he fixed for a taxi to take us shopping yesterday morning. But Linda said she wanted to go alone. I let her. I suppose I should have known she didn't mean to come back.'

'Linda? Who is this Linda?'

'She's the one who answered Uncle Dart's advert. She's a hairdresser from East Grinstead, really, but she said she loved cooking and wanted to come to Scotland.'

Maggie had been looking round the dismal kitchen. She peered into the larder and found it contained two mousetraps and some empty jam jars. She said incredulously, 'Do you mean to say that this Linda went off and left you all on your own?'

Abby shrugged. 'I didn't mind – at least, only a bit when it was dark. But I think she might have sent the taxi back with some food. I looked in Uncle Dart's room in case he left his telephone number or a bar of chocolate, but all I found was the note Linda left. I opened it and read it. And what do you think she told him, Maggie?'

'Tell me about it when you're dressed and have something warm inside you,' said Maggie. 'I'm taking you home.'

When Dart came into the Dunlops' kitchen at noon, the first person he saw was his niece. Abby's freckled face was flushed, and he thought she looked happier than he had seen her for a while. She had been tiresome and argumentative during the summer holidays, and Lady Dulcimer thought the child was still grieving for Antonia. It had been with some thought of relieving his mother and giving Abby a treat that Dart had brought her to Glen Cary ahead of her brothers.

'It's all right,' Abby said rather defensively. 'Honestly. Maggie asked me to come. She's showing me how to make lentil soup. She's training me up so that I can do the cooking, now that Linda has gone with Duncan.'

'Duncan? She said she went to nurse her sick aunt.'

'I know that's what she wrote.' Abby gave a cackle of laughter. 'Some aunt! This Duncan man rang from a pub in Rosyth the night before last, and Linda was gassing away to him for hours. He sounds dire, Uncle Dart. Linda says that he's got black hair all over his chest.'

Dart said nothing while he digested this information. 'So that explains her urgent yearning for the Highlands. The little—' He broke off as Maggie came in.

She directed an unsmiling look at him and said formally, 'My father is waiting to see you in the front room, my lord. Please go through. You know your way.'

'Won't you join us, Maggie?'

'I'll stay in the kitchen with Abby, thank you,' she replied curtly.

428

'She's been on her own for two whole days. If you had troubled to let her know you weren't coming back, you would have found out. I suppose you were too busy enjoying yourself.'

'Are you speaking to me again, Maggie mine,' said Dart, putting an arm round her shoulders and smiling at her in a way that would once have had her swooning.

She looked at him with only the barest twinkle in her eyes. 'I feel a little less like telling you off, if that's what you mean.'

He laughed. 'Well, that's a weight off my mind.'

'And thank you again for letting my dad stay on, milord.' Maggie was indeed deeply thankful. Dart had seen Dr Mac, and between them it was agreed that Ian Dunlop must on no account be moved, and as Dart had hit on the same happy solution as Maggie, there had been no need for her to tackle him.

Dart held her for a moment longer, and then released her, aware that he was not yet winning. An odd girl, this ex-nursery maid of Antonia's, and hard to read. She had given him a real tongue-lashing on that first evening, but when she heard that her father was not going to be turned out, she had smiled and thanked him with radiant sincerity. For a moment, she had even looked quite pretty.

Her looks had gone off badly since he had seen her last. She was too thin and had the faded look of someone who had been ill. He recalled how Antonia had once felt threatened by Maggie's youthful beauty, and had wanted rid of her. Antonia would have had nothing to worry about now. Antonia. He missed her, particularly when he was at Dulcimer. Her death had been a shock. She had been self-centred and sometimes tiresome, but Antonia had added a spice to life.

However, faded or not, in the eyes of Abby and her brothers this Maggie was perfect. Whenever they could, the children dashed down the road to see her, and stayed there until she sent them home along the lochside. This suited Dart well, for it left him free to do just as he chose – to read by the fire, go fishing, or dine with the minister and enjoy a quiet game of chess.

But Maggie's remote air was starting to annoy him. He decided to do something about it. He had never met a woman yet who was immune to a little judicious flattery. But Maggie seemed to be an exception to this rule. When he smiled at her and asked what spell she used to bewitch his niece and nephews, she smiled back at him, but with a look in her eyes that told him that she knew what he was about. It was not quite a brush-off, but near enough.

Piqued, he called at the cottage unannounced, and next day called again. Relaxed and loving with the children, she was a different person, and he began to see why they liked her. In the Dunlops' cottage, Abby was no longer rebellious, lolling about and saying that she was bored. Maggie kept her too busy to be bored, and although the two of them had arguments, they were like old friends sparring comfortably together.

Maggie sent the three children out to feed the hens and ducks, hunting for the warm eggs in the hay barn, exercising the head keeper's dogs. She sent them into the fields in search of mushrooms, taught them to cook and wash up, to carry in logs and hang out the washing. And they seemed to enjoy these chores, and even learned to keep their voices down out of consideration for the invalid next door. Dart found himself drawn into playing Monopoly and racing demon – with none of them talking above a murmur on account of Ian. He noticed a backgammon board on the kitchen dresser, and challenged Maggie to a game. He would let her win. That ought to please her. To his surprise and slight chagrin, she beat him three times with ease.

He eyed her with reluctant respect.

'Who taught you to play, Maggie?'

'An American officer I once worked for.'

'Not Ben Horowitz, by any chance?'

She nodded, her fingers busy with putting the pieces back in their slots. Her face had gone rather pink. He said, probing, 'Ben beat me too, the only time we played. He came to Dulcimer with David only a week before he was killed. A pity, that.'

There was no doubt about it, the ice maiden was actually blushing and her fingers on the backgammon pieces were not quite steady. Had Ben Horowitz's death something to do with her distant manner to other men? He went on, 'I liked Ben. David had been working with him on some hush-hush job, and they were excited about flying together out of the same American air base. One good thing, Ben was killed instantly, unlike David who was badly mangled on the same day.'

She did not look up, but closed the backgammon box and snapped the catches. She had not uttered a word.

He said quietly, 'Were you in love with him?'

Her eyes came up, wide and startled. She drew an audible breath and said rather stiffly, 'In love . . . with Major Horowitz? Certainly not. I only worked for him for a short while.'

He might have questioned her further but the children came in at that moment. He resolved to explore this avenue later.

Miles shot his first grouse, and the one person he wanted to show it to was Maggie, and Abby grew rosy and more confident with each day that passed. Plain Maggie might be, and politely ignoring his efforts to win her over, but there was something about her. It dawned on him that after her father died, she would make a good caretaker at the Lodge. It would be pleasant to find Maggie waiting there when he came to visit.

Abby had other ideas. She cornered him in his bedroom after breakfast. 'Uncle Dart,' she said seriously. 'Do you think, when David comes, that you could talk to him about Maggie?'

'What about her?'

'It's awkward,' Abby said, frowning. 'David was cross when I wanted her to look after us, and told me to leave her alone. I told Maggie, and she said David was quite right, and that she wouldn't want to stay with us.' She raised her eyes to his face, and said unhappily, 'But I don't believe her. She likes us. I know she does, and she might stay, if only someone could persuade David to let her. I think she's afraid of him. So please will you speak to him, Uncle Dart?'

'Why not talk to him yourself?'

'It would only make him cross again. And anyway, I promised Maggie I wouldn't.' She added, blinking back tears, 'She bit my head off worse than David and made me absolutely swear.'

Dart felt he was missing something, but was at least prepared for Maggie when he next went to the cottage. 'Lord Dartmore,' she said. 'The children say that Mr David is coming soon. Exactly when? Do you know?'

He looked at her. She looked plainer than ever, and he sensed tension under that careful air of calm.

He said vaguely, 'David is flying a Spitfire in the Battle of Britain fly-past. After that, he has things to do in London. He may be here by the twentieth.'

'Thank you. That's all I wanted to know.' She turned and left him.

He poured himself a measure of his favourite malt, and sat musing by the fire until well after midnight. Then he took himself to bed.

He slept dreamlessly and deeply, unaware that a crime was being committed that night on the high moor.

Chapter 30

Having established that Mary Dunlop's bones were safe in the cave, Bob and the minister tried to decide what to do next.

Ian Dunlop had dictated and signed an account of Mary Dunlop's accidental murder. He seemed relieved to be done with it, and had drifted back into sleep within minutes. Before he closed his eyes, however, he looked at the minister and said, 'That's it. Now that you have found my Mary, you'll see to it that we're buried together, won't you?'

Later, Maggie ushered the minister out. She said soberly, 'Thank you for reassuring him. He needs to believe that it can be done, Mr Fraser. Could you wait a bit before you give that paper to the police? Dr Mac thinks he'll be gone within days, and I don't want him harried with questions.'

He agreed to delay it. But he had made discreet inquiries, and what he found out about the law and officialdom had made him feel more and more uneasy. There would need to be a death certificate if Mary was to be buried with her husband. The poor girl had been killed nearly a quarter of a century ago, but even after all that time there would have to be an inquest.

He had promised to hold his hand, but the more he thought of laying Ian's confession before the authorities, the less he wanted to do it. The head keeper would be dead, but once that confession was in official hands, the press would surely get wind of it. A twenty-year-old crime of passion! What a story! And Maggie would bear the brunt of it.

'The newspaper boys will be all over the poor lassie, taking photos, and wanting more pictures of Jock's Crag and that plane wing,' said Bob McGill. 'After the summer she's had, burying Jessie Dunlop and nursing that father of hers . . .' He sighed, and added, 'I mind how he used to beat her sore in the old days. Maggie has suffered enough already. She deserves better.'

'She does indeed,' said the minister soberly.

It was only when the bomb disposal crew were actually in the offing that Mr Fraser came out with his outrageous suggestion. They stared at him. They all wanted to help Maggie, but the minister's

432

proposal shocked them into stunned silence.

Mrs Fraser was the first to speak. 'You're not serious, Angus?'

'It would be a criminal offence,' said Dr Mac judicially. He was smoking his usual smelly pipe and there was ash all over his Fair Isle jumper. 'Speaking for myself, I'm not all that keen to go to jail.'

'That won't happen unless we break the eleventh commandment and get found out,' said the minister tranquilly. He turned his beetling gaze upon Bob, who was joiner and undertaker to the two glens. 'Could you manage your end of it, Bob?'

'Ay, I could. But how would you fetch her down?' Bob had fallen off a roof recently. He pointed glumly to his bandaged knee. 'I'm no use to you with this, and the doctor hasn't enough puff for the hills. You're surely not meaning to go alone, minister?'

'Certainly not,' said Mrs Fraser and the doctor in unison. His wife added urgently, 'Angus, have some sense!'

The minister smiled. 'I shall have two volunteers to help me.' And when they protested against employing outsiders, he added, 'Don't worry. These two feel just as strongly as we do about the need for secrecy. When could you have that coffin ready for us, Bob?'

They were an oddly assorted group of felons. They met briefly before going their several ways – a respected minister of the Church of Scotland, Bob McNeil, Dr Mac – and just landed nearby in an RAF plane, David Vorst and Mr James. They came together for an early breakfast next morning with their mission accomplished, tired but soberly content. Mrs Fraser, an accessory after the fact, was dispensing tea from a large earthenware pot. She had waited up for them all night, and felt light-headed with lack of sleep and relief. It seemed that the most difficult part of their unlawful activities was now over.

Her husband looked exhausted. She was not surprised. It was not every man of seventy who could walk five miles through a blustery night and accomplish an almost vertical climb at the end, not to mention the five miles back to the cellar below the kirk.

They had found Bob waiting beside a large, newly made coffin.

'A work of art, that coffin,' said James, when all that remained of Mary Dunlop had been laid to rest on the silk-lined base, her slender bones wrapped in a sheet, and embedded still in some of the peat that had swaddled her for so long. By the stark light of a single electric bulb, they watched Bob fit the first of two lids carefully over her. He screwed it down, and deftly lined the upper part of the coffin with more silk in readiness for the next and larger occupant. The minister said a short prayer, before leading them up the stone steps and out into the windy churchyard.

The doctor joined them for breakfast. He had been with the head keeper, and he told them that Ian's condition had deteriorated in the night. He was now deeply unconscious, and his daughter was sitting with him, holding his hand.

James and David exchanged glances, and got to their feet.

David was expected at Cranwell for a rehearsal of the Battle of Britain fly-past, and an RAF plane was standing by to get him there on time. James watched the aircraft take off, before returning soberly to Glen Cary.

He went to find his goddaughter Maggie.

The funeral of Ian Dunlop was held on the fifteenth of September, the fifth anniversary of the greatest day in the Battle of Britain, when the tide of the battle had at last turned in Britain's favour. Strangely enough, the bomb disposal squad started work on Jock's Crag on the same day. People told each other how glad the head keeper would have been to know that the high moor would be made safe at last.

Some people were disappointed to learn that no live bombs were found. But nobody was sorry to see the KEEP OUT notices taken down and the barbed wire removed. Even Bert Higgins did not mind when he heard that the Dornier wing had been disposed of. He was no longer much interested, for he was in the middle of his first six weeks of training in the army. To most people, getting rid of those things seemed to confirm that the war was truly over. They had come to the end of an era.

There was a similar feeling about Ian Dunlop's send-off. He had been a giant of a man in his prime, an autocrat, even a bit of a bully. The kirk was full to the doors for his funeral service. The minister gave a short address, and said a prayer for the souls of Ian Dunlop and of his greatly loved wife, Mary, whose untimely death had been an enduring grief to him. Mr Fraser looked down at the coffin, and upon Maggie's posy of garden flowers which was its only adornment. Ian and Mary were together now, he said soberly. He prayed that they would rest in peace, and the congregation joined with him to say 'Amen'.

There was some curiosity about Mary, and one or two mourners resolved to ask about her once the burial was over. But by the time the handsome coffin had been lowered into the grave beside the loch, their thoughts had moved on. Ian Dunlop and his wife were dead, and their troubles and griefs had died with them. Like the war, the dead couple belonged to the unhappy past.

James took Maggie away after the funeral. They stayed for three nights and days in a small, comfortable hotel north of Inverness, and talked and talked. James told Maggie about her mother, and Maggie marvelled at the amazing coincidence of herself and him both going to Maple Valley.

'Not such a coincidence,' James said. He explained how the minister had written a letter to Cornelius Vorst in America at Mary Dunlop's instigation, recommending her cousin to his notice. James had started as a bell-hop in the New York Vorst. 'But I can tell you, Maggie,' he added, 'that when you came to Maple Valley and I found myself cast as the villain who had eloped with your mother, that *did* amaze me.'

'I wish you had told me who you were,' she said.

'How could I? You believed that your mother and I had run away together, which I knew to be a lie. I could not reveal myself as your missing godfather without raising all manner of distressing and totally unanswerable questions.'

'I suppose not,' she conceded. 'I'm happy to know, at least, that my mother did not abandon us.'

He nodded. 'I wanted so badly to tell you that. Mary would never have walked out on her children or her husband, however difficult he could be. She was an exceptionally loving, courageous person. To me she was like a sister, my older sister.'

David rang James every night from Glen Cary, asking after Maggie.

'She looks better,' James told him, 'and is already talking of what she will do next. She thinks she might get a job working with handicapped children. I told her that I wanted to take her back with me to Long Island and she could find a job in the States.'

'What did she say to that?'

'She just smiled and thanked me.' He remembered how she had looked afterwards, and added, 'I don't believe she means to go back to America.'

'Why can't she just say yes or no?'

'If you could see how defeated she looks, David, you wouldn't ask that.'

'I want to see her. It's driving me mad not seeing her. I've been halfway round the world looking for her, and you and that other old guard dog at the manse keep holding me off. I only want to *talk* to Maggie, for Pete's sake. Does she know that I'm here?'

'I'm waiting for the right moment to tell her.'

'Well, get a move on. Abby thinks that Maggie is frightened of me, but she can't be, James. I can understand her being mad at me because she never got a letter. Sometimes I feel like killing that stupid niece of Adele's. But why should she be scared? Let me see her! I'm going totally crazy fooling around with the kids when all I want is Maggie.'

'You've waited a long time, another day won't matter.'

'That's what you think! When are you bringing her back to Glen Cary?'

'Whenever Maggie says she's ready, and wants to go back.'

'You don't seem to care what *I* want. Much more of this hanging about and I'll damn well come and fetch her.'

Maggie, meanwhile, was making a list of the things she needed to do at Glen Cary before she left for good. Lists gave a focus for her thoughts. It was time she went back. She would ask James to take her in the morning, for she would have to be gone before David came. Dart had told her he would arrive on Thursday. The cottage would need to be cleaned and ready for the incoming head keeper. That would be her first chore. After that she would say her farewells and go.

They left the hotel early next morning, and were running through Inverness before she discovered that David was already at Glen Cary. She seized James's arm and implored him to drop her off at the railway station.

He glanced at her, saw the stark panic in her face, and said sternly, 'What's this, Maggie? Don't try to tell me you're scared of David. He's looking forward to seeing you again. He was saying so, only last night.'

'No. Of course I'm not scared. It's because . . .' She broke off, for there was no way of telling anyone, even James, why she could not bear to meet David again, or even hear his voice. Particularly not his voice, she thought miserably. She finished lamely, 'I just don't want to see him. I *mustn't* see him.'

He looked at her without speaking.

'Please, Mr James. You said you wanted to help me. Please help me now. I . . . I'm desperate . . .'

She thought he was about to refuse, but instead he suddenly made up his mind. Within a few minutes he had bought her a first-class ticket from Inverness to Edinburgh. The train was about to depart, so they ran together down the platform to an accompaniment of whistles and doors being slammed.

James stood and watched the train go, then hurried into the nearest telephone kiosk. He was lucky enough to get hold of David right away. He told him what had just happened, and where to look for Maggie on the train.

The express train had gone, and the one that Maggie had boarded in such haste was of the leisurely variety, stopping at every halt and station between Inverness and Edinburgh. There had been no time to reach the first-class carriages near the engine, and the corridor was crowded. Mr James had pretty well bundled her on the train as it began to move. She sat down gasping on her small suitcase. After some minutes she started to weep.

A young man in the carriage behind her offered her his seat when he got off at Aviemore. She sat wedged between two large women with brown paper parcels, wishing that she had brought a book so

436

that she could pretend to read it. One of the women patted her hand and asked her if she was all right. Gulping and sniffing, she said that she was fine. She kept her head down, refusing to meet curious eyes, and blew her nose on one of Gran's linen handkerchiefs. Gran had always looked on a handkerchief as essential funeral kit, so there was one in Maggie's bag from the previous week.

Soon the train was running through all too familiar country. Within minutes they would pass the request stop for Glen Cary Halt. Maggie supposed that the train would run straight through. It always did unless someone wanted to board or alight at Glen Cary. But to her dismay she felt it beginning to slow down. It stopped. She held her breath, and buried her tear-wet face into the sodden rag that Gran would undoubtedly have called a disgrace. She prayed that nobody would get on who knew her.

The stationmaster at the Halt was in an indignant mood. Young men had no respect for authority these days. The train was already running late, and he had been about to wave his green flag when there was a shout and a man loped across the railway line – a totally illegal action – and came tearing along the platform, *ordering* him to hold the train. And without a by your leave or the least apology, the madman had opened a door of the first-class section and vanished within.

There were further shouts at the back of the train. An abandoned car behind the level crossing was blocking half the road. A lorry driver was hooting his horn, and people were converging on the abandoned car, trying to move it aside.

Maggie heard the hooting of horns and the shouts but kept her head down and paid no heed. There was a much nearer commotion in the corridor outside, and the next thing she knew, David Vorst was standing over her and grasping her shoulders. His narrowed eyes looked black with rage.

Failing to find her in the first-class carriages where James had told him she would be, he had pushed his way down the long train, growing more desperate with each passing moment, sliding doors, peering in, and hurrying on. Suddenly, there she was! The fact that she was trying to hide behind her handkerchief made him angrier than ever.

He said in a taut voice, 'Maggie! What the hell do you think you're doing?'

She looked up with something between a gasp and a whimper, and he saw that she had been crying. He took one of her hands and started to pull her to her feet. 'You're coming with me,' he said. 'Where's your baggage? The train is about to go.'

Maggie found her voice. 'I'm going to Edinburgh. Leave me be.'

'Like hell I will! You'll come with me and tell me what all this is about.'

The train gave a lurch, and he grabbed at the luggage rack to steady himself. The train was moving, picking up speed. The station master came into sight, red-faced and glaring, and was left behind. A signal box whisked by. In a short time they were running along an embankment, and soon would be crossing the iron bridge over the river. He said angrily, 'Now look what you've done, you fool girl! Your case! Which is it? Show me.'

She put a protective hand over it and said, 'I told you to leave me alone. I'm going to Edinburgh. Who are you to call me a fool? You're going to be stuck on the train until the next stop.'

'You think so?' said David, with a look that boded no good. 'Then think again, Maggie, my love.'

With this, he reached up to the communication cord – 'Penalty for Improper Use, £5' – and pulled it firmly downwards.

'That'll cost you, young man,' said a voice. 'They'll have you in court for it.'

'Leave the poor lass alone. Can't you see she's been greeting . . .'

'Who does he think he is?' demanded another voice.

'The train is late already. Really . . .'

If David heard the chorus of disapproving voices, he paid no heed. As the train slowed down with a prolonged shrieking of brakes and some convulsive jerks, he opened the far side carriage door and heaved Maggie's suitcase through it, before turning back to her. The nearest passengers craned forward, and saw the case bouncing and rolling down the steep heather-covered embankment. It landed up against a wire fence at the bottom, and burst open.

'Now, Maggie . . .'

She had retreated behind the brown paper parcels and was watching him wide-eyed. She stamped her foot. 'You can't do this! Are you drunk or something?'

'Come along,' he said, as though she had not spoken. 'You've wasted enough of my time already.'

'What makes you think you can bully me like this? I told you to leave me be!'

A renewed commotion outside in the corridor informed David that it was time to be going. He lunged forward, grabbed Maggie's wrist, and jerked her past the brown paper parcel ladies and a tweed clad man in lace-up boots. Still holding her, he jumped out of the train on to the cinder track.

'Come, Maggie.'

'No!'

He gave a little laugh. He had more than once had to extract an inanimate fellow airman from a plane in a hurry. There was no help for it. The technique was similar, but his burden this time was neither unconscious nor cooperative. As he swung Maggie out of the train and over his shoulder, she kicked and swore and hammered him with her fists all the way down the steep embankment. And when she saw her case, with its contents spilled out all over the heather, she went for him like a wildcat.

Some of the train passengers were leaning out of the windows by this time, some protesting, many more laughing and enjoying the spectacle. And when the tall abductor finally pinned the girl's flailing hands behind her, and bent to kiss her long and lingeringly on the mouth, the laughter swelled to a rousing crescendo of cheers which echoed and re-echoed down the length of the train, nearly drowning the sound of the engine getting up steam.

They watched the train draw away in silence, both of them breathing fast.

Maggie dropped to her knees, and started to gather up her scattered belongings. David squatted down beside her and helped, and presently snapped the case shut.

He turned to look at her, still kneeling in the heather with her face averted. He put a finger to his cheek, and it came away smeared with blood from where she had scratched him.

'Well, my darling,' he said, and she found that her fears had been well-founded. His voice had lost none of its undermining power. 'James told me that you were a poor beaten thing, to be treated gently. He should have been looking out of the train just now.'

Still she would not look at him. She said in a scolding tone, 'You should be ashamed, pulling the communication cord like that. Apart from the expense, and that's bad enough, think of how people will talk. It's as well I'm leaving. You've made me so ashamed.'

'So you should be. You may have scarred me for life.'

She looked up, and saw the scratch on his lean cheek. 'I never did that!'

'You certainly did.'

'It serves you right for pulling me off the train.'

'How else was I to stop you vanishing again?' he demanded. He looked down at her pale, tear-streaked face and swollen eyelids. She must have been crying all the way from Inverness. His mind went back to the weeks and months of scouring Asia for her, and of his despair when he thought she might be dead. Records of air accidents were often incomplete at that stage of the war, and sometimes nonexistent. The sight of 'Dunlop, M.' on one casualty list had given him a bad few days, until further research revealed that the deceased had been a 43-year-old sergeant in the Burmese police.

He drew a shuddering breath, which had nothing to do with his recent struggles to drag her from the train and carry her kicking and cursing down the embankment. He had been waiting at Glen Cary for

439

days without being allowed to see her, and here she was at last. She was tear-stained and blotched, her mouth swollen as a result of his punitive kisses. Dart had told him cheerfully that Maggie Dunlop had gone off sadly, but to David's eyes she was entirely beautiful.

He was suddenly terrified of losing her again. He said with sudden, blundering anxiety, 'Maggie. Marry me! You will, won't you?'

'So you won't marry me? Why not?'

'It's not fitting, David.'

'That's what you said the first time, but you still haven't told me what you mean.'

'You should know without my having to tell you,' she said, crumbling her morning roll on the plate.

He waited for her to go on.

They had retrieved the car and more or less mollified the station-master by this time, and were sitting in the cheerless station tearoom. This was as far as Maggie would agree to go. She still insisted that she was going to Edinburgh, and he had promised to put her on a train if she first told him why she wanted to go way. David took the precaution of eating two pancakes and some bramble jelly with his stewed station tea. He had missed breakfast at the Lodge, and the stubborn set of Maggie's mouth informed him that this encounter was likely to take a while.

Maggie said crossly, 'If I choose to go to Edinburgh what business is it of yours?'

'James said that you couldn't face meeting me. Even if you were afraid, for some reason, it's not like you to act like a coward.'

She said wearily, 'When I was your driver, I pretended to be brave, but I haven't any energy left for that now. James told me that you . . . you know about my father being a murderer. That's one good reason why I'm no fitting wife for you.'

He was watching her intently. He recalled that James had said that Maggie looked defeated, and had to repress an urge to take her in his arms. But as he had agreed not to touch her, he just said gently, 'That's nonsense. Tell me your next reason, Maggie.'

She sighed. 'It's pretty obvious – or it should be. Think of what your parents and the rest of the family would say if you brought me to Maple Valley as your wife. Mr David and his nursery maid bride? What a laugh there would be in the staff dining room too!'

'If they want to laugh, that's fine by me. And as for my mother, when I told her I was going to marry you, she couldn't have been more delighted.'

'You . . . you told Mrs Vorst that?' said Maggie, horrified. 'You had no right to tell her any such thing. You'll look pretty silly when you have to tell her I turned you down.'

'Yes, won't I just?' he said, smiling at her. 'So why not take pity on me and say you will.'

'Havers,' said Maggie, refusing the invitation of that smile. 'You ought to marry someone like my friend Sophy.'

'Thanks! I'm more likely to wring her neck if we meet. Do you realise that she lost the letter I wrote you from hospital? She found it a couple of weeks ago. When I think of all the time wasted . . .'

Maggie said carefully, 'You wrote?'

'I did. I sent it way back in November. I should have written sooner, but with one thing and another . . .' He paused. This was not the moment to talk of his illness or of Antonia, and how his guilt over her death had reduced his self-esteem to well below rock bottom. 'When you didn't answer, and the RAF told me that you were being posted to India, I assumed you wanted to get away from me.'

Maggie stared at him, and said accusingly, 'You must have wanted to assume it. I never had your letter, but how could you think that I would treat you like that if I had?'

'I was a fool.'

Maggie was looking at him properly for the first time. She said soberly, even though her spirits were trying to take off like a helium balloon, 'We were both foolish. I had hoped so much to hear from you, and when you didn't get in touch I wanted to run away to the other end of the world.'

He returned her look with a glowing one which she knew well, and had never thought to see again. 'That figures. I felt like bumping myself off more than once. But why run away this time, Maggie? Tell me? I truly want to understand.'

She looked at him gravely. 'It nearly killed me getting over you last time. I just couldn't stand the thought of seeing you and breaking my heart all over again.'

'Damn you, Vorst,' said Dart. 'This is the second time you've swiped a girl from under my nose.'

David looked at Dart, and said kindly, 'Didn't Maggie fall for your fatal charm? How irritating for you.'

Maggie had just come down after saying goodnight to the children. Dart put an arm round her shoulders and kissed her warmly. 'You were beginning to get to like me, weren't you, Maggie mine?'

'It was kind of you to take so much trouble. I never quite worked out what it was you wanted.'

Dart looked slightly taken aback by her directness, and by the sparkle of amusement in her grey eyes. He was sufficiently nettled to answer in kind. 'I thought you would make a good caretaker for the Lodge. But Abby said she needed you, and who was I to stand in her way? You know, don't you, that David only proposed

441

to you because the children told him he must.'

'It's nice to be wanted,' said Maggie tranquilly, and kissed him goodnight before David took her hand and led her to his car. He was driving her to the manse where she and her godfather had stayed since her return. This was the last time they would make the journey. Tomorrow they were to be married, and Mrs Fraser had given David strict instructions to get Maggie home before midnight.

Maggie was silent as they travelled down the rough glen road. He brought the car to a halt within sight of the Frasers' house, where for three evenings they had lingered to say their leisurely goodnights.

Maggie said suddenly, 'David. I'd forgotten about Nanny.'

'What about Nanny?'

'She won't like it. She'll think I'm getting too big for my boots.'

'So? You want to call it off because of Nanny? Don't be afraid to say so.'

She said with a choke of laughter, 'I mean it about Nanny. I ought to ring her up at least, and try to make it right with her.'

'Don't forget to ring Trumpet and Vestry while you're about it.'

'David. I wish you would be serious.'

He went on inexorably, 'And how will you face Aunt Effie's dogs if you don't make it right with them. Dogs are worse snobs than humans.'

Maggie, worn down, laughed and said imploringly. 'That's enough. Kiss me goodnight instead of talking nonsense. We cannot please everyone, after all, and Mrs Fraser will be cross if I'm late.'